JUST ENOUGH JEEVES

P. G. WODEHOUSE

Introduction by Robert McCrum

W. W. Norton & Company
New York • London

Originally published in the USA under the title *Jeeves in the Morning*

First published in the USA by Doubleday Doran, 1930

Originally published in the USA under the title *Brinkley Manor*

Printed in the United States of America
First Edition

For information about special discounts for bulk purchases, please contact
W. W. Norton Special Sales at specialsales@wwnorton.com or 800-233-4830

Manufacturing by Courier Westford
Book design by Judith Stagnitto Abbate / Abbate Design
Production manager: Devon Zahn

Library of Congress Cataloging-in-Publication Data

Wodehouse, P. G. (Pelham Grenville), 1881–1975.
Just enough Jeeves / P.G. Wodehouse. — 1st ed.
p. cm.
ISBN 978-0-393-33943-7 (pbk.)
1. Jeeves (Fictitious character)—Fiction. 2. Wooster,
Bertie (Fictitious character)—Fiction. 3. Valets—Fiction.
4. Single men—Fiction. 5. England—Fiction. 6. Humorous stories, English.
I. Title.
PR6045.O53J87 2010
823'.912—dc22

2010029419

W. W. Norton & Company, Inc.
500 Fifth Avenue, New York, N.Y. 10110
www.wwnorton.com

W. W. Norton & Company Ltd.
Castle House, 75/76 Wells Street, London W1T 3QT

1 2 3 4 5 6 7 8 9 0

CONTENTS

INTRODUCTION

When P. G. Wodehouse, one of the comic masters of English literature, died on Valentine's Day 1975, he was famous throughout the English-speaking world for a cast of immortal characters—Psmith, Ukridge, Lord Emsworth, and Mr Mulliner—but most unforgettably for the "mentally negligible" Bertie Wooster and his omniscient manservant Jeeves.

As much as the characters in Jane Austen, every one of Wodehouse's drones, nincompoops and bounders sprang from a small world, "one of the smallest I ever met", in the words of their author. In later life, looking back on the landscape of his youth, Wodehouse would write that "It was bounded on the east by St James's street, on the west by Hyde Park Corner, by Oxford street on the north and by Piccadilly on the south. And now it is not even small, it is non-existent. It has gone with the wind and is one with Nineveh and Tyre. In a word, it has had it."

In some ways Wodehouse's work as a whole is a kind of nonsense elegy for Edwardian England, and few twentieth-century writers, it seems, could be more quintessentially English than P. G. Wodehouse. His name alone appears to guarantee a happy escape into a lost world of upper-class English frivolity: Mayfair lounge lizards; dreamy, pig-loving earls; inscrutable butlers and, of course, those fearsome aunts Agatha and Dahlia.

Yet the truth about Wodehouse is that, in his professional life, he was very much an American, too. He first came to New York, just over a hundred years ago, travelling steerage, on the SS *St Louis*, in the spring of 1904, aged twenty-two. Like many literary Englishmen, he had two jobs. In the mornings he was a columnist on a London evening paper, *The Globe*; for the rest of the working day he was a freelance writer. So he came to the New World in search of copy. Wodehouse fell in love with Manhattan at first sight. "To say that New York came up to its advance billing," he wrote later, "would be the baldest of understatements. Being there was like being in heaven, without going to all the bother and expense of dying."

If that's an emotion shared by many English visitors since those days, then the Manhattan which the young Wodehouse discovered with such enthusiasm is also, strangely, still available today. Greenwich Village is perhaps no longer a "rural paradise", but the Hotel Earle (now the Washington Square Hotel) on Waverly Place at the north-west corner of the square has hardly changed externally since Wodehouse stayed there. Stand outside the hotel on MacDougall Street, and it's not difficult to picture the young journalist with literary aspirations, in heavy boots and tweed jacket, heading off uptown in search of material, or passing down Wooster Street. Now there's a thought. . . .

When Wodehouse returned to London, he discovered that his newly acquired American savvy had transformed his value as a struggling freelance. "After that trip to New York," he recalled, "I was a man who counted. . . . My income rose like a rocketing pheasant." From 1904 until the day he died, Wodehouse perfected the art of selling a literary interpretation of America to British readers, and an affectionate caricature of Britain to an American audience. The frivolous extravagance of the Edwardians became the vapid indolence of the Drones Club in *My Man Jeeves*. Actually, Jeeves, named after an English county cricketer, and now synonymous with British sang-froid, made his first appearance in New York in 1916. The story, entitled "Extricating Young Gussie", was first published in the *Saturday Evening Post*. "I find it curious," Wodehouse once wrote, "now that I have written so much about him, to recall how softly and undramatically Jeeves first entered my little world. On that occasion he spoke just two lines. The first was: 'Mrs Gregson to see you, sir.' The second, 'Very good sir. Which suit will you wear?' It was only some time later . . . that the man's qualities dawned upon me. I still blush to think of the off-hand way I treated him at our first encounter."

Wodehouse had spent twenty years as a professional writer before he hit a winning streak with Jeeves. Thereafter, the unlikely alliance of silly young master and cunning manservant (a classical standby) gave him all he needed. For the rest of his life he could make "musical comedy without music" in a succession of comic arpeggios. Bertie's adventures collected in this volume demonstrate early, middle and late Wodehouse at his best, though you might be hard-pressed to detect much evidence of growing up. Bertie remains a "willowy" twenty-something. Jeeves is always slightly his senior.

The passage of years between *Very Good, Jeeves!* (1930) and *Joy in the Morning* (1947) does not dim Bertie's enthusiasm for fancy dress, or his aversion to matrimony, or Jeeves's dislike of *outre* menswear. This is also an especially perfect collection because it demonstrates Wodehouse's transition from the champagne moments of the stories to the vintage satisfactions of the novels, a progression from *urbs* to *rus*.

In *Very Good, Jeeves!* Bertie is the inveterate clubman, dwelling in Berkeley Mansions, the amiable friend, the loyal school chum and willing partygoer, but above all the proud employer of the all-powerful Jeeves, that supreme arbiter of youthful romantic scrapes. In *Right Ho, Jeeves* Bertie is poised between Mayfair and the countryside. In *Joy in the Morning* the action begins on the road to Aunt Agatha's country seat in Steeple Bumpleigh and takes place exclusively in and around that rural hellhole. As these three Wodehouse classics suggest, not only is his literary career distinguished by its timeless charm, he also pulled off an almost unprecedented run of success throughout the 1920s and 1930s, up to *Joy in the Morning* (1947) and, some would say, beyond. Every new book seemed to surpass its predecessor. During those two decades, moreover, he hit the kind of mid-season form that less gifted writers can only dream about: a perfect union of style and content, exemplified by the three titles you will find in this volume. *Very Good, Jeeves!* is the third in the sequence of story collections that began with *The Inimitable Jeeves* in 1923. Master and servant are now in an almost perfect relationship, one is tempted to say "marriage". Bertie is still inclined to defy Jeeves; and Jeeves, for all his erudite superiority, has come to seem like Bertie's friend and equal. With a Jeeves story straight in his mind, Wodehouse could complete a first draft in three or four days.

Right Ho, Jeeves was also written at top speed in a matter of a few weeks in the summer of 1933 during one of the lowest points in Wodehouse's career. He was being hounded by the tax man, and the book is dedicated to the lawyer who got him off. With a three-act structure, this is probably the Wodehouse novel that many readers know best. The climactic comic set-piece—newt-fancying teetotaller Gussie Fink-Nottle giving away the prizes to the boys of Market Snodsbury Grammar School—is one of the most anthologised in the Wodehouse canon. When the action of the novel begins, Gussie is discovered roaming London in fancy dress, disguised as Mephistopheles, and in love with Madeleine Bassett, to whom Bertie has been engaged, and who (according to Bertie) believes that the stars are "God's daisy chain". Gussie is in town to consult Jeeves on how best to pluck up the courage to propose to Miss Bassett. The quest for love soon carries both Gussie and Bertie to Brinkley Court, Worcestershire, home of Dahlia Travers, Bertie's favourite aunt, editor of *Milady's Boudoir*, the magazine for gentlewomen to which Bertie had once contributed "What the Well-Dressed Man is Wearing". Clothes, once again, play a decisive role in the plot. Bertie has returned from France with a fashionable white mess-jacket, and Jeeves does not approve ("Surely you are not proposing to wear it in England, sir"). A temporary coolness between master and valet ensues, and Bertie must try to resolve the complications of Gussie's wooing without the full benefit of Jeeves's omniscience. But all ends happily ever after. During a triumphant nocturnal finale in the grounds of Brinkley Court sundered hearts are reunited. Gussie's engagement to La Bassett is secured. As Bertie puts it, "Looking at the thing from every angle, I saw that Jeeves had done well".

None of this, however, compares with *Joy in the Morning*, with which this volume begins, described by its author with characteristic modesty as "*the* supreme Jeeves novel of all time". A more brilliant example of Wodehouse's literary escapism is hard to find. Not only does he weave together many of the best characters and themes around the plot of Florence Craye's matrimonial designs on Bertie ("she was one of those intellectual girls, steeped to the gills in serious purpose, who are unable to see a male soul without wanting to get behind it and shove"), it was also conceived and written in Le Touquet during the Phoney War, fully drafted during the Nazi occupation of France, and finally completed in the midst of the global furor surrounding Wodehouse's ill-judged broadcasts from Nazi Berlin. It can't be fanciful to see, in Bertie's "cold gesture" to Florence's boy scout brother Edwin, a sly allusion to the behaviour of Le Touquet's German garrison: "Now, I don't know how you would have made a cold gesture—no doubt people's methods vary—but the way I did it was by raising the right arm in a sort of salute and allowing it to fall to my side."

Joy in the Morning is an anthology of Wodehouse's favourite comic situations (a blazing cottage; a nocturnal confrontation; a fancy dress ball; the midnight resolution), and he achieves the perfect union of plot and style when a running gag about "the fretful porpentine" culminates with a "hidden hand" concealing a hedgehog in Bertie's bed. Almost as satisfying, *Joy in the Morning* also has some of his best lines: "Like a man who, stooping to pluck a nosegay of wild flowers on a railway line, is unexpectedly struck in the small of the back by the Cornish Express" or, "He spun round with a sort of guilty bound, like an adagio dancer surprised while watering the cat's milk".

The novel also conceals a subtle strand of oblique self-justification, a riposte to the critics who had turned on him after the infamous broadcasts: "I mean, it's all very well for a chap to plead that he's an author and expect on the strength of that to get away with conduct which would qualify the ordinary man for a one-way ticket to Colney Hatch, but even an author ought to have had the sense . . ." Wodehouse repeats the teasing references to writers' inability to conduct their own lives: "I doubt", says Bertie at one point, "if you can ever trust an author not to make an ass of himself". The revels come to a harmonious conclusion (Florence will marry 'Stilton' Cheesewright, not Bertie) in which, for once, Jeeves plays only a minor role. With the happy ending secure, Bertie, like his creator, makes a sneaky getaway, with lines reminiscent of a Broadway comedy routine:

> 'How would it be,' I suggested, 'to zoom off immediately, without waiting to pack?'
>
> 'I was about to suggest such a course myself, sir.'
>
> 'It would enable one to avoid tedious explanations.'

'Precisely, sir.'

'Then shift ho, Jeeves,' I said.

As Bertie and Jeeves motor happily back to the beloved metropolis, it is Jeeves, prompted by Bertie, who finds the quotation ("A wheeze. A gag.") that puts the whole thing in a nutshell: "Joy cometh in the morning". The genius of P. G. Wodehouse never fails to lift the spirits.

Robert McCrum
23 May 2010

JUST ENOUGH JEEVES

JOY IN THE MORNING

PART 1

1

After the thing was all over, when peril had ceased to loom and happy endings had been distributed in heaping handfuls and we were driving home with our hats on the side of our heads, having shaken the dust of Steeple Bumpleigh from our tyres, I confessed to Jeeves that there had been moments during the recent proceedings when Bertram Wooster, though no weakling, had come very near to despair.

'Within a toucher, Jeeves.'

'Unquestionably affairs had developed a certain menacing trend, sir.'

'I saw no ray of hope. It looked to me as if the blue bird had thrown in the towel and formally ceased to function. And yet here we are, all boomps-a-daisy. Makes one think a bit, that.'

'Yes, sir.'

'There's an expression on the tip of my tongue which seems to me to sum the whole thing up. Or, rather, when I say an expression, I mean a saying. A wheeze. A gag. What, I believe, is called a saw. Something about Joy doing something.'

'Joy cometh in the morning, sir?'

'That's the baby. Not one of your things, is it?'

'No, sir.'

'Well, it's dashed good,' I said.

And I still think that there can be no neater way of putting in a nutshell the outcome of the super-sticky affair of Nobby Hopwood, Stilton Cheesewright, Florence Craye, my Uncle Percy, J. Chichester Clam, Edwin the

Boy Scout and old Boko Fittleworth—or, as my biographers will probably call it, the Steeple Bumpleigh Horror.

Even before the events occurred which I am about to relate, the above hamlet had come high up on my list of places to be steered sedulously clear of. I don't know if you have ever seen one of those old maps where they mark a spot with a cross and put 'Here be dragons' or 'Keep ye eye skinned for hippogriffs', but I had always felt that some such kindly warning might well have been given to pedestrians and traffic with regard to this Steeple Bumpleigh.

A picturesque settlement, yes. None more so in all Hampshire. It lay embowered, as I believe the expression is, in the midst of smiling fields and leafy woods, hard by a willow-fringed river, and you couldn't have thrown a brick in it without hitting a honeysuckle-covered cottage or beaning an apple-cheeked villager. But you remember what the fellow said—it's not a bally bit of use every prospect pleasing if man is vile, and the catch about Steeple Bumpleigh was that it contained Bumpleigh Hall, which in its turn contained my Aunt Agatha and her second husband.

And when I tell you that this second h. was none other than Percival, Lord Worplesdon, and that he had with him his daughter Florence and his son Edwin, the latter as pestilential a stripling as ever wore khaki shorts and went spooring or whatever it is that these Boy Scouts do, you will understand why I had always declined my old pal Boko Fittleworth's invitations to visit him at the bijou residence he maintained in those parts.

I had also had to be similarly firm with Jeeves, who had repeatedly hinted his wish that I should take a cottage there for the summer months. There was, it appeared, admirable fishing in the river, and he is a man who dearly loves to flick the baited hook. 'No, Jeeves,' I had been compelled to say, 'much though it pains me to put a stopper on your simple pleasures, I cannot take the risk of running into that gang of pluguglies. Safety first.' And he had replied, 'Very good, sir,' and there the matter had rested.

But all the while, unsuspected by Bertram, the shadow of Steeple Bumpleigh was creeping nearer and nearer, and came a day when it tore off its whiskers and pounced.

Oddly enough, the morning on which this major disaster occurred was one that found me completely, even exuberantly, in the pink. No inkling of the soup into which I was to be plunged came to mar my perfect *bien être*. I had slept well, shaved well and shower-bathed well, and it was with a merry cry that I greeted Jeeves as he brought in the coffee and kippers.

'Odd's boddikins, Jeeves,' I said, 'I am in rare fettle this a.m. Talk about exulting in my youth! I feel up and doing, with a heart for any fate, as Tennyson says.'

'Longfellow, sir.'

'Or, if you prefer it, Longfellow. I am in no mood to split hairs. Well, what's the news?'

'Miss Hopwood called while you were still asleep, sir.'

'No, really? I wish I'd seen her.'

'The young lady was desirous of entering your room and rousing you with a wet sponge, but I dissuaded her. I considered it best that your repose should not be disturbed.'

I applauded this watch-dog spirit, showing as it did both the kindly heart and the feudal outlook, but continued to tut-tut a bit at having missed the young pipsqueak, with whom my relations had always been of the matiest. This Zenobia ('Nobby') Hopwood was old Worplesdon's ward, as I believe it is called. A pal of his, just before he stopped ticking over some years previously, had left him in charge of his daughter. I don't know how these things are arranged—no doubt documents have to be drawn up and dotted lines signed on—but, whatever the procedure, the upshot was as I have stated. When all the smoke had cleared away, my Uncle Percy was Nobby's guardian.

'Young Nobby, eh? When did she blow into the great city?' I asked. For, on becoming Uncle Percy's ward, she had of course joined the strength at his Steeple Bumpleigh lair, and it was only rarely nowadays that she came to London.

'Last night, sir.'

'Making a long stay?'

'Only until to-morrow, sir.'

'Hardly worth while sweating up just for a day, I should have thought.'

'I understand that she came because her ladyship desired her company, sir.'

I quailed a bit.

'You don't mean Aunt Agatha's in London?'

'Merely passing through, sir,' replied the honest fellow, calming my apprehensions. 'Her ladyship is on her way to minister to Master Thomas, who has contracted mumps at his school.'

His allusion was to the old relative's son by her first marriage, one of our vilest citizens. Many good judges rank him even higher in England's Rogues' Gallery than her stepson Edwin. I was rejoiced to learn that he had got mumps, and toyed for a moment with a hope that Aunt Agatha would catch them from him.

'And what had Nobby to say for herself?'

'She was regretting that she saw so little of you nowadays, sir.'

'Quite mutual, the agony, Jeeves. There are few better eggs than this Hopwood.'

'She expressed a hope that you might shortly see your way to visiting Steeple Bumpleigh.'

I shook the head.

'Out of the q., Jeeves.'

'The young lady tells me the fish are biting well there just now.'

'No, Jeeves. I'm sorry. Not even if they bite like serpents do I go near Steeple Bumpleigh.'

'Very good, sir.'

He spoke sombrely, and I endeavoured to ease the strain by asking for another cup of coffee.

'Was Nobby alone?'

'No, sir. There was a gentleman with her, who spoke as if he were acquainted with you. Miss Hopwood addressed him as Stilton.'

'Big chap?'

'Noticeably well developed, sir.'

'With a head like a pumpkin?'

'Yes, sir. There was a certain resemblance to the vegetable.'

'It must have been a companion of my earlier years named G. D'Arcy Cheesewright. In our whimsical way we used to call him Stilton. I haven't seen him for ages. He lives in the country somewhere, and to hobnob with Bertram Wooster it is imperative that you stick around the metropolis. Odd, him knowing Nobby.'

'I gathered from the young lady's remarks that Mr Cheesewright is also a resident of Steeple Bumpleigh, sir.'

'Really? It's a small world, Jeeves.'

'Yes, sir.'

'I don't know when I've seen a smaller,' I said, and would have gone more deeply into the subject, but at this juncture the telephone tinkled out a summons, and he shimmered off to answer it. Through the door, which he had chanced to leave ajar, the ear detected a good deal of Yes-my-lord-ing and Very-good-my-lord-ing, seeming to indicate that he had hooked one of the old nobility.

'Who was it?' I asked, as he filtered in again.

'Lord Worplesdon, sir.'

It seems almost incredible to me, looking back, that I should have received this news item with nothing more than a mildly surprised 'Oh, ah?' Amazing, I mean, that I shouldn't have spotted the sinister way in which what you might call the Steeple Bumpleigh note had begun to intrude itself like some creeping fog or miasma, and trembled in every limb, asking myself what this portended. But so it was. The significance of the thing failed to penetrate and, as I say, I oh-ahed with merely a faint spot of surprise.

'The call was for me, sir. His lordship wishes me to go to his office immediately.'

'He wants to see you?'

'Such was the impression I gathered, sir.'

'Did he say why?'

'No, sir. Merely that the matter was of considerable urgency.'

I mused, thoughtfully champing a kipper. It seemed to me that there could be but one solution.

'Do you know what I think, Jeeves? He's in a spot of some kind and needs your counsel.'

'It may be so, sir.'

'I'll bet it's so. He must know all about your outstanding gifts. You can't go on as you have gone on so long, dishing out aid and comfort to all and sundry, without acquiring a certain reputation, if only in the family circle. Grab your hat and race along. I shall be all agog to learn the inside story. What sort of a day is it?'

'Extremely clement, sir.'

'Sunshine and all that?'

'Yes, sir.'

'I thought as much. That must be why I'm feeling so dashed fit. Then I think I'll take myself for an airing. Tell me,' I said, for I was a trifle remorseful at having had to adopt that firm attitude about going to Steeple Bumpleigh and wished to bring back into his life the joy which my refusal to allow him to get in among the local fish had excluded from it, 'is there any little thing I can do for you while I'm out?'

'Sir?'

'Any little gift you would like, I mean?'

'It is extremely kind of you, sir.'

'Not at all, Jeeves. The sky is the limit. State your desire.'

'Well, sir, there has recently been published a new and authoritatively annotated edition of the works of the philosopher Spinoza. Since you are so generous, I would appreciate that very much.'

'You shall have it. It shall be delivered at your door in a plain van without delay. You're sure you've got the name right? Spinoza?'

'Yes, sir.'

'It doesn't sound probable, but no doubt you know best. Spinoza, eh? Is he the Book Society's Choice of the Month?'

'I believe not, sir.'

'Well, he's the only fellow I ever heard of who wasn't. Right ho. I'll see to it instanter.'

And presently, having assembled the hat, the gloves and the neatly rolled u., I sauntered forth.

As I made my way to the bookery, I found my thoughts turning once more, as you may readily imagine, to this highly suggestive business of old Worplesdon. The thing intrigued me. I found it difficult to envisage what possible sort of a jam a man like that could have got himself into.

When, about eighteen months before, news had reached me through well-informed channels that my Aunt Agatha, for many years a widow, or derelict, as I believe it is called, was about to take another pop at matrimony, my first emotion, as was natural in the circumstances, had been a gentle pity for the unfortunate goop slated to step up the aisle with her—she, as you are aware, being my tough aunt, the one who eats broken bottles and conducts human sacrifices by the light of the full moon.

But when details began to come in, and I discovered that the bimbo who had drawn the short straw was Lord Worplesdon, the shipping magnate, this tender commiseration became sensibly diminished. The thing, I felt, would be no walkover. Even if in the fullness of time she wore him down and at length succeeded in making him jump through hoops, she would know she had been in a fight.

For he was hot stuff, this Worplesdon. I had known him all my life. It was he who at the age of fifteen—when I was fifteen, I mean, of course—found me smoking one of his special cigars in the stable yard and chased me a mile across difficult country with a hunting crop. And though with advancing years our relations had naturally grown more formal, I had never been able to think of him without getting goose pimples. Given the choice between him and a hippogriff as a companion for a walking tour, I would have picked the hippogriff every time.

It was not easy to see how such a man of blood and iron could have been reduced to sending out S O S's for Jeeves, and I was reflecting on the possibility of compromising letters in the possession of gold-digging blondes, when I reached my destination and started to lodge my order.

'Good morning, good morning,' I said. 'I want a book.'

Of course, I ought to have known that it's silly to try to buy a book when you go to a book shop. It merely startles and bewilders the inmates. The motheaten old bird who had stepped forward to attend to me ran true to form.

'A book, sir?' he said, with ill-concealed astonishment.

'Spinoza,' I replied, specifying.

This had him rocking back on his heels.

'Did you say Spinoza, sir?'

'Spinoza was what I said.'

He seemed to be feeling that if we talked this thing out long enough as man to man, we might eventually hit upon a formula.

'You do not mean "The Spinning Wheel"?'

'No.'

'It would not be "The Poisoned Pin"?'

'It would not.'

'Or "With Gun and Camera in Little Known Borneo"?' he queried, trying a long shot.

'Spinoza,' I repeated firmly. That was my story, and I intended to stick to it.

He sighed a bit, like one who feels that the situation has got beyond him.

'I will go and see if we have it in stock, sir. But possibly this may be what you are requiring. Said to be very clever.'

He pushed off, Spinoza-ing under his breath in a hopeless sort of way, leaving me clutching a thing called 'Spindrift'.

It looked pretty foul. Its jacket showed a female with a green, oblong face sniffing at a purple lily, and I was just about to fling it from me and start a hunt for that 'Poisoned Pin' of which he had spoken, when I became aware of someone Good-gracious-Bertie-ing and, turning, found that the animal cries proceeded from a tall girl of commanding aspect who had oiled up behind me.

'Good gracious, Bertie! Is it really you?'

I emitted a sharp gurgle, and shied like a startled mustang. It was old Worplesdon's daughter, Florence Craye.

And I'll tell you why, on beholding her, I shied and gurgled as described. I mean, if there's one thing I bar, it's the sort of story where people stagger to and fro, clutching their foreheads and registering strong emotion, and not a word of explanation as to what it's all about till the detective sums up in the last chapter.

Briefly, then, the reason why this girl's popping up had got in amongst me in this fashion was that we had once been engaged to be married, and not so dashed long ago, either. And though it all came out all right in the end, the thing being broken off and self saved from the scaffold at the eleventh hour, it had been an extraordinarily narrow squeak and the memory remained green. The mere mention of her name was still enough to make me call for a couple of quick ones, so you can readily appreciate my agitation at bumping into her like this absolutely in the flesh.

I swayed in the breeze, and found myself a bit stumped for the necessary dialogue.

'Oh, hullo,' I said.

Not good, of course, but the best I could do.

2

Scanning the roster of the females I've nearly got married to in my time, we find the names of some tough babies. The eye rests on that of Honoria Glossop, and a shudder passes through the frame. So it does when we turn to the B's and come upon Madeline Bassett. But, taking everything into consideration and weighing this and that, I have always been inclined to consider Florence Craye the top. In the face of admittedly stiff competition, it is to her that I would award the biscuit.

Honoria Glossop was hearty, yes. Her laugh was like a steam-riveting machine, and from a child she had been a confirmed back-slapper. Madeline Bassett was soppy, true. She had large, melting eyes and thought the stars were God's daisy chain. These are grave defects, but to do this revolting duo justice neither had tried to mould me, and that was what Florence Craye had done from the start, seeming to look on Bertram Wooster as a mere chunk of plasticine in the hands of the sculptor.

The root of the trouble was that she was one of those intellectual girls, steeped to the gills in serious purpose, who are unable to see a male soul without wanting to get behind it and shove. We had scarcely arranged the preliminaries before she was checking up on my reading, giving the bird to 'Blood on the Banisters', which happened to be what I was studying at the moment, and substituting for it a thing called 'Types of Ethical Theory'. Nor did she attempt to conceal the fact that this was a mere pipe opener and that there was worse to come.

Have you ever dipped into 'Types of Ethical Theory'? The volume is still on my shelves. Let us open it and see what it has to offer. Yes, here we are.

> Of the two antithetic terms in the Greek philosophy one only was real and selfsubsisting; that is to say, Ideal Thought as opposed to that which it has to penetrate and mould. The other, corresponding to our Nature, was in itself phenomenal, unreal, without any permanent footing, having no predicates that held true for two moments together; in short, redeemed from negation only by including indwelling realities appearing through.

Right. You will have got the idea, and will, I think, be able to understand why the sight of her made me give at the knees somewhat. Old wounds had been reopened.

None of the embarrassment which was causing the Wooster toes to curl up inside their neat suède shoes like the tendrils of some sensitive plant seemed to be affecting this chunk of the dead past. Her manner, as always, was brisk and aunt-like. Even at the time when I had fallen beneath the spell of that profile of hers, which was a considerable profile and tended to make a man commit himself to statements which he later regretted, I had always felt that she was like someone training on to be an aunt.

'And how are you, Bertie?'

'Oh, fine, thanks.'

'I have just run up to London to see my publisher. Fancy meeting you, and in a book shop, of all places. What are you buying? Some trash, I suppose?'

Her gaze, which had been resting on me in a rather critical and censorious way, as if she was wondering how she could ever have contemplated linking her lot to anything so sub-human, now transferred itself to the volume in my hand. She took it from me, her lip curling in faint disgust, as if she wished she had had a pair of tongs handy.

And then, as she looked at it, her whole aspect suddenly altered. She switched off the curling lip. She smiled a pleased smile. The eye softened. A blush mantled the features. She positively giggled.

'Oh, Bertie!'

The gist got past me. 'Oh, Bertie!' was a thing she had frequently said to me in the days when we had been affianced, but always with that sort of nasty ring in the voice which made you feel that she had been on the point of expressing her exasperation with something a good deal fruitier but had remembered her ancient lineage just in time. This current 'Oh, Bertie!' was quite different. Practically a coo. As it might have been one turtle dove addressing another turtle dove.

'Oh, *Bertie*!' she repeated. 'Well, of course, I must autograph it for you,' she said, and at the same moment all was suddenly made clear to me. I had missed it at first, because I had been concentrating on the girl with the green face, but I now perceived at the bottom of the jacket the words 'By Florence Craye'. They had been half hidden by a gummed-on label which said 'Book Society Choice of the Month'. I saw all, and the thought of how near I had come to marrying a female novelist made everything go black for a bit.

She wrote in the book with a firm hand, thus dishing any prospect that the shop would take it back and putting me seven bob and a tanner down almost, as you might say, before the day had started. Then she said 'Well!' still with that turtle dove timbre in her voice.

'Fancy you buying "Spindrift"!'

Well, one has to say the civil thing, and it may be that in the agitation of the moment I overdid it a bit. I rather think that the impression I must have conveyed, when I assured her that I had made a bee-line for the beastly volume, was that I had been counting the minutes till I could get my hooks on it. At any rate, she came back with a gratified simper.

'I can't tell you how pleased I am. Not just because it's mine, but because I see that all the trouble I took training your mind was not wasted. You have grown to love good literature.'

It was at this point, as if he had entered on cue, that the motheaten bird returned and said they had not got old Pop Spinoza, but could get him for me. He seemed rather depressed about it all, but Florence's eyes lit up as if somebody had pressed a switch.

'Bertie! This is amazing! Do you really read Spinoza?'

It's extraordinary how one yields to that fatal temptation to swank. It undoes the best of us. Nothing, I mean, would have been simpler than to reply that she had got the data twisted and that the authoritatively annotated edition was a present for Jeeves. But, instead of doing the simple, manly, straightforward thing, I had to go and put on dog.

'Oh, rather,' I said, with an intellectual flick of the umbrella. 'When I have a leisure moment, you will generally find me curled up with Spinoza's latest.'

'*Well!*'

A simple word, but as she spoke it a shudder ran through me from brilliantined topknot to rubber shoe sole.

It was the look that accompanied the yip that caused this shudder. It was exactly the same sort of look that Madeline Bassett had given me, that time I went to Totleigh Towers to pinch old Bassett's cow-creamer and she thought I had come because I loved her so much that I couldn't stay away from her side. A frightful, tender, melting look that went through me like a red-hot bradawl through a pat of butter and filled me with a nameless fear.

I wished now I hadn't plugged Spinoza so heartily, and above all I wished I hadn't been caught in the act of apparently buying this blighted 'Spindrift'. I saw that unwittingly I had been giving myself a terrific build-up, causing this girl to see Bertram Wooster with new eyes and to get hep to his hidden depths. It might quite well happen that she would review the position in the light of this fresh evidence and decide that she had made a mistake in breaking off her engagement to so rare a spirit. And once she got thinking along those lines, who knew what the harvest might be?

An imperious urge came upon me to be elsewhere, before I could make a chump of myself further.

'Well, I'm afraid I must be popping,' I said. 'Most important appointment. Frightfully jolly, seeing you again.'

'We ought to see each other more,' she replied, still with that melting look. 'We ought to have some long talks.'

'Oh, rather.'

'A developing mind is so fascinating. Why don't you ever come to the Hall?'

'Oh, well, one gets a bit chained to the metropolis, you know.'

'I should like to show you the reviews of "Spindrift". They are wonderful. Edwin is pasting them in an album for me.'

'I'd love to see them some time. Later on, perhaps. Good-bye.'

'You're forgetting your book.'

'Oh, thanks. Well, toodle-oo,' I said, and fought my way out.

The appointment to which I had alluded was with the barman at the

Bollinger. Seldom, if ever, had I felt in such sore need of a restorative. I headed for my destination like a hart streaking towards cooling streams, when heated in the chase, and was speedily in conference with the dispenser of life savers.

Ten minutes later, feeling considerably better, though still shaken, I was standing in the doorway, twirling my umbrella and wondering what to do next, when my eye was arrested by an odd spectacle.

A certain rumminess had begun to manifest itself across the way.

3

The Bollinger bar conducts its beneficent activities about halfway up Bond Street, and on the other side of the thoroughfare, immediately opposite, there stands a courteous and popular jeweller's, where I generally make my purchases when the question of investing in *bijouterie* arises. In fact, the day being so fine, I was rather thinking of looking in there now and buying a new cigarette case.

It was outside this jeweller's that the odd spectacle was in progress. A bloke of furtive aspect was shimmering to and fro on the threshold of the emporium, his demeanour rather like that of the cat in the adage, which, according to Jeeves, and I suppose he knows, let 'I dare not' wait upon 'I would'. He seemed, that is to say, desirous of entering, but was experiencing some difficulty in making the grade. He would have a sudden dash at it, and then draw back and stand shooting quick glances right and left, as if fearing the scrutiny of the public eye. Over in New York, during the days of Prohibition, I have seen fellows doing the same sort of thing outside speakeasies.

He was a massive bloke, and there was something in his appearance that seemed familiar. Then, as I narrowed my gaze and scanned him more closely, memory did its stuff. That beefy frame . . . That pumpkin-shaped head . . . The face that looked like a slab of pink dough . . . It was none other than my old friend, Stilton Cheesewright. And what he was doing, pirouetting outside jewellery bins, was more than I could understand.

I started across the road with the idea of instituting a probe or quiz, and at the same moment he seemed to summon up a sudden burst of resolution. As I paused to disentangle myself from a passing bus, he picked up his feet, tossed his head in a mettlesome sort of way, and was through the door like a man dashing into a railway-station buffet with only two minutes for a gin and tonic before his train goes.

When I entered the establishment, he was leaning over the counter, his gaze riveted on some species of merchandise which was being shown him by the gentlemanly assistant. To prod him in the hindquarters with my umbrella was with me the work of an instant.

'Ahoy there, Stilton!' I cried.

He spun round with a sort of guilty bound, like an adagio dancer surprised while watering the cat's milk.

'Oh, hullo,' he said.

There was a pause. At a moment like this, with old boyhood friends meeting again after long separation, I mean to say, you might have expected a good deal of animated what-ho-ing and an immediate picking up of the threads. Of this, however, there was a marked absence. The Auld Lang Syne spirit was strong in me, but not, or I was mistaken, equally strong in G. D'Arcy Cheesewright. I have met so many people in my time who have wished that Bertram was elsewhere that I have come to recognize the signs. And it was these signs that this former playmate was now exhibiting.

He drew me away from the counter, shielding it from my gaze with his person, like somebody trying to hide the body.

'I wish you wouldn't go spiking people in the backside with your beastly umbrella,' he said, and one sensed the querulous note. 'Gave me a nasty shock.'

I apologized gracefully, explaining that if you have an umbrella and are fortunate enough to catch an old acquaintance bending, you naturally do not let the opportunity slip, and endeavoured to set him at his ease with genial chit-chat. From the embarrassment he was displaying, I might have been some high official in the police force interrupting him in the middle of a smash and grab raid. His demeanour perplexed me.

'Well, well, well, Stilton,' I said. 'Quite a while since we met.'

'Yes,' he responded, his air that of a man who was a bit sorry it hadn't been longer.

'How's the boy?'

'Oh, all right. How are you?'

'Fine, thanks. As a matter of fact, I'm feeling unusually fizzy.'

'That's good.'

'I thought you'd be pleased.'

'Oh, I am. Well, good-bye, Bertie,' he said, shaking me by the hand. 'Nice to have seen you.'

I looked at him, amazed. Did he really imagine, I asked myself, that I was as easily got rid of as this? Why, experts have tried to get rid of Bertram Wooster and have been forced to admit defeat.

'I'm not leaving you yet,' I assured him.

'Aren't you?' he said, wistfully.

'No, no. Still here. Jeeves tells me you dropped in on me this morning.'

'Yes.'

'Accompanied by Nobby.'

'Yes.'

'You live at Steeple Bumpleigh, too, I hear.'

'Yes.'

'It's a small world.'

'Not so very.'

'Jeeves thinks it is.'

'Well, fairly small, perhaps,' he agreed, making a concession. 'You're sure I'm not keeping you, Bertie?'

'No, no.'

'I thought you might have some date somewhere.'

'Oh, no, not a thing.'

There was another pause. He hummed a few bars of a popular melody, but not rollickingly. He also shuffled his feet quite a bit.

'Been there long?'

'Where?'

'Steeple Bumpleigh.'

'Oh? No, not very long.'

'Like it?'

'Very much.'

'What do you do there?'

'Do?'

'Come, come, you know what I mean by "do". Boko Fittleworth, for instance, writes wholesome fiction for the masses there. My Uncle Percy relaxes there after the day's shipping magnateing. What is your racket?'

A rather odd look came into his map, and he fixed me with a cold and challenging eye, as if daring me to start something. I remembered having seen the same defiant glitter behind the spectacles of a man I met in a country hotel once, just before he told me his name was Snodgrass. It was as if this old companion of mine were on the brink of some shameful confession.

Then he seemed to think better of it.

'Oh, I mess about.'

'Mess about?'

'Yes. Just mess about. Doing this and that, you know.'

There seemed nothing to be gained by pursuing this line of inquiry. It was obvious that he did not intend to loosen up. I passed on, accordingly, to the point which had been puzzling me so much.

'Well, flitting lightly over that,' I said, 'why were you hovering?'

'Hovering?'

'Yes.'

'When?'

'Just now. Outside the shop.'

'I wasn't hovering.'

'You were distinctly hovering. You reminded me of a girl Jeeves was speaking about the other day, who stood with reluctant feet where the brook and river meet. And when I follow you in, I find you buzz-buzzing into the ear of the assistant, plainly making some furtive purchase. What are you buying, Stilton?'

Fixed by my penetrating eye, he came clean. I suppose he saw that further concealment was useless.

'A ring,' he said, in a low, hoarse voice.

'What sort of a ring?' I asked, pressing him.

'An engagement ring,' he muttered, twisting his fingers and in other ways showing that he was fully conscious of his position.

'Are you engaged?'

'Yes.'

'Well, well, well!'

I laughed heartily, as is my custom on these occasions, but on his inquiring in a throaty growl rather like the snarl of the Rocky Mountains timber wolf what the devil I was cackling about, cheesed the mirth. I had always found Stilton intimidating, when stirred. In a weak moment at Oxford, misled by my advisers, I once tried to do a bit of rowing, and Stilton was the bird who coached us from the towing path. I could still recall some of the things he had said about my stomach, which—rightly or wrongly—he considered that I was sticking out. It would seem that when you are a Volga boatman, you aren't supposed to stick your stomach out.

'I always laugh when people tell me they are engaged,' I explained, more soberly.

It did not seem to mollify him—if 'mollify' is the word I want. He continued to glower.

'You have no objection to my being engaged?'

'No, no.'

'Why shouldn't I be engaged?'

'Oh, quite.'

'What do you mean by "Oh, quite"?'

I didn't quite know what I had meant by 'Oh, quite,' unless possibly 'Oh, quite.' I explained this, trying to infuse into my manner a soothing what-is-it, for he appeared to be hotting up.

'I hope you will be very, very happy,' I said.

He thanked me, though not effusively.

'Nice girl, I expect?'

'Yes.'

The response was not what you would call lyrical, but we Woosters can read between the lines. His eyes were rolling in their sockets, and his face had taken on the colour and expression of a devout tomato. I could see that he loved like a thousand of bricks.

A thought struck me.

'It isn't Nobby?'

'No. She's engaged to Boko Fittleworth.'

'What!'

'Yes.'

'I never knew that. He might have told me. Nobby and Boko have hitched up, have they?'

'Yes.'

'Well, well, well! The laughing Love God has been properly up on his toes in and around Steeple Bumpleigh of late, what?'

'Yes.'

'Never an idle moment. Day and night shifts. Your betrothed, I take it, is a resident?'

'Yes. Her name's Craye. Florence Craye.'

'What!'

The word escaped my lips in a sort of yowl, and he started and gave me the raised eyebrow. I suppose it always perplexes the young Romeo to some extent, when fellows begin yowling on being informed of the loved one's identify.

'What's the matter?' he asked, a rather strained note in his voice.

Well, of course, that yowl of mine, as you may well imagine, had been one of ecstasy and relief. I mean, if Florence was all tied up with him, the peril I had been envisaging could be considered to have blown a fuse and ceased to impend. Spinoza or no Spinoza, I felt, this let Bertram out. But I couldn't very well tell him that.

'Oh, nothing,' I said.

'You seem to know her.'

'Oh, yes, we've met.'

'I've never heard her speak of you.'

'No?'

'No. Have you known her long?'

'A certain time.'

'Do you know her well?'

'Pretty well.'

'When you say "Pretty well," you mean—?'

'Fairly well. Tolerably well.'

'How did you come to know her?'

I was conscious of a growing embarrassment. A little more of this, I felt, and he would elicit the fact that his betrothed had once been very near to Bertram—a dashed sight nearer, as we have seen, than Bertram had liked: and no recently engaged bimbo cares to discover that he was not the little woman's first choice. It sort of rubs the bloom off the thing. What he wants to feel is that she spent her time gazing out of the turret window in a yearning spirit till he came galloping up on the white horse.

I temporized, accordingly. I believe the word is 'temporized'. I should have to check up with Jeeves.

'Her ghastly father married my frightful aunt.'

'Is Lady Worplesdon your aunt?'

'And how!'

'You didn't know her before that?'

'Well, yes. Slightly.'

'I see.'

He was still giving me that searching look, like a G-man hobnobbing with a suspect, and I am not ashamed to confess that I wiped a bead of persp. from the brow with the ferule of my umbrella. That embarrassment, to which I have referred, was still up and doing—in fact, more so than ever.

I could see now what I had failed to spot before, that in thinking of him as a Romeo I had made an incorrect diagnosis. The bird whose name ought to have sprung to my mind was Othello. In this Cheesewright, it was plain, I had run up against one of those touchy lovers who go about the place in a suspicious and red-eyed spirit, eager to hammer the stuffing out of such of the citizenry as they suppose to be or to have been in any sense matey with the adored object. It would, in short, require but a sketchy outline of the facts relating to self and Florence to unleash the cave man within him.

'When I say "slightly",' I hastened to add, 'I mean, of course, that we were just acquaintances.'

'Just acquaintances, eh?'

'Just.'

'You simply happened to meet her once or twice?'

'That's right. You put it in a nutshell.'

'I see. The reason I ask is that it seemed to me, when I told you she was engaged to me, that your manner was peculiar—'

'It always is before lunch.'

'You started—'

'Touch of cramp.'

'And uttered an exclamation. As if the news had come as an unpleasant shock to you.'

'Oh, no.'

'You're sure it didn't?'

'Not a bit.'

'In fact, you were mere acquaintances?'

'Mere to the core.'

'Still, it's strange that she has never mentioned you.'

'Well, pip-pip,' I said, changing the subject, and withdrew.

4

It was a grave and thoughtful Bertram Wooster who started to amble back to the old flat. I was feeling a bit weak, too. During the recent scene I had run the gamut of the emotions, as I believe it is called, and that always takes it out of one.

My first reaction to Stilton's revelation had, as I have indicated, been relief, and of course I was still rolling the eyes up to Heaven in silent thankfulness a goodish bit. But it is seldom that the Woosters think only of self, and I now found the contemplation of the dreadful thing which had come upon this man filling me almost to the brim with pity and terror. It seemed to me that a Save Stilton Cheesewright movement ought to be got under way immediately. For though he wasn't what you would call absolutely one of my bosom pals, like Boko Fittleworth, one has one's human feelings. I remembered how the iron had entered into my gizzard when I was faced with the prospect of being led to the altar by Florence Craye.

One could see, of course, how the tragedy had occurred. It was the poor blister's pathetic desire to do his soul a bit of good that had landed him in this awful predicament. As is so often the case with these stolid, beefy birds, he had always had a yearning for higher things.

This whole business of jacking up the soul is one that varies according to what Jeeves calls the psychology of the individual, some being all for it, others not. You take me, for instance. I don't say I've got much of a soul, but, such as it is, I'm perfectly satisfied with the little chap. I don't want people fooling about with it. 'Leave it alone,' I say. 'Don't touch it. I like it the way it is.'

But with Stilton it was different. Buttonhole him and offer to give his soul a shot in the arm, and you found in him a receptive audience and a disciple ready to try anything once. Florence must have seemed to him just what the doctor ordered, and he had probably quite enjoyed thumbing the pages of 'Types of Ethical Theory', feeling, no doubt, that this was the stuff to give the troops.

But—and this was the reflection that furrowed the brow—how long would this last? I mean to say, he might be liking the set-up, but, as I saw it, the time would come when he would examine his soul, note how it had sprouted and say, 'Fine. That's enough to be going on with. Let's call it a day,' only to discover that he was inextricably entangled with a girl who had merely started. It was from this fate, which is sometimes called the bitter awakening, that I wanted to rescue him.

How to do it was, of course, a problem, and many chaps in my place would, I suppose, have been nonplussed. But my brain was working like a buzz saw this morning, and the two snifters at the Bollinger had put a keen edge on it. By the time I was latch-keying my way into the flat I had placed my finger on the solution. The thing to do, I saw, was to write a strong note to Nobby Hopwood, outlining the situation and urging her to draw Stilton aside and make it quite clear to him what he was up against. Nobby, I reasoned, had known Florence since she was so high, and would consequently be in a position to assemble all the talking points.

Still, just in case she might have overlooked any of them, I carefully pointed out in my communication all Florence's defects, considered not only as a prospective bride but as a human being. I put my whole heart into the thing, and it was with an agreeable feeling of duty done and a kindly act accomplished that I took it round the corner and dropped it in the pillar box.

When I got back, I found Jeeves once more in residence. He had returned from his mission and was fooling about at some domestic task in the dining-room. I gave him a hail, and he floated in.

'Jeeves,' I said, 'you remember Mr Cheesewright, who called this morning?'

'Yes, sir.'

'I ran into him just now, buying an engagement ring. He is betrothed.'

'Indeed, sir?'

'Yes. And do you know who to? Lady F. Craye.'

'Indeed, sir?'

We exchanged a meaning glance. Or, rather, two meaning glances, I giving him one and he giving me the other. There was no need for words. Jeeves is familiar with every detail of the Wooster—Craye imbroglio, having been constantly at my side right through that critical period in my affairs. As a matter of fact, as I have recorded elsewhere in the archives, it was he who got me out of the thing.

'And what's so poignant, Jeeves, if that's the word I want, is that he seems to like it.'

'Indeed, sir?'

'Yes. Rather pleased about it all than otherwise, it struck me. It reminded me of those lines in the poem—"See how the little how-does-it-go tum tumty tiddly push." Perhaps you remember the passage?'

'"Alas, regardless of their fate, the little victims play," sir.'

'Quite. Sad, Jeeves.'

'Yes, sir.'

'He must be saved from himself, of course, and fortunately I have the situation well in hand. I have taken all the necessary steps, and anticipate a happy and successful issue. And now,' I said, turning to the other matter on the agenda paper, 'tell me about Uncle Percy. You saw him?'

'Yes, sir.'

'Was he in the market for aid and counsel?'

'Yes, sir.'

'I knew I was right. What was it? Blackmail? Does he want you to pinch damaging correspondence from the peroxided? Has some quick-thinking adventuress got him in her toils?'

'Oh, no, sir. I am sure his lordship's private life is above reproach.'

I weighed this in the light of the known facts.

'I'm not so dashed sure about that. It depends what you call above reproach. He once chased me over a measured mile, showing great accuracy with the hunting crop. At a moment, too, when, being half-way through my first cigar, I was in urgent need of quiet and repose. To my mind, a man capable of that would be capable of anything. Well, if it wasn't blackmail, what was the trouble?'

'His lordship finds himself in a somewhat difficult position, sir.'

'What's biting him?'

He did not reply for a space. A wooden expression had crept into his features, and his eyes had taken on the look of cautious reserve which you see in those of parrots, when offered half a banana by a stranger of whose *bona fides* they are not convinced. It meant that he had come over all discreet, as he sometimes does, and I hastened to assure him that he might speak freely.

'You know me, Jeeves. The silent tomb.'

'The matter is highly confidential, sir. It should not be allowed to go further.'

'Wild horses shall not drag it from me. Not that I suppose they'll try.'

'Well, then, sir, his lordship informs me that he is in the process of concluding the final details of a business agreement of great delicacy and importance.'

'And he wanted you to vet the thing for snags?'

'Not precisely that, sir. But he desired my advice.'

'They all come to you, Jeeves, don't they—from the lowest to the highest?'

'It is kind of you to say so, sir.'

'Did he mention what the b. a. of great d. and i. was?'

'No, sir. But, of course, one has read the papers.'

'I haven't.'

'You do not study the financial pages, sir?'

'Never give them a glance.'

'They have been devoting considerable space of late to rumours of a merger or combination which is said to be impending between his lordship's Pink Funnel Line and an equally prominent shipping firm of the United States of America, sir. It is undoubtedly to this that his lordship was guardedly alluding.'

The information did not make me leap about to any extent.

'Going to team up, are they, these nautical tycoons?'

'So it is supposed, sir.'

'Well, God bless them.'

'Yes, sir.'

'I mean, why shouldn't they?'

'Exactly, sir.'

'Well, what's his difficulty?'

'A somewhat tense situation has arisen, sir. The negotiations would appear to have arrived at a point where it is essential that his lordship shall meet and confer with the gentleman conducting the pourparlers on behalf of the American organization. On the other hand, it is vital that he shall not be seen in the latter's society, for such a meeting would instantly be accepted in the City as conclusive proof that the fusion of interests was about to take place, with immediate reactions on the respective shares of the two concerns.'

I began to see daylight. There have been mornings, after some rout or revel at the Drones, when this sort of thing would merely have caused the head to throb, but to-day, as I have said, I was feeling exceptionally bright.

'They would go up, you mean?'

'A sharp rise would be inevitable, sir.'

'And Uncle Percy views such a prospect with concern?'

'Yes, sir.'

'His idea being to collect a parcel cheap before the many-headed can horn in and spoil the market?'

'Precisely, sir. *Rem acu tetigisti*.'

'*Rem*—?'

'*Acu tetigisti*, sir. A Latin expression. Literally, it means "You have touched the matter with a needle," but a more idiomatic rendering would be—'

'Put my finger on the nub?'

'Exactly, sir.'

'Yes, I get it now. You have clarified the situation. Getting right down to it, these two old buzzards have got to foregather in secret and require a hideout.'

'Precisely, sir. And, of course, the movements of both gentlemen are being closely watched by representatives of the financial press.'

'I suppose this mystic sort of stuff goes on all the time in the world of commerce?'

'Yes, sir.'

'One understands and sympathizes.'

'Yes, sir.'

'Though one dislikes the idea of Uncle Percy getting any richer. Already, he has the stuff in gobs. However, bearing in mind the fact that he is an uncle by marriage, I suppose one ought to espouse his cause. Had you anything to suggest?'

'Yes, sir.'

'I bet you had.'

'It occurred to me that such a meeting might well take place unobserved, if the two parties were to arrange to come together beneath the roof of some remote country cottage.'

I mused.

'You mean a cottage in the country somewhere?'

'You have interpreted me exactly, sir.'

'I don't think much of that, Jeeves. You must be losing your grip.'

'Sir?'

'Well, to name but one objection, how can you go to the owner of a country cottage, whom you don't know from Adam, and ask him to let you and your pals plot in the parlour?'

'It would be necessary, of course, that the proprietor of the establishment should be no stranger to his lordship.'

'He would have to be somebody who knew Uncle Percy, you mean?'

'Precisely, sir.'

'But, Jeeves, my dear old soul, don't you see that that makes it still worse? Use the bean. In that case, the chap says to himself, "Hullo! Old Worplesdon having secret meetings with mystery men? Come, come, what's all this? I'll bet this means that that merger I've been reading about so much is going to come off." And he nips out and phones his broker to start buying those shares and to keep on buying till he's blue in the face. Thus wrecking all Uncle Percy's carefully laid plans and rendering him sicker than mud. You follow me, Jeeves?'

'Completely, sir. I had not overlooked that contingency. The occupant of the cottage would, of course, have to be some gentleman whom his lordship could trust.'

'Such as—?'

'Well, yourself, sir.'

'But—sorry to have to rub it in like this, but it's only kind to remove the scales from your eyes—I haven't got a cottage.'

'Yes, sir.'

'I don't get you, Jeeves.'

'His lordship is placing one of his own at your disposal, sir. He instructed me to say that he wishes you to proceed to-morrow to Steeple Bumpleigh—'

'Steeple Bumpleigh!'

'— where you will find a small but compact residence awaiting you, in perfect condition for immediate occupation. It is delightfully situated not far from the river—'

It needed no more than that word 'river' to tell me what had occurred. On his good mornings, I don't suppose there are more than a handful of men in the W.1 postal district of London swifter to spot oompus-boompus than Bertram Wooster, and this was one of my particularly good mornings. I saw the whole hideous plot.

'Jeeves,' I said, 'you have done the dirty on me.'

'I am sorry, sir. It seemed the only solution of his lordship's problem. I feel sure, sir, that when you see the residence in question, your prejudice against Steeple Bumpleigh will be overcome. I speak, of course, only from hearsay, but I understand from his lordship that it is replete with every modern convenience. It contains one large master's bedroom, a well-appointed sitting-room, water both hot and cold—'

'The usual domestic offices?' I said. And I meant it to sting.

'Yes, sir. Furthermore, you will be quite adjacent to Mr Fittleworth.'

'And you will be quite adjacent to your fish.'

'Why, yes, sir. The point had not occurred to me, but now that you mention it that is certainly so. I should find a little fishing most enjoyable, if you could spare me from time to time while we are at Wee Nooke.'

'Did you say "Wee Nooke"?'

'Yes, sir.'

'Spelled, I'll warrant, with an "e"?'

'Yes, sir.'

I breathed heavily through the nostrils.

'Well, listen to me, Jeeves. The thing's off. You understand? Off. Spelled with an o and two f's. I'm dashed if I'm going to be made a—what's the word?'

'Sir?'

'Catspaw. Though why catspaw? I mean, what have cats got to do with it?'

'The expression derives from the old story of the cat, the monkey and the chestnuts, sir. It appears—'

'Skip it, Jeeves. This is no time for chewing the fat about the animal kingdom. And if it's the story about where the monkey puts the nuts, I know it and it's very vulgar. Getting back to the *res*, I absolutely, positively and totally refuse to go to Steeple Bumpleigh.'

'Well, of course, sir, it is perfectly open to you to adopt the attitude you indicate, but—'

He paused, massaging the chin. I saw his point.

'Uncle Percy would look askance, you mean?'

'Yes, sir.'

'And might report the matter to Aunt Agatha?'

'Precisely, sir. And her ladyship, when incensed, can be noticeably unpleasant.'

'*Rem acu tetigisti*,' I said, moodily. 'All right, start packing.'

5

It has been well said of Bertram Wooster by those who enjoy his close acquaintance that if there is one quality more than another that distinguishes him, it is his ability to keep the lip stiff and upper and make the best of things. Though crushed to earth, as the expression is, he rises again—not absolutely in mid-season form, perhaps, but perkier than you would expect and with an eye alert for silver linings.

Waking next morning to another day and thumbing the bell for the cup of tea, I found myself, though still viewing the future with concern, considerably less down among the wines and spirits than I had been yestreen. The flesh continued to creep briskly at the thought of entering the zone of influence of Uncle Percy and loved ones, but I was able to discern one reasonably brightish spot in the set-up.

'You did say, Jeeves,' I said, touching on this as he entered with the steaming Bohea, 'that Aunt Agatha would not be at Steeple Bumpleigh to greet me on my arrival?'

'Yes, sir. Her ladyship expects to be absent for some little time.'

'If she's going to remain with young Thos till they've demumped him, it may well be that she will be away during the whole of my sojourn.'

'Quite conceivably, sir.'

'That is a substantial bit of goose.'

'Yes, sir. And I am happy to be able to indicate another. In the course of her visit yesterday, Miss Hopwood mentioned a fancy dress ball which, it appears, is to take place at East Wibley, the market town adjacent to Steeple Bumpleigh. You will enjoy that, sir.'

'I shall, indeed,' I assented, for as a dancer I out-Fred the nimblest Astaire, and fancy dress binges have always been my dish. 'When does it come to a head?'

'To-morrow night, I understand, sir.'

'Well, I must say this has brightened the horizon considerably. When I have breakfasted, I will go out and buy a costume. Sindbad the Sailor, don't you think?'

'That should prove most effective, sir.'

'Not forgetting the ginger whiskers that go with it.'

'Precisely, sir. They are of the essence.'

'If you've finished the packing, you can cram it into the small suitcase.'

'Very good, sir.'

'We'll drive down, of course.'

'Possibly it would be best, sir, if I were to make the journey by train.'

'A bit haughty, this exclusiveness, is it not, Jeeves?'

'I should have mentioned, sir, that Miss Hopwood rang up, hoping that you would be able to accommodate her in your car. Assuming that I should be falling in with your wishes in doing so, I took the responsibility of replying that you would be quite agreeable.'

'I see. Yes, that's all right.'

'Her ladyship has also telephoned.'

'Aunt Agatha?'

'Yes, sir.'

'No rot, I trust, about having changed her mind and decided not to rally round young Thos?'

'Oh, no, sir. It was merely to leave a message, saying that she wishes you to call in at Aspinall's in Bond Street before you leave, and secure a brooch which she purchased there yesterday.'

'She does, does she? Why me?' I asked, speaking with a touch of acerbity, for I rather resented this seeming inability on the relative's part to distinguish between a nephew and a district messenger boy.

'I understand that the trinket is a present for Lady Florence, sir, who is celebrating her birthday to-day. Her ladyship wishes you to convey it to its destination personally, realizing that, should she entrust it to the ordinary channels, the gift will be delayed in its arrival beyond the essential date.'

'You mean, if she posts it, it won't get there in time?'

'Precisely, sir.'

'I see. Yes, there's something in that.'

'Her ladyship appeared a little dubious as to your ability to carry through the commission without mishap—'

'Ho!'

'—but I assured her that it was well within your scope.'

'I should think so,' I said, piqued. I balanced a thoughtful lump of sugar on the teaspoon. 'So it's Lady Florence's birthday, is it?' I said, pondering. 'This opens up a social problem on which I should be glad to have your opinion. Ought I to weigh in with a present?'

'No, sir.'

'Not necessary, you think?'

'No, sir. Not after what has occurred.'

I was glad to hear him say so. I mean, while one wants on all occasions to do the *preux* thing, it is a tricky business, this bestowing of gifts, and apt to put ideas into a girl's head. Coming on top of 'Spindrift' and Spinoza, the merest bottle of scent at this juncture might well have set such a seal upon my glamour as to cause the beasel to decide to return Stilton to store and make other arrangements.

'Well, I defer to your judgement, Jeeves. No present for La Craye, then.'

'No, sir.'

'But, while on this subject, we shall shortly have to be nosing round for one for La Hopwood.'

'Sir?'

'A wedding gift. She's gone and got engaged to Boko Fittleworth.'

'Indeed, sir? I am sure I wish the young lady and gentleman every happiness.'

'Well spoken, Jeeves. Me, too. The projected union, I may say at once, is one that has my complete approval. Which is not always the case when a pal puts the banns up.'

'No, sir.'

'Too often on such occasions one feels, as I feel so strongly with regard to poor old Stilton, that the kindly thing to do would be to seize the prospective bridegroom's trousers in one's teeth and draw him back from danger, as faithful dogs do to their masters on the edge of precipices on dark nights.'

'Yes, sir.'

'But in the present case I have no such misgivings. Each of the contracting parties, in my opinion, has picked a winner, and it is with a light heart that I shall purchase the necessary fish slice. I am even prepared, if desired, to be best man and make a speech at the wedding breakfast, and one cannot say more than that.'

'No, sir.'

'Right ho, Jeeves,' I said, flinging back the bedclothes and rising from the couch. 'Unchain the eggs and bacon. I will be with you in a moment.'

After I had broken the fast and smoked a soothing cigarette, I sallied forth, for I had a busy morning before me. I popped in at Aspinall's and pocketed the brooch, and thence repaired to the establishment of the Cohen Bros. in Covent Garden, well known among the cognoscenti as the Mecca for the discriminating seeker after fancy dress costumes. They were fortunately able to supply me with the required Sindbad, the last they had in stock, and a visit to a near-by theatrical wiggery put me in possession of an admirable set of ginger whiskers, thus giving me a full hand.

The car was at the door on my return, a suitcase of feminine aspect in its rumble. This seemed to indicate that Nobby had arrived, and as I had expected I found her in the sitting-room, sipping a refresher.

It having been some considerable time since we had foregathered, there ensued, of course, a certain period of leaping about and fraternizing. Then, having put away a refresher myself, I escorted her to the car and bunged her in. Jeeves, following my instructions, had placed the small suitcase with the Sindbad in it beneath the front seat, so that it should be under my personal eye, and we were thus all set. I trod on the self-starter and we began the journey, Jeeves standing on the pavement, seeing us off like an archbishop blessing pilgrims, his air that of one who would shortly be following by train with the heavy luggage.

Though sorry to be deprived of this right-hand man's society, for his conversation always tends to elevate and instruct, I was glad to get Nobby alone. I wanted to hear all about this pending merger with Boko. Each being a valued member of my entourage, the news that they were affianced had interested me strangely.

I am never much of a lad for chatting in traffic, and until I had eased the vehicle out of the congested districts I remained strong and silent, the lips tense, the eyes keen. But when we were bowling along the Portsmouth Road, with nothing to distract the attention, I got down to it.

6

So you and Boko are planning to leap in among the orange blossoms?' I said. 'I had the news from Stilton yesterday, and was much stirred.'

'I hope you approve?'

'Thoroughly. Nice work, in my opinion. I think you're both on to a good thing, and would be well advised to push it along with the utmost energy. I have always considered you an extremely sound young potato.'

She thanked me for these kind words, and I assured her that the tribute was well deserved.

'As for Boko,' I proceeded, 'one of the best, of course. I could tell you things about Boko which would drive it well into your nut that you have picked a winner.'

'You don't have to.'

Her voice was soft and tender, like that of a hen crooning over its egg, and it was easy to see that, as far as she was concerned, Cupid's dart had done its stuff. I gave the wheel a twiddle, to avoid a casual dog, and went into my questionnaire. I always like to know all the facts on these occasions.

'When did you arrange this match?'

'About a week ago.'

'But you felt it coming on before that, I take it?'

'Oh, yes. Directly we met.'

'When was that?'

'At the end of May.'

'It was love at first sight, was it?'

'It was.'

'On his side, also?'

'On his side, also.'

Well, I could readily understand Boko falling in love at first sight with Nobby, of course, for she is a girl liberally endowed with oomph. But how she could have fallen in love at first sight with Boko beat me. The first sight of Boko reveals to the beholder an object with a face like an intellectual parrot. Furthermore, as is the case with so many of the younger literati, he dresses like a tramp cyclist, affecting turtleneck sweaters and grey flannel bags with a patch on the knee and conveying a sort of general suggestion of having been left out in the rain overnight in an ash can. The only occasion on which I have ever seen Jeeves really rattled was when he met Boko for the first time. He winced visibly and tottered off to the kitchen, no doubt to pull himself together with cooking sherry.

I mentioned this to Nobby, and she said she knew what I meant.

'You would think he was the sort of man who would have to grow on a girl—gradually, as it were—wouldn't you? But no. There was one startled moment when I wondered if I was seeing things, and then—bang—like a thunderbolt.'

'As quick as that, was it?'

'Yes.'

'And his reactions were similar?'

'Yes.'

'Well, here's something I don't understand. You say you met in May, and we are now in July. Why did he take such a dickens of a time wooing you?'

'He didn't exactly woo me.'

'How do you mean, not exactly? A man either woos or he does not woo. There can be no middle course.'

'There were reasons why he couldn't let himself go.'

'You speak in riddles, young Nobby. Still, so long as he got round to it eventually. And when are the bells going to ring out in the little village church?'

'I don't know if they ever are.'

'Eh?'

'Uncle Percy doesn't seem to think so.'

'What do you mean?'

'He disapproves of the match.'

'What!'

I was astounded. It seemed to me for an instant that she must be pulling the Wooster leg. Then, scrutinizing her closely, I noted that the lips were tight and the brow clouded. This young Hopwood is a blue-eyed little half portion with, normally, an animated dial. The dial to which I refer was now contorted with anguish, as if she had just swallowed a bad oyster.

'You don't mean that?'

'I do.'

'Egad!' I said.

For this was serious. Nobby, you see, was peculiarly situated. As often occurs, I believe, when Girl A becomes the ward of Bloke B, a clause had been inserted in the contract to the effect that there must be no rot about her marrying without the big chief's consent till she was twenty-one or forty-one or something. So if Uncle Percy really had an anti-Boko complex, he was in a position to bung a spanner into the works with no uncertain hand.

I couldn't get it.

'But why? The man must be cuckoo. Boko is one of our most eligible young bachelors. He makes pots of money with his pen. You see his stuff everywhere. That play he had on last year was a substantial hit. And they were saying at the Drones the other day that he's had an offer to go to Hollywood. Has he?'

'Yes.'

'Well, then.'

'Oh, I know all that. But what you're overlooking is the fact that Uncle Percy is the sort of man who is suspicious of writers. He doesn't believe in their solvency. He's been in business all his life, and he can't imagine anybody having any real money except a business man.'

'But he must know Boko's dashed near being a celebrity. He's had his photograph in the *Tatler*.'

'Yes, but Uncle Percy has the idea that an author's success is here to-day and gone to-morrow. Boko may be doing all right now, but he feels that his earning capacity may go phut at any moment. I suppose he pictures himself having to draw him out of the bread line a year or two from now and support him and me and half a dozen little Boko's for the rest of our lives. And then, of course, he was prejudiced against the poor darling from the start.'

'Because of those trousers?'

'They may have helped, perhaps.'

'The man's an ass. Boko's a writer. He must know that writers are allowed a wide latitude. Besides, though I wouldn't care to have Jeeves hear me say so, trousers aren't everything.'

'But the real reason was that he thought Boko was a butterfly.'

I couldn't follow her. She had me fogged. Anything less like a butterfly than good old Boko I've never set eyes on.

'A butterfly?'

'Yes. Flitting from flower to flower and sipping.'

'And he doesn't like butterflies?'

'Not when they flit and sip.'

'What on earth has put the extraordinary idea into his head that Boko's a flitting sipper?'

'Well, you see, when he arrived in Steeple Bumpleigh, he was engaged to Florence.'

'What!'

'It was she who made him settle there. That was what I meant when I said that he couldn't woo me, as you call it, with any real abandon at first. Being engaged to Florence sort of hampered him.'

I was amazed. I nearly ran over a hen in my emotion.

'Engaged to Florence? He never told me.'

'You haven't seen him for some time.'

'No, that's true. Well, I'll be dashed. Did you know that I was once engaged to Florence?'

'Of course.'

'And now Stilton is.'

'Yes.'

'How absolutely extraordinary. It's like one of those great race movements you read about.'

'I suppose it's her profile that does it. She has a lovely profile.'

'Seen from the left.'

'Seen from the right, too.'

'Well, yes, in a measure, seen from the right, too. But would that account for it? I mean, in these busy days you can't spend your whole time dodging round a girl, trying to see her sideways. I still maintain that this tendency on the part of the populace to get engaged to Florence is inexplicable. And that made Uncle Percy a bit frosty to Boko?'

'Glacial.'

'I see. One understands his point of view, of course. He frowns on this in and out running. Florence yesterday, you today. I suppose he thinks you are just another of the flowers that Boko is flitting in on for sipping purposes.'

'I suppose so.'

'And, in addition, he doubts his earning capacity.'

'Yes.'

I pondered. If Uncle Percy really thought that Boko was a butterfly that might go broke at any moment, Love's young dream had unquestionably stubbed its toe. I mean, an oofy butterfly is bad enough. But it can at least pay the rent. I could well imagine a man of conservative views recoiling from one which might come asking for handouts for the rest of its life.

A thought occurred to me. With that Wooster knack of looking on the bright side, I saw that all was not yet lost.

'How old do you have to be before you can marry without Uncle Percy's kayo?'

'Twenty-one.'

'How old are you now?'

'Twenty.'

'Well, there you are, then. I knew that if we looked close enough we should find that the sun was still shining. You've only got to wait another year, and there you are.'

'Yes. But Boko leaves for Hollywood next month. I don't know how you feel about this dream man of mine, but to me, and I have studied his character with loving care, he doesn't seem the sort of person to be allowed to go to Hollywood without a wife at his side to distract his attention from the local fauna.'

Her outlook shocked me, causing me to put a bit of austere top-spin on my next crack.

'There can be no love where there is not perfect trust.'

'Who told you that?'

'Jeeves, I think. It sounds like one of his things.'

'Well, Jeeves is wrong. There jolly well can be love without perfect trust, and don't you forget it. I love Boko distractedly, but at the thought of him going to Hollywood without me I come over all faint. He wouldn't mean to let me down. I don't suppose he would even know he was doing it. But one morning I should get an apologetic cable saying that he couldn't quite explain how it had happened, but that he had inadvertently got married last night, and had I anything to suggest. It's his sweet, impulsive nature. He can't say No. I believe that's how he came to get engaged to Florence.'

I frowned meditatively. Now that she had outlined the position of affairs, I could see that the situation was a tricky one.

'Then what's the procedure?'

'I don't know.'

I frowned another meditative one.

'Something must be done.'

'But what?'

I had an idea. It is often like that with the Woosters. They appear baffled, and then suddenly—*bingo!*—an inspiration.

'Leave this to me,' I said.

What had crossed my mind was the thought that by establishing myself at Wee Nooke on his behalf, I was doing Uncle Percy a dashed good turn—so dashed that if he had a spark of gratitude in his composition he ought to be all over me. I could picture him clasping my hand and saying that thanks to me that merger had come off and was there any reward I cared to ask, for he could deny me nothing.

'What you need here,' I said, 'is the suave intervention of a polished man of the world, a silver-tongued orator who will draw Uncle Percy aside and plead your cause, softening his heart and making him take the big, broad view. I'll attend to it.'

'You?'

'In person. Within the next day or two.'

'Oh, Bertie!'

'It will be a pleasure to put in a word for you. I anticipate notable results. I shall probably play on the old crumb as on a stringed instrument.'

She registered girlish joy.

'Bertie, you're a lamb!'

'Maybe you're right. A touch of the lamb, perhaps.'

'It's a wonderful idea. You see, you've known Boko so long.'

'Virtually from the egg.'

'You'll be able to think of all sorts of things to say about him. Did he ever save your life, when you were a boy?'

'Not that I remember.'

'You could say he did.'

'I doubt if it would go well. Uncle Percy was none too keen on me at that epoch. It would be more likely to strike a chord if I told him that Boko had repeatedly tried to assassinate me, when I was a boy. However, leave it to me. I'll find words.'

All this while, of course, the old two-seater had been humming along towards Steeple Bumpleigh with the needle in the sixties, and at this point Nobby notified me that we were approaching our destination.

'Those chimneys through the trees are the Hall. You see that little lane to the left. You go down it, and you come to Boko's place. Yours is about half a mile beyond it, up another sort of side turning. You really will plead with Uncle Percy?'

'Like billy-o.'

'You won't weaken?'

'Not a chance.'

'Of course, it's just possible that you may not have to. You see, I thought that if Boko and Uncle Percy could really get together, Uncle Percy might learn to love him. So, though it wasn't easy, I arranged that Boko should give him lunch to-day. I do hope everything has gone all right. A lot depends on how Boko behaved. I mean, up till now, whenever they have met, he has always been so stiff in his manner. I begged him with tears in my eyes to let himself go and be bright and genial, and he promised he would try. So I'm hoping for the best.'

'Me, too,' I said, and—if I remember correctly—patted her little hand. I then drove to the Hall and decanted her at its gates, assuring her that, even if Boko had failed to fascinate at the midday meal, I would see to it that everything came out all right. With a final cheery wave of the hand, I backed the car and headed for the lane of which she had spoken.

All this talking had, of course, left me with a well defined thirst, and it seemed to me, despite a householder's natural desire to take possession as soon as possible, that my first move had better be to stop off at Boko's and touch him for the needful. I assumed that the whitewashed cottage standing on the river bank must be the Bokeries, for Nobby had indicated that I had to pass it on my way to Wee Nooke.

I hove to alongside, accordingly, and noting that one of the windows at the side was open I approached it and whistled.

A hoarse shout from within and a small china ornament whizzing past my head informed me that my old friend was at home.

7

The passing of the china ornament, which had come within an ace of copping me on the napper, drew from my lips a sharp 'Oi!' and as if in answer to the cry Boko now appeared at the window. His hair was disordered and his face flushed, presumably with literary composition. In appearance, as I have indicated, this man of letters is a cross between a comedy juggler and a parrot that has been dragged through a hedge backwards, and you never catch him at his nattiest in the workshop. I took it that I had interrupted him at a difficult point in a chapter.

He had been glaring at me through horn-rimmed spectacles, but now, as he perceived who it was that stood without, the flame faded behind the lenses, to be replaced by a look of astonishment.

'Good Lord, Bertie! Is that you?'

I assured him that such was the case, and he apologized for having bunged china ornaments at me.

'Why did you imitate the note of the lesser screech owl?' he said, rebukingly. 'I thought you were young Edwin. He comes sneaking round here, trying to do me acts of kindness, and that is always how he announces his presence. I am never without a certain amount of ammunition handy on the desk. Where on earth did you spring from?'

'The metropolis. I've just arrived.'

'Well, you might have had the sense to send a wire. I'd have killed the fatted calf.'

I saw that he was under a misapprehension.

'I haven't come to stay with you. I'm hanging out at a cottage which they tell me is a little farther down the road.'

'Wee Nooke?'

'That's right.'

'Have you taken Wee Nooke?'

'Yes.'

'What made you suddenly decide to do that?'

I had foreseen that some explanation of my presence might be required, and was ready with my story. My lips being sealed, of course, on the real reason which had brought me to Steeple Bumpleigh, it was necessary to dissemble.

'Jeeves thought he would like to do a bit of fishing. And,' I added, making the thing more plausible, 'they tell me a fancy dress dance is breaking out in these parts to-morrow night. Well, you know me when I hear rumours of these entertainments. The war horse and the bugle. And now,' I said, licking the lips, 'how about a cooling drink? The journey has left me a little parched.'

I climbed through the window, and sank into a chair, while he went off to fetch the ingredients. Presently he returned with the jingling tray, and after we had done a bit of stag-at-eve-ing and exchanged some desultory remarks about this and that, I did the civil thing by congratulating him on his engagement.

'I was saying to Nobby, whom I drove down here in my car, how extraordinary it was that any girl should have fallen in love with you at first sight. I wouldn't have thought it could be done.'

'It came as quite a surprise to me, too. You could have knocked me down with a feather.'

'I don't wonder. Still, all sorts of unlikely people do seem to excite the spark of passion. Look at my Aunt Agatha.'

'Ah.'

'And Stilton.'

'You know about Stilton?'

'I ran into him in a jeweller's, buying the ring, and he told me of his fearful predicament.'

'Sooner him than me.'

'Just how I feel. Nobby thinks it's Florence's profile that does it.'

'Quite possibly.'

There was a silence, broken only by the musical sound of us having another go at the elixir. Then he heaved a sigh and said that life was rummy, to which I assented that in many respects it was very rummy.

'Take my case,' he said. 'Did Nobby tell you what the position was?'

'About Uncle Percy gumming the works, you mean? Oh, rather.'

'A nice bit of box fruit, what?'

'So it struck me. Decidedly. The heart bled.'

'Fancy having to get anyone's consent to your getting married in this enlightened age! The thing's an anachronism. Why, you can't use it as a motive for a story even in a woman's magazine nowadays. Doesn't your Aunt Dahlia run some sort of women's rag?'

'"Milady's Boudoir". Sixpence weekly. I once contributed an article to it on What the Well-Dressed Man is Wearing.'

'Well, I've never read "Milady's Boudoir", but I have no doubt it is the lowest dregs of the publishing world. Yet if I were to submit a story to your aunt about a girl who couldn't marry a fellow without some blasted head of the family's consent, she would hoot at it. That is to say, I am not allowed to turn an honest penny by using this complication in my work, but it is jolly well allowed to come barging in and ruining my life. A pretty state of things!'

'What happens if you go ahead regardless?'

'I believe I get jugged. Or is that only when you marry a ward in Chancery without the Lord Chancellor hoisting the All Right flag?'

'You have me there. We could ask Jeeves.'

'Yes, Jeeves would know. Have you brought him?'

'He's following with the heavy luggage.'

'How is he these days?'

'Fine.'

'Brain all right?'

'Colossal.'

'Then he may be able to think of some way out of this mess.'

'We shan't need Jeeves. I am handling the whole thing. I'm going to get hold of Uncle Percy and plead your cause.'

'You?'

'Oddly enough, that's what Nobby said. In the same surprised tone.'

'But I thought the man scared you stiff.'

'He does. But I've been able to do him a good turn, and my drag with him is now substantial.'

'Well, that's fine,' he said, brightening. 'Snap into it, Bertie. But,' he added, coming unbrightened again, 'you've got a tough job.'

'Oh, I don't know.'

'I do. After what happened at lunch to-day.'

I was conscious of a sudden, quick concern.

'Your lunch with Uncle Percy?'

'That's the one.'

'Didn't it go well?'

'Not too well.'

'Nobby was anticipating that it would bring home the bacon.'

'Ha! God bless her optimistic little soul.'

I gave him one of my keen looks. There was a sombre expression on his map. The nose was wiggling in an overwrought way. It was easy to perceive that pain and anguish racked the brow.

'Tell me all,' I said.

He unshipped a heavy sigh.

'You know, Bertie, the whole idea was a mistake from the start. She should never have brought us together. And, if she had to bring us together, she ought not to have told me to be bright and genial. You know about her wanting me to be bright and genial?'

'Yes. She said you were inclined to be a bit stiff in your manner with Uncle Percy.'

'I am always stiff in my manner with elderly gentlemen who snort like foghorns when I appear and glare at me as if I were somebody from Moscow distributing Red propaganda. It's the sensitive, highly strung artist in me. Old Hardened Arteries does not like me.'

'So Nobby said. She thinks it's because he regards you as a butterfly. My personal view is that it's those grey flannel bags of yours.'

'What's wrong with them?'

'The patch on the knee, principally. It creates a bad impression. Haven't you another pair?'

'Who do you think I am? Beau Brummel?'

I forbore to pursue the subject.

'Well, go on.'

'Where was I?'

'You were saying you made a bloomer in trying to be bright and genial.'

'Ah, yes. That's right. I did. And this is how it came about. You see, the first thing a man has to ask himself, when he is told to be bright and genial, is "How bright? How genial?" Shall he, that is to say, be just a medium ray of sunshine, or shall he go all out and shoot the works? I thought it over, and decided to bar nothing and be absolutely rollicking. And that, I see now, is where I went wrong.'

He paused, and remained for a space in thought. I could see that some painful memory was engaging his attention.

'I wonder, Bertie,' he said, coming to the surface at length, 'if you were present one day at the Drones when Freddie Widgeon sprang those Joke Goods on the lunchers there?'

'Joke Goods?'

'The things you see advertised in toy-shop catalogues as handy for breaking the ice and setting the table in a roar. You know. The Plate Lifter. The Dribble Glass. The Surprise Salt Shaker.'

'Oh, those?'

I laughed heartily. I remembered the occasion well. Catsmeat Potter-Pirbright was suffering from a hangover at the moment, and I shall not readily forget his emotion when he picked up his roll and it squeaked and a rubber mouse ran out of it. Strong men had to rally round with brandy.

And then I stopped laughing heartily. The frightful significance of his words hit me, and I started as if somebody had jabbed a red-hot skewer through the epidermis.

'You aren't telling me you worked those off on Uncle Percy?'

'Yes, Bertie. That is what I did.'

'Golly!'

'That about covers it.'

I groaned a hollow one. The heart had sunk. One has, of course, to make allowances for writers, all of them being more or less loony. Look at Shakespeare, for instance. Very unbalanced. Used to go about stealing ducks. Nevertheless, I couldn't help feeling that in springing Joke Goods on the guardian of the girl he loved Boko had carried an author's natural goofiness too far. Even Shakespeare might have hesitated to go to such lengths.

'But why?'

'I suppose the idea at the back of my mind was that I ought to show him my human side.'

'Did he take it big?'

'Pretty big.'

'He didn't like it?'

'No. I can answer that question without reservation. He did not like it.'

'Has he forbidden you the house?'

'You don't have to forbid people houses after looking at them as he looked at me over the Surprise Salt Shaker. The language of the eyes is enough. Do you know the Surprise Salt Shaker? You joggle it, and out comes a spider. The impression I received was that he was allergic to spiders.'

I rose. I had heard enough.

'I'll be pushing along,' I said, rather faintly.

'What's your hurry?'

'I ought to be going to Wee Nooke. Jeeves will be arriving at any moment with the luggage, and I shall have to get settled in.'

'I see. I would come with you, only I am in the act of composing a well-expressed letter of apology to my Lord Worplesdon. I had better finish it, though it may not be needed, if all you say about being in a position to plead with him is true. Plead well, Bertie. Pitch it strong. Let the golden phrases come rolling out like honey. For, as I say, I don't think you've got an easy job on your hands. Eloquence beyond the ordinary will be required. And, by the way. Not a word to Nobby about that lunch. The facts will have to be broken to her gently and by degrees, if at all.'

My mood, as I set a course for Wee Nooke, was, as you may well suppose, a good deal less effervescent than it had been. The idea of pleading with Uncle Percy had lost practically all its fascination.

There rose before me a vision of this relative by marriage, as he would probably appear directly I mentioned Boko's name—the eyes glaring, the moustache bristling and the *tout ensemble* presenting a strong resemblance to a short-tempered tiger of the jungle which has just seen its peasant shin up a tree. And while it would be going too far, perhaps, to say that Bertram Wooster shuddered, a certain coolness of the feet unquestionably existed.

I was trying to hold the thought that, once that merger had gone through, joy would most likely reign so supreme that the old bounder would look even on Boko with the eye of kindliness, when there came the ting of a bicycle bell, and a voice called my name, Woostering with such vehemence that I immediately braked the car and glanced round. The sight I saw smote me like a blow.

Heaving alongside was Stilton Cheesewright, and on his face, as he alighted from his bicycle and confronted me, there was about as unpleasant a look as ever caught me in the eyeball. It was a look pregnant with amazement and hostility. A Gorblimey-what's-this-blighter-doing-here look. The sort of look, in fine, which the heroine of a pantomime gives the Demon King when he comes popping up out of a trap at her elbow. And I could follow what was passing in his mind as clearly as if it had been broadcast on a nation-wide hook-up.

All along, I had been far from comfortable when speculating as to what this Othello's reactions would be on discovering me in the neighbourhood. The way in which he had received the information that I was an old acquaintance of Florence's had shown that his thoughts had been given a morbid turn, causing him to view Bertram with suspicion, and I had been afraid that he was going to place an unfortunate construction on my sudden arrival in her vicinity. It was almost inevitable, I mean, that the thing should smack, in his view, far too strongly of Young Lochinvar coming out of the West. And, of course, my lips being sealed, I couldn't explain.

A delicate and embarrassing situation.

And yet, amazing though you will find the statement, what was causing me to goggle at him with saucer eyes was not this look that told me that my fears had been well founded, but the fact that the face attached to it was topped by a policeman's helmet. The burly frame, moreover, was clad in a policeman's uniform, and on the feet one noted the regulation official boots or beetle crushers which go to complete the panoply of the awful majesty of the Law.

In a word, Stilton Cheesewright had suddenly turned into a country copper, and I could make nothing of it.

8

I started at the man.

'Stap my vitals, Stilton,' I cried, in uncontrollable astonishment. 'Why the fancy dress?'

He, too, had a question to ask.

'What the hell are you doing here, you bloodstained Wooster?'

I held up a hand. This was no time for side issues.

'Why are you got up like a policeman?'

'I am a policeman.'

'A policeman?'

'Yes.'

'When you say "policeman",' I queried, groping, 'do you mean "policeman"?'

'Yes.'

'You're a policeman?'

'Yes, blast you. Are you deaf? I'm a policeman.'

I grasped it now. He was a policeman. And, my mind flashing back to yesterday's encounter in the jewellery bin, I realized what had made his manner furtive and evasive when I had asked him what he did at Steeple Bumpleigh. He had shrunk from revealing the truth, fearing lest I might be funny at his expense—as, indeed, I would have been, extraordinarily funny. Even now, though the gravity of the situation forbade their utterance, I was thinking of at least three priceless cracks I could make.

'What about it? Why shouldn't I be a policeman?'

'Oh, rather.'

'Half the men you know go into the police nowadays.'

I nodded. This was undoubtedly true. Since they started that College at Hendon, the Force has become congested with one's old buddies. I remember Barmy Fotheringay-Phipps describing to me with gestures his emotions on being pinched in Leicester Square one Boat Race night by his younger brother George. And much the same thing happened to Freddie Widgeon at Hurst Park in connection with his cousin Cyril.

'Yes,' I said, spotting a flaw, 'but in London.'

'Not necessarily.'

'With the idea of getting into Scotland Yard and rising to great heights in their profession.'

'That's what I'm going to do.'

'Get into Scotland Yard?'

'Yes.'

'Rise to great heights?'

'Yes.'

'Well, I shall watch your future progress with considerable interest,' I said.

But I spoke dubiously. At Eton, Stilton had been Captain of the Boats, and he had also rowed assiduously for Oxford. His entire formative years, therefore, as you might say, had been spent in dipping an oar into the water, giving it a shove and hauling it out again. Only a pretty dumb brick would fritter away his golden youth doing that sort of thing—which, in addition to being silly, is also the deuce of a sweat—and Stilton Cheesewright was a pretty dumb brick. A fine figure of a young fellow as far northwards as the neck, but above that solid concrete. I could not see him as a member of the Big Four. Far more likely that he would end up as one of those Scotland Yard bunglers who used, if you remember, always to be getting into Sherlock Holmes's hair.

However, I didn't say so. As a matter of fact, I didn't say anything, for I was too busy pondering on this new and unforeseen development. I was profoundly thankful that Jeeves had voted against my giving Florence a birthday present. Such a gift, if Stilton heard of it, would have led to his tearing me limb from limb or, at the best, summoning me for failing to abate a smoky chimney. You can't be too careful how you stir up policemen.

I had succeeded in sidetracking his question for a space, but I knew that the respite would be merely temporary. They train these cops to stick to the point. I was not surprised, therefore, when he now repeated it. I'm not saying I didn't wish he hadn't. All I'm saying is that I wasn't surprised.

'Well, to blazes with all that. You haven't told me what you are doing in Steeple Bumpleigh.'

I temporized.

'Oh, just making a passing sojourn,' I said nonchalantly, the old, careless Bertram Wooster.

'You mean you've come to stay?'

'For a while. Somewhere over yonder is my little nest. I hope you will frequently drop in, when off duty.'

'And what made you suddenly decide to come taking little nests in these parts?'

I went into my routine.

'Jeeves wanted to do a bit of fishing.'

'Oh?'

'Yes. He tells me it is admirable here. You find the hook, and the fish do the rest.'

For quite a while he had been staring at me in an unpleasant, boiled sort of way, the brows drawn, the eyes bulging in their sockets. The austerity of his gaze now became intensified. Except for the fact that he hadn't taken out a notebook and a stub of pencil, he might have been questioning some rat of the underworld as to where he had been on the night of June the twenty-fifth.

'I see. That is your statement, is it? Jeeves wanted to do a bit of fishing?'

'That's right.'

'Oh? Well, I'll tell you what you wanted to do, young blasted Wooster. A bit of snake in the grassing.'

I affected not to have grabbed the gist, though in reality I had got it nicely.

'Snake in the whatting?'

'Grassing.'

'I don't follow you.'

'Then I'll make it clearer. You've come here to sneak round Florence.'

'My dear chap!'

He ground a tooth or two. It was plain that he was in dangerous mood.

'I may as well tell you,' he resumed, 'that I was not at all satisfied with your evidence—with what you said when I saw you yesterday. You stated that you had known Florence—'

'Just one moment, Stilton. Sorry to interrupt, but do we bandy a woman's name?'

'Yes, we do, and ruddy well keep on bandying it.'

'Oh, right ho. I just wanted to know.'

'You stated that you had known Florence only slightly. "Pretty well" was the exact expression you used, and it seemed to me that your manner was suspicious. So when I got back, I saw her and questioned her about you. She confessed that you and she had once been engaged.'

I moistened the lips with the tip of the tongue. I am never at my best *tête à tête* with the constabulary. They always seem somehow to quell my manly spirit. It may be the helmet that does it, or possibly the boots. And, of course, when one of the *gendarmerie* is accusing you of trying to pinch his girl, the embarrassment deepens. At moment of going to press, with Stilton's eyes boring holes through me, I had begun to feel like Eugene Aram just before they put the gyves on his wrists. I don't know if you remember the passage? 'Ti-tum-ti-tum ti-tumty tum, ti-tumty tumty mist (I think it's mist), and Eugene Aram walked between, with gyves upon his wrist.'

I cleared the throat, and endeavoured to speak with a winning frankness.

'Why, yes. That's right. It all comes back to me. We were. Long ago.'

'Not so long ago.'

'Well, it seems like long ago.'

'Oh?'

'Yes.'

'Is that so?'

'Positively.'

'The whole thing's over, eh?'

'Definitely.'

'Nothing between you now?'

'Not a thing.'

'Then how do you account for the fact that she gives you a copy of her novel and writes "To Bertie, with love from Florence" in it?'

I tottered. And at the same time, I'm bound to confess, I found myself feeling a new respect for Stilton. At first, if you recollect, when he had spoken of rising to great heights at Scotland Yard, I had thought lightly of his chances. It seemed to me now that he must have the makings of a very hot detective indeed.

'You had the book with you when you came into that jeweller's shop. You left it on the counter, and I looked inside.'

I revised my views about his sleuthing powers. Not so hot, after all. Sherlock Holmes, if you remember, always said that it was a mistake for a detective to explain his methods.

'Well?'

I laughed lightly. At least, I tried to. As a matter of fact, the thing came out more like a death rattle.

'Oh, that was rather amusing.'

'All right. Go on. Make me laugh.'

'I was in the book shop, and she came in—'

'You had an assignation with her in a book shop?'

'No, no. Just an accidental meeting.'

'I see. And you've come down here to arrange another.'

'Good Lord, no.'

'Do you seriously expect me to believe that you aren't trying to steal her from me?'

'Nothing could be farther from my thoughts, old man.'

'Don't call me "old man".'

'Right ho, if you don't like it. The whole thing, officer, is one of those absurd misunderstandings. As I was starting to tell you, I was in this book shop—'

Here he interrupted me, damning the book shop with a good deal of heartiness.

'I'm not interested in the book shop. The point is that you have come down here to make a snake in the grass of yourself, and I'm not going to have it. I have just one thing to say to you, Wooster. Get out!'

'But—'

'Push off. Remove your beastly presence. Pop back to your London residence and stay there. And do it quick.'

'But I can't.'

'What do you mean?'

Well, as I said before, my lips were sealed. But the Woosters are swift thinkers.

'Old Boko,' I explained. 'I am acting for him in a rather delicate matter. As you possibly may know, my Uncle Percy is endeavouring to put the bee on his union with Nobby, and I have promised the young couple that I will plead for them. This will, of course, involve my remaining *in statu*—what is it?'

'Pah!'

'No, not pah. *Quo*. That's the word I'm trying to think of. You can't plead with an uncle by marriage unless you're *in statu quo*.'

It seemed to me a pretty good and reasonable explanation, and I was distressed, accordingly, to observe that he was sneering unpleasantly.

'I don't believe a word of it. You plead? What's the good of you pleading? As if anything you could say would have any weight with anybody. I repeat—clear out. Otherwise—'

He didn't mention what would happen otherwise, but the menacing way in which he hopped on his bicycle and pedalled off spoke louder than words. I don't think I have ever seen anyone pedal with a more sinister touch to the ankle work.

I was still looking after him, feeling a little weak, when from the opposite or Wee Nooke direction there came the ting of another bicycle bell and, swiveling round, I perceived Florence approaching. As perfect an instance of one damn' thing after another as I have ever experienced.

In sharp contradistinction to those of Stilton, her eyes were shining with a welcoming light. She hopped off as she reached the car, and flashed a bright smile at me.

'Oh, here you are, Bertie. I have just been putting a few flowers in Wee Nooke for you.'

I thanked her, but with a sinking heart. I hadn't liked that smile, and I didn't like the idea of her sweating about strewing flowers in my path. The note struck seemed to me altogether too matey. Then I reminded myself that if she was betrothed to Stilton there could be no real cause for alarm.

After all, her father had married my aunt, which made us sort of cousins, and there was nothing necessarily sinister in a bit of cousinly bustling about. Blood, I mean to say, when you come right down to it, being thicker than water.

'Frightfully decent of you,' I said. 'I've just been having a chat with Stilton.'

'Stilton?'

'Your affianced.'

'Oh, D'Arcy? Why do you call him Stilton?'

'Boyish nickname. We were at school together.'

'Oh? Then perhaps you can tell me if he was always such a perfect imbecile as he is to-day.'

I didn't like this. It didn't seem the language of love.

'In what sense do you use the word "imbecile"?'

'I use it as the only possible description of a man who, with a wealthy uncle willing and anxious to do everything for him, deliberately elects to become a common constable.'

'Why did he?' I asked. 'Become a common constable, I mean.'

'He says that every man ought to stand on his own feet and earn a living.'

'Conscientious.'

'Rubbish.'

'You don't think it does him credit?'

'No, I don't. I think he's a perfect idiot.'

There was a pause. It was plain that his behaviour rankled, and it seemed to me what was required here was a strong boost for the young copper. For I need scarcely say that, now that I was face to face again with this girl, all thought of carrying on with the promotion of that Save Stilton Cheesewright campaign was farther from my mind than ever.

'I should have thought you would have been rather bucked about it all. As giving evidence of Soul, I mean.'

'Soul?'

'It shows he's got a great soul.'

'I should be extremely surprised to find that he has any soul above those great, clodhopping boots he wears. He is just pigheaded. I have reasoned with him over and over again. His uncle wants him to stand for Parliament and is prepared to pay all his expenses and to finance him generously for the rest of his life, but no, he just looks mulish and talks about earning his living. I am sick and tired of the whole thing, and I really don't know what I shall do about it. Well, good-bye, Bertie, I must be getting along,' she concluded abruptly, as if she found the subject too painful to dwell on, and was off—just at the very moment when I had remembered that it was her birthday and that I had a brooch in my pocket to deliver to her from Aunt Agatha.

I could have called her back, I suppose, but somehow didn't feel in the mood. Her words had left me shaking in every limb. The revelation of the flimsiness of the foundations on which the Florence—Stilton romance appeared to be founded had appalled me, and I had to remain *in statu quo* and smoke a couple of cigarettes before I felt strong enough to resume my journey.

Then, feeling a little better and trying to tell myself that this was just a passing tiff and that matters would speedily adjust themselves, I pushed on and in another couple of minutes was coming to anchor abaft Wee Nooke.

9

Wee Nooke proved to be a decentish little shack, situated in agreeable surroundings. A bit Ye Olde, but otherwise all right. It had a thatched roof and a lot of those windows with small leaded panes, and there was a rockery in the front garden. It looked, in short, as I subsequently learned was the case, as if it had formerly been inhabited by an elderly female of good family who kept cats.

I had walked in and deposited the small suitcase in the hall, when, as I stood gazing about me and inhaling the fug which always seems to linger about these antique interiors, I became aware that there was more in this joint than met the eye. In a word, I suddenly found myself speculating on the possibility of it not only being fuggy, but haunted.

What started this train of thought was the fact that odd noises were in progress somewhere near at hand, here a bang and there a crash, suggesting the presence of a poltergeist or what not.

The sounds seemed to proceed from the other side of a door at the end of the hall, and I was hastening thither to investigate, for I was dashed if I was going to have poltergeists lounging about the place as if it belonged to them, when I took a toss over a pail which had been placed in the fairway. And I had just picked myself up, rubbing the spot, when the door opened and there entered a small boy with a face like a ferret. He was wearing the uniform of a Boy Scout, and I had no difficulty, in spite of the fact that his features were liberally encrusted with dirt, in identifying him as Florence's little brother Edwin—the child at whom Boko Fittleworth was accustomed to throw china ornaments.

'Oh, hullo, Bertie,' he said, grinning all over his loathsome face.

'Hullo, you frightful young squirt,' I responded civilly. 'What are you doing here?'

'Tidying up.'

I touched on a point of absorbing interest.

'Was it you who left that bally pail there?'

'Where?'

'In the middle of the hall.'

'Coo! Yes, I remember now. I put it there to be out of the way.'

'I see. Well, you'll be amused to learn that I've nearly broken my leg.'

He started. A fanatic gleam came into his eyes. He looked like a boy confronted with an unexpected saucer of ice cream.

'I say! Have you really? This is a bit of bunce. I can give you first aid.'

'No, you jolly well can't.'

'But if you've bust your leg—'

'I haven't bust my leg.'

'You said you had.'

'A mere figure of speech.'

'Well, you may have sprained your ankle.'

'I haven't sprained my ankle.'

'I can do first aid for contusions.'

'I haven't any contusions. Stand back!' I cried, for I was prepared to defend myself with iron resolution.

There was a pause. His manner was that of one who finds the situation at a deadlock. My spirited attitude had plainly disconcerted him.

'Can't I bandage you?'

'You'll get a thick ear, if you try.'

'You may get gangrene.'

'I anticipate no such contingency.'

'You'll look silly if you get gangrene.'

'No, I shan't. I shall look fine.'

'I knew a chap who bumped his leg, and it turned black and had to be cut off at the knee.'

'You do seem to mix with the most extraordinary people.'

'I could turn the cold tap on it.'

'No, you couldn't.'

Again, that baffled air came into his demeanour. I had nonplussed him.

'Then I'll be getting back to the kitchen,' he said. 'I'm going to do the chimney. It needs a jolly good cleaning out. This place would have been in a fearful mess, if it hadn't been for me,' he added, with a smugness which jarred upon my sensibilities.

'How do you mean, if it hadn't been for you?' I riposted, in my keen way. 'I'll bet you've been spreading ruin and desolation on all sides.'

'I've been tidying up,' he said, with a touch of pique. 'Florence put some flowers for you in the sitting-room.'

'I know. She told me.'

'I fetched the water. Well, I'll go and do that chimney, shall I?'

'Do it, if it pleases you, till your eyes bubble,' I said, and dismissed him with a cold gesture.

Now, I don't know how you would have made a cold gesture—no doubt people's methods vary—but the way I did it was by raising the right arm in a sort of salute and allowing it to fall to my side. And, as it fell, I became aware of something missing. The coat pocket against which the wrist impinged should have contained a small, solid object—to wit, the package containing the brooch which Aunt Agatha had told me to convey to Florence for her birthday. And it didn't. The pocket was empty.

And at the same moment the kid Edwin said 'Coo!' and stooped, and came up holding the thing.

'Did you drop this?' he asked.

Any doubts that may have lingered in the child's mind as to my having broken my leg must have been dispelled by the spring I made. I flew through the air with the greatest of ease. A panther could not have moved more nippily. I wrenched the thing from his grasp, and once more pocketed it.

He seemed intrigued.

'What was it?'

'A brooch. Birthday present for Florence.'

'Shall I take it to her?'

'No, thanks.'

'I will, if you like.'

'No, thanks.'

'It would save you trouble.'

Had the circumstances been other than they were, I might have found this benevolence of his cloying—so much so, indeed, as to cause me to kick him in the pants. But he had rendered me so signal a service that I merely smiled warmly at the young blister, a thing I hadn't done for years.

'No, thanks,' I said. 'I don't let it out of my hands. I will run across and deliver it this evening. Well, well, young Edwin,' I continued affably, 'a smart piece of work, that. They train you sprouts to keep your eyes open. Tell me, how have you been all this while? All right? No colds, colics or other juvenile ailments? Splendid. I should hate to feel that you had been suffering in any way. It was decent of you to suggest putting my leg under the tap. Greatly appreciated. I wish I had a drink to offer you. You must come up and see me some time, when I am more settled.'

And on this cordial note our interview terminated. I tottered out into the garden, and for a space stood leaning on the front gate, for my spine was still feeling a bit jellified and I needed support.

I say my spine had become as jelly, and if you knew my Aunt Agatha you would agree that so it jolly well might.

This relative is a woman who, like Napoleon, if it was Napoleon, listens to no excuses for failure, however sound. If she gives you a brooch to take to a stepdaughter, and you lose it, it is no sort of use trying to tell her that the whole thing was an Act of God, caused by your tripping over unforeseen pails and having the object jerked out of your pocket. Pawn though you may have been in the hands of Fate, you get put through it just the same.

If I had not recovered this blighted trinket, I should never have heard the last of it. The thing would have marked an epoch. World-shaking events would have been referred to as having happened 'about the time Bertie lost that brooch' or 'just after Bertie made such an idiot of himself over Florence's birthday present'. Aunt Agatha is like an elephant—not so much to look at, for in appearance she resembles more a well-bred vulture, but because she never forgets.

Leaning on the gate, I found myself seething with kindly feelings towards young Edwin. I wondered how I could ever have gone so astray in my judgement as to consider him a ferret-faced little son of a what not. And I was just going on to debate in my mind the idea of buying him some sort of a gift as a reward for his admirable behaviour, when there was a loud explosion and, turning, I saw that Wee Nooke had gone up in flames.

It gave me quite a start.

10

Well, everybody enjoys a good fire, of course, and for a while it was in a purely detached and appreciative spirit that I stood eyeing the holocaust. I felt that this was going to be value for money. Already the thatched roof was well ablaze, and it seemed probable that before long the whole edifice, being the museum piece it was, all dry rot and what not, would spit on its hands and really get down to it. And so, as I say, for about the space of two shakes of a duck's tail I stood watching it with quiet relish.

Then, putting a bit of a damper on the festivities, there came floating into my mind a rather disturbing thought—to wit, that the last I had seen of young Edwin, he had been seeping back into the kitchen. Presumably, therefore, he was still on the premises, and the conclusion to which one was forced was that, unless somebody took prompt steps through the proper channels, he was likely ere long to be rendered unfit for human consumption. This was followed by a second and still more disturbing thought that the only person in a position to do the necessary spot of fireman-save-my-child-ing was good old Wooster.

I mused. I suppose you would call me a fairly intrepid man, taken by and large, but I'm bound to admit I wasn't any too keen on the thing. Apart from anything else, my whole attitude towards the stripling who was faced with the prospect of being grilled on both sides had undergone another quick change.

When last heard from, if you remember, I had been thinking kindly thoughts of young Edwin and even going to the length of considering buying him some inexpensive present. But now I found myself once more viewing him with the eye of censure. I mean to say, it was perfectly obvious to the meanest intelligence that it was owing to some phonus-bolonus on his part that the conflagration had been unleashed, and I was conscious of a strong disposition to leave well alone.

It being, however, one of those situations where *noblesse* more or less *obliges*, I decided that I had better do the square thing, and I had torn off my coat and flung it from me and was preparing to plunge into the burning building, though still feeling that it was a bit thick having to get myself all charred up to gratify a kid who would be far better cooked to a cinder, when he emerged. His face was black, and he hadn't any eyebrows, but in other respects appeared reasonably bobbish. Indeed, he seemed entertained rather than alarmed by what had occurred.

'Coo!' he said, in a pleased sort of voice. 'Bit of a bust up, wasn't it?'

I eyed him sternly.

'What the dickens have you been playing at, you abysmal young louse?' I demanded. 'What was that explosion?'

'That was the kitchen chimney. It was full of soot, so I shoved some gunpowder up it. And I think I may have used too much. Because there was a terrific bang and everything sort of caught fire. Coo! It didn't half make me laugh.'

'Why didn't you pour water on the flames?'

'I did. Only it turned out to be paraffin.'

I clutched the brow. I was deeply moved. It had just come home to me that this blazing pyre was the joint which was supposed to be the Wooster G.H.Q., and the householder spirit had awoken in me. Every impulse urged me to give the little snurge six of the best with a bludgeon. But you can't very well slosh a child who has just lost his eyebrows. Besides, I hadn't a bludgeon.

'Well, you've properly messed things up,' I said.

'It didn't all work out quite the way I meant,' he admitted. 'But I wanted to do my last Friday's act of kindness.'

At these words, all was suddenly made plain to me. It was so long since I had seen the young poison sac that I had forgotten the kink in his psychology which made him such a menace to society.

This Edwin, I now recalled, was one of those thorough kids who spare no effort. He had the same serious outlook on life as his sister Florence. And when he joined the Boy Scouts, he did so, resolved not to shirk his responsibilities. The programme called for a daily act of kindness, and he went at it in a grave and earnest spirit. Unfortunately, what with one thing and another, he was always dropping behind schedule, and would then set such a clip to try and catch up with himself that any spot in which he happened to be functioning rapidly became a perfect hell for man and beast. It was so at the house in Shropshire where I had first met him, and it was evidently just the same now.

It was with a grave face and a thoughtful tooth chewing the lower lip that I picked up my coat and donned it. A weaker man, contemplating the fact that he was trapped in a locality containing not only Florence Craye, Police Constable Cheesewright and Uncle Percy, but also Edwin doing acts of kindness, would probably have given at the knees. And I am not so sure I might not have done so myself, had not my mind been diverted by a frightful discovery, so ghastly that I uttered a hoarse cry and all thoughts of Florence, Stilton, Uncle Percy and Edwin were wiped from my mind.

I had just remembered that my suitcase with the Sindbad the Sailor costume in it was in the Wee Nooke front hall, and the flames leaping ever nearer.

There was no hesitation, no vacillating about my movements now. When it had been a matter of risking my life to save Boy Scouts, I may have stood scratching the chin a bit, but this was different. I needed that Sindbad. Only by retrieving it would I be able to attend the fancy dress ball at East Wibley to-morrow night, the one bright spot in a dark and sticky future. Well, I suppose I could have popped up to London and got something else, but probably a mere Pierrot, and my whole heart was set on the Sindbad and the ginger whiskers.

Edwin was saying something about fire brigades, and I right-hoed absently. Then, snapping into it like a jack rabbit, I commended my soul to God, and plunged in.

Well, as it turned out, I needn't have worried. It is true that there was a certain amount of smoke in the hall, billowing hither and thither in murky clouds, but nothing to bother a man who had often sat to leeward of Catsmeat Potter-Pirbright when he was enjoying one of those cigars of his. In a few minutes, it was plain, the whole place would be a cheerful blaze, but for the nonce conditions were reasonably normal.

It is no story, in short, of a jolly-nearly-fried-to-a-crisp Bertram Wooster that I have to tell, but rather of a Bertram Wooster who just scooped up the old suitcase, whistled a gay air and breezed out without a mark on him. I may have coughed once or twice, but nothing more.

But though peril might have failed to get off the mark inside the house, it was very strong on the wing outside. The first thing I saw, as I emerged, was Uncle Percy standing at the gate. And as Edwin had now vanished, presumably in search of fire brigades, I was alone with him in the great open spaces—a thing I've always absolutely barred being from the days of childhood.

'Oh, hullo, Uncle Percy,' I said. 'Good afternoon, good afternoon.'

A casual passer-by, hearing the words and noting the hearty voice in which they had been spoken, might have been deceived into supposing that Bertram was at his ease. Such, however, was far from being the case. Whether anyone was ever at his ease in the society of this old Gawd-help-us, I cannot say, but I definitely was not. The spine, and I do not attempt to conceal the fact, had become soluble in the last degree.

You may wonder at this, arguing that as I was not responsible for the disaster which had come upon us, I had nothing to fear. But a longish experience has taught me that on these occasions innocence pays no dividends. Pure as the driven snow though he may be, or even purer, it is the man on the spot who gets the brickbats.

My civil greeting elicited no response. He was staring past me at the little home, now beyond any possible doubt destined to be a total loss. Edwin might return with all the fire brigades in Hampshire, but nothing was going to prevent Wee Nooke winding up as a heap of ashes.

'What?' he said, speaking thickly, as if the soul were bruised, as I imagine to have been the case. 'What? What? What? What . . . ?'

I saw that, unless checked, this was going to take some time.

'There's been a fire,' I said.

'What do you mean?'

Well, I didn't see how I could have put it much clearer.

'A fire,' I repeated, waving a hand in the direction of the burning edifice, as much as to tell him to take a glance for himself. 'How are you, Uncle Percy? You're looking fine.'

He wasn't, as a matter of fact, nor did this attempt to ease the strain by giving him the old oil have the desired effect. He directed at me a kind of frenzied glare, containing practically nil in the way of an uncle's love, and spoke in a sort of hollow, despairing voice.

'I might have known! My best friends would have warned me what would come of letting a lunatic like you loose in the place. I ought to have guessed that the first thing you would do—before so much as unpacking—would be to set the whole damned premises ablaze.'

'Not me,' I said, wishing to give credit where credit was due. 'Edwin.'

'Edwin? My son?'

'Yes, I know,' I said sympathetically. 'Too bad. Yes, he's your son, all right. He's been tidying up.'

'You can't start a fire by tidying up.'

'You can if you use gunpowder.'

'Gunpowder?'

'He appears to have touched off a keg or two in the kitchen chimney, to correct a disposition on its part to harbour soot.'

Well, I had naturally supposed, as anyone would have supposed, that this frank explanation would have set me right, causing him to dismiss me without a stain on my character, and that the rather personal note which had crept into his remarks would instantly have been switched off. What I had anticipated was that he would issue an apology for that crack of his about lunatics, which I would gracefully accept, and that we would then get together like two old buddies and shake our heads over the impulsiveness of the younger generation.

Not a bit of it, however. He continued to bend upon me the accusing gaze which I had disliked so much from the start.

'Why the devil did you give the boy gunpowder?'

I saw that he had still got the wrong angle.

'I didn't give the boy gunpowder.'

'Only a congenital idiot would give a boy gunpowder. There's not a man in England, except you, who wouldn't know what would happen if you gave a boy gunpowder. Do you realize what you have done? The sole reason for your coming here was that I should have a place where I could meet an old friend and discuss certain matters of interest, and now look at it. I ask you. Look at it.'

'Not too good,' I was forced to concede, as the roof fell in, sending up a shower of sparks and causing a genial glow to play about our cheeks.

'I suppose it never occurred to you to throw water on the flames?'

'It did to Edwin. Only he used paraffin.'

He started, staring at me incredulously.

'You tried to put the fire out with paraffin? You ought to be certified, and as soon as I can collect a couple of doctors, I'll have it seen to.'

What was making this conversation so difficult was, as you have probably spotted, the apparent impossibility of getting the old ass to sort out the principals in the affair and assign to each his respective role. He was one of those men you meet sometimes who only listen to about two words of any observation addressed to them. I suppose he had got that way through presiding at board meetings and constantly chipping in and squelching shareholders in the middle of sentences.

Once more, I tried to drive it home to him that it was Edwin who had done all the what you might call heavy work, Bertram having been throughout merely an innocent bystander, but it didn't penetrate. He was left with the settled conviction that I and the child had got together, forming a quorum, and after touching off the place with gunpowder had nursed the conflagration along with careful injections of paraffin, each encouraging each, as you might say, on the principle that it is team-work that tells.

When he finally pushed off, instructing me to send Jeeves along to him the moment he arrived, he was reiterating the opinion that I ought not to be at large, and wishing—though here I definitely could not see eye to eye with him—that I was ten years younger, so that he could have got after me with that hunting crop of his. He then withdrew, leaving me to my meditations.

These, as you may suppose, were not of the juiciest. However, they didn't last long, for I don't suppose I had been meditating more than about a couple of minutes when a wheezing, rattling sound made itself heard off-stage and there entered left upper centre a vehicle which could only have been a station taxi. There was luggage on it, and looking more closely I saw Jeeves protruding from the side window.

The weird old object—the cab, I mean, not Jeeves—came to a halt at the gate. Jeeves paid it off, the luggage was dumped by the roadside, and he was at liberty to get into conference with the young master, not an instant too soon for the latter. I had need of his sympathy, encouragement and advice. I also wanted to tick him off a bit for letting me in for all this.

11

'Jeeves,' I said, getting right down to it in the old Wooster way, 'here's a nice state of things!'

'Sir?'

'Hell's foundations have been quivering.'

'Indeed, sir?'

'The curse has come upon me. As I warned you it would, if I ever visited Steeple Bumpleigh. You have long been familiar with my views on this leper colony. Have I not repeatedly said that, what though the spicy breezes blow soft o'er Steeple Bumpleigh, the undersigned deemed it wisest to give it the complete miss in baulk?'

'Yes, sir.'

'Very well, Jeeves. Perhaps you will listen to me another time. However, let us flit lightly over the recriminations and confine ourselves to the facts. You notice our little home has been gutted?'

'Yes, sir. I was just observing it.'

'Edwin did that. There's a lad, Jeeves. There's a boy who makes you feel that what this country wants is somebody like King Herod. Started in with gunpowder and carried on with paraffin. Just cast your eye over those smouldering ruins. You would scarcely have thought it possible, would you, that one frail child in a sport shirt and khaki shorts could have accomplished such devastation. Yet he did it, Jeeves, and did it on his head. You understand what this means?'

'Yes, sir.'

'He has properly put the kybosh on the trysting-place of Uncle Percy and his nautical pal. You'll have to think again.'

'Yes, sir. His lordship is fully alive to the fact that in the existing circumstances a meeting at Wee Nooke will not be feasible.'

'You've seen him, then?'

'He was emerging from the lane, as I entered it, sir.'

'Did he tell you he wants you to go and hobnob with him at your earliest convenience?'

'Yes, sir. Indeed, he insists on my taking up my residence at the Hall.'

'So as to be handy, in case you have a sudden inspiration?'

'No doubt that was in his lordship's mind, sir.'

'Was I invited?'

'No, sir.'

Well, I hadn't expected to be. Nevertheless, I was conscious of a pang.

'We part, then, for the nonce, do we?'

'I fear so, sir.'

'You taking the high road, and self taking the low road, as it were?'

'Yes, sir.'

'I shall miss you, Jeeves.'

'Thank you, sir.'

'Who was the chap who was always beefing about losing gazelles?'

'The poet Moore, sir. He complained that he had never nursed a dear gazelle, to glad him with its soft black eye, but when it came to know him well and love him, it was sure to die.'

'It's the same with me. I am a gazelle short. You don't mind me alluding to you as a gazelle, Jeeves?'

'Not at all, sir.'

'Well, that's that, then. I suppose I had better go and stay with Boko.'

'I was about to suggest it, sir. I am sure Mr Fittleworth will be most happy to accommodate you.'

'I think so. I hope so. Only recently, he was speaking about killing fatted calves. But to return to Uncle Percy and the old salt from America, have you any ideas on the subject of bringing them together?'

'Not at the moment, sir.'

'Well, bend the bean to it, because it's important. You remember me telling you that Boko and young Nobby were betrothed?'

'Yes, sir.'

'She can't marry without Uncle Percy's consent.'

'Indeed, sir?'

'Not till she's twenty-one. Legal stuff. And here's the nub, Jeeves. I haven't time to give you the full details now, but Boko, the silly ass, has been making a silly ass of himself, with the result that he has—what's the word that means making somebody froth at the mouth and chew pieces out of the carpet?'

'"Alienate", sir, is, I think, the verb for which you are groping.'

'That's it. Alienate. Well, as I say, I've no time to give you the inside story now, but Boko has played the goat and alienated Uncle Percy, and not a smell of a guardian's blessing is the latter prepared to give him. So you see what I mean about this meeting. It is vital that it takes place at the earliest possible date.'

'In order that his lordship may be brought to a more amiable frame of mind?'

'Exactly. If that merger comes off, the milk of human kindness will slosh about in him like the rising tide, swamping all animosity. Or don't you think so?'

'Undoubtedly, in my opinion, sir.'

'That's what I felt. And that is why you found me moody just now, Jeeves. I had just concluded an unpleasant interview with Uncle Percy, in the course of which he came out openly as not one of my admirers, thinking—incorrectly—that I had played an impressive part in the recent spot of arson.'

'He wronged you, sir?'

'Completely. I had nothing to do with it. I was a mere cipher in the affair. Edwin attended to the whole thing. But that was what he thought, and he blinded and stiffed with a will.'

'Unfortunate, sir.'

'Most. Of course, for the actual vote of censure that was passed I care little. A few poohs and a tush about cover that. Bertram Wooster is not a man who minds a few harsh words. He laughs lightly and snaps the fingers. It is wholly immaterial to me what the old bounder thinks of me, and in any case he didn't say a tithe of the things Aunt Agatha would have got off in similar circumstances. But the point is that I had promised Nobby that I would plead for her loved one, and what was saddening me when you came along was the thought that my potentialities in that direction had become greatly diminished. As far as Uncle Percy is concerned, I am not the force I was. So push that meeting along.'

'I will certainly use every endeavour, sir. I fully appreciate the situation.'

'Right. Now, what else have I to tell you? Oh, yes. Stilton.'

'Mr Cheesewright?'

'Police Constable Cheesewright, Jeeves. Stilton turns out to be the village bluebottle.'

He seemed surprised, and I didn't wonder. To him, of course, on the occasion when they had met at the flat, Stilton had been a mere, ordinary, tweed-suited popper-in. I mean, no uniform, no helmet and not a suggestion of any regulation boots.

'A policeman, sir?'

'Yes, and a nasty, vindictive policeman, too. With him, also, I have been having an unpleasant interview. He resents my presence here.'

'I suppose a great many young gentlemen enter the Force nowadays, sir.'

'I wish one fewer had. It is a tricky business falling foul of the constabulary, Jeeves.'

'Yes, sir.'

'I shall have to employ ceaseless vigilance, so as to give him no loophole for exercising his official powers. No drunken revels at the village pub.'

'No, sir.'

'One false step, and he'll swoop on me like the—who was it who came down like a wolf on the fold?'

'The Assyrian, sir.'

'That's right. Well, that is what I have been through since I saw you last. First Stilton, then Edwin, then the fire, and finally Uncle Percy—all in about half an hour. It just shows what Steeple Bumpleigh can do, when it starts setting about you. And, oh my gosh, I was forgetting. You know the brooch?'

'Sir?'

'Aunt Agatha's brooch.'

'Oh, yes, sir.'

'I lost it. Oh, it's all right. I found it again. But what I mean is, picture my embarrassment. My heart stood still.'

'I can readily imagine it, sir. But you have it safely now?'

'Oh, rather,' I said, dipping a hand into the pocket. 'Or, rather,' I went on, bringing it out again with ashen face and bulging eyes. 'Oh, rather not. Jeeves,' I said, 'you will scarcely credit this, but the bally thing has gone again!'

It occasionally happens, and I have had to tell him off for doing so, that this man receives announcements that the young master's world is rocking about him with a mere 'Most disturbing, sir.' But now it was plain that he recognized that the thing was too big for that. I don't think he paled, and he certainly didn't say 'Golly!' or anything of that nature, but he came as near as he ever does to what they call in the movies 'the quick take 'um'. There was concern in his eyes, and if it hadn't been that his views are rigid in the matter of the correct etiquette between employee and employer, I have an idea that he would have patted me on the shoulder.

'This is a serious disaster, sir.'

'You are informing me, Jeeves!'

'Her ladyship will be vexed.'

'I can picture her screaming with annoyance.'

'Can you think where you could have dropped it, sir?'

'That's just what I'm trying to do. Wait, Jeeves,' I said, closing my eyes. 'Let me brood.'

I brooded.

'Oh, my gosh!'

'Sir?'

'I've got it.'

'The brooch, sir?'

'No, Jeeves, not the brooch. I mean I've reconstructed the scene and have now spotted where I must have parted company with it. Here's the sequence. The place caught fire, and I suddenly remembered I had left the small suitcase in the hall. I need scarcely remind you of its contents. My Sindbad the Sailor costume.'

'Ah, yes, sir.'

'Don't say "Ah, yes," Jeeves. Just keep on listening. I suddenly remembered, I repeat, that I had left the small suitcase in the hall. Well, you know me. To think is to act. I was inside, gathering it up, without a moment's delay. This involved stooping. This stooping must have caused the thing to fall out of my pocket.'

'Then it would still be in the hall, sir.'

'Yes. And take a look at the hall!'

We both took a look at it. I shook my head. He shook his. Wee Nooke was burning lower now, but its interior was still something which only Shadrach, Meshach and Abednego could have entered with any genuine enjoyment.

'No hope of getting it, if it's there.'

'No, sir.'

'Then what's to be done?'

'May I brood, sir?'

'Certainly, Jeeves.'

'Thank you, sir.'

He passed into the silence, and I filled in the time by thinking of what Aunt Agatha was going to say. I did not look forward to getting in touch with her. In fact, it almost seemed as if another of my quick trips to America would be rendered necessary. About the only advantage of having an aunt like her is that it makes one travel, thus broadening the mind and enabling one to see new faces.

And I was just saying to myself 'Young man, go West,' when, happening to glance at the thinker, I observed that his face was wearing the brainy expression which always signifies that there is a hot one coming along.

'Yes, Jeeves?'

'I think I have hit on quite a simple solution of your difficulty, sir.'

'Let me have it, Jeeves, and speedily.'

'What I would suggest, sir, is that I take the car, drive to London, call at the emporium where her ladyship made her purchase and procure another brooch in place of the one that is missing.'

I weighed this. It sounded promising. Hope began to burgeon.

'You mean, put on an understudy?'

'Yes, sir.'

'Delivering it to addressee as the original?'

'Precisely, sir.'

I went on weighing. And the more I did so, the fruitier the idea seemed.

'Yes, I see what you mean. The mechanism is much the same as that which you employed in the case of Aunt Agatha's dog McIntosh.'

'Not dissimilar, sir.'

'There we were in the position of being minus an Aberdeen terrier, when we should have been plus an Aberdeen terrier. You reasoned correctly that all members of this particular canine family look very much alike, and rang in a ringer with complete success.'

'Yes, sir.'

'Would the same system work with brooches?'

'I think so, sir.'

'Is one brooch just like another brooch?'

'Not invariably, sir. But a few words of inquiry will enable me to obtain a description of the lost trinket and to ascertain the price which her ladyship paid for it. I shall thus be enabled to return with something virtually indistinguishable from the original.'

I was convinced. It was as if a heavy weight had been removed from my soul. I have mentioned that a short while back he had seemed to be thinking of patting me on the shoulder. It was now all I could do to restrain myself from patting him on his.

'A winner, Jeeves!'

'Thank you, sir.'

'*Rem*—what is it again?'

'*Acu tetigisti*, sir.'

'I might have known that you would find the way.'

'I am gratified to feel that I enjoy your confidence, sir.'

'I have an account at Aspinall's, so you can tell them to chalk it up on the slate.'

'Very good, sir.'

'Buzz off instanter.'

'There is ample time, sir. I shall be able to reach London long before the establishment closes for the day. Before proceeding thither, I think it would be best for me to stop at Mr Fittleworth's residence, apprise him of what has occurred, deposit the luggage and warn him of your coming.'

'Is "warn" the word?'

'"Inform" I should have said, sir.'

'Well, don't cut it too fine. The sands are running out, remember. That brooch must be in recipient's hands to-night. What one aims at is to have it lying alongside her plate at the dinner-table.'

'I shall undoubtedly be able to reach Steeple Bumpleigh on my return journey at about the dinner hour, sir.'

'Right ho, Jeeves. I know I can rely on you to run to time. First stop, Boko's, then. I, meanwhile, will be nosing round here. There is just a chance that I may have dropped the thing somewhere in the open. I can't remember exactly how the sight of that fire affected me, but I have no doubt that I sprang up and down a bit—quite nimbly enough to jerk packages out of pockets.'

Of course, I didn't think so, really. My original theory that I had become unbrooched while picking up the suitcase persisted. But on these occasions the instinct is to turn every stone and leave no avenue unexplored.

I nosed round, accordingly, scanning the turf and even going so far as to feel about in the rockery. As I had foreseen, no dice. It wasn't long before I gave it up and started to stroll along to Boko's. And I had just reached his gate, when there was the ting of bicycle bell—I noted as a curious phenomenon that the denizens of Steeple Bumpleigh seemed to do practically nothing but ride about on bicycles, tinging bells—and I saw Nobby approaching.

I hastened to meet her, for she was just the girl I wanted to get in touch with. I was anxious to thresh out with her the whole topic of Stilton and his love life.

PART 2

12

She dismounted with lissome grace, beaming welcomingly. Since I had last seen her, she had washed off the stains of travel and changed her frock and was looking spruce and dapper. Why she should have bothered to smarten herself up, when she was only going to meet a bird in patched grey flannel trousers and a turtleneck sweater, I was at a loss to understand, but girls will, of course, be girls.

'Hullo, Bertie,' she said. 'Are you paying a neighbourly call on Boko?'

I replied that that was about what it amounted to, but added that first I required a few moments of her valuable time.

'Listen, Nobby,' I said.

She didn't, of course. I've never met a girl yet who did. Say 'Listen' to any member of the delicately nurtured sex, and she takes it as a cue to start talking herself. However, as the subject she introduced proved to be the very one I had been planning to ventilate, the desire to beat her brains out with a brick was not so pronounced as it would otherwise have been.

'What have you been doing to inflame Stilton, Bertie? I met him just now and asked if he had seen you, and he turned vermilion and gnashed every tooth in his head. I don't think I've ever seen a more incandescent copper.'

'He didn't explain?'

'No. He simply pedalled on furiously, as if he had been competing in a six-day bicycle race and had just realized he was dropping behind the leaders. What was the trouble?'

I tapped her on the arm with a grave forefinger.

'Nobby,' I said, 'there has been a bit of a mix-up. What's that word that begins with "con"?'

'Con?'

'I've heard Jeeves use it. There's a cat in it somewhere.'

'What on earth are you drivelling about?'

'Concatenation,' I said, getting it. 'Owing to an unfortunate concatenation of circumstances, Stilton is viewing me with concern. He has got the idea rooted in his bean that I've come down here to try to steal Florence from him.'

'Have you?'

'My dear young blister,' I said, with some impatience, 'would anybody want to steal Florence? Do use your intelligence. But, as I say, this unfortunate concatenation has led him to suspect the worst.'

And in a few simple words I gave her the run of the scenario, featuring the Young Lochinvar aspect of the matter. When I had finished, she made one of those foolish remarks which do so much to confirm a man in his conviction that women as a sex should be suppressed.

'You should have told him you were guiltless of the charge.'

I tut-tutted impatiently.

'I did tell him I was guiltless of the charge, and a fat lot he believed me. He continued to hot up, finally reaching a condition of so much Fahrenheit that I was surprised he didn't run me in on the spot. In which connection, you might have told me he was a cop.'

'I forgot to.'

'It would have spared me a very disconcerting shock. When I heard someone calling my name and looked round and saw him cycling towards me in the complete rig-out of a rural policeman, I nearly got the vapours.'

She laughed—a solo effort. Nothing in the prevailing circumstances made me feel like turning it into a duet.

'Poor old Stilton!'

'Yes, that's all very well, but—'

'I think it's rather sporting of him, wanting to earn his living, instead of sitting on the knee of that uncle of his and helping himself out of his pockets.'

'I dare say, but—'

'Florence doesn't. And it's rather funny, because it was she who turned his thoughts in that direction. She talked Socialism to him, and made him read Karl Marx. He's very impressionable.'

I agreed with her there. I had never forgotten the time at Oxford when somebody temporarily converted him to Buddhism. It led to a lot of unpleasantness with the authorities, I recall, he immediately starting to cut chapel and go and meditate beneath the nearest thing the neighbourhood could provide to a bo tree.

'She's furious now, and says he was a fool to take her literally.'

She paused, in order to laugh again, and I seized the opportunity to get a word in edgeways.

'Exactly. As you state, she is furious. And that's just the aspect of the matter that I want to discuss. I could put up with a green-eyed Stilton, a Stilton who turns vermilion and gnashes the molars at the mention of my name. I don't say it could ever be pleasant, going about knowing that the Force was gnashing its teeth at you, but one learns to take the rough with the smooth. The real trouble is that I believe Florence is weakening on him.'

'What makes you think that?'

'She's just been talking to me about him. She used the expression "pig-headed", and said she was sick and tired of the whole thing and really didn't know what she was going to do about it. Her whole attitude seemed to me that of a girl on the very verge of giving her heart-throb the raspberry and returning the ring and presents. You spot the frightful menace?'

'You mean that if she breaks it off with Stilton, she may consider taking you on again?'

'That's what I mean. The peril is appalling. Owing to another unfortunate concatenation of circumstances, my stock has recently gone up with her to a fearful extent, and anything may happen at any moment.'

And I briefly outlined the Spindrift-Spinoza affair. When I had concluded, a meditative look came into her face.

'Do you know, Bertie,' she said, 'I've often thought that, of all the multitude Florence has been engaged to, you were the one she really wanted?'

'Oh, my gosh!'

'It's your fault for being so fascinating.'

'I dare say, but too late to do anything about that now.'

'Still, I don't see what you've got to worry about. If she proposes to you, just blush a little and smile tremulously and say "I'm sorry—so, so sorry. You have paid me the greatest compliment a woman can pay a man. But it cannot be. So shall we be pals—just real pals?" That'll fix her.'

'It won't do anything of the sort. You know what Florence is like. Propose, forsooth! She'll just notify me that the engagement is on again, like a governess telling a young charge to eat his spinach. And if you think I've got the force of character to come back with a *nolle prosequi*—'

'With a what?'

'One of Jeeves's gags. It means roughly "Nuts to you!" If, I say, you think I'm capable of asserting myself and giving her the bird, you greatly overestimate the Wooster fortitude. She must be reconciled to Stilton. It is the only way. Listen, Nobby. I wrote you a letter yesterday, giving my views on Florence and urging you to employ every means in your power to open Stilton's eyes to what he was in for. Have you read it?'

'Every syllable. It gripped me tremendously. I never knew you had such a vivid prose style. It reminded me of Ernest Hemingway. You don't by any chance write under the name of Ernest Hemingway, do you?'

I shook the head.

'No. The only thing I've ever written was an article for "Milady's Boudoir" on What the Well-Dressed Man is Wearing. It appeared under my own name. But what I want to say is, pay no attention to that letter. I am now wholeheartedly in favour of the match. The wish to save Stilton has left me. The chap I have my eye on for saving purposes is B. Wooster. When chatting with Florence, therefore, boost Stilton in every possible way. Make her see what a prize she has got. And if you have any influence with him, endeavour to persuade him to chuck all this policeman nonsense and stand for Parliament, as she wants him to.'

'I'd love to see Stilton in Parliament.'

'So would I, if it means healing this rift.'

'Wouldn't he be a scream!'

'Not necessarily. There are bigger fatheads than Stilton among our legislators—dozens of them. They would probably shove him in the Cabinet. So push it along, young Nobby.'

'I'll do what I can. But Stilton isn't the easiest person to persuade, once the trend of his mind has set in any direction. You remember the deaf adder?'

'What deaf adder?'

'The one that stopped its ear, and would not listen to the voice of the charmers, charming never so wisely. That's Stilton. However, as I say, I'll do what I can. And now let's go and rout Boko out. I'm dying to hear what happened at that lunch of his.'

'You haven't seen Uncle Percy, then?'

'Not yet. He was out. Why?'

'Oh, nothing. I was only thinking that, if you had, you would have got an eye-witness's report from him,' I said, and was conscious of a pang of pity for my old friend and a hope that by this time he would have succeeded in thinking up a reasonably good story to cover the binge in question.

The sound of a typewriter greeted us as we crossed the threshold, indicating that Boko was still at work on that letter to Uncle Percy. It ceased abruptly as Nobby yoo-hooed, and when we passed on into the sitting-room, he was hastily dropping a sheet of paper into the basket.

'Oh, hullo, darling,' he said brightly. Watching him bound from his chair and fold Nobby in a close embrace, the casual observer would have supposed him to have had nothing on his mind except the hair which he had apparently not brushed for days. 'I was just roughing out a *morceau*.'

'Oh, angel, have we interrupted the flow?'

'Not at all, not a-tall.'

'I was so anxious to hear how the lunch went off.'

'Of course, of course. I'll tell you all about it. By the way, Bertie, Jeeves delivered your effects. They are in the spare room. Delighted to put you up, of course. Too bad about that fire.'

'What fire?' asked Nobby.

'Jeeves tells me that Edwin has succeeded in burning Wee Nooke to the ground. Correct, Bertie?'

'Quite correct. It was his last Friday's act of kindness.'

'What a shame!' said Nobby, with a womanly sympathy that well became her.

Boko, however, looked on the bright side.

'Personally,' he said, 'I consider that Bertie has got off lightly. He appears not to have been even singed. A burned house is a mere bagatelle. Generally, when Edwin is trying to catch up with his acts of kindness, human life is imperilled. The mind flits back to the time when he mended my egg boiler. Occasionally, when I am much occupied with a job of work, sparing no effort to give my public of my best, I rise early, before my housekeeper turns up in the morning. On these occasions, it is my practice to boil myself a refreshing egg, using one of those patent machines for the purpose. You know the sort of thing I mean. It rings an alarm, hopes you've slept well, pours water on the coffee, lights a flame underneath and gets action on the egg. Well, the day after Edwin had fixed some trifling flaw in the apparatus, the egg was scarcely in position when it flew at me like a bullet, catching me on the tip of the nose and knocking me base over apex. I bled for hours. So I maintain that if you got off with a mere fire that destroyed your house, you are sitting pretty.'

Nobby speculated as to the chances of somebody some day murdering Edwin, and we agreed that the hour must eventually produce the man.

'And now,' said Boko, still with that strange brightness which, knowing the facts, I could not but admire, 'you will want to hear all about the lunch. Well, it was a great success.'

'Darling!'

'Yes, a notable success. I think I have made an excellent start.'

'Were you bright?'

'Very bright.'

'And genial?'

'The word understates it.'

'Angel!' said Nobby, and kissed him about fifteen times in rapid succession.

'Yes,' said Boko, 'I think I have got him on the run. It is difficult to tell with a man like that, who conceals his emotions behind a poker face, but I believe he's weakening. And we never expected him to fall on my neck right away, did we? It was agreed that the lunch was merely to prepare the soil.'

'What did you talk about?'

'Oh, this and that. The subject of spiders, I remember, was one that came up.'

'Spiders?'

'He seemed interested in spiders.'

'I never knew that.'

'Just a side of his character which he hasn't happened to reveal to you,

I suppose. And then, of course, after talking of this and that, we talked of that and this.'

'There weren't any awkward pauses?'

'I didn't notice any. No, he rather prattled on, as it were, especially towards the end.'

'Did you tell him what a lot of money you were making?'

'Oh, yes, I touched on that.'

'I hope you explained that you were a steady young fellow and were bound to go on making it? That's what worries him. He thinks you may blow up at any moment.'

'Like Wee Nooke.'

'You see, when he was a young man, just starting in the shipping business, Uncle Percy used to go about with rather a rackety set in London, and he knew a lot of writers who made quite a bit from time to time and spent it all in a couple of days and then had to live on what they could borrow. My darling father was one of them.'

This was news to me. I had never pictured Uncle Percy as a bird who had gone about with rackety sets as a young man. In fact, I had never pictured him as ever having been a young man at all. It's always the way. If an old buster has a bristling moustache, a solid, lucrative business and the manners of a bear aroused while hibernating, you do not probe into his past and ask yourself whether he, too, in his day may not have been one of the boys.

'I covered that point,' said Boko. 'It was one of the first I stressed. The modern author, I told him, is keen and hardheaded. He is out for the stuff, and when he gets it he salts it away.'

'That ought to have pleased him.'

'Oh, it did.'

'Then everything's fine.'

'Splendid.'

'All we need now is for Bertie to do his act.'

'Exactly. The future hinges on Bertie.'

'When he pleads—'

'Ah, I didn't mean quite that. I'm afraid you are not abreast of the quick rush and swirl of recent events. I doubt if it would be any good for Bertie to plead now. His name has become mud.'

'Mud?'

'"Mud", I think, is the *mot juste*, Bertie?'

I was obliged to concede that this was more or less so.

'Uncle Percy,' I explained, 'has got it into his head that I aided and encouraged Edwin in his fire-bug activities. This has put me back in the betting a good bit, considered as a pleader. I should find it difficult now to sway him like a reed.'

'Then where are we?' said Nobby, registering anguish.

Boko patted her encouragingly on the shoulder.

'We're all right. Don't you worry.'

'But if Bertie can't plead—'

'Ah, but you're forgetting how versatile he is. What you are overlooking is the scullery-window-breaking side of his nature. That is what is going to see us through. Brooding tensely over this business, I have had an idea, and it is a pippin. Suppose, I said to myself, I were to save the heavy's home from being looted by a midnight marauder, that would make him feel I had the right stuff in me, I fancy. He would say "Egad! A fine young fellow, this Fittleworth!" would he not?'

'I suppose so.'

'You speak doubtfully.'

'I was only thinking that there isn't much chance of that happening. There hasn't been a burglary in Steeple Bumpleigh for centuries. Stilton was complaining about it only the other day. He said the place gave an ambitious young copper no scope.'

'These things can be arranged.'

'How do you mean?'

'It only needs a little organization. There is going to be a burglary in Steeple Bumpleigh this very night. Bertie will attend to it.'

There was only one comment to make on this, and I made it.

'Hey!' I cried.

'Don't interrupt, Bertie,' said Boko reprovingly. 'It prevents one marshalling one's thoughts. Here in a nutshell is the scheme I have evolved. Somewhere in the small hours, Bertie and I make our way to the Hall. We approach the scullery window. He busts it. I raise the alarm. He pops off—'

'Ah!' I said. It was the first point he had mentioned of which I found myself approving.

'—while I stay on, to accept the plaudits of all and be fawned on. I don't see how it can fail. The one thing a sturdy householder of the Worplesdon type dislikes is having the house he is holding broken into, and anyone who nips such a venture in the bud creeps straight into his heart. Before the night is out, I expect to have him promising to dance at our wedding.'

'Darling! It's wonderful!'

It was Nobby who said that, not me. I was still chewing the lower lip in open concern. I should have remembered, I was telling myself, that that play of Boko's, to which I alluded earlier, had been one of those mystery thrillers, and that it was only natural that some such set-up as this should have occurred to his diseased mind.

I mean to say, you get a chap whose thoughts run persistently in the direction of screams in the night and lights going out and mysterious hands appearing through the wall and people rushing about shouting 'Here comes The Shadow!' and it is inevitable that that will be the sort of stuff he will dish out in an emergency. I resolved there and then that I would put in a firm *nolle prosequi*. Nobody is more anxious than Bertram Wooster to lend a helping hand to Love's young dream, but there are limits to what he is prepared to sign on for, and sharply defined limits, at that.

Nobby's joyous animation had died away a bit. Like me, she was chewing the lip.

'Yes, it's wonderful. But—'

'I don't like to hear that word "but".'

'I was only going to say, How do you explain?'

'Explain?'

'Your being there to raise alarms and be fawned on.'

'Perfectly simple. My love for you is the talk of Steeple Bumpleigh. What more natural than that I should have come to stand beneath your window, gazing up at it?'

'I see! And then you heard a noise—'

'A curious noise that sounded like the splintering of glass. And I popped round the house to investigate, and there was a bounder smashing the scullery window.'

'Of course!'

'I knew you would see it.'

'Then everything depends on Bertie.'

'Everything.'

'You don't think he'll object?'

'I wish you wouldn't say things like that. You'll hurt his feelings. You don't realize the sort of fellow Bertie is. His nerve is like chilled steel, and when it is a question of helping a pal, he sticks at nothing.'

Nobby drew a deep breath.

'He's wonderful, isn't he?'

'He stands alone.'

'I've always been devoted to Bertie. When I was a child, he once gave me threepennyworth of acid drops.'

'Generous to a fault. These splendid fellows always are.'

'How I admired him!'

'Me, too. I don't know a man I admire more.'

'Doesn't he remind you rather of Sir Galahad?'

'The name was on the tip of my tongue.'

'Of course, he wouldn't dream of not doing his bit.'

'Of course not. All settled, eh, Bertie?'

It's odd what a few kind words will do. Until now, I had, as I say, been all ready with the *nolle prosequi*, and had indeed opened my lips to shoot it across with all the emphasis at my disposal. But as I caught Nobby's eye, fixed on me in a devout sort of way, and at the same time was conscious of Boko shaking my hand and kneading my shoulder, something seemed to check me. I mean, there really didn't seem to be any way of *nolle-prosequi*-ing without spoiling the spirit of the party.

'Oh, rather,' I said. 'Absolutely.'

But not blithely. Not with any real chirpiness.

13

No, not with any real chirpiness. And this shortage of c., I must confess, continued to make its presence felt right up to zero hour. All through the quiet evenfall, the frugal dinner and the long, weary waiting for midnight to strike on the village clock, I was conscious of a growing concern. And when the moment arrived and Boko and self passed through the silent gardens of Bumpleigh Hall on our way to start the doings, it was going stronger than ever.

Boko was in gay and effervescent mood, speaking from time to time in a low but enthusiastic voice of the beauties of Nature and drawing my attention in a cautious whisper to the agreeable niffiness of the flowers past which we flitted, but it was far different with Bertram. Bertram, and I do not attempt to conceal it, was not at his fizziest. His spine crawled, and his heart was bowed down with weight of woe. The word of a Wooster was pledged; I had placed my services at the disposal of the young couple and there was no question of my doing a quick sneak and edging out of the enterprise, but nothing was going to make me like it.

I think I have mentioned before my dislike for creeping about strange gardens in the dark. Too many painful episodes in my past have been connected with other people's dark gardens, notably the time when circumstances compelled me to slide out in the small hours and ring the fire bell at Brinkley Court and that other occasion when Roberta Wickham induced me against my better judgement to climb a tree and drop a flowerpot through the roof of a greenhouse, in order to create a diversion which would enable her cousin Clementina, who was A.W.O.L. from her school, to ooze back into it unobserved.

Of all these experiences, the last named had been, to date, the most soul searing, because it had culminated in the sudden appearance of a policeman saying 'What's all this?' And it was the thought that there might quite possibly be a repetition of this routine, and the realization that if a policeman did come muscling in now it would be Stilton, that curdled the blood and made me feel a dry, fluttering feeling in the pit of the stomach, as if I had swallowed a heaping tablespoonful of butterflies.

So pronounced was this sensation that I found myself clutching Boko's arm in ill-concealed panic and drawing him beneath a passing tree.

'Boko,' I gurgled, 'what about Stilton? Have you considered the Stilton angle?'

'Eh?'

'Suppose he's on duty at night? Suppose he's prowling? Suppose he suddenly pops out at us, complete with whistle and notebook?'

'Nonsense.'

'It would be an awful thing to be pinched by a chap you were boys together with. And he would spring to the task. He's got it in for me.'

'Nonsense, nonsense,' said Boko, continuing debonair to the gills. 'You mustn't allow your thoughts to take this morbid trend, Bertie. These tremors are unworthy of you. Don't you worry about Stilton. You have only to look at him—that clear eye, those rosy cheeks—to know that he is a man who makes a point of getting his regular eight hours. Early to bed and early to rise, is his slogan. Stilton is tucked up between the sheets, sleeping like a little child, and won't start functioning again till his alarm clock explodes at seven-thirty.'

Well, that was all right, as far as it went. His reasoning was specious, and did much to reassure me. Stilton's cheeks unquestionably were rosy. But it was only for a moment that I was strengthened. After all, I reflected, Stilton was merely a part of the menace. Even leaving him out of it, there was the Uncle Percy-Aunt Agatha side of the business. You couldn't get away from it that these gardens and messuages whose privacy we were violating belonged to the former, and that the latter had a joint interest in them. I might, that is to say, be safe from the dragon, but what about the hippogriffs? That was the question I asked myself. What price the hippogriffs?

If anything were to go wrong, if this frightful binge on which I had embarked were in the slightest detail to slip a cog, what would be the upshot? I'll tell you what would jolly well be the upshot. Not only should I be placed in the position of having to explain to a slavering uncle, justly incensed at being deprived of his beauty sleep, why I was going about the place breaking his scullery windows, but the whole story would be told to Aunt Agatha on her return with a wealth of detail, and then what?

Far less serious offences on my part in the past had brought the old relative leaping after me with her hatchet like a Red Indian on the war-path, howling for my blood.

I mentioned this to Boko as we fetched up at journey's end, and he patted me on the shoulder. Well meant, no doubt, and a kindly gesture, but one that accomplished little or nothing in the way of stiffening my *morale*.

'If you're copped,' said Boko, 'just pass it off.'

'Pass it off?'

'That's right. Nonchalantly. Got the treacle?'

I said I had got the treacle.

'And the paper?'

'Yes.'

'Then I'll take a stroll for ten minutes. That will give you eight minutes to screw your courage to the sticking-point, one minute to break window and one to make getaway.'

This treacle idea was Boko's. He had insisted upon it as an indispensable adjunct to the proceedings, claiming that it would lend the professional touch at which we were aiming. According to him, and he is a chap who has studied these things, the knowledgeable burglar's first act is to equip himself with treacle and brown paper. He glues the latter to the window by means of the former, and then hauls off and busts the glass with a sharp buffet of the fist.

What a way to earn a living! I suppose I must have used up quite three minutes of my ten in meditating on these hardy fellows and wondering what made them go in for such an exacting life work. Large profits, no doubt, and virtually no overhead, but think what they must have to spend on nerve specialists and rest cures. Some sort of tonic alone must form a heavy item of a burglar's expenses.

I could have gone on for quite a while musing along these lines, but was obliged to dismiss the subject from my mind, for time was passing and I might expect Boko's return at any minute. And I shrank from the prospect of having to explain to him that I had been frittering away in daydreaming the moments which should have been earmarked for action.

Feeling, therefore, that if the thing was to be smacked into, 'twere well 'twere smacked into quickly, as Shakespeare says, I treacled the paper and attached it to the window. All that now remained to be done was to deliver the sharp buffet. And it was at this point that I suddenly came over all cat-in-the-adage-y. The chilliness of the feet became intensified, and I began to hover, as Stilton had done outside that jeweller's shop.

I had thought, while watching him on that occasion, that he had accomplished what you might call the last word in backing and filling, but I now realized that he had merely scratched the surface. Compared with mine at this juncture, Stilton's hovering could scarcely be termed hovering at all. I moved towards my objective and away from my objective, and some of the time I moved sideways. To an observer, had one been present, it might have seemed that I was trying out the intricate steps of some rhythmic dance.

Finally, however, stiffening the sinews and summoning up all the splendid Wooster courage, I made a quick forward movement and was in the act of raising my fist, when it was as if a stick of dynamite had been touched off beneath me. The hair rose in a solid mass, and every nerve in the body stood straight up, curling at the ends. There have been moments in his career, many of them, when Bertram Wooster has not felt at his ease, but this one was the top.

From somewhere above, a voice had spoken.

'Coo!' it said. 'Who's there?'

If it hadn't been for that 'Coo!' I might have supposed it the voice of Conscience. As it was, I was enabled to ticket it correctly as that of young blasted Edwin. Glued against the wall, as if I had been a bit of treacled paper, I could just see him leaning out of an adjacent window. And when I reflected that, after all I had gone through, I was now being set upon by

Boy Scouts, I don't mind admitting that the iron entered into my soul. Very bitter, the whole thing.

After he had said 'Who's there?' he was silent for a space, as if pausing for a reply, though you would have thought even a cloth-headed kid like that would have known that it's hopeless to expect burglars to keep the conversation going.

'Who's that?' he said, at length.

I maintained a prudent reserve. He then said 'I can see you all right,' but in an uncertain voice which told me he was lying in his teeth. The one thing that was serving to buoy me up and still the fluttering heart-strings at this most unpleasant moment was the fact that it was a dark night, without a moon or any rot of that sort. Stars, yes. Moon, no. A lynx might have seen me, but only a lynx, and it would have had to be a pretty sharpsighted lynx, at that.

My silence seemed to discourage him. These one-sided conversations always flag fairly quickly. He brooded over the scene a bit longer—Jeeves would have spotted a resemblance to the Blessed Damozel gazing out from the gold bar of heaven—then drew his head in, and I was alone at last.

Not, however, for long. A moment later, Boko hove alongside.

'All set?' he asked, in a hearty voice that seemed to boom through the garden like a costermonger calling attention to his brussels sprouts, and I grabbed him feverishly, begging him to pipe down a bit.

'Not so loud!'

'What's the matter?'

'Edwin.'

'Edwin?'

'He just poked his foul head out of a window and wanted to know who was there.'

'Did you tell him?'

'No.'

'Excellent. Very wise move. He's probably gone to sleep again.'

'Boy Scouts never sleep.'

'Of course they do. In droves. Have you smashed the window?'

'No.'

'Why not?'

'Because of Edwin.'

He clicked his tongue, causing me to quiver from stem to stern. To me, a little nervous at the moment, as I have shown, it sounded like a mass meeting of Spanish dancers playing the castanets.

'You mustn't let yourself be diverted from the task in hand by trifles, Bertie. I can't help wondering if you're taking this thing with the proper seriousness. I may be wrong, but there seems to me something frivolous in your attitude. Do pull yourself together and try to remember what this means to Nobby and me.'

'But I can't smash windows, with Edwin lurking above.'

'Of course you can. I can't see your difficulty. Pay no attention whatever to Edwin. If he is on the alert, so much the better. It will all help when the moment comes for me to put on my act. His story will support mine. I'll give you another ten minutes, and then I really must insist on a little action. Got a cigarette?'

'No.'

'Then I shall simply have to go on smoking mine. That's what it amounts to,' said Boko, and breezed off.

Now, reading the above splash of dialogue, you will have noticed something. I don't know if you happen to know the meaning of the French expression *sang-froid*, but, if you do, you can scarcely have failed to observe to what an extraordinary extent the recent Fittleworth had been exhibiting this quality. While I trembled and twittered, he remained as cool and calm as a turbot on ice, and it now occurred to me that the reason for this might very possibly be that he was keeping on the move.

It helps on these occasions to be able to circulate freely instead of standing on point duty outside scullery windows, and it was quite on the cards, I felt, that a short stroll might do something towards keying up my sagging nervous system. With this end in view, I wandered off round the house.

Any hope I may have entertained, however, that the vibrating ganglions would cease to quiver and the fluttering feeling in the pit of the stomach simmer down was shattered before I had gone a dozen yards. A dim figure suddenly loomed up before me in the darkness, causing me to leap perhaps five feet in the air and utter a sharp yip.

My composure was somewhat restored—not altogether, but somewhat—when the dim f. spoke, and I recognized Jeeves's voice.

14

'Good evening, sir,' he said.

'Good evening, Jeeves,' I responded.

'You gave me quite a start, sir.'

'Nothing to the one you gave me. I thought the top of my head had come off.'

'I am sorry to have been the cause of your experiencing any discomfort, sir. I was unable to herald my approach, the encounter being quite unforeseen. You are up late, sir.'

'Yes.'

'One could scarcely desire more delightful conditions for a nocturnal ramble.'

'That is your view, is it?'

'It is indeed, sir. I always feel that nothing is so soothing as a walk in a garden at night.'

'Ha!'

'The cool air. The scent of growing things. That is tobacco plant which you can smell, sir.'

'Is it?'

'The stars, sir.'

'Stars?'

'Yes, sir.'

'What about them?'

'I was merely directing your attention to them, sir. Look how the floor of heaven is thick inlaid with patines of bright gold.'

'Jeeves—'

'There's not the smallest orb which thou beholdest, sir, but in his motion like an angel sings, still quiring to the young-eyed cherubims.'

'Jeeves—'

'Such harmony is in immortal souls. But whilst this muddy vesture of decay doth grossly close it in, we cannot hear it.'

'Jeeves—'

'Sir?'

'You couldn't possibly switch it off, could you?'

'Certainly, sir, if you wish it.'

'I'm not in the mood.'

'Very good, sir.'

'You know how one isn't, sometimes.'

'Yes, sir. I quite understand. I procured the brooch, sir.'

'Brooch?'

'The one which you wished me to purchase in place of the trinket lost in the fire, sir. Lady Florence's birthday present.'

'Oh, ah.' It will give you some rough indication of how what he had called this nocturnal ramble of mine had affected me, when I say that I had completely forgotten about the damn' thing. 'You got it, eh?'

'Yes, sir.'

'And handed it in?'

'Yes, sir.'

'Good. That's off my mind, then. And, believe me, Jeeves, the more I can get off my mind at this juncture, the better I shall like it, because it's already loaded down well above the Plimsoll mark.'

'I am sorry to hear that, sir.'

'Do you know why I'm prowling about this garden?'

'I was hoping that you might enlighten me, sir.'

'I will. This is no careless saunter on which you find me engaged, Jeeves, but an enterprise whose consequences may well stagger humanity.'

He listened attentively while I sketched out the events which had led up to the tragedy, interrupting only with a respectful intake of the breath as I spoke of Uncle Percy, Boko and the Joke Goods. It was plain that my story had gripped him.

'An eccentric young gentleman, Mr Fittleworth, sir,' was his comment, as I concluded.

'Loony to the eyebrows,' I agreed.

'The scheme which he has formulated is not, however, without its ingenuity. His lordship would undoubtedly be most grateful to anyone whom he supposed to have foiled a raid on the premises on this particular night. I happen to be aware that, despite her ladyship's repeated instructions to him to attend to the matter, he forgot to post the letter renewing his burglary insurance.'

'How do you know that?'

'I had the facts from his lordship in person, sir. Ascertaining that I was about to drive to London this afternoon, he gave me the communication to dispatch in the metropolitan area, so that it should reach its destination to-morrow morning by the first delivery. His emotion, as he urged me not to fail him and alluded to what her ladyship would say if she ever discovered his negligence, was very noticeable. He shook visibly.'

I was amazed.

'You don't mean he's scared of Aunt Agatha?'

'Intensely, sir.'

'A tough bird like him? Practically a bucko mate of a tramp steamer?'

'Even bucko mates stand in awe of the captains of their vessels, sir.'

'Well, you absolutely astound me. I should have thought that if ever there was a bimbo who was master in his own home, that bimbo was Percival, Lord Worplesdon.'

'I am inclined to doubt whether the gentleman exists who could be master in a home that contained her ladyship, sir.'

'Perhaps you're right.'

'Yes, sir.'

I breathed deeply. For the first time since Boko had outlined the night's programme, I was conscious of a relaxation of the strain. It would be paltering with the truth to say that even now Bertram Wooster looked forward with any actual relish to busting that scullery window, but it was stimulating to feel that the action was likely to produce solid results.

'Then you think this scheme of Boko's will drag home the gravy?'

'Quite conceivably, sir.'

'That's a comfort.'

'On the other hand—'

'Oh, golly, Jeeves. What's wrong now?'

'I was merely about to say that Mr Fittleworth has selected a somewhat unfortunate moment for his enterprise, sir. It tends to clash with his lordship's arrangements.'

'How do you mean?'

'By an unfortunate coincidence, his lordship will in a few moments from now be proceeding to the potting shed to confer with Mr Chichester Clam.'

'Chichester Clam?'

'Yes, sir.'

I shook the head.

'I think the strain to which I have been subjected must have affected my hearing. You sound to me just as if you were saying Chichester Clam.'

'Yes, sir. Mr J. Chichester Clam, managing director of the Clam Line.'

'What on earth's a clam line?'

'The shipping line, sir, which, if you remember, is on the eve of being merged with his lordship's Pink Funnel.'

I got it at last.

'You mean the chap Uncle Percy is trying to get together with? The ancient mariner from America?'

'Precisely, sir. Owing to the conflagration at Wee Nooke, it became necessary to think of some other spot where the two gentlemen could meet and discuss their business without fear of interruption.'

'And you chose the potting shed?'

'Yes, sir.'

'God bless you, Jeeves.'

'Thank you, sir.'

'Is this bird in the potting shed now?'

'I should be disposed to imagine so, sir. When I motored to London this afternoon, it was with instructions from his lordship to establish telephonic communication with Mr Clam at his hotel and urge him to hasten to Steeple Bumpleigh and be in the potting shed half an hour after midnight. The gentleman expressed complete understanding and agreement, and assured me that he would drive down in good time to keep the appointment.'

I could not repress a pang of gentle pity for this hand across the sea. Born and brought up in America, he would, of course, not have the slightest idea of the sort of place Steeple Bumpleigh was and what he was letting himself in for in going there. I couldn't, offhand, say what Steeple Bumpleigh was saving up for Chichester Clam, but obviously he was headed for a sticky evening.

I saw, too, what Jeeves meant about Boko having selected an unfortunate moment for his enterprise.

'Half an hour after midnight? It must be nearly that now.'

'Exactly that, sir.'

'Then Uncle Percy will be manifesting himself at any moment.'

'If I am not mistaken, sir, this would be his lordship whom you can hear approaching.'

And, sure enough, from somewhere to the nor'-nor'-east there came the sound of some solid object shuffling through the night.

I inhaled in quick concern.

'Egad, Jeeves!'

'Sir?'

''Tis he!'

'Yes, sir.'

I mused a moment.

'Well,' I said, though not liking the prospect and wishing that the civility could have been avoided, 'I suppose I'd better pass the time of day. What ho,' I continued, as he came abreast. 'What ho, what ho!'

I must say the results were not unpleasing—to a man, I mean, who, like myself, had twice to-night been forced to skip like the high hills on finding himself unexpectedly addressed from the shadows. Watching the relative soar skywards with a wordless squeak, obviously startled out of a year's growth, I was conscious of a distinct sensation of getting a bit of my own back. I felt that, whatever might befall, I was at least that much to the good.

In introducing this uncle by marriage, I showed him to be a man who, in moments of keen emotion, had a tendency to say 'What?' and keep on saying it. He did so now.

'What? What? What? What? What?' he ejaculated, making five in all. 'What?' he added, bringing it up to the round half dozen.

'Lovely evening, Uncle Percy,' I said, hoping by the exercise of suavity to keep the conversation on an amicable plane. 'Jeeves and I were just talking about the stars. What was it you said about the stars, Jeeves?'

'I alluded to the fact that there was not the smallest orb which did not sing in its motion like an angel, still quiring to the young-eyed cherubims, sir.'

'That's right. Worth knowing, that, eh, Uncle Percy?'

During these exchanges, the relative had been going on saying 'What?' in a sort of strangled voice, as if still finding it a bit hard to cope with the pressure of events. He now came forward and peered at me, feasting the eyes as far as was possible in the uncertain light.

'You!' he said, with a kind of gasp, like some strong swimmer in his agony. 'What the devil are you doing here?'

'Just sauntering.'

'Then go and saunter somewhere else, damn it.'

The Woosters are quick to take a hint, and are generally able to spot when our presence is not desired. Reading between the lines, I could see that he was wishing me elsewhere.

'Right ho, Uncle Percy,' I said, still maintaining the old suavity, and was about to withdraw, when another of those voices which seemed to be so common in these parts spoke in my immediate rear, causing me to equal, if not to improve upon, the old relative's recent standing high jump.

'What's all this?' it said, and with what is sometimes called a sickening qualm I perceived that it was Stilton who had joined our little group. Boko had been completely wrong about the man. Rosy though his cheeks may have been, here was no eight-hour slumberer, who had to be brought to life by alarm clocks, but a vigilant guardian of the peace who was always up and doing, working while others slept.

Stilton was looking gruesomely official. His helmet gleamed in the starlight. His regulation boots had settled themselves solidly into the turf. I rather think he had got his notebook out.

'What's all this?' he repeated.

I suppose Uncle Percy was still feeling a bit edgy. Nothing else could have explained the crisp, mouth-filling expletive which now proceeded from him like a shot out of a gun. It sounded to me like something he must have picked up from one of the sea captains in his employment. These rugged mariners always have excellent vocabularies, and no doubt they frequently drop in at the office on their return from a voyage and teach him something new.

'What the devil do you mean, what's all this? And who the devil are you to come trespassing in my grounds, asking what's all this? What's all this yourself? What,' proceeded Uncle Percy, warming to his work, 'are you doing here, you great oaf? I suppose you're just sauntering, too? Good God! I try to enjoy a quiet stroll in my garden, and before I can so much as inhale a breath of air I find it crawling with nephews and policemen. I come out to be alone with Nature, and the first thing I know I can't move for the crowd. What is this place? Piccadilly Circus? Hampstead Heath on Bank Holiday? The spot chosen for the annual outing of the police force?'

I saw his point. Nothing is more annoying to a man who is seeking privacy than to discover that, without knowing it, he has thrown his grounds open to the public. In addition to which, of course, Chichester Clam was waiting for him in the potting shed.

The acerbity of his tone had not been lost on Stilton. Well, I mean to say, it couldn't very well have been. That expletive alone would have been enough to tell him that he was not a welcome visitor. I could see that he was piqued. His was in many ways a haughty spirit, and it was plain that he resented this brusqueness. From the fact that the top of his helmet moved sharply in the direction of the stars, I knew that he had drawn himself to his full height.

He found himself, however, in a somewhat embarrassing position. He could not come back with anything really snappy, Uncle Percy being a Justice of the Peace and, as such, able to put it across him like the dickens if he talked out of his turn. Besides being his future father-in-law. He was compelled, accordingly, to temper his resentment with a modicum of reserve and to take it out in stiffness of manner.

'I am sorry—'

'No use being sorry. Thing is not to do it, blast it.'

'— to intrude—'

'Then stop intruding.'

'— but I am here in the performance of my duty.'

'What do you mean? Never heard such nonsense.'

'I received a telephone call just now, desiring me to proceed to the Hall immediately.'

'Telephone call? Telephone call? What rot! At this time of night? Who telephoned you?'

I suppose that stiff, official manner is difficult to keep up. Quite a bit of a strain, probably. At any rate, Stilton now lapsed from it.

'Young ruddy Edwin,' he replied sullenly.

'My son Edwin?'

'Yes. He said he had seen a burglar in the grounds.'

A spasm seemed to pass through Uncle Percy. The word 'burglar' had plainly touched a chord. He spun round with a passionate gesture.

'Jeeves!'

'M'lord?'

'Did you post that letter?'

'Yes, m'lord.'

'Phew!' said Uncle Percy, and mopped his brow.

He was still mopping it, when there came the sound of galloping feet and somebody started giving tongue in the darkness.

'Hi! Hi! Hi! Wake up, everybody. Turn out the guard. I've caught a burglar in the potting shed.'

The voice was Boko's, and with another pang of pity I realized that J. Chichester Clam's troubles had begun. He knew now what happened to people who came to Steeple Bumpleigh.

15

In the brief interval which elapsed before Boko sighted us and came to join our little circle, I fell to musing on this Clam and thinking how different he must be finding all this from what he had been accustomed to.

Here, I mean to say, was one of those solid business men who are America's pride, whose lives are as regular and placid as that of a bug in a rug. On my visits to New York I had met dozens of them, so I could envisage without difficulty a typical Clam day.

Up in the morning bright and early at his Long Island home. The bath. The shave. The eggs. The cereal. The coffee. The drive to the station. The 8.15. The cigar. The *New York Times*. The arrival at the Pennsylvania terminus. The morning's work. The lunch. The afternoon's work. The cocktail. The 5.50. The drive from the station. The return home. The kiss for the wife and tots, the pat for the welcoming dog. The shower. The change into something loose. The well-earned dinner. The quiet evening. Bed.

That was the year in, year out routine of a man like Chichester Clam, Sundays and holidays excepted, and it was one ill calculated to fit him for the raw excitements and jungle conditions of Steeple Bumpleigh. Steeple Bumpleigh must have come upon him as a totally new experience, causing him to wonder what had hit him—like a man who, stooping to pluck a nosegay of wild flowers on a railway line, is unexpectedly struck in the small of the back by the Cornish Express. As he now sat in the potting shed, listening to Boko's view halloos, he was probably convinced that all this must be that Collapse of Civilization, of which he had no doubt so often spoken at the Union League Club.

In spite of the floor of heaven being thick inlaid with patines of bright gold, it was, as I have said, a darkish night, not easy to see things in. The visibility was, however, quite good enough to enable one to perceive that Boko was pretty pleased with himself. Indeed, it would not be overstating it to say that he had got it right up his nose. That this was so was borne in upon me by the fact that he started right away calling Uncle Percy 'my dear Worplesdon'—a thing which in his calmer moments he wouldn't have done on a bet.

'Ah, my dear Worplesdon,' he said, having peered into the relative's face and identified him, 'so you're up and about, are you? Capital, capital. Stilton, too? And Jeeves? And Bertie? Fine. Between the five of us, we ought to be well able to overpower the miscreant. I don't know if you were listening to what I was saying just now, but I've locked a burglar up in the potting shed.'

He spoke these words with the air of a man getting ready to receive the thanks of the nation, tapping Uncle Percy's chest the while as if to suggest that the latter was a lucky chap to have Boko Fittleworths working day and night in his interests. It did not surprise me to observe the relative's growing restiveness under the treatment.

'Will you stop prodding me, sir!' he cried, plainly stirred. 'What's all this nonsense about burglars?'

Boko seemed taken aback. One could see that he was feeling that this was not quite the tone.

'Nonsense, Worplesdon?'

'How do you know the fellow's a burglar?'

'My dear Worplesdon! Would anybody but a burglar be lurking in potting sheds at this time of night? But, if you still need convincing, let me tell you that I was passing the scullery window just now, and I noticed that it was covered with a piece of brown paper.'

'Brown paper?'

'Brown paper. Pretty sinister, eh?'

'Why?'

'My dear Worplesdon, it proves to the hilt the man's criminal intentions. You are possibly not aware of it, but when these fellows plan to enter a house and snaffle contents, they always stick a bit of brown paper on a window with treacle and then smash it with a blow of the fist. It's the regular procedure. The fragments of glass adhere to the paper, and they are thus enabled to climb in without mincing themselves into hash. Oh, no, my dear Worplesdon, there can be no doubt concerning the scoundrel's guilty purpose. I bottled him up in the nick of time. I heard something moving in the potting shed, peeped in, saw a dark form, and slammed the door and fastened it, thus laying him a dead stymie and foiling all his plans.'

This statement drew a word of professional approbation from the sleepless guardian of the law.

'Good work, Boko.'

'Thanks, Stilton.'

'You showed great presence of mind.'

'Nice of you to say so.'

'I'll go and pinch him.'

'Just what I was about to suggest.'

'Has he a gun?'

'I don't know. You'll soon find out.'

'I don't care if he has.'

'The right spirit.'

'I shall just make a quick spring—'

'That's the idea.'

'—and disarm him.'

'We will hope so. We will certainly hope so. Yes, let us hope for the best. Still, whatever happens, you will have the satisfaction of knowing that you have done your duty.'

Throughout these exchanges, starting at the words 'Good work' and continuing right through to the tab line 'done your duty', Uncle Percy had been exhibiting much of the frank perturbation of a cat on hot bricks. Nor could one blame him. He had invited J. Chichester Clam for a quiet talk in the potting shed, and the thought of constables making quick springs at him must have been a very bitter one. You can't conduct delicate business negotiations with that sort of thing going on. In his agony of spirit, he now began saying 'What?' again, leading Boko to apply that patronizing finger to his brisket once more.

'It's quite all right, my dear Worplesdon,' said Boko, tapping like a woodpecker. 'Have no concern about Stilton. He won't get hurt. At least, I don't think so. One may be wrong, of course. Anyway, he is paid to take these risks. Ah, Florence,' he added, addressing the daughter of the house, who had just come alongside in a dressing-gown, with her hair in curling pins.

It was plain that Florence was not her usual calm and equable self. When she spoke, one noted a testiness.

'Never mind the "Ah, Florence." What is going on out here? What is all this noise and disturbance? I was woken up by someone shouting.'

'Me,' said Boko, and even in the uncertain light I could see that he was smirking. I doubt if in all Hampshire that night you could have found a fellow more thoroughly satisfied with himself. He had got it firmly rooted in his mind that he was the popular hero, beloved of all—little knowing that Uncle Percy's favourite reading would have been his name on a tombstone. Rather saddening, the whole thing.

'Well, I wish you wouldn't. It is perfectly impossible to sleep, with people romping all over the garden.'

'Romping? I was catching a burglar.'

'Catching a burglar?'

'You never spoke a truer word. A great desperate brute of a midnight marauder, who may or may not be armed to the teeth. That question we shall be able to answer better after Stilton has got together with him.'

'But how did you catch a burglar?'

'Oh, it's just a knack.'

'I mean, what were you doing here at this time of night?'

It was as if Uncle Percy had been waiting for someone to come along and throw him just that cue.

'Exactly,' he cried, having snorted the snort of a lifetime. 'The very thing I want to know. The precise question I was about to ask myself. What the devil are you doing here? I am not aware that I invited you to infest my private grounds and go charging about them like a buffalo, making an appalling din and rendering peace and quiet impossible. You have a garden of your own, I believe? If you must behave like a buffalo, kindly go and do so there. And the idea of locking people in my potting shed! I never heard of anything so officious in my life.'

'Officious?'

'Yes, damned officious.'

Boko was patently stunned. One sensed that thoughts about birds biting the hand that fed them were racing through his mind. He stuttered a while before speaking.

'Well!' he said, at length, having ceased to imitate a motor bicycle. 'Well, I'm dashed! Well, I must say! Well, I'm blowed! Officious, eh? That is the attitude you take, is it? Ha! One desires no thanks, of course, for these little good turns one does people—at some slight inconvenience to oneself, one might perhaps mention—but I should have thought that in the circumstances one was entitled to expect at least decent civility. Jeeves!'

'Sir?'

'What did Shakespeare say about ingratitude?'

'"Blow, blow, thou winter wind," sir, "thou art not so unkind as man's ingratitude." He also alludes to the quality as "thou marble-hearted fiend".'

'And he wasn't so dashed far wrong! I brood over this house like a guardian angel, sacrificing my sleep and leisure to its interests. I sweat myself to the bone, catching burglars—'

Uncle Percy tuned in again.

'Burglars, indeed! All silly nonsense. The man is probably some harmless wayfarer, who has taken refuge in my potting shed from the storm—'

'What storm?'

'Never mind what storm.'

'There isn't a storm.'

'All right, all right!'

'It's a lovely night. No suggestion of a storm.'

'All right, all *right*! We aren't talking about the weather. We're talking about this poor waif in my potting shed. I say he is probably just some homeless wayfarer, and I refuse to persecute the unfortunate fellow. What harm has he done? All the riff-raff for miles around have been using my garden as if it were their own, so who shouldn't he? This is Liberty Hall, damn it—or seems to be.'

'So you don't think he's a burglar?'

'No, I do not.'

'Worplesdon, you're a silly ass. How about the brown paper? What price the treacle?'

'Damn the treacle. Curse the brown paper. And how dare you call me a silly ass? Jeeves!'

'M'lord?'

'Here's ten shillings. Go and give it to the poor chap and let him go. Tell him to buy himself a warm bed and supper.'

'Very good, m'lord.'

Boko uttered a sharp, yapping sound, like a displeased hyena.

'And, Jeeves!' he said.

'Sir?'

'When he's got the warm bed, better tuck him up and see that he has a hot water bottle.'

'Very good, sir.'

'Ten shillings, eh? Supper, egad? Warm bed, forsooth? Well, this lets me out,' said Boko. 'I wash my hands of the whole affair. This is the last occasion on which you may expect my help when you have burglars in this loony bin. Next time they come flocking round, I shall pat them on the back and hold the ladder for them.'

He strode off into the darkness, full to the brim of dudgeon, and I can't say I was much surprised. The way things had panned out had been enough to induce dudgeon in the mildest of men, let alone a temperamental young author, accustomed to calling on his publishers and raising hell at the smallest provocation.

But though seeing his viewpoint, I mourned. In fact, I would go further, I groaned in spirit. The tender Wooster heart had been deeply touched by the non-smooth running of the course of the Boko-Nobby true love, and I had hoped that to-night's rannygazoo would have culminated in a thorough sweetening of Uncle Percy and a consequent straightening out of the tangle.

Instead of which, this impulsive scrivener had gone and deposited himself lower down among the wines and spirits than ever. If the betting against his scooping in a guardian's consent had been about four to one up to this point, it could scarcely be estimated now at anything shorter than a hundred to eight—and even at that generous price I doubt if the punters would have invested.

I was just wondering whether it would be any use my putting in a soothing word, and feeling on the whole perhaps not, when there came to my ears a low whistle, which may or may not have been the note of the lesser screech owl, and I observed something indistinct but apparently feminine bobbing about behind a distant tree. Everything seeming to point to this being Nobby, I detached myself from the main body and oiled off in her direction.

My surmise was correct. It was Nobby, in a dressing-gown but not curling pins. Apparently, with her style of hair you don't use them. She was fizzing with excitement and the desire to learn the latest hot news.

'I didn't like to join the party,' she said, after the preliminary what-hoes had been exchanged. 'Uncle Percy would have sent me to bed. How's it coming along, Bertie?'

It wrenched the heart-strings to have to ladle out bad tidings to the eager young prune, but the painful task could not be avoided.

'Not too well,' I replied sombrely.

As I had foreseen, the statement got right in amongst her. She uttered a stricken yowl.

'Not too well?'

'No.'

'What went wrong?'

'It would be better to ask what went right. The enterprise was a flop from start to finish.'

She sharp-exclamationed, and I saw that she was giving me one of those unpleasant, suspicious looks.

'I suppose you fell down on your end of the thing?'

'Nothing of the kind. I did all that man could have done. But there was one of those unfortunate concatenations of circumstances, which led to what we had anticipated would be a nice little night's work for the two of us becoming a mob scene. We were just getting on with it most satisfactorily, when the gardens and messuages became a seething mass of Uncle Percys, Jeeveses, Stiltons, Florences and what not. It dished our aims completely. And I am sorry to say that Boko did not show himself at his best.'

'What do you mean?'

'He would keep calling Uncle Percy "my dear Worplesdon". You can't address a man like that as "my dear Worplesdon" for long without something cracking under the strain. Heated words ensued, quite a few being contributed by Boko. The scene, a most painful one, concluded with him calling Uncle Percy a silly ass and turning on his heel and stalking off. I fear his standing with the above has hit a new low.'

She moaned softly, and I considered for a moment the idea of patting her head. Not much use, though, I felt on consideration, and gave it a miss.

'I did think I could have trusted Boko not to make an ass of himself just for once,' she murmured with a wild regret.

'I doubt if you can ever trust an author not to make an ass of himself,' I responded gravely.

'Golly, I'll tick him off for this! Which way did he go, when he turned on his heel?'

'Somewhere in that direction.'

'Wait till I find him!' she cried, baying like an undersized bloodhound, and was gone with the wind.

It was perhaps a couple of ticks later, or three, that Jeeves came shimmering up.

'A disturbing evening, sir,' he said. 'I released Mr Clam.'

'Never mind about Clam. Clam leaves me cold. The chap I'm worrying about is Boko.'

'Ah, yes, sir.'

'Silly idiot, alienating Uncle Percy like that.'

'Yes, sir. It was a pity that the young gentleman's manner should not have been more conciliatory.'

'He's sunk, unless you can think of some way of healing the breach.'

'Yes, sir.'

'Get hold of him, Jeeves.'

'Yes, sir.'

'Confer with him.'

'Yes, sir.'

'Strain the bean to the utmost in order to hit upon some solution.'

'Very good, sir.'

'You will find him somewhere out there in the silent night. At least, it won't be so dashed silent, because Nobby will be telling him what she thinks of him. Circle around till you hear a raised soprano voice, and that will be the spot to head for.'

He popped off, as desired, and I started to do a bit of pacing to and fro, knitting the brows. I had been knitting them for about five minutes, when something loomed up in the offing and I saw that it was Boko, come to play a return date.

16

Boko was looking subdued and chastened, as if his soul had been passed through the wringer. He wore the unmistakable air of a man who has just been properly told where he gets off by the girl of his dreams and has not yet reassembled the stunned faculties.

'Hullo, Bertie,' he said, in a sort of hushed, saintlike voice.

'Pip-pip, Boko.'

'Some night!'

'Considerable.'

'You haven't a flask on you, have you?'

'No.'

'A pity. One should always carry a flask about in case of emergencies. Saint Bernard dogs do it in the Alps. Fifty million Saint Bernard dogs can't be wrong. I have just passed through a great emotional experience, Bertie.'

'Did Nobby find you?'

He gave a little shiver.

'I've just been chatting with her.'

'I had a sort of idea you had.'

'It shows in my appearance, does it? Yes, I suppose it would. It wasn't you who told her about those Joke Goods, was it?'

'Of course not.'

'Somebody did.'

'Uncle Percy, probably.'

'That's true. She would have asked him how the lunch came out.

Yes, I imagine that was the authoritative source from which she had her information.'

'So she touched on the Joke Goods?'

'Oh, yes. Yes, she touched on them. Her conversation dealt partly with them and partly with what happened to-night. She was at no loss for words on either theme. You're absolutely sure you haven't a flask?'

'Quite, I'm afraid.'

'Ah, well,' said Boko, and relapsed into silence for a while, emerging from it to ask me in a wondering sort of voice where girls picked up these expressions.

'What expressions?'

'I couldn't repeat them, with gentlemen present. I suppose they learn them at their finishing schools.'

'She gave you beans, did she?'

'With no niggardly hand. It was an extraordinary feeling, standing there while she put me through it. One had a dazed sensation of something small and shrill whirling about one, seething with fury. Like being attacked by a Pekinese.'

'I've never been attacked by a Pekinese.'

'Well, ask the man who has. He'll tell you. Every moment, I was expecting to get a nasty nip in the ankle.'

'How did it all end?'

'Oh, I got away with my life. Still, what's life?'

'Life's all right.'

'Not if you've lost the girl you love.'

'Have you lost the girl you love?'

'That's what I'm trying to figure out. I can't make up my mind. It all depends what construction you place on the words "I never want to see or speak to you again in this world or the next, you miserable fathead."'

'Did she say that?'

'Among other things.'

I saw that the time had come to soothe and encourage.

'I wouldn't let that worry me, Boko.'

He seemed surprised.

'You wouldn't?'

'No. She didn't mean it.'

'Didn't mean it?'

'Of course not.'

'Just said it for something to say? Making conversation, as it were?'

'Well, I'll tell you, Boko. I've made a pretty deep study of the sex, observing them in all their moods, and the conclusion I've come to is that when they shoot their heads off in the manner described, little attention need be paid to the subject matter.'

'You would advise ignoring it?'

'Absolutely. Dismiss it from the mind.'

He was silent for a moment. When he spoke, it was on a note of hope.

'There's one thing, of course. She used to love me. As recently as this afternoon. Dearly. She said so. One's got to remember that.'

'She still does.'

'You really feel that, do you?'

'Of course.'

'In spite of calling me a miserable fathead?'

'Certainly. You are a miserable fathead.'

'That's true.'

'You can't go by what a girl says, when she's giving you the devil for making a chump of yourself. It's like Shakespeare. Sounds well, but doesn't mean anything.'

'Your view, then, is that the old affection still lingers?'

'Definitely. Dash it, man, if she could love you in spite of those grey flannel trousers of yours, it isn't likely that any mere acting of the goat on your part will have choked her off. Love is indestructible. Its holy flame burneth for ever.'

'Who told you that?'

'Jeeves.'

'He ought to know.'

'He does. You can bank on Jeeves.'

'That's right. You can, can't you? You're a great comfort, Bertie.'

'I try to be, Boko.'

'You give me hope. You raise me from the depths.'

He had perked up considerably. He wasn't actually squaring his shoulders and sticking his chin out, but the morale had plainly stiffened. And I have an idea that in another minute or two he might have become almost jaunty, had there not cut through the night air at this juncture a feminine voice, calling his name.

'Boko!'

He shook like an aspen.

'Yes, darling?'

'Come here. I want you.'

'Coming, darling. Oh, my God!' I heard him whisper. 'An encore!'

He tottered off, and I was left to ponder over the trend of affairs.

I may say at once that I viewed the situation without concern. To Boko, who had actually been in the ring with the young geezer while she was exploding in all directions, it had naturally seemed that the end of the world had come and Judgement Day set in with unusual severity. But to me, the cool and level-headed bystander, the whole thing had been pure routine. One shrugged the shoulders and recognized it for what it was—viz. pure apple sauce.

Love's silken bonds are not broken just because the female half of the sketch takes umbrage at the loony behaviour of the male partner and slips it across him in a series of impassioned speeches. However devoutly a girl may worship the man of her choice, there always comes a time when she feels an irresistible urge to haul off and let him have it in the neck. I suppose if the young lovers I've known in my time were placed end to end—difficult to manage, of course, but what I mean is just suppose they were—they would reach half-way down Piccadilly. And I couldn't think of a single dashed one who hadn't been through what Boko had been through to-night.

Already, I felt, the second phase had probably set in, where the female lovebird weeps on the male lovebird's chest and says she's sorry she was cross. And that my surmise was correct was proved by Boko's demeanour, as he rejoined me some minutes later. Even in the dim light, you could see that he was feeling like a million dollars. He walked as if on air, and the whole soul had obviously expanded, like a bath sponge placed in water.

'Bertie.'

'Hullo?'

'Still there?'

'On the spot.'

'It's all right, Bertie.'

'She loves you still?'

'Yes.'

'Good.'

'She wept on my chest.'

'Fine.'

'And said she was sorry she had been cross. I said "There, there!" and everything is once more gas and gaiters.'

'Splendid.'

'I felt terrific.'

'I bet you did.'

'She withdrew the words "miserable fathead".'

'Good.'

'She said I was the tree on which the fruit of her life hung.'

'Fine.'

'And apparently it was all a mistake when she told me she never wanted to see or speak to me again in this world or the next. She does. Frequently.'

'Splendid.'

'I clasped her to me, and kissed her madly.'

'I bet you did.'

'Jeeves, who was present, was much affected.'

'Oh, Jeeves was there?'

'Yes. He and Nobby had been discussing plans and schemes.'

'For sweetening Uncle Percy?'

'Yes. For, of course, that still has to be done.'

I looked grave. Not much use, of course, in that light.

'It's going to be difficult—'

'Not a bit.'

'—after your not only addressing him as "my dear Worplesdon" but also calling him a silly ass.'

'Not a bit, Bertie, not a bit. Jeeves has come across with one of his ripest suggestions.'

'He has?'

'What a man!'

'Ah!'

'I often say there's nobody like Jeeves.'

'And well you may.'

'Have you ever noticed how his head sticks out at the back?'

'Often.'

'That's where the brain is. Packed away behind the ears.'

'Yes. What's his idea?'

'Briefly this. He thinks it would make an excellent impression and enable me to recover the lost ground, if I stuck up for old Worplesdon.'

'Stuck him up? I don't get that. With a gun, do you mean?'

'I didn't say "stuck up". Stuck up for.'

'Oh, stuck up for?'

'That's right. Stuck up for. In other words, he advises me to take the old boy's part—protect him, as it were.'

'Protect Uncle Percy?'

'Oh, I know it sounds bizarre. But Jeeves thinks it will work.'

'I still don't get it.'

'It's perfectly simple, really. Look here. Suppose some great blustering brute of a chap barges into old Worplesdon's study at ten sharp to-morrow morning and starts ballyragging him like the dickens, calling him every name under the sun and generally making himself thoroughly offensive. I'm waiting outside the study window, and at the psychological moment I stick my head in and in a quiet, reproving voice, say "Stop, Bertie!—"'

'Bertie?'

'The chap's name is Bertie. But don't interrupt. I'll lose the thread. I stick my head in and say "Stop, Bertie! You are strangely forgetting yourself. I cannot stand by and listen to you abusing a man I admire and respect as highly as Lord Worplesdon. Lord Worplesdon and I may have had our differences—the fault was mine and I am heartily sorry for it—but I have never deviated from the opinion that it is an honour to know him. And when I hear you calling him a—"'

I am pretty quick. Already, I had spotted the nature of the frightful scheme.

'You want me to go into Uncle Percy's lair and call him names?'

'At ten sharp. Most important, that. We shall have to synchronize to the second. Nobby tells me he always spends the morning in his study, no doubt writing stinkers to the captains of his ships.'

'And you bob up and tick me off for ticking him off?'

'That's the idea. It can hardly fail to show me in a sympathetic light, causing him to warm to me and feel that I'm a pretty good chap, after all. There he will be, I mean to say, cowering in his chair, while you stand over him, shaking your finger in his face—'

The vision conjured up by these words was so ghastly that I staggered and would have fallen, had I not clutched at a tree.

'You say Jeeves suggested that?'

'As I told you, just like a flash.'

'He must be tight.'

A stiffness crept into Boko's manner.

'I don't understand you, Bertie. I rank the scheme among his very subtlest efforts. It seems to me one of those simple stratagems, all the more effective for their simplicity, which can hardly drop a stitch. Coming in at the moment when you are intimidating old Worplesdon, and throwing the whole weight of my sympathy and support on his side, I shall—'

There are moments when we Woosters can be very firm—adamant is perhaps the word—and one of these is when we are asked to intimidate men like Uncle Percy.

'I'm sorry, Boko.'

'Sorry? Why?'

'Include me out.'

'What!'

'Nothing doing.'

He leaned forward, the better to stare incredulously into my face. The man seemed stunned.

'Bertie!'

'Yes, I know. But I repeat—nothing doing.'

'Nothing doing?'

'Nothing doing.'

A pleading note came into his voice, the same sort of note I've sometimes heard in Bingo Little's, when asking a bookie to take the broad, spacious view and wait for his money till Wednesday week.

'But, Bertie, you're fond of Nobby?'

'Of course.'

'Of course you are, or you would never have given her that threepennyworth of acid drops. And you don't, I take it, dispute the fact that you and I were at school together? Of course, you don't. When I thought I heard you say you wouldn't sit in, I must have misunderstood you.'

'You didn't.'

'I didn't?'

'No.'

'You refuse to do your bit?'

'I do.'

'You—I want to get this straight—you really decline to play your part—your simple, easy part—in this enterprise?'

'That's right.'

'This *is* Bertie Wooster speaking?'

'It is.'

'The Bertie Wooster I was at school with?'

'That's right.'

He drew in his breath with a sort of whistle.

'Well, if anybody had told me this would happen, I wouldn't have believed it. I would have laughed mockingly. Bertie Wooster let me down? No, no, I would have said—not Bertie, who was not only at school with me but is at this very moment bursting with my meat.'

This was a nasty one. I wasn't actually bursting with his meat, of course, because there hadn't been such a frightful lot of it, but I saw what it meant. For an instant, when he put it like that, I nearly weakened. Then I thought of Uncle Percy 'cowering in his chair'—cowering in his chair, my foot!—and was strong again.

'I'm sorry, Boko.'

'So am I, Bertie. Sorry and disappointed. Sick at heart is the expression that leaps to the lips. Well, I suppose I shall have to go and break the news to Nobby. Golly, how she'll cry!'

I could not repress a pang.

'I don't want to make Nobby cry.'

'You will, though. Gallons.'

He faded away into the darkness, sighing reproachfully, leaving me alone with the stars.

And I was just examining them and wondering what had given Jeeves the idea that they were quiring to the young-eyed cherubims—I couldn't see the slightest indication of such a thing myself—when they suddenly merged, as if they had been Uncle Percy and J. Chichester Clam, and became a jagged sheet of flame.

This was because a hidden hand, creeping up behind me unperceived, had given me the dickens of a slosh with what I assumed to be some blunt instrument. It caught me squarely on the back hair, bringing me to earth with a sharp 'Ouch!'

17

I sat up, rubbing the occiput, and a squeaky voice spoke in my earhole. Eyeing me solicitously, or else gloating over his handiwork, I couldn't tell which, was young blighted Edwin.

'Coo!' he said. 'Is that you, Bertie?'

'Yes, it jolly well is,' I replied with a touch of not unnatural asperity. I mean, life's difficult enough without having Boy Scouts beaning one every other minute, and I was incensed. 'What's the idea? What do you mean, you repellent young boll weevil, by socking me with a dashed great club?'

'It wasn't a club. It was my Scout's stick. Sort of like a hockey stick. Very useful.'

'Comes in handy, does it?'

'Rather! Did it hurt?'

'You may take it as definitely official that it hurt like blazes.'

'Coo! I'm sorry. I mistook you for the burglar. There's one lurking in the grounds. I heard him underneath my window. I said "Who's there?" and he slunk off with horrid imprecations. I say, I'm not having much luck to-night. The last chap I mistook for the burglar turned out to be father.'

'Father?'

'Yes. How was I to know it was him? I never thought he would be wandering about the garden in the middle of the night. I saw a shadowy form crouching down, as if about to spring, and I crept up behind it and—'

'You didn't biff him?'

'Yes. Rather a juicy one.'

I must say my heart leaped up, as Jeeves tells me his does when he beholds a rainbow in the sky. The thought of Uncle Percy stopping a hot one with the trouser seat was pretty stimulating. It had been coming to him for years. I had that sort of awed feeling one gets sometimes, when one has a close-up of the workings of Providence and realizes that nothing is put into this world without a purpose, not even Edwin, and that the meanest creatures have their uses.

'He was a bit shirty about it.'

'It annoyed him, eh?'

'He wanted to give me beans, but Florence wouldn't let him. She said, "Father, you are not to touch him. It was a pure misunderstanding." Florence is very fond of me.'

I raised my eyebrows. A girl, I felt, of strange, even morbid tastes.

'So all he did was to tell me to go to bed.'

'Then why aren't you in bed?'

'Bed? Coo! Not likely. How's your head?'

'Rotten.'

'Does it ache?'

'Of course it aches.'

'Have you got a contusion?'

'Yes, I have.'

'This is where I could give you first aid.'

'No, it isn't.'

'Don't you want first aid?'

'No, I don't. We have threshed all this out before, young Edwin. You know my views.'

'I don't ever seem able to get anyone to let me give them first aid,' he said wistfully. 'And what one needs is lots of practice. What are you doing here, Bertie?'

'Everybody asks me what I'm doing here,' I replied, with a touch of pique. 'Why shouldn't I be here? This place is related to me by ties of blood. If you really want to know, I came here for an after dinner saunter with Boko Fittleworth.'

'I haven't seen Boko.'

'A bit of luck for him.'

'D'Arcy Cheesewright's here.'

'I know.'

'I phoned him after I saw the burglar.'

'I know.'

'Did you know he was engaged to Florence?'

'Yes.'

'I'm not sure it's not off. They were having an awful row just now.'

He spoke lightly, throwing the statement out as if it had been some news item of merely negligible interest, and was probably surprised at the concern which I exhibited.

'What!'

'Yes.'

'An awful row?'

'Yes.'

'What about?'

'I don't know.'

'When you say an awful row, how awful a row do you mean?'

'Well, fairly awful.'

'High words?'

'Pretty high.'

My heart, which had leaped up as described at the bulletin about Uncle Percy's trouser seat, was now down in the basement again. The whole trend of my foreign policy, as I have made abundantly clear, being to promote cordial relations between these two, the information that they had been having even fairly high words was calculated to freeze the blood.

You see, what I was saying apropos of Nobby hauling up her slacks and coming the Pekinese on Boko—all that stuff, if you remember, about girls giving their loved one the devil just for the fun of the thing and to keep the pores open—didn't apply to serious minded females like Florence and the sort of chap Stilton was. It's all a question of what Jeeves calls the psychology of the individual. If Florence and Stilton had gone to the mat and started chewing pieces out of each other, the outlook was unsettled.

'How much of it did you hear?'

'Not much. Because that was when I saw something moving in the darkness and went and biffed it with my Scout's stick, and it turned out to be you.'

This, of course, put a slightly better complexion on things. My first impression had been that he had had a ringside seat all through the conflict. If he had only heard the opening exchanges, it might be that matters had not proceeded too far. Cooler thoughts might have prevailed after his departure, causing the contestants to cheese it before the breach became irreparable. It often happens like that with girls and men of high spirit. They start off with a whoop and a holler, and then, their better selves prevailing, pipe down.

I mentioned this to Edwin, and he seemed to think that there might be something in it. But I noticed that he appeared distrait and not really interested, and after a pause of a few moments, during which I hoped for the best and he twiddled his Scout's stick, he revealed why this was so. He was worrying about a point of procedure.

'I say, Bertie,' he said, 'you know that slosh I gave you.'

I assured him that I had not forgotten it.

'I meant well, you know.'

'That's a comfort.'

'Still, of course, I did sock you, didn't I?'

'You did.'

'You can't get away from that.'

'No.'

'Then here's what I'm wondering. Have I wiped out the act of kindness I did you this afternoon?'

'When you tidied up Wee Nooke?'

'No, I'm afraid that doesn't count, because it didn't work out right. I meant finding that brooch.'

I had to watch my step rather sedulously here. I mean to say, the brooch he had found and the brooch Jeeves had delivered to Florence were supposed to be one and the same brooch, and he must never learn from my lips that I had lost the dashed thing again after he had found it that time in the hall.

'Oh, that?' I said. 'Yes, that was a Grade A act of kindness.'

'I know. But do you think it still counts?'

'Oh, rather.'

'In spite of my socking you?'

'Unquestionably.'

'Coo! Then I'm all square up to last Thursday.'

'You mean last Friday.'

'Thursday.'

'Friday.'

'Thursday.'

'Friday, you fatheaded young faulty reasoner,' I said, with some heat, for his inability to keep the score correctly was annoying me as much as that 'We are seven' stuff must have annoyed the poet—I forget his name—who got talking figures with another child. 'Listen. Your last Friday's act of kindness would have been the tidying up of Wee Nooke. Right. But owing to the unfortunate sequel that has to be scratched off the list. You admit that, don't you? Well, that makes the finding of the brooch your last Friday's act of kindness. Perfectly simple, if you'll only use the little grey cells a bit.'

'Yes, but you haven't got it right.'

'I have got it right. Listen—'

'I mean, you're talking about the first time I found the brooch. What I'm talking about is the second time. That counts as well.'

I couldn't follow him.

'How do you mean, the second time? You didn't find it twice.'

'Yes, I did. The first time was when you dropped it in the hall, you remember. Then I went off to clean the kitchen chimney. Then there was that explosion, and I came out, and you were standing on the lawn in your shirt sleeves. You had taken off your coat and chucked it away.'

'Oh my gosh!'

What with the stress of this and that, I had completely forgotten that coat sequence. It all came back to me now, and a cold hand seemed to clutch at my heart. I could see where he was heading.

'I suppose the brooch must have fallen out of your pocket, because when you had gone into the house I saw it lying there. And I thought it would be an act of kindness if I saved you trouble by taking it to Florence.'

I gazed at him dully. With a lack-lustre eye is, I believe, the expression.

'So you took it to Florence?'

'Yes.'

'Saying it was a present from me?'

'Yes.'

'Did she seem pleased?'

'Frightfully. Coo!'

He vanished abruptly, like an eel going into mud, and I was aware of the approach of someone breathing heavily.

It did not need the child's impulsive dash into the shadows to tell me that this stertorous newcomer was Florence.

18

Florence was obviously in the grip of some powerful emotion. She quivered gently, as if in the early stages of palsy, and her face, as far as I could gather from the sketchy view I was able to obtain of it, was pale and set, like the white of a hardboiled egg.

'D'Arcy Cheesewright,' she said, getting right off the mark without so much as a preliminary 'What ho, there,' 'is an obstinate, mulish, pigheaded, overbearing, unimaginative, tyrannical jack in office!'

Her words froze me to the core. I was conscious of a sense of frightful peril. Owing to young Edwin's infernal officiousness, this pancake had been in receipt only a few hours earlier of a handsome diamond brooch, ostensibly a present from Bertram W., and now, right on top of it, she had had a falling out with Stilton, so substantial that it took her six distinct adjectives to describe him. When a girl uses six derogatory adjectives in her attempt to paint the portrait of the loved one, it means something. One may indicate a merely temporary tiff. Six is big stuff.

I didn't like the way things were shaping. I didn't like it at all. It seemed to me that what she must be saying to herself was 'Look here upon this picture and on this,' as it were. I mean to say, on the one hand, a suave, knightly donor of expensive brooches; on the other, an obstinate, mulish, pigheaded, overbearing, unimaginative, tyrannical jack in office. If you were a girl, which would you prefer to link your lot with? Exactly.

I felt that I must spare no effort to plead Stilton's cause, to induce her to overlook whatever it was he had done to make her go about breathing like an asthma patient and scattering adjectives all over the place. The time had come for me to be eloquent and persuasive as never before, pouring oil on the troubled waters with a liberal hand, emptying the jug if necessary.

'Oh, dash it!' I cried.

'What do you mean by "Oh, dash it"?'

'Just "Oh, dash it!" Sort of protest, if you follow me.'

'You do not agree with me?'

'I think you've misjudged him.'

'I have not.'

'Splendid fellow, Stilton.'

'He is nothing of the kind.'

'Wouldn't you say he was the sort of chap who has made England what it is?'

'No.'

'No?'

'I said no.'

'Yes, that's right. So you did.'

'He is a mere uncouth Cossack.'

A cossack, I knew, was one of those things clergymen wear, and I wondered why she thought Stilton was like one. An inquiry into this would have been fraught with interest, but before I could institute it she had continued.

'He has been abominably rude, not only to me but to father. Just because father would not allow him to arrest the man in the potting shed.'

A bright light shone upon me. Her words had made clear the root of the trouble. I had, if you remember, edged away from the Stilton-Florence-Uncle Percy group just after the last named had put the presidential veto on the able young officer's scheme of pinching J. Chichester Clam, and had, accordingly, not been there to hear Stilton's comments. These, it was now evident, must have been on the fruity side. Stilton, as I have indicated, is a man of strong passions—one who, when annoyed, does not mince his words.

My mind went back to that time at Oxford, when I had gone in for rowing and had drawn him as a coach. If what he had said to Uncle Percy had been even remotely in the same class as his remarks on that occasion with reference to my stomach, I could see that relations must inevitably have got pretty strained, and my heart sank as I visualized the scene.

'He said father was shackling the police and that it was men like him, grossly lacking in any sense of civic duty, who were the cause of the ever-growing crime wave. He said that father was a menace to the community and would be directly responsible if half the population of Steeple Bumpleigh were murdered in their beds.'

'You don't think he spoke laughingly?'

'No, I do not think he spoke laughingly.'

'With a twinkle in his eye, I mean.'

'There was not the slightest suggestion of any twinkle in his eye.'

'You might have missed it. It's a dark night.'

'Please do not be utterly absurd, Bertie. I have sufficient intelligence, I hope, to be able to recognize a vile exhibition of bad temper when I see it. His tone was most offensive. "And you," he said, looking at father as if he were some sort of insect, "call yourself a Justice of the Peace. Faugh!"'

'Fore? Like at golf?'

'F-a-u-g-h.'

'Oh, ah.'

I was beginning to be almost sorry for Uncle Percy, as far as it is possible to be sorry for a man like that. I mean, there was no getting away from it that it hadn't been a big evening for the poor old bloke. First, Boko with his 'My dear Worplesdon'; then Edwin with his hockey stick; and now Stilton with his 'Faughs'. One of those nights you look back to with a shudder.

'His behaviour was a revelation to me. It laid bare a brutal, inhuman side of his character, of the existence of which I had never till then had a suspicion. There was something positively horrible in the fury he exhibited, when he realized that he was not to be allowed to arrest the man. He was like some malignant wild beast deprived of its prey.'

It was plain that Stilton's stock was in or approaching the cellar, and I did what I could to stop the slump.

'Still, it showed zeal, what?'

'Tchah!'

'And zeal, after all, when you come right down to it, is what he draws his weekly envelope for.'

'Don't talk to me about zeal. It was revolting. And when I said that father was quite right, he turned on me like a tiger.'

Although by this time, as you may well imagine, I was rocking on my base and becoming more and more a prey to alarm and despondency, I couldn't help admiring Stilton for his intrepid courage. Circumstances had so arranged themselves as to extract most of the stuffing from what had been a closeish boyhood friendship, but I had to respect a man capable of turning on Florence like a tiger. I would hardly have thought Attila the Hun could have done it, even if at the peak of his form.

All the same, I wished he hadn't. Oh, I was saying to myself, that the voice of Prudence had whispered in his ear. It was so vital to my interests that the mutual love of these two should continue unimpaired, and already much of the gilt, I feared, must have been rubbed off the gingerbread of their romance. Love is a sensitive plant, which needs cherishing and fostering. This cannot be done by turning on girls like tigers.

'I told him that modern enlightened thought held that imprisonment merely brutalizes the criminal.'

'And what did he say to that?'

'"Oh, yes?"'

'Ah, he agreed with you.'

'He did nothing of the kind. He spoke in a most unpleasant, sneering voice. "It does, does it?" he said. And I said "Yes, it does." He then said something about modern enlightened thought which I cannot repeat.'

I wondered what this had been. Evidently something red hot, for it was clear that it still rankled like a boil on the back of the neck. Her fists, I saw, were clenched, and she had started to tap her foot on the ground—sure indications that the soul is fed to the eye teeth. Florence is one of those girls who look on modern enlightened thought as a sort of personal buddy, and receive with an ill grace cracks at its expense.

I groaned in spirit. The way things were shaping, I was expecting her to say next that she had broken off the engagement.

And that was just what she did say.

'Of course, I broke off the engagement instantly.'

In spite of the fact that, as I say, I had practically known it was coming, I skipped like the high hills.

'You broke off the engagement?'

'Yes.'

'Oh, I say, you shouldn't have done that.'

'Why not?'

'Sterling chap like Stilton.'

'He is nothing of the kind.'

'You ought to forget those cruel words he spoke. You should make allowances.'

'I don't understand you.'

'Well, look at it from the poor old buster's point of view. Stilton, you must bear in mind, entered the police force hoping for rapid advancement.'

'Well?'

'Well, of course, the men up top don't advance a young rozzer rapidly unless he comes through with something so spectacular as to make them draw in their breath with an awed "Lord love a duck!" For weeks, months perhaps, he has been chafing like a caged eagle at the frightful law-abidingness of this place, hoping vainly for even a collarless dog or a decent drunk and disorderly that he could get his teeth into, and the sudden arrival of a burglar must have seemed to him manna from heaven. Here, he must have said to himself, was where at last he made his presence felt. And just as he was hitching up his sleeves and preparing to take his big opportunity, Uncle Percy goes and puts him on the leash. It was enough to upset any cop. Naturally he forgot himself and spoke with a generous strength. But he never means what he says in moments of heat. You should have heard him once at Oxford, talking to me about sticking out my stomach while toiling at the oar. You would have thought he loathed my stomach and its contents. Yet only a few hours later we were dining *vis-à-vis* at the Clarendon—clear soup, turbot and a saddle of mutton, I remember—and he was amiability itself. You'll find it's just the same now. I'll bet remorse is already gnawing him, and nobody is sorrier than he for having said nasty things about modern enlightened thought. He loves you devotedly. This is official. I happen to know. So what I would suggest is that you go to him and tell him that all is forgotten and forgiven. Only thus can you avoid making a bloomer, the memory of which will haunt you through the years. If you give Stilton the bum's rush, you'll kick yourself practically incessantly for the rest of your life. The whitest man I know.'

I paused, partly for breath and partly because I felt I had said enough. I stood there, waiting for her reply, wishing I had a throat lozenge to suck.

Well, I don't know what reaction I had expected on her part—possibly the drooping of the head and the silent tear, as the truth of my words filtered through her system; possibly some verbal statement to the effect that I had spoken a mouthful. What I had definitely not expected was that she would kiss me, and with a heartiness that nearly dropped me in my tracks.

'Bertie, you are extraordinary!' She laughed, a thing I couldn't have done, if handsomely paid. 'So quixotic. It is what I love in you. Nobody hearing you would dream that it is your dearest wish to marry me yourself.'

I tried to utter, but could not. The tongue had got all tangled up with the uvula, and the brain seemed paralysed. I was feeling the same stunned feeling which, I imagine, Chichester Clam must have felt as the door of the potting shed slammed and he heard Boko starting to yodel without—a nightmare sensation of being but a helpless pawn in the hands of Fate.

She passed an arm through mine, and began to explain, like a governess instructing a backward pupil in the rudiments of simple arithmetic.

'Do you think I have not understood? My dear Bertie, I am not blind. When I broke off our engagement, I naturally supposed that you would forget—or perhaps that you would be angry and resentful and think hard, bitter thoughts of me. To-night, I realized how wrong I had been. It was that brooch you gave me that opened my eyes to your real feelings. There was no need for you to have given me a birthday present at all, unless you wanted me to know that you still cared. And to give me one so absurdly expensive . . . Of course, I knew at once what you were trying to tell me. It all fitted in so clearly with the other things you had said. About your reading Spinoza, for instance. You had lost me, as you thought, but you still went on studying good literature for my sake. And I found you in that book shop buying my novel. I can't tell you how it touched me. And as the result of that chance meeting you could not keep yourself from coming to Steeple Bumpleigh, so that you might be near me once more. And to-night, you crept out, to stand beneath my window in the starlight . . . No, let us have no more misunderstandings. I am thankful that I should have seen the meaning of your shy overtures in time, and that I should have had the real D'Arcy Cheesewright revealed to me before it was too late. I will be your wife, Bertie.'

There didn't seem much to say to this except 'Oh, thanks.' I said it, and the interview terminated. She kissed me again, expressed her preference for a quiet wedding, with just a few relations and intimate friends, and beetled off.

19

It was not immediately that I, too, departed. The hour was late, and my bed awaited me *chez* Boko, but for a considerable time I remained rooted to the spot, staring dazedly into the darkness. Winged creatures of the night came bumping into the old face and bumping off again, while others used the back stretches of my neck as a skating rink, but I did not even raise a hand to interfere with their revels. This awful thing that had come upon me had practically turned me into a pillar of salt. I doubt if the moth, or whatever it was that was doing Swedish exercises in and around my left ear, had the remotest notion that it had parked itself on the person of a once vivacious young clubman. A tree, it probably thought, or possibly even the living rock.

Presently, however, life returned to the rigid limbs, and I started to plod my weary way down the drive and out of the gate, eventually reaching Boko's door. It was open, and I heaved myself through. There was a light along the passage, and heading for it I won through to the sitting-room.

Boko was in an armchair, with his feet on the mantelpiece and his hand clasping a glass. The sight of another glass and a siphon and decanter drew me to the table like a magnet. The sloshing of the liquid seemed to rouse mine host from a reverie, causing him for the first time to become aware of my presence.

'Help yourself,' he said.

'Thanks, old man.'

'Though I'm surprised you have the heart to drink, after what has occurred to-night.'

He spoke coldly, and there was a distinct aloofness in his manner as he reached out and refilled his glass. He eyed me for a moment as if I had been a caterpillar in some salad of which he was about to partake, and resumed.

'I saw Nobby.'

'Oh, yes?'

'As I anticipated, she cried buckets.'

'I'm sorry.'

'So you should be. Yours was the hand that wrenched those pearly drops from her eyes.'

'Oh, dash it!'

'It's no good saying "Oh, dash it!" You have a conscience, I presume? Then it must have informed you that you were directly responsible for the downpour. Well, well, if anybody had told me that Bertie Wooster would let me down—'

'You said that before.'

'And I shall go on saying it. Even unto seventy times seven. One doesn't dismiss a thing like that with a single careless comment. When your whole faith in human nature has been shattered, you are entitled to repeat yourself a bit.'

He laughed a short, mirthless laugh, very rasping and hard on the ears. Then, as if dismissing an unpleasant subject for the time being, he drained his snootful and turned to the matter of my belated return, saying that he had expected me back hours ago.

'When I took you for an after dinner stroll, I didn't think you were going to stay out practically till the arrival of the morning milk. You will have to change these dissolute city ways, if you wish to fit in with the life of a decent English village.'

'I am a bit later than I had anticipated.'

'What kept you?'

'Well, for one thing, I was being biffed over the nut by Edwin with a hockey stick. That took time.'

'What?'

'Yes.'

'He socked you with a hockey stick?'

'Right on the bean.'

'Ah!' said Boko, and seemed to brighten quite a good deal. 'Fine little chap, Edwin. Good stuff in that boy. Got nice ideas.'

The circs being what they were, this absence of the sympathetic note distressed me, filling me with what I have heard Jeeves describe as thoughts that lie too deep for tears. A man in my position wants his friends to rally round him.

'Don't gibe and scoff,' I begged. 'I want sympathy, Boko—sympathy and advice. Do you know what?'

'What?'

'I'm engaged to Florence.'

'What, again? What's become of Stilton?'

'I will tell you the whole ghastly story.'

I suppose the poignant note in my voice stirred his better nature, for he listened gravely and with evidences of human feeling as I related my tragedy. When I had concluded, he shivered and reached out for the decanter, his whole aspect that of a man who needed one quick.

'There but for the grace of God,' he said, in a low voice, 'goes George Webster Fittleworth!'

I pointed out that he was missing the nub.

'Yes, that's all very well, Boko, and I am sure you have my heartiest congratulations, but the basic fact with which we have to deal is that there actually does go Bertram Wooster. Have you nothing to suggest?'

'Is any man safe?' he continued, still musing. 'I did think that the black spot had finally passed into Stilton's possession.'

'So did I.'

'It's a shame it hasn't, because he really loves that girl, Bertie. No doubt you have been feeling a decent pity for Stilton, but I assure you it was wasted. He loves her. And when a man with a head as fat as that loves, it is for ever. You and I would say that it was impossible that anyone should really want to marry this frightful girl, but it is a fact. Did she make you read "Types of Ethical Theory"?'

'Yes.'

'Me, too. It was that that first awoke me to a sense of my peril. But when she slipped it to Stilton, he ate it alive. I don't suppose he understood a word of it, but I repeat, he ate it alive. Theirs would have been an ideal match. Too bad it has blown a fuse. Of course, if Stilton would resign from the Force, a way could readily be paved to an understanding. It's that that is at the root of the trouble.'

Once more, I saw that the nub had eluded him.

'It's not Stilton I'm worrying about, Boko, old man, it's me. I view Stilton with a benevolent eye, and would be glad to see him happily mated, but the really vital question is Where does Bertram get off? How do we extricate poor old Wooster?'

'You really want to be extricated?'

'My dear chap!'

'She would be a good influence in your life, remember. Steadying. Educative.'

'Would you torture me, Boko?'

'Well, how did you extricate yourself, when you were engaged to her last time?'

'It's a long story.'

'Then for goodness' sake don't start it now. All I meant was, could the same technique be employed in the present crisis?'

'I'm afraid not. There was something she wanted me to do for her, and I failed to do it and she gave me the air. These circs could not arise again.'

'I see. Well, it's a pity you can't use the method I did. The Fittleworth System. Simple but efficacious. That would solve all your difficulties.'

'Why can't I use it?'

'Because you don't know what it is.'

'You could tell me.'

He shook his head.

'No, Bertie, not after the extraordinary attitude you have seen fit to take up with regard to my proposals for sweetening your Uncle Percy. The Fittleworth Method—tried and tested, I may say, and proved infallible—can be imparted only to the deserving. It is not a secret I would care to share with any except real friends who are as true as steel.'

'I'm as true as steel, Boko.'

'No, Bertie, you are not as true as steel, or anything like it. You may have shown that by your behaviour to-night. A real eye-opener it has been, causing me to revise my estimate of your friendship from the bottom up. Of course, if you were to reconsider your refusal to chip in on this scheme of Jeeves's and consent, after all, to play your allotted part, I should be delighted to . . . But what's the use of talking about it? You have declined, and that's that. I know your iron will. When you come to a decision, it stays come to.'

I didn't know so much about that. It is true, of course, that I have a will of iron, but it can be switched off if the circumstances seem to demand it. The strong man always knows when to yield and make concessions. I have frequently found myself doing so in my relation with Jeeves.

'You absolutely guarantee this secret method?' I asked earnestly.

'I can only tell you that it produced immediate and gratifying results in my own case. One moment, I was engaged to Florence; the next, I wasn't. As quick as that. It was more like magic than anything I can think of.'

'And you'll tell it me, if I promise to tick Uncle Percy off?'

'I'll tell it you *after* you've ticked him off.'

'Why not now?'

'Just a whim. It's not that I don't trust you, Bertie. It's not that I think that, having learned the Fittleworth secret, you would change your mind about carrying out your end of the contract. But it would be a temptation, and I don't want your pure soul to be sullied by it.'

'But you'll tell me without fail after I've done the deed?'

'Without fail.'

I pondered. It was a fearful choice to have to make. But I did not hesitate long.

'All right, Boko. I'll do it.'

He tapped me affectionately on the chest. It was odd how to-night's events had brought out the chest-tapper in him.

'Splendid fellow!' he said. 'I thought you would. Now, you pop off to bed, so as to get a good night's rest and rise alert and refreshed. I will sit up and rough out a few things for you to say to the old boy. It's no good your trusting to the inspiration of the moment. You must have your material all written out and studied. I doubt, too, if, left to yourself, you would be able to think of anything really adequate. This is one of the occasions when you need the literary touch.'

20

It was but a troubled slumber that I enjoyed that night, much disturbed by dreams of Uncle Percy chasing me with his hunting crop. Waking next morning, I found that though the heart was leaden, the weather conditions were of the best and brightest. The sun shone, the sky was blue, and in the trees outside my window the ear detected the twittering of a covey or platoon of the local fowls of the air.

But though all Nature smiled, there was, as I have indicated, no disposition on the part of Bertram to follow its example. I got no kick from the shining sun, no uplift from the azure firmament, as it is sometimes called: while as for the twittering birds their heartiness in the circumstances seemed overdone and in dubious taste. When you're faced with the sort of ordeal I was faced with, there is but little satisfaction to be derived from the thought that you've got a nice day for it.

My watch showed me that the hour was considerably less advanced than my customary one for springing from between the sheets, and it is possible that, had the burden on the soul been lighter, I might have turned over and got another forty minutes. But the realization of what dark deeds must be done ere this day's sun should have set—or, for the matter of that, ere this day's lunch should have been eaten—forbade sleep. I rose, accordingly, and assembling sponge and towel was about to proceed to the bathroom for a bit of torso sluicing, when my eye was caught by a piece of paper protruding from beneath the door. I picked it up, and found it to be the material which Boko had sat up on the previous night composing for my benefit—the few things, if you remember, which he wanted me to say to Uncle Percy. And as my eye flitted over it, the persp. started out on my brow and I sank back on the bed, appalled. It was as if I had scooped in a snake.

I think that in an earlier chronicle I related how, when a growing boy at my private school, I once sneaked down at dead of night to the study of the headmaster, the Rev. Aubrey Upjohn, in order to pinch a few mixed biscuits from the store which I had been informed that he maintained in the cupboard there; and how, having got well ahead with the work in hand, I discovered that their proprietor was also among those present, seated at his desk regarding my activities with a frosty eye.

The reason I bring this up again is that on the occasion to which I allude, after a brief pause—on my side, of embarrassment, on his of working up steam—the Rev. Aubrey had started to give a sort of character sketch of the young Wooster, which until now I had always looked upon as the last word in scholarly invective. It was the kind of thing a minor prophet of the Old Testament might have thrown together on one of his bilious mornings, and, as I say, I considered it to have set up a mark at which other orators would shoot in vain. I had been wrong. This screed of Boko's left it nowhere. Book began where the Rev. Aubrey Upjohn left off.

Typewritten, with single spaces, I suppose the stuff ran to about six hundred words, and of all those six hundred words I don't think there were more than half a dozen which I could have brought myself to say to a man of Uncle Percy's caliber, unless primed to the back teeth with the raw spirit. And Boko, you will recall, was expecting me to deliver my harangue at ten o'clock in the morning.

To shoot out of my room into his, bubbling over with expostulations and what not, was with me the work of an instant. But the eloquent outburst which I had been planning was rendered null and void by the fact that he was not there, and an injury of an aged female whom I found messing about in the kitchen elicited the information that he had gone for a swim in the river. Repairing thither, I perceived him splashing about in midstream with many a merry cry.

But once more I was obliged to choke back the burning words. A second glance, revealing a pink, porpoise-like object at his side, told me that he was accompanied by Stilton. It was to Steeple Bumpleigh's zealous police constable that the merry cries were addressed, and I deemed it wisest to leave my presence unrevealed. It seemed to me that a chat with Stilton at this particular juncture could be fraught with neither pleasure nor profit.

I pushed along the bank, therefore, pondering deeply, and I hadn't gone far when there came to my ears the swish of a fishing line, and there was Jeeves, harrying the finny denizens like nobody's business. I might have known that his first act on finding himself established in Steeple Bumpleigh would have been to head for the fluid and cast a fly or two.

As it was to this fly-caster that I owed my present hideous predicament, you will not be surprised to learn that my manner, as I came abreast, was on the distant side.

'Ah, Jeeves,' I said.

'Good morning, sir,' he responded. 'A lovely day.'

'Lovely for some of us, perhaps, Jeeves,' I said coldly, 'but not for the Last of the Woosters, who, thanks to you, is faced by a binge beside which all former binges fade into insignificance.'

'Sir?'

'It's no good saying "Sir?" You know perfectly well what I mean. Entirely through your instrumentality, I shall shortly be telling Uncle Percy things about himself which will do something to his knotted and combined locks which at the moment has slipped my memory.'

'Make his knotted and combined locks to part and each particular hair to stand on end like quills upon the fretful porpentine, sir.'

'Porpentine?'

'Yes, sir.'

'That can't be right. There isn't such a thing. However, let that pass. The point is that you have let me in for the ghastly task of ticking Uncle Percy off, and I want to know what you did it for. Was it kind, Jeeves? Was it feudal?'

He registered surprise. Mild surprise, of course. He never goes as far as the other sort. One eyebrow flickered a little, and the tip of the nose moved slightly.

'You are alluding to the suggestion I offered Mr Fittleworth, sir?'

'That is the suggestion I am alluding to, Jeeves.'

'But surely, sir, if you have decided to fall in with the scheme, it was entirely your kind heart that led you to do so? It would have been optional for you to have declined to lend your assistance.'

'Ha!'

'Sir?'

'I said "Ha!" Jeeves. And I meant "Ha!" Do you know what happened last night?'

'So much happened last night, sir.'

'True. Among other things, I got properly biffed over the coconut by young Edwin with his Scout's stick, he thinking I was a burglar.'

'Indeed, sir?'

'We then fell into conversation, and he informed me that he had found the brooch which we assumed to have perished in the flames and had delivered it to Lady Florence, telling her it was a birthday present from me.'

'Indeed, sir?'

'It just turned the scale. She had a frightful row with Stilton, gave him the air for saying derogatory things about modern enlightened thought, and is now betrothed once more to the toad beneath the harrow whom you see before you.'

I thought he was going to say 'Indeed, sir?' again, in which case I might easily have forgotten all the decencies of civilized life and dotted him one. At the last moment, however, he checked the utterance and merely pursed his lips in a grave and sympathetic manner. A vast improvement.

'And the reason I consented to sit in on this scheme of yours was that Boko confided to me last night that he had a simple infallible remedy for getting out of being engaged to this specific girl, and he won't tell me what it is till I have interviewed Uncle Percy.'

'I see, sir.'

'I must learn it at all costs. It's no use my trying the Stilton method and saying nasty things about modern enlightened thought, because I couldn't think of any. It is the Boko way or nothing. You don't happen to know what it was that made Lady Florence sever her relations with him, do you?'

'No, sir. Indeed, it is news to me that Mr Fittleworth was affianced to her ladyship.'

'Oh, yes. He was affianced to her, all right. Post-Wooster, but pre-Stilton. And something occurred, an imbroglio of some description, took place, and the thing was instantly broken off. Just like magic, he said. I gathered that it was something he did. But what could it have been?'

'I fear I am unable to hazard a conjecture, sir. Would you wish me to institute inquiries among the domestic staff at the Hall?'

'An excellent idea, Jeeves.'

'It is possible that some member of that unit may have become cognisant of the facts.'

'The thing was probably the talk of the Housekeeper's Room for days. Sound the butler. Question the cook.'

'Very good, sir.'

'Or try Lady Florence's personal maid. Somebody is sure to know. There's not much that domestic staffs don't become cognisant of.'

'No, sir. One has usually found them well informed.'

'And bear in mind that speed is essential. If you can hand me the data before I see Uncle Percy—that is to say, any time up to ten o'clock, for which hour the kick-off is slated—I shall be in a position to edge out of giving him that straight talk, at the thought of which I don't mind telling you that the flesh creeps. As for the happiness of Boko and soulmate, I am all for giving that a boost, of course, but I feel that it can be done by other and less drastic methods. So lose no time, Jeeves, in instituting those inquiries.'

'Very good, sir.'

'Be at the main gate of the Hall from half-past nine onwards. I shall be arriving about then, and shall expect your report. Try not to fail me, Jeeves. Now is the time for all good men to come to the aid of the party. If I could show you that list Boko drafted out of the things he wants me to say—I unfortunately left it in my room, where it fell from my nerveless fingers—your knotted and combined locks would part all right, believe me. You're sure it's porpentine?'

'Yes, sir.'

'Very odd. But I suppose half the time Shakespeare just shoved down anything that came into his head.'

Having been *en route* for the bathroom at the moment when I buzzed off to seek audience of Boko, I was still, of course, in the ordinary slumberwear of the English gentleman, plus a dressing-gown, and it was some little time, accordingly, after I had returned to the house, before I showed up in the dining-salon. I found Boko there, getting outside a breakfast egg. I asked him if he knew what a porpentine was, and he said to hell with all porpentines and had I got that sheet of instructions all right and, if so, what did I think of it.

To this, my reply was that I certainly had jolly well got it and that it had frozen me to the marrow. No human power, I added, would induce me to pass on to Uncle Percy even a skeleton outline of the document's frightful contents.

'Frightful contents?'

'That was what I said.'

He seemed wounded, and murmured something about the artist and destructive criticism.

'I thought it was particularly good stuff. Crisp, terse and telling. The subject inspired me, and I was under the impression that I had given of my best. Still, if you feel that I stressed the personal note a bit too much, you can modify it here and there, if you like—preserving the substance, of course.'

'As a matter of fact,' I said, thinking it best to prepare him, 'you mustn't be surprised, Boko, if at the last moment I change my plans and decide to give the whole thing a miss.'

'What!'

'I am toying with the idea.'

'Well, I'm blowed! Is this—?'

'Yes, it is.'

'You don't know what I was going to say.'

'Yes, I do. You were going to say "Is this Bertie Wooster speaking?"'

'Quite right. I was. Well, is it?'

'Yes.'

His table talk then took on a rather acid tone, touching disparagingly on so-called friends who, supposed by him hitherto to be staunch and true, turned out to his disappointment to be lily-livered poltroons lacking even the meagre courage of a rabbit.

'Where are the boys of the bulldog breed? That's what I want to know,' he concluded, plainly chagrined. 'Well, you understand clearly what this means. Fail me, and not an inkling of the Fittleworth secret do you get.'

I smiled subtly, and helped myself to a slice of ham. He little knew, I felt.

'I shall watch you walking up the aisle with Florence Craye, and not stir a finger to save you. In fact, you will hear a voice singing "Oh, perfect love" rather louder than the rest of the congregation, and it will be mine. Reconsider, Bertie. That is what I advise.'

'Well, of course,' I said, 'I don't say I will back out of the assignment. I only say I may.'

This calmed him somewhat, and he softened—saying that he was sure that when the hour struck, my better self would prevail. And a bit later, we parted with mutual good wishes.

For it had been arranged that we should proceed to the Hall separately. In his case, Boko felt, not without some reason, that there was need for stealth, lest he be fallen upon and slung out. He proposed, therefore, to circle round the outskirts till he found a gap in the hedge and then approach the study by a circuitous route, keeping well in the shelter of the bushes and not letting a twig snap beneath his feet.

I set out by myself, accordingly, and arriving at the main entrance found Jeeves waiting for me in the drive. It needed but a glance to inform me that the man had good tidings. I can always tell. He doesn't exactly smile on these occasions, because he never does, but the lips twitch slightly at the corners and the eye is benevolent.

I gave tongue eagerly.

'Well, Jeeves?'

'I have the data you require, sir.'

'Splendid fellow! You saw the butler? You probed the cook?'

'Actually, it was from the boy who cleans the knives and boots that I secured the information, sir. A young fellow of the name of Erbut.'

'How did he come to be our special correspondent?'

'It appears that he was actually an eye-witness of the scene, sir, sheltered in the obscurity of a neighbouring bush, where he had been enjoying a surreptitious cigarette. From this point of vantage he was enabled to view the entire proceedings.'

'And what were they? Tell me all, Jeeves, omitting no detail, however slight.'

'Well, sir, the first thing that attracted the lad's attention was the approach of Master Edwin.'

'He comes into it, does he?'

'Yes, sir. His role, as you will see, is an important one. Master Edwin, Erbut reports, was advancing through the undergrowth, his gaze fixed upon the ground. He seemed to be tracking something.'

'Spooring, no doubt. It is a practice to which these Scouts are much addicted.'

'So I understand, sir. His movements, Erbut noted, were being observed with a sisterly indulgence by Lady Florence, who was cutting flowers in an adjacent border.'

'She was watching him, eh?'

'Yes, sir. Simultaneously, Mr Fittleworth appeared, following the young gentleman.'

'Spooring the spoorer?'

'Yes, sir. Erbut describes his manner as keen and purposeful. That, at least, was his meaning, though the actual phrasing of his statement was different. These knives and boots boys seldom express themselves well.'

'I've often noticed it. Rotten vocabularies. Go on, Jeeves. I'm all agog. Boko, you say, was trailing Edwin. Why?'

'That was what Erbut appears to have asked himself, sir.'

'He was mystified?'

'Yes, sir.'

'I don't blame him. I'm mystified myself. I gather, of course, that the plot thickens, but I'm dashed if I can see where it's heading.'

'It was not long before Mr Fittleworth's motives were abundantly clear, sir. As Master Edwin approached the flower bed, he suddenly accelerated his movements—'

'Edwin did?'

'No, sir. Mr Fittleworth. He bounded forward at the young gentleman, and taking advantage of the fact that the latter, in the course of his spooring, had just adopted a stooping posture, proceeded to deliver a forceful kick upon his person—'

'Golly, Jeeves!'

'— causing him to fly through the air and fall at Lady Florence's feet. Her ladyship, horrified and incensed, rebuked Mr Fittleworth sharply, demanding an immediate explanation of this wanton assault. The latter endeavoured to justify his action by accusing Master Edwin of having tampered with his patent egg boiler, so disorganizing the mechanism that a new-laid egg had flown from its base and struck him on the tip of the nose. Her ladyship, however, was unable to see her way to accepting this as a palliation of what had occurred, and shortly afterwards announced that the betrothal was at an end.'

I drew in the breath. The scales had fallen from my eyes. I saw all. So that was the Fittleworth remedy—booting young Edwin! No wonder Boko had spoken of it as simple and efficacious. All you needed was a good stout shoe and a sister's love.

I heard Jeeves cough.

'If you will glance to your left, sir,' he said, 'you will observe that Master Edwin has just entered the drive and is stooping over some object on the ground that appears to have engaged his attention.'

21

I got the gist. The significance of his words was not lost upon me. The grave, encouraging look with which he had accompanied the news bulletin would alone have been enough to enable me to sense the underlying message he was trying to convey. It was the sort of look a Roman father might have given his son, when handing him shield and spear and pushing him off to battle, and it ought, I suppose, to have stirred me like a bugle.

Nevertheless, I found myself hesitating. After that sock on the head he had given me on the previous night, the thought of kicking young Edwin was one that presented many attractions, of course, and there was no question but that the child had been asking for some such little personal attention for years. But there's something rather embarrassing about doing that sort of thing in cold blood. Difficult, I felt, to lead up to it neatly in the course of conversation. ('Hullo, Edwin. How are you? Lovely day. *Biff*.' You see what I mean. Not easy.)

In Boko's case, of course, the whole set-up had been entirely different, for he had been in the grip of the berserk fury which comes upon a man when he is hit on the tip of the nose with new-laid eggs. This had enabled him, so to speak, to get a running start.

And so I fingered the chin dubiously.

'Yes,' I said. 'Yes, there he is, Jeeves—and, as you say, stooping. But do you really advise—'

'I do, sir.'

'What, now?'

'Yes, sir. There is a tide in the affairs of men which, taken at the flood, leads on to fortune. Omitted, all the voyage of their life is bound in shallows and in miseries.'

'Oh, rather. Quite. No argument about that. But—'

'If what you are trying to say, sir, is that it is of the essence that Lady Florence be present, to observe the proceedings as she did in the case of Mr Fittleworth, I fully concur. I would suggest that I go and inform her ladyship that you are waiting on the drive and would be glad of a word with her.'

I still hesitated. It was one of those cases where you approve the broad, general principle of an idea, but can't help being in a bit of a twitter at the prospect of putting it into practical effect. I explained this to Jeeves, and he said that much the same thing had bothered Hamlet.

'Your irresolution is quite understandable, sir. Between the acting of a dreadful thing and the first motion, all the interim is like a phantasma or a hideous dream. The genius and the mortal instruments are then in council; and that state of man, like to a little kingdom, suffers then the nature of an insurrection.'

'Absolutely,' I said. He puts these things well.

'If it would assist you to stiffen the sinews and summon up the blood, sir, may I remind you that it is very nearly ten o'clock, and that only the promptest action along the lines I have indicated can enable you to avoid appearing in his lordship's study at that hour.'

He had found the talking-point. I hesitated no longer.

'You're right, Jeeves. How long do you think it will be necessary to detain young Edwin in conversation before you can bring Lady Florence on stage?'

'Not more than a few minutes, sir. I happen to know that her ladyship is at the moment in her private apartment, engaged upon literary work. There will be but a brief interval before she appears.'

'Then tally ho!'

'Very good, sir.'

He flickered off upon his mission, while I, having summoned up the blood a bit and stiffened the sinews as far as was possible at such short notice, squared the shoulders and headed for where Edwin was squatting. The weather continued uniformly fine. The sun shone, and a blackbird, I remember, was singing in an adjoining thicket. No reason why it shouldn't have been, of course. I mention the fact merely to stress the general peace and tranquillity of everything. And I must say it did strike me as a passing thought that the sort of setting a job like this really needed was a blasted heath at midnight, with a cold wind whistling in the bushes and three witches doing their stuff at the cauldron.

However, one can't have everything, and I doubt if an observer would have noted any diffidence in Bertram's bearing as he advanced upon his prey. Bertram, I rather fancy he would have thought, was in pretty good form.

I hove to at the stripling's side.

'Hullo, young Edwin,' I said.

His gaze had been riveted on the ground, but at the sound of the familiar voice a couple of pink-rimmed eyes came swivelling round in my direction. He looked up at me like a ferret about to pass the time of day with another ferret.

'Hullo, Bertie. I say, Bertie, I did another act of kindness this morning.'

'Oh, yes?'

'I finished pasting the notices of Florence's novel in her album. That puts me all right up to last Wednesday.'

'Good work. You're catching up. And what do you think you're doing now?'

'I'm studying ants. Do you know anything about ants, Bertie?'

'Only from meeting them at picnics.'

'I've been reading up about them. Very interesting.'

'Vastly, I shouldn't wonder.'

I was glad the topic had been introduced, for it promised to be one that would carry us along nicely until Florence's arrival on the scene. It was obvious that the young squirt was bulging with information about these industrious little creatures and asked nothing better than to be allowed to impart it.

'Did you know ants can talk?'

'Talk?'

'In a sort of way. To other ants, of course. They do it by tapping their heads on a leaf. How's your head this morning, Bertie? I nearly forgot to ask.'

'Still on the tender side.'

'I thought it would be. Coo! That was funny last night, wasn't it? I laughed for hours, when I got to bed.'

He emitted a ringing guffaw, and at the raucous sound any spark of compunction that might have been lingering in my bosom was quenched. A boy to whom the raising of a lump the size of a golf ball on the Wooster bean was a subject for heartless mirth deserved all that boot toe could do to him. For the first time, I found myself contemplating the task before me with real fire and enthusiasm—almost, as you might say, in a missionary spirit. I mean, I felt what a world of good a swift kick in the pants would do to this child. It might prove to be the turning-point in his life.

'You laughed, did you?'

'Rather!'

'Ha!' I said, and ground a few teeth.

The maddening thing was, of course, that though I was now keyed up to give of my best, and though the position he had assumed for this ant-studying session of his was the exact position demanded by the run of the scenario, I was debarred from getting action. You might have compared me to a greyhound on the leash. Until Florence came along, I could not fulfil myself. As Jeeves had said, her presence was of the essence. I scanned the horizon for a sight of her, like a shipwrecked mariner hoping for a sail, but she did not appear, and in the meantime we went on talking about ants, Edwin saying that they were members of the Hymenoptera family and self replying, 'Well, well. Quite the nibs, eh?'

'They are characterized by unusual distinctness of the three regions of the body—head, thorax and abdomen—and by the stack or petiole of the abdomen having one or two scales or nodes, so that the abdomen moves very freely on the trunk or thorax.'

'You wouldn't fool me?'

'The female, after laying her eggs, feeds the larvæ with food regurgitated from her stomach.'

'Try to keep it clean, my lad.'

'Both males and females are winged.'

'And why not?'

'But the female pulls off its wings and runs about without them.'

'I question that. I doubt if even an ant would be such an ass.'

'It's quite true. It says so in the book. Have you ever seen ants fight?'

'Not that I remember.'

'They rise on their hind legs and curve the abdomen.'

And, to my consternation and chagrin, whether because it was his intention to illustrate or because he found his squatting position cramping to the limbs, this was just what he did himself. He rose on his hind legs, and stood facing me, curving the abdomen—at the exact moment when I perceived Florence emerging from the house and walking briskly in our direction.

It was a crisis at which a less resourceful man might have supposed that all was lost. But the Woosters are quick thinkers.

'Hullo!' I said.

'What's the matter?'

'Have you dropped a sixpence?'

'No.'

'Somebody has. Look.'

'Where?'

'Under that bush,' I said, and pointed to a shrub of sorts on the edge of the drive.

As you probably conjecture, in saying this I was descending to subterfuge, and anybody knowing Bertram Wooster and his rigid principles might have supposed that such willful tampering with the truth would have caused the blush of shame to mantle his cheek. Not so, however. If there was a flush to be noted, it was the flush of excitement and triumph.

For my subtle appeal to the young blister's cupidity had not failed to achieve its end. Already, he was down on all fours, and if I had posed him with my own hands I could not have obtained better results. His bulging shorts seemed to smile up at me in a sort of inviting, welcoming way.

As Jeeves had rightly said, there is a tide in the affairs of men which, taken at the flood, leads on to fortune. I drew back the leg, and let him have it just where the pants were tightest.

It was a superb effort. Considering that I hadn't kicked anyone since the distant days of school, you might have thought that the machinery would have got rusty. But no. All the old skill still lingered. My timing was perfect, and so was my follow through. He disappeared into the bush, travelling as if out of a gun, and as he did so Florence's voice spoke.

'Ah!' she said.

There was no mistaking the emotion that animated the ejaculation. It was stiff with it. But with a dazed sensation of something having gone wrong I realized that it was not the emotion I had anticipated. Horror was completely absent, nor had there come through anything in the nature of indignation and sisterly resentment. Astounding as it may seem, joy was the predominating note. One might go further and say ecstasy. Her 'Ah!' in short, had been practically equivalent to 'Whoopee!' and I could make nothing of it.

'Thank you, Bertie!' she said. 'It was just what I was going to do myself. Edwin, come here!'

Down in the forest something stirred. It was the prudent child wriggling his way through the bush in a diametrically opposite direction. There came the sound of a faint and distant 'Coo!' and he was gone, leaving not a wrack behind.

Florence was gazing at me, a cordial and congratulatory light in her eyes, a happy smile playing about her lips.

'Thank you, Bertie!' she said again, once more with that wealth of emotion in her voice. 'I would like to skin him! I have just been looking at my album of press clippings, and he has gone and pasted in half the reviews of "Spindrift" wrong side up. I believe he did it on purpose. It's a pity I couldn't catch him, but there it is. I can't tell you how grateful I am, Bertie, for what you did. What gave you the idea?'

'Oh, it just came to me.'

'I understand. A sort of sudden inspiration. The central theme of "Spindrift" came like that. Jeeves says you want to speak to me. Is it something very important?'

'Oh, no. Not important.'

'Then we will keep it till later. I must go back now and see if there isn't some way of floating those clippings off with hot water.'

She hurried away, turning as she entered the house to wave a loving hand, and I was left alone to submit the situation to the analysis it demanded.

I don't know anything that seems to jar the back teeth like having a sure thing come unstuck, and it was with a dull sensation of having been hit in the stomach by a medicine ball, as once happened to me during a voyage to America, that I stood contemplating the future. Not even the fact that in the recent scene this girl had shown a warm, human side to her nature, which I had not suspected that she possessed, could reconcile me to what I was now so unavoidably in for. A Florence capable of wanting to skin Edwin was better, of course, than a Florence susceptible of no such emotion, but no, I couldn't bring myself to like the shape of things to come.

How long I stood brooding there before I became aware of the squeaking that was going on at my side, I cannot say. Quite a time it must have been. For when at length I came out of my reverie, to find that Nobby was endeavouring to attract my attention, I saw that her manner was impatient, like that of one who has been trying to hobnob with a deaf mute and is finding the one-sided conversation weighing upon the spirits.

'Bertie!'

'Oh, sorry. I was musing.'

'Well, stop musing. You'll be late.'

'Late?'

'For Uncle Percy. In the study.'

I have mentioned earlier in this narrative that I am a pretty good silver-lining spotter, and that if there is a bright side to any cataclysm or disaster I seldom fail to put my finger on it sooner or later. Her words reminded me that there was one attached to the present catastrophe. Murky the future might be, what with all those wedding bells and what not which now seemed so inescapable, but at least I was in a position to save something out of the wreck. I could at any rate give Uncle Percy the go-by.

'Oh, that?' I said. 'That's off.'

'Off?'

'My reward for sitting in on the scheme,' I explained, 'was to have been the learning of the Fittleworth secret process for getting out of being engaged to Florence. I have learned it, and it is a wash-out. I, therefore, hand in my portfolio.'

'You mean you won't help us?'

'In some other way, to be decided on later, certainly. But not by inflaming Uncle Percy.'

'Oh, Bertie!'

'And it's no good saying, "Oh, Bertie!"'

She looked at me with bulging eyes, and it seemed for an instant as if those pearly drops, of which Boko had spoken so eloquently, were about to start functioning once more. But there was good stuff in the Hopwoods. The dam did not burst.

'But I don't understand.'

I explained in some detail what had occurred.

'Boko,' I concluded, 'claimed that this secret remedy of his was infallible. It is not. So unless he has something else to suggest—'

'But he has. I mean, I have.'

'You?'

'You want Florence to break off the engagement?'

'I do.'

'Well, go and talk to Uncle Percy, and I'll show her that letter you wrote me, saying what you thought of her. That'll work it.'

I started. In fact, I leaped about a foot.

'Golly!'

'Don't you agree?'

'Well, I'm dashed!'

I don't know when I've been so affected. I had forgotten all about that letter, but now, as its burning phrases came back to me, hope, which I had thought dead, threw off the winding sheet and resumed business at the old stand. The Fittleworth method might have failed, but there was no question that the Hopwood remedy would bring home the bacon.

'Nobby!'

'Think on your feet!'

'You promise you'll show Florence that letter?'

'Faithfully. If you will give Uncle Percy the treatment.'

'Is Boko at his post?'

'Sure to be by now.'

'Then out of my way! Here we go!'

And, moving as if on wings, I flitted to the house, plunged across the threshold, shot down the passage that led to the relative's sanctum and dived in.

PART 3

22

Uncle Percy's study, to which this was of course my first visit, proved to be what they call on the stage a 'rich interior', liberally equipped with desks, chairs, tables, carpets and all the usual fixings. Books covered one side of it, and on the opposite wall there hung a large picture showing nymphs, or something similar, sporting with what, from the look of them and the way they were behaving, I took to be fauns. One also noted a terrestrial globe, some bowls of flowers, a stuffed trout, a cigar humidor, and a bust which might have been that of the late Mr Gladstone.

In short, practically the only thing you could think of that could have been in the room, but wasn't, was Uncle Percy. He was not seated in the chair behind the desk, nor was he pacing the carpet, twiddling the globe, sniffing the flowers, reading the books, admiring the stuffed trout or taking a gander at the nymphs and fauns. Not a glimpse of him met the eye, and this total absence of uncles, so different from what I had been led to expect, brought me up with a bit of a turn.

It's a rummy feeling, when you've got yourself all braced for the fray and suddenly discover that the fray hasn't turned up. Rather like treading on the last stair when it isn't there. I stood chewing the lip in some perplexity, wondering what to do for the best.

The scent of a robust cigar, still lingering in the air, showed that he must have been on the spot quite recently, and the open French windows suggested that he had popped out into the garden, there possibly to wrestle with the problems which were weighing on his mind—notably, no doubt, that of how the dickens life at Steeple Bumpleigh being what it was, he was to obtain an uninterrupted five minutes with Chichester Clam. And what I was debating within myself was whether to follow him or to remain in *status quo* till he came back.

Much depended, of course, on how long he was going to be. I mean, it wasn't as if the mood of fiery resolution in which I had hurled myself across the threshold was a thing which would last indefinitely. Already, the temperature of the feet had become sensibly lowered, and I was conscious of an emptiness behind the diaphragm and a disposition to gulp. Postpone the fixture for even another minute or two, and the evil would spread to such an extent that the relative, when he eventually showed up, would find a Bertram out of whom all the sawdust had trickled—a Wooster capable of nothing better than a mild 'Yes, Uncle Percy,' and 'No, Uncle Percy.'

Looking at it from every angle, therefore, it seemed that it would be best to go and tackle him in the great open spaces, where Boko by this time was presumably lurking. And I had reached the French windows, and was about to pass through, though with little or no relish for what lay before me, when my attention was arrested by the sound of raised voices. They came from a certain distance, and the actual wording of the dialogue escaped the eardrum, but from the fact that they were addressing each other as 'My dear Worplesdon' and 'You blot', I divined that they belonged—respectively—to Boko and the seigneur of Bumpleigh Hall.

A moment later, my conjecture was proved correct. A little procession came into view, crossing the strip of lawn outside the study. Heading it was Boko, looking less debonair than I have sometimes seen him. Following him came a man of garden-eresque appearance, armed with a pitchfork and accompanied by a dog of uncertain breed. The rear was brought up by Uncle Percy, waving a cigar menacingly like the angel expelling Adam from the Garden of Eden.

It was he who seemed to be doing most of the talking. From time to time, Boko would look around, as if about to say something, but whatever eloquence he may have been intending was checked by the expression on the face of the dog, which was that of one fit for treasons, stratagems and spoils, and the fact that the pitchfork to which I have alluded was almost touching the seat of his trousers.

Half-way across the lawn, Uncle Percy detached himself from the convoy and came stumping rapidly towards me, puffing emotionally at his cigar. Boko and his new friends continued in the direction of the drive.

After the painful shock, inevitable on seeing an old friend given the push from enclosed premises, my first thought, as you may have surmised, had been that there was nothing to keep me. The whole essence of the scheme to which I had consented to lend my services had been that Boko should be within earshot while I was making my observations to Uncle Percy, and nothing was clearer than that by the time the latter reached his sanctum he would have drifted away like thistledown.

I shot off, accordingly, not standing upon the order of my going but going at once, as the fellow said, and was making good progress when, as I approached the door, I suddenly observed that there hung over it a striking portrait of Aunt Agatha, from the waist upwards. In making my entrance, I had, of course, missed this, but there it had been all the time, and now it caught my eye and halted me in my tracks as if I had run into a lamppost.

It was the work of one of those artists who reveal the soul of the sitter, and it had revealed so much of Aunt Agatha's soul that for all practical purposes it might have been that danger to traffic in person. Indeed, I came within an ace of saying 'Oh, hullo!' at the same moment when I could have sworn it said 'Bertie!' in that compelling voice which had so often rung in my ears and caused me to curl up in a ball in the hope that a meek subservience would enable me to get off lightly.

The weakness was, of course, merely a temporary one. A moment later, Bertram was himself again. But the pause had been long enough to allow Uncle Percy to come clumping into the room, and escape was now impossible. I remained, therefore, and stood shooting my cuffs, trusting that the action would induce fortitude. It does sometimes.

Uncle Percy appeared to be soliloquizing.

'I trod on him! *Trod* on him! There he was, nestling in the grass, and I trod on him! It's not enough that the fellow comes roaming my grounds uninvited at all hours of the night. He comes also by day, and reclines in my personal grass. No keeping him out, apparently. He oozes into the place like oil.'

Here, for the first time, he seemed to become aware of a nephew's presence.

'Bertie!'

'Oh, hullo, Uncle Percy.'

'My dear fellow! Just the chap I wanted to see.'

To say that I was surprised at this remark would be to portray my emotions but feebly. It absolutely knocked me endways.

I mean, consider the facts. Man and boy, I had known this old buzzard a matter of fifteen years, and not once during that period had he even hinted that my society held any attraction for him. In fact, on most of the occasions when we had foregathered, he had rather gone out of his way to indicate that the reverse was the case. I have already alluded to the episode of the hunting crop, and there had been other similar passages through the course of the years.

I have, I think, made it sufficiently clear that few harder eggs ever stepped out of the saucepan than this Percival, Lord Worplesdon. Rugged sea captains, accustomed to facing gales in the Western Ocean without a tremor, quivered like blancmanges when hauled up before him in his office and asked why the devil they had—or had not—ported the helm or spliced the main-brace during their latest voyage in his service. In disposition akin to a more than ordinarily short-tempered snapping turtle, he resembled in appearance a malevolent Aubrey Smith, and usually, when one encountered him, gave the impression of being just about to foam at the mouth.

Yet now he was gazing at me in a manner which, when you came to look closely and got past the bristling moustache, revealed itself as not only part human, but actually kindly. From the pain in the neck generally induced by the sight of Bertram Wooster he appeared to be absolutely free.

'Who, me?' I said, weakly, my amazement such that I was compelled to support myself against the terrestrial globe.

'Yes, you. The very fellow. Have a drink, Bertie.'

I said something about it being a bit early, but he pooh-poohed the suggestion.

'It's never too early to have a drink, if you've been wading ankle deep in blasted Fittleworths. I was taking a stroll with my cigar, my mind deeply occupied with vital personal problems, and my foot came down on something squashy, and there the frightful chap was, reclining in the lush grass by the lake as if he had been a dashed field-mouse or something. If I had had a weak heart, it might have been the end of me.'

I couldn't help mourning for Boko. I could picture what must have occurred. Making his way snakily towards the study window, he had heard Uncle Percy's approach and had taken cover, little knowing that a moment later the latter's number eleven foot was about to descend upon what—from the fact that the other had described it as squashy—must have been some tender portion of his anatomy. A nasty jar for the poor chap. A nasty jar for Uncle Percy, too, of course. In fact, one of those situations where the heart bleeds for both the party of the first part and the party of the second part.

'Fittleworth!' He shot an accusing glance at me. 'Friend of yours, isn't he?'

'Oh, bosom.'

'You would do well to choose your friends more carefully,' he said, with the first lapse from that strange benevolence of his which he had yet shown.

I suppose this was really the moment for embarking upon an impassioned defence of Boko, stressing his admirable qualities. Not being able to think of any, however, I remained silent, and he carried on.

'But never mind him. My gardening staff is seeing him off the premises, with strict orders to jab him in the seat of his pants with a pitchfork if he dares to offer the slightest resistance. I venture to think that these grounds will see less of him in the future. And, by George, that is what Bumpleigh Hall wants, to make it an earthly Paradise—fewer and better Fittleworths. Have a cigar, Bertie.'

'I don't think so, thanks.'

'Nonsense. I can't understand this in and out policy of yours with regard to my cigars. When I don't want you to smoke them, you do—remember that hunting crop, eh, ha, ha?—and when I do want you to smoke them, you don't. All silly nonsense. Put this in your face, you young rascal,' he said, producing from the humidor something that looked like a torpedo, 'and let's have no more of this "I don't think so, thanks." I want you to be all relaxed and comfortable, because I have something very important to consult you about. Ah, bring it here, Maple.'

On the cue 'It's never too early to have a drink,' I should have mentioned, he had pressed the bell, causing the butler to appear and book instruction. The latter had now re-entered with a half-bot from the oldest bin, and it was while genially uncorking this that the relative resumed his remarks.

'Yes, never mind Fittleworth,' he repeated, handing me a foaming goblet. 'Let us dismiss him from our thoughts. I have other things to talk out. First and foremost . . . Cheerio, Bertie.'

'Cheerio,' I said, faintly.

'Success to crime.'

'Skin off your nose,' I responded, still on the dazed side.

'Mud in your eye,' said this extraordinary changeling. 'First and foremost,' he proceeded, passing a rapid glassful down the hatch, 'I wish to express my appreciation of your spectacularly admirable conduct on the drive just now. I met Edwin out there, and he told me you had kicked him. A thing I've been wanting to do for years, but never had the nerve.'

Here he rose from his chair with outstretched hand, shook mine warmly and reseated himself.

'Thinking over some of our recent meetings, Bertie,' he said—I don't say softly, because he couldn't speak softly, but as softly as a chap who found it so difficult to speak softly could speak, 'I fancy you may have run away with the idea that I was a bad-tempered, cross-grained old fellow. I believe I spoke harshly to you last night. You must overlook it. You must make allowances. You can't judge a man with a son like Edwin by the same standards as men who haven't got a son like Edwin. Did you happen to hear that he got me squarely with that infernal Scout's stick of his last night?'

'Me, too.'

'Right on the—'

'He got me on the head.'

'Thinking I was a burglar, or some such nonsense. And when I wanted to take steps, Florence wouldn't let me. You can imagine how I felt when I learned that you had kicked him. I wish I had seen it. Still, I gathered enough from his story to tell me that you behaved with notable gallantry and resource, and I don't mind admitting, my boy, that the thing has completely revolutionized my opinion of you. For years I have been looking on you as a mere lackadaisical, spiritless young man about town. I see now how wrong I was. You have shown yourself to be possessed of the highest executive qualities, and I have decided that you are the chap to advise me in the crisis which has arisen in my affairs. I am in a painful dilemma,

Bertie. It is absolutely essential that . . . But perhaps you have heard about it from Jeeves?'

'He did give me a sort of outline.'

'Chichester Clam?'

'Yes.'

'My vital need for meeting him in secret session?'

'Yes.'

'That clears the ground then. Never mind why it is so urgent for me to meet Chichester Clam in secret session. So long as you understand that it is, that is all that matters. He was the man in the potting shed last night.'

'Yes.'

'You know that, do you? It was Jeeves's suggestion, and a very good one, too. In fact, if it hadn't been for that revolting Fittleworth . . . But don't let me get on to the subject of Fittleworth. I want to keep calm. Yes, Clam was in the potting shed. Curious fellow.'

'Oh, yes?'

'Most curious. I wonder how I can describe him to you. Ever seen a fawn?'

'Like the chaps in that picture?'

'No, not that sort of faun. I mean the animal. The timid fawn that shivers and shakes and at the slightest suspicion of danger starts like a . . . like a fawn. That's Clam. Not to look at, I don't mean. He's stouter than the average fawn, and he wears horn-rimmed spectacles, which, of course, fawns don't. I'm referring to his character and disposition. You agree with me?'

I reminded him that, owing to the fact that I had never had the pleasure of making his acquaintance, Clam's psychology was a sealed book to me.

'That's true. I was forgetting. Well, that's what he's like. A fawn. Nervous. Quivering. Gets the wind up at the slightest provocation. Came out of that potting shed, I understand, shaking like a leaf and saying "Never again!" Yes, every drop of his manly courage had evaporated, and any scheme which we may devise for a future meeting will have to be a good one, a foolproof one, a scheme which even he can see involves him in no peril. Odd, this neurotic tendency in the American business man. Can you account for it? No? I can. Too much coffee.'

'Coffee?'

'That and the New Deal. Over in America, it appears, life for the business man is one long series of large cups of coffee, punctuated with shocks from the New Deal. He drinks a quart of coffee, and gets a nasty surprise from the New Deal. To pull himself together, he drinks another quart of coffee, and along comes another nasty surprise from the New Deal. He staggers off, calling feebly for more coffee, and . . . Well, you see what I mean. Vicious circle. No nervous system could stand it. Chichester Clam's nerves are in ruins. He wants to take the next boat to New York. Knows he will be wrecking the business deal of a lifetime by doing so, but says he doesn't care, just so long as he gets God's broad, deep Atlantic Ocean in between him and the English potting shed. A most extraordinary prejudice he seems to have taken against potting sheds, so keep steadily in your mind the fact that whatever you may have to suggest must be totally free from anything in the nature of a potting-shed angle. What have you to suggest, Bertie?'

To this, of course, there was but one reply.

'I think we'd better consult Jeeves.'

'I have consulted Jeeves, and he says he's baffled.'

I shot out an aghastish puff of smoke. The thing seemed incredible.

'Jeeves says he's baffled?'

'Told me so himself. That's why I've come to you. Fresh mind.'

'When did he say that?'

'Last night.'

I saw that all was not lost.

'Ah, but he's had a refreshing sleep since then, and you know how a spot of sleep picks you up. And, by Jove, Uncle Percy, I'll tell you something I've just remembered. Early this morning I came upon him fishing in the river.'

'What of it?'

'The fact is tremendously significant. I didn't actually question him on the subject, but a man of his caliber would be bound to have caught a few. No doubt, he had them for breakfast. In which case, his faculties will have been greatly stimulated. Probably by now he's at the top of his form again, with his brain humming like a dynamo.'

It was plain that the relative found himself infected by my enthusiasm.

In obvious excitement, he put the wrong end of his cigar in his mouth, singeing his moustache at the corner.

'I never thought of that,' he said, having cursed a bit.

'That often happens with Jeeves.'

'Is that so?'

'Most of his major triumphs have been accomplished on fish.'

'You don't say?'

'Absolutely. The phosphorus, you know.'

'Of course.'

'Even a single sardine will sometimes do the trick. Can you lay your hand on him?'

'I'll ring for Maple. Oh, Maple,' he said, as the butler fetched up at journey's end, 'send Jeeves to me.'

'Very good, m'lord.'

'And another half-bottle, I think, don't you, Bertie?'

'Just as you say, Uncle Percy.'

'It would be rash not to have it. You have no conception how it shakes a man, bringing his foot down on what he thinks is solid ground and finding it's Fittleworth. Another of the same, Maple.'

'Very good, m'lord.'

During the stage wait, which was not of long duration, the old relative filled in with some *ad lib* stuff about Boko, mostly about how much he disliked his face. Then the door opened again to admit a procession headed by the half-bottle on a salver. This was followed by Maple, who in his turn was followed by Jeeves. Maple withdrew, and Uncle Percy got down to it.

'Jeeves.'

'M'lord?'

'Did you catch any fish this morning?'

'Two, m'lord.'

'Have 'em for breakfast?'

'Yes, m'lord.'

'Splendid. Capital. Excellent. Then come along. Hark for'ard.'

'M'lord?'

'I was telling his lordship how fish always gingered up your thought processes,' I explained. 'He is rather expecting that you may now have something constructive to suggest in re another meeting with Chichester Clam.'

'I am sorry, sir. I have used every endeavour to hit upon a solution of the problem confronting his lordship, but I regret to say that my efforts have not been crowned with success.'

'A wash-out, he says,' I construed, for Uncle Percy's benefit.

Uncle Percy said he had hoped for better things. Jeeves said he had, too.

'Any good offering you a glass of bubbly? Might buck you up.'

'I fear not, m'lord. Alcohol has a sedative rather than a stimulating effect on me.'

'In that case, nothing to be done, I suppose. All right, Jeeves. Thanks.'

A fairly sombre silence fell upon the room for some moments, after the man's departure. I gave the terrestrial globe a twirl. Uncle Percy stared at the stuffed trout.

'Well, that's that, what?' I said, at length.

'Eh?'

'I mean, if Jeeves is baffled, hope would appear to be more or less dead.'

To my surprise, he did not agree with me. His eye flashed fire. I had underestimated the fighting spirit of these blokes who have made large fortunes in the shipping business. You may depress them for a while, but you can't keep them down.

'Nonsense, nonsense. Nothing of the kind. Jeeves isn't the only man in this house with a head on his shoulders. Anyone who could conceive the idea of kicking Edwin and carry it out as brilliantly as you did is not to be beaten by a simple problem like this. I am relying on you, Bertie. Chichester Clam—how to meet him? Don't give it up. Think again.'

'Shall I go and brood a bit on the drive?'

'Brood wherever you like, all over the grounds.'

'Right ho,' I said, and took a meditative departure.

I had scarcely closed the door and started to push along the passage, when Nobby appeared, as if out of a trap.

23

She came leaping towards me, like Lady Macbeth coming to get first-hand news from the guest-room.

'Well?' she said, getting her hooks on my arm with girlish animation. 'I'm nearly expiring with excitement and suspense, Bertie. Did everything go off all right? I listened at the door for a bit, but it was so difficult to hear what was going on. All that came through was Uncle Percy's voice rumbling like thunder, and occasionally a bleat from you.'

I would have denied, and with some warmth, this charge that I had bleated, but she gave me no opportunity to speak.

'And what puzzled me was that, according to the programme, it should have been your voice rumbling like thunder and an occasional bleat from Uncle Percy. And I couldn't hear Boko at all. He might just as well not have been there.'

I winced. It seemed to be my constant task to have to dash the cup of joy from this young geezer's lips, and I didn't like it any more than I had the first time. However, I forced myself to give her the works.

'Boko wasn't there.'

'Not there?'

'No.'

'But the whole point—'

'I know. But he was unavoidably detained by a gardener with a pitchfork and a dog which seemed to me to have a dash of the wolf-hound in him.'

And in a few sympathetic words I related how the light of her life had become less than the dust beneath Uncle Percy's gent's Oxfords and had been slung off the premises with all his music still within him.

A hard, set look came into her face.

'So Boko's made an ass of himself *again*?'

'I wouldn't call it actually making an ass of himself this time. More accurate, don't you think, to chalk him up as the helpless prey of destiny?'

'He could have rolled out of the way.'

'Not very easily. Uncle Percy's foot covers a wide area.'

She seemed to see the justice of this. Her map softened, and she asked if the poor darling had been hurt.

I weighed this.

'His physical injuries, I imagine, were slight. He seemed to be navigating under his own steam. Spiritually, he did not appear to be doing so well.'

'Poor lamb! He's so sensitive. What would you say his standing was now with Uncle Percy?'

'Lowish.'

'This has put the lid on things, you think?'

'To some extent, yes. But,' I said, glad to be able to drop a word of comfort, 'there is just a chance that, wind and weather permitting, the sun will ere long peep through the clouds. All depends on how the Wooster brain responds to the spurring it is going to get in the next half-hour or so.'

'What do you mean?'

'Rummy things have been happening, Nobby. You will recall how I tried the Fittleworth patent process for getting out of being engaged to Florence.'

'By kicking Edwin?'

'By, as you say, kicking Edwin. It has produced a bountiful harvest.'

'But you told me it hadn't worked.'

'Not in the way I had anticipated. But there has been an amazing by-product. Uncle Percy, informed of my activities, is all over me. For years, apparently, he has wanted to kick the young gumboil himself, but Florence has always stayed his foot.'

'I never knew that.'

'No doubt he has worn the mask. But the yearning was there, and it reached fever-point last night, when Edwin, sneaking up behind him, let him have it in the pants with his Scout's stick. So you can understand how he felt on learning that I had rushed in where he had feared to tread. It revolutionized his whole outlook. He shook my hand, gave me a cigar, pressed drink on me, and I am now his trusted friend and adviser. He thinks the world of me.'

'Yes, but—'

'You spoke?'

'I was only going to say that that's splendid and wonderful and marvellous, and I hope you will be very, very happy, but what I want is for him to think the world of Boko.'

'I am coming to that. Does the old relative ever speak to you of his affairs?'

'Only to tell me not to come bothering him now, because he's busy.'

'Then you wouldn't have heard of an American tycoon named J. Chichester Clam, with whom he has got to have a secret meeting in order to complete an important deal. Mysterious commercial stuff. He has asked me to think out some way of arranging this meeting. If I do, you will be on velvet.'

'How do you make that out?'

'Well, dash it, already I am practically Uncle Percy's ewe lamb. That will make me still ewer. He will be able to deny me nothing. I shall be in a position to melt his heart—'

'Oh, golly, yes. I see now.'

'—and get you and Boko fixed up. Then you show Florence that letter of mine, and that will get me fixed up.'

'But, Bertie, this is stupendous.'

'Yes, the prospects are of the rosiest, provided—'

'Provided what?'

'Well, provided I can think of a way of arranging this secret meeting, which at the moment of going to press I'm absolutely dashed if I can.'

'There are millions of ways.'

'Name three.'

'Why, you could . . . No, I see what you mean . . . It is difficult. I know. Ask Jeeves.'

'We have asked Jeeves. He says he's baffled.'

'Baffled? Jeeves?'

'I know. It came as a great shock to me. Chap was full of fish, too.'

'Then what are you going to do?'

'I told Uncle Percy I would brood.'

'Perhaps Boko would have something to suggest.'

Here, I was obliged to be firm.

'I bet he would,' I said, 'and I bet it would be something which would land us so deeply in the soup that it would require a dredging outfit to get us out again. I love Boko like a brother, but what I always feel about the dear old bird is that it's wisest not to stir him.'

She agreed with this, admitting that if there was a way of making things worse than they were Boko would unquestionably find it.

'I'm going to see him,' she said suddenly, after taking time out for a few moments in order to knit the brow.

'Boko?'

'Jeeves. I don't believe all this stuff about him being baffled.'

'He said he was.'

'I don't care. I don't believe it. Have you ever known Jeeves to be baffled?'

'Very seldom.'

'Well, then,' she said, and legged it for the staff quarters, leaving me to pass from the hall—I rather think with bowed head—and move out into the open. Here for a space I pondered.

How long I pondered, I cannot say. When the bean is tensely occupied, it is difficult to keep tab on the passage of time. I am unable to state, therefore, whether it was ten minutes later or more like twenty when I emerged from a profound reverie to discover that Jeeves was in my midst. I had had no inkling of his approach, but then one very often hasn't. He has a way of suddenly materializing at one's side like one of those Indian blokes who shoot their astral bodies to and fro, going into thin air in Rangoon and reassembling the parts in Calcutta. I think it's done with mirrors.

Nobby was also there, looking pretty dashed pleased with herself.

'I told you so,' she said.

'Eh?'

'About Jeeves being baffled. I knew there must be some mistake. He isn't baffled at all.'

I stared at the man, astonished. True, he was looking in rare intellectual form, what with his head sticking out at the back and all the acumen gleaming from his eyes, but he had stated so definitely to Uncle Percy and self that he had been laid a stymie.

'Not baffled?'

'No. He was only fooling. He's got a terrific idea.'

'How much does he know of recent developments?'

'I've just been bringing him up to date.'

'You have been apprised of the failure of the Fittleworth system, Jeeves?'

'Yes, sir. And also of your *rapprochement* with his lordship.'

'My what with his lordship?'

'*Rapprochement*, sir. A French expression. I confess that I experienced no little surprise on finding you on such excellent terms, but Miss Hopwood's explanation has rendered everything perfectly clear.'

'And you really have a scheme for bringing Uncle Percy and Clam together?'

'Yes, sir. I must confess that in our recent interview I intentionally misled his lordship. Realizing how vital it was to the interests of Mr Fittleworth and Miss Hopwood that you should be in a position to use your influence on their behalf, I thought it better that the suggestion should appear to emanate from you.'

'So that you can become more than ever the ewe lamb,' explained Nobby.

I nodded. His meaning had not escaped me. If you analysed it, it was the old Bacon and Shakespeare gag. Bacon, as you no doubt remember, wrote Shakespeare's stuff for him and then, possibly because he owed the latter money or it may be from sheer good nature, allowed him to take the credit for it. I mentioned this to Jeeves, and he said that perhaps an even closer parallel was that of Cyrano de Bergerac.

'The nature of the scheme which I have evolved, I should begin by saying, sir, renders the laying of it before his lordship a matter of some little delicacy, and it may be that a certain finesse will be required to induce him to fall in with it.'

'One of those schemes, is it?'

'Yes, sir. So, if I might make the suggestion, I think it would be best if you were to leave the matter in my hands.'

'You mean, let you sell it to him?'

'Precisely, sir. I would, of course, stress the fact that you were its originator and myself merely the go-between or emissary.'

'Just as you feel, Jeeves. You know best. And what is this scheme?'

'Briefly this, sir. I see no reason why his lordship and Mr Clam should not meet in perfect secrecy and safety at the fancy dress dance which is to take place to-night at the East Wibley Town Hall.'

I was absolutely staggered. I had clean forgotten that those East Wibley doings were scheduled for to-night. Which, when you reflect how keenly I had been looking forward to them, will give you some idea of the extent to which the fierce rush of life at Steeple Bumpleigh had disorganized my faculties.

'Isn't that a ball of fire?' said Nobby, enthusiastically.

I could not wholly subscribe to this.

'I spot a fatal flaw.'

'What do you mean, a flaw?'

'Well, try this on your pianola. Where, at such short notice, can Uncle Percy procure a costume? He can't go without one. Fancy dress, I take it, is obligatory. In other words, we come up against the snag the Wedding Guest ran into.'

'Which Wedding Guest? The one who beat his breast?'

'No, the chap in the parable, who was invited to a wedding but, having omitted to dress the part, got slung out on his ear like—'

I had been about to say 'like Boko from the precincts of Bumpleigh Hall', but refrained, fearing lest it might wound. But even without the addition my remorselessly logical words struck home.

'Oh, golly! I had forgotten about the upholstery. How do you get around that, Jeeves?'

'Quite simply, miss. I fear it will be necessary for you to lend his lordship your Sindbad the Sailor costume, sir.'

I uttered a stricken cry, like a cat to whom the suggestion has been made that she part with her new-born kitten.

'My God, Jeeves!'

'I fear so, sir.'

'But, dash it, that means I won't be able to attend the function.'

'I fear not, sir.'

'Well, why do you want to attend the rotten function?' demanded Nobby.

I gnawed the lower lip.

'You feel that this is absolutely essential, Jeeves? Think well.'

'Quite essential, sir. It may be a little difficult to persuade his lordship to take part in a frivolous affair of this nature, owing to his fear of what her ladyship would say, should she learn of it, and I am relying on the ginger whiskers which go with the costume to turn the scale. In placing the proposition before his lordship, I shall lay great stress on the completeness of the disguise which these will afford, preventing recognition by any acquaintance whom he may chance to encounter in the course of the festivities.'

I nodded. He was right. I decided to make the great sacrifice. The Woosters are seldom deaf to the voice of Reason, even if it involves draining the bitter cup.

'True, Jeeves. The keenest eye could not pierce those whiskers.'

'No, sir.'

'So be it, then. I will donate the costume.'

'Thank you, sir. Then I will be seeing his lordship immediately.'

'Heaven speed your efforts, Jeeves.'

'Thank you, sir.'

'Same here, Jeeves.'

'Thank you, miss.'

He shimmered off, and I turned to Nobby, with a sigh, saying that this was a blow and I would not attempt to conceal it. And once more she asked me why I was so keen on attending what she described as a footling country dance.

'Well, for one thing, I had set my heart on knocking East Wibley's eye out with that Sindbad. You've never seen me as Sindbad the Sailor, have you, Nobby?'

'No.'

'You haven't lived. But,' I proceeded, 'there is another angle, and I wish it had floated into my mind before Jeeves popped off, because I should like his views on it. If Uncle Percy meets Chichester Clam at this orgy and all goes well, he will, of course, be in malleable mood. But the point is, do these malleable moods last? By the following morning, may he not have simmered down? In order to strike while the iron is hot, both I and Boko ought to be there—I to seize the psychological moment for approaching Uncle Percy on your behalf and Boko to carry on from where I leave off.'

She saw what I meant.

'Yes, that wants thinking out.'

'If you don't mind, I'll pace up and down a bit.'

I did so, and was still hard at it, when Nobby's voice hailed me, and I saw that Jeeves had returned from his mission. Joining them at my best speed, I found him looking modestly triumphant.

'His lordship has consented, sir.'

'Good. But—'

'I am to proceed to London without delay, in order to see Mr Clam and secure his co-operation.'

'Quite. But—'

'Meanwhile, Miss Hopwood has drawn my attention to the point which you have raised, sir, and I am in cordial agreement with your view that both yourself and Mr Fittleworth should be present at the dance. What I would suggest, sir, is that Mr Fittleworth drives me to the metropolis in his car, starting as soon as possible in order that we may return in good time. While I am interviewing Mr Clam, Mr Fittleworth can be purchasing the necessary costumes. I think this meets your difficulty, sir?'

I brooded for a moment. The scheme did, as he had said, meet my difficulty. The only thing that was bothering me was whether an essentially delicate matter like the selection of fancy dress costumes could be left safely in the hands of a bird like Boko. He was the sort of chap who might quite easily come back with a couple of Pierrots.

'Wouldn't it be better if I drove you to London?'

'No, sir. I think that you should remain, in order to keep his lordship's courage screwed to the sticking-place. His acceptance of the scheme was not obtained without considerable trouble. He would agree, and then he would glance at the portrait of her ladyship which hangs above the study door and demur once more. Left to himself, without constant exhortation and encouragement, I fear he might yet change his mind.'

I saw what he meant.

'Something in that, Jeeves. A bit jumpy, is he?'

'Extremely so, sir.'

I could not blame the old bird. I have already described my own emotions on catching the eye of that portrait of Aunt Agatha.

'Right ho, Jeeves.'

'Very good, sir. I would recommend constant allusions to the efficacy of the whiskers. As I had anticipated, it was they that turned the scale. Would Mr Fittleworth be at his residence now, miss? Then I will proceed thither at once.'

24

Jeeves's prediction that Uncle Percy would require constant exhortation and encouragement, to prevent him issuing an eleventh hour *nolle prosequi* and ducking out of the assignment he had undertaken, was abundantly fulfilled, and I must say I found the task of holding his hand and shooting pep into him a bit wearing. As the long day wore on, I began to understand why prize-fighters' managers, burdened with the job of bringing their men to the scratch, are always fairly careworn birds, with lined faces and dark circles under the eyes.

I could not but feel that it was ironical that the old relative should have spoken disparagingly of fawns as a class, sneering at their timidity in that rather lofty and superior manner, for he himself could have walked straight into a gathering of these animals, and no questions asked. There were moments, as he sat gazing at that portrait of Aunt Agatha over the study door, when he would have made even an unusually jumpy fawn look like Dangerous Dan McGrew.

Take it for all in all, therefore, it was a relief when, towards the quiet evenfall, the telephone rang and the following dialogue took place.

UNCLE PERCY: What? What? What-what-what? What? What? . . . Oh, hullo, Clam.

CLAM (OFF STAGE): Quack, quack, quack, quack, quack, quack, quack, quack (about a minute and a half of this, in all).

UNCLE PERCY: Fine, good. Splendid. I'll look out for you, then.

'Clam,' he said, replacing the receiver. 'Says he's heart and soul in favour of the scheme, and is coming to the ball as Edward the Confessor.'

I nodded understandingly. I thought Clam's choice was good.

'A bearded bozo, was he not, this Edward?' I asked.

'To the eyebrows,' said Uncle Percy. 'Those were the days when the world was a solid mass of beavers. I shall keep my eye open for something that looks like a burst horsehair sofa, and that will be Clam.'

'Then you've really definitely and finally decided to attend the binge?'

'With bells on, my dear boy, with bells on. You might not think it, to look at me now, but there was a time when no Covent Garden ball was complete without me. I used to have the girls flocking round me like flies about a honeypot. Between ourselves, it was owing to the fact that I got thrown out of a Covent Garden ball and taken to Vine Street Police Station in the company of a girl who, if memory serves me aright, was named Tottie that I escaped—that I had the misfortune not to marry your aunt thirty years earlier than I did.'

'Really?'

'I assure you. We had just got engaged at the time, and she broke it off within three minutes of reading my press notices in the evening papers. I was too late, of course, for the morning sheets, but the midday specials of the evening ones did me proud, and she was a little upset about it all. That is why I am so particularly anxious that no hint of to-night's doings shall reach her ears. Your aunt is a wonderful woman, Bertie . . . can't think what I should do without her . . . but—well, you know how it is.'

I said I knew how it was.

'So I trust that all will be well and that she will never learn of the dark deeds which have been done in her absence. I think I have the mechanics of the thing fairly well planned out. I shall sneak down the back stairs, muffled to the eyes in an overcoat, and tool over to East Wibley on my old push bicycle. It's only half a dozen miles. No flaws in that?'

'None that I can spot.'

'Of course, if Florence saw me—'

'She won't.'

'Or Edwin.'

'Not a chance.'

'Or Maple.'

I was distressed to note this resurgence of the old fawn complex just when everything had seemed hotsy-totsy, and addressed myself without delay to the task of putting a stopper on it. And eventually I succeeded. By the time I had finished pointing out that nothing was more unlikely than that Florence should be roaming the back stairs at such an hour, that Edwin was bound to take a day or two off from his spooring after the treatment I had administered that morning, and that Maple, if encountered, could readily be squared with a couple of quid, he bucked up enormously, and I left him trying out dance steps on the study floor.

Well, of course, you can't ginger up an uncle by marriage from shortly after breakfast to about five in the afternoon without paying the toll a bit. All this exhortation and encouragement had, as you may well imagine, taken it out of me not a little, inducing a limpness of the limbs and a sort of general feeling of stickiness. I don't say I was perspiring at every pore, but I felt in need of a thorough rinse: and, the river being at my very door, this was easy to obtain. A quarter of an hour later, I might have been observed breasting the waves, clad in a bathing suit from Boko's store.

In fact, I was observed, and by none other than G. D'Arcy Cheesewright. Doing the Australian crawl back to the bank after a refreshing plunge and holding on to a bush while I brushed the moisture from my eyes, I glanced up and saw him standing above me.

It was an embarrassing moment. I don't know when you feel less at ease than when encountering a bloke to whose *fiancée* you have just got engaged.

'Oh, hullo, Stilton,' I said. 'Coming in?'

'Not while you are polluting the water.'

'I'm just coming out.'

'Then I'll let it run a bit and perhaps it will be all right.'

His words alone would have been enough to inform a man of my quick intelligence that he was not unmixedly pro-Bertram, and as I climbed out and slid into the bath robe he gave me a look which drove the thing home. I have already, in another place, described at some length these looks of his, and I may say that this one was fully up to the sample he had given me outside Wee Nooke on the previous day.

However, if there is a chance that suavity will ease a situation, the Woosters always give it a buzz.

'Nice day,' I said. 'Pretty country, this.'

'Ruined by the people you meet.'

'Trippers, you mean?'

'No, I don't mean trippers. I refer to snakes in the grass.'

It would be absurd to say that his attitude was encouraging, but I persevered.

'Talking of grass,' I said, 'Boko was in that of Bumpleigh Hall this morning, and Uncle Percy trod on him.'

'I wish he had broken your neck.'

'I wasn't there.'

'I thought you said your uncle trod on you.'

'You don't listen, Stilton. I said he trod on Boko.'

'Oh Boko? Good Lord!' he cried, with honest heat. 'With a fellow like you around, he treads on Boko! What on earth was the use of treading on Boko?'

There was a pause, during which he tried to catch my eye and I tried to avoid his. Stilton's eye, even in repose, is nothing to write home about, being a sort of hard blue and rather bulging. In moments of emotion, it tends to protrude even farther, like that of an irascible snail, the general effect being rather displeasing.

Presently, he spoke again.

'I've just seen Florence.'

My embarrassment increased. I had been hoping that the topic might have been avoided. But Stilton is one of those rugged, forthright chaps who don't avoid topics.

'Oh, yes?' I said. 'Florence, eh?'

'She says she's going to marry you.'

I was liking this less and less.

'Oh, yes,' I said. 'Yes, I believe there is some idea of a union.'

'What do you mean, some idea? It's all fixed for September.'

'September?' I quavered, trembling from head to foot a bit. I hadn't had a notion that the curse was slated to come upon me so dashed quick.

'So she says,' he responded moodily. 'I'd like to break your neck. But I can't, because I'm in uniform.'

'Yes, there's that. One doesn't want one of these unpleasant police scandals, does one?'

There was another pause. He was looking at me in a sort of yearning way.

'Gosh!' he murmured, almost dreamily. 'I wish there was something I could pinch you for!'

'Come, come, Stilton. Is this the tone?'

'I'd love to see you cowering in the dock, with me giving evidence against you.'

He was silent for a space, and I could see that he was still gloating over the vision he had conjured up. Then he asked me rather abruptly if I had finished with the river, and I said I had.

'Then in about five minutes or so I might take a chance and go in,' he said.

It was, as you may well imagine, in pretty fairly melancholy mood that I donned the bath robe and made my way back to the house. There's always something about the going phut of an old friendship that tends to lower the spirits. It was many years since this Cheesewright and I had started what I believe is known as plucking the gowans fine, and there had been a time when we had plucked them rather assiduously. But his attitude at the recent get-together had made it plain that the close season for gowans had now set in, and, as I say, it rather saddened me.

Shoving on the shirt and bags with an unshed tear in the eye, I trickled along to the sitting-room to see if Boko had returned from his mission to London. I found him sitting in an armchair with Nobby on his lap, seeming in admirable spirits.

'Come in, Bertie, come in,' he cried jovially. 'Jeeves is in the kitchen, brewing a dish of tea. You will join us in a cup?'

Inclining my head in assent to this suggestion, I addressed Nobby on a point of pre-eminent interest.

'Nobby,' I said, 'I have just seen Stilton, and he informs me that Florence has fixed the nuptials for a shockingly early date—viz. September. It is vital, therefore, that you lose no time in showing her that letter of mine.'

'If everything goes all right to-night, she will be skimming through it to-morrow morning over her early cup of tea.'

Relieved, I turned to Boko.

'Did you get the costumes?'

'Of course I got the costumes. What the dickens do you think I sweated up to London for? Two in all, one for self and one for you, the finest the Bros. Cohen could supply. Mine is a Cavalier. A rather sex-appealy wig goes with it. Yours—'

'Yes, what about mine?'

He hesitated a moment.

'You'll like yours. It's a Pierrot.'

I uttered a cry of chagrin. Boko, like all my circle, is well acquainted with my views on going to fancy dress dances as a Pierrot. I consider it roughly equivalent to shooting a sitting bird.

'Oh, is it?' I said, speaking with quiet firmness. 'Well, I'm jolly well going to have the Cavalier.'

'You can't, Bertie, old man. It wouldn't fit you. It was built for a shortish, squarish reveler like me. You are tall and slim and elegant. "Elegant" is the word?' he said, putting it up to Nobby.

'Just the word,' she assented.

'Another good adjective would be "willowy". Or "sylphlike". Gosh, I wish I had a figure like yours, Bertie. You don't know what you've got.'

'Yes, I do,' I riposted, coldly ignoring the salve. 'I've got a ruddy Pierrot costume. A Wooster going to a fancy dress ball as a Pierrot!' I said, and laughed shortly.

Boko shot Nobby off his knee and rose and began patting my shoulder. I suppose he could see that I was in dangerous mood.

'You need have no qualms about appearing in this Pierrot, Bertie,' he said soothingly. 'Where you have gone astray is in supposing that it is an ordinary Pierrot. Far from it. I doubt if, strictly speaking, you could call it a Pierrot at all. For one thing, it is mauve in colour. For another . . . But I'll show it to you, and I'll bet you go dancing about the house, clapping your hands.'

He reached for the suitcase which lay in the foreground, opened it, pulled out its contents and stared at them, aghast. So did I. So did Nobby. We all stared at them, aghast.

They consisted of what appeared to be a football suit. There was a pair of blue shorts, a pair of purple stockings and a crimson jersey.

Across the chest of the jersey, in large white letters, ran the legend 'BORSTAL ROVERS'.

25

It was some moments before any of us broke what I believe is called the pregnant silence. Then Nobby spoke.

'Do either of you see what I see?' she asked, in a sort of hushed, awed voice.

My own was dull and toneless.

'If what you see is a gent's footballing outfit,' I replied, 'that is what is impressing itself on the Wooster retina.'

'With "Borstal Rovers" written across the jersey?'

'Right across the jersey.'

'In large white letters?'

'In very large white letters. I am waiting,' I said, coldly, 'for an explanation, Fittleworth.'

Nobby uttered a passionate cry.

'I can give you the explanation. Boko has gone and made an ass of himself *again*!'

Cringing beneath her flaming eye, the wretched man broke into a storm of protest.

'I haven't! I swear I haven't, darling!'

'Come, come, Boko,' I said, sternly. I had no wish to grind the man into the dust, but he had the wages of sin coming to him. 'A Cavalier costume and a mauve—if your story is to be credited—Pierrot have changed, while in your custody, into a football kit belonging apparently to an athlete who turns out for the Borstal Rovers, though I wouldn't have said offhand that there was such a team. Someone has blundered, and all the evidence points to you.'

Boko had tottered to a chair, and was sitting in it with his head in his hands. He emitted a sudden yip.

'Catsmeat!' he cried. 'I see it all. It was that chump, Catsmeat. Before starting to return here,' he proceeded, looking up and looking quickly down again as his eye collided with Nobby's, 'I stopped in at the Drones to get one for the road. Catsmeat Potter-Pirbright was there. We fell into conversation, and it turned out that he, too, was going to a fancy dress binge to-night. We chatted for a while of this and that, and then he looked at his watch and found that he had only just time to catch his train, and buzzed off. What happened is obvious. Rendered cock-eyed by haste, he took my suitcase in mistake for his own. And if you're going to make out that that was my fault,' said Boko, speaking now with some spirit, 'then all I can say is that there's no justice in the world and that it's a fat lot of use being as innocent as the driven snow.'

This appeal to our better feelings was not without its effect. Nobby flung herself into his arms, cooing over him to a considerable extent, and even I was compelled to admit that he had been more sinned against than sinning.

'Still, it's all right,' said Boko, now definitely chirpy once more. 'Catsmeat and I are about the same build, so I can wear this number. I would prefer, of course, not to have to flaunt myself before East Wibley as a member of the Borstal Rovers, but one realizes that this is not a time when one can pick and choose. Yes, I can take it.'

I mentioned a point which he appeared to have overlooked.

'And how about me? I've got to be there, too, to pave the way for you with Uncle Percy. A lot of solid talking will be required before it will be any use you approaching him. If I'm not at this East Wibley orgy, you might just as well stay at home.'

My words, as I had anticipated, produced a marked sensation. Nobby gave a sort of distraught hiccough, like a bull-pup choking on a rubber bone, and Boko confessed with a moody oath that he hadn't thought of that.

'Think of it now,' I said. 'Or, better,' I went on, as the door opened, 'ask

Jeeves what his views on the matter are. You will probably have something to suggest, eh, Jeeves?'

'Sir?'

'A snag has arisen in our path, an Act of God having left us a costume short,' I explained, 'and we are frankly baffled.'

He placed the tea-tray on the table, and listened with respectful interest while we laid the facts before him.

'Might I take a short walk, sir,' he said, when we had finished, 'and think the problem over?'

'Certainly, Jeeves,' I replied, concealing a slight pang of disappointment, for I had hoped that he might have come across with an immediate solution. 'By all means take a short walk. You will find us here on your return.'

He oiled off, and we settled down to an informal debate, in which the note of hope was conspicuous by its a. It could scarcely escape the attention of three keen minds like ours that what looked like dishing us was the matter of time. It was now well past five o'clock, which rendered out of the question the idea of another quick dash to the metropolis and a second visit to the establishment of the Bros. Cohen. Zealous though they are in their self-chosen task of supplying the populace with clothing, there comes a moment when these merchants call it a day and put up the shutters. Not even by exceeding the speed limit all the way could a driver, starting from Steeple Bumpleigh now, reach the emporium in time to do business. Long ere he could arrive, the Bros. and their corps of assistants would have retired to their various residences and be relaxing over good books.

And as for the chance of securing anything in the nature of a costume in Steeple Bumpleigh, that, it seemed to us, could be ruled out altogether. At the beginning of this chronicle, I gave a brief description of this hamlet, showing it to be rich in honeysuckle-covered cottages and apple-cheeked villagers, but that let it out. It had only one shop, that so ably conducted by Mrs Greenless opposite the Jubilee watering-trough: and this, after it had supplied you with string, pink sweets, sides of bacon, tinned goods and *Old Moore's Almanac*, was a spent force.

Taking it for all in all, accordingly, the situation seemed pretty bleak. When I tell you that the best suggestion was the one advanced by Boko, that I should strip to a loin-cloth and smear myself with boot polish and go to the dance as a Zulu chief, you will see how little constructive progress had been made by the time the door opened and Jeeves was once more in our midst.

There is something about the mere sight of this number-nine-size-hatted man that seldom fails to jerk the beholder from despondency's depths in times of travail. Although Reason told us that he couldn't possibly have formulated a scheme for dragging home the gravy, we hailed him eagerly.

'Well?' I said.

'Well?' said Boko.

'Well?' said Nobby.

'Any luck, Jeeves?' I asked.

He inclined the coconut.

'Yes, sir. I am happy to say that I have been successful in finding a solution to the problem confronting you.'

'Gosh!' cried Nobby, stunned to the core.

'Egad!' cried Boko, the same.

'Well, I'm blowed!' I ejaculated, ibid. 'You have? I wouldn't have thought it possible. Would you, Boko?'

'I certainly wouldn't.'

'Or you, Nobby?'

'Not in a million years.'

'Well, there it is. That's Jeeves. Where others merely smite the brow and clutch the hair, he acts. Napoleon was the same.'

Boko shook his head.

'You can't class Napoleon with Jeeves.'

'Like putting up a fairish selling-plater against a classic yearling,' agreed Nobby.

'Napoleon had his moments,' I urged.

'On a very limited scale compared with Jeeves,' said Boko. 'I have nothing against Napoleon, but I cannot see him sauntering out into Steeple Bumpleigh at half-past five in the afternoon and coming back ten minutes later with a costume for a fancy dress ball. And this, you say, is what you have accomplished, Jeeves?'

'Yes, sir.'

'Well, I don't know how you feel about it, Bertie,' said Boko, 'but to me the thing looks like a ruddy miracle. Where is this costume, Jeeves?'

'I have placed it on the bed in Mr Wooster's room, sir.'

'But where on earth did you get it?'

'I found it, sir.'

'Found it? Just lying around, do you mean?'

'Yes, sir. On the bank of the river.'

I don't know why it was, unless possibly because we Woosters are a bit quicker than other men, but at these words a sudden, horrible suspicion shot through me like a dose of salts, numbing the nerve centres and turning the blood to ice.

'Jeeves,' I faltered, 'this thing . . . this what-you-may-call-it . . . this costume of which you speak . . . what is it?'

'A policeman's uniform, sir.'

I collapsed into a chair as if the lower limbs had been mown off with a scythe. The s. had been well founded.

'It has occurred to me since that it may possibly have been the property of Mr Cheesewright, sir. I observed him disporting himself in the water not far away.'

I rose from the chair. It wasn't an easy thing to do, but I managed it.

'Jeeves,' I said, or perhaps it would be *mot juster* to say I thundered, 'you will go and restore that dashed uniform to its bally owner instanter!'

Boko and Nobby, who had been slapping each other's backs in the foreground, halted in mid-slap and stared at me, Boko as if he couldn't believe his ears, Nobby as if she couldn't believe hers.

'Restore it?' cried Nobby.

'To its bally owner?' gasped Boko. 'I simply fail to follow you, Bertie.'

'Me, too,' said Nobby. 'If you had been a Israelite in the wilderness, you wouldn't have passed up your plateful of manna, would you?'

'Exactly,' said Boko. 'Here, at the eleventh hour, just when the total downfall of all our hopes and dreams seemed to stare us in the eyeball because we were unable to lay our hooks on a fancy dress costume, an admirable costume has been sent from Heaven, as you might say, and you appear to be suggesting that we shall give it the go-by. You can't realize what you are saying. Reflect, Bertie. Consider.'

I preserved my iron front.

'That uniform,' I said, 'goes back to its proprietor by special messenger at the earliest possible date. My dear Boko, my good Nobby, have you the slightest conception of the bitterly anti-Wooster sentiments which prevail in Stilton's bosom? The man specifically stated to me not half an hour ago that his dearest wish was to catch Bertram bending. Let him discover that I have been pinching his uniforms, and I can hope for no mercy. Three months in the second division will be the best I can expect.'

Nobby started to say something about three months soon passing, but Boko shushed her.

'Why on earth should he discover anything of the sort?' he said. 'You aren't proposing to parade Steeple Bumpleigh day in and day out in this uniform. You're only going to wear it to-night.'

I corrected this view.

'I am not going to wear it to-night.'

'Oh, aren't you?' cried Nobby. 'Well, then, I'm jolly well not going to show that letter of yours to Florence.'

'Good girl,' said Boko. 'Well spoken, young light of my life. Laugh that off, Bertie.'

I made no endeavour to do so. Her words had chilled the spine. I don't suppose there is a man living who is swifter than Bertram Wooster to perceive when someone has got him by the short hairs, and it was clear to me that this was what had happened now. However fearful the perils that confronted me if I accepted Jeeves's loathsome gift, they must be faced.

A moment's struggle for utterance, and I bowed the onion and right-hoed.

'Splendid fellow!' said Boko. 'I knew you would see the light.'

'Bertie's always so reasonable,' said Nobby.

'Clear-thinking chap. Very level-headed,' agreed Boko. 'Then we're all set, eh? You come to the ball—of which in such a costume you can scarcely fail to be the belle—and you lurk till you have ascertained that old Worplesdon has had a satisfactory conference with Clam. If all has gone well, you buttonhole him and give me a build up. As soon as he is in melting mood, you give me the high sign, and I carry on from there, while you come home and turn in with an easy mind. I doubt if the whole thing—your part of it—will take more than half an hour. And now I think I had better be stepping along and taking Stilton a raincoat. No doubt he has a spare uniform at his residence, but one would like to get him there without causing comment. We can't have chaps roaming the countryside in the nude. All right for the Riviera, no doubt, but thank God we have a stricter code in Steeple Bumpleigh.'

He pushed off, taking Nobby with him, and I turned to Jeeves, who during these exchanges had been standing completely motionless, looking like a stuffed owl, his habit on occasions when he is among those present but has not been invited to join in the chit-chat.

'Jeeves,' I said.

'Sir?' he responded, coming to life in a deferential sort of way.

I did not mince my words.

'Well, Jeeves,' I said, and my face was hard and cold, 'you appreciate the set-up, I trust? Thanks to you, I am as properly up against it as I can remember being in the course of a not uneventful career. My position, as I see it, is roughly that of one who has removed a favourite cub from the custody of a rather more than usually short-tempered tigress, and is obliged to carry it on his person in the animal's immediate neighbourhood. I am not a weak man, Jeeves, but when I think of what will happen if Stilton cops me while I am draped in that uniform, it makes my knotted and combined locks . . . what was that gag of yours?'

'Part, sir, and each particular hair—'

'Stand on end, wasn't it?'

'Yes, sir. Like quills upon the fretful porpentine.'

'That's right. And that brings me back to it. What the dickens is a porpentine?'

'A porcupine, sir.'

'Oh, a *porcupine*? Why didn't you say that at first? It's been worrying me all day. Well, that, as I say, is the posish, Jeeves, and it is you who have brought it about.'

'I acted from the best motives, sir. It seemed to me that at all costs it was essential that you take part in to-night's festivities.'

I saw his point. If there's one thing the Woosters are, it's fairminded. We writhe, but we are just.

'Yes,' I assented with a moody nod, 'I suppose you meant well. And no doubt, in a sense, you did the right and judicious thing. But you can't get away from it that mine is a fearful predicament. One false step, and Stilton will be on the back of my neck, shouting for Justices of the Peace to come and sentence me to a long spell in the cooler. And, apart from that, has it occurred to you that this Cheesewright is about forty inches more round the chest and eight inches more round the head than me? Clad in his uniform, and especially wearing his helmet, I shall look like a Keystone Kop. Why, dash it, I'd rather go to this binge as the meanest Pierrot. Still, I suppose my bally preferences don't count.'

'I fear not, sir. For know, rash youth—if you will pardon me, sir—the expression is Mr Bernard Shaw's, not my own . . . For know, rash youth, that in this star crost world Fate drives us all to find our chiefest good in what we can, and not in what we would.'

Again, I saw his point.

'Quite,' I responded. 'Yes, I suppose the bullet must be bitten. Right ho, Jeeves,' I said, summoning to my aid all the splendid Wooster fortitude, 'lead me to it.'

26

It had been Boko's idea that he and I should make the journey to East Wibley in his car, he at the wheel, I at his side, so that if there were any minor details to be settled which we had overlooked, we could get them ironed out before arrival, thus achieving a perfect preparedness and avoiding any chance of last minute stymies.

To this suggestion, though admitting its basic soundness, I demurred. In fact, when I say I demurred, I ought to put it stronger. I more or less recoiled in horror. I had been Boko's passenger on a previous occasion, and it was not an experience one would wish to repeat. Put an author in the driver's seat of a car, and his natural goofiness seems to become intensified. Not only did Boko persistently overtake on blind corners, but he did it with a dreamy, faraway look in his eyes, telling one the plot of his next novel the while and not infrequently removing both hands from the wheel in order to drive home some dramatic point with gestures.

Another reason why I preferred to travel in the Wooster two-seater was that I was naturally anxious to get home and out of that uniform as speedily as possible. And, of course, it would be necessary, if all went well, for Boko to linger on and talk turkey to Uncle Percy.

My qualms regarding spending the evening in Stilton's plumage had in no way diminished with the passage of time. I still viewed the ordeal with concern.

Boko, returning from his errand of mercy to the zealous officer, had reported that the latter had seemed a bit upset about it all and inclined to suspect me of being the motivating force behind the outrage. To this,

Boko had rather cleverly replied by saying that it was far more likely to have been young Edwin who had done the horrid deed. There comes a moment, he had pointed out, in the life of every Boy Scout when he suddenly feels fed up with doing acts of kindness and allows his human side to get uppermost. On such occasions, the sight of a policeman's uniform lying on the river bank would, he maintained, call to such a Scout like deep calling to deep and prove practically irresistible. He told me he thought he had lulled Stilton's suspicions, all right.

This, of course, was all very well, as far as it went, but I could not conceal it from myself that if Stilton were to see me wearing the uniform, his suspicions would pretty damn' soon come unlulled. He might or might not have what it takes to make a man a master-mind of Scotland Yard, but he unquestionably had sufficient intelligence, should such a contingency occur, to put two and two together, as the expression is. I mean to say, a policeman who has had his uniform pinched and later in the day comes on someone swathed in it is practically bound to fall into a certain train of thought.

'No, Boko,' I said. 'I proceed to the tryst under my own steam, and I come away the moment I have completed my share in the proceedings, driving like the wind.'

And so it was arranged.

Well, of course, it being so essential for me to get to the scene of operations in good time, you might have known what would happen. At about the half-way mark, the old two-seater suddenly faded out, coming to a placid standstill in prettily wooded country miles from anywhere. And as I don't know the first thing about fixing a car, my talents being limited to twisting the wheel and tooting the tooter, I had to wait there till the United States Marines arrived.

These took the shape—at about a quarter to twelve—of a kindly bird in a lorry who, on being hailed, put everything right with a careless twiddle of the fingers so rapidly that he had occasion to spit only twice from start to finish. I thanked him, flung him a purse of gold and proceeded on my way, fetching up at journey's end just as the local clocks were striking midnight.

The interior of the East Wibley Town Hall presented a gay and fairylike appearance. Coloured lanterns hung from the roof, there was a good deal of smilax here and there, and on all sides the eye detected fair women and brave men. One of the latter, a footballer in the striking colours of the Borstal Rovers, detached himself from the throng and arrested my progress, full of recriminations.

'Bertie, you outstanding louse,' said Boko, for it was he, 'where the devil have you been? I was expecting you hours ago.'

I explained the reasons for my delay, and he said peevishly that I was just the sort of chap whose car would break down when every moment was precious, adding that it was a lucky thing that it hadn't been me they sent to bring the good news from Aix to Ghent, because, if it had been, Ghent would have got it first in the Sunday papers.

'It's going to be touch and go, Bertie,' he proceeded. 'A wholly unforeseen situation has arisen. Old Worplesdon has gone to earth in the bar and is lowering the stuff by the pailful.'

'But that's fine,' I said. 'The significance of his actions has probably escaped you, but I can read between the lines. It means that he has seen Clam and that everything is satisfactorily fixed up.'

He clicked his tongue impatiently.

'Of course it does. But the frightful danger is that at any moment he may pass completely out, and then where are we?'

I saw what he meant, and it was as if a hand of ice had been placed on my heart. No wonder he had used the words, 'frightful danger'. The peril was hideous. Our whole plan of strategy called for an Uncle Percy in whom the neap tide of the milk of human kindness was at its height. A blind and speechless Uncle P., stacked up against the wall in a corner of the bar like an umbrella in an umbrella stand, would defeat all our aims.

'Go to him without a second's delay,' said Boko, urgently. 'Pray Heaven it may not be too late!'

The words had scarcely left his lips before I was skimming barwards like a greyhound released from the slips. And it was with profound relief that I saw that I was in time. Uncle Percy had not passed out. He was still up and doing, playing the genial host to a platoon of friends and admirers who had plainly come to look on him in the light of a public drinking fountain.

I was just starting to head in his direction, when the band struck up another tune and his pals swallowed theirs quick and streamed out, leaving the old relative leaning back in his chair with his feet on the table. I lost no time in stepping up and fraternizing.

'What ho, Uncle Percy,' I said.

'Ah, Bertie,' he replied. He shut one eye and scrutinized me narrowly. 'I am right,' he queried, 'in supposing that that is Bertram Wooster rattling about inside that helmet?'

'It is,' I replied shortly. The uniform and helmet were proving even roomier than I had feared they would be, and I was about fed up with them. The almost universal merriment which had greeted me, as I passed through the crowd of revelers, had been hard to bear. The Woosters are not accustomed to getting the horse's laugh when they lend their presence to fancy dress dances.

'It doesn't fit. It's too large. You should change your hatter, or your armourer, or whatever it is. Still, be that as it may, tiddly-om-pom-pom. Sit down and have some of this disgusting champagne, Bertie. I'll join you.'

I thought it best to speak the word in season.

'Haven't you had enough, Uncle Percy?'

He weighed this.

'If what you mean by that question is, am I stinko,' he replied, 'in a broad, general sense you are right. I *am* stinko. But everything is relative, Bertie . . . You, for instance, are my relative, and I am your relative . . . and the point I want to make is that I am not one bit as stinko as I'm going to be later on. This is a night for unstinted rejoicing, my dear boy, and if you think I am not going to rejoice—and unstintedly, at that—then I reply "Watch me!" That is all I say. Watch me!'

The spectacle of an uncle, even if only an uncle by marriage, going down for the third time in a sea of dance champagne can never be an agreeable one. But though I mourned as a nephew, I'm bound to say I found myself pretty bucked in my capacity of ambassador for Boko. Pie-eyed, even plastered, this man might be, but there was no mistaking his geniality. It was like something out of Dickens, and I saw that he was going to be clay in my hands.

'I've seen Clam,' he proceeded.

'You have?'

'With the naked eye. And I refuse to believe that Edward the Confessor really looked like that. Nobody presenting such an obscene appearance as

J. Chichester Clam could possibly have held the throne of England for five minutes. Lynching parties would have been organized, knights sent out to cope with the nuisance with battleaxes.'

'Is everything all right?'

'Everything's fine, except that I am beginning to see two of you. And one was ample.'

'I mean, you've had your conference?'

'Oh, our conference? Yes, we had that, and I don't mind telling you, if you can hear me from inside that helmet, that I put it all over him. When he looks at that agreement we sketched out on the back of the wine list—an agreement, I may mention, legally witnessed by the chap behind the bar and impossible to get out of—he'll realize that he's practically given me his bally shipping line. That is why I say—and with all the emphasis at my disposal—tiddly-om-pom-pom. Fill your glass, Bertie. Don't spare the vitriol.'

I felt that a word of praise would not be amiss. However mellowed a man may be, it never hurts to mellow him a bit more by giving him the old oil.

'Smooth work, Uncle Percy.'

'You may well say so, my boy.'

'There can't be many fellows about with brains like yours.'

'There aren't.'

'Very creditable to you, the whole thing. I mean, considering your condition.'

'You allude to my being tight? Quite, quite. But I wasn't tight when I was dealing with Clam. Though my shoes were. I seem,' he said, his lips contorted by a spasm of pain, 'to have come out in a pair of shoes about eleven sizes too small, and they're nipping me like nobody's business. I'm going to look for a quiet spot where I can take them off for a bit.'

I drew my breath in sharply. I had seen the way. I suppose this is how great generals win battles, by suddenly spotting the right course to pursue and immediately pulling up their socks and snapping into it.

You see, what I had been alive to all along had been the danger that this man, as soon as I switched the conversation to the subject of Boko, would turn on his heel and stalk off, leaving me flat. Catch him with his shoes off, and this problem would not arise. An uncle by marriage with only socks on finds it dashed difficult to turn on his heel, especially if he's sitting in a car. And it was into a car that I proposed to decant this Percy.

'What you want,' I said, 'is to go and sit in a car.'

'I haven't got a car. I tooled over on my push bike, and a hell of a sweat it was, taxing the unaccustomed calf muscles like billy-o.'

'I'll find a car.'

'Not that rotten little two-seater of yours, I trust? I shall require space. I want to stretch my legs out and relax. The calves are still throbbing.'

'No, this is a bigger, better car altogether. The property of a friend of mine.'

'Will he object to my taking my shoes off?'

'Not a bit.'

'Excellent. Lead the way, then, my boy. Before starting, however, I had better procure another quart of this gooseberry cider and take it along.'

'If you think it advisable.'

'Not merely advisable. Imperative. One doesn't want to lose a moment.'

I had no difficulty in spotting Boko's car. It was a thing about the size of a young tank, which he had bought second-hand in his less oofy days and refused to part with because its admirable solidity served him so well in the give and take of traffic. He told me once that it brushed ordinary sports models aside like flies, and that his money would be on it even in the event of a collision with an omnibus.

I ushered the old relative into its cavernous depths, and he removed the shoes. Not till he was safely reclining on his spine, twiddling his toes out of the window, so that the cool night air could play on them, did I start to bring up the big item on the agenda paper.

'So you slipped it across Clam, did you, Uncle Percy?' I said. 'Splendid. Capital. And after accomplishing so notable a business triumph you are, I take it, feeling pretty benevolent towards your fellow men?'

'I love them all,' he said handsomely. 'I look on the entire human species with a kindly and indulgent eye.'

'Well, that's fine.'

'Always excepting, of course, the foe of that species, the hellhound Fittleworth.'

This wasn't so good.

'Would you make exceptions, Uncle Percy? On a night like this?'

'On this or any other night, and also by day. Fittleworth! Invites me to lunch—'

'I know. He told me.'

'— and wantonly causes spiders to emerge from the salt cellar.'

'I know. But—'

'Roams my grounds, officiously locking my business associates in potting sheds—'

'I know. Quite. But—'

'And, to top it all off, lurks in my grass like a ruddy grasshopper, so that I can't stir a step without treading on him. When I reflect that I have not dissected Fittleworth, limb by limb, and danced on his remains, my moderation astounds me. Don't talk to me about Fittleworth.'

'But that's just what I want to talk about. I want to plead his cause. You are aware, Uncle Percy,' I said, bunging a bit of a tremolo into the old voice, 'that he loves young Nobby.'

'So I have been informed, dash his cheek.'

'It would be an ideal match. You and he may not always have seen eye to eye in such matters as spiders in salt cellars, but you can't get away from it that he is one of the hottest of England's younger litterateurs. He earns more per annum than a Cabinet Minister.'

'He ought to be ashamed of himself, if he didn't. Have you ever met a Cabinet Minister? I know dozens, and not one of them that wouldn't be grossly overpaid at thirty shillings a week.'

'He could support Nobby in the style to which she is accustomed.'

'No, he couldn't. Ask me why not.'

'Why not?'

'Because I'm jolly well not going to let him.'

'But he loves, Uncle Percy.'

'Has he got an Uncle Percy?'

I saw that unless prompt steps were taken, we should be getting muddled.

'When I say He loves, Uncle Percy,' I explained, 'I don't mean he loves, verb transitive, Uncle Percy, accusative. I mean he loves, comma, Uncle Percy, exclamation mark.'

Even while uttering the words, I had had a fear lest I might be making the thing a shade too complex for one in the relative's condition. And so it proved.

'Bertie,' he said, gravely, 'I should have watched you more carefully. You're tighter than I am.'

'No, no.'

'Then just go over that observation of yours again slowly. I would be the last man to dispute that my faculties are a little blurred, but—'

'I only said, that he loved, and shoved in an "Uncle Percy" at the end of my remarks.'

'Addressing me, you mean?'

'Yes.'

'In the vocative, as it were?'

'That's right.'

'Now we've got it straight. And where does it get us? Just where we were before. You say he loves my ward, Zenobia. I reply, "All right, let him, and I hope he has a fine day for it. But I'm dashed if he's going to marry her." I take my position as guardian of that girl pretty seriously. You might say I regard it as a sacred trust. When confiding her to my care, I remember, her poor old father, as fine a fellow as ever stepped, though too fond of pink gin, clasped my hand and said, "Watch her like a hawk, Percy, old boy, or she'll go marrying some bally blot on the landscape." And I said, "Roddy, old man"—his name was Roderick—"just slip a clause in the lease, saying that she's got to get my consent first, and you need have no further uneasiness." And what happens? First thing you know, up pops probably the worst blot any landscape was ever afflicted with. But he finds me ready, my boy. He finds me ready and prepared. There is my authority in black and white, and I intend to exercise it.'

'But her father wasn't thinking of a chap like Boko.'

'There are limits to every man's imagination.'

'Boko's a frightfully good egg.'

'He is nothing of the kind. Good egg, forsooth! Tell me a single thing this Fittleworth has ever done that entitles him to consideration and respect.'

I thought for a moment. And when the Woosters think for a moment, they generally spear something good.

'It may be news to you,' I said, 'that he once kicked Edwin.'

This got home. His mouth opened, and his feet twitched, as if stirred by a passing zephyr.

'Is this true?'

'Ask Florence. Ask the knives and boots boy.'

'Well, I'm dashed.'

He sat for a while, deep in thought. I could see that the revelation had made a deep impression.

'I confess,' he said at length, raising the bottle to his lips and swallowing about a third of its contents, 'that what you tell me causes me to look on the fellow with a somewhat kindlier eye. Yes, to some extent, I admit, it has modified my views regarding him. It just shows that there is good in all of us.'

'Then on consideration—'

He shook his head.

'No, Bertie, I cannot consent to this match. Look at it from my point of view. The fellow lives at my very doors. Give him an excuse like being married to my ward, and he would always be popping in. Every time I took a stroll in my garden, I should be watching my step in case he happened to be hiding in the grass. Every time he came to lunch, my eyes would be riveted on the salt cellar. No nervous system could stand it.'

I saw the talking point.

'But you haven't heard the latest, Uncle Percy. Boko leaves next month for Hollywood. Do you realize that America is three thousand miles away, and that Hollywood is three thousand miles on the other side of America?'

He started.

'Is it?'

'Absolutely.'

He sat for a moment twiddling his fingers.

'I make that six thousand miles.'

'That's right.'

'Six thousand miles,' he said, rolling the words round his tongue. 'Why, this alters everything. You think Zenobia loves him?'

'Devotedly.'

'Odd. Strange. And his financial position is as sound as you suggest?'

'Sounder. Editors scream like frightened children when his agent looks in to talk terms for a new contract.'

'And about Hollywood. You're sure your figures are right? Six thousand miles?'

'A bit more, if anything.'

'Well, then, really, dash it, in that case—'

I saw that the iron was hot, and that the moment had come for Boko to strike it.

'I'll send him to you,' I said, 'and you can have a talk and rough out the arrangements. No need for you to move. This is his car. By Jove, Uncle Percy, you'll be thankful for this later on, when you realize what a bit of a goose you're handing two young hearts in springtime.'

'Tiddly-om-pom-pom,' said the relative, waving a cordial toe and once more applying his lips to the bot.

I did not let the g. grow under the feet. Hastening back to the ballroom, I sorted Boko out from the revelers, and sent him off with many a hearty 'Tails up' and 'God speed'. Then, unleashing the two-seater, I drove home, thankful that a sticky bit of business had been safely concluded.

My first act, on reaching journey's end, was, of course, to tear off the uniform. Having crept to the river bank and consigned it to the dark waters, which might or might not eventually cast it up on some distant shore whence it would be returned to its owner, I whizzed back to my room and darted into bed.

It was not immediately that the tired eyelids closed in sleep, for some hidden hand had placed a hedgehog between the sheets—practically, you might say, a fretful porpentine. Assuming this to be Boko's handiwork, I was strongly inclined to transfer it to his couch. Reflecting, however, that while this would teach him a much needed lesson it would be a bit tough on the porpentine, I took the latter out into the garden and loosed it into the grass.

Then, the day's work done, I turned in and soon sank into a dreamless slumber.

27

The sun was high in the heavens, or fairly high, when I awoke next morning. From behind the closed door of Boko's sleeping apartment there proceeded a rhythmic sound like the sawing of wood, indicating that he had not yet sprung from his bed. I would have liked to waken him and ask if all was well, but refrained. No doubt, I felt, he had returned at a late hour and needed an extra bit of what I have heard Jeeves call tired Nature's sweet restorer. I donned the bathing suit and bath robe, and started off for the river, and I hadn't more than shoved my nose outside the garden gate when along came Nobby on her bicycle.

It would have been plain even to the most casual observer that Nobby was in the pink. Her eyes were shining like twin stars as the expression is, and she greeted me with one of the heartiest pip-pips that ever proceeded from female throat.

'Hullo, Bertie,' she cried. 'I say, Bertie, isn't everything super-colossal!'

'I think so,' I replied. 'I hope so. I left Uncle Percy in malleable mood, and Boko was just going to confer with him. All should have gone well.'

'Then you haven't heard? Didn't Boko tell you?'

'I haven't seen him yet. Our waking moments have not synchronized. When he got back, I was asleep, and when I got up, he was asleep.'

'Oh, I see. Well, he came round in the small hours and threw gravel at my window and made his report. Everything went like a breeze.'

'It did?'

'According to Boko, the thing was a love feast. Uncle Percy sent him back to the bar for another bottle of champagne, and they split it like a couple of sailors on shore leave.'

'And he's given his consent?'

'Definitely, Boko says. He's so grateful to you for all you have done, Bertie. So am I. I could kiss you.'

'Just as you wish,' I assented civilly, and she did so. Then she legged it for the house, and I proceeded on my way to the river.

My mood, as I clove its crystal waters, was, as you may imagine, pretty uplifted. Nobby's story had left no room for doubt that happy endings had come popping up like rabbits. I had forgotten to ask her when she was going to show that letter to Florence, but no doubt this would be done in the course of the morning, releasing me from my honourable obligations. And, as for her and Boko, it was well within the bounds of possibility that before nightfall they would be united in the bonds of holy wedlock. Boko had made no secret of the fact that for many a day past he had had the licence tucked away in the drawer of his desk, ready to do its stuff the moment the starter's pistol went.

In addition to this, Stilton's uniform was floating on its way to the sea, and absolutely nothing to prove that it and Bertram had ever been in any way connected. It was just possible that some inkling of the truth might come to the promising young copper, causing him to regard me, when we next met, with sullen suspicion and even to go so far as to grind his teeth: but as for his assembling a telling weight of evidence which would land me in the dock and subsequently in the lowest dungeon beneath the castle moat, not a hope.

It was, accordingly, with no uncertain feeling that this was the maddest, merriest day of all the glad new year that I returned to the house, where genial smells from the dining-room greeted the nostrils and caused me to dress like a streak. Entering the food zone a few moments later, I found Boko restoring his tissues, with Nobby sitting on the end of the table, drinking in his every word.

'Ah, Bertie,' said Boko. 'Good morning, Bertie. Now you're here, I'd better start again.'

He did so, and for some minutes held me spellbound. Even though

I had heard the outline of the plot from Nobby and so knew how it all came out in the end, I hung upon his lips from start to finish.

'You didn't get his consent in writing?' I asked, as he concluded.

'Well, no,' he admitted. 'It never occurred to me. But if what is in your mind is that he may try to back out of it, don't worry. You have no conception, Bertie, literally no conception of the chumminess which exists between us. Hands were shaken, and backs slapped. He was all over me like a bedspread. Well, to give you some idea, he said he wished he had a son like me.'

'Well, considering he's got a son like Edwin, that isn't saying much.'

'Don't be a wet blanket, Bertie. Don't try to cast a gloom on this wonderful morning. Another thing he said was that he hoped I would be very successful in Hollywood and would remain working there for many years—in fact, indefinitely. One sees what he meant, of course. Like others, he has long chafed at the rottenness of motion pictures and is relying on me to raise the standard.'

'You will, angel,' said Nobby.

'You betcher,' said Boko, swilling coffee.

The meal proceeded on its pleasant course. A less kindly man than Bertram Wooster might have struck a jarring note by bringing up the matter of that porpentine in my bed, but I refrained from this. Instead, I asked what became of Uncle Percy at the close of the proceedings.

'I suppose he pushed home on his push bike,' said Boko. 'What did you do with Stilton's uniform?'

I explained that I had committed it to the deep, and he said I could not have made a wiser move. And he was just starting to be dashed funny about my last night's outer crust, when I stopped him with an imperious gesture.

Out of the corner of my eye, I had seen something large and blue turning in at the garden gate. A moment later, there came the sound of feet crunching on gravel, and the *timbre* and volume of the noise was such that only regulation official boots could have caused it. I was not surprised when in due season the torso and helmeted head of Stilton were framed in the open window. And more profoundly than ever I congratulated myself on the shrewdness and foresight which had led me to bung that uniform into the river.

'Ah, Stilton,' I said, and, what is more, I said it airily. The keenest ear could not have detected that the conscience was not as clean as a whistle. One prefers, of course, on all occasions to be stainless and above reproach, but, failing that, the next best thing is unquestionably to have got rid of the body

Boko, who is always a perfect host, bade the newcomer a cheery good morning, and asked him to keep his mouth open and he would throw a sardine into it. But apparently the latter had already breakfasted, for he declined the invitation with a petulant jerk of the head.

'Ho!' he said.

Touching for a moment on this matter of policemen and the word 'Ho'. I have an idea that the first thing they teach the young recruit on joining the Force is how to utter this ejaculation. I've never met a rozzer yet who didn't say it, and they all say it in just the same way. Inevitably one is led to assume a course of schooling.

'So there you are, you blasted Wooster!'

Speculating, as I had done from time to time since the previous evening, on the probable demeanour of this painstaking young officer when next he should catch sight of me, I had never anticipated that it would be elfin. I had budgeted for the dark frown, the flushed face and the hard and bulging eye. And there they all were, precisely as foreshadowed, and they found me ready to cope with them.

I preserved my aplomb.

'Yes, here I am,' I responded, buttering a nonchalant slice of toast. 'Where else would I be, my dear Stilton? This, thanks to Boko's princely hospitality, is where I am living.'

'Ho!' said Stilton. 'Well, you won't be living here much longer, because you're bally well coming along with me.'

Boko looked at me, and raised his eyebrows. I looked at Boko, and raised my eyebrows. Nobby looked at us both, and raised her eyebrows. Then we looked at Stilton, and all raised our eyebrows. It was one of those big eyebrow-raising mornings.

'Coming along with you? Surely, Stilton,' said Boko, 'you do not use that expression in a technical sense?'

'Yes, I do.'

'You have come to arrest Bertie?'

'Yes, I have.'

'What for?'

'Pinching my uniform.'

Nobby turned to me in girlish astonishment.

'Have you been pinching Stilton's uniform, Bertie?'

'Certainly not.'

'How lucky.'

'Extremely fortunate.'

'Because I suppose you could get about three months for a thing like that.'

'Besides the shame of it all,' I pointed out. 'If I ever feel the temptation to commit this rash act, I must fight against it. Not that I imagine I shall.'

'Pretty unlikely,' Nobby agreed. 'I mean, what on earth would you want a policeman's uniform for?'

'Exactly,' I said. 'You have touched the matter with a needle.'

'Done what?'

'One of Jeeves's gags,' I explained. '*Rem* something. Latin stuff.'

Boko, who had been frowning thoughtfully, went more deeply into the matter.

'I believe I know what's on Stilton's mind,' he said. 'I don't think I told you, but yesterday, while he was bathing, somebody snitched his uniform, which he had left lying on the bank. Did I mention it?'

'Not to my recollection,' said Nobby.

'Nor to mine,' I said, shaking the bean.

'Odd,' said Boko. 'I suppose it slipped my mind.'

'Things do,' said Nobby.

'Frequently,' I agreed.

'Well, that's what happened, and one can't blame him for wanting to bring the criminal to justice. But why he has got this extraordinary idea that it was Bertie who was responsible for the foul outrage is more than I can understand. I told you yesterday, Stilton, that the hidden hand was almost certainly young Edwin's.'

'Yes, and I've just been tackling him about it. He denies it categorically.'

'And you accept his word?'

'Yes, I do. He has an alibi.'

'Well, you perfect chump,' cried Nobby, 'don't you know that that dishes him? Haven't you ever read any detective stories? Ask Lord Peter Wimsey what an alibi amounts to.'

'Or Monsieur Poirot,' I suggested.

'Yes. Or Reggie Fortune, or Inspector French, or Nero Wolfe. I can't understand a man of your intelligence falling for that alibi stuff.'

'Incredible,' I said. 'The oldest trick in the game.'

'Trot along and bust it, is my advice, Stilton,' said Boko.

One might have expected a cop to wilt beneath all this, but it speedily became plain that the Cheesewrights were made of sterner stuff.

'If you want to know why I accept young Edwin's alibi,' said Stilton, allowing his eyes to bulge a bit farther from the parent sockets, 'it's because it's supported by the vicar, the vicar's wife, the curate, the curate's sister, the doctor, the doctor's aunt, a scoutmaster, fifteen assorted tradesmen and forty-seven Boy Scouts. It appears that the doctor was giving a lecture on First Aid in the village hall yesterday evening, and Edwin was the chap who went on the platform and was illustrated on. At the moment when my uniform was pinched, he was lying on a table, swathed in bandages, showing what you have to do to a bloke with a fractured thigh bone.'

This, I admit, spiked our guns to no little extent. Nobby did say that it might have been an accomplice cunningly disguised to look like Edwin, but you could see that it was simply a suggestion.

'Yes,' said Boko, at length, 'that does seem to let Edwin out. But I still don't see where you get this extraordinary idea that Bertie is the culprit.'

'I'll tell you that, too,' said Stilton, plainly resolved to keep nothing from us. 'Edwin, questioned, had an amazing story to relate. He stated that, going to accused's bedroom later in the evening to put a hedgehog in his bed—'

'Ha!' I exclaimed, and gave Boko a penitent look, remorseful that even in thought I should have wronged my kind host.

'— he saw the uniform there. And I met a chap this morning who had been an extra waiter at the fancy dress ball at East Wibley last night, and he informs me that there was a loathsome-looking object taking part in the festivities, dressed in a policeman's uniform six sizes too large for him. I am ready to step along, Wooster, if you are.'

It seemed to me a fair cop, as I believe the expression is, and I saw nothing to be gained by postponing the inevitable. I rose, and wiped the lips with the napkin, like a French aristocrat informed that the tumbrel is at the door.

Boko's hat, however, was still in the ring.

'Just a minute, Stilton,' he said. 'Not so fast, officer. Have you a warrant?'

The question seemed to discompose Stilton.

'Why, I . . . Er, no.'

'Must have a warrant,' said Boko. 'You can't make a summary arrest on a serious charge like this.'

The momentary weakness passed. Stilton was himself again.

'I don't believe it,' he said stoutly. 'I think you're talking through your hat. Still, I'll go to the station and ask the sergeant.'

He vanished, and Boko became brisk and efficient.

'You'll have to leg it, Bertie,' he said, 'and without a second's delay. Get your car, drive to London and go abroad. They won't be watching the ports yet. Better look in on the Cohen Bros. *en route* and buy a false moustache.'

It isn't often that I would care to allow this borderline case's counsel to rule my actions, but on this occasion it seemed to me that his advice was good. I had been thinking along the same lines myself. Oh, as a matter of fact, I had just been saying to myself at that very moment, for the wings of a dove. Briefly requesting him to get hold of Jeeves and tell him to follow with the personal effects, I streaked for the garage.

And I was just about to fling wide the gates, when there suddenly came from the other side of the door the sound of a hoarse voice, and I paused, astounded. Unless the ears had deceived me, there was a human soul inside the edifice.

It spoke again, and what enabled me to get abreast and identify the thorax from which it proceeded was the fact that one caught the name 'Fittleworth', preceded by a number of qualifying adjectives of a rugged and rather Elizabethan nature. In a flash, I got the whole set-up.

Driving away from the East Wibley Town Hall at the conclusion of the recent festivities, Boko must inadvertently have taken Uncle Percy with him. He had sped homewards with a song on his lips, and all unknown to him, overlooked while getting a spot of tired Nature's sweet restorer in the back of the car, the old relative had come along for the ride.

28

I drew in the breath with a startled whoosh, and for some moments stood rooted to the s., the brow furrowed, the eyes bulging. To say that this thing had come upon me like a sock behind the ear from a stuffed eelskin would be in no wise to overstate the facts. As I stood there with my ear against the door, listening to what was filtering through the woodwork, it is not too much to say that melancholy marked me for its own.

Consider the posish, I mean. The one thing that was of the essence was that Boko should keep this man a thing of sweetness and light, and it was absurd to suppose that this could be done by locking him up all night in garages in the costume of Sindbad the Sailor. A man of generous spirit, like Uncle Percy, inevitably chafes at such treatment.

He was chafing now. I could hear him. The tone of his observations left no room for misunderstanding. They were not the obiter dicta of one who, when released, would laugh heartily at the amusing little misunderstanding, but rather of a man whose earnest endeavour it would be to skin the person responsible for his incarceration.

Indeed, it was upon this very point that he had now begun to touch. And not only was he resolved to skin Boko. He stressed in unmistakable terms his intention of doing it lingeringly and with a blunt knife. In short, it was abundantly clear that, however beautiful might have been the friendship which had been started overnight between his host and himself, it had now taken a bad toss and definitely come unstuck.

I found myself frankly unable to cope with the situation. It was one of those which seemed to call imperiously for a word or two of advice from

Jeeves. And I was just regretting that he was not there, when a gentle cough in my rear told me that he was. It was as if some sort of telepathy, if that's the word I want, had warned him that the young master had lost his grip and could do with twopennyworth of feudal assistance.

'Jeeves!' I cried, and clutched him by the coat sleeve, like a lost child hooking on to its mother. When I had finished pouring my tale into his receptive ear, it was plain that he had not failed to grasp the nub.

'Most disturbing, sir,' he said.

'Most,' I responded.

I refrained from wounding him with any word of censure and rebuke, but I could not but feel, as I have so frequently felt before, that a spot of leaping about and eyeball-rolling would have been more in keeping with the gravity of the situation. If Jeeves has a fault, as I think I have already mentioned, it is that he is too prone merely to tut at times when you would prefer to see his knotted and combined locks do a bit of parting.

'His lordship, you gather, sir, is incensed?'

I could answer that one.

'Yes, Jeeves. His remarks, as far as I was able to catch them, were unquestionably those of a man a good deal steamed up. What is the Death of the Thousand Cuts?'

'It is a penal sentence in vogue in Chinese police courts for minor offences. Roughly equivalent to our fourteen days with the option of a fine. Why do you ask, sir?'

'Uncle Percy happened to mention it in passing. It's one of the things he is planning to do to Boko when they get together. Good Lord, Jeeves!' I exclaimed.

'Sir?'

The reason I had exclaimed as above was that this mention of police courts and penal sentences had suddenly reminded me of my own position. For a brief space, the mind, occupied with this business of uncles in garages, had slid away from the fact that I was a fugitive from a chain gang.

'You haven't heard the latest. Stilton. He has found out about that uniform and has gone off to get warrants and things.'

'Indeed, sir?'

'Yes. Young Edwin, creeping into my room last night in order to insinuate a hedgehog into my bed, saw the thing lying there, and went and squealed to Stilton, the degraded little copper's nark. Only by making an immediate getaway can I hope to escape undergoing the utmost rigours of the Law. You see the frightful dilemma I'm on the horns of. My car's in the garage. To get it, I shall have to open the door. And opening the door involves having Uncle Percy come popping out like a cork out of a bottle.'

'You shrink from an encounter with his lordship, sir?'

'Yes, Jeeves. I shrink from an encounter with his lordship. Oh, I know what you are going to say. You are about to point out that it was Boko who lodged him in the coop, not me.'

'Precisely, sir. You are armed so strong in honesty that his lordship's displeasure will pass by you as the idle wind, which you respect not.'

'I dare say. But have you ever removed a wounded puma from a trap?'

'No, sir. I have not had that experience.'

'Well, anyone will tell you that on such occasions the animal does not pause to pick and choose. It just goes baldheaded for the nearest innocent bystander in sight.'

'I appreciate your point, sir. It might be better if you were to return to the house and allow me to extricate his lordship.'

His nobility stunned me.

'Would you, Jeeves?'

'Certainly, sir.'

'Pretty white of you.'

'Not at all, sir.'

'You could turn the key, shout "All clear," and then run like a rabbit.'

'I would prefer to linger on the scene, sir, in the hope of doing something to smooth his lordship's wounded feelings.'

'With honeyed words, you mean?'

'Precisely, sir.'

I drew a deep breath.

'You wouldn't consider at least climbing a tree?'

'No, sir.'

I drew another one.

'Well, all right, if you say so. You know best. Carry on, then, Jeeves.'

'Very good, sir. I will bring your car to the front door, so that you will be enabled to make an immediate start. I will follow later in the day with the suitcases.'

It was some slight consolation to me in this dark hour to reflect, as I tooled back to the house, that the news I was bearing would, if he were still eating sardines, cause those sardines to turn to ashes in Boko's mouth. I am not a vindictive man, but I was feeling in no amiable frame of mind towards this literary screwball. I mean, it's all very well for a chap to plead that he's an author and expect on the strength of that to get away with conduct which would qualify the ordinary man for a one-way ticket to Colney Hatch, but even an author, I felt—and I think with justice—ought to have had the sense to glance through his car before he locked it up for the night, to make sure there weren't any shipping magnates dozing in the back seat.

As it happened, he was past the sardines phase. He was lolling in his chair in quiet enjoyment of the after-breakfast pipe, while Nobby, at his side, did the crossword puzzle in the morning paper. At the sight of Bertram, both expressed surprise.

'Why, hullo!' said Nobby.

'Haven't you gone yet?' said Boko.

'No, I haven't,' I replied, and laughed a hard, mirthless one.

It caused Boko to frown disapprovingly.

'What's the idea of coming here and trilling with laughter?' he asked austerely. 'You must try to get it into your head, my lad, that this is not the time for that sort of thing. Don't you realize your position? Unless you're across the Channel by nightfall, you haven't a hope. Where's your car?'

'In the garage.'

'Then get it out of the garage.'

'I can't,' I said, letting him have it right in the gizzard. 'Uncle Percy's there.'

And in a few crisp words I slipped him the lowdown.

I had anticipated that my statement would get in amongst him a bit, and this expectation was fulfilled. Man and boy, I have seen a good many lower jaws fall, but never one that shot down with such a sudden swoop as his. It was surprising that the thing didn't come off its hinges.

'But how was he in my car? He can't have been in my car. Why didn't I notice him?'

This, of course, was susceptible of a ready explanation.

'Because you're a fathead.'

Nobby, who since the initial spilling of the beans had been sitting bolt upright in her chair with gleaming eyes, making little gulping noises and chewing the lower lip with pearly teeth, endorsed this.

'Fathead,' she concurred, speaking in a strange, strangled voice, 'is right. Of all—'

Preoccupied though Boko was, there must have penetrated to his consciousness some inkling of what the harvest would be, were she permitted to get going and really start hauling up her slacks. He strove to head her off with a tortured gesture.

'Just a minute, darling.'

'Of all the—'

'Yes, yes.'

'Of all the gibbering—'

'Quite, quite. But half a second, angel. Bertie and I are threshing out an important point. Let me just try to envisage what happened after you left last night, Bertie. Here is the sequence, as I recall it. I had my talk with old Worplesdon, and, as I told you, secured a guardian's blessing: and then—yes, then I went back to the ballroom to tread the measure for a while.'

'Of all the gibbering, half-witted—'

'Exactly, exactly. But don't interrupt the flow of my thoughts, precious. I'm trying to get this thing straight. I danced a saraband or two, and then looked in at the bar for a moment. I wanted to get a snootful and muse over my happiness. And I was doing this, when it suddenly occurred to me that Nobby was probably tossing sleeplessly on her pillow, dying to hear how everything had come out, and I felt that I must get home immediately and go and bung gravel at her window. I raced back to the car, accordingly, sprang to the wheel and drove off. I see now why I didn't notice old Worplesdon. Obviously, the man by that time had passed out and was lying on the floor. Well, dash it, a chap in my frame of mind, all joy and ecstasy and excitement, with his soul full to the brim of tender thoughts of the girl he loved, couldn't be expected to go over the floor of his car with a magnifying-glass, on the chance that there might be Worplesdons there. Naturally, not observing him, I assumed that he had gone off on his push bike. Would you have had me borrow a couple of bloodhounds and search the *tonneau* from end to end? I'm sure you understand everything now, darling, and will be the first to withdraw the adjective "gibbering". Oh, I am not angry,' said Boko, 'in fact, not even surprised that in the heat of the moment you should have spoken as you did. Just so long as you realize that I am innocent, blameless . . .'

At this juncture there was a confused noise without, and Uncle Percy crossed the threshold, moving well. A moment later, Jeeves shimmered in his wake.

Having become so accustomed during our hobnobbings of the previous day to seeing this uncle by marriage in genial and comradely mood, I had almost forgotten how like the Assyrian swooping down on the fold he could look, when deeply stirred. And that he was so now rather leaped to the eye. The ginger whiskers which go with the costume of Sindbad the Sailor obscured his countenance to a great extent, rendering it difficult to note the full play of expression on the features, but one was able to observe his eyes, and that was enough to be going on with. Fixed on Boko with an unwinking glare, they had the effect of causing that unhappy purveyor of wholesome literature for the masses to recoil at least a dozen feet. And he would undoubtedly have gone farther, had he not fetched up against the wall.

Jeeves had spoke of his intention of trying to smooth the ruffled Worplesdon feelings with honeyed words. Whether he hadn't been allowed to get one in edgeways, or whether he had tried a few and they hadn't been honeyed enough, I was not in a position to say. But the fact was patent that the above feelings were still as ruffled as dammit, and that Hampshire contained at this moment no hotter-under-the-collar shipping magnate.

Proof of this was given by his opening speech, which consisted of the word 'What', repeated over and over again as if fired from a machine-gun. It was always this uncle's practice, as I have mentioned, to what-what-what rather freely in moments of emotion, and he did not deviate from it on this occasion.

'What?' he said, in part, continuing to focus the eye on Boko. 'What-what-what-what-what-what-what-what?'

Here he paused, as if for a reply, and I think Boko did the wrong thing by asking him if he would like a sardine. The question, seeming to touch an exposed nerve, caused a sheet of flame to shoot from his eyes.

'Sardine?' he said, with a bitter intonation. 'Sardine? Sardine? Sardine?'

'You'll feel better, when you've had some breakfast,' said Nobby, pulling a quick ministering-angel-thou.

Uncle Percy opposed this view.

'I shall not. The only thing that can make me feel better is to thrash that pie-faced young wart-hog Fittleworth within an inch of his life. Bertie, get me a horsewhip.'

I pursed the lips dubiously.

'I don't believe we have one,' I said. 'Are there any horsewhips on the premises, Boko?'

'No, no horsewhips,' the latter responded, now trying to get through the wall.

Uncle Percy snorted.

'What a house! Jeeves.'

'M'lord?'

'Go over to the Hall and bring me my horsewhip with the ivory handle.'

'Yes, m'lord.'

'I think it's in my study. If not, hunt about for it.'

'Very good, m'lord. No doubt her ladyship will be able to inform me of the instrument's whereabouts.'

He spoke so casually that it was perhaps three seconds by the stop-watch before Uncle Percy got the gist. When he did, he started, like one jabbed in the fleshy parts with a sudden bradawl.

'Her . . . what?'

'Her ladyship, m'lord.'

'Her ladyship?'

'Yes, m'lord.'

Uncle Percy had crumpled like a wet sock. He sank into a chair, and clutched the marmalade jar, as if for support. His eyes popped out of his head, and waved about on their stalks.

'But her ladyship—'

'—returned unexpectedly late last night, m'lord.'

29

I don't know if the name of Lot's wife is familiar to you, and if you were told about her rather remarkable finish. I may not have got the facts right, but the story, as I heard it, was that she was advised not to look round at something or other or she would turn into a pillar of salt, so, naturally imagining that they were simply pulling her leg, she looked round, and—*bing*—a pillar of salt. And the reason I mention this now is that the very same thing seemed to have happened to Uncle Percy. Crouching there with his fingers riveted to the marmalade jar, he appeared to have turned into a pillar of salt. If it hadn't been that the ginger whiskers were quivering gently, you would have said that life had ceased to animate the rigid limbs.

'It appears that Master Thomas is now out of danger, m'lord, and no longer has need of her ladyship's ministrations.'

The whiskers contined to quiver, and I didn't blame them. I knew just how the old relative must be feeling, for, as I have already indicated, he had made no secret when chatting with me of his apprehensions concerning the shape of things to come, should Aunt Agatha ever learn that he had been attending fancy dress dances in her absence.

The poignant drama of it all had not escaped Nobby, either.

'Golly, Uncle Percy,' she said, a womanly pity in her voice that became her well, 'this is a bit awkward, is it not? You'll have to devote a minute or two, when you see her, to explaining why you were out all night, won't you?'

Her words had the effect of bringing the unhappy man out of his trance or coma as if she had touched off a stick of dynamite under him. He moved, he stirred, he seemed to feel the rush of life along his keel.

'Jeeves,' he said hoarsely.

'M'lord?'

'Jeeves.'

'M'lord?'

Uncle Percy shoved out his tongue about an inch, moistening the lips with the tip of it. It was plain that he was finding it no easy matter to get speech over the larynx.

'Her ladyship, Jeeves . . . Tell me . . . Is she . . . Has she . . . Is she by any chance aware of my absence?'

'Yes, m'lord. She was apprised of it by the head housemaid. I left them in conference. "You tell me his lordship's bed *has not been slept in*?" her ladyship was saying. Her agitation was most pronounced.'

I caught Uncle Percy's eye. It had swivelled round at me with a dumb, pleading look in it, as if saying that suggestions would be welcomed.

'How would it be,' I said—well, one had to say something, 'if you told her the truth?'

'The truth?' he repeated dazedly, and you could see he thought the idea a novel one.

'That you went to the ball to confer with Clam.'

He shook his head.

'I could never convince your aunt that I had gone to a fancy dress ball from purely business motives. Women are so prone to think the worst.'

'Something in that.'

'And it's no good trying to make them see reason, because they talk so damn' quick. No,' said Uncle Percy, 'this is the end. I can only set my teeth and take my medicine like an English gentleman.'

'Unless, of course, Jeeves has something to suggest.'

This perked him up for an instant. Then the drawn, haggard look came back into his face, and he shook the lemon again, slowly and despondently.

'Impossible. The situation is beyond Jeeves.'

'No situation is beyond Jeeves,' I said, with quiet rebuke. 'In fact,' I went on, scrutinizing the man closely, 'I believe something is fermenting now inside that spacious bean. Am I wrong, Jeeves, in supposing that I can see the light of inspiration in your eye?'

'No, sir. You are quite correct. I think that I may perhaps be able to offer a satisfactory solution of his lordship's difficulty.'

Uncle Percy inhaled sharply. An awed look came into the unoccupied areas of his face. I heard him murmur something under his breath about fish.

'You mean that, Jeeves?'

'Yes, m'lord.'

'Then let us have it,' I said, feeling rather like some impresario of performing fleas who watches the star member of his troupe advance to the footlights. 'What is this solution of which you speak?'

'Well, sir, it occurred to me that as his lordship has, as I understand, given his consent to the union of Mr Fittleworth and Miss Hopwood—'

Uncle Percy uttered an animal cry.

'I haven't! Or, if I did, I've withdrawn it.'

'Very good, m'lord. In that case, I have nothing to suggest.'

There was a silence. One could sense the struggle proceeding in Uncle Percy's bosom. I saw him look at Boko, and quiver. Then a strong shudder passed through the frame, and I knew he was recalling what Jeeves had said about Aunt Agatha's agitation being most pronounced. When Aunt Agatha's agitation is pronounced, she has a way of drawing her eyebrows together and making her nose look like an eagle's beak. Strong men have quailed at the spectacle, repeatedly.

'May as well hear what you've got to say, I suppose,' he said, at length.

'Quite,' I agreed. 'No harm in having a—what, Jeeves?'

'Academic discussion, sir.'

'Thank you, Jeeves.'

'Not at all, sir.'

'Carry on, then.'

'Very good, sir. It merely occurred to me that, had his lordship consented to the union, nothing would have been more natural than that he should have visited Mr Fittleworth at his house for the purpose of talking the matter over and making arrangements for the wedding. Immersed in this absorbing subject, his lordship would quite understandably have lost count of time—'

I yipped intelligently. I had got the set-up.

'And when he looked at his watch and found how late it was—'

'Precisely, sir. When his lordship looked at his watch and found how late it was, Mr Fittleworth hospitably suggested that he should pass the remainder of the night beneath his roof. His lordship agreed that this would be the most convenient course, and so it was arranged.'

I looked at Uncle Percy, confidently expecting the salvo of applause, and was amazed to find him shaking the bean once more.

'It wouldn't work,' he said.

'Why on earth not? It's a pip.'

He kept on oscillating the lozenge.

'No, Bertie, the scheme is not practical. Your aunt, my dear boy, is a suspicious woman. She probes beneath the surface and asks questions. And the first one she would ask on this occasion would be, Why, merely in order to discuss wedding arrangements with my ward's future husband, did I dress up as Sindbad the Sailor? You can see for yourself how awkward that question would be, and how difficult to answer.'

The point was well taken.

'A snag, Jeeves. Can you get round it?'

'Quite easily, sir. Before returning to the Hall, his lordship could borrow a suit of clothes from you, sir.'

'Of course he could. Clad in the herring-bone tweed which is in the cupboard in my bedroom, Uncle Percy, you could look Aunt Agatha in the eye without a tremor.'

I dare say you have frequently, when strolling in your garden, seen a parched flower beneath a refreshing downpour. It was of such a flower that Uncle Percy now irresistibly reminded me. He seemed to swell and burgeon, as it were, and the strained eyes lost that resemblance to the under side of a dead fish which had been so noticeable since the beginning of this sequence.

'Good Lord!' he exclaimed. 'You're quite right. So I could. Jeeves,' he went on, emotionally, 'you must have that brain of yours pickled and presented to some national museum.'

'Very good, m'lord.'

'When you've done with it, of course. Come on, Bertie, action, action! Ho for the herring-bone tweed!'

'This way, Uncle Percy,' I said, and we started for the door, to find our path barred by Boko. He was looking a bit green about the gills, but firm and resolute.

'Just a minute,' said Boko. 'Not so jolly fast, if you don't mind. How about that guardian's blessing? Do I cop?'

'Of course you do, old bird,' I said soothingly. 'That's all budgeted for in the estimates, Uncle Percy?'

'Eh? What?'

'The guardian's b. You're dishing that out?'

Once more there was that silent struggle. Then he nodded sombrely.

'It seems unavoidable.'

'It is unavoidable.'

'Then I won't try to avoid it.'

'Okay, Boko, you're all set.'

'Good,' said Boko. 'I'll just have that in writing, if you don't mind, my dear Worplesdon. I don't want to carp or criticize, but there's been a lot of in-and-out running about this business to present date, and one would welcome a few words in black and white. You will find pen and ink on the table in the corner. Sing out, my dear Worplesdon, if the nib doesn't suit you, and I will provide you with another.'

Uncle Percy went to the table in the corner, and took pen in hand. It would be too much to say that his demeanour, as he did so, was rollicking. I fancy that up to this moment he had been entertaining a faint hope that, if his luck held, he might somehow derive the benefits from Jeeves's scheme without having to sit in on its drawbacks. However, as I say, he took pen in hand and, having scribbled for a minute or so, handed the result to Boko, who read it through and handed it to Nobby, who read it through and tucked it away with a satisfied 'Okay-doke' in some safe deposit in the recesses of her costume.

She had scarcely done so, when heavy, official footsteps sounded without, and Stilton came clumping in.

You will scarcely believe me, but it is a fact that I had been so tensely gripped by the drama of the last quarter of an hour that the Stilton angle had been completely expunged from my mind, and it was only now, as I watched him heave to, that the thought of the Wooster personal peril came back to me. The first thing he did on entering the room was to give me one of those looks of his, and it chilled my insides like a quart of ice cream.

I had a shot at an airy 'Ah, there you are, Stilton,' but my heart was not in it, and it elicited no response except a short 'Ho!' Having got off this 'Ho!' which, as I have explained, was in the nature of a sort of signature tune, he addressed himself to Boko.

'You were right about that warrant,' he said. 'The sergeant says I've got to have one. I've brought it along. It has to be signed by a Justice of the Peace.' Here, for the first time, he appeared to become aware of Uncle Percy's identity, which, of course, had been shrouded from him by the whiskers. 'Why, hullo, Lord Worplesdon,' he said, 'you're just the man I was looking for. If you will shove your name on the dotted line, we can go ahead. So you went to that fancy dress ball last night?' he said, giving him the eye.

I think he had merely intended to be chatty and to show a kindly interest, as it were, in the relative's affairs, but he had said the wrong thing. Uncle Percy stiffened haughtily.

'What do you mean, I went to the fancy dress ball last night? I did nothing of the kind, and I shall be glad if you will refrain from making loose statements of that description. Went to the fancy dress ball, indeed! What fancy dress ball? Where? It is news to me that there has been a fancy dress ball.'

His generous indignation seemed to take Stilton aback.

'Oh, sorry,' he said. 'I just thought . . . The costume, I mean.'

'And what about the costume? If my ward and her future husband are planning an evening of amateur theatricals and asked me as a personal favour to put on the costume of Sindbad the Sailor, to see if I was the type for the part, is it so singular that I should good-humouredly have acceded to their wishes? And is it any business of yours? Does it entitle you to jump to idiotic conclusions about fancy dress balls? Have I got to explain every simple little action of mine to every flatfooted copper who comes along and can't keep his infernal nose out of my business?'

These were not easy questions to answer, and the best Stilton could do was to shuffle his feet and say 'Oh, ah.'

'Well, anyway,' he said, after a rather painful pause, changing the subject and getting back to the *res*, 'would you mind signing this warrant?'

'Warrant? What warrant? What's it all about? What's all this nonsense about warrants?'

There was a sound in the background like a distant sheep coughing gently on a mountainside. Jeeves sailing into action.

'If I might explain, your lordship. It appears that in the course of yesterday afternoon the officer's uniform was purloined as he bathed in the river. He accuses Mr Wooster of the crime.'

'Mr Wooster? Bertie? My nephew?'

'Yes, m'lord. To me, a most bizarre theory. One seeks in vain for a motive which could plausibly have led Mr Wooster to perpetrate such an outrage. The constable, I understand, alleges that Mr Wooster desired the uniform in order to be able to attend the fancy dress ball.'

This seemed to interest Uncle Percy.

'There really was a fancy dress ball, was there?'

'Yes, m'lord. At the neighbouring town of East Wibley.'

'Odd. I never heard about it.'

'A very minor affair, m'lord, I gather. Not at all the sort of entertainment in which a gentleman of Mr Wooster's position would condescend to participate.'

'Of course not. I wouldn't have gone to it myself. Just one of those potty little country affairs, eh?'

'Precisely, m'lord. Nobody, knowing Mr Wooster, would suppose for a moment that he would waste his sweetness on such desert air.'

'Eh?'

'A quotation, m'lord. The poet Gray.'

'Ah. But you say the officer sticks to it that he did?'

'Yes, m'lord. It is fortunate, therefore, that your lordship passed the night in this house, and so is able to testify that Mr Wooster never left the premises.'

'Dashed fortunate. Settles the whole thing.'

I never know, when I am telling a story where a couple of fellows are talking and a third fellow is trying to shove his oar in, whether to interpolate the last named's gulps and gurgles in the run of the dialogue or to wait till it's all over and then chalk up these gulps and gurgles to their utterer's score. I think it works out smoother the second way, and that is why, in recording the above exchanges, I have left out Stilton's attempts to chip in. All through this Jeeves—Worplesdon exchange of ideas he had been trying to catch the Speaker's eye, only to be 'Tchah'-ed and 'Be quiet, officer'-ed by Uncle Percy. A lull in the conversation having occurred at the word 'thing', he was now able to speak his piece.

'I tell you the accused Wooster did pinch my uniform!' he cried, his eyes bulging more than ever and his cheeks a pretty scarlet.

'It was seen on his bed by the witness Edwin.'

Things were going so well that I felt equal to raising the eyebrows and coming through with a light, amused laugh.

'Edwin, Uncle Percy! One smiles, does one not?'

The relative backed me up nobly.

'Smiles? Certainly one smiles. Like the dickens. Are you trying to tell me,' he said, letting Stilton have the eye in no uncertain measure, 'that this preposterous accusation of yours is based on the unsupported word of my son Edwin? I can scarcely credit it. Can you, Jeeves?'

'Most extraordinary, m'lord. But possibly the officer is not aware that Mr Wooster inflicted a personal assault upon Master Edwin yesterday, and so does not realize how biased any statement on the part of the young gentleman regarding Mr Wooster must inevitably be.'

'Don't make excuses for him. The man's a fool. And I should like to say,' said Uncle Percy, swelling like a balloon and starting to give Stilton the strong remarks from the bench, 'that we have had in my opinion far too much of late of these wild and irresponsible accusations on the part of the police. A deplorable spirit is creeping into the Force, and as long as I remain a Justice of the Peace I shall omit no word or act to express my strongest disapproval of it. I shall stamp it out, root and branch, and see to it that the liberty of the subject is not placed in jeopardy by officers of the Law who so far forget their—yes, dash it, their sacred obligations as to bring trumped-up charges right and left in a selfish desire to secure promotion. I have nothing further to add except to express my profound regret that you should have been subjected to this monstrous persecution, Bertie.'

'Quite all right, Uncle Percy.'

'It is not all right. It is outrageous. I advise you in future, officer, to be careful, very careful. And as for that warrant of yours, you can take it and stick it . . . However, that is neither here nor there.'

It was good stuff. Indeed, I can't remember ever having heard better, except once, when I was a stripling and Aunt Agatha was ticking me off for breaking a valuable china vase with my catapult. I confidently expected Stilton to cower beneath it like a worm in a thunderstorm. But he didn't. it was plain that he burned, not with shame and remorse but with the baffled fury of the man who, while not quite abreast of the run of the scenario, realizes that dirty work is afoot at the crossroads and that something swift is being slipped across him.

'Ho!' he said, and paused for a moment to wrestle with his feelings. Then, with generous emotion: 'It's a bally conspiracy,' he cried. 'It's a low-down, hornswoggling plot to defeat the ends of justice. For the last time, Lord Worplesdon, will you sign this warrant?'

Nothing could have been more dignified than Uncle Percy's demeanour. He drew himself up, and his voice was quiet and cold.

'I have already indicated what you can do with that warrant. I think, officer, that it would be well if you were to go and sleep it off. For the kindest interpretation which I can place upon your extraordinary behaviour is that you are intoxicated. Bertie, show the constable the door.'

I showed Stilton the door, and he took a sort of dazed look at it, as if it was the first time he had seen the bally thing. Then he navigated slowly through, and disappeared, not even pausing to say 'Ho' over his shoulder. The impression I received was that his haughty spirit was at last crushed. Presently we heard the sound of his violin cases tramping away down the garden path.

'And now, my boy,' said Uncle Percy, as the last echoes died away, 'for the herring-bone tweed. Also a bath and a shave and a cup of strong black coffee with perhaps the merest suspicion of brandy in it. And perhaps it would be as well, when I am ready to start for the Hall, if you were to accompany me, to add your testimony to mine regarding my spending last night under this roof. You will not falter, will you? You will support my statement, will you not, in a strong resonant voice, carrying conviction in every syllable? Nothing on these occasions creates so unfortunate an impression as the pause for thought, the hesitating utterance, the nervous twiddling of the fingers. Above all things, remember not to stand on one leg. Right, my boy. Let us go.'

I escorted him to my room, dug out the suit, showed him the bathroom and left him to it. When I got back to the dining-room, Boko had gone, but Nobby was still there, chatting with Jeeves. She greeted me warmly.

'Boko's gone to fetch his car,' she said. 'We're going to run up to London and get married. Wonderful how everything has come out, isn't it? I thought Uncle Percy was terrific.'

'Most impressive,' I agreed.

'And what words that tongue could utter could give even a sketchy idea of how one feels about you, Jeeves.'

'I am deeply gratified, miss, if I have been able to give satisfaction.'

'I've said it before, and I'll say it again—there's nobody like you.'

'Thank you very much, miss.'

I think this might have gone on for some time, for Nobby was plainly filled to the back teeth with girlish enthusiasm, but at this point I interrupted. I would be the last man ever to deprive Jeeves of his meed of praise, but I had a question of compelling interest to put.

'Have you shown Florence that letter of mine, Nobby?' I asked.

A sudden cloud came over her eager map, and she made a clicking noise.

'I knew there was something I had forgotten. Oh, Bertie, I'm so sorry.'

'Sorry?' I said, filled with a nameless fear.

'I've been meaning to tell you. When I got up this morning, I couldn't find that letter anywhere, and I was looking for it, when Edwin came along and told me he had done an act of kindness last night by tidying my room. I think he must have destroyed the letter. He generally does destroy all correspondence when he tidies rooms. I'm most awfully sorry, but I expect you'll find some other way of coping with Florence. Ask Jeeves. He's sure to think of something. Ah,' she said, as a booming voice came from the great open spaces, 'there's Boko calling me. Good-bye, Bertie. Good-bye, Jeeves. I must rush.'

She was gone with the wind, and I turned to Jeeves with a pale, set face.

'Yes, sir.'

'Can you think of a course to pursue?'

'No, sir.'

'You are baffled?'

'For the moment, sir, unquestionably. I fear that Miss Hopwood overestimated my potentialities.'

'Come, come, Jeeves. It is not like you to be a . . . what's the word . . . it's on the tip of my tongue.'

'Defeatist, sir?'

'That's right. It is not like you to be a defeatist. Don't give it up. Go and brood in the kitchen. There may be some fish there. Did you notice any, when you were there yesterday?'

'Only a tin of anchovy paste, sir.'

My heart sank a bit. Anchovy paste is a slender reed on which to lean in a major crisis. Still, it was fish within the meaning of the act, and no doubt contained its quota of phosphorus.

'Go and wade into it.'

'Very good, sir.'

'Don't spare the stuff. Dig it out with a spoon,' I said, and dismissed him with a moody gesture.

Moody was the word which would have described my aspect, as a few moments later I left the house and proceeded to the garden, feeling in need of a bit of air. I had kept up a brave front, but I had little real hope that anchovy paste would bring home the bacon. As I stood at the garden gate, staring sombrely before me, I was at a pretty low ebb.

I mean to say, I had been banking everything on that letter. I had counted on it to destroy the Wooster glamour in Florence's eyes. And, lacking it, I couldn't see how she was going to be persuaded that I was not a king among men. Not for the first time, I found myself musing bitterly on young Edwin, the *fons et origo*—a Latin expression—of all my troubles.

And I was just regretting that we were not in China, where it would have been a simple matter to frame up something against the child, thus putting him in line for the Death of the Thousand Cuts, when my reverie was interrupted by the ting of a bicycle bell, and Stilton came wheeling up.

After what had passed, of course, it was not agreeable to be closeted with this vindictive copper, and I am not ashamed to say that I backed a pace. In fact, I would probably have gone on backing, had he not reached out a hand like a ham and grabbed me by the slack of my coat.

'Stand still, you blasted object,' he said. 'I have something to say to you.'

'You couldn't write?'

'No, I could not write. Don't wriggle. Listen.'

I could see that the man was wrestling with some strong emotion, and could only hope that it was not homicidal. The eyes were glittering, and the face flushed.

'Listen,' he said again. 'You know that engagement of yours?'

'To Florence?'

'To Florence. It's off.'

'Off?'

'Off,' said Stilton.

A sharp exclamation passed my lips. I clutched at the gate for support. The sun, which a moment before had gone behind a cloud, suddenly came shooting out like a rabbit and started shining like the dickens. On every side, it seemed to me, birds began to tootle their songs of joy. It will give you some rough indication of my feelings when I tell you that not only did all Nature become beautiful, but even for an instant Stilton.

Through a sort of pink mist, I heard myself asking faintly what he meant. The question caused him to frown with some impatience.

'You can understand words of one syllable, can't you? I tell you your engagement is off. Florence is going to marry me. I met her, as I came away from this pest house, and had it out with her. After that revolting exhibition of fraud and skullduggery in there, I had decided to resign from the Force, and I told her so. It removed the only barrier there had ever been between us. Questioned, she broke down and came clean, admitting that she had always loved me, and had got engaged to you merely to score off me for something I had said about modern enlightened thought. I withdrew the remark, and she fell into my arms. She seemed not to like the idea of breaking the news to you, so I said I would do it. "And if young blasted Wooster has anything to say," I told her, "I will twist his head off and ram it down his throat." Have you anything to say, Wooster?'

I paused for a moment to listen to the tootling birds. Then I raised the map, and allowed the beaming sun to play on it.

'Not a thing,' I assured him.

'You realize the position? She has returned you to store. No ruddy wedding bells for you.'

'Quite.'

'Good. You will be leaving here fairly soon, I take it?'

'Almost at once.'

'Good,' said Stilton, and sprang on his bicycle as if it had been a mettlesome charger.

Nor did I linger. I did the distance from the gate to the kitchen in about three seconds flat. From the window of the bathroom, as I passed, there came the voice of Uncle Percy as he sluiced the frame. He was singing some gay air. A sea chanty, probably, which he had learned from Clam or one of the captains in his employment.

Jeeves was pacing the kitchen floor, deep in thought. He looked round, as I entered, and his manner was apologetic.

'It appears, sir, I regret to say, that there is no anchovy paste. It was finished yesterday.'

I didn't actually slap him on the back, but I gave him the dickens of a beaming smile.

'Never mind the anchovy paste, Jeeves. It will not be required. I've just seen Stilton. A reconciliation has taken place between him and Lady Florence, and they are once more headed for the altar rails. So, there being nothing to keep us in Steeple Bumpleigh, let's go.'

'Very good, sir. The car is at the door.'

I paused.

'Oh, but, dash it, we can't.'

'Sir?'

'I've just remembered I promised Uncle Percy to go to the Hall with him and help him cope with Aunt Agatha.'

'Her ladyship is not at the Hall, sir.'

'What! But you said she was.'

'Yes, sir. I fear I was guilty of a subterfuge. I regretted the necessity, but it seemed to me essential in the best interests of all concerned.'

I goggled at the man.

'Egad, Jeeves!'

'Yes, sir.'

Faintly from the distance there came the sound of Uncle Percy working through his chanty.

'How would it be,' I suggested, 'to zoom off immediately, without waiting to pack?'

'I was about to suggest such a course myself, sir.'

'It would enable one to avoid tedious explanations.'

'Precisely, sir.'

'Then shift ho, Jeeves,' I said.

It was as we were about half-way between Steeple Bumpleigh and the old metrop, that I mentioned that there was an expression on the tip of my tongue which seemed to me to sum up the nub of the recent proceedings.

'Or, rather, when I say an expression, I mean a saying. A wheeze. A gag. What, I believe, is called a saw. Something about Joy . . .'

But we went into all that before, didn't we?

VERY GOOD, JEEVES!

TO E. PHILLIPS OPPENHEIM

CONTENTS

PREFACE

The question of how long an author is to be allowed to go on recording the adventures of any given character or characters is one that has frequently engaged the attention of thinking men. The publication of this book brings it once again into the foreground of national affairs.

It is now some fourteen summers since, an eager lad in my early thirties, I started to write Jeeves stories: and many people think this nuisance should now cease. Carpers say that enough is enough. Cavillers say the same. They look down the vista of the years and see these chronicles multiplying like rabbits, and the prospect appals them. But against this must be set the fact that writing Jeeves stories gives me a great deal of pleasure and keeps me out of the public-houses.

At what conclusion, then, do we arrive? The whole thing is undoubtedly very moot.

From the welter of recrimination and argument one fact emerges—that we have here the third volume of a series. And what I do feel very strongly is that, if a thing is worth doing, it is worth doing well and thoroughly. It is perfectly possible, no doubt, to read *Very Good, Jeeves!* as a detached effort—or, indeed, not to read it at all: but I like to think that this country contains men of spirit who will not rest content till they have dug down into the old oak chest and fetched up the sum necessary for the purchase of its two predecessors—*The Inimitable Jeeves* and *Carry On, Jeeves!* Only so can the best results be obtained. Only so will allusions in the present volume to incidents occurring in the previous volumes become intelligible, instead of mystifying and befogging.

We do you these two books at the laughable price of half-a-crown apiece, and the method of acquiring them is simplicity itself.

All you have to do is to go to the nearest bookseller, when the following dialogue will take place:

YOURSELF: Good morning, Mr Bookseller.

BOOKSELLER: Good morning, Mr Everyman.

YOURSELF: I want *The Inimitable Jeeves* and *Carry On, Jeeves!*

BOOKSELLER: Certainly, Mr Everyman. You make the easy payment of five shillings, and they will be delivered at your door in a plain van.

YOURSELF: Good morning, Mr Bookseller.

BOOKSELLER: Good morning, Mr Everyman.

Or take the case of a French visitor to London, whom, for want of a better name, we will call Jules St Xavier Popinot. In this instance the little scene will run on these lines:

AU COIN DE LIVRES

POPINOT: Bon jour, Monsieur le marchand de livres.

MARCHAND: Bon jour, Monsieur. Quel beau temps aujourdhui, n'est-ce-pas?

POPINOT: Absolument. Eskervous avez le *Jeeves Inimitable* et le *Continuez, Jeeves!* du maitre Vodeouse?

MARCHAND: Mais certainement, Monsieur.

POPINOT: Donnez-moi les deux, s'il vous plait.

MARCHAND: Oui, par exemple, morbleu. Et aussi la plume, l'encre, et la tante du jardinière?

POPINOT: Je m'en fiche de cela. Je désire seulement le Vodeouse.

MARCHAND: Pas de chemises, de cravats, ou le tonic pour les cheveux?

POPINOT: Seulement le Vodeouse, je vous assure.

MARCHAND: Parfaitement, Monsieur. Deux-et-six pour chaque bibelot—exactement cinq roberts.

POPINOT: Bon jour, Monsieur.

MARCHAND: Bon jour, Monsieur.

As simple as that.

See that the name 'Wodehouse' is on every label.

P. G. W.

1

JEEVES AND THE IMPENDING DOOM

It was the morning of the day on which I was slated to pop down to my Aunt Agatha's place at Woollam Chersey in the county of Herts for a visit of three solid weeks; and, as I seated myself at the breakfast table, I don't mind confessing that the heart was singularly heavy. We Woosters are men of iron, but beneath my intrepid exterior at that moment there lurked a nameless dread.

'Jeeves,' I said, 'I am not the old merry self this morning.'

'Indeed, sir?'

'No, Jeeves. Far from it. Far from the old merry self.'

'I am sorry to hear that, sir.'

He uncovered the fragrant eggs and b., and I pronged a moody forkful.

'Why—this is what I keep asking myself, Jeeves,—why has my Aunt Agatha invited me to her country seat?'

'I could not say, sir.'

'Not because she is fond of me.'

'No, sir.'

'It is a well-established fact that I give her a pain in the neck. How it happens I cannot say, but every time our paths cross, so to speak, it seems to be a mere matter of time before I perpetrate some ghastly floater and have her hopping after me with her hatchet. The result being that she regards me as a worm and an outcast. Am I right or wrong, Jeeves?'

'Perfectly correct, sir.'

'And yet now she has absolutely insisted on my scratching all previous engagements and buzzing down to Woollam Chersey. She must have some sinister reason of which we know nothing. Can you blame me, Jeeves, if the heart is heavy?'

'No, sir. Excuse me, sir, I fancy I heard the front-door bell.'

He shimmered out, and I took another listless stab at the e. and bacon.

'A telegram, sir,' said Jeeves, re-entering the presence.

'Open it, Jeeves, and read contents. Who is it from?'

'It is unsigned, sir.'

'You mean there's no name at the end of it?'

'That is precisely what I was endeavouring to convey, sir.'

'Let's have a look.'

I scanned the thing. It was a rummy communication. Rummy. No other word.

As follows:

Remember when you come here absolutely vital meet perfect strangers.

We Woosters are not very strong in the head, particularly at breakfast-time; and I was conscious of a dull ache between the eyebrows.

'What does it mean, Jeeves?'

'I could not say, sir.'

'It says "come here". Where's here?'

'You will notice that the message was handed in at Woollam Chersey, sir.'

'You're absolutely right. At Woollam, as you very cleverly spotted, Chersey. This tells us something, Jeeves.'

'What, sir?'

'I don't know. It couldn't be from my Aunt Agatha, do you think?'

'Hardly, sir.'

'No; you're right again. Then all we can say is that some person unknown, resident at Woollam Chersey, considers it absolutely vital for me to meet perfect strangers. But why should I meet perfect strangers, Jeeves?'

'I could not say, sir.'

'And yet, looking at it from another angle, why shouldn't I?'

'Precisely, sir.'

'Then what it comes to is that the thing is a mystery which time alone can solve. We must wait and see, Jeeves.'

'The very expression I was about to employ, sir.'

I hit Woollam Chersey at about four o'clock, and found Aunt Agatha in her lair, writing letters. And, from what I know of her, probably offensive letters, with nasty postscripts. She regarded me with not a fearful lot of joy.

'Oh, there you are, Bertie.'

'Yes, here I am.'

'There's a smut on your nose.'

I plied the handkerchief.

'I am glad you have arrived so early. I want to have a word with you before you meet Mr Filmer.'

'Who?'

'Mr Filmer, the Cabinet Minister. He is staying in the house. Surely even you must have heard of Mr Filmer?'

'Oh, rather,' I said, though as a matter of fact the bird was completely unknown to me. What with one thing and another, I'm not frightfully up in the personnel of the political world.

'I particularly wish you to make a good impression on Mr Filmer.'

'Right-ho.'

'Don't speak in that casual way, as if you supposed that it was perfectly natural that you would make a good impression upon him. Mr Filmer is a serious-minded man of high character and purpose, and you are just the type of vapid and frivolous wastrel against which he is most likely to be prejudiced.'

Hard words, of course, from one's own flesh and blood, but well in keeping with past form.

'You will endeavour, therefore, while you are here not to display yourself in the *rôle* of a vapid and frivolous wastrel. In the first place, you will give up smoking during your visit.'

'Oh, I say!'

'Mr Filmer is president of the Anti-Tobacco League. Nor will you drink alcoholic stimulants.'

'Oh, dash it!'

'And you will kindly exclude from your conversation all that is suggestive of the bar, the billiard-room, and the stage-door. Mr Filmer will judge you largely by your conversation.'

I rose to a point of order.

'Yes, but why have I got to make an impression on this—on Mr Filmer?'

'Because,' said the old relative, giving me the eye, 'I particularly wish it.'

Not, perhaps, a notably snappy come-back as come-backs go; but it was enough to show me that that was more or less that; and I beetled out with an aching heart.

I headed for the garden, and I'm dashed if the first person I saw wasn't young Bingo Little.

Bingo Little and I have been pals practically from birth. Born in the same village within a couple of days of one another, we went through kindergarten, Eton, and Oxford together; and, grown to riper years we have enjoyed in the old metrop. full many a first-class binge in each other's society. If there was one fellow in the world, I felt, who could alleviate the horrors of this blighted visit of mine, that bloke was young Bingo Little.

But how he came to be there was more than I could understand. Some time before, you see, he had married the celebrated authoress, Rosie M. Banks; and the last I had seen of him he had been on the point of accompanying her to America on a lecture tour. I distinctly remembered him cursing rather freely because the trip would mean his missing Ascot.

Still, rummy as it might seem, here he was. And aching for the sight of a friendly face, I gave tongue like a bloodhound.

'Bingo!'

He spun round; and, by Jove, his face wasn't friendly after all. It was what they call contorted. He waved his arms at me like a semaphore.

''Sh!' he hissed. 'Would you ruin me?'

'Eh?'

'Didn't you get my telegram?'

'Was that *your* telegram?'

'Of course it was my telegram.'

'Then why didn't you sign it?'

'I did sign it.'

'No, you didn't. I couldn't make out what it was all about.'

'Well, you got my letter.'

'What letter?'

'My letter.'

'I didn't get any letter.'

'Then I must have forgotten to post it. It was to tell you that I was down here tutoring your Cousin Thomas, and that it was essential that, when we met, you should treat me as a perfect stranger.'

'But why?'

'Because, if your aunt supposed that I was a pal of yours, she would naturally sack me on the spot.'

'Why?'

Bingo raised his eyebrows.

'Why? Be reasonable, Bertie. If you were your aunt, and you knew the sort of chap you were, would you let a fellow you knew to be your best pal tutor your son?'

This made the old head swim a bit, but I got his meaning after awhile, and I had to admit that there was much rugged good sense in what he said. Still, he hadn't explained what you might call the nub or gist of the mystery.

'I thought you were in America,' I said.

'Well, I'm not.'

'Why not?'

'Never mind why not. I'm not.'

'But why have you taken a tutoring job?'

'Never mind why. I have my reasons. And I want you to get it into your head, Bertie—to get it right through the concrete—that you and I must not be seen hobnobbing. Your foul cousin was caught smoking in the shrubbery the day before yesterday, and that has made my position pretty tottery, because your aunt said that, if I had exercised an adequate surveillance over him, it couldn't have happened. If, after that, she finds out I'm a friend of yours, nothing can save me from being shot out. And it is vital that I am not shot out.'

'Why?'

'Never mind why.'

At this point he seemed to think he heard somebody coming, for he suddenly leaped with incredible agility into a laurel bush. And I toddled along to consult Jeeves about these rummy happenings.

'Jeeves,' I said, repairing to the bedroom, where he was unpacking my things, 'you remember that telegram?'

'Yes, sir.'

'It was from Mr Little. He's here, tutoring my young Cousin Thomas.'

'Indeed, sir?'

'I can't understand it. He appears to be a free agent, if you know what I mean; and yet would any man who was a free agent wantonly come to a house which contained my Aunt Agatha?'

'It seems peculiar, sir.'

'Moreover, would anybody of his own free-will and as a mere pleasure-seeker tutor my Cousin Thomas, who is notoriously a tough egg and a fiend in human shape?'

'Most improbable, sir.'

'These are deep waters, Jeeves.'

'Precisely, sir.'

'And the ghastly part of it all is that he seems to consider it necessary, in order to keep his job, to treat me like a long-lost leper. Thus killing my only chance of having anything approaching a decent time in this abode of desolation. For do you realize, Jeeves, that my aunt says I mustn't smoke while I'm here?'

'Indeed, sir?'

'Nor drink.'

'Why is this, sir?'

'Because she wants me—for some dark and furtive reason which she will not explain—to impress a fellow named Filmer.'

'Too bad, sir. However, many doctors, I understand, advocate such abstinence as the secret of health. They say it promotes a freer circulation of the blood and insures the arteries against premature hardening.'

'Oh, do they? Well, you can tell them next time you see them that they are silly asses.'

'Very good, sir.'

And so began what, looking back along a fairly eventful career, I think I can confidently say was the scaliest visit I have ever experienced in the course of my life. What with the agony of missing the life-giving cocktail before dinner; the painful necessity of being obliged, every time I wanted a quiet cigarette, to lie on the floor in my bedroom and puff the smoke up the chimney; the constant discomfort of meeting Aunt Agatha round unexpected corners; and the fearful strain on the morale of having to chum with the Right Hon. A. B. Filmer, it was not long before Bertram was up against it to an extent hitherto undreamed of.

I played golf with the Right Hon. every day, and it was only by biting the Wooster lip and clenching the fists till the knuckles stood out white under the strain that I managed to pull through. The Right Hon. punctuated some of the ghastliest golf I have ever seen with a flow of conversation which, as far as I was concerned, went completely over the top; and, all in all, I was beginning to feel pretty sorry for myself when, one night as I was in my room listlessly donning the soup-and-fish in preparation for the evening meal, in trickled young Bingo and took my mind off my own troubles.

For when it is a question of a pal being in the soup, we Woosters no longer think of self; and that poor old Bingo was knee-deep in the bisque was made plain by his mere appearance—which was that of a cat which has just been struck by a half-brick and is expecting another shortly.

'Bertie,' said Bingo, having sat down on the bed and diffused silent gloom for a moment, 'how is Jeeves's brain these days?'

'Fairly strong on the wing, I fancy. How is the grey matter, Jeeves? Surging about pretty freely?'

'Yes, sir.'

'Thank Heaven for that,' said young Bingo, 'for I require your soundest counsel. Unless right-thinking people take strong steps through the proper channels, my name will be mud.'

'What's wrong, old thing?' I asked, sympathetically.

Bingo plucked at the coverlet.

'I will tell you,' he said. 'I will also now reveal why I am staying in this pest-house, tutoring a kid who requires not education in the Greek and Latin languages but a swift slosh on the base of the skull with a black-jack. I came here, Bertie, because it was the only thing I could do. At the last moment before she sailed to America, Rosie decided that I had better stay behind and look after the Peke. She left me a couple of hundred quid to see me through till her return. This sum, judiciously expended over the period of her absence, would have been enough to keep Peke and self in moderate affluence. But you know how it is.'

'How what is?'

'When someone comes slinking up to you in the club and tells you that some cripple of a horse can't help winning even if it develops lumbago and the botts ten yards from the starting-post. I tell you, I regarded the thing as a cautious and conservative investment.'

'You mean you planked the entire capital on a horse?'

Bingo laughed bitterly.

'If you could call the thing a horse. If it hadn't shown a flash of speed in the straight, it would have got mixed up with the next race. It came in last, putting me in a dashed delicate position. Somehow or other I had to find the funds to keep me going, so that I could win through till Rosie's return without her knowing what had occurred. Rosie is the dearest girl in the world; but if you were a married man, Bertie, you would be aware that the best of wives is apt to cut up rough if she finds that her husband has dropped six weeks' housekeeping money on a single race. Isn't that so, Jeeves?'

'Yes, sir. Women are odd in that respect.'

'It was a moment for swift thinking. There was enough left from the wreck to board the Peke out at a comfortable home. I signed him up for six weeks at the Kosy Komfort Kennels at Kingsbridge, Kent, and tottered out, a broken man, to a tutoring job. I landed the kid Thomas. And here I am.'

It was a sad story, of course, but it seemed to me that, awful as it might be to be in constant association with my Aunt Agatha and young Thos, he had got rather well out of a tight place.

'All you have to do,' I said, 'is to carry on here for a few weeks more, and everything will be oojah-cum-spiff.'

Bingo barked bleakly.

'A few weeks more! I shall be lucky if I stay two days. You remember I told you that your aunt's faith in me as a guardian of her blighted son was shaken a few days ago by the fact that he was caught smoking. I now find that the person who caught him smoking was the man Filmer. And ten minutes ago young Thomas told me that he was proposing to inflict some hideous revenge on Filmer for having reported him to your aunt. I don't know what he is going to do, but if he does it, out I inevitably go on my left ear. Your aunt thinks the world of Filmer, and would sack me on the spot. And three weeks before Rosie gets back!'

I saw all.

'Jeeves,' I said.

'Sir?'

'I see all. Do you see all?'

'Yes, sir.'

'Then flock round.'

'I fear, sir—'

Bingo gave a low moan.

'Don't tell me, Jeeves,' he said, brokenly, 'that nothing suggests itself.'

'Nothing at the moment, I regret to say, sir.'

Bingo uttered a stricken woofle like a bull-dog that has been refused cake.

'Well, then, the only thing I can do, I suppose,' he said sombrely, 'is not to let the pie-faced little thug out of my sight for a second.'

'Absolutely,' I said. 'Ceaseless vigilance, eh, Jeeves?'

'Precisely, sir.'

'But meanwhile, Jeeves,' said Bingo in a low, earnest voice, 'you will be devoting your best thought to the matter, won't you?'

'Most certainly, sir.'

'Thank you, Jeeves.'

'Not at all, sir.'

I will say for young Bingo that, once the need for action arrived, he behaved with an energy and determination which compelled respect. I suppose there was not a minute during the next two days when the kid

Thos was able to say to himself, 'Alone at last!' But on the evening of the second day Aunt Agatha announced that some people were coming over on the morrow for a spot of tennis, and I feared that the worst must now befall.

Young Bingo, you see, is one of those fellows who, once their fingers close over the handle of a tennis racket, fall into a sort of trance in which nothing outside the radius of the lawn exists for them. If you came up to Bingo in the middle of a set and told him that panthers were devouring his best friend in the kitchen garden, he would look at you and say, 'Oh, ah?' or words to that effect. I knew that he would not give a thought to young Thomas and the Right Hon. till the last ball had bounced, and, as I dressed for dinner that night, I was conscious of an impending doom.

'Jeeves,' I said, 'have you ever pondered on Life?'

'From time to time, sir, in my leisure moments.'

'Grim, isn't it, what?'

'Grim, sir?'

'I mean to say, the difference between things as they look and things as they are.'

'The trousers perhaps a half-inch higher, sir. A very slight adjustment of the braces will effect the necessary alteration. You were saying, sir?'

'I mean, here at Woollam Chersey we have apparently a happy, care-free country-house party. But beneath the glittering surface, Jeeves, dark currents are running. One gazes at the Right Hon. wrapping himself round the salmon mayonnaise at lunch, and he seems a man without a care in the world. Yet all the while a dreadful fate is hanging over him, creeping nearer and nearer. What exact steps do you think the kid Thomas intends to take?'

'In the course of an informal conversation which I had with the young gentleman this afternoon, sir, he informed me that he had been reading a romance entitled *Treasure Island*, and had been much struck by the character and actions of a certain Captain Flint. I gathered that he was weighing the advisability of modelling his own conduct on that of the Captain.'

'But, good heavens, Jeeves! If I remember *Treasure Island*, Flint was the bird who went about hitting people with a cutlass. You don't think young Thomas would bean Mr Filmer with a cutlass?'

'Possibly he does not possess a cutlass, sir.'

'Well, with anything.'

'We can but wait and see, sir. The tie, if I might suggest it, sir, a shade more tightly knotted. One aims at the perfect butterfly effect. If you will permit me—'

'What do ties matter, Jeeves, at a time like this? Do you realize that Mr Little's domestic happiness is hanging in the scale?'

'There is no time, sir, at which ties do not matter.'

I could see the man was pained, but I did not try to heal the wound. What's the word I want? Preoccupied. I was too preoccupied, don't you know. And distrait. Not to say careworn.

I was still careworn when, next day at half-past two, the revels commenced on the tennis lawn. It was one of those close, baking days, with thunder rumbling just round the corner; and it seemed to me that there was a brooding menace in the air.

'Bingo,' I said, as we pushed forth to do our bit in the first doubles, 'I wonder what young Thos will be up to this afternoon, with the eye of authority no longer on him?'

'Eh?' said Bingo, absently. Already the tennis look had come into his face, and his eye was glazed. He swung his racket and snorted a little.

'I don't see him anywhere,' I said.

'You don't what?'

'See him.'

'Who?'

'Young Thos.'

'What about him?'

I let it go.

The only consolation I had in the black period of the opening of the tourney was the fact that the Right Hon. had taken a seat among the spectators and was wedged in between a couple of females with parasols. Reason told me that even a kid so steeped in sin as young Thomas would hardly perpetrate any outrage on a man in such a strong strategic position. Considerably relieved, I gave myself up to the game, and was in the act of putting it across the local curate with a good deal of vim when there was a roll of thunder and the rain started to come down in buckets.

We all stampeded for the house, and had gathered in the drawing-room for tea, when suddenly Aunt Agatha, looking up from a cucumber-sandwich, said:

'Has anybody seen Mr Filmer?'

It was one of the nastiest jars I have ever experienced. What with my fast serve zipping sweetly over the net and the man of God utterly unable to cope with my slow bending return down the centre-line, I had for some little time been living, as it were, in another world. I now came down to earth with a bang: and my slice of cake, slipping from my nerveless fingers, fell to the ground and was wolfed by Aunt Agatha's spaniel, Robert. Once more I seemed to become conscious of an impending doom.

For this man Filmer, you must understand, was not one of those men who are lightly kept from the tea-table. A hearty trencherman, and particularly fond of his five o'clock couple of cups and bite of muffin, he had until this afternoon always been well up among the leaders in the race for the food-trough. If one thing was certain, it was that only the machinations of some enemy could be keeping him from being in the drawing-room now, complete with nose-bag.

'He must have got caught in the rain and be sheltering somewhere in the grounds,' said Aunt Agatha. 'Bertie, go out and find him. Take a raincoat to him.'

'Right-ho!' I said. My only desire in life now was to find the Right Hon. And I hoped it wouldn't be merely his body.

I put on a raincoat and tucked another under my arm, and was sallying forth, when in the hall I ran into Jeeves.

'Jeeves,' I said, 'I fear the worst. Mr Filmer is missing.'

'Yes, sir.'

'I am about to scour the grounds in search of him.'

'I can save you the trouble, sir. Mr Filmer is on the island in the middle of the lake.'

'In this rain? Why doesn't the chump row back?'

'He has no boat, sir.'

'Then how can he be on the island?'

'He rowed there, sir. But Master Thomas rowed after him and set his boat adrift. He was informing me of the circumstances a moment ago, sir. It appears that Captain Flint was in the habit of marooning people on islands, and Master Thomas felt that he could pursue no more judicious course than to follow his example.'

'But, good Lord, Jeeves! The man must be getting soaked.'

'Yes, sir. Master Thomas commented upon that aspect of the matter.'

It was a time for action.

'Come with me, Jeeves!'

'Very good, sir.'

I buzzed for the boathouse.

My Aunt Agatha's husband, Spenser Gregson, who is on the Stock Exchange, had recently cleaned up to an amazing extent in Sumatra Rubber; and Aunt Agatha, in selecting a country estate, had lashed out on an impressive scale. There were miles of what they call rolling parkland, trees in considerable profusion well provided with doves and what not cooing in no uncertain voice, gardens full of roses, and also stables, outhouses, and messuages, the whole forming a rather fruity *tout ensemble*. But the feature of the place was the lake.

It stood to the east of the house, beyond the rose garden, and covered several acres. In the middle of it was an island. In the middle of the island was a building known as the Octagon. And in the middle of the Octagon, seated on the roof and spouting water like a public fountain, was the Right Hon. A. B. Filmer. As we drew nearer, striking a fast clip with self at the oars and Jeeves handling the tiller-ropes, we heard cries of gradually increasing volume, if that's the expression I want; and presently, up aloft, looking from a distance as if he were perched on top of the bushes, I located the Right Hon. It seemed to me that even a Cabinet Minister ought to have had more sense than to stay right out in the open like that when there were trees to shelter under.

'A little more to the right, Jeeves.'

'Very good, sir.'

I made a neat landing.

'Wait here, Jeeves.'

'Very good, sir. The head gardener was informing me this morning, sir, that one of the swans had recently nested on this island.'

'This is no time for natural history gossip, Jeeves,' I said, a little severely, for the rain was coming down harder than ever and the Wooster trouser-legs were already considerably moistened.

'Very good, sir.'

I pushed my way through the bushes. The going was sticky and took about eight and elevenpence off the value of my Sure-Grip tennis shoes in the first two yards: but I persevered, and presently came out in the open and found myself in a sort of clearing facing the Octagon.

This building was run up somewhere in the last century, I have been told, to enable the grandfather of the late owner to have some quiet place out of earshot of the house where he could practise the fiddle. From what I know of fiddlers, I should imagine that he had produced some fairly frightful sounds there in his time: but they can have been nothing to the ones that were coming from the roof of the place now. The Right Hon., not having spotted the arrival of the rescue-party, was apparently trying to make his voice carry across the waste of waters to the house; and I'm not saying it was not a good sporting effort. He had one of those highish tenors, and his yowls seemed to screech over my head like shells.

I thought it about time to slip him the glad news that assistance had arrived, before he strained a vocal cord.

'Hi!' I shouted, waiting for a lull.

He poked his head over the edge.

'Hi!' he bellowed, looking in every direction but the right one, of course.

'Hi!'

'Hi!'

'Hi!'

'Hi!'

'Oh!' he said, spotting me at last.

'What-ho!' I replied, sort of clinching the thing. I suppose the conversation can't be said to have touched a frightfully high level up to this moment; but probably we should have got a good deal brainier very shortly—only just then, at the very instant when I was getting ready to say something good, there was a hissing noise like a tyre bursting in a nest of cobras, and out of the bushes to my left there popped something so large and white and active that, thinking quicker than I have ever done in my puff, I rose like a rocketing pheasant, and, before I knew what I was doing, had begun to climb for life. Something slapped against the wall about an inch below my right ankle, and any doubts I may have had about remaining below vanished. The lad who bore 'mid snow and ice the banner with the strange device 'Excelsior!' was the model for Bertram.

'Be careful!' yipped the Right Hon.

I was.

Whoever built the Octagon might have constructed it especially for this sort of crisis. Its walls had grooves at regular intervals which were just right for the hands and feet, and it wasn't very long before I was parked up on the roof beside the Right Hon., gazing down at one of the largest and shortest-tempered swans I had ever seen. It was standing below, stretching up a neck like a hosepipe, just where a bit of brick, judiciously bunged, would catch it amidships.

I bunged the brick and scored a bull's-eye.

The Right Hon. didn't seem any too well pleased.

'Don't tease it!' he said.

'It teased me,' I said.

The swan extended another eight feet of neck and gave an imitation of steam escaping from a leaky pipe. The rain continued to lash down with what you might call indescribable fury, and I was sorry that in the agitation inseparable from shinning up a stone wall at practically a second's notice I had dropped the raincoat which I had been bringing with me for my fellow-rooster. For a moment I thought of offering him mine, but wiser counsels prevailed.

'How near did it come to getting you?' I asked.

'Within an ace,' replied my companion, gazing down with a look of marked dislike. 'I had to make a very rapid spring.'

The Right Hon. was a tubby little chap who looked as if he had been poured into his clothes and had forgotten to say 'When!' and the picture he conjured up, if you know what I mean, was rather pleasing.

'It is no laughing matter,' he said, shifting the look of dislike to me.

'Sorry.'

'I might have been seriously injured.'

'Would you consider bunging another brick at the bird?'

'Do nothing of the sort. It will only annoy him.'

'Well, why not annoy him? He hasn't shown such a dashed lot of consideration for our feelings.'

The Right Hon. now turned to another aspect of the matter.

'I cannot understand how my boat, which I fastened securely to the stump of a willow-tree, can have drifted away.'

'Dashed mysterious.'

'I begin to suspect that it was deliberately set loose by some mischievous person.'

'Oh, I say, no, hardly likely, that. You'd have seen them doing it.'

'No, Mr Wooster. For the bushes form an effective screen. Moreover, rendered drowsy by the unusual warmth of the afternoon, I dozed off for some little time almost immediately I reached the island.'

This wasn't the sort of thing I wanted his mind dwelling on, so I changed the subject.

'Wet, isn't it, what?' I said.

'I had already observed it,' said the Right Hon. in one of those nasty, bitter voices. 'I thank you, however, for drawing the matter to my attention.'

Chit-chat about the weather hadn't gone with much of a bang, I perceived. I had a shot at Bird Life in the Home Counties.

'Have you ever noticed,' I said, 'how a swan's eyebrows sort of meet in the middle?'

'I have had every opportunity of observing all that there is to observe about swans.'

'Gives them a sort of peevish look, what?'

'The look to which you allude has not escaped me.'

'Rummy,' I said, rather warming to my subject, 'how bad an effect family life has on a swan's disposition.'

'I wish you would select some other topic of conversation than swans.'

'No, but, really, it's rather interesting. I mean to say, our old pal down there is probably a perfect ray of sunshine in normal circumstances. Quite the domestic pet, don't you know. But purely and simply because the little woman happens to be nesting—'

I paused. You will scarcely believe me, but until this moment, what with all the recent bustle and activity, I had clean forgotten that, while we were treed up on the roof like this, there lurked all the time in the background one whose giant brain, if notified of the emergency and requested to flock round, would probably be able to think up half-a-dozen schemes for solving our little difficulties in a couple of minutes.

'Jeeves!' I shouted.

'Sir?' came a faint respectful voice from the great open spaces.

'My man,' I explained to the Right Hon. 'A fellow of infinite resource and sagacity. He'll have us out of this in a minute. Jeeves!'

'Sir?'

'I'm sitting on the roof.'

'Very good, sir.'

'Don't say "Very good". Come and help us. Mr Filmer and I are treed, Jeeves.'

'Very good, sir.'

'Don't keep saying "Very good". It's nothing of the kind. The place is alive with swans.'

'I will attend to the matter immediately, sir.'

I turned to the Right Hon. I even went so far as to pat him on the back. It was like slapping a wet sponge.

'All is well,' I said. 'Jeeves is coming.'

'What can he do?'

I frowned a trifle. The man's tone had been peevish, and I didn't like it.

'That,' I replied with a touch of stiffness, 'we cannot say until we see him in action. He may pursue one course, or he may pursue another. But on one thing you can rely with the utmost confidence—Jeeves will find a way. See, here he comes stealing through the undergrowth, his face shining with the light of pure intelligence. There are no limits to Jeeves's brain-power. He virtually lives on fish.'

I bent over the edge and peered into the abyss.

'Look out for the swan, Jeeves.'

'I have the bird under close observation, sir.'

The swan had been uncoiling a further supply of neck in our direction; but now he whipped round. The sound of a voice speaking in his rear seemed to affect him powerfully. He subjected Jeeves to a short, keen scrutiny; and then, taking in some breath for hissing purposes, gave a sort of jump and charged ahead.

'Look out, Jeeves!'

'Very good, sir.'

Well, I could have told that swan it was no use. As swans go, he may have been well up in the ranks of the intelligentsia; but, when it came to pitting his brains against Jeeves, he was simply wasting his time. He might just as well have gone home at once.

Every young man starting life ought to know how to cope with an angry swan, so I will briefly relate the proper procedure. You begin by picking up the raincoat which somebody has dropped; and then, judging the distance to a nicety, you simply shove the raincoat over the bird's head; and, taking the boathook which you have prudently brought with you, you insert it underneath the swan and heave. The swan goes into a bush and starts trying to unscramble itself; and you saunter back to your boat, taking with you any friends who may happen at the moment to be sitting on roofs in the vicinity. That was Jeeves's method, and I cannot see how it could have been improved upon.

The Right Hon. showing a turn of speed of which I would not have believed him capable, we were in the boat in considerably under two ticks.

'You behaved very intelligently, my man,' said the Right Hon. as we pushed away from the shore.

'I endeavour to give satisfaction, sir.'

The Right Hon. appeared to have said his say for the time being. From that moment he seemed to sort of huddle up and meditate. Dashed absorbed he was. Even when I caught a crab and shot about a pint of water down his neck he didn't seem to notice it.

It was only when we were landing that he came to life again.

'Mr Wooster.'

'Oh, ah?'

'I have been thinking of that matter of which I spoke to you some time back—the problem of how my boat can have got adrift.'

'I didn't like this.

'The dickens of a problem,' I said. 'Better not bother about it any more. You'll never solve it.'

'On the contrary, I have arrived at a solution, and one which I think is the only feasible solution. I am convinced that my boat was set adrift by the boy Thomas, my hostess's son.'

'Oh, I say, no! Why?'

'He had a grudge against me. And it is the sort of thing only a boy, or one who is practically an imbecile, would have thought of doing.'

He legged it for the house; and I turned to Jeeves, aghast. Yes, you might say aghast.

'You heard, Jeeves?'

'Yes, sir.'

'What's to be done?'

'Perhaps Mr Filmer, on thinking the matter over, will decide that his suspicions are unjust.'

'But they aren't unjust.'

'No, sir.'

'Then what's to be done?'

'I could not say, sir.'

I pushed off rather smartly to the house and reported to Aunt Agatha that the Right Hon. had been salved; and then I toddled upstairs to have a hot bath, being considerably soaked from stem to stern as the result of my rambles. While I was enjoying the grateful warmth, a knock came at the door.

It was Purvis, Aunt Agatha's butler.

'Mrs Gregson desires me to say, sir, that she would be glad to see you as soon as you are ready.'

'But she has seen me.'

'I gather that she wishes to see you again, sir.'

'Oh, right-ho.'

I lay beneath the surface for another few minutes; then, having dried the frame, went along the corridor to my room. Jeeves was there, fiddling about with underclothing.

'Oh, Jeeves,' I said, 'I've just been thinking. Oughtn't somebody to go and give Mr Filmer a spot of quinine or something? Errand of mercy, what?'

'I have already done so, sir.'

'Good. I wouldn't say I like the man frightfully, but I don't want him to get a cold in the head.' I shoved on a sock. 'Jeeves,' I said, 'I suppose you know that we've got to think of something pretty quick? I mean to say, you realize the position? Mr Filmer suspects young Thomas of doing exactly what he did do, and if he brings home the charge Aunt Agatha will undoubtedly fire Mr Little, and then Mrs Little will find out what Mr Little has been up to, and what will be the upshot and outcome, Jeeves? I will tell you. It will mean that Mrs Little will get the goods on Mr Little to an extent to which, though only a bachelor myself, I should say that no wife ought to get the goods on her husband if the proper give and take of married life—what you might call the essential balance, as it were—is to be preserved. Women bring these things up, Jeeves. They do not forget and forgive.'

'Very true, sir.'

'Then how about it?'

'I have already attended to the matter, sir.'

'You have?'

'Yes, sir. I had scarcely left you when the solution of the affair presented itself to me. It was a remark of Mr Filmer's that gave me the idea.'

'Jeeves, you're a marvel!'

'Thank you very much, sir.'

'What was the solution?'

'I conceived the notion of going to Mr Filmer and saying that it was you who had stolen his boat, sir.'

The man flickered before me. I clutched a sock in a feverish grip.

'Saying—what?'

'At first Mr Filmer was reluctant to credit my statement. But I pointed out to him that you had certainly known that he was on the island—a fact which he agreed was highly significant. I pointed out, furthermore, that you were a light-hearted young gentleman, sir, who might well do such a thing as a practical joke. I left him quite convinced, and there is now no danger of his attributing the action to Master Thomas.'

I gazed at the blighter spellbound.

'And that's what you consider a neat solution?' I said.

'Yes, sir. Mr Little will now retain his position as desired.'

'And what about me?'

'You are also benefited, sir.'

'Oh, I am, am I?'

'Yes, sir. I have ascertained that Mrs Gregson's motive in inviting you to this house was that she might present you to Mr Filmer with a view to your becoming his private secretary.'

'What!'

'Yes, sir. Purvis, the butler, chanced to overhear Mrs Gregson in conversation with Mr Filmer on the matter.'

'Secretary to that superfatted bore! Jeeves, I could never have survived it.'

'No, sir. I fancy you would not have found it agreeable. Mr Filmer is scarcely a congenial companion for you. Yet, had Mrs Gregson secured the position for you, you might have found it embarrassing to decline to accept it.'

'Embarrassing is right!'

'Yes, sir.'

'But I say, Jeeves, there's just one point which you seem to have overlooked. Where exactly do I get off?'

'Sir?'

'I mean to say, Aunt Agatha sent word by Purvis just now that she wanted to see me. Probably she's polishing up her hatchet at this very moment.'

'It might be the most judicious plan not to meet her, sir.'

'But how can I help it?'

'There is a good, stout waterpipe running down the wall immediately outside this window, sir. And I could have the two-seater waiting outside the park gates in twenty minutes.'

I eyed him with reverence.

'Jeeves,' I said, 'you are always right. You couldn't make it five, could you?'

'Let us say ten, sir.'

'Ten it is. Lay out some raiment suitable for travel, and leave the rest to me. Where is this waterpipe of which you speak so highly?'

2

THE INFERIORITY COMPLEX OF OLD SIPPY

I checked the man with one of my glances. I was astounded and shocked.

'Not another word, Jeeves,' I said. 'You have gone too far. Hats, yes. Socks, yes. Coats, trousers, shirts, ties, and spats, absolutely. On all these things I defer to your judgement. But when it comes to vases, no.'

'Very good, sir.'

'You say that this vase is not in harmony with the appointments of the room—whatever that means, if anything. I deny this, Jeeves, *in toto*. I like this vase. I call it decorative, striking, and, all in all, an exceedingly good fifteen bob's worth.'

'Very good, sir.'

'That's that, then. If anybody rings up, I shall be closeted during the next hour with Mr Sipperley at the offices of *The Mayfair Gazette*.'

I beetled off with a fairish amount of restrained hauteur, for I was displeased with the man. On the previous afternoon, while sauntering along the Strand, I had found myself wedged into one of those sort of alcove places where fellows with voices like fog-horns stand all day selling things by auction. And, though I was still vague as to how exactly it had happened, I had somehow become the possessor of a large china vase with crimson dragons on it. And not only dragons, but birds, dogs, snakes, and a thing that looked like a leopard. This menagerie was now stationed on a bracket over the door of my sitting-room.

I liked the thing. It was bright and cheerful. It caught the eye. And that was why, when Jeeves, wincing a bit, had weighed in with some perfectly gratuitous art-criticism, I ticked him off with no little vim. *Ne sutor ultra* whatever-it-is, I would have said to him, if I'd thought of it. I mean to say, where does a valet get off, censoring vases? Does it fall within his province to knock the young master's chinaware? Absolutely not, and so I told him.

I was still pretty heartily hipped when I reached the office of *The Mayfair Gazette*, and it would have been a relief to my feelings to have decanted my troubles on to old Sippy, who, being a very dear old pal of mine, would no doubt have understood and sympathized. But when the office-boy had slipped me through into the inner cubbyhole where the old lad performed his editorial duties, he seemed so preoccupied that I hadn't the heart.

All these editor blokes, I understand, get pretty careworn after they've been at the job for awhile. Six months before, Sippy had been a cheery cove, full of happy laughter; but at that time he was what they call a free-lance, bunging in a short story here and a set of verses there and generally enjoying himself. Ever since he had become editor of this rag, I had sensed a change, so to speak.

To-day he looked more editorial then ever; so, shelving my own worries for the nonce, I endeavoured to cheer him up by telling him how much I had enjoyed his last issue. As a matter of fact, I hadn't read it, but we Woosters do not shrink from subterfuge when it is a question of bracing up a buddy.

The treatment was effective. He showed animation and verve.

'You really liked it?'

'Red-hot, old thing.'

'Full of good stuff, eh?'

'Packed.'

'That poem—Solitude?'

'What a gem!'

'A genuine masterpiece.'

'Pure tabasco. Who wrote it?'

'It was signed,' said Sippy, a little coldly.

'I keep forgetting names.'

'It was written,' said Sippy, 'by Miss Gwendolen Moon. Have you ever met Miss Moon, Bertie?'

'Not to my knowledge. Nice girl?'

'My God!' said Sippy.

I looked at him keenly. If you ask my Aunt Agatha she will tell you—in fact, she is quite likely to tell you even if you don't ask her—that I am a vapid and irreflective chump. Barely sentient, was the way she once described me: and I'm not saying that in a broad, general sense she isn't right. But there is one department of life in which I am Hawkshaw the detective in person. I can recognize Love's Young Dream more quickly than any other bloke of my weight and age in the Metropolis. So many of my pals have copped it in the past few years that now I can spot it a mile off on a foggy day. Sippy was leaning back in his chair, chewing a piece of indiarubber with a far-off look in his eyes, and I formed my diagnosis instantly.

'Tell me all, laddie,' I said.

'Bertie, I love her.'

'Have you told her so?'

'How can I?'

'I don't see why not. Quite easy to bring into the general conversation.'

Sippy groaned hollowly.

'Do you know what it is, Bertie, to feel the humility of a worm?'

'Rather! I do sometimes with Jeeves. But today he went too far. You will scarcely credit it, old man, but he had the crust to criticize a vase which—'

'She is so far above me.'

'Tall girl?'

'Spiritually. She is all soul. And what am I? Earthy.'

'Would you say that?'

'I would. Have you forgotten that a year ago I did thirty days without the option for punching a policeman in the stomach on Boat-Race night?'

'But you were whiffled at the time.'

'Exactly. What right has an inebriated jail-bird to aspire to a goddess?'

My heart bled for the poor old chap.

'Aren't you exaggerating things a trifle, old lad?' I said. 'Everybody who has had a gentle upbringing gets a bit sizzled on Boat-Race night, and the better element nearly always have trouble with the gendarmes.'

He shook his head.

'It's no good, Bertie. You mean well, but words are useless. No, I can but worship from afar. When I am in her presence a strange dumbness comes over me. My tongue seems to get entangled with my tonsils. I could no more muster up the nerve to propose to her than . . . Come in!' he shouted.

For, just as he was beginning to go nicely and display a bit of eloquence, a knock had sounded on the door. In fact, not so much a knock as a bang—or even a slosh. And there now entered a large, important-looking bird with penetrating eyes, a Roman nose, and high cheek-bones. Authoritative. That's the word I want. I didn't like his collar, and Jeeves would have had a thing or two to say about the sit of his trousers; but, nevertheless, he was authoritative. There was something compelling about the man. He looked like a traffic-policeman.

'Ah, Sipperley!' he said.

Old Sippy displayed a good deal of agitation. He had leaped from his chair, and was now standing in a constrained attitude, with a sort of pop-eyed expression on his face.

'Pray be seated, Sipperley,' said the cove. He took no notice of me. After one keen glance and a brief waggle of the nose in my direction, he had washed Bertram out of his life. 'I have brought you another little offering—ha! Look it over at your leisure, my dear fellow.'

'Yes, sir,' said Sippy.

'I think you will enjoy it. But there is just one thing. I should be glad, Sipperley, if you would give it a leetle better display, a rather more prominent position in the paper than you accorded to my "Landmarks of Old Tuscany". I am quite aware that in a weekly journal space is a desideratum, but one does not like one's efforts to be—I can only say pushed away in a back corner among advertisements of bespoke tailors and places of amusement.' He paused, and a nasty gleam came into his eyes. 'You will bear this in mind, Sipperley?'

'Yes, sir,' said Sippy.

'I am greatly obliged, my dear fellow,' said the cove, becoming genial again. 'You must forgive my mentioning it. I would be the last person to attempt to dictate the—ha!—editorial policy, but— Well, good afternoon, Sipperley. I will call for your decision at three o'clock to-morrow.'

He withdrew, leaving a gap in the atmosphere about ten feet by six. When this had closed in, I sat up.

'What was it?' I said.

I was startled to observe poor old Sippy apparently go off his onion. He raised his hands over his head, clutched his hair, wrenched it about for a while, kicked a table with great violence, and then flung himself into his chair.

'Curse him!' said Sippy. 'May he tread on a banana-skin on his way to chapel and sprain both ankles!'

'Who was he?'

'May he get frog-in-the-throat and be unable to deliver the end-of-term sermon!'

'Yes, but who was he?'

'My old head master, Bertie,' said Sippy.

'Yes, but, my dear old soul—'

'Head master of my old school.' He gazed at me in a distraught sort of way. 'Good Lord! Can't you understand the position?'

'Not by a jugful, laddie.'

Sippy sprang from his chair and took a turn or two up and down the carpet.

'How do you feel,' he said, 'when you meet the head master of your old school?'

'I never do. He's dead.'

'Well, I'll tell you how I feel. I feel as if I were in the Lower Fourth again, and had been sent up by my form-master for creating a disturbance in school. That happened once, Bertie, and the memory still lingers. I can recall as if it were yesterday knocking at old Waterbury's door and hearing him say, "Come in!" like a lion roaring at an early Christian, and going in and shuffling my feet on the mat and him looking at me and me explaining—and then, after what seemed a lifetime, bending over and receiving six of the juiciest on the old spot with a cane that bit like an adder. And whenever he comes into my office now the old wound begins to trouble me, and I just say, "Yes, sir," and "No, sir," and feel like a kid of fourteen.'

I began to grasp the posish. The whole trouble with these fellows like Sippy, who go in for writing, is that they develop the artistic temperament, and you never know when it is going to break out.

'He comes in here with his pockets full of articles on "The Old School Cloisters" and "Some Little-Known Aspects of Tacitus", and muck like that, and I haven't the nerve to refuse them. And this is supposed to be a paper devoted to the lighter interests of Society.'

'You must be firm, Sippy. Firm, old thing.'

'How can I, when the sight of him makes me feel like a piece of chewed blotting-paper? When he looks at me over that nose, my *morale* goes blue at the roots and I am back at school again. It's persecution, Bertie. And the next thing that'll happen is that my proprietor will spot one of those articles, assume with perfect justice that, if I can print that sort of thing, I must be going off my chump, and fire me.'

I pondered. It was a tough problem.

'How would it be—?' I said.

'That's no good.'

'Only a suggestion,' I said.

'Jeeves,' I said, when I got home, 'surge round!'

'Sir?'

'Burnish the old bean. I have a case that calls for one of your best efforts. Have you ever heard of a Miss Gwendolen Moon?'

'Authoress of *Autumn Leaves. 'Twas on an English June*, and other works. Yes, sir.'

'Great Scott, Jeeves, you seem to know everything.'

'Thank you very much, sir.'

'Well, Mr Sipperley is in love with Miss Moon.'

'Yes, sir.'

'But fears to speak.'

'It is often the way, sir.'

'Deeming himself unworthy.'

'Precisely, sir.'

'Right! But that is not all. Tuck that away in a corner of the mind, Jeeves, and absorb the rest of the facts. Mr Sipperley, as you are aware, is the editor of a weekly paper devoted to the interests of the lighter Society. And now the head master of his old school has started calling at the office and unloading on him junk entirely unsuited to the lighter Society. All clear?'

'I follow you perfectly, sir.'

'And this drip Mr Sipperley is compelled to publish, much against his own wishes, purely because he lacks the nerve to tell the man to go to blazes. The whole trouble being, Jeeves, that he has got one of those things that fellows do get—it's on the tip of my tongue.'

'An inferiority complex, sir?'

'Exactly. An inferiority complex. I have one myself with regard to my Aunt Agatha. You know me, Jeeves. You know that if it were a question of volunteers to man the lifeboat, I would spring to the task. If anyone said, "Don't go down the coal-mine, daddy," it would have not the slightest effect on my resolution—'

'Undoubtedly, sir.'

'And yet—and this is where I want you to follow me very closely, Jeeves—when I hear that my Aunt Agatha is out with her hatchet and moving in my direction, I run like a rabbit. Why? Because she gives me an inferiority complex. And so it is with Mr Sipperley. He would, if called upon, mount the deadly breach, and do it without a tremor; but he cannot bring himself to propose to Miss Moon, and he cannot kick his old head master in the stomach and tell him to take his beastly essays on "The Old School Cloisters" elsewhere, because he has an inferiority complex. So what about it, Jeeves?'

'I fear I have no plan which I could advance with any confidence on the spur of the moment, sir.'

'You want time to think, eh?'

'Yes, sir.'

'Take it, Jeeves, take it. You may feel brainier after a night's sleep. What is it Shakespeare calls sleep, Jeeves?'

'Tired Nature's sweet restorer, sir.'

'Exactly. Well, there you are, then.'

… … …

You know, there's nothing like sleeping on a thing. Scarcely had I woken up next morning when I discovered that, while I slept, I had got the whole binge neatly into order and worked out a plan Foch might have been proud of. I rang the bell for Jeeves to bring me my tea.

I rang again. But it must have been five minutes before the man showed up with the steaming.

'I beg your pardon, sir,' he said, when I reproached him. 'I did not hear the bell. I was in the sitting-room, sir.'

'Ah?' I said, sucking down a spot of the mixture. 'Doing this and that, no doubt?'

'Dusting your new vase, sir.'

My heart warmed to the fellow. If there's one person I like, it's the chap who is not too proud to admit it when he's in the wrong. No actual statement to that effect had passed his lips, of course, but we Woosters can read between the lines. I could see that he was learning to love the vase.

'How does it look?'

'Yes, sir.'

A bit cryptic, but I let it go.

'Jeeves,' I said.

'Sir?'

'That matter we were in conference about yestereen.'

'The matter of Mr Sipperley, sir?'

'Precisely. Don't worry yourself any further. Stop the brain working. I shall not require your services. I have found the solution. It came on me like a flash.'

'Indeed, sir?'

'Just like a flash. In a matter of this kind, Jeeves, the first thing to do is to study—what's the word I want?'

'I could not say, sir.'

'Quite a common word—though long.'

'Psychology, sir?'

'The exact noun. It is a noun?'

'Yes, sir.'

'Spoken like a man! Well, Jeeves, direct your attention to the psychology of old Sippy. Mr Sipperley, if you follow me, is in the position of a man from whose eyes the scales have not fallen. The task that faced me, Jeeves, was to discover some scheme which would cause those scales to fall. You get me?'

'Not entirely, sir.'

'Well, what I'm driving at is this. At present this head master bloke, this Waterbury, is tramping all over Mr Sipperley because he is hedged about with dignity, if you understand what I mean. Years have passed; Mr Sipperley now shaves daily and is in an important editorial position; but he can never forget that this bird once gave him six of the juiciest. Result: an inferiority complex. The only way to remove that complex, Jeeves, is to arrange that Mr Sipperley shall see this Waterbury in a thoroughly undignified position. This done, the scales will fall from his eyes. You must see that for yourself, Jeeves. Take your own case. No doubt there are a number of your friends and relations who look up to you and respect you greatly. But suppose one night they were to see you, in an advanced state of intoxication, dancing the Charleston in your underwear in the middle of Piccadilly Circus?'

'The contingency is remote, sir.'

'Ah, but suppose they did. The scales would fall from their eyes, what?'

'Very possibly, sir.'

'Take another case. Do you remember a year or so ago the occasion when my Aunt Agatha accused the maid at that French hotel of pinching her pearls, only to discover that they were still in her drawer?'

'Yes, sir.'

'Whereupon she looked the most priceless ass. You'll admit that.'

'Certainly I have seen Mrs Spenser Gregson appear to greater advantage than at that moment, sir.'

'Exactly. Now follow me like a leopard. Observing my Aunt Agatha in her downfall; watching her turn bright mauve and listening to her being told off in liquid French by a whiskered hotel proprietor without coming back with so much as a single lift of the eyebrows, I felt as if the scales had fallen from my eyes. For the first time in my life, Jeeves, the awe with which this woman had inspired me from childhood's days left me. It came back later, I'll admit; but at the moment I saw my Aunt Agatha for what she was—not, as I had long imagined, a sort of man-eating fish at the very mention of whose name strong men quivered like aspens, but a poor goop who had just dropped a very serious brick. At that moment, Jeeves, I could have told her precisely where she got off; and only a too chivalrous regard for the sex kept me from doing so. You won't dispute that?'

'No, sir.'

'Well, then, my firm conviction is that the scales will fall from Mr Sipperley's eyes when he sees this Waterbury, this old head master, stagger into his office covered from head to foot with flour.'

'Flour, sir?'

'Flour, Jeeves.'

'But why should he pursue such a course, sir?'

'Because he won't be able to help it. The stuff will be balanced on top of the door, and the force of gravity will do the rest. I propose to set a booby-trap for this Waterbury, Jeeves.'

'Really, sir, I would scarcely advocate—'

I raised my hand.

'Peace, Jeeves! There is more to come. You have not forgotten that Mr Sipperley loves Miss Gwendolen Moon, but fears to speak. I bet you'd forgotten that.'

'No, sir.'

'Well, then, my belief is that, once he finds he has lost his awe of this Waterbury, he will be so supremely braced that there will be no holding him. He will rush right off and bung his heart at her feet, Jeeves.'

'Well, sir—'

'Jeeves,' I said, a little severely, 'whenever I suggest a plan or scheme or course of action, you are too apt to say "Well, sir," in a nasty tone of voice. I do not like it, and it is a habit you should check. The plan or scheme or course of action which I have outlined contains no flaw. If it does, I should like to hear it.'

'Well, sir—'

'Jeeves!'

'I beg your pardon, sir. I was about to remark that, in my opinion, you are approaching Mr Sipperley's problems in the wrong order.'

'How do you mean; the wrong order?'

'Well, I fancy sir, that better results would be obtained by first inducing

Mr Sipperley to offer marriage to Miss Moon. In the event of the young lady proving agreeable, I think that Mr Sipperley would be in such an elevated frame of mind that he would have no difficulty in asserting himself with Mr Waterbury.'

'Ah, but you are then stymied by the question—How is he to be induced?'

'It had occurred to me, sir, that, as Miss Moon is a poetess and of a romantic nature, it might have weight with her if she heard that Mr Sipperley had met with a serious injury and was mentioning her name.'

'Calling for her brokenly, you mean?'

'Calling for her, as you say, sir, brokenly.'

I sat up in bed, and pointed at him rather coldly with the teaspoon.

'Jeeves,' I said, 'I would be the last man to accuse you of dithering, but this is not like you. It is not the old form, Jeeves. You are losing your grip. It might be years before Mr Sipperley had a serious injury.'

'There is that to be considered, sir.'

'I cannot believe that it is you, Jeeves, who are meekly suggesting that we should suspend all activities in this matter year after year, on the chance that some day Mr Sipperley may fall under a truck or something. No! The programme will be as I have sketched it out, Jeeves. After breakfast, kindly step out, and purchase about a pound and a half of the best flour. The rest you may leave to me.'

'Very good, sir.'

The first thing you need in matters of this kind, as every general knows, is a thorough knowledge of the terrain. Not know the terrain, and where are you? Look at Napoleon and that sunken road at Waterloo. Silly ass!

I had a thorough knowledge of the terrain of Sippy's office, and it ran as follows. I won't draw a plan, because my experience is that, when you're reading one of those detective stories and come to the bit where the author draws a plan of the Manor, showing room where body was found, stairs leading to passageway, and all the rest of it, one just skips. I'll simply explain in a few brief words.

The offices of *The Mayfair Gazette* were on the first floor of a mouldy old building off Covent Garden. You went in at a front door and ahead of you was a passage leading to the premises of Bellamy Bros, dealers in seeds and garden produce. Ignoring the Bros Bellamy, you proceeded upstairs and found two doors opposite you. One, marked Private, opened into Sippy's editorial sanctum. The other—sub-title: Inquiries—shot you into a small room where an office-boy sat, eating peppermints and reading the adventures of Tarzan. If you got past the office-boy, you went through another door and there you were in Sippy's room, just as if you had nipped through the door marked Private. Perfectly simple.

It was over the door marked Inquiries that I proposed to suspend the flour.

Now, setting a booby-trap for a respectable citizen like a head master (even of an inferior school to your own) is not a matter to be approached lightly and without careful preparation. I don't suppose I've ever selected a lunch with more thought than I did that day. And after a nicely-balanced meal, preceded by a couple of dry Martinis, washed down with half a bot. of a nice light, dry champagne, and followed by a spot of brandy, I could have set a booby-trap for a bishop.

The only really difficult part of the campaign was to get rid of the office-boy; for naturally you don't want witnesses when you're shoving bags of flour on doors. Fortunately, every man has his price, and it wasn't long before I contrived to persuade the lad that there was sickness at home and he was needed at Cricklewood. This done, I mounted a chair and got to work.

It was many, many years since I had tackled this kind of job, but the old skill came back as good as ever. Having got the bag so nicely poised that a touch on the door would do all that was necessary, I skipped down from my chair, popped off through Sippy's room, and went into the street. Sippy had not shown up yet, which was all to the good, but I knew he usually trickled in at about five to three. I hung about in the street, and presently round the corner came the bloke Waterbury. He went in at the front door, and I started off for a short stroll. It was no part of my policy to be in the offing when things began to happen.

It seemed to me that, allowing for wind and weather, the scales should have fallen from old Sippy's eyes by about three-fifteen, Greenwich mean time; so, having prowled around Covent Garden among the spuds and cabbages for twenty minutes or so, I retraced my steps and pushed up the stairs. I went in at the door marked Private, fully expecting to see old Sippy, and conceive of my astonishment and chagrin when I found on entering only the bloke Waterbury. He was seated at Sippy's desk, reading a paper, as if the place belonged to him.

And, moreover, there was of flour on his person not a trace.

'Great Scott!' I said.

It was a case of the sunken road, after all. But, dash it, how could I have been expected to take into consideration the possibility that this cove, head master though he was, would have had the cold nerve to walk into Sippy's private office instead of pushing in a normal and orderly manner through the public door?

He raised the nose, and focused me over it.

'Yes?'

'I was looking for old Sippy.'

'Mr Sipperley has not yet arrived.'

He spoke with a good deal of pique, seeming to be a man who was not used to being kept waiting.

'Well, how is everything?' I said, to ease things along.

He started reading again. He looked up as if he found me pretty superfluous.

'I beg your pardon?'

'Oh, nothing.'

'You spoke.'

'I only said "How is everything?" don't you know.'

'How is what?'

'Everything.'

'I fail to understand you.'

'Let it go,' I said.

I found a certain difficulty in boosting along the chit-chat. He was not a responsive cove.

'Nice day,' I said.

'Quite.'

'But they say the crops need rain.'

He had buried himself in his paper once more, and seemed peeved this time on being lugged to the surface.

'What?'

'The crops.'

'The crops?'

'Crops.'

'What crops?'

'Oh, just crops.'

He laid down his paper.

'You appear to be desirous of giving me some information about crops. What is it?'

'I hear they need rain.'

'Indeed?'

That concluded the small-talk. He went on reading, and I found a chair and sat down and sucked the handle of my stick. And so the long day wore on.

It may have been some two hours later, or it may have been about five minutes, when there became audible in the passage outside a strange wailing sound, as of some creature in pain. The bloke Waterbury looked up. I looked up.

The wailing came closer. It came into the room. It was Sippy, singing.

'—I love you. That's all that I can say. I love you, I lo-o-ve you. The same old—'

He suspended the chant, not too soon for me.

'Oh, hullo!' he said.

I was amazed. The last time I had seen old Sippy, you must remember, he had had all the appearance of a man who didn't know it was loaded. Haggard. Drawn face. Circles under the eyes. All that sort of thing. And now, not much more than twenty-four hours later, he was simply radiant. His eyes sparkled. His mobile lips were curved in a happy smile. He looked as if he had been taking as much as will cover a sixpence every morning before breakfast for years.

'Hullo, Bertie!' he said. 'Hullo, Waterbury old man! Sorry I'm late.'

The bloke Waterbury seemed by no means pleased at this cordial form of address. He froze visibly.

'You are exceedingly late. I may mention that I have been waiting for upwards of half an hour, and my time is not without its value.'

'Sorry, sorry, sorry, sorry, sorry,' said Sippy, jovially. 'You wanted to see me about that article on the Elizabethan dramatists you left here yesterday, didn't you? Well, I've read it, and I'm sorry to say, Waterbury, my dear chap, that it's N.G.'

'I beg your pardon?'

'No earthly use to us. Quite the wrong sort of stuff. This paper is supposed to be all light Society interest. What the *débutante* will wear for Goodwood, you know, and I saw Lady Betty Bootle in the Park yesterday—she is, of course, the sister-in-law of the Duchess of Peebles, "Cuckoo" to her intimates—all that kind of rot. My readers don't want stuff about Elizabethan dramatists.'

'Sipperley—!'

Old Sippy reached out and patted him in a paternal manner on the back.

'Now listen, Waterbury,' he said, kindly. 'You know as well as I do that I hate to turn down an old pal. But I have my duty to the paper. Still, don't be discouraged. Keep trying, and you'll do fine. There is a lot of promise in your stuff, but you want to study your market. Keep your eyes open and see what editors need. Now, just as a suggestion, why not have a dash at a light, breezy article on pet dogs. You've probably noticed that the pug, once so fashionable, has been superseded by the Peke, the griffon, and the Sealyham. Work on that line and—'

The bloke Waterbury navigated towards the door.

'I have no desire to work on that line, as you put it,' he said, stiffly. 'If you do not require my paper on the Elizabethan dramatists I shall no doubt be able to find another editor whose tastes are more in accord with my work.'

'The right spirit absolutely, Waterbury,' said Sippy, cordially. 'Never give in. Perseverance brings home the gravy. If you get an article accepted, send another article to that editor. If you get an article refused, send that article to another editor. Carry on, Waterbury. I shall watch your future progress with considerable interest.'

'Thank you,' said the bloke Waterbury, bitterly. 'This expert advice should prove most useful.'

He biffed off, banging the door behind him, and I turned to Sippy, who was swerving about the room like an exuberant snipe.

'Sippy—'

'Eh? What? Can't stop, Bertie, can't stop. Only looked in to tell you the news. I'm taking Gwendolen to tea at the Carlton. I'm the happiest man in the world, Bertie. Engaged, you know. Betrothed. All washed up and signed on the dotted line. Wedding, June the first, at eleven a.m. sharp, at St Peter's, Eaton Square. Presents should be delivered before the end of May.'

'But, Sippy! Come to roost for a second. How did this happen? I thought—'

'Well, it's a long story. Much too long to tell you now. Ask Jeeves. He came along with me, and is waiting outside. But when I found her bending over me, weeping, I knew that a word from me was all that was needed. I took her little hand in mine and—'

'What do you mean, bending over you? Where?'

'In your sitting-room.'

'Why?'

'Why what?'

'Why was she bending over you?'

'Because I was on the floor, ass. Naturally a girl would bend over a fellow who was on the floor. Good-bye, Bertie. I must rush.'

He was out of the room before I knew he had started. I followed at a high rate of speed, but he was down the stairs before I reached the passage. I legged it after him, but when I got into the street it was empty.

No, not absolutely empty. Jeeves was standing on the pavement, gazing dreamily at a brussels sprout which lay in the fairway.

'Mr Sipperley has this moment gone, sir,' he said, as I came charging out.

I halted and mopped the brow.

'Jeeves,' I said, 'what has been happening?'

'As far as Mr Sipperley's romance is concerned, sir, all, I am happy to report, is well. He and Miss Moon have arrived at a satisfactory settlement.'

'I know. They're engaged. But how did it happen?'

'I took the liberty of telephoning to Mr Sipperley in your name, asking him to come immediately to the flat, sir.'

'Oh, that's how he came to be at the flat? Well?'

'I then took the liberty of telephoning to Miss Moon and informing her that Mr Sipperley had met with a nasty accident. As I anticipated, the young lady was strongly moved and announced her intention of coming to see Mr Sipperley immediately. When she arrived, it required only a few moments to arrange the matter. It seems that Miss Moon has long loved Mr Sipperley, sir, and—'

'I should have thought that, when she turned up and found he hadn't had a nasty accident, she would have been thoroughly pipped at being fooled.'

'Mr Sipperley had had a nasty accident, sir.'

'He had?'

'Yes, sir.'

'Rummy coincidence. I mean, after what you were saying this morning.'

'Not altogether, sir. Before telephoning to Miss Moon, I took the further liberty of striking Mr Sipperley a sharp blow on the head with one of your golf-clubs, which was fortunately lying in a corner of the room. The putter, I believe, sir. If you recollect, you were practicing with it this morning before you left.'

I gaped at the blighter. I had always known Jeeves for a man of infinite sagacity, sound beyond belief on any question of ties or spats; but never before had I suspected him capable of strong-arm work like this. It seemed to open up an entirely new aspect of the fellow. I can't put it better than by saying that, as I gazed at him, the scales seemed to fall from my eyes.

'Good heavens, Jeeves!'

'I did it with the utmost regret, sir. It appeared to me the only course.'

'But look here, Jeeves. I don't get this. Wasn't Mr Sipperley pretty shirty when he came to and found that you had been soaking him with putters?'

'He was not aware that I had done so, sir. I took the precaution of waiting until his back was momentarily turned.'

'But how did you explain the bump on his head?'

'I informed him that your new vase had fallen on him, sir.'

'Why on earth would he believe that? The vase would have been smashed.'

'The vase was smashed, sir.'

'What!'

'In order to achieve verisimilitude, I was reluctantly compelled to break it, sir. And in my excitement, sir, I am sorry to say I broke it beyond repair.'

I drew myself up.

'Jeeves!' I said.

'Pardon me, sir, but would it not be wiser to wear a hat? There is a keen wind.'

I blinked.

'Aren't I wearing a hat?'

'No, sir.'

I put up a hand and felt the lemon. He was perfectly right.

'Nor I am! I must have left it in Sippy's office. Wait here, Jeeves, while I fetch it.'

'Very good, sir.'

'I have much to say to you.'

'Thank you, sir.'

I galloped up the stairs and dashed in at the door. And something squashy fell on my neck, and the next minute the whole world was a solid mass of flour. In the agitation of the moment I had gone in at the wrong door; and what it all boils down to is that, if any more of my pals get inferiority complexes, they can jolly well get rid of them for themselves. Bertram is through.

3

JEEVES AND THE YULE-TIDE SPIRIT

The letter arrived on the morning of the sixteenth. I was pushing a bit of breakfast into the Wooster face at the moment and, feeling fairly well-fortified with coffee and kippers, I decided to break the news to Jeeves without delay. As Shakespeare says, if you're going to do a thing you might just as well pop right at it and get it over. The man would be disappointed, of course, and possibly even chagrined: but, dash it all, a splash of disappointment here and there does a fellow good. Makes him realize that life is stern and life is earnest.

'Oh, Jeeves,' I said.

'Sir?'

'We have here a communication from Lady Wickham. She has written inviting me to Skeldings for the festives. So you will see about bunging the necessaries together. We repair thither on the twenty-third. Plenty of white ties, Jeeves, also a few hearty country suits for use in the daytime. We shall be there some little time, I expect.'

There was a pause. I could feel he was directing a frosty gaze at me, but I dug into the marmalade and refused to meet it.

'I thought I understood you to say, sir, that you proposed to visit Monte Carlo immediately after Christmas.'

'I know. But that's all off. Plans changed.'

'Very good, sir.'

At this point the telephone bell rang, tiding over very nicely what had threatened to be an awkward moment. Jeeves unhooked the receiver.

'Yes? . . . Yes, madam . . . Very good, madam. Here is Mr Wooster.' He handed me the instrument. 'Mrs Spenser Gregson, sir.'

You know, every now and then I can't help feeling that Jeeves is losing his grip. In his prime it would have been with him the work of a moment to have told Aunt Agatha that I was not at home. I gave him one of those reproachful glances, and took the machine.

'Hullo?' I said. 'Yes? Hullo? Hullo? Bertie speaking. Hullo? Hullo? Hullo?'

'Don't keep on saying Hullo,' yipped the old relative in her customary curt manner. 'You're not a parrot. Sometimes I wish you were, because then you might have a little sense.'

Quite the wrong sort of tone to adopt towards a fellow in the early morning, of course, but what can one do?

'Bertie, Lady Wickham tells me she has invited you to Skeldings for Christmas. Are you going?'

'Rather!'

'Well, mind you behave yourself. Lady Wickham is an old friend of mine.'

I was in no mood for this sort of thing over the telephone. Face to face, I'm not saying, but at the end of a wire, no.

'I shall naturally endeavour, Aunt Agatha,' I replied stiffly, 'to conduct myself in a manner befitting an English gentleman paying a visit—'

'What did you say? Speak up. I can't hear.'

'I said Right-ho.'

'Oh? Well, mind you do. And there's another reason why I particularly wish you to be as little of an imbecile as you can manage while at Skeldings. Sir Roderick Glossop will be there.'

'What!'

'Don't bellow like that. You nearly deafened me.'

'Did you say Sir Roderick Glossop?'

'I did.'

'You don't mean Tuppy Glossop?'

'I mean Sir Roderick Glossop. Which was my reason for saying Sir Roderick Glossop. Now, Bertie, I want you to listen to me attentively. Are you there?'

'Yes. Still here.'

'Well, then, listen. I have at last succeeded, after incredible difficulty, and in face of all the evidence, in almost persuading Sir Roderick that you are not actually insane. He is prepared to suspend judgement until he has seen you once more. On your behaviour at Skeldings, therefore—'

But I had hung up the receiver. Shaken. That's what I was. S. to the core.

Stop me if I've told you this before: but, in case you don't know, let me just mention the facts in the matter of this Glossop. He was a formidable old bird with a bald head and out-size eyebrows, by profession a loony-doctor. How it happened, I couldn't tell you to this day, but I once got engaged to his daughter, Honoria, a ghastly dynamic exhibit who read Nietzsche and had a laugh like waves breaking on a stern and rock-bound coast. The fixture was scratched owing to events occurring which convinced the old boy that I was off my napper; and since then he has always had my name at the top of his list of 'Loonies I have Lunched With'.

It seemed to me that even at Christmas time, with all the peace on earth and goodwill towards men that there is knocking about at that season, a reunion with this bloke was likely to be tough going. If I hadn't had more than one particularly good reason for wanting to go to Skeldings, I'd have called the thing off.

'Jeeves,' I said, all of a twitter, 'do you know what? Sir Roderick Glossop is going to be at Lady Wickham's.'

'Very good, sir. If you have finished breakfast, I will clear away.'

Cold and haughty. No symp. None of the rallying-round spirit which one likes to see. As I had anticipated, the information that we were not going to Monte Carlo had got in amongst him. There is a keen sporting streak in Jeeves, and I knew he had been looking forward to a little flutter at the tables.

We Woosters can wear the mask. I ignored his lack of decent feeling.

'Do so, Jeeves,' I said proudly, 'and with all convenient speed.'

... ...

Relations continued pretty fairly strained all through the rest of the week. There was a frigid detachment in the way the man brought me my dollop of tea in the mornings. Going down to Skeldings in the car on the afternoon of the twenty-third, he was aloof and reserved. And before dinner on the first night of my visit he put the studs in my dress-shirt in what I can only call a marked manner. The whole thing was extremely painful, and it seemed to me, as I lay in bed on the morning of the twenty-fourth, that the only step to take was to put the whole facts of the case before him and trust to his native good sense to effect an understanding.

I was feeling considerably in the pink that morning. Everything had gone like a breeze. My hostess, Lady Wickham, was a beaky female built far too closely on the lines of my Aunt Agatha for comfort, but she had seemed matey enough on my arrival. Her daughter, Roberta, had welcomed me with a warmth which, I'm bound to say, had set the old heart-strings fluttering a bit. And Sir Roderick, in the brief moment we had had together, appeared to have let the Yule Tide Spirit soak into him to the most amazing extent. When he saw me, his mouth sort of flickered at one corner, which I took to be his idea of smiling, and he said 'Ha, young man!' Not particularly chummily, but he said it: and my view was that it practically amounted to the lion lying down with the lamb.

So, all in all, life at this juncture seemed pretty well all to the mustard, and I decided to tell Jeeves exactly how matters stood.

'Jeeves,' I said, as he appeared with the steaming.

'Sir?'

'Touching on this business of our being here, I would like to say a few words of explanation. I consider that you have a right to the facts.'

'Sir?'

'I'm afraid scratching that Monte Carlo trip has been a bit of a jar for you, Jeeves.'

'Not at all, sir.'

'Oh, yes, it has. The heart was set on wintering in the world's good old Plague Spot, I know. I saw your eye light up when I said we were due for a visit there. You snorted a bit and your fingers twitched. I know, I know.

And now that there has been a change of programme the iron has entered into your soul.'

'Not at all, sir.'

'Oh, yes, it has. I've seen it. Very well, then, what I wish to impress upon you, Jeeves, is that I have not been actuated in this matter by any mere idle whim. It was through no light and airy caprice that I accepted this invitation to Lady Wickham's. I have been angling for it for weeks, prompted by many considerations. In the first place, does one get the Yule-tide spirit at a spot like Monte Carlo?'

'Does one desire the Yule-tide spirit, sir?'

'Certainly one does. I am all for it. Well, that's one thing. Now here's another. It was imperative that I should come to Skeldings for Christmas, Jeeves, because I knew that young Tuppy Glossop was going to be here.'

'Sir Roderick Glossop, sir?'

'His nephew. You may have observed hanging about the place a fellow with light hair and a Cheshire-cat grin. That is Tuppy, and I have been anxious for some time to get to grips with him. I have it in for that man of wrath. Listen to the facts, Jeeves, and tell me if I am not justified in planning a hideous vengeance.' I took a sip of tea, for the mere memory of my wrongs had shaken me. 'In spite of the fact that young Tuppy is the nephew of Sir Roderick Glossop, at whose hands, Jeeves, as you are aware, I have suffered much, I fraternized with him freely, both at the Drones Club and elsewhere. I said to myself that a man is not to be blamed for his relations, and that I would hate to have my pals hold my Aunt Agatha, for instance, against me. Broad-minded, Jeeves, I think?'

'Extremely, sir.'

'Well, then, as I say, I sought this Tuppy out, Jeeves, and hobnobbed, and what do you think he did?'

'I could not say, sir.'

'I will tell you. One night after dinner at the Drones he betted me I wouldn't swing myself across the swimming-bath by the ropes and rings. I took him on and was buzzing along in great style until I came to the last ring. And then I found that this fiend in human shape had looped it back against the rail, thus leaving me hanging in the void with no means of getting ashore to my home and loved ones. There was nothing for it but to drop into the water. He told me that he had often caught fellows that way:

and what I maintain, Jeeves, is that, if I can't get back at him somehow at Skeldings—with all the vast resources which a country-house affords at my disposal—I am not the man I was.'

'I see, sir.'

There was still something in his manner which told me that even now he lacked complete sympathy and understanding, so, delicate though the subject was, I decided to put all my cards on the table.

'And now, Jeeves, we come to the most important reason why I had to spend Christmas at Skeldings. Jeeves,' I said, diving into the old cup once more for a moment and bringing myself out wreathed in blushes, 'the fact of the matter is, I'm in love.'

'Indeed, sir?'

'You've seen Miss Roberta Wickham?'

'Yes, sir.'

'Very well, then.'

There was a pause, while I let it sink in.

'During your stay here, Jeeves,' I said, 'you will, no doubt, be thrown a good deal together with Miss Wickham's maid. On such occasions, pitch it strong.'

'Sir?'

'You know what I mean. Tell her I'm rather a good chap. Mention my hidden depths. These things get round. Dwell on the fact that I have a kind heart and was runner-up in the Squash Handicap at the Drones this year. A boost is never wasted, Jeeves.'

'Very good, sir. But—'

'But what?'

'Well, sir—'

'I wish you wouldn't say "Well, sir" in that soupy tone of voice. I have had to speak of this before. The habit is one that is growing upon you. Check it. What's on your mind?'

'I hardly like to take the liberty—'

'Carry on, Jeeves. We are always glad to hear from you, always.'

'What I was about to remark, if you will excuse me, sir, was that I would scarcely have thought Miss Wickham a suitable—'

'Jeeves,' I said coldly, 'if you have anything to say against that lady, it had better not be said in my presence.'

'Very good, sir.'

'Or anywhere else, for that matter. What is your kick against Miss Wickham?'

'Oh, really, sir!'

'Jeeves, I insist. This is a time for plain speaking. You have beefed about Miss Wickham. I wish to know why.'

'It merely crossed my mind, sir, that for a gentleman of your description Miss Wickham is not a suitable mate.'

'What do you mean by a gentleman of my description?'

'Well, sir—'

'Jeeves!'

'I beg your pardon, sir. The expression escaped me inadvertently. I was about to observe that I can only asseverate—'

'Only what?'

'I can only say that, as you have invited my opinion—'

'But I didn't.'

'I was under the impression that you desired to canvass my views on the matter, sir.'

'Oh? Well, let's have them, anyway.'

'Very good, sir. Then briefly, if I may say so, sir, though Miss Wickham is a charming young lady—'

'There, Jeeves, you spoke an imperial quart. What eyes!'

'Yes, sir.'

'What hair!'

'Very true, sir.'

'And what *espièglerie*, if that's the word I want.'

'The exact word, sir.'

'All right, then. Carry on.'

'I grant Miss Wickham the possession of all these desirable qualities, sir. Nevertheless, considered as a matrimonial prospect for a gentleman of your description, I cannot look upon her as suitable. In my opinion Miss Wickham lacks seriousness, sir. She is too volatile and frivolous. To qualify as Miss Wickham's husband, a gentleman would need to possess a commanding personality and considerable strength of character.'

'Exactly!'

'I would always hesitate to recommend as a life's companion a young lady with quite such a vivid shade of red hair. Red hair, sir, in my opinion, is dangerous.'

I eyed the blighter squarely.

'Jeeves,' I said, 'you're talking rot.'

'Very good, sir.'

'Absolute drivel.'

'Very good, sir.'

'Pure mashed potatoes.'

'Very good, sir.'

'Very good, sir—I mean very good Jeeves, that will be all,' I said.

And I drank a modicum of tea, with a good deal of hauteur.

It isn't often that I find myself able to prove Jeeves in the wrong, but by dinner-time that night I was in a position to do so, and I did it without delay.

'Touching on that matter we were touching on, Jeeves,' I said, coming in from the bath and tackling him as he studied the shirt, 'I should be glad if you would give me your careful attention for a moment. I warn you that what I am about to say is going to make you look pretty silly.'

'Indeed, sir?'

'Yes, Jeeves. Pretty dashed silly it's going to make you look. It may lead you to be rather more careful in future about broadcasting these estimates of yours of people's characters. This morning, if I remember rightly, you stated that Miss Wickham was volatile, frivolous and lacking in seriousness. Am I correct?'

'Quite correct, sir.'

'Then what I have to tell you may cause you to alter that opinion. I went for a walk with Miss Wickham this afternoon: and, as we walked, I told her about what young Tuppy Glossop did to me in the swimming-bath at the Drones. She hung upon my words, Jeeves, and was full of sympathy.'

'Indeed, sir?'

'Dripping with it. And that's not all. Almost before I had finished, she was suggesting the ripest, fruitiest, brainiest scheme for bringing young Tuppy's grey hairs in sorrow to the grave that anyone could possibly imagine.'

'That is very gratifying, sir.'

'Gratifying is the word. It appears that at the girls' school where Miss Wickham was educated, Jeeves, it used to become necessary from time to time for the right-thinking element of the community to slip it across certain of the baser sort. Do you know what they did, Jeeves?'

'No, sir.'

'They took a long stick, Jeeves, and—follow me closely here—they tied a darning-needle to the end of it. Then at dead of night, it appears, they sneaked privily into the party of the second part's cubicle and shoved the needle through the bedclothes and punctured her hot-water bottle. Girls are much subtler in these matters than boys, Jeeves. At my old school one would occasionally heave a jug of water over another bloke during the night-watches, but we never thought of effecting the same result in this particularly neat and scientific manner. Well, Jeeves, that was the scheme which Miss Wickham suggested I should work on young Tuppy, and that is the girl you call frivolous and lacking in seriousness. Any girl who can think up a wheeze like that is my idea of a helpmeet. I shall be glad, Jeeves, if by the time I come to bed to-night you have waiting for me in this room a stout stick with a good sharp darning needle attached.'

'Well, sir—'

I raised my hand.

'Jeeves,' I said. 'Not another word. Stick, one, and needle, darning, good, sharp, one, without fail in this room at eleven-thirty to-night.'

'Very good, sir.'

'Have you any idea where young Tuppy sleeps?'

'I could ascertain, sir.'

'Do so, Jeeves.'

In a few minutes he was back with the necessary informash.

'Mr Glossop is established in the Moat Room, sir.'

'Where's that?'

'The second door on the floor below this, sir.'

'Right ho, Jeeves. Are the studs in my shirt?'

'Yes, sir.'

'And the links also?'

'Yes, sir.'

'Then push me into it.'

... ...

The more I thought about this enterprise which a sense of duty and good citizenship had thrust upon me, the better it seemed to me. I am not a vindictive man, but I felt, as anybody would have felt in my place, that if fellows like young Tuppy are allowed to get away with it the whole fabric of Society and Civilization must inevitably crumble. The task to which I had set myself was one that involved hardship and discomfort, for it meant sitting up till well into the small hours and then padding down a cold corridor, but I did not shrink from it. After all, there is a lot to be said for family tradition. We Woosters did our bit in the Crusades.

It being Christmas Eve, there was, as I had foreseen, a good deal of revelry and what not. First, the village choir surged round and sang carols outside the front door, and then somebody suggested a dance, and after that we hung around chatting of this and that, so that it wasn't till past one that I got to my room. Allowing for everything, it didn't seem that it was going to be safe to start my little expedition till half-past two at the earliest: and I'm bound to say that it was only the utmost resolution that kept me from snuggling into the sheets and calling it a day. I'm not much of a lad now for late hours.

However, by half-past two everything appeared to be quiet. I shook off the mists of sleep, grabbed the good old stick-and-needle and toddled off along the corridor. And presently, pausing outside the Moat Room, I turned the handle, found the door wasn't locked, and went in.

I suppose a burglar—I mean a real professional who works at the job six nights a week all the year round—gets so that finding himself standing in the dark in somebody else's bedroom means absolutely nothing to him. But for a bird like me, who has had no previous experience, there's a lot to be said in favour of washing the whole thing out and closing the door gently and popping back to bed again. It was only by summoning up all the old bull-dog courage of the Woosters, and reminding myself that, if I let this opportunity slip another might never occur, that I managed to stick out what you might call the initial minute of the binge. Then the weakness passed, and Bertram was himself again.

At first when I beetled in, the room had seemed as black as a coal-cellar: but after a bit things began to lighten. The curtains weren't quite drawn over the window and I could see a trifle of the scenery here and there. The bed was opposite the window, with the head against the wall and the end where the feet were jutting out towards where I stood, thus rendering it possible after one had sown the seed, so to speak, to make a quick getaway. There only remained now the rather tricky problem of locating the old hot-water bottle. I mean to say, the one thing you can't do if you want to carry a job like this through with secrecy and dispatch is to stand at the end of a fellow's bed, jabbing the blankets at random with a darning-needle. Before proceeding to anything in the nature of definite steps, it is imperative that you locate the bot.

I was a good deal cheered at this juncture to hear a fruity snore from the direction of the pillows. Reason told me that a bloke who could snore like that wasn't going to be awakened by a trifle. I edged forward and ran a hand in a gingerly sort of way over the coverlet. A moment later I had found the bulge. I steered the good old darning-needle on to it, gripped the stick, and shoved. Then, pulling out the weapon, I sidled towards the door, and in another moment would have been outside, buzzing for home and the good night's rest, when suddenly there was a crash that sent my spine shooting up through the top of my head and the contents of the bed sat up like a jack-in-the-box and said:

'Who's that?'

It just shows how your most careful strategic moves can be the very ones that dish your campaign. In order to facilitate the orderly retreat according to plan I had left the door open, and the beastly thing had slammed like a bomb.

But I wasn't giving much thought to the causes of the explosion, having other things to occupy my mind. What was disturbing me was the discovery that, whoever else the bloke in the bed might be, he was not young Tuppy. Tuppy has one of those high, squeaky voices that sound like the tenor of the village choir failing to hit a high note. This one was something in between the last Trump and a tiger calling for breakfast after being on a diet for a day or two. It was the sort of nasty, rasping voice you hear shouting 'Fore!' when you're one of a slow foursome on the links and are holding up a couple of retired colonels. Among the qualities it lacked were kindliness, suavity and that sort of dove-like cooing note which makes a fellow feel he has found a friend.

I did not linger. Getting swiftly off the mark, I dived for the door-handle and was off and away, banging the door behind me. I may be a chump in many ways, as my Aunt Agatha will freely attest, but I know when and when not to be among those present.

And I was just about to do the stretch of corridor leading to the stairs in a split second under the record time for the course, when something brought me up with a sudden jerk. One moment, I was all dash and fire and speed; the next, an irresistible force had checked me in my stride and was holding me straining at the leash, as it were.

You know, sometimes it seems to me as if Fate were going out of its way to such an extent to snooter you that you wonder if it's worth while continuing to struggle. The night being a trifle chillier than the dickens, I had donned for this expedition a dressing-gown. It was the tail of this infernal garment that had caught in the door and pipped me at the eleventh hour.

The next moment the door had opened, light was streaming through it, and the bloke with the voice had grabbed me by the arm.

It was Sir Roderick Glossop.

The next thing that happened was a bit of a lull in the proceedings. For about three and a quarter seconds or possibly more we just stood there, drinking each other in, so to speak, the old boy still attached with a limpet-like grip to my elbow. If I hadn't been in a dressing-gown and he in pink pyjamas with a blue stripe, and if he hadn't been glaring quite so much as if he were shortly going to commit a murder, the tableau would have looked rather like one of those advertisements you see in the magazines, where the experienced elder is patting the young man's arm, and saying to him, 'My boy, if you subscribe to the Mutt-Jeff Correspondence School of Oswego, Kan., as I did, you may some day, like me, become Third Assistant Vice-President of the Schenectady Consolidated Nail-File and Eyebrow Tweezer Corporation.'

'You!' said Sir Roderick finally. And in this connection I want to state that it's all rot to say you can't hiss a word that hasn't an 's' in it. The way he pushed out that 'You!' sounded like an angry cobra, and I am betraying no secrets when I mention that it did me no good whatsoever.

By rights, I suppose, at this point I ought to have said something. The best I could manage, however, was a faint, soft bleating sound. Even on ordinary social occasions, when meeting this bloke as man to man and with a clear conscience, I could never be completely at my ease: and now those eyebrows seemed to pierce me like a knife.

'Come in here,' he said, lugging me into the room. 'We don't want to wake the whole house. Now,' he said, depositing me on the carpet and closing the door and doing a bit of eyebrow work, 'kindly inform me what is this latest manifestation of insanity?'

It seemed to me that a light and cheery laugh might help the thing along. So I had a pop at one.

'Don't gibber!' said my genial host. And I'm bound to admit that the light and cheery hadn't come out quite as I'd intended.

I pulled myself together with a strong effort.

'Awfully sorry about all this,' I said in a hearty sort of voice. 'The fact is, I thought you were Tuppy.'

'Kindly refrain from inflicting your idiotic slang on me. What do you mean by the adjective "tuppy"?'

'It isn't so much an adjective, don't you know. More of a noun, I should think, if you examine it squarely. What I mean to say is, I thought you were your nephew.'

'You thought I was my nephew? Why should I be my nephew?'

'What I'm driving at is, I thought this was his room.'

'My nephew and I changed rooms. I have a great dislike for sleeping on an upper floor. I am nervous about fire.'

For the first time since this interview had started, I braced up a trifle. The injustice of the whole thing stirred me to such an extent that for a moment I lost that sense of being a toad under the harrow which had been cramping my style up till now. I even went so far as to eye this pink-pyjamaed poltroon with a good deal of contempt and loathing. Just because he had this craven fear of fire and this selfish preference for letting Tuppy be cooked instead of himself should the emergency occur, my nicely-reasoned plans had gone up the spout. I gave him a look, and I think I may even have snorted a bit.

'I should have thought that your man-servant would have informed you,' said Sir Roderick, 'that we contemplated making this change. I met him shortly before luncheon and told him to tell you.'

I reeled. Yes, it is not too much to say that I reeled. This extraordinary statement had taken me amidships without any preparation, and it staggered me. That Jeeves had been aware all along that this old crumb would be the occupant of the bed which I was proposing to prod with darning-needles and had let me rush upon my doom without a word of warning was almost beyond belief. You might say I was aghast. Yes, practically aghast.

'You told Jeeves that you were going to sleep in this room?' I gasped.

'I did. I was aware that you and my nephew were on terms of intimacy, and I wished to spare myself the possibility of a visit from you. I confess that it never occurred to me that such a visit was to be anticipated at three o'clock in the morning. What the devil do you mean,' he barked, suddenly hotting up, 'by prowling about the house at this hour? And what is that thing in your hand?'

I looked down, and found that I was still grasping the stick. I give you my honest word that, what with the maelstrom of emotions into which his revelation about Jeeves had cast me, the discovery came as an absolute surprise.

'This?' I said. 'Oh, yes.'

'What do you mean, "Oh, yes"? What is it?'

'Well, it's a long story—'

'We have the night before us.'

'It's this way. I will ask you to picture me some weeks ago, perfectly peaceful and inoffensive, after dinner at the Drones, smoking a thoughtful cigarette and—'

I broke off. The man wasn't listening. He was goggling in a rapt sort of way at the end of the bed, from which there had now begun to drip on to the carpet a series of drops.

'Good heavens!'

'—thoughtful cigarette and chatting pleasantly of this and that—'

I broke off again. He had lifted the sheets and was gazing at the corpse of the hot-water bottle.

'Did you do this?' he said in a low, strangled sort of voice.

'Er—yes. As a matter of fact, yes. I was just going to tell you—'

'And your aunt tried to persuade me that you were not insane!'

'I'm not. Absolutely not. If you'll just let me explain.'

'I will do nothing of the kind.'

'It all began—'

'Silence!'

'Right-ho.'

He did some deep-breathing exercises through the nose.

'My bed is drenched!'

'The way it all began—'

'Be quiet!' He heaved somewhat for awhile. 'You wretched, miserable idiot,' he said, 'kindly inform me which bedroom you are supposed to be occupying?'

'It's on the floor above. The Clock Room.'

'Thank you. I will find it.'

He gave me the eyebrow.

'I propose,' he said, 'to pass the remainder of the night in your room, where, I presume, there is a bed in a condition to be slept in. You may bestow yourself as comfortably as you can here. I will wish you good-night.'

He buzzed off, leaving me flat.

Well, we Woosters are old campaigners. We can take the rough with the smooth. But to say that I liked the prospect now before me would be paltering with the truth. One glance at the bed told me that any idea of sleeping there was out. A goldfish could have done it, but not Bertram. After a bit of a look round, I decided that the best chance of getting a sort of night's rest was to doss as well as I could in the arm-chair. I pinched a couple of pillows off the bed, shoved the hearth-rug over my knees, and sat down and started counting sheep.

But it wasn't any good. The old lemon was sizzling much too much to admit of anything in the nature of slumber. This hideous revelation of the blackness of Jeeves's treachery kept coming back to me every time I nearly succeeded in dropping off: and, what's more, it seemed to get colder and colder as the long night wore on. I was just wondering if I would ever get to sleep again in this world when a voice at my elbow said 'Good-morning, sir,' and I sat up with a jerk.

I could have sworn I hadn't so much as dozed off for even a minute, but apparently I had. For the curtains were drawn back and daylight was coming in through the window and there was Jeeves standing beside me with a cup of tea on a tray.

'Merry Christmas, sir!'

I reached out a feeble hand for the restoring brew. I swallowed a mouthful or two, and felt a little better. I was aching in every limb and the dome felt like lead, but I was now able to think with a certain amount of clearness, and I fixed the man with a stony eye and prepared to let him have it.

'You think so, do you?' I said. 'Much, let me tell you, depends on what you mean by the adjective "merry". If, moreover, you suppose that it is going to be merry for you, correct that impression. Jeeves,' I said, taking another half-oz of tea and speaking in a cold, measured voice, 'I wish to ask you one question. Did you or did you not know that Sir Roderick Glossop was sleeping in this room last night?'

'Yes, sir.'

'You admit it!'

'Yes, sir.'

'And you didn't tell me!'

'No, sir. I thought it would be more judicious not to do so.'

'Jeeves—'

'If you will allow me to explain, sir.'

'Explain!'

'I was aware that my silence might lead to something in the nature of an embarrassing contretemps, sir—'

'You thought that, did you?'

'Yes, sir.'

'You were a good guesser,' I said, sucking down further Bohea.

'But it seemed to me, sir, that whatever might occur was all for the best.'

I would have put in a crisp word or two here, but he carried on without giving me the opp.

'I thought that possibly, on reflection, sir, your views being what they are, you would prefer your relations with Sir Roderick Glossop and his family to be distant rather than cordial.'

'My views? What do you mean, my views?'

'As regards a matrimonial alliance with Miss Honoria Glossop, sir.'

Something like an electric shock seemed to zip through me. The man had opened up a new line of thought. I suddenly saw what he was driving at, and realized all in a flash that I had been wronging this faithful fellow. All the while I supposed he had been landing me in the soup, he had really been steering me away from it. It was like those stories one used to read as a kid about the traveller going along on a dark night and his dog grabs him by the leg of his trousers and he says 'Down, sir! What are you doing, Rover?' and the dog hangs on and he gets rather hot under the collar and curses a bit but the dog won't let him go and then suddenly the moon shines through the clouds and he finds he's been standing on the edge of a precipice and one more step would have— well, anyway, you get the idea: and what I'm driving at is that much the same sort of thing seemed to have been happening now.

It's perfectly amazing how a fellow will let himself get off his guard and ignore the perils which surround him. I give you my honest word, it had never struck me till this moment that my Aunt Agatha had been scheming to get me in right with Sir Roderick so that I should eventually be received back into the fold, if you see what I mean, and subsequently pushed off on Honoria.

'My God, Jeeves!' I said, paling.

'Precisely, sir.'

'You think there was a risk?'

'I do, sir. A very grave risk.'

A disturbing thought struck me.

'But, Jeeves, on calm reflection won't Sir Roderick have gathered by now that my objective was young Tuppy and that puncturing his hot-water bottle was just one of those things that occur when the Yule-tide spirit is abroad—one of those things that have to be overlooked and taken with the indulgent smile and the fatherly shake of the head? I mean to say, Young Blood and all that sort of thing? What I mean is he'll realize that I wasn't trying to snooter him, and then all the good work will have been wasted.'

'No, sir. I fancy not. That might possibly have been Sir Roderick's mental reaction, had it not been for the second incident.'

'The second incident?'

'During the night, sir, while Sir Roderick was occupying your bed, somebody entered the room, pierced his hot-water bottle with some sharp instrument, and vanished in the darkness.'

I could make nothing of this.

'What! Do you think I walked in my sleep?'

'No, sir. It was young Mr Glossop who did it. I encountered him this morning, sir, shortly before I came here. He was in cheerful spirits and inquired of me how you were feeling about the incident. Not being aware that his victim had been Sir Roderick.'

'But, Jeeves, what an amazing coincidence!'

'Sir?'

'Why, young Tuppy getting exactly the same idea as I did. Or, rather, as Miss Wickham did. You can't say that's not rummy. A miracle, I call it.'

'Not altogether, sir. It appears that he received the suggestion from the young lady.'

'From Miss Wickham?'

'Yes, sir.'

'You mean to say that, after she had put me up to the scheme of puncturing Tuppy's hot-water bottle, she went away and tipped Tuppy off to puncturing mine?'

'Precisely, sir. She is a young lady with a keen sense of humour, sir.'

I sat there, you might say stunned. When I thought how near I had come to offering the heart and hand to a girl capable of double-crossing a strong man's honest love like that, I shivered.

'Are you cold, sir?'

'No, Jeeves. Just shuddering.'

'The occurrence, if I may take the liberty of saying so, sir, will perhaps lend colour to the view which I put forward yesterday that Miss Wickham, though in many respects a charming young lady—'

I raised the hand.

'Say no more, Jeeves,' I replied. 'Love is dead.'

'Very good, sir.'

I brooded for a while.

'You've seen Sir Roderick this morning, then?'

'Yes, sir.'

'How did he seem?'

'A trifle feverish, sir.'

'Feverish?'

'A little emotional, sir. He expressed a strong desire to meet you, sir.'

'What would you advise?'

'If you were to slip out by the back entrance as soon as you are dressed, sir, it would be possible for you to make your way across the field without being observed and reach the village, where you could hire an automobile to take you to London. I could bring on your effects later in your own car.'

'But London, Jeeves? Is any man safe? My Aunt Agatha is in London.'

'Yes, sir.'

'Well, then?'

He regarded me for a moment with a fathomless eye.

'I think the best plan, sir, would be for you to leave England, which is not pleasant at this time of the year, for some little while. I would not take the liberty of dictating your movements, sir, but as you already have accommodation engaged on the Blue Train for Monte Carlo for the day after to-morrow—'

'But you cancelled the booking?'

'No, sir.'

'I thought you had.'

'No, sir.'

'I told you to.'

'Yes, sir. It was remiss of me, but the matter slipped my mind.'

'Oh?'

'Yes, sir.'

'All right, Jeeves. Monte Carlo ho, then.'

'Very good, sir.'

'It's lucky, as things have turned out, that you forgot to cancel that booking.'

'Very fortunate indeed, sir. If you will wait here, sir, I will return to your room and procure a suit of clothes.'

4

JEEVES AND THE SONG OF SONGS

Another day had dawned all hot and fresh and, in pursuance of my unswerving policy at that time, I was singing 'Sonny Boy' in my bath, when there was a soft step without and Jeeves's voice came filtering through the woodwork.

'I beg your pardon, sir.'

I had just got to that bit about the Angels being lonely, where you need every ounce of concentration in order to make the spectacular finish, but I signed off courteously.

'Yes, Jeeves? Say on.'

'Mr Glossop, sir.'

'What about him?'

'He is in the sitting-room, sir.'

'Young Tuppy Glossop?'

'Yes, sir.'

'In the sitting-room?'

'Yes, sir.'

'Desiring speech with me?'

'Yes, sir.'

'H'm!'

'Sir?'

'I only said H'm.'

And I'll tell you why I said H'm. It was because the man's story had interested me strangely. The news that Tuppy was visiting me at my flat, at an hour when he must have known that I would be in my bath and consequently in a strong strategic position to heave a wet sponge at him, surprised me considerably.

I hopped out with some briskness and, slipping a couple of towels about the limbs and torso, made for the sitting-room. I found young Tuppy at the piano, playing 'Sonny Boy' with one finger.

'What ho!' I said, not without a certain hauteur.

'Oh, hullo, Bertie,' said young Tuppy. 'I say, Bertie, I want to see you about something important.'

It seemed to me that the bloke was embarrassed. He had moved to the mantelpiece, and now he broke a vase in rather a constrained way.

'The fact is, Bertie, I'm engaged.'

'Engaged?'

'Engaged,' said young Tuppy, coyly dropping a photograph frame into the fender. 'Practically, that is.'

'Practically?'

'Yes. You'll like her, Bertie. Her name is Cora Bellinger. She's studying for Opera. Wonderful voice she has. Also dark, flashing eyes and a great soul.'

'How do you mean, practically?'

'Well, it's this way. Before ordering the trousseau, there is one little point she wants cleared up. You see, what with her great soul and all that, she has a rather serious outlook on life: and the one thing she absolutely bars is anything in the shape of hearty humour. You know, practical joking and so forth. She said if she thought I was a practical joker she would never speak to me again. And unfortunately she appears to have heard about that little affair at the Drones—I expect you have forgotten all about that, Bertie?'

'I have not!'

'No, no, not forgotten exactly. What I mean is, nobody laughs more heartily at the recollection than you. And what I want you to do, old man, is to seize an early opportunity of taking Cora aside and categorically denying that there is any truth in the story. My happiness, Bertie, is in your hands, if you know what I mean.'

Well, of course, if he put it like that, what could I do? We Woosters have our code.

'Oh, all right,' I said, but far from brightly.

'Splendid fellow!'

'When do I meet this blighted female?'

'Don't call her "this blighted female", Bertie, old man. I have planned all that out. I will bring her round here to-day for a spot of lunch.'

'What!'

'At one-thirty. Right. Good. Fine. Thanks. I knew I could rely on you.'

He pushed off, and I turned to Jeeves, who had shimmered in with the morning meal.

'Lunch for three to-day, Jeeves,' I said.

'Very good, sir.'

'You know, Jeeves, it's a bit thick. You remember my telling you about what Mr Glossop did to me that night at the Drones?'

'Yes, sir.'

'For months I have been cherishing dreams of getting a bit of my own back. And now, so far from crushing him into the dust, I've got to fill him and fiancée with rich food and generally rally round and be the good angel.'

'Life is like that, sir.'

'True, Jeeves. What have we here?' I asked, inspecting the tray.

'Kippered herrings, sir.'

'And I shouldn't wonder,' I said, for I was in thoughtful mood, 'if even herrings haven't troubles of their own.'

'Quite possibly, sir.'

'I mean, apart from getting kippered.'

'Yes, sir.'

'And so it goes on, Jeeves, so it goes on.'

I can't say I exactly saw eye to eye with young Tuppy in his admiration for the Bellinger female. Delivered on the mat at one-twenty-five, she proved to be an upstanding light-heavy-weight of some thirty summers, with a commanding eye and a square chin which I, personally, would have steered clear of. She seemed to me a good deal like what Cleopatra would have been after going in too freely for the starches and cereals. I don't know why it is, but women who have anything to do with Opera, even if they're only studying for it, always appear to run to surplus poundage.

Tuppy, however, was obviously all for her. His whole demeanour, both before and during lunch, was that of one striving to be worthy of a noble soul. When Jeeves offered him a cocktail, he practically recoiled as from a serpent. It was terrible to see the change which love had effected in the man. The spectacle put me off my food.

At half-past two, the Bellinger left to go to a singing lesson. Tuppy trotted after her to the door, bleating and frisking a goodish bit, and then came back and looked at me in a goofy sort of way.

'Well, Bertie?'

'Well, what?'

'I mean, isn't she?'

'Oh, rather,' I said, humouring the poor fish.

'Wonderful eyes?'

'Oh, rather.'

'Wonderful figure?'

'Oh, quite.'

'Wonderful voice?'

Here I was able to intone the response with a little more heartiness. The Bellinger, at Tuppy's request, had sung us a few songs before digging in at the trough, and nobody could have denied that her pipes were in great shape. Plaster was still falling from the ceiling.

'Terrific,' I said.

Tuppy sighed, and, having helped himself to about four inches of whisky and one of soda, took a deep, refreshing draught.

'Ah!' he said. 'I needed that.'

'Why didn't you have it at lunch?'

'Well, it's this way,' said Tuppy. 'I have not actually ascertained what Cora's opinions are on the subject of the taking of slight snorts from time to time, but I thought it more prudent to lay off. The view I took was that laying off would seem to indicate the serious mind. It is touch-and-go, as you might say, at the moment, and the smallest thing may turn the scale.'

'What beats me is how on earth you expect to make her think you've got a mind at all—let alone a serious one.'

'I have my methods.'

'I bet they're rotten.'

'You do, do you?' said Tuppy warmly. 'Well, let me tell you, my lad, that that's exactly what they're anything but. I am handling this affair with consummate generalship. Do you remember Beefy Bingham who was at Oxford with us?'

'I ran into him only the other day. He's a parson now.'

'Yes. Down in the East End. Well, he runs a Lads' Club for the local toughs—you know the sort of thing—cocoa and back-gammon in the reading-room and occasional clean, bright entertainments in the Oddfellows' Hall: and I've been helping him. I don't suppose I've passed an evening away from the back-gammon board for weeks. Cora is extremely pleased. I've got her to promise to sing on Tuesday at Beefy's next clean, bright entertainment.'

'You have?'

'I absolutely have. And now mark my devilish ingenuity, Bertie. I'm going to sing, too.'

'Why do you suppose that's going to get you anywhere?'

'Because the way I intend to sing the song I intend to sing will prove to her that there are great deeps in my nature, whose existence she has not suspected. She will see that rough, unlettered audience wiping the tears out of its bally eyes and she will say to herself "What ho! The old egg really has a soul!" For it is not one of your mouldy comic songs, Bertie. No low buffoonery of that sort for me. It is all about Angels being lonely and what not—'

I uttered a sharp cry.

'You don't mean you're going to sing "Sonny Boy"?'

'I jolly well do.'

I was shocked. Yes, dash it, I was shocked. You see, I held strong views on "Sonny Boy". I considered it a song only to be attempted by a few of the elect in the privacy of the bathroom. And the thought of it being murdered in open Oddfellows' Hall by a man who could treat a pal as young Tuppy had treated me that night at the Drones sickened me. Yes, sickened me.

I hadn't time, however, to express my horror and disgust, for at this juncture Jeeves came in.

'Mrs Travers has just rung up on the telephone, sir. She desired me to say that she will be calling to see you in a few minutes.'

'Contents noted, Jeeves,' I said. 'Now listen, Tuppy—'

I stopped. The fellow wasn't there.

'What have you done with him, Jeeves?' I asked.

'Mr Glossop has left, sir.'

'Left? How can he have left? He was sitting there—'

'That is the front door closing now, sir.'

'But what made him shoot off like that?'

'Possibly Mr Glossop did not wish to meet Mrs Travers, sir.'

'Why not?'

'I could not say, sir. But undoubtedly at the mention of Mrs Travers' name he rose very swiftly.'

'Strange, Jeeves.'

'Yes, sir.'

I turned to a subject of more moment.

'Jeeves,' I said, 'Mr Glossop proposes to sing "Sonny Boy" at an entertainment down in the East End next Tuesday.'

'Indeed, sir?'

'Before an audience consisting mainly of costermongers, with a sprinkling of whelk-stall owners, purveyors of blood-oranges, and minor pugilists.'

'Indeed, sir?'

'Make a note to remind me to be there. He will infallibly get the bird, and I want to witness his downfall.'

'Very good, sir.'

'And when Mrs Travers arrives, I shall be in the sitting-room.'

Those who know Bertram Wooster best are aware that in his journey through life he is impeded and generally snootered by about as scaly a platoon of aunts as was ever assembled. But there is one exception to the general ghastliness—viz., my Aunt Dahlia. She married old Tom Travers the year Bluebottle won the Cambridgeshire, and is one of the best. It is always a pleasure to me to chat with her, and it was with a courtly geniality that I rose to receive her as she sailed over the threshold at about two-fifty-five.

She seemed somewhat perturbed, and snapped into the agenda without delay. Aunt Dahlia is one of those big, hearty women. She used to go in a lot for hunting, and she generally speaks as if she had just sighted a fox on a hillside half a mile away.

'Bertie,' she cried, in the manner of one encouraging a bevy of hounds to renewed efforts. 'I want your help.'

'And you shall have it, Aunt Dahlia,' I replied suavely. 'I can honestly say that there is no one to whom I would more readily do a good turn than yourself; no one to whom I am more delighted to be—'

'Less of it,' she begged, 'less of it. You know that friend of yours, young Glossop?'

'He's just been lunching here.'

'He has, has he? Well, I wish you'd poisoned his soup.'

'We didn't have soup. And, when you describe him as a friend of mine, I wouldn't quite say the term absolutely squared with the facts. Some time ago, one night when we had been dining together at the Drones—'

At this point Aunt Dahlia—a little brusquely, it seemed to me—said that she would rather wait for the story of my life till she could get it in book-form. I could see now that she was definitely not her usual sunny self, so I shelved my personal grievances and asked what was biting her.

'It's that young hound Glossop,' she said.

'What's he been doing?'

'Breaking Angela's heart.' (Angela. Daughter of above. My cousin. Quite a good egg.)

'Breaking Angela's heart?'

'Yes . . . Breaking . . . Angela's . . . HEART!'

'You say he's breaking Angela's heart?'

She begged me in rather a feverish way to suspend the vaudeville cross-talk stuff.

'How's he doing that?' I asked.

'With his neglect. With his low, callous, double-crossing duplicity.'

'Duplicity is the word, Aunt Dahlia,' I said. 'In treating of young Tuppy Glossop, it springs naturally to the lips. Let me just tell you what he did to me one night at the Drones. We had finished dinner—'

'Ever since the beginning of the season, up till about three weeks ago, he was all over Angela. The sort of thing which, when I was a girl, we should have described as courting—'

'Or wooing?'

'Wooing or courting, whichever you like.'

'Whichever *you* like, Aunt Dahlia,' I said courteously.

'Well, anyway, he haunted the house, lapped up daily lunches, danced with her half the night, and so on, till naturally the poor kid, who's quite off her oats about him, took it for granted that it was only a question of time before he suggested that they should feed for life out of the same crib. And now he's gone and dropped her like a hot brick, and I hear he's infatuated with some girl he met at a Chelsea tea-party—a girl named—now, what was it?'

'Cora Bellinger.'

'How do you know?'

'She was lunching here to-day.'

'He brought her?'

'Yes.'

'What's she like?'

'Pretty massive. In shape, a bit on the lines of the Albert Hall.'

'Did he seem very fond of her?'

'Couldn't take his eyes off the chassis.'

'The modern young man,' said Aunt Dahlia, 'is a congenital idiot and wants a nurse to lead him by the hand and some strong attendant to kick him regularly at intervals of a quarter of an hour.'

I tried to point out the silver lining.

'If you ask me, Aunt Dahlia,' I said, 'I think Angela is well out of it. This Glossop is a tough baby. One of London's toughest. I was trying to tell you just now what he did to me one night at the Drones. First having got me in sporting mood with a bottle of the ripest, he betted I wouldn't swing myself across the swimming-bath by the ropes and rings. I knew I could do it on my head, so I took him on, exulting in the fun, so to speak. And when I'd done half the trip and was going as strong as dammit, I found he had looped the last rope back against the rail, leaving me no alternative but to drop into the depths and swim ashore in correct evening costume.'

'He did?'

'He certainly did. It was months ago, and I haven't got really dry yet. You wouldn't want your daughter to marry a man capable of a thing like that?'

'On the contrary, you restore my faith in the young hound. I see that there must be lots of good in him, after all. And I want this Bellinger business broken up, Bertie.'

'How?'

'I don't care how. Any way you please.'

'But what can I do?'

'Do? Why, put the whole thing before your man Jeeves. Jeeves will find a way. One of the most capable fellers I ever met. Put the thing squarely up to Jeeves and tell him to let his mind play round the topic.'

'There may be something in what you say, Aunt Dahlia,' I said thoughtfully.

'Of course there is,' said Aunt Dahlia. 'A little thing like this will be child's play to Jeeves. Get him working on it, and I'll look in to-morrow to hear the result.'

With which, she biffed off, and I summoned Jeeves to the presence.

'Jeeves,' I said, 'you have heard all?'

'Yes, sir.'

'I thought you would. My Aunt Dahlia has what you might call a carrying voice. Has it ever occurred to you that, if all other sources of income failed, she could make a good living calling the cattle home across the Sands of Dee?'

'I had not considered the point, sir, but no doubt you are right.'

'Well, how do we go? What is your reaction? I think we should do our best to help and assist.'

'Yes, sir.'

'I am fond of my Aunt Dahlia and I am fond of my cousin Angela. Fond of them both, if you get my drift. What the misguided girl finds to attract her in young Tuppy, I cannot say, Jeeves, and you cannot say. But apparently she loves the man—which shows it can be done, a thing I wouldn't have believed myself—and is pining away like—'

'Patience on a monument, sir.'

'Like Patience, as you very shrewdly remark, on a monument. So we must cluster round. Bend your brain to the problem, Jeeves. It is one that will tax you to the uttermost.'

Aunt Dahlia blew in on the morrow, and I rang the bell for Jeeves. He appeared looking brainier than one could have believed possible—sheer intellect shining from every feature—and I could see at once that the engine had been turning over.

'Speak, Jeeves,' I said.

'Very good, sir.'

'You have brooded?'

'Yes, sir.'

'With what success?'

'I have a plan, sir, which I fancy may produce satisfactory results.'

'Let's have it,' said Aunt Dahlia.

'In affairs of this description, madam, the first essential is to study the psychology of the individual.'

'The what of the individual?'

'The psychology, madam.'

'He means the psychology,' I said. 'And by psychology, Jeeves, you imply—?'

'The natures and dispositions of the principals in the matter, sir.'

'You mean, what they're like?'

'Precisely, sir.'

'Does he talk like this to you when you're alone, Bertie?' asked Aunt Dahlia.

'Sometimes. Occasionally. And, on the other hand, sometimes not. Proceed, Jeeves.'

'Well, sir, if I may say so, the thing that struck me most forcibly about Miss Bellinger when she was under my observation was that hers was a somewhat hard and intolerant nature. I could envisage Miss Bellinger applauding success. I could not so easily see her pitying and sympathizing with failure. Possibly you will recall, sir, her attitude when Mr Glossop endeavoured to light her cigarette with his automatic lighter? I thought

I detected a certain impatience at his inability to produce the necessary flame.'

'True, Jeeves. She ticked him off.'

'Precisely, sir.'

'Let me get this straight,' said Aunt Dahlia, looking a bit fogged. 'You think that, if he goes on trying to light her cigarettes with his automatic lighter long enough, she will eventually get fed up and hand him the mitten? Is that the idea?'

'I merely mentioned the episode, madam, as an indication of Miss Bellinger's somewhat ruthless nature.'

'Ruthless,' I said, 'is right. The Bellinger is hard-boiled. Those eyes. That chin. I could read them. A woman of blood and iron, if ever there was one.'

'Precisely, sir. I think, therefore, that, should Miss Bellinger be a witness of Mr Glossop appearing to disadvantage in public, she would cease to entertain affection for him. In the event, for instance, of his failing to please the audience on Tuesday with his singing—'

I saw daylight.

'By Jove, Jeeves! You mean if he gets the bird, all will be off?'

'I shall be greatly surprised if such is not the case, sir.'

I shook my head.

'We cannot leave this thing to chance, Jeeves. Young Tuppy, singing "Sonny Boy", is the likeliest prospect for the bird that I can think of—but, no—you must see for yourself that we can't simply trust to luck.'

'We need not trust to luck, sir. I would suggest that you approach your friend, Mr Bingham, and volunteer your services as a performer at his forthcoming entertainment. It could readily be arranged that you sang immediately before Mr Glossop. I fancy, sir, that, if Mr Glossop were to sing "Sonny Boy" directly after you, too, had sung "Sonny Boy", the audience would respond satisfactorily. By the time Mr Glossop began to sing, they would have lost their taste for that particular song and would express their feelings warmly.'

'Jeeves,' said Aunt Dahlia, 'you're a marvel!'

'Thank you, madam.'

'Jeeves,' I said, 'you're an ass!'

'What do you mean, he's an ass?' said Aunt Dahlia hotly. 'I think it's the greatest scheme I ever heard.'

'Me sing "Sonny Boy" at Beefy Bingham's clean, bright entertainment? I can see myself!'

'You sing it daily in your bath, sir. Mr Wooster,' said Jeeves, turning to Aunt Dahlia, 'has a pleasant, light baritone—'

'I bet he has,' said Aunt Dahlia.

I froze the man with a look.

'Between singing "Sonny Boy" in one's bath, Jeeves, and singing it before a hall full of assorted blood-orange merchants and their young, there is a substantial difference.'

'Bertie,' said Aunt Dahlia, 'you'll sing, and like it!'

'I will not.'

'Bertie!'

'Nothing will induce—'

'Bertie,' said Aunt Dahlia firmly, 'you will sing "Sonny Boy" on Tuesday, the third *prox.*, and sing it like a lark at sunrise, or may an aunt's curse—'

'I won't!'

'Think of Angela!'

'Dash Angela!'

'Bertie!'

'No, I mean, hang it all!'

'You won't?'

'No, I won't.'

'That is your last word, is it?'

'It is. Once and for all, Aunt Dahlia, nothing will induce me to let out so much as a single note.'

And so that afternoon I sent a pre-paid wire to Beefy Bingham, offering my services in the cause, and by nightfall the thing was fixed up. I was billed to perform next but one after the intermission. Following me, came Tuppy. And, immediately after him, Miss Cora Bellinger, the well-known operatic soprano.

'Jeeves,' I said that evening—and I said it coldly—'I shall be obliged if you will pop round to the nearest music-shop and procure me a copy of

"Sonny Boy". It will now be necessary for me to learn both verse and refrain. Of the trouble and nervous strain which this will involve, I say nothing.'

'Very good, sir.'

'But this I do say—'

'I had better be starting immediately, sir, or the shop will be closed.'

'Ha!' I said.

And I meant it to sting.

Although I had steeled myself to the ordeal before me and had set out full of the calm, quiet courage which makes men do desperate deeds with careless smiles, I must admit that there was a moment, just after I had entered the Oddfellows' Hall at Bermondsey East and run an eye over the assembled pleasure-seekers, when it needed all the bull-dog pluck of the Woosters to keep me from calling it a day and taking a cab back to civilization. The clean, bright entertainment was in full swing when I arrived, and somebody who looked as if he might be the local undertaker was reciting 'Gunga Din'. And the audience, though not actually chi-yiking in the full technical sense of the term, had a grim look which I didn't like at all. The mere sight of them gave me the sort of feeling Shadrach, Meshach and Abednego must have had when preparing to enter the burning, fiery furnace.

Scanning the multitude, it seemed to me that they were for the nonce suspending judgement. Did you ever tap on the door of one of those New York speakeasy places and see the grille snap back and a Face appear? There is one long, silent moment when its eyes are fixed on yours and all your past life seems to rise up before you. Then you say that you are a friend of Mr Zinzinheimer and he told you they would treat you right if you mentioned his name, and the strain relaxes. Well, these costermongers and whelk-stallers appeared to me to be looking just like that Face. Start something, they seemed to say, and they would know what to do about it. And I couldn't help feeling that my singing 'Sonny Boy' would come, in their opinion, under the head of starting something.

'A nice, full house, sir,' said a voice at my elbow. It was Jeeves, watching the proceedings with an indulgent eye.

'You here, Jeeves?' I said, coldly.

'Yes, sir. I have been present since the commencement.'

'Oh?' I said. 'Any casualties yet?'

'Sir?'

'You know what I mean, Jeeves,' I said sternly, 'and don't pretend you don't. Anybody got the bird yet?'

'Oh, no, sir.'

'I shall be the first, you think?'

'No, sir. I see no reason to expect such a misfortune. I anticipate that you will be well received.'

A sudden thought struck me.

'And you think everything will go according to plan?'

'Yes, sir.'

'Well, I don't,' I said. 'And I'll tell you why I don't. I've spotted a flaw in your beastly scheme.'

'A flaw, sir?'

'Yes. Do you suppose for a moment that, if when Mr Glossop hears me singing that dashed song, he'll come calmly on a minute after me and sing it too? Use your intelligence, Jeeves. He will perceive the chasm in his path and pause in time. He will back out and refuse to go on at all.'

'Mr Glossop will not hear you sing, sir. At my advice, he has stepped across the road to the Jug and Bottle, an establishment immediately opposite the hall, and he intends to remain there until it is time for him to appear on the platform.'

'Oh?' I said.

'If I might suggest it, sir, there is another house named the Goat and Grapes only a short distance down the street. I think it might be a judicious move—'

'If I were to put a bit of custom in their way?'

'It would ease the nervous strain of waiting, sir.'

I had not been feeling any too pleased with the man for having let me in for this ghastly binge, but at these words, I'm bound to say, my austerity softened a trifle. He was undoubtedly right. He had studied the psychology of the individual, and it had not led him astray. A quiet ten minutes at the Goat and Grapes was exactly what my system required. To buzz off there and inhale a couple of swift whisky-and-sodas was with Bertram Wooster the work of a moment.

The treatment worked like magic. What they had put into the stuff, besides vitriol, I could not have said; but it completely altered my outlook on life. That curious, gulpy feeling passed. I was no longer conscious of the sagging sensation at the knees. The limbs ceased to quiver gently, the tongue became loosened in its socket, and the backbone stiffened. Pausing merely to order and swallow another of the same, I bade the barmaid a cheery good night, nodded affably to one or two fellows in the bar whose faces I liked, and came prancing back to the hall, ready for anything.

And shortly afterwards I was on the platform with about a million bulging eyes goggling up at me. There was a rummy sort of buzzing in my ears, and then through the buzzing I heard the sound of a piano starting to tinkle: and, commending my soul to God, I took a good, long breath and charged in.

Well, it was a close thing. The whole incident is a bit blurred, but I seem to recollect a kind of murmur as I hit the refrain. I thought at the time it was an attempt on the part of the many-headed to join in the chorus, and at the moment it rather encouraged me. I passed the thing over the larynx with all the vim at my disposal, hit the high note, and off gracefully into the wings. I didn't come on again to take a bow. I just receded and oiled round to where Jeeves awaited me among the standees at the back.

'Well, Jeeves,' I said, anchoring myself at his side and brushing the honest sweat from the brow, 'they didn't rush the platform.'

'No, sir.'

'But you can spread it about that that's the last time I perform outside my bath. My swan-song, Jeeves. Anybody who wants to hear me in future must present himself at the bathroom door and shove his ear against the keyhole. I may be wrong, but it seemed to me that towards the end they were hotting up a trifle. The bird was hovering in the air. I could hear the beating of its wings.'

'I did detect a certain restlessness, sir, in the audience. I fancy they had lost their taste for that particular melody.'

'Eh?'

'I should have informed you earlier, sir, that the song had already been sung twice before you arrived.'

'What!'

'Yes, sir. Once by a lady and once by a gentleman. It is a very popular song, sir.'

I gaped at the man. That, with this knowledge, he could calmly have allowed the young master to step straight into the jaws of death, so to speak, paralysed me. It seemed to show that the old feudal spirit had passed away altogether. I was about to give him my views on the matter in no uncertain fashion, when I was stopped by the spectacle of young Tuppy lurching on to the platform.

Young Tuppy had the unmistakable air of a man who has recently been round to the Jug and Bottle. A few cheery cries of welcome, presumably from some of his backgammon-playing pals who felt that blood was thicker than water, had the effect of causing the genial smile on his face to widen till it nearly met at the back. He was plainly feeling about as good as a man can feel and still remain on his feet. He waved a kindly hand to his supporters, and bowed in a regal sort of manner, rather like an Eastern monarch acknowledging the plaudits of the mob.

Then the female at the piano struck up the opening bars of 'Sonny Boy', and Tuppy swelled like a balloon, clasped his hands together, rolled his eyes up at the ceiling in a manner denoting Soul, and began.

I think the populace was too stunned for the moment to take immediate steps. It may seem incredible, but I give you my word that young Tuppy got right through the verse without so much as a murmur. Then they all seemed to pull themselves together.

A costermonger, roused, is a terrible thing. I had never seen the proletariat really stirred before, and I'm bound to say it rather awed me. I mean, it gave you some idea of what it must have been like during the French Revolution. From every corner of the hall there proceeded simultaneously the sort of noise which you hear, they tell me, at one of those East End boxing places when the referee disqualifies the popular favourite and makes the quick dash for life. And then they passed beyond mere words and began to introduce the vegetable motive.

I don't know why, but somehow I had got it into my head that the first thing thrown at Tuppy would be a potato. One gets these fancies. It was, however, as a matter of fact, a banana, and I saw in an instant that the choice had been made by wiser heads than mine. These blokes who have grown up from childhood in the knowledge of how to treat a dramatic entertainment that doesn't please them are aware by a sort of instinct just what to do for the best, and the moment I saw that banana splash on Tuppy's shirt-front I realized how infinitely more effective and artistic it was than any potato could have been.

Not that the potato school of thought had not also its supporters. As the proceedings warmed up, I noticed several intelligent-looking fellows who threw nothing else.

The effect on young Tuppy was rather remarkable. His eyes bulged and his hair seemed to stand up, and yet his mouth went on opening and shutting, and you could see that in a dazed, automatic way he was still singing 'Sonny Boy'. Then, coming out of his trance, he began to pull for the shore with some rapidity. The last seen of him, he was beating a tomato to the exit by a short head.

Presently the tumult and the shouting died. I turned to Jeeves.

'Painful, Jeeves,' I said. 'But what would you?'

'Yes, sir.'

'The surgeon's knife, what?'

'Precisely, sir.'

'Well, with this happening beneath her eyes, I think we may definitely consider the Glossop-Bellinger romance off.'

'Yes, sir.'

At this point old Beefy Bingham came out on to the platform.

'Ladies and gentlemen,' said old Beefy.

I supposed that he was about to rebuke his flock for the recent expression of feeling. But such was not the case. No doubt he was accustomed by now to the wholesome give-and-take of these clean, bright entertainments and had ceased to think it worth while to make any comment when there was a certain liveliness.

'Ladies and gentlemen,' said old Beefy, 'the next item on the programme was to have been Songs by Miss Cora Bellinger, the well-known operatic soprano. I have just received a telephone-message from Miss Bellinger, saying that her car has broken down. She is, however, on her way here in a cab and will arrive shortly. Meanwhile, our friend Mr Enoch Simpson will recite "Dangerous Dan McGrew".'

I clutched at Jeeves.

'Jeeves! You heard?'

'Yes, sir.'

'She wasn't there!'

'No, sir.'

'She saw nothing of Tuppy's Waterloo.'

'No, sir.'

'The whole bally scheme has blown a fuse.'

'Yes, sir.'

'Come, Jeeves,' I said, and those standing by wondered, no doubt, what had caused that clean-cut face to grow so pale and set. 'I have been subjected to a nervous strain unparalleled since the days of the early Martyrs. I have lost pounds in weight and permanently injured my entire system. I have gone through an ordeal, the recollection of which will make me wake up screaming in the night for months to come. And all for nothing. Let us go.'

'If you have no objection, sir, I would like to witness the remainder of the entertainment.'

'Suit yourself, Jeeves,' I said moodily. 'Personally, my heart is dead and I am going to look in at the Goat and Grapes for another of their cyanide specials and then home.'

It must have been about half-past ten, and I was in the old sitting-room sombrely sucking down a more or less final restorative, when the front-door bell rang, and there on the mat was young Tuppy. He looked like a man who has passed through some great experience and stood face to face with his soul. He had the beginnings of a black eye.

'Oh, hullo, Bertie,' said young Tuppy.

He came in, and hovered about the mantelpiece as if he were looking for things to fiddle with and break.

'I've just been singing at Beefy Bingham's entertainment,' he said after a pause.

'Oh?' I said. 'How did you go?'

'Like a breeze,' said young Tuppy. 'Held them spellbound.'

'Knocked 'em, eh?'

'Cold,' said young Tuppy. 'Not a dry eye.'

And this, mark you, a man who had had a good upbringing and had, no doubt, spent years at his mother's knee being taught to tell the truth.

'I suppose Miss Bellinger is pleased?'

'Oh, yes. Delighted.'

'So now everything's all right?'

'Oh, quite.'

Tuppy paused.

'On the other hand, Bertie—'

'Yes?'

'Well, I've been thinking things over. Somehow I don't believe Miss Bellinger is the mate for me, after all.'

'You don't?'

'No, I don't.'

'Why don't you?'

'Oh, I don't know. These things sort of flash on you. I respect Miss Bellinger, Bertie. I admire her. But—er—well, I can't help feeling now that a sweet, gentle girl—er—like your cousin Angela, for instance, Bertie, would—er—in fact—well, what I came round for was to ask if you would 'phone Angela and find out how she reacts to the idea of coming out with me to-night to the Berkeley for a segment of supper and a spot of dancing.'

'Go ahead. There's the 'phone.'

'No, I'd rather you asked her, Bertie. What with one thing and another, if you paved the way—You see, there's just a chance that she may be—I mean, you know how misunderstandings occur—and—well, what I'm driving at, Bertie, old man, is that I'd rather you surged round and did a bit of paving, if you don't mind.'

I went to the 'phone and called up Aunt Dahlia's.

'She says come right along,' I said.

'Tell her,' said Tuppy in a devout sort of voice, 'that I will be with her in something under a couple of ticks.'

He had barely biffed, when I heard a click in the keyhole and a soft padding in the passage without.

'Jeeves,' I called.

'Sir?' said Jeeves, manifesting himself.

'Jeeves, a remarkably rummy thing has happened. Mr Glossop has just been here. He tells me that it is all off between him and Miss Bellinger.'

'Yes, sir.'

'You don't seem surprised.'

'No, sir. I confess I had anticipated some such eventuality.'

'Eh? What gave you that idea?'

'It came to me, sir, when I observed Miss Bellinger strike Mr Glossop in the eye.'

'Strike him!'

'Yes, sir.'

'In the eye?'

'The right eye, sir.'

I clutched the brow.

'What on earth made her do that?'

'I fancy she was a little upset, sir, at the reception accorded to her singing.'

'Great Scott! Don't tell me she got the bird, too?'

'Yes, sir.'

'But why? She's got a red-hot voice.'

'Yes, sir. But I think the audience resented her choice of a song.'

'Jeeves!' Reason was beginning to do a bit of tottering on its throne. 'You aren't going to stand there and tell me that Miss Bellinger sang "Sonny Boy", too!'

'Yes, sir. And—rashly, in my opinion—brought a large doll on to the platform to sing it to. The audience affected to mistake it for a ventriloquist's dummy, and there was some little disturbance.'

'But, Jeeves, what a coincidence!'

'Not altogether, sir. I ventured to take the liberty of accosting Miss Bellinger on her arrival at the hall and recalling myself to her recollection. I then said that Mr Glossop had asked me to request her that as a particular favour to him—the song being a favourite of his—she would sing "Sonny

Boy". And when she found that you and Mr Glossop had also sung the song immediately before her, I rather fancy that she supposed that she had been made the victim of a practical pleasantry by Mr Glossop. Will there be anything further, sir?'

'No, thanks.'

'Good night, sir.'

'Good night, Jeeves,' I said reverently.

5

EPISODE OF THE DOG McINTOSH

I was jerked from the dreamless by a sound like the rolling of distant thunder; and, the mists of sleep clearing away, was enabled to diagnose this and trace it to its source. It was my Aunt Agatha's dog, McIntosh, scratching at the door. The above, an Aberdeen terrier of weak intellect, had been left in my charge by the old relative while she went off to Aix-les-Bains to take the cure, and I had never been able to make it see eye to eye with me on the subject of early rising. Although a glance at my watch informed me that it was barely ten, here was the animal absolutely up and about.

I pressed the bell, and presently in shimmered Jeeves, complete with tea-tray and preceded by dog, which leaped upon the bed, licked me smartly in the right eye, and immediately curled up and fell into a deep slumber. And where the sense is in getting up at some ungodly hour of the morning and coming scratching at people's doors, when you intend at the first opportunity to go to sleep again, beats me. Nevertheless, every day for the last five weeks this loony hound had pursued the same policy, and I confess I was getting a bit fed.

There were one or two letters on the tray; and, having slipped a refreshing half-cupful into the abyss, I felt equal to dealing with them. The one on top was from my Aunt Agatha.

'Ha!' I said.

'Sir?'

'I said "Ha!" Jeeves. And I meant "Ha!" I was registering relief. My Aunt Agatha returns this evening. She will be at her town residence between the hours of six and seven, and she expects to find McIntosh waiting for her on the mat.'

'Indeed, sir? I shall miss the little fellow.'

'I, too, Jeeves. Despite his habit of rising with the milk and being hearty before breakfast, there is sterling stuff in McIntosh. Nevertheless, I cannot but feel relieved at the prospect of shooting him back to the old home. It has been a guardianship fraught with anxiety. You know what my Aunt Agatha is. She lavishes on that dog a love which might better be bestowed on a nephew: and if the slightest thing had gone wrong with him while I was *in loco parentis*; if, while in my charge, he had developed rabies or staggers or the botts, I should have been blamed.'

'Very true, sir.'

'And, as you are aware, London is not big enough to hold Aunt Agatha and anybody she happens to be blaming.'

I had opened the second letter, and was giving it the eye.

'Ha!' I said.

'Sir?'

'Once again "Ha!" Jeeves, but this time signifying mild surprise. This letter is from Miss Wickham.'

'Indeed, sir?'

I sensed—if that is the word I want—the note of concern in the man's voice, and I knew he was saying to himself 'Is the young master about to slip?' You see, there was a time when the Wooster heart was to some extent what you might call ensnared by this Roberta Wickham, and Jeeves had never approved of her. He considered her volatile and frivolous and more or less of a menace to man and beast. And events, I'm bound to say, had rather borne out his view.

'She wants me to give her lunch to-day.'

'Indeed, sir?'

'And two friends of hers.'

'Indeed, sir?'

'Here. At one-thirty.'

'Indeed, sir?'

I was piqued.

'Correct this parrot-complex, Jeeves,' I said, waving a slice of bread-and-butter rather sternly at the man. 'There is no need for you to stand there saying "Indeed, sir?" I know what you're thinking, and you're wrong. As far as Miss Wickham is concerned, Bertram Wooster is chilled steel. I see no earthly reason why I should not comply with this request. A Wooster may have ceased to love, but he can still be civil.'

'Very good, sir.'

'Employ the rest of the morning, then, in buzzing to and fro and collecting provender. The old King Wenceslas touch, Jeeves. You remember? Bring me fish and bring me fowl—'

'Bring me flesh and bring me wine, sir.'

'Just as you say. You know best. Oh, and roly-poly pudding, Jeeves.'

'Sir?'

'Roly-poly pudding with lots of jam in it. Miss Wickham specifically mentions this. Mysterious, what?'

'Extremely, sir.'

'Also oysters, ice-cream, and plenty of chocolates with that goo-ey, slithery stuff in the middle. Makes you sick to think of it, eh?'

'Yes, sir.'

'Me, too. But that's what she says. I think she must be on some kind of diet. Well, be that as it may, see to it, Jeeves, will you?'

'Yes, sir.'

'At one-thirty of the clock.'

'Very good, sir.'

'Very good, Jeeves.'

At half-past twelve I took the dog McIntosh for his morning saunter in the Park; and, returning at about one-ten, found young Bobbie Wickham in the sitting-room, smoking a cigarette and chatting to Jeeves, who seemed a bit distant, I thought.

I have an idea I've told you about this Bobbie Wickham. She was the red-haired girl who let me down so disgracefully in the sinister affair of Tuppy Glossop and the hot-water bottle, that Christmas when I went to stay at Skeldings Hall, her mother's place in Hertfordshire. Her mother is Lady Wickham, who writes novels which, I believe, command a ready sale among those who like their literature pretty sloppy. A formidable old bird, rather like my Aunt Agatha in appearance. Bobbie does not resemble her, being constructed more on the lines of Clara Bow. She greeted me cordially as I entered—in fact, so cordially that I saw Jeeves pause at the door before buffing off to mix the cocktails and shoot me the sort of grave, warning look a wise old father might pass out to the effervescent son on seeing him going fairly strong with the local vamp. I nodded back, as much as to say 'Chilled steel!' and he oozed out, leaving me to play the sparkling host.

'It was awfully sporting of you to give us this lunch, Bertie,' said Bobbie.

'Don't mention it, my dear old thing,' I said. 'Always a pleasure.'

'You got all the stuff I told you about?'

'The garbage, as specified, is in the kitchen. But since when have you become a roly-poly pudding addict?'

'That isn't for me. There's a small boy coming.'

'What!'

'I'm awfully sorry,' she said, noting my agitation. 'I know just how you feel, and I'm not going to pretend that this child isn't pretty near the edge. In fact, he has to be seen to be believed. But it's simply vital that he be cosseted and sucked up to and generally treated as the guest of honour, because everything depends on him.'

'How do you mean?'

'I'll tell you. You know mother?'

'Whose mother?'

'My mother.'

'Oh, yes. I thought you meant the kid's mother.'

'He hasn't got a mother. Only a father, who is a big theatrical manager in America. I met him at a party the other night.'

'The father?'

'Yes, the father.'

'Not the kid?'

'No, not the kid.'

'Right. All clear so far. Proceed.'

'Well, mother—my mother—has dramatized one of her novels, and when I met this father, this theatrical manager father, and, between ourselves, made rather a hit with him, I said to myself, "Why not?"'

'Why not what?'

'Why not plant mother's play on him.'

'Your mother's play?'

'Yes, not his mother's play. He is like his son, he hasn't got a mother, either.'

'These things run in families, don't they?'

'You see, Bertie, what with one thing and another, my stock isn't very high with mother just now. There was that matter of my smashing up the car—oh, and several things. So I thought, here is where I get a chance to put myself right. I cooed to old Blumenfeld—'

'Name sounds familiar.'

'Oh, yes, he's a big man over in America. He has come to London to see if there's anything in the play line worth buying. So I cooed to him a goodish bit and then asked him if he would listen to mother's play. He said he would, so I asked him to come to lunch and I'd read it to him.'

'You're going to read your mother's play—here?' I said, paling.

'Yes.'

'My God!'

'I know what you mean,' she said. 'I admit it's pretty sticky stuff. But I have an idea that I shall put it over. It all depends on how the kid likes it. You see, old Blumenfeld, for some reason, always banks on his verdict. I suppose he thinks the child's intelligence is exactly the same as an average audience's and—'

I uttered a slight yelp, causing Jeeves, who had entered with cocktails, to look at me in a pained sort of way. I had remembered.

'Jeeves!'

'Sir?'

'Do you recollect, when we were in New York, a dish-faced kid of the name of Blumenfeld who on a memorable occasion snootered Cyril Bassington-Bassington when the latter tried to go on the stage?'

'Very vividly, sir.'

'Well, prepare yourself for a shock. He's coming to lunch.'

'Indeed, sir?'

'I'm glad you can speak in that light, careless way. I only met the young stoup of arsenic for a few brief minutes, but I don't mind telling you the prospect of hobnobbing with him again makes me tremble like a leaf.'

'Indeed, sir?'

'Don't keep saying "Indeed, sir?" You have seen this kid in action and you know what he's like. He told Cyril Bassington-Bassington, a fellow to whom he had never been formally introduced, that he had a face like a fish. And this not thirty seconds after their initial meeting. I give you fair warning that, if he tells me I have a face like a fish, I shall clump his head.'

'Bertie!' cried the Wickham, contorted with anguish and apprehension and what not.

'Yes, I shall.'

'Then you'll simply ruin the whole thing.'

'I don't care. We Woosters have our pride.'

'Perhaps the young gentleman will not notice that you have a face like a fish, sir,' suggested Jeeves.

'Ah! There's that, of course.'

'But we can't just trust to luck,' said Bobbie. 'It's probably the first thing he will notice.'

'In that case, miss,' said Jeeves, 'it might be the best plan if Mr Wooster did not attend the luncheon.'

I beamed on the man. As always, he had found the way.

'But Mr Blumenfeld will think it so odd.'

'Well, tell him I'm eccentric. Tell him I have these moods, which come upon me quite suddenly, when I can't stand the sight of people. Tell him what you like.'

'He'll be offended.'

'Not half so offended as if I socked his son on the upper maxillary bone.'

'I really think it would be the best plan, miss.'

'Oh, all right,' said Bobbie. 'Push off, then. But I wanted you to be here to listen to the play and laugh in the proper places.'

'I don't suppose there are any proper places,' I said. And with these words I reached the hall in two bounds, grabbed a hat, and made for the street. A cab was just pulling up at the door as I reached it, and inside it were Pop Blumenfeld and his foul son. With a slight sinking of the old heart, I saw that the kid had recognized me.

'Hullo!' he said.

'Hullo!' I said.

'Where are you off to?' said the kid.

'Ha, ha!' I said, and legged it for the great open spaces.

I lunched at the Drones, doing myself fairly well and lingering pretty considerably over the coffee and cigarettes. At four o'clock I thought it would be safe to think about getting back; but, not wishing to take any chances, I went to the 'phone and rang up the flat.

'All clear, Jeeves?'

'Yes, sir.'

'Blumenfeld junior nowhere about?'

'No, sir.'

'Not hiding in any nook or cranny, what?'

'No, sir.'

'How did everything go off?'

'Quite satisfactorily, I fancy, sir.'

'Was I missed?'

'I think Mr Blumenfeld and young Master Blumenfeld were somewhat surprised at your absence, sir. Apparently they encountered you as you were leaving the building.'

'They did. An awkward moment, Jeeves. The kid appeared to desire speech with me, but I laughed hollowly and passed on. Did they comment on this at all?'

'Yes, sir. Indeed, young Master Blumenfeld was somewhat outspoken.'

'What did he say?'

'I cannot recall his exact words, sir, but he drew a comparison between your mentality and that of a cuckoo.'

'A cuckoo, eh?'

'Yes, sir. To the bird's advantage.'

'He did, did he? Now you see how right I was to come away. Just one crack like that out of him face to face, and I should infallibly have done his upper maxillary a bit of no good. It was wise of you to suggest that I should lunch out.'

'Thank you, sir.'

'Well, the coast being clear, I will now return home.'

'Before you start, sir, perhaps you would ring Miss Wickham up. She instructed me to desire you to do so.'

'You mean she asked you to ask me?'

'Precisely, sir.'

'Right-ho. And the number?'

'Sloane 8090. I fancy it is the residence of Miss Wickham's aunt, in Eaton Square.'

I got the number. And presently young Bobbie's voice came floating over the wire. From the *timbre* I gathered that she was extremely bucked.

'Hullo? Is that you, Bertie?'

'In person. What's the news?'

'Wonderful. Everything went off splendidly. The lunch was just right. The child stuffed himself to the eyebrows and got more and more amiable, till by the time he had had his third go of ice-cream he was ready to say that any play—even one of mother's—was the goods. I fired it at him before he could come out from under the influence, and he sat there absorbing it in a sort of gorged way, and at the end old Blumenfeld said "Well, sonny, how about it?" and the child gave a sort of faint smile, as if he was thinking about roly-poly pudding, and said "O.K., pop," and that's all there was to it. Old Blumenfeld has taken him off to the movies, and I'm to look in at the Savoy at five-thirty to sign the contract. I've just been talking to mother on the 'phone, and she's quite consumedly braced.'

'Terrific!'

'I knew you'd be pleased. Oh, Bertie, there's just one other thing. You remember saying to me once that there wasn't anything in the world you wouldn't do for me?'

I paused a trifle warily. It is true that I had expressed myself in some such terms as she had indicated, but that was before the affair of Tuppy and the hot-water bottle, and in the calmer frame of mind induced by that episode I wasn't feeling quite so spacious. You know how it is. Love's flame flickers and dies, Reason returns to her throne, and you aren't nearly as ready to hop about and jump through hoops as in the first pristine glow of the divine passion.

'What do you want me to do?'

'Well, it's nothing I actually want you to do. It's something I've done that I hope you won't be sticky about. Just before I began reading the play, that dog of yours, the Aberdeen terrier, came into the room. The child Blumenfeld was very much taken with it and said he wished he had a dog like that, looking at me in a meaning sort of way. So naturally, I had to say "Oh, I'll give you this one!"'

I swayed somewhat.

'You . . . You . . . What was that?'

'I gave him the dog. I knew you wouldn't mind. You see, it was vital to keep cosseting him. If I'd refused, he would have cut up rough and all that roly-poly pudding and stuff would have been thrown away. You see—'

I hung up. The jaw had fallen, the eyes were protruding. I tottered from the booth and, reeling out of the club, hailed a taxi. I got to the flat and yelled for Jeeves.

'Jeeves!'

'Sir?'

'Do you know what?'

'No, sir.'

'The dog . . . my Aunt Agatha's dog . . . McIntosh . . .'

'I have not seen him for some little while, sir. He left me after the conclusion of luncheon. Possibly he is in your bedroom.'

'Yes, and possibly he jolly dashed well isn't. If you want to know where he is, he's in a suite at the Savoy.'

'Sir?'

'Miss Wickham has just told me she gave him to Blumenfeld junior.'

'Sir?'

'Gave him to Jumenfeld blunior, I tell you. As a present. As a gift. With warm personal regards.'

'What was her motive in doing that, sir?'

I explained the circs. Jeeves did a bit of respectful tongue-clicking.

'I have always maintained, if you will remember, sir,' he said, when I had finished, 'that Miss Wickham, though a charming young lady—'

'Yes, yes, never mind about that. What are we going to do? That's the point. Aunt Agatha is due back between the hours of six and seven. She will find herself short one Aberdeen terrier. And, as she will probably have been considerably sea-sick all the way over, you will readily perceive, Jeeves, that, when I break the news that her dog has been given away to a total stranger, I shall find her in no mood of gentle charity.'

'I see, sir. Most disturbing.'

'What did you say it was?'

'Most disturbing, sir.'

I snorted a trifle.

'Oh?' I said. 'And I suppose, if you had been in San Francisco when the earthquake started, you would just have lifted up your finger and said "Tweet, tweet! Shush, shush! Now, now! Come, come!" The English language, they used to tell me at school, is the richest in the world, crammed full from end to end with about a million red-hot adjectives. Yet the only one you can find to describe this ghastly business is the adjective "disturbing". It is not disturbing, Jeeves. It is . . . what's the word I want?'

'Cataclysmal, sir?'

'I shouldn't wonder. Well, what's to be done?'

'I will bring you a whisky-and-soda, sir.'

'What's the good of that?'

'It will refresh you, sir. And in the meantime, if it is your wish, I will give the matter consideration.'

'Carry on.'

'Very good, sir. I assume that it is not your desire to do anything that may in any way jeopardize the cordial relations which now exist between Miss Wickham and Mr and Master Blumenfeld?'

'Eh?'

'You would not, for example, contemplate proceeding to the Savoy Hotel and demanding the return of the dog?'

It was a tempting thought, but I shook the old onion firmly. There are things which a Wooster can do and things which, if you follow me, a Wooster cannot do. The procedure which he had indicated would undoubtedly have brought home the bacon, but the thwarted kid would have been bound to turn nasty and change his mind about the play. And, while I didn't think that any drama written by Bobbie's mother was likely to do the theatre-going public much good, I couldn't dash the cup of happiness, so to speak, from the blighted girl's lips, as it were. *Noblesse oblige* about sums the thing up.

'No, Jeeves,' I said. 'But if you can think of some way by which I can oil privily into the suite and sneak the animal out of it without causing any hard feelings, spill it.'

'I will endeavour to do so, sir.'

'Snap into it, then, without delay. They say fish are good for the brain. Have a go at the sardines and come back and report.'

'Very good, sir.'

It was about ten minutes later that he entered the presence once more.

'I fancy, sir—'

'Yes, Jeeves?'

'I rather fancy, sir, that I have discovered a plan of action.'

'Or scheme.'

'Or scheme, sir. A plan of action or scheme which will meet the situation. If I understood you rightly, sir, Mr and Master Blumenfeld have attended a motion-picture performance?'

'Correct.'

'In which case, they should not return to the hotel before five-fifteen?'

'Correct once more. Miss Wickham is scheduled in at five-thirty to sign the contract.'

'The suite, therefore, is at present unoccupied.'

'Except for McIntosh.'

'Except for McIntosh, sir. Everything, accordingly, must depend on whether Mr Blumenfeld left instructions that, in the event of her arriving before he did, Miss Wickham was to be shown straight up to the suite, to await his return.'

'Why does everything depend on that?'

'Should he have done so, the matter becomes quite simple. All that is necessary is that Miss Wickham shall present herself at the hotel at five o'clock. She will go up to the suite. You will also have arrived at the hotel at five, sir, and will have made your way to the corridor outside the suite. If Mr and Master Blumenfeld have not returned, Miss Wickham will open the door and come out and you will go in, secure the dog, and take your departure.'

I stared at the man.

'How many tins of sardines did you eat, Jeeves?'

'None, sir. I am not fond of sardines.'

'You mean, you thought of this great, this ripe, this amazing scheme entirely without the impetus given to the brain by fish?'

'Yes, sir.'

'You stand alone, Jeeves.'

'Thank you, sir.'

'But I say!'

'Sir?'

'Suppose the dog won't come away with me? You know how meagre his intelligence is. By this time, especially when he's got used to a new place, he may have forgotten me completely and will look on me as a perfect stranger.'

'I had thought of that, sir. The most judicious move will be for you to sprinkle your trousers with aniseed.'

'Aniseed?'

'Yes, sir. It is extensively used in the dog-stealing industry.'

'But, Jeeves . . . dash it . . . aniseed?'

'I consider it essential, sir.'

'But where do you get the stuff?'

'At any chemist's, sir. If you will go out now and procure a small bottle, I will be telephoning to Miss Wickham to apprise her of the contemplated arrangements and ascertain whether she is to be admitted to the suite.'

I don't know what the record is for popping out and buying aniseed, but I should think I hold it. The thought of Aunt Agatha getting nearer and nearer to the Metropolis every minute induced a rare burst of speed. I was back at the flat so quick that I nearly met myself coming out.

Jeeves had good news.

'Everything is perfectly satisfactory, sir. Mr Blumenfeld did leave instructions that Miss Wickham was to be admitted to his suite. The young lady is now on her way to the hotel. By the time you reach it, you will find her there.'

You know, whatever you may say against old Jeeves—and I, for one, have never wavered in my opinion that his views on shirts for evening wear are hidebound and reactionary to a degree—you've got to admit that the man can plan a campaign. Napoleon could have taken his correspondence course. When he sketches out a scheme, all you have to do is to follow it in detail, and there you are.

On the present occasion everything went absolutely according to plan. I had never realized before that dog-stealing could be so simple, having always regarded it rather as something that called for the ice-cool brain and the nerve of steel. I see now that a child can do it, if directed by Jeeves. I got to the hotel, sneaked up the stairs, hung about in the corridor trying to look like a potted palm in case anybody came along, and presently the door of the suite opened and Bobbie appeared, and suddenly, as I approached, out shot McIntosh, sniffing passionately, and the next moment his nose was up against my Spring trouserings and he was drinking me in with every evidence of enjoyment. If I had been a bird that had been dead about five days, he could not have nuzzled me more heartily. Aniseed isn't a scent that I care for particularly myself, but it seemed to speak straight to the deeps in McIntosh's soul.

The connection, as it were, having been established in this manner, the rest was simple. I merely withdrew, followed by the animal in the order named. We passed down the stairs in good shape, self reeking to heaven and animal inhaling the bouquet, and after a few anxious moments were safe in a cab, homeward bound. As smooth a bit of work as London had seen that day.

Arrived at the flat, I handed McIntosh to Jeeves and instructed him to shut him up in the bathroom or somewhere where the spell cast by my trousers would cease to operate. This done, I again paid the man a marked tribute.

'Jeeves,' I said, 'I have had occasion to express the view before, and I now express it again fearlessly—you stand in a class of your own.'

'Thank you very much, sir. I am glad that everything proceeded satisfactorily.'

'The festivities went like a breeze from start to finish. Tell me, were you always like this, or did it come on suddenly?'

'Sir?'

'The brain. The grey matter. Were you an outstandingly brilliant boy?'

'My mother thought me intelligent, sir.'

'You can't go by that. My mother thought *me* intelligent. Anyway, setting that aside for the moment, would a fiver be any use to you?'

'Thank you very much, sir.'

'Not that a fiver begins to cover it. Figure to yourself, Jeeves—try to envisage, if you follow what I mean, the probable behaviour of my Aunt Agatha if I had gone to her between the hours of six and seven and told her that McIntosh had passed out of the picture. I should have had to leave London and grow a beard.'

'I can readily imagine, sir, that she would have been somewhat perturbed.'

'She would. And on the occasions when my Aunt Agatha is perturbed heroes dive down drain-pipes to get out of her way. However, as it is, all has ended happily . . . Oh, great Scott!'

'Sir?'

I hesitated. It seemed a shame to cast a damper on the man just when he had extended himself so notably in the cause, but it had to be done.

'You've overlooked something, Jeeves.'

'Surely not, sir?'

'Yes, Jeeves, I regret to say that the late scheme or plan of action, while gilt-edged as far as I am concerned, has rather landed Miss Wickham in the cart.'

'In what way, sir?'

'Why don't you see that, if they know that she was in the suite at the time of the outrage, the Blumenfelds, father and son, will instantly assume that she was mixed up in McIntosh's disappearance, with the result that in their pique and chagrin they will call off the deal about the play? I'm surprised at you not spotting that, Jeeves. You'd have done much better to eat those sardines, as I advised.'

I waggled the head rather sadly, and at this moment there was a ring at the front-door bell. And not an ordinary ring, mind you, but one of those resounding peals that suggest that somebody with a high blood-pressure and a grievance stands without. I leaped in my tracks. My busy afternoon had left the old nervous system not quite in mid-season form.

'Good Lord, Jeeves!'

'Somebody at the door, sir.'

'Yes.'

'Probably Mr Blumenfeld, senior, sir.'

'What!'

'He rang up on the telephone, sir, shortly before you returned, to say that he was about to pay you a call.'

'You don't mean that?'

'Yes, sir.'

'Advise me, Jeeves.'

'I fancy the most judicious procedure would be for you to conceal yourself behind the settee, sir.'

I saw that his advise was good. I had never met this Blumenfeld socially, but I had seen him from afar on the occasion when he and Cyril Bassington-Bassington had had their falling out, and he hadn't struck me then as a bloke with whom, if in one of his emotional moods, it would be at all agreeable to be shut up in a small room. A large, round, fat, overflowing bird, who might quite easily, if stirred, fall on a fellow and flatten him to the carpet.

So I nestled behind the settee, and in about five seconds there was a sound like a mighty, rushing wind and something extraordinarily substantial bounded into the sitting-room.

'This guy Wooster,' bellowed a voice that had been strengthened by a lifetime of ticking actors off at dress-rehearsals from the back of the theatre. 'Where is he?'

Jeeves continued suave.

'I could not say, sir.'

'He's sneaked my son's dog.'

'Indeed, sir?'

'Walked into my suite as cool as dammit and took the animal away.'

'Most disturbing, sir.'

'And you don't know where he is?'

'Mr Wooster may be anywhere, sir. He is uncertain in his movements.'

The bloke Blumenfeld gave a loud sniff.

'Odd smell here!'

'Yes, sir?'

'What is it?'

'Aniseed, sir.'

'Aniseed?'

'Yes, sir. Mr Wooster sprinkles it on his trousers.'

'Sprinkles it on his trousers?'

'Yes, sir.'

'What on earth does he do that for?'

'I could not say, sir. Mr Wooster's motives are always somewhat hard to follow. He is eccentric.'

'Eccentric? He must be a loony.'

'Yes, sir.'

'You mean he is?'

'Yes, sir!'

There was a pause. A long one.

'Oh?' said old Blumenfeld, and it seemed to me that a good deal of what you might call the vim had gone out of his voice.

He paused again.

'Not *dangerous*?'

'Yes, sir, when roused.'

'Er—what rouses him chiefly?'

'One of Mr Wooster's peculiarities is that he does not like the sight of gentlemen of full habit, sir. They seem to infuriate him.'

'You mean, fat men?'

'Yes, sir.'

'Why?'

'One cannot say, sir.'

There was another pause.

'*I'm* fat!' said old Blumenfeld in a rather pensive sort of voice.

'I would not have ventured to suggest it myself, sir, but as you say so . . . You may recollect that, on being informed that you were to be a member of the luncheon party, Mr Wooster, doubting his power of self-control, refused to be present.'

'That's right. He went rushing out just as I arrived. I thought it odd at the time. My son thought it odd. We both thought it odd.'

'Yes, sir. Mr Wooster, I imagine, wished to avoid any possible unpleasantness, such as has occurred before . . . With regard to the smell of aniseed, sir, I fancy I have now located it. Unless I am mistaken it proceeds from behind the settee. No doubt Mr Wooster is sleeping there.'

'Doing what?'

'Sleeping, sir.'

'Does he often sleep on the floor?'

'Most afternoons, sir. Would you desire me to wake him?'

'No!'

'I thought you had something that you wished to say to Mr Wooster, sir.'

Old Blumenfeld drew a deep breath. 'So did I,' he said. 'But I find I haven't. Just get me alive out of here, that's all I ask.'

I heard the door close, and a little while later the front door banged. I crawled out. It hadn't been any too cosy behind the settee, and I was glad to be elsewhere. Jeeves came trickling back.

'Gone, Jeeves?'

'Yes, sir.'

I bestowed an approving look on him.

'One of your best efforts, Jeeves.'

'Thank you, sir.'

'But what beats me is why he ever came here. What made him think that I had sneaked McIntosh away?'

'I took the liberty of recommending Miss Wickham to tell Mr Blumenfeld that she had observed you removing the animal from his suite, sir. The point which you raised regarding the possibility of her being suspected of complicity in the affair, had not escaped me. It seemed to me that this would establish her solidly in Mr Blumenfeld's good opinion.'

'I see. Risky, of course, but possibly justified. Yes, on the whole, justified. What's that you've got there?'

'A five-pound note, sir.'

'Ah, the one I gave you?'

'No, sir. The one Mr Blumenfeld gave me.'

'Eh? Why did he give you a fiver?'

'He very kindly presented it to me on my handing him the dog, sir.'

I gaped at the man.

'You don't mean to say—?'

'Not McIntosh, sir. McIntosh is at present in my bedroom. This was another animal of the same species which I purchased at the shop in Bond Street during your absence. Except to the eye of love, one Aberdeen terrier looks very much like another Aberdeen terrier, sir. Mr Blumenfeld, I am happy to say, did not detect the innocent subterfuge.'

'Jeeves,' I said—and I am not ashamed to confess that there was a spot of chokiness in the voice—'there is none like you, none.'

'Thank you very much, sir.'

'Owing solely to the fact that your head bulges in unexpected spots, thus enabling you to do about twice as much bright thinking in any given time as any other two men in existence, happiness, you might say, reigns supreme. Aunt Agatha is on velvet, I am on velvet, the Wickhams, mother and daughter, are on velvet, the Blumenfelds, father and son, are on velvet. As far as the eye can reach, a solid mass of humanity, owing to you, all on velvet. A fiver is not sufficient, Jeeves. If I thought the world thought that Bertram Wooster thought a measly five pounds an adequate reward for such services as yours, I should never hold my head up again. Have another?'

'Thank you, sir.'

'And one more?'

'Thank you very much, sir.'

'And a third for luck?'

'Really, sir, I am exceedingly obliged. Excuse me, sir, I fancy I heard the telephone.'

He pushed out into the hall, and I heard him doing a good deal of the 'Yes, madam,' 'Certainly, madam!' stuff. Then he came back.

'Mrs Spenser Gregson on the telephone, sir.'

'Aunt Agatha?'

'Yes, sir. Speaking from Victoria Station. She desires to communicate with you with reference to the dog McIntosh. I gather that she wishes to hear from your own lips that all is well with the little fellow, sir.'

I straightened the tie. I pulled down the waistcoat. I shot the cuffs. I felt absolutely all-righto.

'Lead me to her,' I said.

6

THE SPOT OF ART

I was lunching at my Aunt Dahlia's, and despite the fact that Anatole, her outstanding cook, had rather excelled himself in the matter of the bill-of-fare, I'm bound to say the food was more or less turning to ashes in my mouth. You see, I had some bad news to break to her—always a prospect that takes the edge off the appetite. She wouldn't be pleased, I knew, and when not pleased Aunt Dahlia, having spent most of her youth in the hunting-field, has a crispish way of expressing herself.

However, I supposed I had better have a dash at it and get it over.

'Aunt Dahlia,' I said, facing the issue squarely.

'Hullo?'

'You know that cruise of yours?'

'Yes.'

'That yachting-cruise you are planning?'

'Yes.'

'That jolly cruise in your yacht in the Mediterranean to which you so kindly invited me and to which I have been looking forward with such keen anticipation?'

'Get on, fathead, what about it?'

I swallowed a chunk of *côtelette-suprême-aux-choux-fleurs* and slipped her the distressing info'.

'I'm frightfully sorry, Aunt Dahlia,' I said, 'but I shan't be able to come.'

As I had foreseen, she goggled.

'What!'

'I'm afraid not.'

'You poor, miserable hell-hound, what do you mean, you won't be able to come?'

'Well, I won't.'

'Why not?'

'Matters of the most extreme urgency render my presence in the Metropolis imperative.'

She sniffed.

'I supposed what you really mean is that you're hanging round some unfortunate girl again?'

I didn't like the way she put it, but I admit I was stunned by her penetration, if that's the word I want. I mean the sort of thing detectives have.

'Yes, Aunt Dahlia,' I said, 'you have guessed my secret. I do indeed love.'

'Who is she?'

'A Miss Pendlebury. Christian name, Gwladys. She spells it with a "w".'

'With a "g", you mean.'

'With a "w" *and* a "g".'

'Not Gwladys?'

'That's it.'

The relative uttered a yowl.

'You sit there and tell me you haven't enough sense to steer clear of a girl who calls herself Gwladys? Listen, Bertie,' said Aunt Dahlia earnestly, 'I'm an older woman than you are—well, you know what I mean—and I can tell you a thing or two. And one of them is that no good can come of association with anything labelled Gwladys or Ysobel or Ethyl or Mabelle or Kathryn. But particularly Gwladys. What sort of girl is she?'

'Slightly divine.'

'She isn't that female I saw driving you at sixty miles p.h. in the Park the other day. In a red two-seater?'

'She did drive me in the Park the other day. I thought it rather a hopeful sign. And her Widgeon Seven is red.'

Aunt Dahlia looked relieved.

'Oh well, then, she'll probably break your silly fat neck before she can get you to the altar. That's some consolation. Where did you meet her?'

'At a party in Chelsea. She's an artist.'

'Ye gods!'

'And swings a jolly fine brush, let me tell you. She's painted a portrait of me. Jeeves and I hung it up in the flat this morning. I have an idea Jeeves doesn't like it.'

'Well, if it's anything like you I don't see why he should. An artist! Calls herself Gwladys! And drives a car in the sort of way Segrave would if he were pressed for time.' She brooded awhile. 'Well, it's all very sad, but I can't see why you won't come on the yacht.'

I explained.

'It would be madness to leave the metrop. at this juncture,' I said. 'You know what girls are. They forget the absent face. And I'm not at all easy in my mind about a certain cove of the name of Lucius Pim. Apart from the fact that he's an artist, too, which forms a bond, his hair waves. One must never discount wavy hair, Aunt Dahlia. Moreover, this bloke is one of those strong, masterful men. He treats Gwladys as if she were less than the dust beneath his taxi wheels. He criticizes her hats and says nasty things about her chiaroscuro. For some reason, I've often noticed, this always seems to fascinate girls, and it has sometimes occurred to me that, being myself more the parfait gentle knight, if you know what I mean, I am in grave danger of getting the short end. Taking all these things into consideration, then, I cannot breeze off to the Mediterranean, leaving this Pim a clear field. You must see that?'

Aunt Dahlia laughed. Rather a nasty laugh. Scorn in its *timbre*, or so it seemed to me.

'I shouldn't worry,' she said. 'You don't suppose for a moment that Jeeves will sanction the match?'

I was stung.

'Do you imply, Aunt Dahlia,' I said—and I can't remember if I rapped the table with the handle of my fork or not, but I rather think I did—'that

I allow Jeeves to boss me to the extent of stopping me marrying somebody I want to marry?'

'Well, he stopped you wearing a moustache, didn't he? And purple socks. And soft-fronted shirts with dress-clothes.'

'That is a different matter altogether.'

'Well, I'm prepared to make a small bet with you, Bertie. Jeeves will stop this match.'

'What absolute rot!'

'And if he doesn't like that portrait, he will get rid of it.'

'I never heard such dashed nonsense in my life.'

'And, finally, you wretched, pie-faced wambler, he will present you on board my yacht at the appointed hour. I don't know how he will do it, but you will be there, all complete with yachting-cap and spare pair of socks.'

'Let us change the subject, Aunt Dahlia,' I said coldly.

Being a good deal stirred up by the attitude of the flesh-and-blood at the luncheon-table, I had to go for a bit of a walk in the Park after leaving, to soothe the nervous system. By about four-thirty the ganglions had ceased to vibrate, and I returned to the flat. Jeeves was in the sitting-room, looking at the portrait.

I felt a trifle embarrassed in the man's presence, because just before leaving I had informed him of my intention to scratch the yacht-trip, and he had taken it on the chin a bit. You see, he had been looking forward to it rather. From the moment I had accepted the invitation, there had been a sort of nautical glitter in his eye, and I'm not sure I hadn't heard him trolling Chanties in the kitchen. I think some ancestor of his must have been one of Nelson's tars or something, for he has always had the urge of the salt sea in his blood. I have noticed him on liners, when we were going to America, striding the deck with a sailorly roll and giving the distinct impression of being just about to heave the main-brace or splice the binnacle.

So, though I had explained my reasons, taking the man fully into my confidence and concealing nothing, I knew that he was distinctly peeved; and my first act, on entering, was to do the cheery a bit. I joined him in front of the portrait.

'Looks good, Jeeves, what?'

'Yes, sir.'

'Nothing like a spot of art for brightening the home.'

'No, sir.'

'Seems to lend the room a certain—what shall I say—'

'Yes, sir.'

The responses were all right, but his manner was far from hearty, and I decided to tackle him squarely. I mean, dash it. I mean, I don't know if you have ever had your portrait painted, but if you have you will understand my feelings. The spectacle of one's portrait hanging on the wall creates in one a sort of paternal fondness for the thing: and what you demand from the outside public is approval and enthusiasm—not the curling lip, the twitching nostril, and the kind of supercilious look which you see in the eye of a dead mackerel. Especially is this so when the artist is a girl for whom you have conceived sentiments deeper and warmer than those of ordinary friendship.

'Jeeves,' I said, 'you don't like this spot of art.'

'Oh, yes, sir.'

'No. Subterfuge is useless. I can read you like a book. For some reason this spot of art fails to appeal to you. What do you object to about it?'

'Is not the colour-scheme a trifle bright, sir?'

'I had not observed it, Jeeves. Anything else?'

'Well, in my opinion, sir, Miss Pendlebury has given you a somewhat too hungry expression.'

'Hungry?'

'A little like that of a dog regarding a distant bone, sir.'

I checked the fellow.

'There is no resemblance whatever, Jeeves, to a dog regarding a distant bone. The look to which you allude is wistful and denotes Soul.'

'I see, sir.'

I proceeded to another subject.

'Miss Pendlebury said she might look in this afternoon to inspect the portrait. Did she turn up?'

'Yes, sir.'

'But has left?'

'Yes, sir.'

'You mean she's gone, what?'

'Precisely, sir.'

'She didn't say anything about coming back, I suppose?'

'No, sir. I received the impression that it was not Miss Pendlebury's intention to return. She was a little upset, sir, and expressed a desire to go to her studio and rest.'

'Upset? What was she upset about?'

'The accident, sir.'

I didn't actually clutch the brow, but I did a bit of mental brow-clutching, as it were.

'Don't tell me she had an accident!'

'Yes, sir.'

'What sort of accident?'

'Automobile, sir.'

'Was she hurt?'

'No, sir. Only the gentleman.'

'What gentleman?'

'Miss Pendlebury had the misfortune to run over a gentleman in her car almost immediately opposite this building. He sustained a slight fracture of the leg.'

'Too bad! But Miss Pendlebury is all right?'

'Physically, sir, her condition appeared to be satisfactory. She was suffering a certain distress of mind.'

'Of course, with her beautiful, sympathetic nature. Naturally. It's a hard world for a girl, Jeeves, with fellows flinging themselves under the wheels of her car in one long, unending stream. It must have been a great shock to her. What became of the chump?'

'The gentleman, sir?'

'Yes.'

'He is in your spare bedroom, sir.'

'What!'

'Yes, sir.'

'In my spare bedroom?'

'Yes, sir. It was Miss Pendlebury's desire that he should be taken there.

She instructed me to telegraph to the gentleman's sister, sir, who is in Paris, advising her of the accident. I also summoned a medical man, who gave it as his opinion that the patient should remain for the time being *in statu quo*.'

'You mean, the corpse is on the premises for an indefinite visit?'

'Yes, sir.'

'Jeeves, this is a bit thick!'

'Yes, sir.'

And I meant it, dash it. I mean to say, a girl can be pretty heftily divine and ensnare the heart and what not, but she's no right to turn a fellow's flat into a morgue. I'm bound to say that for a moment passion ebbed a trifle.

'Well, I suppose I'd better go and introduce myself to the blighter. After all, I am his host. Has he a name?'

'Mr Pim, sir.'

'Pim!'

'Yes, sir. And the young lady addressed him as Lucius. It was owing to the fact that he was on his way here to examine the portrait which she had painted that Mr Pim happened to be in the roadway at the moment when Miss Pendlebury turned the corner.'

I headed for the spare bedroom. I was perturbed to a degree. I don't know if you have ever loved and been handicapped in your wooing by a wavy-haired rival, but one of the things you don't want in such circs is the rival parking himself on the premises with a broken leg. Apart from anything else, the advantage the position gives him is obviously terrific. There he is, sitting up and toying with a grape and looking pale and interesting, the object of the girl's pity and concern, and where do you get off, bounding about the place in morning costume and spats and with the rude flush of health on the cheek? It seemed to me that things were beginning to look pretty mouldy.

I found Lucius Pim lying in bed, draped in a suit of my pyjamas, smoking one of my cigarettes, and reading a detective story. He waved the cigarette at me in what I considered a dashed patronizing manner.

'Ah, Wooster!' he said.

'Not so much of the "Ah, Wooster!"' I replied brusquely. 'How soon can you be moved?'

'In a week or so, I fancy.'

'In a week!'

'Or so. For the moment, the doctor insists on perfect quiet and repose. So forgive me, old man, for asking you not to raise your voice. A hushed whisper is the stuff to give the troops. And now, Wooster, about this accident. We must come to an understanding.'

'Are you sure you can't be moved?'

'Quite. The doctor said so.'

'I think we ought to get a second opinion.'

'Useless, my dear fellow. He was most emphatic, and evidently a man who knew his job. Don't worry about my not being comfortable here. I shall be quite all right. I like this bed. And now, to return to the subject of this accident. My sister will be arriving to-morrow. She will be greatly upset. I am her favourite brother.'

'You are?'

'I am.'

'How many of you are there?'

'Six.'

'And you're her favourite?'

'I am.'

It seemed to me that the other five must be pretty fairly sub-human, but I didn't say so. We Woosters can curb the tongue.

'She married a bird named Slingsby. Slingsby's Superb Soups. He rolls in money. But do you think I can get him to lend a trifle from time to time to a needy brother-in-law?' said Lucius Pim bitterly. 'No, sir! However, that is neither here nor there. The point is that my sister loves me devotedly: and, this being the case, she might try to prosecute and persecute and generally bite pieces out of poor little Gwladys if she knew that it was she who was driving the car that laid me out. She must never know, Wooster. I appeal to you as a man of honour to keep your mouth shut.'

'Naturally.'

'I'm glad you grasp the point so readily, Wooster. You are not the fool people take you for.'

'Who takes me for a fool?'

The Pim raised his eyebrows slightly.

'Don't people?' he said. 'Well, well. Anyway, that's settled. Unless I can think of something better I shall tell my sister that I was knocked down by a car which drove on without stopping and I didn't get its number. And now perhaps you had better leave me. The doctor made a point of quiet and repose. Moreover, I want to go on with this story. The villain has just dropped a cobra down the heroine's chimney, and I must be at her side. It is impossible not to be thrilled by Edgar Wallace. I'll ring if I want anything.'

I headed for the sitting-room. I found Jeeves there, staring at the portrait in rather a marked manner, as if it hurt him.

'Jeeves,' I said, 'Mr Pim appears to be a fixture.'

'Yes, sir.'

'For the nonce, at any rate. And to-morrow we shall have his sister, Mrs Slingsby, of Slingsby's Superb Soups, in our midst.'

'Yes, sir. I telegraphed to Mrs Slingsby shortly before four. Assuming her to have been at her hotel in Paris at the moment of the telegram's delivery, she will no doubt take a boat early to-morrow afternoon, reaching Dover—or, should she prefer the alternative route, Folkestone—in time to begin the railway journey at an hour which will enable her to arrive in London at about seven. She will possibly proceed first to her London residence—'

'Yes, Jeeves,' I said, 'yes. A gripping story, full of action and human interest. You must have it set to music some time and sing it. Meanwhile, get this into your head. It is imperative that Mrs Slingsby does not learn that it was Miss Pendlebury who broke her brother in two places. I shall require you, therefore, to approach Mr Pim before she arrives, ascertain exactly what tale he intends to tell, and be prepared to back it up in every particular.'

'Very good, sir.'

'And now, Jeeves, what of Miss Pendlebury?'

'Sir?'

'She's sure to call to make inquiries.'

'Yes, sir.'

'Well, she mustn't find me here. You know all about women, Jeeves?'

'Yes, sir.'

'Then tell me this. Am I not right in supposing that if Miss Pendlebury is in a position to go into the sick-room, take a long look at the interesting invalid, and then pop out, with the memory of that look fresh in her mind, and get a square sight of me lounging about in sponge-bag trousers, she will draw damaging comparisons? You see what I mean? Look on this picture and on that—the one romantic, the other not . . . Eh?'

'Very true, sir. It is a point which I had intended to bring to your attention. An invalid undoubtedly exercises a powerful appeal to the motherliness which exists in every woman's heart, sir. Invalids seem to stir their deepest feelings. The poet Scott has put the matter neatly in the lines—"Oh, Woman in our hours of ease uncertain, coy, and hard to please . . . When pain and anguish rack the brow—"'

I held up a hand.

'At some other time, Jeeves,' I said, 'I shall be delighted to hear you say your piece, but just now I am not in the mood. The position being as I have outlined, I propose to clear out early to-morrow morning and not to reappear until nightfall. I shall take the car and dash down to Brighton for the day.'

'Very good, sir.'

'It is better so, is it not, Jeeves?'

'Indubitably, sir.'

'I think so, too. The sea breezes will tone up my system, which sadly needs a dollop of toning. I leave you in charge of the old home.'

'Very good, sir.'

'Convey my regrets and sympathy to Miss Pendlebury and tell her I have been called away on business.'

'Yes, sir.'

'Should the Slingsby require refreshment, feed her in moderation.'

'Very good, sir.'

'And, in poisoning Mr Pim's soup, don't use arsenic, which is readily detected. Go to a good chemist and get something that leaves no traces.'

I sighed, and cocked an eye at the portrait.

'All this is very wonky, Jeeves.'

'Yes, sir.'

'When that portrait was painted, I was a happy man.'

'Yes, sir.'

'Ah, well, Jeeves!'

'Very true, sir.'

And we left it at that.

… … …

It was lateish when I got back on the following evening. What with a bit of ozone-sniffing, a good dinner, and a nice run home in the moonlight with the old car going as sweet as a nut, I was feeling in pretty good shape once more. In fact, coming through Purley, I went so far as to sing a trifle. The spirit of the Woosters is a buoyant spirit, and optimism had begun to reign again in the W. bosom.

The way I looked at it was, I saw I had been mistaken in assuming that a girl must necessarily love a fellow just because he has broken a leg. At first, no doubt, Gwladys Pendlebury would feel strangely drawn to the Pim when she saw him lying there a more or less total loss. But it would not be long before other reflections crept in. She would ask herself if she were wise in trusting her life's happiness to a man who hadn't enough sense to leap out of the way when he saw a car coming. She would tell herself that, if this sort of thing had happened once, who knew that it might not go on happening again and again all down the long years. And she would recoil from a married life which consisted entirely of going to hospitals and taking her husband fruit. She would realize how much better off she would be, teamed up with a fellow like Bertram Wooster, who, whatever his faults, at least walked on the pavement and looked up and down a street before he crossed it.

It was in excellent spirits, accordingly, that I put the car in the garage, and it was with a merry Tra-la on my lips that I let myself into the flat as Big Ben began to strike eleven. I rang the bell and presently, as if he had divined my wishes, Jeeves came in with siphon and decanter.

'Home again, Jeeves,' I said, mixing a spot.

'Yes, sir.'

'What has been happening in my absence? Did Miss Pendlebury call?'

'Yes, sir. At about two o'clock.'

'And left?'

'At about six, sir.'

I didn't like this so much. A four-hour visit struck me as a bit sinister. However, there was nothing to be done about it.

'And Mrs Slingsby?'

'She arrived shortly after eight and left at ten, sir.'

'Ah? Agitated?'

'Yes, sir. Particularly when she left. She was very desirous of seeing you, sir.'

'Seeing me?'

'Yes, sir.'

'Wanted to thank me brokenly, I suppose, for so courteously allowing her favourite brother a place to have his game legs in. Eh?'

'Possibly, sir. On the other hand, she alluded to you in terms suggestive of disapprobation, sir.'

'She—what?'

'"Feckless idiot" was one of the expressions she employed, sir.'

'Feckless idiot?'

'Yes, sir.'

I couldn't make it out. I simply couldn't see what the woman had based her judgement on. My Aunt Agatha has frequently said that sort of thing about me, but she has known me from a boy.

'I must look into this, Jeeves. Is Mr Pim asleep?'

'No, sir. He rang the bell a moment ago to inquire if we had not a better brand of cigarette in the flat.'

'He did, did he?'

'Yes, sir.'

'The accident doesn't seem to have affected his nerve.'

'No, sir.'

I found Lucius Pim sitting propped up among the pillows, reading his detective story.

'Ah, Wooster,' he said. 'Welcome home. I say, in case you were worrying, it's all right about that cobra. The hero had got at it without the villain's knowledge and extracted its poison-fangs. With the result that when it fell down the chimney and started trying to bite the heroine its efforts were null and void. I doubt if a cobra has ever felt so silly.'

'Never mind about cobras.'

'It's no good saying "Never mind about cobras",' said Lucius Pim in a gentle, rebuking sort of voice. 'You've jolly well *got* to mind about cobras, if they haven't had their poison-fangs extracted. Ask anyone. By the way, my sister looked in. She wants to have a word with you.'

'And I want to have a word with her.'

'"Two minds with but a single thought". What she wants to talk to you about is this accident of mine. You remember that story I was to tell her? About the car driving on? Well the understanding was, if you recollect, that I was only to tell it if I couldn't think of something better. Fortunately, I thought of something much better. It came to me in a flash as I lay in bed looking at the ceiling. You see, that driving-on story was thin. People don't knock fellows down and break their legs and go driving on. The thing wouldn't have held water for a minute. So I told her you did it.'

'What!'

'I said it was you who did it in your car. Much more likely. Makes the whole thing neat and well-rounded. I knew you would approve. At all costs we have got to keep it from her that I was outed by Gwladys. I made it as easy for you as I could, saying that you were a bit pickled at the time and so not to be blamed for what you did. Some fellows wouldn't have thought of that. Still,' said Lucius Pim with a sigh, 'I'm afraid she's not any too pleased with you.'

'She isn't, isn't she?'

'No, she is not. And I strongly recommend you, if you want anything like a pleasant interview to-morrow, to sweeten her a bit overnight.'

'How do you mean, sweeten her?'

'I'd suggest you sent her some flowers. It would be a graceful gesture. Roses are her favourites. Shoot her in a few roses—Number Three, Hill Street is the address—and it may make all the difference. I think it my duty to inform you, old man, that my sister Beatrice is rather a tough egg, when roused. My brother-in-law is due back from New York at any moment, and the danger, as I see it, is that Beatrice, unless sweetened, will get at him and make him bring actions against you for torts and malfeasances and what not and get thumping damages. He isn't over-fond of me and, left to himself, would rather approve than otherwise of people who broke my legs: but he's crazy about Beatrice and will do anything she asks him to. So my advice is, Gather ye rose-buds, while ye may and bung them in to Number Three, Hill Street. Otherwise, the case of Slingsby *v.* Wooster will be on the calendar before you can say "What-ho".'

I gave the fellow a look. Lost on him, of course.

'It's a pity you didn't think of all that before,' I said. And it wasn't so much the actual words, if you know what I mean, as the way I said it.

'I thought of it all right,' said Lucius Pim. 'But, as we were both agreed that at all costs—'

'Oh, all right,' I said. 'All right, all right.'

'You aren't annoyed?' said Lucius Pim, looking at me with a touch of surprise.

'Oh, no!'

'Splendid,' said Lucius Pim, relieved. 'I knew you would feel that I had done the only possible thing. It would have been awful if Beatrice had found out about Gwladys. I daresay you have noticed, Wooster, that when women find themselves in a position to take a running kick at one of their own sex they are twice as rough on her as they would be on a man. Now, you, being of the male persuasion, will find everything made nice and smooth for you. A quart of assorted roses, a few smiles, a tactful word or two, and she'll have melted before you know where you are. Play your cards properly, and you and Beatrice will be laughing merrily and having a game of Round and Round the Mulberry Bush together in about five minutes. Better not let Slingsby's Soups catch you at it, however. He's very jealous where Beatrice is concerned. And now you'll forgive me, old chap, if I send you away. The doctor says I ought not to talk too much for a day or two. Besides, it's time for bye-bye.'

The more I thought it over, the better that idea of sending those roses looked. Lucius Pim was not a man I was fond of—in fact, if I had had to choose between him and a cockroach as a companion for a walking-tour, the cockroach would have had it by a short head—but there was no doubt that he had outlined the right policy. His advice was good, and I decided to follow it. Rising next morning at ten-fifteen, I swallowed a strengthening breakfast and legged it off to that flower-shop in Piccadilly. I couldn't leave the thing to Jeeves. It was essentially a mission that demanded the personal touch. I laid out a couple of quid on a sizeable bouquet, sent it with my card to Hill Street, and then looked in at the Drones for a brief refresher. It is a thing I don't often do in the morning, but this threatened to be rather a special morning.

It was about noon when I got back to the flat. I went into the sitting-room and tried to adjust the mind to the coming interview. It had to be faced, of course, but it wasn't any good my telling myself that it was going to be one of those jolly scenes the memory of which cheer you up as you sit toasting your toes at the fire in your old age. I stood or fell by the roses. If they sweetened the Slingsby, all would be well. If they failed to sweeten her, Bertram was undoubtedly for it.

The clock ticked on, but she did not come. A late riser, I took it, and was slightly encouraged by the reflection. My experience of women has been that the earlier they leave the hay the more vicious specimens they are apt to be. My Aunt Agatha, for instance, is always up with the lark, and look at her.

Still, you couldn't be sure that this rule always worked, and after a while the suspense began to get in amongst me a bit. To divert the mind, I fetched the old putter out of its bag and began to practice putts into a glass. After all, even if the Slingsby turned out to be all that I had pictured her in my gloomier moments, I should have improved my close-to-the-hole work on the green and be that much up, at any rate.

It was while I was shaping for a rather tricky shot that the front-door bell went.

I picked up the glass and shoved the putter behind the settee. It struck me that if the woman found me engaged on what you might call a frivolous pursuit she might take it to indicate lack of remorse and proper feeling. I straightened the collar, pulled down the waistcoat, and managed to fasten on the face a sort of sad half-smile which was welcoming without being actually jovial. It looked all right in the mirror, and I held it as the door opened.

'Mr Slingsby,' announced Jeeves.

And, having spoken these words, he closed the door and left us alone together.

For quite a time there wasn't anything in the way of chit-chat. The shock of expecting Mrs Slingsby and finding myself confronted by something entirely different—in fact, not the same thing at all—seemed to have affected the vocal cords. And the visitor didn't appear to be disposed to make light conversation himself. He stood there looking strong and silent. I suppose you have to be like that if you want to manufacture anything in the nature of a really convincing soup.

Slingsby's Superb Soups was a Roman Emperor-looking sort of bird, with keen, penetrating eyes and one of those jutting chins. The eyes seemed to be fixed on me in a dashed unpleasant stare and, unless I was mistaken, he was grinding his teeth a trifle. For some reason he appeared to have taken a strong dislike to me at sight, and I'm bound to say this rather puzzled me. I don't pretend to have one of those Fascinating Personalities which you get from studying the booklets advertised in the back pages of the magazines, but I couldn't recall another case in the whole of my career where a single glimpse of the old map had been enough to make anyone look as if he wanted to foam at the mouth. Usually, when people meet me for the first time, they don't seem to know I'm there.

However, I exerted myself to play the host.

'Mr Slingsby?'

'That is my name.'

'Just got back from America?'

'I landed this morning.'

'Sooner than you were expected, what?'

'So I imagine.'

'Very glad to see you.'

'You will not be long.'

I took time off to do a bit of gulping. I saw now what had happened. This bloke had been home, seen his wife, heard the story of the accident, and had hastened round to the flat to slip it across me. Evidently those roses had not sweetened the female of the species. The only thing to do now seemed to be to take a stab at sweetening the male.

'Have a drink?' I said.

'No!'

'A cigarette?'

'No!'

'A chair?'

'No!'

I went into the silence once more. These non-drinking, non-smoking non-sitters are hard birds to handle.

'Don't grin at me, sir!'

I shot a glance at myself in the mirror, and saw what he meant. The sad half-smile *had* slopped over a bit. I adjusted it, and there was another pause.

'Now, sir,' said the Superb Souper. 'To business. I think I need scarcely tell you why I am here.'

'No. Of course. Absolutely. It's about that little matter—'

He gave a snort which nearly upset a vase on the mantelpiece.

'Little matter? So you consider it a little matter, do you?'

'Well—'

'Let me tell you, sir, that when I find that during my absence from the country a man has been annoying my wife with his importunities I regard it as anything but a little matter. And I shall endeavour,' said the Souper, the eyes gleaming a trifle brighter as he rubbed his hands together in a hideous, menacing way, 'to make you see the thing in the same light.'

I couldn't make head or tail of this. I simply couldn't follow him. The lemon began to swim.

'Eh?' I said. 'Your wife?'

'You heard me.'

'There must be some mistake.'

'There is. You made it.'

'But I don't know your wife.'

'Ha!'

'I've never even met her.'

'Tchah!'

'Honestly, I haven't.'

'Bah!'

He drank me in for a moment.

'Do you deny you sent her flowers?'

I felt the heart turn a double somersault. I began to catch his drift.

'Flowers!' he proceeded. 'Roses, sir. Great, fat, beastly roses. Enough of them to sink a ship. Your card was attached to them by a small pin—'

His voice died away in a sort of gurgle, and I saw that he was staring at something behind me. I spun round, and there, in the doorway—I hadn't seen it open, because during the last spasm of dialogue I had been backing cautiously towards it—there in the doorway stood a female. One glance was enough to tell me who she was. No woman could look so like Lucius Pim who hadn't the misfortune to be related to him. It was Sister Beatrice, the tough egg. I saw all. She had left home before the flowers had arrived: she had sneaked, unsweetened, into the flat, while I was fortifying the system at the Drones: and here she was.

'Er—' I said.

'Alexander!' said the female.

'Goo!' said the Souper. Or it may have been 'Coo'.

Whatever it was, it was in the nature of a battle-cry or slogan of war. The Souper's worst suspicions had obviously been confirmed. His eyes shone with a strange light. His chin pushed itself out another couple of inches. He clenched and unclenched his fingers once or twice, as if to make sure that they were working properly and could be relied on to do a good, clean job of strangling. Then, once more observing 'Coo!' (or 'Goo!'), he sprang forward, trod on the golf-ball I had been practising putting with, and took one of the finest tosses I have ever witnessed. The purler of a lifetime. For a moment the air seemed to be full of arms and legs, and then, with a thud that nearly dislocated the flat, he made a forced landing against the wall.

And, feeling I had had about all I wanted, I oiled from the room and was in the act of grabbing my hat from the rack in the hall, when Jeeves appeared.

'I fancied I heard a noise, sir,' said Jeeves.

'Quite possibly,' I said. 'It was Mr Slingsby.'

'Sir?'

'Mr Slingsby practicing Russian dances,' I explained. 'I rather think he has fractured an assortment of limbs. Better go in and see.'

'Very good, sir.'

'If he is the wreck I imagine, put him in my room and send for the doctor. The flat is filling up nicely with the various units of the Pim family and its connections, eh, Jeeves?'

'Yes, sir.'

'I think the supply is about exhausted, but should any aunts or uncles by marriage come along and break their limbs, bed them out on the Chesterfield.'

'Very good, sir.'

'I, personally, Jeeves,' I said, opening the front door and pausing on the threshold, 'am off to Paris. I will wire you the address. Notify me in due course when the place is free from Pims and completely purged of Slingsbys, and I will return. Oh, and Jeeves.'

'Sir?'

'Spare no effort to mollify these birds. They think—at least, Slingsby (female) thinks, and what she thinks to-day he will think to-morrow—that it was I who ran over Mr Pim in my car. Endeavour during my absence to sweeten them.'

'Very good, sir.'

'And now perhaps you had better be going in and viewing the body. I shall proceed to the Drones, where I shall lunch, subsequently catching the two o'clock train at Charing Cross. Meet me there with an assortment of luggage.'

It was a matter of three weeks or so before Jeeves sent me the 'All clear' signal. I spent the time pottering pretty perturbedly about Paris and environs. It is a city I am fairly fond of, but I was glad to be able to return to the old home. I hopped on to a passing aeroplane and a couple of hours later was bowling through Croydon on my way to the centre of things. It was somewhere down in the Sloane Square neighbourhood that I first caught sight of the posters.

A traffic block had occurred, and I was glancing idly this way and that, when suddenly my eye was caught by something that looked familiar. And then I saw what it was.

Pasted on a blank wall and measuring about a hundred feet each way was an enormous poster, mostly red and blue. At the top of it were the words:

SLINGSBY'S SUPERB SOUPS

and at the bottom:

SUCCULENT AND STRENGTHENING

And, in between, me. Yes, dash it, Bertram Wooster in person. A reproduction of the Pendlebury portrait, perfect in every detail.

It was the sort of thing to make a fellow's eyes flicker, and mine flickered. You might say a mist seemed to roll before them. Then it lifted, and I was able to get a good long look before the traffic moved on.

Of all the absolutely foul sights I have ever seen, this took the biscuit with ridiculous ease. The thing was a bally libel on the Wooster face, and yet it was as unmistakable as if it had had my name under it. I saw now what Jeeves had meant when he said that the portrait had given me a hungry look. In the poster this look had become one of bestial greed. There I sat absolutely slavering through a monocle about six inches in circumference at a plateful of soup, looking as if I hadn't had a meal for weeks. The whole thing seemed to take one straight away into a different and a dreadful world.

I woke from a species of trance or coma to find myself at the door of the block of flats. To buzz upstairs and charge into the home was with me the work of a moment.

Jeeves came shimmering down the hall, the respectful beam of welcome on his face.

'I am glad to see you back, sir.'

'Never mind about that,' I yipped. 'What about—?'

'The posters, sir? I was wondering if you might have observed them.'

'I observed them!'

'Striking, sir?'

'Very striking. Now, perhaps you'll kindly explain—'

'You instructed me, if you recollect, sir, to spare no effort to mollify Mr Slingsby.'

'Yes, but—'

'It proved a somewhat difficult task, sir. For some time Mr Slingsby, on the advice and owing to the persuasion of Mrs Slingsby, appeared to be resolved to institute an action in law against you—a procedure which I knew you would find most distasteful.'

'Yes, but—'

'And then, the first day he was able to leave his bed, he observed the portrait, and it seemed to me judicious to point out to him its possibilities as an advertising medium. He readily fell in with the suggestion and, on my assurance that, should he abandon the projected action in law, you would willingly permit the use of the portrait, he entered into negotiations with Miss Pendlebury for the purchase of the copyright.'

'Oh? Well, I hope she's got something out of it, at any rate?'

'Yes, sir. Mr Pim, acting as Miss Pendlebury's agent, drove, I understand, an extremely satisfactory bargain.'

'He acted as her agent, eh?'

'Yes, sir. In his capacity as fiancé to the young lady, sir.'

'Fiancé!'

'Yes, sir.'

It shows how the sight of that poster had got into my ribs when I state that, instead of being laid out cold by this announcement, I merely said 'Ha!' or 'Ho!' or it may have been 'H'm'. After the poster, nothing seemed to matter.

'After that poster, Jeeves,' I said, 'nothing seems to matter.'

'No, sir?'

'No, Jeeves. A woman has tossed my heart lightly away, but what of it?'

'Exactly, sir.'

'The voice of Love seemed to call to me, but it was a wrong number. Is that going to crush me?'

'No, sir.'

'No, Jeeves. It is not. But what does matter is this ghastly business of my face being spread from end to end of the Metropolis with the eyes fixed on a plate of Slingsby's Superb Soup. I must leave London. The lads at the Drones will kid me without ceasing.'

'Yes, sir. And Mrs Spenser Gregson—'

I paled visibly. I hadn't thought of Aunt Agatha and what she might have to say about letting down the family prestige.

'You don't mean to say she has been ringing up?'

'Several times daily, sir.'

'Jeeves, flight is the only resource.'

'Yes, sir.'

'Back to Paris, what?'

'I should not recommend the move, sir. The posters are, I understand, shortly to appear in that city also, advertising the *Bouillon Suprême*. Mr Slingsby's products command a large sale in France. The sight would be painful for you, sir.'

'Then where?'

'If I might make a suggestion, sir, why not adhere to your original intention of cruising in Mrs Travers' yacht in the Mediterranean? On the yacht you would be free from the annoyance of these advertising displays.'

The man seemed to me to be drivelling.

'But the yacht started weeks ago. It may be anywhere by now.'

'No, sir. The cruise was postponed for a month owing to the illness of Mr Travers' chef, Anatole, who contracted influenza. Mr Travers refused to sail without him.'

'You mean they haven't started?'

'Not yet, sir. The yacht sails from Southampton on Tuesday next.'

'Why, then, dash it, nothing could be sweeter.'

'No, sir.'

'Ring up Aunt Dahlia and tell her we'll be there.'

'I ventured to take the liberty of doing so a few moments before you arrived, sir.'

'You did?'

'Yes, sir. I thought it probable that the plan would meet with your approval.'

'It does! I've wished all along I was going on that cruise.'

'I, too, sir. It should be extremely pleasant.'

'The tang of the salt breezes, Jeeves!'

'Yes, sir.'

'The moonlight on the water!'

'Precisely, sir.'

'The gentle heaving of the waves!'

'Exactly, sir.'

I felt absolutely in the pink. Gwladys—pah! The posters—bah! That was the way I looked at it.

'Yo-ho-ho, Jeeves!' I said, giving the trousers a bit of a hitch.

'Yes, sir.'

'In fact, I will go further. Yo-ho-ho and a bottle of rum!'

'Very good, sir. I will bring it immediately.'

7

JEEVES AND THE KID CLEMENTINA

It has been well said of Bertram Wooster by those who know him best that, whatever other sporting functions he may see fit to oil out of, you will always find him battling to his sixteen handicap at the annual Golf tournament of the Drones Club. Nevertheless, when I heard that this year they were holding it at Bingley-on-Sea, I confess I hesitated. As I stood gazing out of the window of my suite at the Splendide on the morning of the opening day, I was not exactly a-twitter, if you understand me, but I couldn't help feeling I might have been rather rash.

'Jeeves,' I said, 'now that we have actually arrived, I find myself wondering if it was quite prudent to come here.'

'It is a pleasant spot, sir.'

'Where every prospect pleases,' I agreed. 'But though the spicy breezes blow fair o'er Bingley-on-Sea, we must never forget that this is where my Aunt Agatha's old friend, Miss Mapleton, runs a girl's school. If the relative knew I was here, she would expect me to call on Miss Mapleton.'

'Very true, sir.'

I shivered somewhat.

'I met her once, Jeeves. 'Twas on a summer's evening in my tent, the day

I overcame the Nervii. Or, rather, at lunch at Aunt Agatha's a year ago come Lammas Eve. It is not an experience I would willingly undergo again.'

'Indeed, sir?'

'Besides, you remember what happened last time I got into a girls' school?'

'Yes, sir.'

'Secrecy and silence, then. My visit here must be strictly incog. If Aunt Agatha happens to ask you where I spent this week, tell her I went to Harrogate for the cure.'

'Very good, sir. Pardon me, sir, are you proposing to appear in those garments in public?'

Up to this point our conversation had been friendly and cordial, but I now perceived that the jarring note had been struck. I had been wondering when my new plus-fours would come under discussion, and I was prepared to battle for them like a tigress for her young.

'Certainly, Jeeves,' I said. 'Why? Don't you like them?'

'No, sir.'

'You think them on the bright side?'

'Yes, sir.'

'A little vivid, they strike you as?'

'Yes, sir.'

'Well, I think highly of them, Jeeves,' I said firmly.

There already being a certain amount of chilliness in the air, it seemed to me a suitable moment for springing another item of information which I had been keeping from him for some time.

'Er—Jeeves,' I said.

'Sir?'

'I ran into Miss Wickham the other day. After chatting of this and that, she invited me to join a party she is getting up to go to Antibes this summer.'

'Indeed, sir?'

He now looked definitely squiggle-eyed. Jeeves, as I think I have mentioned before, does not approve of Bobbie Wickham.

There was what you might call a tense silence. I braced myself for an exhibition of the good old Wooster determination. I mean to say, one has got to take a firm stand from time to time. The trouble with Jeeves is that he tends occasionally to get above himself. Just because he has surged round and—I admit it freely—done the young master a bit of good in one or two crises, he has a nasty way of conveying the impression that he looks on Bertram Wooster as a sort of idiot child who, but for him, would conk in the first chukka. I resent this.

'I have accepted, Jeeves,' I said in a quiet, level voice, lighting a cigarette with a careless flick of the wrist.

'Indeed, sir?'

'You will like Antibes.'

'Yes, sir?'

'So shall I.'

'Yes, sir?'

'That's settled, then.'

'Yes, sir.'

I was pleased. The firm stand, I saw, had done its work. It was plain that the man was crushed beneath the iron heel—cowed, if you know what I mean.

'Right-ho, then, Jeeves.'

'Very good, sir.'

I had not expected to return from the arena until well on in the evening, but circumstances so arranged themselves that it was barely three o'clock when I found myself back again. I was wandering moodily to and fro on the pier, when I observed Jeeves shimmering towards me.

'Good afternoon, sir,' he said. 'I had not supposed that you would be returning quite so soon, or I would have remained at the hotel.'

'I had not supposed that I would be returning quite so soon myself, Jeeves,' I said, sighing somewhat. 'I was outed in the first round, I regret to say.'

'Indeed, sir? I am sorry to hear that.'

'And, to increase the mortification of defeat, Jeeves, by a blighter who had not spared himself at the luncheon-table and was quite noticeably sozzled. I couldn't seem to do anything right.'

'Possibly you omitted to keep your eye on the ball with sufficient assiduity, sir?'

'Something of that nature, no doubt. Anyway, here I am, a game and popular loser and . . .' I paused, and scanned the horizon with some interest. 'Great Scott, Jeeves! Look at that girl just coming on to the pier. I never saw anybody so extraordinarily like Miss Wickham. How do you account for these resemblances?'

'In the present instance, sir, I attribute the similarity to the fact that the young lady *is* Miss Wickham.'

'Eh?'

'Yes, sir. If you notice, she is waving to you now.'

'But what on earth is she doing down here?'

'I am unable to say, sir.'

His voice was chilly and seemed to suggest that, whatever had brought Bobbie Wickham to Bingley-on-Sea, it could not, in his opinion, be anything good. He dropped back into the offing, registering alarm and despondency, and I removed the old Homburg and waggled it genially.

'What-ho!' I said.

Bobbie came to anchor alongside.

'Hullo, Bertie,' she said. 'I didn't know you were here.'

'I am,' I assured her.

'In mourning?' she asked, eyeing the trouserings.

'Rather natty, aren't they?' I said, following her gaze. 'Jeeves doesn't like them, but then he's notoriously hidebound in the matter of leg-wear. What are you doing in Bingley?'

'My cousin Clementina is at school here. It's her birthday and I thought I would come down and see her. I'm just off there now. Are you staying here to-night?'

'Yes. At the Splendide.'

'You can give me dinner there if you like.'

Jeeves was behind me, and I couldn't see him, but at these words I felt his eye slap warningly against the back of my neck. I knew what it was that he was trying to broadcast—viz. that it would be tempting Providence to mix with Bobbie Wickham even to the extent of giving her a bite to eat. Dashed absurd, was my verdict. Get entangled with young Bobbie in the intricate life of a country-house, where almost anything can happen, and I'm not saying. But how any doom or disaster could lurk behind the simple pronging of a spot of dinner together, I failed to see. I ignored the man.

'Of course. Certainly. Rather. Absolutely,' I said.

'That'll be fine. I've got to get back to London to-night for revelry of sorts at the Berkeley, but it doesn't matter if I'm a bit late. We'll turn up at about seven-thirty, and you can take us to the movies afterwards.'

'We? Us?'

'Clementina and me.'

'You don't mean you intend to bring your ghastly cousin?'

'Of course I do. Don't you want the child to have a little pleasure on her birthday? And she isn't ghastly. She's a dear. She won't be any trouble. All you'll have to do is take her back to the school afterwards. You can manage that without straining a sinew, can't you?'

I eyed her keenly.

'What does it involve?'

'How do you mean, what does it involve?'

'The last time I was lured into a girls' school, a headmistress with an eye like a gimlet insisted on my addressing the chain-gang on Ideals and the Life To Come. This will not happen to-night?'

'Of course not. You just go to the front door, ring the bell, and bung her in.'

I mused.

'That would appear to be well within our scope. Eh, Jeeves?'

'I should be disposed to imagine so, sir.'

The man's tone was cold and soupy: and, scanning his face, I observed on it an 'If-you-would-only-be-guided-by-me' expression which annoyed me intensely. There are moments when Jeeves looks just like an aunt.

'Right,' I said, ignoring him once more—and rather pointedly, at that. 'Then I'll expect you at seven-thirty. Don't be late. And see,' I added, just to show the girl that beneath the smiling exterior I was a man of iron, 'that the kid has her hands washed and does not sniff.'

I had not, I confess, looked forward with any great keenness to hobnobbing with Bobbie Wickham's cousin Clementina, but I'm bound to admit that she might have been considerably worse. Small girls as a rule, I have noticed, are inclined, when confronted with me, to giggle a good deal. They snigger and they stare. I look up and find their eyes glued on me in an incredulous manner, as if they were reluctant to believe that I was really true. I suspect them of being in the process of memorizing any little peculiarities of deportment that I may possess, in order to reproduce them later for the entertainment of their fellow-inmates.

With the kid Clementina there was nothing of this description. She was a quiet, saintlike child of about thirteen—in fact, seeing that this was her birthday, exactly thirteen—and her gaze revealed only silent admiration. Her hands were spotless; she had not a cold in the head; and at dinner, during which her behaviour was unexceptionable, she proved a sympathetic listener, hanging on my lips, so to speak, when with the aid of a fork and two peas I explained to her how my opponent that afternoon had stymied me on the tenth.

She was equally above criticism at the movies, and at the conclusion of the proceedings thanked me for the treat with visible emotion. I was pleased with the child, and said as much to Bobbie while assisting her into her two-seater.

'Yes, I told you she was a dear,' said Bobbie, treading on the self-starter in preparation for the dash to London. 'I always insist that they misjudge her at that school. They're always misjudging people. They misjudged me when I was there.'

'Misjudge her? How?'

'Oh, in various ways. But, then, what can you expect of a dump like St Monica's?'

I started.

'St Monica's?'

'That's the name of the place.'

'You don't mean the kid is at Miss Mapleton's school?'

'Why shouldn't she be?'

'But Miss Mapleton is my Aunt Agatha's oldest friend.'

'I know. It was your Aunt Agatha who got mother to send me there when I was a kid.'

'I say,' I said earnestly, 'when you were there this afternoon you didn't mention having met me down here?'

'No.'

'That's all right.' I was relieved. 'You see, if Miss Mapleton knew I was in Bingley, she would expect me to call. I shall be leaving to-morrow morning, so all will be well. But, dash it,' I said, spotting the snag, 'how about to-night?'

'What about to-night?'

'Well, shan't I have to see her? I can't just ring the front-door bell, sling the kid in, and leg it. I should never hear the last of it from Aunt Agatha.'

Bobbie looked at me in an odd, meditative sort of way.

'As a matter of fact, Bertie,' she said, 'I had been meaning to touch on that point. I think, if I were you, I wouldn't ring the front-door bell.'

'Eh? Why not?'

'Well, it's like this, you see. Clementina is supposed to be in bed. They sent her there just as I was leaving this afternoon. Think of it! On her birthday—right plumb spang in the middle of her birthday—and all for putting sherbet in the ink to make it fizz!'

I reeled.

'You aren't telling me that this foul kid came out without leave?'

'Yes, I am. That's exactly it. She got up and sneaked out when nobody was looking. She had set her heart on getting a square meal. I suppose I really ought to have told you right at the start, but I didn't want to spoil your evening.'

As a general rule, in my dealings with the delicately-nurtured, I am the soul of knightly chivalry—suave, genial and polished. But I can on occasion say the bitter, cutting thing, and I said it now.

'Oh?' I said.

'But it's all right.'

'Yes,' I said, speaking, if I recollect, between my clenched teeth, 'nothing could be sweeter, could it? The situation is one which it would be impossible to view with concern, what? I shall turn up with the kid, get looked at through steel-rimmed spectacles by the Mapleton, and after an agreeable five minutes shall back out, leaving the Mapleton to go to her escritoire and write a full account of the proceedings to my Aunt Agatha. And, contemplating what will happen after that, the imagination totters. I confidently expect my Aunt Agatha to beat all previous records.'

The girl clicked her tongue chidingly.

'Don't make such heavy weather, Bertie. You must learn not to fuss so.'

'I must, must I?'

'Everything's going to be all right. I'm not saying it won't be necessary to exercise a little strategy in getting Clem into the house, but it will be perfectly simple, if you'll only listen carefully to what I'm going to tell you. First, you will need a good long piece of string.'

'String?'

'String. Surely even you know what string is?'

I stiffened rather haughtily.

'Certainly,' I replied. 'You mean string.'

'That's right. String. You take this with you—'

'And soften the Mapleton's heart by doing tricks with it, I suppose?'

Bitter, I know. But I was deeply stirred.

'You take this string with you,' proceeded Bobbie patiently, 'and when you get into the garden you go through it till you come to a conservatory near the house. Inside it you will find a lot of flower-pots. How are you on recognizing a flower-pot when you see one, Bertie?'

'I am thoroughly familiar with flower-pots. If, as I suppose, you mean those sort of pot things they put flowers in.'

'That's exactly what I do mean. All right, then. Grab an armful of these flower-pots and go round the conservatory till you come to a tree. Climb this, tie a string to one of the pots, balance it on a handy branch which you will find overhangs the conservatory, and then, having stationed Clem near the front door, retire into the middle distance and jerk the string. The flower-pot will fall and smash the glass, someone in the house will hear the noise and come out to investigate, and while the door is open and nobody near Clem will sneak in and go up to bed.'

'But suppose no one comes out?'

'Then you repeat the process with another pot.'

It seemed sound enough.

'You're sure it will work?'

'It's never failed yet. That's the way I always used to get in after lock-up when I was at St Monica's. Now, you're sure you've got it clear, Bertie? Let's have a quick run-through to make certain, and then I really must be off. String.'

'String.'

'Conservatory.'

'Or greenhouse.'

'Flower-pot.'

'Flower-pot.'

'Tree. Climb. Branch. Climb down. Jerk. Smash. And then off to beddy-bye. Got it?'

'I've got it. But,' I said sternly, 'let me tell you just one thing—'

'I haven't time. I must rush. Write to me about it, using one side of the paper only. Good-bye.'

She rolled off, and after following her with burning eyes for a moment I returned to Jeeves, who was in the background showing the kid Clementina how to make a rabbit with a pocket handkerchief. I drew him aside. I was feeling a little better now, for I perceived that an admirable opportunity had presented itself for putting the man in his place and correcting his view that he is the only member of our establishment with brains and resource.

'Jeeves,' I said, 'you will doubtless be surprised to learn that something in the nature of a hitch has occurred.'

'Not at all, sir.'

'No?'

'No, sir. In matters where Miss Wickham is involved, I am, if I may take the liberty of saying so, always on the alert for hitches. If you recollect, sir, I have frequently observed that Miss Wickham, while a charming young lady, is apt—'

'Yes, yes, Jeeves. I know.'

'What would the precise nature of the trouble be this time, sir?'

I explained the circs.

'The kid is A.W.O.L. They sent her to bed for putting sherbet in the ink, and in bed they imagine her to have spent the evening. Instead of which, she was out with me, wolfing the eight-course table-d'hôte dinner at seven and six, and then going on to the Marine Plaza to enjoy an entertainment on the silver screen. It is our task to get her back into the house without anyone knowing. I may mention, Jeeves, that the school in which this young excrescence is serving her sentence is the one run by my Aunt Agatha's old friend, Miss Mapleton.'

'Indeed, sir?'

'A problem, Jeeves, what?'

'Yes, sir.'

'In fact, one might say a pretty problem?'

'Undoubtedly, sir. If I might suggest—'

I was expecting this. I raised a hand.

'I do not require any suggestions, Jeeves. I can handle this matter myself.'

'I was merely about to propose—'

I raised the hand again.

'Peace, Jeeves. I have the situation well under control. I have had one of my ideas. It may interest you to hear how my brain worked. It occurred to me, thinking the thing over, that a house like St Monica's would be likely to have near it a conservatory containing flower-pots. Then, like a flash, the whole thing came to me. I propose to procure some string, to tie it to a flower-pot, to balance the pot on a branch—there will, no doubt, be a tree near the conservatory with a branch overhanging it—and to retire to a distance, holding the string. You will station yourself with the kid near the front door, taking care to keep carefully concealed. I shall then jerk the string, the pot will smash the glass, the noise will bring someone out, and while the front door is open you will shoot the kid in and leave the rest to her personal judgement. Your share in the proceedings, you will notice, is simplicity itself—mere routine-work—and should not tax you unduly. How about it?'

'Well, sir—'

'Jeeves, I have had occasion before to comment on this habit of yours of saying "Well, sir" whenever I suggest anything in the nature of a ruse or piece of strategy. I dislike it more every time you do it. But I shall be glad to hear what possible criticism you can find to make.'

'I was merely about to express the opinion, sir, that the plan seems a trifle elaborate.'

'In a place as tight as this you have got to be elaborate.'

'Not necessarily, sir. The alternative scheme which I was about to propose—'

I shushed the man.

'There will be no need for alternative schemes, Jeeves. We will carry on along the lines I have indicated. I will give you ten minutes' start. That will enable you to take up your position near the front door and self to collect the string. At the conclusion of that period I will come along and do all the difficult part. So no more discussion. Snap into it, Jeeves.'

'Very good, sir.'

I felt pretty bucked as I tooled up the hill to St Monica's and equally bucked as I pushed open the front gate and stepped into the dark garden. But, just as I started to cross the lawn, there suddenly came upon me a rummy sensation as if all my bones had been removed and spaghetti substituted, and I paused.

I don't know if you have ever had the experience of starting off on a binge filled with a sort of glow of exhilaration, if that's the word I want, and then, without a moment's warning, having it disappear as if somebody had pressed a switch. That is what happened to me at this juncture, and a most unpleasant feeling it was—rather like when you take one of those express elevators in New York at the top of the building and discover, on reaching the twenty-seventh floor, that you have carelessly left all your insides up on the thirty-second, and too late now to stop and fetch them back.

The truth came to me like a bit of ice down the neck. I perceived that I had been a dashed sight too impulsive. Purely in order to score off Jeeves, I had gone and let myself in for what promised to be the mouldiest ordeal of a lifetime. And the nearer I got to the house, the more I wished that I had been a bit less haughty with the man when he had tried to outline that alternative scheme of his. An alternative scheme was just what I felt I could have done with, and the more alternative it was the better I would have liked it.

At this point I found myself at the conservatory door, and a few moments later I was inside, scooping up the pots.

Then ho, for the tree, bearing 'mid snow and ice the banner with the strange device 'Excelsior!'

I will say for that tree that it might have been placed there for the purpose. My views on the broad, general principle of leaping from branch to branch in a garden belonging to Aunt Agatha's closest friend remained unaltered; but I had to admit that, if it was to be done, this was undoubtedly the tree to do it on. It was a cedar of sorts; and almost before I knew where I was, I was sitting on top of the world with the conservatory roof gleaming below me. I balanced the flower-pot on my knee and began to tie the string round it.

And, as I tied, my thoughts turned in a moody sort of way to the subject of Woman.

I was suffering from a considerable strain of the old nerves at the moment, of course, and, looking back, it may be that I was too harsh; but the way I felt in that dark, roosting hour was that you can say what you like, but the more a thoughtful man has to do with women, the more extraordinary it seems to him that such a sex should be allowed to clutter up the earth.

Women, the way I looked at it, simply wouldn't do. Take the females who were mixed up in this present business. Aunt Agatha, to start with, better known as the Pest of Pont Street, the human snapping-turtle. Aunt Agatha's closest friend, Miss Mapleton, of whom I can only say that on the single occasion on which I had met her she had struck me as just the sort of person who would be Aunt Agatha's closest friend. Bobbie Wickham, a girl who went about the place letting the pure in heart in for the sort of thing I was doing now. And Bobbie Wickham's cousin Clementina, who, instead of sticking sedulously to her studies and learning to be a good wife and mother, spent the springtime of her life filling inkpots with sherbet—

What a crew! What a crew!

I mean to say, what a *crew*!

I had just worked myself up into rather an impressive state of moral indignation, and was preparing to go even further, when a sudden bright light shone upon me from below and a voice spoke.

'Ho!' it said.

It was a policeman. Apart from the fact of his having a lantern, I knew it was a policeman because he had said 'Ho!' I don't know if you recollect my telling you of the time I broke into Bingo Little's house to pinch the dictaphone record of the mushy article his wife had written about him and sailed out of the study window right into the arms of the Force? On that occasion the guardian of the Law had said 'Ho!' and kept on saying it, so evidently policemen are taught this as part of their training. And after all, it's not a bad way of opening conversation in the sort of circs in which they generally have to chat with people.

'You come on down out of that,' he said.

I came on down. I had just got the flower-pot balanced on its branch, and I left it there, feeling rather as if I had touched off the time-fuse of a bomb. Much seemed to me to depend on its stability and poise, as it were. If it continued to balance, an easy nonchalance might still get me out of this delicate position. If it fell, I saw things being a bit hard to explain. In fact, even as it was, I couldn't see my way to any explanation which would be really convincing.

However, I had a stab at it.

'Ah, officer,' I said.

It sounded weak. I said it again, this time with the emphasis on the 'Ah!' It sounded weaker than ever. I saw that Bertram would have to do better than this.

'It's all right, officer,' I said.

'All right, is it?'

'Oh, yes. Oh, yes.'

'What you doing up there?'

'Me, officer?'

'Yes, you.'

'Nothing, sergeant.'

'Ho!'

We eased into the silence, but it wasn't one of those restful silences that occur in talks between old friends. Embarrassing. Awkward.

'You'd better come along with me,' said the gendarme.

The last time I had heard those words from a similar source had been in Leicester Square one Boat Race night when, on my advice, my old pal Oliver Randolph Sipperley had endeavoured to steal a policeman's helmet at a moment when the policeman was inside it. On that occasion they had been addressed to young Sippy, and they hadn't sounded any too good, even so. Addressed to me, they more or less froze the marrow.

'No, I say, dash it!' I said.

And it was at this crisis, when Bertram had frankly shot his bolt and could only have been described as nonplussed, that a soft step sounded beside us and a soft voice broke the silence.

'Have you got them, officer? No, I see. It is Mr Wooster.'

The policeman switched the lantern round.

'Who are you?'

'I am Mr Wooster's personal gentleman's gentleman.'

'Whose?'

'Mr Wooster's.'

'Is this man's name Wooster?'

'This gentleman's name is Mr Wooster. I am in his employment as gentleman's personal gentleman.'

I think the cop was awed by the man's majesty of demeanour, but he came back strongly.

'Ho!' he said. 'Not in Miss Mapleton's employment?'

'Miss Mapleton does not employ a gentleman's personal gentleman.'

'Then what are you doing in her garden?'

'I was in conference with Miss Mapleton inside the house, and she desired me to step out and ascertain whether Mr Wooster had been successful in apprehending the intruders.'

'What intruders?'

'The suspicious characters whom Mr Wooster and I had observed passing through the garden as we entered it.'

'And what were you doing entering it?'

'Mr Wooster had come to pay a call on Miss Mapleton, who is a close friend of his family. We noticed suspicious characters crossing the lawn. On perceiving these suspicious characters, Mr Wooster despatched me to warn and reassure Miss Mapleton, he himself remaining to investigate.'

'I found him up a tree.'

'If Mr Wooster was up a tree, I have no doubt he was actuated by excellent motives and had only Miss Mapleton's best interests at heart.'

The policeman brooded.

'Ho!' he said. 'Well, if you want to know, I don't believe a word of it. We had a telephone call at the station saying there was somebody in Miss Mapleton's garden, and I found this fellow up a tree. It's my belief you're both in this, and I'm going to take you in to the lady for identification.'

Jeeves inclined his head gracefully.

'I shall be delighted to accompany you, officer, if such is your wish. And I feel sure that in this connection I may speak for Mr Wooster also. He too, I am confident, will interpose no obstacle in the way of your plans. If you consider that circumstances have placed Mr Wooster in a position that may be termed equivocal, or even compromising, it will naturally be his wish to exculpate himself at the earliest possible—'

'Here!' said the policeman, slightly rattled.

'Officer?'

'Less of it.'

'Just as you say, officer.'

'Switch it off and come along.'

'Very good, officer.'

I must say that I have enjoyed functions more than that walk to the front door. It seemed to me that the doom had come upon me, so to speak, and I thought it hard that a gallant effort like Jeeves's, well reasoned and nicely planned, should have failed to click. Even to me his story had rung almost true in spots, and it was a great blow that the man behind the lantern had not sucked it in without question. There's no doubt about it, being a policeman warps a man's mind and ruins that sunny faith in his fellow human beings which is the foundation of a lovable character. There seems no way of avoiding this.

I could see no gleam of light in the situation. True, the Mapleton would identify me as the nephew of her old friend, thus putting the stopper on the stroll to the police station and the night in the prison cell, but, when you came right down to it, a fat lot of use that was. The kid Clementina was presumably still out in the night somewhere, and she would be lugged in and the full facts revealed, and then the burning glance, the few cold words and the long letter to Aunt Agatha. I wasn't sure that a good straight term of penal servitude wouldn't have been a happier ending.

So, what with one consideration and another, the heart, as I toddled in through the front door, was more or less bowed down with weight of woe. We went along the passage and into the study, and there, standing behind a desk with the steel-rimmed spectacles glittering as nastily as on the day when I had seen them across Aunt Agatha's luncheon-table, was the boss in person. I gave her one swift look, then shut my eyes.

'Ah!' said Miss Mapleton.

Now, uttered in a certain way—dragged out, if you know what I mean, and starting high up and going down into the lower register, the word 'Ah!' can be as sinister and devastating as the word 'Ho!' In fact, it is a very moot question which is the scalier. But what stunned me was that this wasn't the way she had said it. It had been, or my ears deceived me, a genial 'Ah!'. A matey 'Ah!'. The 'Ah!' of one old buddy to another. And this startled me so much that, forgetting the dictates of prudence, I actually ventured to look at her again. And a stifled exclamation burst from Bertram's lips.

The breath-taking exhibit before me was in person a bit on the short side. I mean to say, she didn't tower above one, or anything like that. But, to compensate for this lack of inches, she possessed to a remarkable degree that sort of quiet air of being unwilling to stand any rannygazoo which females who run schools always have. I had noticed the same thing when in *statu pupillari*, in my old head master, one glance from whose eye had invariably been sufficient to make me confess all. Sergeant-majors are like that, too. Also traffic-cops and some post office girls. It's something in the way they purse up their lips and look through you.

In short, through years of disciplining the young—ticking off Isabel and speaking with quiet severity to Gertrude and that sort of thing—Miss Mapleton had acquired in the process of time rather the air of a female lion-tamer; and it was this air which had caused me after the first swift look to shut my eyes and utter a short prayer. But now, though she still resembled a lion-tamer, her bearing had most surprisingly become that of a chummy lion-tamer—a tamer who, after tucking the lions in for the night, relaxes in the society of the boys.

'So you did not find them, Mr Wooster?' she said. 'I am sorry. But I am none the less grateful for the trouble you have taken, nor lacking in appreciation of your courage. I consider that you have behaved splendidly.'

I felt the mouth opening feebly and the vocal cords twitching, but I couldn't manage to say anything. I was simply unable to follow her train of thought. I was astonished. Amazed. In fact, dumbfounded about sums it up.

The hell-hound of the Law gave a sort of yelp, rather like a wolf that sees its Russian peasant getting away.

'You identify this man, ma'am?'

'Identify him? In what way identify him?'

Jeeves joined the symposium.

'I fancy the officer is under the impression, madam, that Mr Wooster was in your garden for some unlawful purpose. I informed him that Mr Wooster was the nephew of your friend, Mrs Spenser Gregson, but he refused to credit me.'

There was a pause. Miss Mapleton eyed the constable for an instant as if she had caught him sucking acid-drops during the Scripture lesson.

'Do you mean to tell me, officer,' she said, in a voice that hit him just under the third button of the tunic and went straight through to the spinal column, 'that you have had the imbecility to bungle this whole affair by mistaking Mr Wooster for a burglar?'

'He was up a tree, ma'am.'

'And why should he not be up a tree? No doubt you had climbed the tree in order to watch the better, Mr Wooster?'

I could answer that. The first shock over, the old sang-froid was beginning to return.

'Yes. Rather. That's it. Of course. Certainly. Absolutely,' I said. 'Watch the better. That's it in a nutshell.'

'I took the liberty of suggesting that to the officer, madam, but he declined to accept the theory as tenable.'

'The officer is a fool,' said Miss Mapleton. It seemed a close thing for a moment whether or not she would rap him on the knuckles with a ruler. 'By this time, no doubt, owing to his idiocy, the miscreants have made good their escape. And it is for this,' said Miss Mapleton, 'that we pay rates and taxes!'

'Awful!' I said.

'Iniquitous.'

'A bally shame.'

'A crying scandal,' said Miss Mapleton.

'A grim show,' I agreed.

In fact, we were just becoming more like a couple of lovebirds than anything, when through the open window there suddenly breezed a noise.

I'm never at my best at describing things. At school, when we used to do essays and English composition, my report generally read 'Has little or no ability, but does his best,' or words to that effect. True, in the course of years I have picked up a vocabulary of sorts from Jeeves, but even so I'm not nearly hot enough to draw a word-picture that would do justice to that extraordinarily hefty crash. Try to imagine the Albert Hall falling on the Crystal Palace, and you will have got the rough idea.

All four of us, even Jeeves, sprang several inches from the floor. The policeman uttered a startled 'Ho!'

Miss Mapleton was her calm masterful self again in a second.

'One of the men appears to have fallen through the conservatory roof,' she said. 'Perhaps you will endeavour at the eleventh hour to justify your existence, officer, by proceeding there and making investigations.'

'Yes, ma'am.'

'And try not to bungle matters this time.'

'No, ma'am.'

'Please hurry, then. Do you intend to stand there gaping all night?'

'Yes, ma'am. No, ma'am. Yes, ma'am.'

It was pretty to hear him.

'It is an odd coincidence, Mr Wooster,' said Miss Mapleton, becoming instantly matey once more as the outcast removed himself. 'I had just finished writing a letter to your aunt when you arrived. I shall certainly reopen it to tell her how gallantly you have behaved to-night. I have not in the past entertained a very high opinion of the modern young man, but you have caused me to alter it. To track these men unarmed through a dark garden argues courage of a high order. And it was most courteous of you to think of calling upon me. I appreciate it. Are you making a long stay in Bingley?'

This was another one I could answer.

'No,' I said. 'Afraid not. Must be in London to-morrow.'

'Perhaps you could lunch before your departure?'

'Afraid not. Thanks most awfully. Very important engagement that I can't get out of. Eh, Jeeves?'

'Yes, sir.'

'Have to catch the ten-thirty train, what?'

'Without fail, sir.'

'I am sorry,' said Miss Mapleton. 'I had hoped that you would be able to say a few words to my girls. Some other time perhaps?'

'Absolutely.'

'You must let me know when you are coming to Bingley again.'

'When I come to Bingley again,' I said, 'I will certainly let you know.'

'If I remember your plans correctly, sir, you are not likely to be in Bingley for some little time, sir.'

'Not for some considerable time, Jeeves,' I said.

The front door closed. I passed a hand across the brow.

'Tell me all, Jeeves,' I said.

'Sir?'

'I say, tell me all. I am fogged.'

'It is quite simple, sir. I ventured to take the liberty, on my own responsibility, of putting into operation the alternative scheme which, if you remember, I wished to outline to you.'

'What was it?'

'It occurred to me, sir, that it would be most judicious for me to call at the back door and desire an interview with Miss Mapleton. This, I fancied, would enable me, while the maid had gone to convey my request to Miss Mapleton, to introduce the young lady into the house unobserved.'

'And did you?'

'Yes, sir. She proceeded up the back stairs and is now safely in bed.'

I frowned. The thought of the kid Clementina jarred upon me.

'She is, is she?' I said. 'A murrain on her, Jeeves, and may she be stood in the corner next Sunday for not knowing her Collect. And then you saw Miss Mapleton?'

'Yes, sir.'

'And told her that I was out in the garden, chivvying burglars with my bare hands?'

'Yes, sir.'

'And had been on my way to call upon her?'

'Yes, sir.'

'And now she's busy adding a postscript to her letter to Aunt Agatha, speaking of me in terms of unstinted praise.'

'Yes, sir.'

I drew a deep breath. It was too dark for me to see the superhuman intelligence which must have been sloshing about all over the surface of the man's features. I tried to, but couldn't make it.

'Jeeves,' I said, 'I should have been guided by you from the first.'

'It might have spared you some temporary unpleasantness, sir.'

'Unpleasantness is right. When that lantern shone up at me in the silent night, Jeeves, just as I had finished poising the pot, I thought I had unshipped a rib. Jeeves!'

'Sir?'

'That Antibes expedition is off.'

'I am glad to hear it, sir.'

'If young Bobbie Wickham can get me into a mess like this in a quiet spot like Bingley-on-Sea, what might she not be able to accomplish at a really lively resort like Antibes?'

'Precisely, sir. Miss Wickham, as I have sometimes said, though a charming—'

'Yes, yes, Jeeves. There is no necessity to stress the point. The Wooster eyes are definitely opened.'

I hesitated.

'Jeeves.'

'Sir?'

'Those plus-fours.'

'Yes, sir?'

'You may give them to the poor.'

'Thank you very much, sir.'

I sighed.

'It is my heart's blood, Jeeves.'

'I appreciate the sacrifice, sir. But, once the first pang of separation is over, you will feel much easier without them.'

'You think so?'

'I am convinced of it, sir.'

'So be it, then, Jeeves,' I said, 'so be it.'

8

THE LOVE THAT PURIFIES

There is a ghastly moment in the year, generally about the beginning of August, when Jeeves insists on taking a holiday, the slacker, and legs it off to some seaside resort for a couple of weeks, leaving me stranded. This moment had now arrived, and we were discussing what was to be done with the young master.

'I had gathered the impression, sir,' said Jeeves, 'that you were proposing to accept Mr Sipperley's invitation to join him at his Hampshire residence.'

I laughed. One of those bitter, rasping ones.

'Correct, Jeeves. I was. But mercifully I was enabled to discover young Sippy's foul plot in time. Do you know what?'

'No, sir.'

'My spies informed me that Sippy's fiancée, Miss Moon, was to be there. Also his fiancée's mother, Mrs Moon, and his fiancée's small brother, Master Moon. You see the hideous treachery lurking behind the invitation? You see the man's loathsome design? Obviously my job was to be the task of keeping Mrs Moon and little Sebastian Moon interested and amused while Sippy and his blighted girl went off for the day, roaming the pleasant woodlands and talking of this and that. I doubt if anyone has ever had a narrower escape. You remember little Sebastian?'

'Yes, sir.'

'His goggle eyes? His golden curls?'

'Yes, sir.'

'I don't know why it is, but I've never been able to bear with fortitude anything in the shape of a kid with golden curls. Confronted with one, I feel the urge to step on him or drop things on him from a height.'

'Many strong natures are affected in the same way, sir.'

'So no *chez* Sippy for me. Was that the front-door bell ringing?'

'Yes, sir.'

'Somebody stands without.'

'Yes, sir.'

'Better go and see who it is.'

'Yes, sir.'

He oozed off, to return a moment later bearing a telegram. I opened it, and a soft smile played about the lips.

'Amazing how often things happen as if on a cue, Jeeves. This is from my Aunt Dahlia, inviting me down to her place in Worcestershire.'

'Most satisfactory, sir.'

'Yes. How I came to overlook her when searching for a haven, I can't think. The ideal home from home. Picturesque surroundings. Company's own water, and the best cook in England. You have not forgotten Anatole?'

'No, sir.'

'And above all, Jeeves, at Aunt Dahlia's there should be an almost total shortage of blasted kids. True, there is her son Bonzo, who, I take it, will be home for the holidays, but I don't mind Bonzo. Buzz off and send a wire, accepting.'

'Yes, sir.'

'And then shove a few necessaries together, including golf-clubs and tennis racquet.'

'Very good, sir. I am glad that matters have been so happily adjusted.'

… … …

I think I have mentioned before that my Aunt Dahlia stands alone in the grim regiment of my aunts as a real good sort and a chirpy sportsman. She is the one, if you remember, who married old Tom Travers and, with the assistance of Jeeves, lured Mrs Bingo Little's French cook, Anatole, away from Mrs B. L. and into her own employment. To visit her is always a pleasure. She generally has some cheery birds staying with her, and there is none of that rot about getting up for breakfast which one is sadly apt to find at country-houses.

It was, accordingly, with unalloyed lightness of heart that I edged the two-seater into the garage at Brinkley Court, Worc., and strolled round to the house by way of the shrubbery and the tennis-lawn, to report arrival. I had just got across the lawn when a head poked itself out of the smoking-room window and beamed at me in an amiable sort of way.

'Ah, Mr Wooster,' it said. 'Ha, ha!'

'Ho, ho!' I replied, not to be outdone in the courtesies.

It had taken me a couple of seconds to place this head. I now perceived that it belonged to a rather moth-eaten septuagenarian of the name of Anstruther, an old friend of Aunt Dahlia's late father. I had met him at her house in London once or twice. An agreeable cove, but somewhat given to nervous breakdowns.

'Just arrived?' he asked, beaming as before.

'This minute,' I said, also beaming.

'I fancy you will find our good hostess in the drawing-room.'

'Right,' I said, and after a bit more beaming to and fro I pushed on.

Aunt Dahlia was in the drawing-room, and welcomed me with gratifying enthusiasm. She beamed, too. It was one of those big days for beamers.

'Hullo, ugly,' she said. 'So here you are. Thank heaven you were able to come.'

It was the right tone, and one I should be glad to hear in others of the family circle, notably my Aunt Agatha.

'Always a pleasure to enjoy your hosp., Aunt Dahlia,' I said cordially. 'I anticipate a delightful and restful visit. I see you've got Mr Anstruther staying here. Anybody else?'

'Do you know Lord Snettisham?'

'I've met him, racing.'

'He's here, and Lady Snettisham.'

'And Bonzo, of course?'

'Yes. And Thomas.'

'Uncle Thomas?'

'No, he's in Scotland. Your cousin Thomas.'

'You don't mean Aunt Agatha's loathly son?'

'Of course I do. How many cousin Thomases do you think you've got, fathead? Agatha has gone to Homburg and planted the child on me.'

I was visibly agitated.

'But, Aunt Dahlia! Do you realize what you've taken on? Have you an inkling of the sort of scourge you've introduced into your home? In the society of young Thos., strong men quail. He is England's premier fiend in human shape. There is no devilry beyond his scope.'

'That's what I have always gathered from the form book,' agreed the relative. 'But just now, curse him, he's behaving like something out of a Sunday School story. You see, poor old Mr Anstruther is very frail these days, and when he found he was in a house containing two small boys he acted promptly. He offered a prize of five pounds to whichever behaved best during his stay. The consequence is that, ever since, Thomas has had large white wings sprouting out of his shoulders.' A shadow seemed to pass across her face. She appeared embittered. 'Mercenary little brute!' she said. 'I never saw such a sickeningly well-behaved kid in my life. It's enough to make one despair of human nature.'

I couldn't follow her.

'But isn't that all to the good?'

'No, it's not.'

'I can't see why. Surely a smug, oily Thos. about the house is better than a Thos., raging hither and thither and being a menace to society? Stands to reason.'

'It doesn't stand to anything of the kind. You see, Bertie, this Good Conduct prize has made matters a bit complex. There are wheels within wheels. The thing stirred Jane Snettisham's sporting blood to such an extent that she insisted on having a bet on the result.'

A great light shone upon me. I got what she was driving at.

'Ah!' I said. 'Now I follow. Now I see. Now I comprehend. She's betting on Thos., is she?'

'Yes. And naturally, knowing him, I thought the thing was in the bag.'

'Of course.'

'I couldn't see myself losing. Heaven knows I have no illusions about my darling Bonzo. Bonzo is, and has been from the cradle, a pest. But to back him to win a Good Conduct contest with Thomas seemed to me simply money for jam.'

'Absolutely.'

'When it comes to devilry, Bonzo is just a good, ordinary selling-plater. Whereas Thomas is a classic yearling.'

'Exactly. I don't see that you have any cause to worry, Aunt Dahlia. Thos. can't last. He's bound to crack.'

'Yes. But before that the mischief may be done.'

'Mischief?'

'Yes. There is dirty work afoot, Bertie,' said Aunt Dahlia gravely. 'When I booked this bet, I reckoned without the hideous blackness of the Snettishams' souls. Only yesterday it came to my knowledge that Jack Snettisham had been urging Bonzo to climb on the roof and boo down Mr Anstruther's chimney.'

'No!'

'Yes. Mr Anstruther is very frail, poor old fellow, and it would have frightened him into a fit. On coming out of which, his first action would have been to disqualify Bonzo and declare Thomas the winner by default.'

'But Bonzo did not boo?'

'No,' said Aunt Dahlia, and a mother's pride rang in her voice. 'He firmly refused to boo. Mercifully, he is in love at the moment, and it has quite altered his nature. He scorned the tempter.'

'In love? Who with?'

'Lilian Gish. We had an old film of hers at the Bijou Dream in the village a week ago, and Bonzo saw her for the first time. He came out with a pale, set face, and ever since has been trying to lead a finer, better life. So the peril was averted.'

'That's good.'

'Yes. But now it's my turn. You don't suppose I am going to take a thing like that lying down, do you? Treat me right, and I am fairness itself: but try any of this nobbling of starters, and I can play that game, too. If this Good Conduct contest is to be run on rough lines, I can do my bit as well as anyone. Far too much hangs on the issue for me to handicap myself by remembering the lessons I learned at my mother's knee.'

'Lot of money involved?'

'Much more than mere money. I've betted Anatole against Jane Snettisham's kitchen-maid.'

'Great Scott! Uncle Thomas will have something to say if he comes back and finds Anatole gone.'

'And won't he say it!'

'Pretty long odds you gave her, didn't you? I mean, Anatole is famed far and wide as a hash-slinger without peer.'

'Well, Jane Snettisham's kitchen-maid is not to be sneezed at. She is very hot stuff, they tell me, and good kitchen-maids nowadays are about as rare as original Holbeins. Besides, I had to give her a shade the best of the odds. She stood out for it. Well, anyway, to get back to what I was saying, if the opposition are going to place temptations in Bonzo's path, they shall jolly well be placed in Thomas's path, too, and plenty of them. So ring for Jeeves and let him get his brain working.'

'But I haven't brought Jeeves.'

'You haven't brought Jeeves?'

'No. He always takes his holiday at this time of year. He's down at Bognor for the shrimping.'

Aunt Dahlia registered deep concern.

'Then send for him at once! What earthly use do you suppose you are without Jeeves, you poor ditherer?'

I drew myself up a trifle—in fact, to my full height. Nobody has a greater respect for Jeeves than I have, but the Wooster pride was stung.

'Jeeves isn't the only one with brains,' I said coldly. 'Leave this thing to me, Aunt Dahlia. By dinner-time to-night I shall hope to have a fully matured scheme to submit for your approval. If I can't thoroughly encompass this Thos., I'll eat my hat.'

'About all you'll get to eat if Anatole leaves,' said Aunt Dahlia in a pessimistic manner which I did not like to see.

I was brooding pretty tensely as I left the presence. I have always had a suspicion that Aunt Dahlia, while invariably matey and bonhomous and seeming to take pleasure in my society, has a lower opinion of my intelligence than I quite like. Too often it is her practice to address me as 'fathead', and if I put forward any little thought or idea or fancy in her hearing it is apt to be greeted with the affectionate but jarring guffaw. In our recent interview she had hinted quite plainly that she considered me negligible in a crisis which, like the present one, called for initiative and resource. It was my intention to show her how greatly she had underestimated me.

To let you see the sort of fellow I really am, I got a ripe, excellent idea before I had gone half-way down the corridor. I examined it for the space of one and a half cigarettes, and could see no flaw in it, provided—I say, provided old Mr Anstruther's notion of what constituted bad conduct squared with mine.

The great thing on these occasions, as Jeeves will tell you, is to get a toe-hold on the psychology of the individual. Study the individual, and you will bring home the bacon. Now, I had been studying young Thos. for years, and I knew his psychology from caviare to nuts. He is one of those kids who never let the sun go down on their wrath, if you know what I mean. I mean to say, do something to annoy or offend or upset this juvenile thug, and he will proceed at the earliest possible opp. to wreak a hideous vengeance upon you. Only the previous summer, for instance, it having been drawn to his attention that the latter had reported him for smoking, he had marooned a Cabinet Minister on an island in the lake, at Aunt Agatha's place in Hertfordshire—in the rain, mark you, and with no company but that of one of the nastiest-minded swans I have ever encountered. Well, I mean!

So now it seemed to me that a few well-chosen taunts, or jibes, directed at his more sensitive points, must infallibly induce in this Thos. a frame of mind which would lead to his working some sensational violence upon me. And, if you wonder that I was willing to sacrifice myself to this frightful extent in order to do Aunt Dahlia a bit of good, I can only say that we Woosters are like that.

The one point that seemed to me to want a spot of clearing up was this: viz., would old Mr Anstruther consider an outrage perpetrated on the person of Bertram Wooster a crime sufficiently black to cause him to rule Thos. out of the race? Or would he just give a senile chuckle and mumble something about boys being boys? Because, if the latter, the thing was off. I decided to have a word with the old boy and make sure.

He was still in the smoking-room, looking very frail over the morning *Times*. I got to the point at once.

'Oh, Mr Anstruther,' I said. 'What-ho!'

'I don't like the way the American market is shaping,' he said. 'I don't like this strong Bear movement.'

'No?' I said. 'Well, be that as it may, about this Good Conduct prize of yours?'

'Ah, you have heard of that, eh?'

'I don't quite understand how you are doing the judging.'

'No? It is very simple. I have a system of daily marks. At the beginning of each day I accord the two lads twenty marks apiece. These are subject to withdrawal either in small or large quantities according to the magnitude of the offence. To take a simple example, shouting outside my bedroom in the early morning would involve a loss of three marks,—whistling two. The penalty for a more serious lapse would be correspondingly greater. Before retiring to rest at night I record the day's marks in my little book. Simple, but, I think, ingenious, Mr Wooster?'

'Absolutely.'

'So far the result has been extremely gratifying. Neither of the little fellows has lost a single mark, and my nervous system is acquiring a tone which, when I learned that two lads of immature years would be staying in the house during my visit, I confess I had not dared to anticipate.'

'I see,' I said. 'Great work. And how do you react to what I might call general moral turpitude?'

'I beg your pardon?'

'Well, I mean when the thing doesn't affect you personally. Suppose one of them did something to me, for instance? Set a booby-trap or something? Or, shall we say, put a toad or so in my bed?'

He seemed shocked at the very idea.

'I would certainly in such circumstances deprive the culprit of a full ten marks.'

'Only ten?'

'Fifteen, then.'

'Twenty is a nice, round number.'

'Well, possibly even twenty. I have a peculiar horror of practical joking.'

'Me, too.'

'You will not fail to advise me, Mr Wooster, should such an outrage occur?'

'You shall have the news before anyone,' I assured him.

And so out into the garden, ranging to and fro in quest of young Thos. I knew where I was now. Bertram's feet were on solid ground.

I hadn't been hunting long before I found him in the summerhouse, reading an improving book.

'Hullo,' he said, smiling a saintlike smile.

This scourge of humanity was a chunky kid whom a too indulgent public had allowed to infest the country for a matter of fourteen years. His nose was snub, his eyes green, his general aspect that of one studying to be a gangster. I had never liked his looks much, and with a saintlike smile added to them they became ghastly to a degree.

I ran over in my mind a few assorted taunts.

'Well, young Thos.,' I said. 'So there you are. You're getting as fat as a pig.'

It seemed as good an opening as any other. Experience had taught me that if there was a subject on which he was unlikely to accept persiflage in a spirit of amused geniality it was this matter of his bulging tum. On the last occasion when I made a remark of this nature, he had replied to me, child though he was, in terms which I would have been proud to have had in my own vocabulary. But now, though a sort of wistful gleam did flit for a moment into his eyes, he merely smiled in a more saintlike manner than ever.

'Yes, I think I have been putting on a little weight,' he said gently. 'I must try and exercise a lot while I'm here. Won't you sit down, Bertie?' he asked, rising. 'You must be tired after your journey. I'll get you a cushion. Have you cigarettes? And matches? I could bring you some from the smoking-room. Would you like me to fetch you something to drink?'

It is not too much to say that I felt baffled. In spite of what Aunt Dahlia had told me, I don't think that until this moment I had really believed there could have been anything in the nature of a genuinely sensational change in this young plugugly's attitude towards his fellows.

But now, hearing him talk as if he were a combination of Boy Scout and delivery wagon, I felt definitely baffled. However, I stuck at it in the old bull-dog way.

'Are you still at that rotten kids' school of yours?' I asked.

He might have been proof against jibes at his *embonpoint*, but it seemed to me incredible that he could have sold himself for gold so completely as to lie down under taunts directed at his school. I was wrong. The money-lust evidently held him in its grip. He merely shook his head.

'I left this term. I'm going to Pevenhurst next term.'

'They wear mortar-boards there, don't they?'

'Yes.'

'With pink tassels?'

'Yes.'

'What a priceless ass you'll look!' I said, but without much hope. And I laughed heartily.

'I expect I shall,' he said, and laughed still more heartily.

'Mortar-boards!'

'Ha, ha!'

'Pink tassels!'

'Ha, ha!'

I gave the thing up.

'Well, teuf-teuf,' I said moodily, and withdrew.

A couple of days later I realized that the virus had gone even deeper than I had thought. The kid was irredeemably sordid.

It was old Mr Anstruther who sprang the bad news.

'Oh, Mr Wooster,' he said, meeting me on the stairs as I came down after a refreshing breakfast. 'You were good enough to express an interest in this little prize for Good Conduct which I am offering.'

'Oh, ah?'

'I explained to you my system of marking, I believe. Well, this morning I was impelled to vary it somewhat. The circumstances seemed to me to demand it. I happened to encounter our hostess's nephew, the boy Thomas, returning to the house, his aspect somewhat weary, it appeared to me, and travel-stained. I inquired of him where he had been at that early hour—it was not yet breakfast-time—and he replied that he had heard you mention overnight a regret that you had omitted to order the *Sporting*

Times to be sent to you before leaving London, and he had actually walked all the way to the railway-station, a distance of more than three miles, to procure it for you.'

The old boy swam before my eyes. He looked like two old Mr Anstruthers, both flickering at the edges.

'What!'

'I can understand your emotion, Mr Wooster. I can appreciate it. It is indeed rarely that one encounters such unselfish kindliness in a lad of his age. So genuinely touched was I by the goodness of heart which the episode showed that I have deviated from my original system and awarded the little fellow a bonus of fifteen marks.'

'Fifteen!'

'On second thoughts, I shall make it twenty. That, as you yourself suggested, is a nice, round number.'

He doddered away, and I bounded off to find Aunt Dahlia.

'Aunt Dahlia,' I said, 'matters have taken a sinister turn.'

'You bet your Sunday spats they have,' agreed Aunt Dahlia emphatically. 'Do you know what happened just now? That crook Snettisham, who ought to be warned off the turf and hounded out of his clubs, offered Bonzo ten shillings if he would burst a paper bag behind Mr Anstruther's chair at breakfast. Thank heaven the love of a good woman triumphed again. My sweet Bonzo merely looked at him and walked away in a marked manner. But it just shows you what we are up against.'

'We are up against worse than that, Aunt Dahlia,' I said. And I told her what had happened.

She was stunned. Aghast, you might call it.

'*Thomas* did that?'

'Thos. in person.'

'Walked six miles to get you a paper?'

'Six miles and a bit.'

'The young hound! Good heavens, Bertie, do you realize that he may go on doing these Acts of Kindness daily—perhaps twice a day? Is there no way of stopping him?'

'None that I can think of. No, Aunt Dahlia, I must confess it. I am baffled. There is only one thing to do. We must send for Jeeves.'

'And about time,' said the relative churlishly. 'He ought to have been here from the start. Wire him this morning.'

There is good stuff in Jeeves. His heart is in the right place. The acid test does not find him wanting. Many men in his position, summoned back by telegram in the middle of their annual vacation, might have cut up rough a bit. But not Jeeves. On the following afternoon in he blew, looking bronzed and fit, and I gave him the scenario without delay.

'So there you have it, Jeeves,' I said, having sketched out the facts. 'The problem is one that will exercise your intelligence to the utmost. Rest now, and to-night, after a light repast, withdraw to some solitary place and get down to it. Is there any particularly stimulating food or beverage you would like for dinner? Anything that you feel would give the old brain just that extra fillip? If so, name it.'

'Thank you very much, sir, but I have already hit upon a plan which should, I fancy, prove effective.'

I gazed at the man with some awe.

'Already?'

'Yes, sir.'

'Not *already*?'

'Yes, sir.'

'Something to do with the psychology of the individual?'

'Precisely, sir.'

I shook my head, a bit discouraged. Doubts had begun to creep in.

'Well, spring it, Jeeves,' I said. 'But I have not much hope. Having only just arrived, you cannot possibly be aware of the frightful change that has taken place in young Thos. You are probably building on your knowledge of him, when last seen. Useless, Jeeves. Stirred by the prospect of getting his hooks on five of the best, this blighted boy has become so dashed virtuous that his armour seems to contain no chink. I mocked at his waistline and sneered at his school and he merely smiled in a pale, dying-duck sort of way. Well, that'll show you. However, let us hear what you have to suggest.'

'It occurred to me, sir, that the most judicious plan in the circumstances would be for you to request Mrs Travers to invite Master Sebastian Moon here for a short visit.'

I shook the onion again. The scheme sounded to me like apple sauce, and Grade A apple sauce, at that.

'What earthly good would that do?' I asked, not without a touch of asperity. 'Why Sebastian Moon?'

'He has golden curls, sir.'

'What of it?'

'The strongest natures are sometimes not proof against long golden curls.'

Well, it was a thought, of course. But I can't say I was leaping about to any great extent. It might be that the sight of Sebastian Moon would break down Thos.'s iron self-control to the extent of causing him to inflict mayhem on the person, but I wasn't any too hopeful.

'It may be so, Jeeves.'

'I do not think I am too sanguine, sir. You must remember that Master Moon, apart from his curls, has a personality which is not uniformly pleasing. He is apt to express himself with a breezy candour which I fancy Master Thomas might feel inclined to resent in one some years his junior.'

I had had a feeling all along that there was a flaw somewhere, and now it seemed to me that I had spotted it.

'But, Jeeves. Granted that little Sebastian is the pot of poison you indicate, why won't he act just as forcibly on young Bonzo as on Thos.? Pretty silly we should look if our nominee started putting it across him. Never forget that already Bonzo is twenty marks down and falling back in the betting.'

'I do not anticipate any such contingency, sir. Master Travers is in love, and love is a very powerful restraining influence at the age of thirteen.'

'H'm.' I mused. 'Well, we can but try, Jeeves.'

'Yes, sir.'

'I'll get Aunt Dahlia to write to Sippy to-night.'

I'm bound to say that the spectacle of little Sebastian when he arrived two days later did much to remove pessimism from my outlook. If ever there was a kid whose whole appearance seemed to call aloud to any right-minded boy to lure him into a quiet spot and inflict violence upon him, that kid was undeniably Sebastian Moon. He reminded me strongly of Little Lord Fauntleroy. I marked young Thos.'s demeanour closely at the moment of their meeting and, unless I was much mistaken, there came into his eyes the sort of look which would come into those of an Indian chief—Chinchagook, let us say, or Sitting Bull—just before he started reaching for his scalping-knife. He had the air of one who is about ready to begin.

True, his manner as he shook hands was guarded. Only a keen observer could have detected that he was stirred to his depths. But I had seen, and I summoned Jeeves forthwith.

'Jeeves,' I said, 'if I appeared to think poorly of that scheme of yours, I now withdraw my remarks. I believe you have found the way. I was noticing Thos. at the moment of impact. His eyes had a strange gleam.'

'Indeed, sir?'

'He shifted uneasily on his feet and his ears wiggled. He had, in short, the appearance of a boy who was holding himself in with an effort almost too great for his frail body.'

'Yes, sir?'

'Yes, Jeeves. I received a distinct impression of something being on the point of exploding. To-morrow I shall ask Aunt Dahlia to take the two warts for a country ramble, to lose them in some sequestered spot, and to leave the rest to Nature.'

'It is a good idea, sir.'

'It is more than a good idea, Jeeves,' I said. 'It is a pip.'

You know, the older I get the more firmly do I become convinced that there is no such thing as a pip in existence. Again and again have I seen the apparently sure thing go phut, and now it is rarely indeed that I can be lured from my aloof skepticism. Fellows come sidling up to me at the Drones and elsewhere, urging me to invest on some horse that can't lose even if it gets struck by lightning at the starting-post, but Bertram Wooster shakes his head. He has seen too much of life to be certain of anything.

If anyone had told me that my Cousin Thos., left alone for an extended period of time with a kid of the superlative foulness of Sebastian Moon, would not only refrain from cutting off his curls with a pocket-knife and chasing him across country into a muddy pond but would actually return home carrying the gruesome kid on his back because he had got a blister on his foot, I would have laughed scornfully. I knew Thos. I knew his work. I had seen him in action. And I was convinced that not even the prospect of collecting five pounds would be enough to give him pause.

And yet what happened? In the quiet evenfall, when the little birds were singing their sweetest and all Nature seemed to whisper of hope and happiness, the blow fell. I was chatting with old Mr Anstruther on the terrace when suddenly round a bend in the drive the two kids hove in view. Sebastian, seated on Thos.'s back, his hat off and his golden curls floating on the breeze, was singing as much as he could remember of a comic song, and Thos., bowed down by the burden but carrying on gamely, was trudging along, smiling that bally saintlike smile of his. He parked the kid on the front steps and came across to us.

'Sebastian got a nail in his shoe,' he said in a low, virtuous voice. 'It hurt him to walk, so I gave him a piggy-back.'

I heard old Mr Anstruther draw in his breath sharply.

'All the way home?'

'Yes, sir.'

'In this hot sunshine?'

'Yes, sir.'

'But was he not very heavy?'

'He was a little, sir,' said Thos., uncorking the saintlike once more. 'But it would have hurt him awfully to walk.'

I pushed off. I had had enough. If ever a septuagenarian looked on the point of handing out another bonus, that septuagenarian was old Mr Anstruther. He had the unmistakable bonus glitter in his eye. I withdrew, and found Jeeves in my bedroom messing about with ties and things.

He pursed the lips a bit on hearing the news.

'Serious, sir.'

'Very serious, Jeeves.'

'I had feared this, sir.'

'Had you? I hadn't. I was convinced Thos. would have massacred young Sebastian. I banked on it. It just shows what the greed for money will do. This is a commercial age, Jeeves. When I was a boy, I would cheerfully have forfeited five quid in order to deal faithfully with a kid like Sebastian. I would have considered it money well spent.'

'You are mistaken, sir, in your estimate of the motives actuating Master Thomas. It was not a mere desire to win five pounds that caused him to curb his natural impulses.'

'Eh?'

'I have ascertained the true reason for his change of heart, sir.'

I felt fogged.

'Religion, Jeeves?'

'No, sir. Love.'

'Love?'

'Yes, sir. The young gentleman confided in me during a brief conversation in the hall shortly after luncheon. We had been speaking for a while on neutral subjects, when he suddenly turned a deeper shade of pink and after some slight hesitation inquired of me if I did not think Miss Greta Garbo the most beautiful woman at present in existence.'

I clutched the brow.

'Jeeves! Don't tell me Thos. is in love with Greta Garbo?'

'Yes, sir. Unfortunately such is the case. He gave me to understand that it had been coming on for some time, and her last picture settled the issue. His voice shook with an emotion which it was impossible to misread. I gathered from his observations, sir, that he proposes to spend the remainder of his life trying to make himself worthy of her.'

It was a knock-out. This was the end.

'This is the end, Jeeves,' I said. 'Bonzo must be a good forty marks behind by now. Only some sensational and spectacular outrage upon the public weal on the part of young Thos. could have enabled him to wipe out the lead. And of that there is now, apparently, no chance.'

'The eventuality does appear remote, sir.'

I brooded.

'Uncle Thomas will have a fit when he comes back and finds Anatole gone.'

'Yes, sir.'

'Aunt Dahlia will drain the bitter cup to the dregs.'

'Yes, sir.'

'And, speaking from a purely selfish point of view, the finest cooking I have ever bitten will pass out of my life for ever, unless the Snettishams invite me in some night to take pot luck. And that eventuality is also remote.'

'Yes, sir.'

'Then the only thing I can do is square the shoulders and face the inevitable.'

'Yes, sir.'

'Like some aristocrat of the French Revolution popping into the tumbrel, what? The brave smile. The stiff upper lip.'

'Yes, sir.'

'Right-ho, then. Is the shirt studded?'

'Yes, sir.'

'The tie chosen?'

'Yes, sir.'

'The collar and evening underwear all in order?'

'Yes, sir.'

'Then I'll have a bath and be with you in two ticks.'

It is all very well to talk about the brave smile and the stiff upper lip, but my experience—and I daresay others have found the same—is that they are a dashed sight easier to talk about than actually to fix on the face. For the next few days, I'm bound to admit, I found myself, in spite of every effort, registering gloom pretty consistently. For, as if to make things tougher than they might have been, Anatole at this juncture suddenly developed a cooking streak which put all his previous efforts in the shade.

Night after night we sat at the dinner-table, the food melting in our mouths, and Aunt Dahlia would look at me and I would look at Aunt Dahlia, and the male Snettisham would ask the female Snettisham in a ghastly, gloating sort of way if she had ever tasted such cooking and the female Snettisham would smirk at the male Snettisham and say she never had in all her puff, and I would look at Aunt Dahlia and Aunt Dahlia would look at me and our eyes would be full of unshed tears, if you know what I mean.

And all the time old Mr Anstruther's visit drawing to a close.

The sands running out, so to speak.

And then, on the very last afternoon of his stay, the thing happened.

It was one of those warm, drowsy, peaceful afternoons. I was up in my bedroom, getting off a spot of correspondence which I had neglected of late, and from where I sat I looked down on the shady lawn, fringed with its gay flower-beds. There was a bird or two hopping about, a butterfly or so fluttering to and fro, and an assortment of bees buzzing hither and thither. In a garden-chair sat old Mr Anstruther, getting his eight hours. It was a sight which, had I had less on my mind, would no doubt have soothed the old soul a bit. The only blot on the landscape was Lady Snettisham, walking among the flower-beds and probably sketching out future menus, curse her.

And so for a time everything carried on. The birds hopped, the butterflies fluttered, the bees buzzed, and old Mr Anstruther snored—all in accordance with the programme. And I worked through a letter to my tailor to the point where I proposed to say something pretty strong about the way the right sleeve of my last coat bagged.

There was a tap on the door, and Jeeves entered, bringing the second post. I laid the letters listlessly on the table beside me.

'Well, Jeeves,' I said sombrely.

'Sir?'

'Mr Anstruther leaves to-morrow.'

'Yes, sir.'

I gazed down at the sleeping septuagenarian.

'In my young days, Jeeves,' I said, 'however much I might have been in love, I could never have resisted the spectacle of an old gentleman asleep like that in a deck-chair. I would have done *something* to him, no matter what the cost.'

'Indeed, sir?'

'Yes. Probably with a pea-shooter. But the modern boy is degenerate. He has lost his vim. I suppose Thos. is indoors on this lovely afternoon, showing Sebastian his stamp-album or something. Ha!' I said, and I said it rather nastily.

'I fancy Master Thomas and Master Sebastian are playing in the stable-yard, sir. I encountered Master Sebastian not long back and he informed me he was on his way thither.'

'The motion-pictures, Jeeves,' I said, 'are the curse of the age. But for them, if Thos. had found himself alone in a stable-yard with a kid like Sebastian—'

I broke off. From some point to the south-west, out of my line of vision, there had proceeded a piercing squeal.

It cut through the air like a knife, and old Mr Anstruther leaped up as if it had run into the fleshy part of his leg. And the next moment little Sebastian appeared, going well and followed at a short interval by Thos., who was going even better. In spite of the fact that he was hampered in his movements by a large stable-bucket which he bore in his right hand, Thos. was running a great race. He had almost come up with Sebastian, when the latter, with great presence of mind, dodged behind Mr Anstruther, and there for a moment the matter rested.

But only for a moment. Thos., for some reason plainly stirred to the depths of his being, moved adroitly to one side and, poising the bucket for an instant, discharged its contents. And Mr Anstruther, who had just moved to the same side, received, as far as I could gather from a distance, the entire consignment. In one second, without any previous training or upbringing, he had become the wettest man in Worcestershire.

'Jeeves!' I cried.

'Yes, indeed, sir,' said Jeeves, and seemed to me to put the whole thing in a nutshell.

Down below, things were hotting up nicely. Old Mr Anstruther may have been frail, but he undoubtedly had his moments. I have rarely seen a man of his years conduct himself with such a lissome abandon. There was a stick lying beside the chair, and with this in hand he went into action like a two-year-old. A moment later, he and Thos. had passed out of the picture round the side of the house, Thos. cutting out a rare pace but, judging from the sounds of anguish, not quite good enough to distance the field.

The tumult and the shouting died; and, after gazing for a while with considerable satisfaction at the Snettisham, who was standing there with a sand-bagged look watching her nominee pass right out of the betting, I turned to Jeeves. I felt quietly triumphant. It is not often that I score off him, but now I had scored in no uncertain manner.

'You see, Jeeves,' I said, 'I was right and you were wrong. Blood will tell. Once a Thos., always a Thos. Can the leopard change his spots or the Ethiopian his what-not? What was that thing they used to teach us at school about, expelling Nature?'

'You may expel Nature with a pitchfork, sir, but she will always return? In the original Latin—'

'Never mind about the original Latin. The point is that I told you Thos. could not resist those curls, and he couldn't. You would have it that he could.'

'I do not fancy it was the curls that caused the upheaval, sir.'

'Must have been.'

'No, sir. I think Master Sebastian had been speaking disparagingly of Miss Garbo.'

'Eh? Why would he do that?'

'I suggested that he should do so, sir, not long ago when I encountered him on his way to the stable-yard. It was a move which he was very willing to take, as he informed me that in his opinion Miss Garbo was definitely inferior both in beauty and talent to Miss Clara Bow, for whom he has long nourished a deep regard. From what we have just witnessed, sir, I imagine that Master Sebastian must have introduced the topic into the conversation at an early point.'

I sank into a chair. The Wooster system can stand just so much.

'Jeeves!'

'Sir?'

'You tell me that Sebastian Moon, a stripling of such tender years that he can go about the place with long curls without causing mob violence, is in love with Clara Bow?'

'And has been for some little time, he gave me to understand, sir.'

'Jeeves, this Younger Generation is hot stuff.'

'Yes, sir.'

'Were you like that in your day?'

'No, sir.'

'Nor I, Jeeves. At the age of fourteen I once wrote to Marie Lloyd for her autograph, but apart from that my private life could bear the strictest investigation. However, that is not the point. The point is, Jeeves, that once more I must pay you a marked tribute.'

'Thank you very much, sir.'

'Once more you have stepped forward like the great man you are and spread sweetness and light in no uncertain measure.'

'I am glad to have given satisfaction, sir. Would you be requiring my services any further?'

'You mean you wish to return to Bognor and its shrimps? Do so, Jeeves, and stay there another fortnight, if you wish. And may success attend your net.'

'Thank you very much, sir.'

I eyed the man fixedly. His head stuck out at the back, and his eyes sparkled with the light of pure intelligence.

'I am sorry for the shrimp that tries to pit its feeble cunning against you, Jeeves,' I said.

And I meant it.

9

JEEVES AND THE OLD SCHOOL CHUM

In the autumn of the year in which Yorkshire Pudding won the Manchester November Handicap, the fortunes of my old pal Richard ('Bingo') Little seemed to have reached their—what's the word I want? He was, to all appearances, absolutely on plush. He ate well, slept well, was happily married; and, his Uncle Wilberforce having at last handed in his dinner-pail, respected by all, had come into possession of a large income and a fine old place in the country about thirty miles from Norwich. Buzzing down there for a brief visit, I came away convinced that, if ever a bird was sitting on top of the world, that bird was Bingo.

I had to come away because the family were shooting me off to Harrogate to chaperone my Uncle George, whose liver had been giving him the elbow again. But, as we sat pushing down the morning meal on the day of my departure, I readily agreed to play a return date as soon as ever I could fight my way back to civilization.

'Come in time for the Lakenham races,' urged young Bingo. He took aboard a second cargo of sausages and bacon, for he had always been a good trencherman and the country air seemed to improve his appetite. 'We're going to motor over with a luncheon basket, and more or less revel.'

I was just about to say that I would make a point of it, when Mrs Bingo, who was opening letters behind the coffee-apparatus, suddenly uttered a pleased yowl.

'Oh, sweetie-lambkin!' she cried.

Mrs B., if you remember, before her marriage, was the celebrated female novelist, Rosie M. Banks, and it is in some such ghastly fashion that she habitually addresses the other half of the sketch. She has got that way, I take it, from a lifetime of writing heart-throb fiction for the masses. Bingo doesn't seem to mind. I suppose, seeing that the little woman is the author of such outstanding bilge as *Mervyn Keene, Clubman*, and *Only A Factory Girl*, he is thankful it isn't anything worse.

'Oh, sweetie-lambkin, isn't that lovely?'

'What?'

'Laura Pyke wants to come here.'

'Who?'

'You must have heard me speak of Laura Pyke. She was my dearest friend at school. I simply worshipped her. She always had such a wonderful mind. She wants us to put her up for a week or two.'

'Right-ho. Bung her in.'

'You're sure you don't mind?'

'Of course not. Any pal of yours—'

'Darling!' said Mrs Bingo, blowing him a kiss.

'Angel!' said Bingo, going on with the sausages. All very charming, in fact. Pleasant domestic scene, I mean. Cheery give-and-take in the home and all that. I said as much to Jeeves as we drove off.

'In these days of unrest, Jeeves,' I said, 'with wives yearning to fulfil themselves and husbands slipping round the corner to do what they shouldn't, and the home, generally speaking, in the melting-pot, as it were, it is nice to find a thoroughly united couple.'

'Decidedly agreeable, sir.'

'I allude to the Bingos—Mr and Mrs.'

'Exactly, sir.'

'What was it the poet said of couples like the Bingeese?'

'"Two minds with but a single thought, two hearts that beat as one," sir.'

'A dashed good description, Jeeves.'

'It has, I believe, given uniform satisfaction, sir.'

And yet, if I had only known, what I had been listening to that a.m. was the first faint rumble of the coming storm. Unseen, in the background, Fate was quietly slipping the lead into the boxing-glove.

I managed to give Uncle George a miss at a fairly early date and, leaving him wallowing in the waters, sent a wire to the Bingos, announcing my return. It was a longish drive and I fetched up at my destination only just in time to dress for dinner. I had done a quick dash into the soup and fish and was feeling pretty good at the prospect of a cocktail and the well-cooked, when the door opened and Bingo appeared.

'Hello, Bertie,' he said. 'Ah, Jeeves.'

He spoke in one of those toneless voices: and, catching Jeeves's eye as I adjusted the old cravat, I exchanged a questioning glance with it. From its expression I gathered that the same thing had struck him that had struck me—viz., that our host, the young Squire, was none too chirpy. The brow was furrowed, the eye lacked that hearty sparkle, and the general bearing and demeanour were those of a body discovered after being several days in the water.

'Anything up, Bingo?' I asked, with the natural anxiety of a boyhood friend. 'You have a mouldy look. Are you sickening for some sort of plague?'

'I've got it.'

'Got what?'

'The plague.'

'How do you mean?'

'She's on the premises now,' said Bingo, and laughed in an unpleasant, hacking manner, as if he were missing on one tonsil.

I couldn't follow him. The old egg seemed to me to speak in riddles.

'You seem to me, old egg,' I said, 'to speak in riddles. Don't you think he speaks in riddles, Jeeves?'

'Yes, sir.'

'I'm talking about the Pyke,' said Bingo.

'What pike?'

'Laura Pyke. Don't you remember—?'

'Oh, ah. Of course. The school chum. The seminary crony. Is she still here?'

'Yes, and looks like staying for ever. Rosie's absolutely potty about her. Hangs on her lips.'

'The glamour of the old days still persists, eh?'

'I should say it does,' said young Bingo. 'This business of schoolgirl friendships beats me. Hypnotic is the only word. I can't understand it. Men aren't like that. You and I were at school together, Bertie, but, my gosh, I don't look on you as a sort of mastermind.'

'You don't?'

'I don't treat your lightest utterance as a pearl of wisdom.'

'Why not?'

'Yet Rosie does with this Pyke. In the hands of the Pyke she is mere putty. If you want to see what was once a first-class Garden of Eden becoming utterly ruined as a desirable residence by the machinations of a Serpent, take a look round this place.'

'Why what's the trouble?'

'Laura Pyke,' said young Bingo with intense bitterness, 'is a food crank, curse her. She says we all eat too much and eat it too quickly and, anyway, ought not to be eating it at all but living on parsnips and similar muck. And Rosie, instead of telling the woman not to be a fathead, gazes at her in wide-eyed admiration, taking it in through the pores. The result is that the cuisine of this house has been shot to pieces, and I am starving on my feet. Well, when I tell you that it's weeks since a beefsteak pudding raised its head in the home, you'll understand what I mean.'

At this point the gong went. Bingo listened with a moody frown.

'I don't know why they still bang that damned thing,' he said. 'There's nothing to bang it for. By the way, Bertie, would you like a cocktail?'

'I would.'

'Well, you won't get one. We don't have cocktails any more. The girl friend says they corrode the stomachic tissues.'

I was appalled. I had had no idea that the evil had spread as far as this.

'No cocktails!'

'No. And you'll be dashed lucky if it isn't a vegetarian dinner.'

'Bingo,' I cried, deeply moved, 'you must act. You must assert yourself. You must put your foot down. You must take a strong stand. You must be master in the home.'

He looked at me. A long, strange look.

'You aren't married, are you, Bertie?'

'You know I'm not.'

'I should have guessed it, anyway. Come on.'

Well, the dinner wasn't absolutely vegetarian, but when you had said that you had said everything. It was sparse, meagre, not at all the jolly, chunky repast for which the old tum was standing up and clamouring after its long motor ride. And what there was of it was turned to ashes in the mouth by the conversation of Miss Laura Pyke.

In happier circs, and if I had not been informed in advance of the warped nature of her soul, I might have been favourably impressed by this female at the moment of our meeting. She was really rather a good-looking girl, a bit strong in the face but nevertheless quite reasonably attractive. But had she been a thing of radiant beauty, she could never have clicked with Bertram Wooster. Her conversation was of a kind which would have queered Helen of Troy with any right-thinking man.

During dinner she talked all the time, and it did not take me long to see why the iron had entered into Bingo's soul. Practically all she said was about food and Bingo's tendency to shovel it down in excessive quantities, thereby handing the lemon to his stomachic tissues. She didn't seem particularly interested in my stomachic tissues, rather giving the impression that if Bertram burst it would be all right with her. It was on young Bingo that she concentrated as the brand to be saved from the burning. Gazing at him like a high priestess at the favourite, though erring, disciple, she told him all the things that were happening to his inside because he would insist on eating stuff lacking in fat-soluble vitamins. She spoke freely of proteins, carbohydrates, and the physiological requirements of the average individual. She was not a girl who believed in mincing her words, and a racy little anecdote she told about a man who refused to eat prunes had the effect of causing me to be a non-starter for the last two courses.

'Jeeves,' I said, on reaching the sleeping chamber that night, 'I don't like the look of things.'

'No, sir?'

'No, Jeeves, I do not. I view the situation with concern. Things are worse than I thought they were. Mr Little's remarks before dinner may have given you the impression that the Pyke merely lectured on food-reform in a general sort of way. Such, I now find, is not the case. By way of illustrating her theme, she points to Mr Little as the awful example. She criticizes him, Jeeves.'

'Indeed, sir?'

'Yes. Openly. Keeps telling him he eats too much, drinks too much, and gobbles his food. I wish you could have heard a comparison she drew between him and the late Mr Gladstone, considering them in the capacity of food chewers. It left young Bingo very much with the short end of the stick. And the sinister thing is that Mrs Bingo approves. Are wives often like that? Welcoming criticism of the lord and master, I mean?'

'They are generally open to suggestions from the outside public with regard to the improvement of their husbands, sir.'

'That is why married men are wan, what?'

'Yes, sir.'

I had had the foresight to send the man downstairs for a plate of biscuits. I bit a representative specimen thoughtfully.

'Do you know what I think, Jeeves?'

'No, sir.'

'I think Mr Little doesn't realize the full extent of the peril which threatens his domestic happiness. I'm beginning to understand this business of matrimony. I'm beginning to see how the thing works. Would you care to hear how I figure it out, Jeeves?'

'Extremely, sir.'

'Well, it's like this. Take a couple of birds. These birds get married, and for a while all is gas and gaiters. The female regards her mate as about the best thing that ever came a girl's way. He is her king, if you know what I mean. She looks up to him and respects him. Joy, as you might say, reigns supreme. Eh?'

'Very true, sir.'

'Then gradually, by degrees—little by little, if I may use the expression—

disillusionment sets in. She sees him eating a poached egg, and the glamour starts to fade. She watches him mangling a chop, and it continues to fade. And so on and so on, if you follow me, and so forth.'

'I follow you perfectly, sir.'

'But mark this, Jeeves. This is the point. Here we approach the nub. Usually it is all right, because, as I say, the disillusionment comes gradually and the female has time to adjust herself. But in the case of young Bingo, owing to the indecent outspokenness of the Pyke, it's coming in a rush. Absolutely in a flash, without any previous preparation, Mrs Bingo is having Bingo presented to her as a sort of human boa-constrictor full of unpleasantly jumbled interior organs. The picture which the Pyke is building up for her in her mind is that of one of those men you see in restaurants with three chins, bulging eyes, and the veins starting out on the forehead. A little more of this, and love must wither.'

'You think so, sir?'

'I'm sure of it. No affection can stand the strain. Twice during dinner to-night the Pyke said things about young Bingo's intestinal canal which I shouldn't have thought would have been possible in mixed company even in this lax post-War era. Well, you see what I mean. You can't go on knocking a man's intestinal canal indefinitely without causing his wife to stop and ponder. The danger, as I see it, is that after a bit more of this Mrs Little will decide that tinkering is no use and that the only thing to do is to scrap Bingo and get a newer model.'

'Most disturbing, sir.'

'Something must be done, Jeeves. You must act. Unless you can find some way of getting this Pyke out of the woodwork, and that right speedily, the home's number is up. You see, what makes matters worse is that Mrs Bingo is romantic. Women like her, who consider the day ill-spent if they have not churned out five thousand words of superfatted fiction, are apt even at the best of times to yearn a trifle. The ink gets into their heads. I mean to say, I shouldn't wonder if right from the start Mrs Bingo hasn't had a sort of sneaking regret that Bingo isn't one of those strong, curt, Empire-building kind of Englishmen she puts into her books, with sad, unfathomable eyes, lean, sensitive hands, and riding-boots. You see what I mean?'

'Precisely, sir. You imply that Miss Pyke's criticisms will have been instrumental in moving the hitherto unformulated dissatisfaction from the subconscious to the conscious mind.'

'Once again, Jeeves?' I said, trying to grab it as it came off the bat, but missing it by several yards.

He repeated the dose.

'Well, I daresay you're right,' I said. 'Anyway, the point is, P.M.G. Pyke must go. How do you propose to set about it?'

'I fear I have nothing to suggest at the moment, sir.'

'Come, come, Jeeves.'

'I fear not, sir. Possibly after I have seen the lady—'

'You mean, you want to study the psychology of the individual and what not?'

'Precisely, sir.'

'Well, I don't know how you're going to do it. After all, I mean, you can hardly cluster round the dinner-table and drink in the Pyke's small talk.'

'There is that difficulty, sir.'

'Your best chance, it seems to me, will be when we go to the Lakenham races on Thursday. We shall feed out of a luncheon-basket in God's air, and there's nothing to stop you hanging about and passing the sandwiches. Prick the ears and be at your most observant then, is my advice.'

'Very good, sir.'

'Very good, Jeeves. Be there, then, with the eyes popping. And, meanwhile, dash downstairs and see if you can dig up another instalment of these biscuits. I need them sorely.'

The morning of the Lakenham races dawned bright and juicy. A casual observer would have said that God was in His Heaven and all right with the world. It was one of those days you sometimes get lateish in the autumn when the sun beams, the birds toot, and there is a bracing tang in the air that sends the blood beetling briskly through the veins.

Personally, however, I wasn't any too keen on the bracing tang. It made me feel so exceptionally fit that almost immediately after breakfast I found myself beginning to wonder what there would be for lunch. And the thought of what there probably would be for lunch, if the Pyke's influence made itself felt, lowered my spirits considerably.

'I fear the worst, Jeeves,' I said. 'Last night at dinner Miss Pyke threw out the remark that the carrot was the best of all vegetables, having an astonishing effect on the blood and beautifying the complexion. Now, I am all for anything that bucks up the Wooster blood. Also, I would like to give the natives a treat by letting them take a look at my rosy, glowing cheeks. But not at the expense of lunching on raw carrots. To avoid any rannygazoo, therefore, I think it will be best if you add a bit for the young master to your personal packet of sandwiches. I don't want to be caught short.'

'Very good, sir.'

At this point, young Bingo came up. I hadn't seen him look so jaunty for days.

'I've just been superintending the packing of the lunch-basket, Bertie,' he said. 'I stood over the butler and saw that there was no nonsense.'

'All pretty sound?' I asked, relieved.

'All indubitably sound.'

'No carrots?'

'No carrots,' said young Bingo. 'There's ham sandwiches,' he proceeded, a strange, soft light in his eyes, 'and tongue sandwiches and potted meat sandwiches and game sandwiches and hard-boiled eggs and lobster and a cold chicken and sardines and a cake and a couple of bottles of Bollinger and some old brandy—'

'It has the right ring,' I said. 'And if we want a bite to eat after that, of course we can go to the pub.'

'What pub?'

'Isn't there a pub on the course?'

'There's not a pub for miles. That's why I was so particularly careful that there should be no funny work about the basket. The common where these races are held is a desert without an oasis. Practically a death-trap. I met a fellow the other day who told me he got there last year and unpacked his basket and found that the champagne had burst and, together with the salad dressing, had soaked into the ham, which in its turn had got mixed up with the gorgonzola cheese, forming a sort of paste. He had had rather a bumpy bit of road to travel over.'

'What did he do?'

'Oh, he ate the mixture. It was the only course. But he said he could still taste it sometimes, even now.'

... ...

In ordinary circs I can't say I should have been any too braced at the news that we were going to split up for the journey in the following order—Bingo and Mrs Bingo in their car and the Pyke in mine, with Jeeves sitting behind in the dickey. But, things being as they were, the arrangement had its points. It meant that Jeeves would be able to study the back of her head and draw his deductions, while I could engage her in conversation and let him see for himself what manner of female she was.

I started, accordingly, directly we had rolled off and all through the journey until we fetched up at the course she gave of her best. It was with considerable satisfaction that I parked the car beside a tree and hopped out.

'You were listening, Jeeves?' I said gravely.

'Yes, sir.'

'A tough baby?'

'Undeniably, sir.'

Bingo and Mrs Bingo came up.

'The first race won't be for half an hour,' said Bingo. 'We'd better lunch now. Fish the basket out, Jeeves, would you mind?'

'Sir?'

'The luncheon-basket,' said Bingo in a devout sort of voice, licking his lips slightly.

'The basket is not in Mr Wooster's car, sir.'

'What!'

'I assumed that you were bringing it in your own, sir.'

I have never seen the sunshine fade out of anybody's face as quickly as it did out of Bingo's. He uttered a sharp, wailing cry.

'Rosie!'

'Yes, sweetie-pie?'

'The bunch! The lasket!'

'What, darling?'

'The luncheon-basket!'

'What about it, precious?'

'It's been left behind!'

'Oh, has it?' said Mrs Bingo.

I confess she had never fallen lower in my estimation. I had always known her as a woman with as healthy an appreciation of her meals as any of my acquaintance. A few years previously, when my Aunt Dahlia had stolen her French cook, Anatole, she had called Aunt Dahlia some names in my presence which had impressed me profoundly. Yet now, when informed that she was marooned on a bally prairie without bite or sup, all she could find to say was, 'Oh, has it?' I had never fully realized before the extent to which she had allowed herself to be dominated by the deleterious influence of the Pyke.

The Pyke, for her part, touched an even lower level.

'It is just as well,' she said, and her voice seemed to cut Bingo like a knife. 'Luncheon is a meal better omitted. If taken, it should consist merely of a few muscatels, bananas and grated carrots. It is a well-known fact—'

And she went on to speak at some length of the gastric juices in a vein far from suited to any gathering at which gentlemen were present.

'So, you see, darling,' said Mrs Bingo, 'you will really feel ever so much better and brighter for not having eaten a lot of indigestible food. It is much the best thing that could have happened.'

Bingo gave her a long, lingering look.

'I see,' he said. 'Well, if you will excuse me, I'll just go off somewhere where I can cheer a bit without exciting comment.'

I perceived Jeeves withdrawing in a meaning manner, and I followed him, hoping for the best. My trust was not misplaced. He had brought enough sandwiches for two. In fact, enough for three. I whistled to Bingo, and he came slinking up, and we restored the tissues in a makeshift sort of way behind a hedge. Then Bingo went off to interview bookies about the first race, and Jeeves gave a cough.

'Swallowed a crumb the wrong way?' I said.

'No, sir, I thank you. It is merely that I desired to express a hope that I had not been guilty of taking a liberty, sir.'

'How?'

'In removing the luncheon-basket from the car before we started, sir.'

I quivered like an aspen. I stared at the man. Aghast. Shocked to the core.

'You, Jeeves?' I said, and I should rather think Cæsar spoke in the same sort of voice on finding Brutus puncturing him with the sharp instrument. 'You mean to tell me it was you who deliberately, if that's the word I want—?'

'Yes, sir. It seemed to me the most judicious course to pursue. It would not have been prudent, in my opinion, to have allowed Mrs Little, in her present frame of mind, to witness Mr Little eating a meal on the scale which he outlined in his remarks this morning.'

I saw his point.

'True, Jeeves,' I said thoughtfully. 'I see what you mean. If young Bingo has a fault, it is that, when in the society of a sandwich, he is apt to get a bit rough. I've picnicked with him before, many a time and oft, and his method of approach to the ordinary tongue or ham sandwich rather resembles that of the lion, the king of beasts, tucking into an antelope. Add lobster and cold chicken, and I admit the spectacle might have been something of a jar for the consort . . . Still . . . all the same . . . nevertheless—'

'And there is another aspect of the matter, sir.'

'What's that?'

'A day spent without nourishment in the keen autumnal air may induce in Mrs Little a frame of mind not altogether in sympathy with Miss Pyke's views on diet.'

'You mean, hunger will gnaw and she'll be apt to bite at the Pyke when she talks about how jolly it is for the gastric juices to get a day off?'

'Exactly, sir.'

I shook the head. I hated to damp the man's pretty enthusiasm, but it had to be done.

'Abandon the idea, Jeeves,' I said. 'I fear you have not studied the sex as I have. Missing her lunch means little or nothing to the female of the species. The feminine attitude towards lunch is notoriously airy and casual. Where you have made your bloomer is in confusing lunch with tea. Hell, it is well known, has no fury like a woman who wants her tea and can't get it. At such times the most amiable of the sex become mere bombs which a spark may ignite. But lunch, Jeeves, no. I should have thought you would have known that—a bird of your established intelligence.'

'No doubt you are right, sir.'

'If you could somehow arrange for Mrs Little to miss her tea . . . but these are idle dreams, Jeeves. By tea-time she will be back at the old home, in the midst of plenty. It only takes an hour to do the trip. The last race is over shortly after four. By five o'clock Mrs Little will have her feet tucked under the table and will be revelling in buttered toast. I am sorry, Jeeves, but your scheme was a wash-out from the start. No earthly. A dud.'

'I appreciate the point you have raised, sir. What you say is extremely true.'

'Unfortunately. Well, there it is. The only thing to do seems to be to get back to the course and try to skin a bookie or two and forget.'

Well, the long day wore on, so to speak. I can't say I enjoyed myself much. I was distrait, if you know what I mean. Preoccupied. From time to time assorted clusters of spavined local horses clumped down the course with farmers on top of them, but I watched them with a languid eye. To get into the spirit of one of these rural meetings, it is essential that the subject have a good, fat lunch inside him. Subtract the lunch, and what ensues? Ennui. Not once but many times during the afternoon I found myself thinking hard thoughts about Jeeves. The man seemed to me to be losing his grip. A child could have told him that that footling scheme of his would not have got him anywhere.

I mean to say, when you reflect that the average woman considers she has lunched luxuriously if she swallows a couple of macaroons, half a chocolate éclair and a raspberry vinegar, is she going to be peevish because you do her out of a midday sandwich? Of course not. Perfectly ridiculous. Too silly for words. All that Jeeves had accomplished by his bally trying to be clever was to give me a feeling as if foxes were gnawing my vitals and a strong desire for home.

It was a relief, therefore, when, as the shades of evening were beginning to fall, Mrs Bingo announced her intention of calling it a day and shifting.

'Would you mind very much missing the last race, Mr Wooster?' she asked.

'I am all for it,' I replied cordially. 'The last race means little or nothing in my life. Besides, I am a shilling and sixpence ahead of the game, and the time to leave off is when you're winning.'

'Laura and I thought we would go home. I feel I should like an early cup of tea. Bingo says he will stay on. So I thought you could drive our car, and he would follow later in yours, with Jeeves.'

'Right-ho.'

'You know the way?'

'Oh yes. Main road as far as that turning by the pond, and then across country.'

'I can direct you from there.'

I sent Jeeves to fetch the car, and presently we were bowling off in good shape. The short afternoon had turned into a rather chilly, misty sort of evening, the kind of evening that sends a fellow's thoughts straying off in the direction of hot Scotch-and-water with a spot of lemon in it. I put the foot firmly on the accelerator, and we did the five or six miles of main road in quick time.

Turning eastward at the pond, I had to go a bit slower, for we had struck a wildish stretch of country where the going wasn't so good. I don't know any part of England where you feel so off the map as on the by-roads of Norfolk. Occasionally we would meet a cow or two, but otherwise we had the world pretty much to ourselves.

I began to think about that drink again, and the more I thought the better it looked. It's rummy how people differ in this matter of selecting the beverage that is to touch the spot. It's what Jeeves would call the psychology of the individual. Some fellows in my position might have voted for a tankard of ale, and the Pyke's idea of a refreshing snort was, as I knew from what she had told me on the journey out, a cupful of tepid pip-and-peel water or, failing that, what she called the fruit-liquor. You make this, apparently, by soaking raisins in cold water and adding the juice of a lemon. After which, I suppose, you invite a couple of old friends in and have an orgy, burying the bodies in the morning.

Personally, I had no doubts. I never wavered. Hot Scotch-and-water was the stuff for me—stressing the Scotch, if you know what I mean, and going fairly easy on the H_2O. I seemed to see the beaker smiling at me across the misty fields, beckoning me on, as it were, and saying 'Courage, Bertram! It will not be long now!' And with renewed energy I bunged the old foot down on the accelerator and tried to send the needle up to sixty.

Instead of which, if you follow my drift, the bally thing flickered for a moment to thirty-five and then gave the business up as a bad job. Quite suddenly and unexpectedly, no one more surprised than myself, the car let out a faint gurgle like a sick moose and stopped in its tracks. And there we were, somewhere in Norfolk, with darkness coming on and a cold wind that smelled of guano and dead mangold-wurzels playing searchingly about the spinal column.

The back-seat drivers gave tongue.

'What's the matter? What has happened? Why don't you go on? What are you stopping for?'

I explained.

'I'm not stopping. It's the car.'

'Why has the car stopped?'

'Ah!' I said, with a manly frankness that became me well. 'There you have me.'

You see, I'm one of those birds who drive a lot but don't know the first thing about the works. The policy I pursue is to get aboard, prod the self-starter, and leave the rest to Nature. If anything goes wrong, I scream for an A.A. scout. It's a system that answers admirably as a rule, but on the present occasion it blew a fuse owing to the fact that there wasn't an A.A. scout within miles. I explained as much to the fair cargo and received in return a 'Tchah!' from the Pyke that nearly lifted the top of my head off. What with having a covey of female relations who have regarded me from childhood as about ten degrees short of a half-wit, I have become rather a connoisseur of 'Tchahs', and the Pyke's seemed to me well up in Class A, possessing much of the *timbre* and *brio* of my Aunt Agatha's.

'Perhaps I can find out what the trouble is,' she said, becoming calmer. 'I understand cars.'

She got out and began peering into the thing's vitals. I thought for a moment of suggesting that its gastric juices might have taken a turn for the worse owing to lack of fat-soluble vitamins, but decided on the whole not. I'm a pretty close observer, and it didn't seem to me that she was in the mood.

And yet, as a matter of fact, I should have been about right, at that. For after fiddling with the engine for awhile in a discontented sort of way the female was suddenly struck with an idea. She tested it, and it was proved correct. There was not a drop of petrol in the tank. No gas. In other words, a complete lack of fat-soluble vitamins. What it amounted to was that the job now before us was to get the old bus home purely by will-power.

Feeling that, from whatever angle they regarded the regrettable occurrence, they could hardly blame me, I braced up a trifle—in fact, to the extent of a hearty 'Well, well, well!'

'No petrol,' I said. 'Fancy that.'

'But Bingo told me he was going to fill the tank this morning,' said Mrs Bingo.

'I suppose he forgot,' said the Pyke. 'He would!'

'What do you mean by that?' said Mrs Bingo, and I noted in her voice a touch of what-is-it.

'I mean he is just the sort of man who would forget to fill the tank,' replied the Pyke, who also appeared somewhat moved.

'I should be very much obliged, Laura,' said Mrs Bingo, doing the heavy loyal-little-woman stuff, 'if you would refrain from criticizing my husband.'

'Tchah!' said the Pyke.

'And don't say "Tchah!"' said Mrs Bingo.

'I shall say whatever I please,' said the Pyke.

'Ladies, ladies!' I said. 'Ladies, ladies, ladies!'

It was rash. Looking back, I can see that. One of the first lessons life teaches us is that on these occasions of back-chat between the delicately-nurtured a man should retire into the offing, curl up in a ball, and imitate the prudent tactics of the opossum, which, when danger is in the air, pretends to be dead, frequently going to the length of hanging out crêpe and instructing its friends to stand round and say what a pity it all is. The only result of my dash at the soothing intervention was that the Pyke turned on me like a wounded leopardess.

'Well!' she said. 'Aren't you proposing to do anything, Mr Wooster?'

'What can I do?'

'There's a house over there. I should have thought it would be well within even your powers to go and borrow a tin of petrol.'

I looked. There was a house. And one of the lower windows was lighted, indicating to the trained mind the presence of a ratepayer.

'A very sound and brainy scheme,' I said ingratiatingly. 'I will first honk a little on the horn to show we're here, and then rapid action.'

I honked, with the most gratifying results. Almost immediately a human form appeared in the window. It seemed to be waving its arms in a matey and welcoming sort of way. Stimulated and encouraged, I hastened to the front door and gave it a breezy bang with the knocker. Things, I felt, were moving.

The first bang produced no result. I had just lifted the knocker for the encore, when it was wrenched out of my hand. The door flew open, and there was a bloke with spectacles on his face and all round the spectacles an expression of strained anguish. A bloke with a secret sorrow.

I was sorry he had troubles, of course, but, having some of my own, I came right down to the agenda without delay.

'I say . . .' I began.

The bloke's hair was standing up in a kind of tousled mass, and at this juncture, as if afraid it would not stay like that without assistance, he ran a hand through it. And for the first time I noted that the spectacles had a hostile gleam.

'Was that you making that infernal noise?' he asked.

'Er—yes,' I said. 'I did toot.'

'Toot once more—just once,' said the bloke, speaking in a low, strangled voice, 'and I'll shred you up into little bits with my bare hands. My wife's gone out for the evening and after hours of ceaseless toil I've at last managed to get the baby to sleep, and you come along making that hideous din with your damned horn. What do you mean by it, blast you?'

'Er—'

'Well, that's how matters stand,' said the bloke, summing up. 'One more toot—just one single, solitary suggestion of the faintest shadow or suspicion of anything remotely approaching a toot—and may the Lord have mercy on your soul.'

'What I want,' I said, 'is petrol.'

'What you'll get,' said the bloke, 'is a thick ear.'

And, closing the door with the delicate caution of one brushing flies off a sleeping Venus, he passed out of my life.

Women as a sex are always apt to be a trifle down on the defeated warrior. Returning to the car, I was not well received. The impression seemed to be that Bertram had not acquitted himself in a fashion worthy of his Crusading ancestors. I did my best to smooth matters over, but you know how it is. When you've broken down on a chilly autumn evening miles from anywhere and have missed lunch and look like missing tea as well, mere charm of manner can never be a really satisfactory substitute for a tinful of the juice.

Things got so noticeably unpleasant, in fact, that after a while, mumbling something about getting help, I sidled off down the road. And, by Jove, I hadn't gone half a mile before I saw lights in the distance and there, in the middle of this forsaken desert, was a car.

I stood in the road and whooped as I had never whooped before.

'Hi!' I shouted. 'I say! Hi! Half a minute! Hi! Ho! I say! Ho! Hi! Just a second if you don't mind.'

The car reached me and slowed up. A voice spoke.

'Is that you, Bertie?'

'Hullo, Bingo! Is that you? I say, Bingo, we've broken down.'

Bingo hopped out.

'Give us five minutes, Jeeves,' he said, 'and then drive slowly on.'

'Very good, sir.'

Bingo joined me.

'We aren't going to walk, are we?' I asked. 'Where's the sense?'

'Yes, walk, laddie,' said Bingo, 'and warily withal. I want to make sure of something. Bertie, how were things when you left? Hotting up?'

'A trifle.'

'You observed symptoms of a row, a quarrel, a parting of brass rags between Rosie and the Pyke?'

'There did seem a certain liveliness.'

'Tell me.'

I related what had occurred. He listened intently.

'Bertie,' he said as we walked along, 'you are present at a crisis in your old friend's life. It may be that this vigil in a broken-down car will cause Rosie to see what you'd have thought she ought to have seen years ago—viz.: that the Pyke is entirely unfit for human consumption and must be cast into outer darkness where there is wailing and gnashing of teeth. I am not betting on it, but stranger things have happened. Rosie is the sweetest girl in the world, but, like all women, she gets edgy towards tea-time. And to-day, having missed lunch . . . Hark!'

He grabbed my arm, and we paused. Tense. Agog. From down the road came the sound of voices, and a mere instant was enough to tell us that it was Mrs Bingo and the Pyke talking things over.

I had never listened in on a real, genuine female row before, and I'm bound to say it was pretty impressive. During my absence, matters appeared to have developed on rather a spacious scale. They had reached the stage now where the combatants had begun to dig into the past and rake up old scores. Mrs Bingo was saying that the Pyke would never have got into the hockey team at St Adela's if she hadn't flattered and fawned upon the captain in a way that it made Mrs Bingo, even after all these years, sick to think of. The Pyke replied that she had refrained from mentioning it until now, having always felt it better to let bygones be bygones, but that if Mrs Bingo supposed her to be unaware that Mrs Bingo had won the Scripture prize by taking a list of the Kings of Judah into the examination room, tucked into her middy-blouse, Mrs Bingo was vastly mistaken.

Furthermore, the Pyke proceeded, Mrs Bingo was also labouring under an error if she imagined that the Pyke proposed to remain a night longer under her roof. It had been in a moment of weakness, a moment of mistaken kindliness, supposing her to be lonely and in need of intellectual society, that the Pyke had decided to pay her a visit at all. Her intention now was, if ever Providence sent them aid and enabled her to get out of this beastly car and back to her trunks, to pack those trunks and leave by the next train, even if that train was a milk-train, stopping at every station. Indeed, rather than endure another night at Mrs Bingo's, the Pyke was quite willing to walk to London.

To this, Mrs Bingo's reply was long and eloquent and touched on the fact that in her last term at St Adela's a girl named Simpson had told her (Mrs Bingo) that a girl named Waddesley had told her (the Simpson) that the Pyke, while pretending to be a friend of hers (the Bingo's), had told her (the Waddesley) that she (the Bingo) couldn't eat strawberries and cream without coming out in spots, and, in addition, had spoken in the most catty manner about the shape of her nose. It could all have been condensed, however, into the words 'Right-ho'.

It was when the Pyke had begun to say that she had never had such a hearty laugh in her life as when she read the scene in Mrs Bingo's last novel where the heroine's little boy dies of croup that we felt it best to call the meeting to order before bloodshed set in. Jeeves had come up in the car, and Bingo, removing a tin of petrol from the dickey, placed it in the shadows at the side of the road. Then we hopped on and made the spectacular entry.

'Hullo, hullo hullo,' said Bingo brightly. 'Bertie tells me you've had a breakdown.'

'Oh, Bingo!' cried Mrs Bingo, wifely love thrilling in every syllable. 'Thank goodness you've come.'

'Now, perhaps,' said the Pyke, 'I can get home and do my packing. If Mr Wooster will allow me to use his car, his man can drive me back to the house in time to catch the six-fifteen.'

'You aren't leaving us?' said Bingo.

'I am,' said the Pyke.

'Too bad,' said Bingo.

She climbed in beside Jeeves and they popped off. There was a short silence after they had gone. It was too dark to see her, but I could feel Mrs Bingo struggling between love of her mate and the natural urge to say something crisp about his forgetting to fill the petrol tank that morning. Eventually nature took its course.

'I must say, sweetie-pie,' she said, 'it was a little careless of you to leave the tank almost empty when we started to-day. You promised me you would fill it, darling.'

'But I did fill it, darling.'

'But, darling, it's empty.'

'It can't be, darling.'

'Laura said it was.'

'The woman's an ass,' said Bingo. 'There's plenty of petrol. What's wrong is probably that the sprockets aren't running true with the differential gear. It happens that way sometimes. I'll fix it in a second. But I don't want you to sit freezing out here while I'm doing it. Why not go to that house over there and ask them if you can't come in and sit down for ten minutes? They might give you a cup of tea, too.'

A soft moan escaped Mrs Bingo.

'Tea!' I heard her whisper.

I had to bust Bingo's daydream.

'I'm sorry, old man,' I said, 'but I fear the old English hospitality which you outline is off. That house is inhabited by a sort of bandit. As unfriendly a bird as I ever met. His wife's out and he's just got the baby to sleep, and this has darkened his outlook. Tap even lightly on his front door and you take your life into your hands.'

'Nonsense,' said Bingo. 'Come along.'

He banged the knocker, and produced an immediate reaction.

'Hell!' said the Bandit, appearing as if out of a trap.

'I say,' said young Bingo, 'I'm just fixing our car outside. Would you object to my wife coming in out of the cold for a few minutes?'

'Yes,' said the Bandit, 'I would.'

'And you might give her a cup of tea.'

'I might,' said the Bandit, 'but I won't.'

'You won't?'

'No. And for heaven's sake don't talk so loud. I know that baby. A whisper sometimes does it.'

'Let us get this straight,' said Bingo. 'You refuse to give my wife tea?'

'Yes.'

'You would see a woman starve?'

'Yes.'

'Well, you jolly well aren't going to,' said young Bingo. 'Unless you go straight to your kitchen, put the kettle on, and start slicing bread for the buttered toast, I'll yell and wake the baby.'

The Bandit turned ashen.

'You wouldn't do that?'

'I would.'

'Have you no heart?'

'No.'

'No human feeling?'

'No.'

The Bandit turned to Mrs Bingo. You could see his spirit was broken.

'Do your shoes squeak?' he asked humbly.

'No.'

'Then come on in.'

'Thank you,' said Mrs Bingo.

She turned for an instant to Bingo, and there was a look in her eyes that one of those damsels in distress might have given the knight as he shot his cuffs and turned away from the dead dragon. It was a look of adoration, of almost reverent respect. Just the sort of look, in fact, that a husband likes to see.

'Darling!' she said.

'Darling!' said Bingo.

'Angel!' said Mrs Bingo.

'Precious!' said Bingo. 'Come along, Bertie, let's get at that car.'

He was silent till he had fetched the tin of petrol and filled the tank and screwed the cap on again. Then he drew a deep breath.

'Bertie,' he said, 'I am ashamed to admit it, but occasionally in the course of a lengthy acquaintance there have been moments when I have temporarily lost faith in Jeeves.'

'My dear chap!' I said, shocked.

'Yes, Bertie, there have. Sometimes my belief in him has wobbled. I have said to myself, "Has he the old speed, the ancient vim?" I shall never say it again. From now on, childlike trust. It was his idea, Bertie, that if a couple of women headed for tea suddenly found the cup snatched from their lips, so to speak, they would turn and rend one another. Observe the result.'

'But, dash it, Jeeves couldn't have known that the car would break down.'

'On the contrary. He let all the petrol out of the tank when you sent him to fetch the machine—all except just enough to carry it well into the wilds beyond the reach of human aid. He foresaw what would happen. I tell you, Bertie, Jeeves stands alone.'

'Absolutely.'

'He's a marvel.'

'A wonder.'

'A wizard.'

'A stout fellow,' I agreed. 'Full of fat-soluble vitamins.'

'The exact expression,' said young Bingo. 'And now let's go and tell Rosie the car is fixed, and then home to the tankard of ale.'

'Not the tankard of ale, old man,' I said firmly. 'The hot Scotch-and-water with a spot of lemon in it.'

'You're absolutely right,' said Bingo. 'What a flair you have in these matters, Bertie. Hot Scotch-and-water it is.'

10

INDIAN SUMMER OF AN UNCLE

Ask anyone at the Drones, and they will tell you that Bertram Wooster is a fellow whom it is dashed difficult to deceive. Old Lynx-Eye is about what it amounts to. I observe and deduce. I weight the evidence and draw my conclusions. And that is why Uncle George had not been in my midst more than about two minutes before I, so to speak, saw all. To my trained eye the thing stuck out a mile.

And yet it seemed so dashed absurd. Consider the facts, if you know what I mean.

I mean to say, for years, right back to the time when I first went to school, this bulging relative had been one of the recognized eyesores of London. He was fat then, and day by day in every way has been getting fatter ever since, till now tailors measure him just for the sake of the exercise. He is what they call a prominent London clubman—one of those birds in tight morning-coats and grey toppers whom you see toddling along St James's Street on fine afternoons, puffing a bit as they make the grade. Slip a ferret into any good club between Piccadilly and Pall Mall, and you would start half a dozen Uncle Georges.

He spends his time lunching and dining at the Buffers and, between meals, sucking down spots in the smoking-room and talking to anyone who will listen about the lining of his stomach. About twice a year his liver lodges a formal protest and he goes off to Harrogate or Carlsbad to get planed down. Then back again and on with the programme. The last bloke in the world, in short, who you would think would ever fall a victim to the divine pash. And yet, if you will believe me, that was absolutely the strength of it.

This old pestilence blew in on me one morning at about the hour of the after-breakfast cigarette.

'Oh, Bertie,' he said.

'Hullo?'

'You know those ties you've been wearing. Where did you get them?'

'Blucher's, in the Burlington Arcade.'

'Thanks.'

He walked across to the mirror and stood in front of it, gazing at himself in an earnest manner.

'Smut on your nose?' I asked courteously.

Then I suddenly perceived that he was wearing a sort of horrible simper, and I confess it chilled the blood to no little extent. Uncle George, with face in repose, is hard enough on the eye. Simpering, he goes right above the odds.

'Ha!' he said.

He heaved a long sigh, and turned away. Not too soon, for the mirror was on the point of cracking.

'I'm not so old,' he said, in a musing sort of voice.

'So old as what?'

'Properly considered, I'm in my prime. Besides, what a young and inexperienced girl needs is a man of weight and years to lean on. The sturdy oak, not the sapling.'

It was at this point that, as I said above, I saw all.

'Great Scott, Uncle George!' I said. 'You aren't thinking of getting married?'

'Who isn't?' he said.

'You aren't,' I said.

'Yes, I am. Why not?'

'Oh, well—'

'Marriage is an honourable state.'

'Oh, absolutely.'

'It might make you a better man, Bertie.'

'Who says so?'

'I say so. Marriage might turn you from a frivolous young scallywag into—er—a non-scallywag. Yes, confound you, I *am* thinking of getting married, and if Agatha comes sticking her oar in I'll—I'll—well, I shall know what to do about it.'

He exited on the big line, and I rang the bell for Jeeves. The situation seemed to me one that called for a cosy talk.

'Jeeves,' I said.

'Sir?'

'You know my Uncle George?'

'Yes, sir. His lordship has been familiar to me for some years.'

'I don't mean do you know my Uncle George. I mean do you know what my Uncle George is thinking of doing?'

'Contracting a matrimonial alliance, sir.'

'Good Lord! Did he tell you?'

'No, sir. Oddly enough, I chance to be acquainted with the other party in the matter.'

'The girl?'

'The young person, yes, sir. It was from her aunt, with whom she resides, that I received the information that his lordship was contemplating matrimony.'

'Who is she?'

'A Miss Platt, sir. Miss Rhoda Platt. Of Wistaria Lodge, Kitchener Road, East Dulwich.'

'Young?'

'Yes, sir.'

'The old fathead!'

'Yes, sir. The expression is one which I would, of course, not have ventured to employ myself, but I confess to thinking his lordship somewhat ill-advised. One must remember, however, that it is not unusual to find gentlemen of a certain age yielding to what might be described as a sentimental urge. They appear to experience what I may term a sort of Indian summer, a kind of temporarily renewed youth. The phenomenon is particularly noticeable, I am given to understand, in the United States of America among the wealthier inhabitants of the city of Pittsburgh. It is notorious, I am told, that sooner or later, unless restrained, they always endeavour to marry chorus-girls. Why this should be so, I am at a loss to say, but—'

I saw that this was going to take some time. I tuned out.

'From something in Uncle George's manner, Jeeves, as he referred to my Aunt Agatha's probable reception of the news, I gather that this Miss Platt is not of the *noblesse*.'

'No, sir. She is a waitress at his lordship's club.'

'My God! The proletariat!'

'The lower middle classes, sir.'

'Well, yes, by stretching it a bit, perhaps. Still, you know what I mean.'

'Yes, sir.'

'Rummy thing, Jeeves,' I said thoughtfully, 'this modern tendency to marry waitresses. If you remember, before he settled down, young Bingo Little was repeatedly trying to do it.'

'Yes, sir.'

'Odd!'

'Yes, sir.'

'Still, there it is, of course. The point to be considered now is, What will Aunt Agatha do about this? You know her, Jeeves. She is not like me. I'm broad-minded. If Uncle George wants to marry waitresses, let him, say I. I hold that the rank is but the penny stamp—'

'Guinea stamp, sir.'

'All right, guinea stamp. Though I don't believe there is such a thing. I shouldn't have thought they came higher than five bob. Well, as I was saying, I maintain that the rank is but the guinea stamp and a girl's a girl for all that.'

'"For *a'* that", sir. The poet Burns wrote in the North British dialect.'

'Well, "a' that", then, if you prefer it.'

'I have no preference in the matter, sir. It is simply that the poet Burns—'

'Never mind about the poet Burns.'

'No, sir.'

'Forget the poet Burns.'

'Very good, sir.'

'Expunge the poet Burns from your mind.'

'I will do so immediately, sir.'

'What we have to consider is not the poet Burns but the Aunt Agatha. She will kick, Jeeves.'

'Very probably, sir.'

'And, what's worse, she will lug me into the mess. There is only one thing to be done. Pack the toothbrush and let us escape while we may, leaving no address.'

'Very good, sir.'

At this moment the bell rang.

'Ha!' I said. 'Someone at the door.'

'Yes, sir.'

'Probably Uncle George back again. I'll answer it. You go and get ahead with the packing.'

'Very good, sir.'

I sauntered along the passage, whistling carelessly, and there on the mat was Aunt Agatha. Herself. Not a picture.

A nasty jar.

'Oh, hullo!' I said, it seeming but little good to tell her I was out of town and not expected back for some weeks.

'I wish to speak to you, Bertie,' said the Family Curse. 'I am greatly upset.'

She legged it into the sitting-room and volplaned into a chair. I followed, thinking wistfully of Jeeves packing in the bedroom. That suitcase would not be needed now. I knew what she must have come about.

'I've just seen Uncle George,' I said, giving her a lead.

'So have I,' said Aunt Agatha, shivering in a marked manner. 'He called on me while I was still in bed to inform me of his intention of marrying some impossible girl from South Norwood.'

'East Dulwich, the *cognoscenti* inform me.'

'Well, East Dulwich, then. It is the same thing. But who told you?'

'Jeeves.'

'And how, pray, does Jeeves come to know all about it?'

'There are very few things in this world, Aunt Agatha,' I said gravely, 'that Jeeves doesn't know all about. He's met the girl.'

'Who is she?'

'One of the waitresses at the Buffers.'

I had expected this to register, and it did. The relative let out a screech rather like the Cornish Express going through a junction.

'I take it from your manner, Aunt Agatha,' I said, 'that you want this thing stopped.'

'Of course it must be stopped.'

'Then there is but one policy to pursue. Let me ring for Jeeves and ask his advice.'

Aunt Agatha stiffened visibly. Very much the *grande dame* of the old *régime*.

'Are you seriously suggesting that we should discuss this intimate family matter with your manservant?'

'Absolutely. Jeeves will find the way.'

'I have always known that you were an imbecile, Bertie,' said the flesh-and-blood, now down at about three degrees Fahrenheit, 'but I did suppose that you had some proper feeling, some pride, some respect for your position.'

'Well, you know what the poet Burns says.'

She squelched me with a glance.

'Obviously the only thing to do,' she said, 'is to offer this girl money.'

'Money?'

'Certainly. It will not be the first time your uncle has made such a course necessary.'

We sat for a bit, brooding. The family always sits brooding when the subject of Uncle George's early romance comes up. I was too young to be actually in on it at the time, but I've had the details frequently from many sources, including Uncle George. Let him get even the slightest bit pickled, and he will tell you the whole story, sometimes twice in an evening. It was a barmaid at the Criterion, just before he came into the title. Her name was Maudie and he loved her dearly, but the family would have none of it. They dug down into the sock and paid her off. Just one of those human-interest stories, if you know what I mean.

I wasn't so sold on this money-offering scheme.

'Well, just as you like, of course,' I said, 'but you're taking an awful chance. I mean, whenever people do it in novels and plays, they always get the dickens of a welt. The girl gets the sympathy of the audience every time. She just draws herself up and looks at them with clear, steady eyes, causing them to feel not a little cheesey. If I were you, I would sit tight and let Nature take its course.'

'I don't understand you.'

'Well, consider for a moment what Uncle George looks like. No Greta Garbo, believe me. I should simply let the girl go on looking at him. Take it from me, Aunt Agatha, I've studied human nature and I don't believe there's a female in the world who could see Uncle George fairly often in those waistcoats he wears without feeling that it was due to her better self to give him the gate. Besides, this girl sees him at meal-times, and Uncle George with head down among the food-stuffs is a spectacle which—'

'If it is not troubling you too much, Bertie, I should be greatly obliged if you would stop drivelling.'

'Just as you say. All the same, I think you're going to find it dashed embarrassing, offering this girl money.'

'I am not proposing to do so. *You* will undertake the negotiations.'

'Me?'

'Certainly. I should think a hundred pounds would be ample. But I will give you a blank cheque, and you are at liberty to fill it in for a higher sum if it becomes necessary. The essential point is that, cost what it may, your uncle must be released from this entanglement.'

'So you're going to shove this off on me?'

'It is quite time you did something for the family.'

'And when she draws herself up and looks at me with clear, steady eyes, what do I do for an encore?'

'There is no need to discuss the matter any further. You can get down to East Dulwich in half an hour. There is a frequent service of trains. I will remain here to await your report.'

'But, listen!'

'Bertie, you will go and see this woman immediately.'

'Yes, but dash it!'

'Bertie!'

I threw in the towel.

'Oh, right-ho, if you say so.'

'I do say so.'

'Oh, well, in that case, right-ho.'

I don't know if you have ever tooled off to East Dulwich to offer a strange female a hundred smackers to release your Uncle George. In case you haven't, I may tell you that there are plenty of things that are lots better fun. I didn't feel any too good driving to the station. I didn't feel any too good in the train. And I didn't feel any too good as I walked to Kitchener Road. But the moment when I felt least good was when I had actually pressed the front-door bell and a rather grubby-looking maid had let me in and shown me down a passage and into a room with pink paper on the walls, a piano in the corner and a lot of photographs on the mantelpiece.

Barring a dentist's waiting-room, which it rather resembles, there isn't anything that quells the spirit much more than one of these suburban parlours. They are extremely apt to have stuffed birds in glass cases standing about on small tables, and if there is one thing which gives the man of sensibility that sinking feeling it is the cold, accusing eye of a ptarmigan or whatever it may be that has had its interior organs removed and sawdust substituted.

There were three of these cases in the parlour of Wistaria Lodge, so that, wherever you looked, you were sure to connect. Two were singletons, the third a family group, consisting of a father bullfinch, a mother bullfinch, and little Master Bullfinch, the last-named of whom wore an expression that was definitely that of a thug, and did more to damp my *joie de vivre* than all the rest of them put together.

I had moved to the window and was examining the aspidistra in order to avoid this creature's gaze, when I heard the door open and, turning, found myself confronted by something which, since it could hardly be the girl, I took to be the aunt.

'Oh, what-ho,' I said. 'Good morning.'

The words came out rather roopily, for I was feeling a bit on the stunned side. I mean to say, the room being so small and this exhibit so large, I had got that sensation of wanting air. There are some people who don't seem to be intended to be seen close to, and this aunt was one of them. Billowy curves, if you know what I mean. I should think that in her day she must have been a very handsome girl, though even then on the substantial side. By the time she came into my life, she had taken on a good deal of excess weight. She looked like a photograph of an opera singer of the 'eighties. Also the orange hair and the magenta dress.

However, she was a friendly soul. She seemed glad to see Bertram. She smiled broadly.

'So here you are at last!' she said.

I couldn't make anything of this.

'Eh?'

'But I don't think you had better see my niece just yet. She's just having a nap.'

'Oh, in that case—'

'Seems a pity to wake her, doesn't it?'

'Oh, absolutely,' I said, relieved.

'When you get the influenza, you don't sleep at night, and then if you doze off in the morning—well, it seems a pity to wake someone, doesn't it?'

'Miss Platt has influenza?'

'That's what we think it is. But, of course, you'll be able to say. But we needn't waste time. Since you're here, you can be taking a look at my knee.'

'Your knee?'

I am all for knees at their proper time and, as you might say, in their proper place, but somehow this didn't seem the moment. However, she carried on according to plan.

'What do you think of that knee?' she asked, lifting the seven veils.

Well, of course, one has to be polite.

'Terrific!' I said.

'You wouldn't believe how it hurts me sometimes.'

'Really?'

'A sort of shooting pain. It just comes and goes. And I'll tell you a funny thing.'

'What's that?' I said, feeling I could do with a good laugh.

'Lately I've been having the same pain just here, at the end of the spine.'

'You don't mean it!'

'I do. Like red-hot needles. I wish you'd have a look at it.'

'At your spine?'

'Yes.'

I shook my head. Nobody is fonder of a bit of fun than myself, and I am all for Bohemian camaraderie and making a party go, and all that. But there is a line, and we Woosters know when to draw it.

'It can't be done,' I said austerely. 'Not spines. Knees, yes. Spines, no,' I said.

She seemed surprised.

'Well,' she said, 'you're a funny sort of doctor, I must say.'

I'm pretty quick, as I said before, and I began to see that something in the nature of a misunderstanding must have arisen.

'Doctor?'

'Well, you call yourself a doctor, don't you?'

'Did you think I was a doctor?'

'Aren't you a doctor?'

'No. Not a doctor.'

We had got it straightened out. The scales had fallen from our eyes. We knew where we were.

I had suspected that she was a genial soul. She now endorsed this view. I don't think I have ever heard a woman laugh so heartily.

'Well, that's the best thing!' she said, borrowing my handkerchief to wipe her eyes. 'Did you ever! But, if you aren't the doctor, who are you?'

'Wooster's the name. I came to see Miss Platt.'

'What about?'

This was the moment, of course, when I should have come out with the cheque and sprung the big effort. But somehow I couldn't make it. You know how it is. Offering people money to release your uncle is a scaly enough job at best, and when the atmosphere's not right the shot simply isn't on the board.

'Oh, just came to see her, you know.' I had rather a bright idea. 'My uncle heard she was seedy, don't you know, and asked me to look in and make inquiries,' I said.

'Your uncle?'

'Lord Yaxley.'

'Oh! So you are Lord Yaxley's nephew?'

'That's right. I suppose he's always popping in and out here, what?'

'No. I've never met him.'

'You haven't?'

'No. Rhoda talks a lot about him, of course, but for some reason she's never so much as asked him to look in for a cup of tea.'

I began to see that this Rhoda knew her business. If I'd been a girl with someone wanting to marry me and knew that there was an exhibit like this aunt hanging around the home, I, too, should have thought twice about inviting him to call until the ceremony was over and he had actually signed on the dotted line. I mean to say, a thoroughly good soul—heart of gold beyond a doubt—but not the sort of thing you wanted to spring on Romeo before the time was ripe.

'I suppose you were all very surprised when you heard about it?' she said.

'Surprised is right.'

'Of course, nothing is definitely settled yet.'

'You don't mean that? I thought—'

'Oh, no. She's thinking it over.'

'I see.'

'Of course, she feels it's a great compliment. But then sometimes she wonders if he isn't too old.'

'My Aunt Agatha has rather the same idea.'

'Of course, a title *is* a title.'

'Yes, there's that. What do you think about it yourself?'

'Oh, it doesn't matter what I think. There's no doing anything with girls these days, is there?'

'Not much.'

'What I often say is, I wonder what girls are coming to. Still, there it is.'

'Absolutely.'

There didn't seem much reason why the conversation shouldn't go on for ever. She had the air of a woman who had settled down for the day. But at this point the maid came in and said the doctor had arrived.

I got up.

'I'll be tooling off, then.'

'If you must.'

'I think I'd better.'

'Well, pip pip.'

'Toodle-oo,' I said, and out into the fresh air.

Knowing what was waiting for me at home, I would have preferred to have gone to the club and spent the rest of the day there. But the thing had to be faced.

'Well?' said Aunt Agatha, as I trickled into the sitting-room.

'Well, yes and no,' I replied.

'What do you mean? Did she refuse the money?'

'Not exactly.'

'She accepted it?'

'Well, there, again, not precisely.'

I explained what had happened. I wasn't expecting her to be any too frightfully pleased, and it's as well that I wasn't, because she wasn't. In fact, as the story unfolded, her comments became fruitier and fruitier, and when I had finished she uttered an exclamation that nearly broke a window. It sounded something like 'Gor!' as if she had started to say 'Gorblimey!' and had remembered her ancient lineage just in time.

'I'm sorry,' I said. 'And can a man say more? I lost my nerve. The old *morale* suddenly turned blue on me. It's the sort of thing that might have happened to anyone.'

'I never heard of anything so spineless in my life.'

I shivered, like a warrior whose old wound hurts him.

'I'd be most awfully obliged, Aunt Agatha,' I said, 'if you would not use that word spine. It awakens memories.'

The door opened. Jeeves appeared.

'Sir?'

'Yes, Jeeves?'

'I thought you called, sir.'

'No, Jeeves.'

'Very good, sir.'

There are moments when, even under the eye of Aunt Agatha, I can take the firm line. And now, seeing Jeeves standing there with the light of intelligence simply fizzing in every feature, I suddenly felt how perfectly footling it was to give this preeminent source of balm and comfort the go-by simply because Aunt Agatha had prejudices against discussing family affairs with the staff. It might make her say 'Gor!' again, but I decided to do as we ought to have done right from the start—put the case in his hands.

'Jeeves,' I said, 'this matter of Uncle George.'

'Yes, sir.'

'You know the circs?'

'Yes, sir.'

'You know what we want.'

'Yes, sir.'

'Then advise us. And make it snappy. Think on your feet.'

I heard Aunt Agatha rumble like a volcano just before it starts to set about the neighbours, but I did not wilt. I had seen the sparkle in Jeeves's eye which indicated that an idea was on the way.

'I understand that you have been visiting the young person's home, sir?'

'Just got back.'

'Then you no doubt encountered the young person's aunt?'

'Jeeves, I encountered nothing else but.'

'Then the suggestion which I am about to make will, I feel sure, appeal to you, sir. I would recommend that you confronted his lordship with this woman. It has always been her intention to continue residing with her niece after the latter's marriage. Should he meet her, this reflection might give his lordship pause. As you are aware, sir, she is a kind-hearted woman, but definitely of the people.'

'Jeeves, you are right! Apart from anything else, that orange hair!'

'Exactly, sir.'

'Not to mention the magenta dress.'

'Precisely, sir.'

'I'll ask her to lunch to-morrow, to meet him. You see,' I said to Aunt Agatha, who was still fermenting in the background, 'a ripe suggestion first crack out of the box. Did I or did I not tell you—'

'That will do, Jeeves,' said Aunt Agatha.

'Very good, madam.'

For some minutes after he had gone, Aunt Agatha strayed from the point a bit, confining her remarks to what she thought of a Wooster who could lower the prestige of the clan by allowing menials to get above themselves. Then she returned to what you might call the main issue.

'Bertie,' she said, 'you will go and see this girl again tomorrow, and this time you will do as I told you.'

'But, dash it! With this excellent alternative scheme, based firmly on the psychology of the individual—'

'That is quite enough, Bertie. You heard what I said. I am going. Good-bye.'

She buzzed off, little knowing of what stuff Bertram Wooster was made. The door had hardly closed before I was shouting for Jeeves.

'Jeeves,' I said, 'the recent aunt will have none of your excellent alternative schemes, but none the less I propose to go through with it unswervingly. I consider it a ball of fire. Can you get hold of this female and bring her here for lunch to-morrow?'

'Yes, sir.'

'Good. Meanwhile, I will be 'phoning Uncle George. We will do Aunt Agatha good despite herself. What is it the poet says, Jeeves?'

'The poet Burns, sir?'

'Not the poet Burns. Some other poet. About doing good by stealth.'

'"These little acts of unremembered kindness", sir?'

'That's it in a nutshell, Jeeves.'

I suppose doing good by stealth ought to give one a glow, but I can't say I found myself exactly looking forward to the binge in prospect. Uncle George by himself is a mouldy enough luncheon companion, being extremely apt to collar the conversation and confine it to a description of his symptoms, he being one of those birds who can never be brought to believe that the general public isn't agog to hear all about the lining of his stomach. Add the aunt, and you have a little gathering which might well dismay the stoutest. The moment I woke, I felt conscious of some impending doom, and the cloud, if you know what I mean, grew darker all the morning. By the time Jeeves came in with the cocktails, I was feeling pretty low.

'For two pins, Jeeves,' I said, 'I would turn the whole thing up and leg it to the Drones.'

'I can readily imagine that this will prove something of an ordeal, sir.'

'How did you get to know these people, Jeeves?'

'It was through a young fellow of my acquaintance, sir, Colonel Mainwaring-Smith's personal gentleman's gentleman. He and the young person had an understanding at the time, and he desired me to accompany him to Wistaria Lodge and meet her.'

'They were engaged?'

'Not precisely engaged, sir. An understanding.'

'What did they quarrel about?'

'They did not quarrel, sir. When his lordship began to pay his addresses, the young person, naturally flattered, began to waver between love and ambition. But even now she has not formally rescinded the understanding.'

'Then, if your scheme works and Uncle George edges out, it will do your pal a bit of good?'

'Yes, sir. Smethurst—his name is Smethurst—would consider it a consummation devoutly to be wished.'

'Rather well put, that, Jeeves. Your own?'

'No, sir. The Swan of Avon, sir.'

An unseen hand without tootled on the bell, and I braced myself to play the host. The binge was on.

'Mrs Wilberforce, sir,' announced Jeeves.

'And how I'm to keep a straight face with you standing behind and saying "Madam, can I tempt you with a potato?" is more than I know,' said the aunt, sailing in, looking larger and pinker and matier than ever. 'I know him, you know,' she said, jerking a thumb after Jeeves. 'He's been round and taken tea with us.'

'So he told me.'

She gave the sitting-room the once-over.

'You've got a nice place here,' she said. 'Though I like more pink about. It's so cheerful. What's that you've got there? Cocktails?'

'Martini with a spot of absinthe,' I said, beginning to pour.

She gave a girlish squeal.

'Don't you try to make me drink that stuff! Do you know what would happen if I touched one of those things? I'd be racked with pain. What they do to the lining of your stomach!'

'Oh, I don't know.'

'I do. If you had been a barmaid as long as I was, you'd know, too.'

'Oh—er—were you a barmaid?'

'For years, when I was younger than I am. At the Criterion.'

I dropped the shaker.

'There!' she said, pointing the moral. 'That's through drinking that stuff. Makes your hand wobble. What I always used to say to the boys was, "Port, if you like. Port's wholesome. I appreciate a drop of port myself. But these new-fangled messes from America, no." But they would never listen to me.'

I was eyeing her warily. Of course, there must have been thousands of barmaids at the Criterion in its time, but still it gave one a bit of a start. It was years ago that Uncle George's dash at a mesalliance had occurred—long before he came into the title—but the Wooster clan still quivered at the name of the Criterion.

'Er—when you were at the Cri.,' I said, 'did you ever happen to run into a fellow of my name?'

'I've forgotten what it is. I'm always silly about names.'

'Wooster.'

'Wooster! When you were there yesterday I thought you said Foster. Wooster! Did I run into a fellow named Wooster? Well! Why, George Wooster and me—Piggy, I used to call him—were going off to the registrar's, only his family heard of it and interfered. They offered me a lot of money to give him up, and, like a silly girl, I let them persuade me. If I've wondered once what became of him, I've wondered a thousand times. Is he a relation of yours?'

'Excuse me,' I said. 'I just want a word with Jeeves.'

I legged it for the pantry.

'Jeeves!'

'Sir?'

'Do you know what's happened?'

'No, sir.'

'This female—'

'Sir?'

'She's Uncle George's barmaid!'

'Sir?'

'Oh, dash it, you must have heard of Uncle George's barmaid. You know all the family history. The barmaid he wanted to marry years ago.'

'Ah, yes, sir.'

'She's the only woman he ever loved. He's told me so a million times. Every time he gets to the fourth whisky-and-potash, he always becomes maudlin about this female. What a dashed bit of bad luck! The first thing we know, the call of the past will be echoing in his heart. I can feel it, Jeeves. She's just his sort. The first thing she did when she came in was to start talking about the lining of her stomach. You see the hideous significance of that, Jeeves? The lining of his stomach is Uncle George's favourite topic of conversation. It means that he and she are kindred souls. This woman and he will be like—'

'Deep calling to deep, sir?'

'Exactly.'

'Most disturbing, sir.'

'What's to be done?'

'I could not say, sir.'

'I'll tell you what I'm going to do—'phone him and say the lunch is off.'

'Scarcely feasible, sir. I fancy that is his lordship at the door now.'

And so it was. Jeeves let him in, and I followed him as he navigated down the passage to the sitting-room. There was a stunned silence as he went in, and then a couple of the startled yelps you hear when old buddies get together after long separation.

'Piggy!'

'Maudie!'

'Well, I never!'

'Well, I'm dashed!'

'Did you ever!'

'Well, bless my soul!'

'Fancy you being Lord Yaxley!'

'Came into the title soon after we parted.'

'Just to think!'

'You could have knocked me down with a feather!'

I hung about in the offing, now on this leg, now on that. For all the notice they took of me, I might just have well been the late Bertram Wooster, disembodied.

'Maudie, you don't look a day older, dash it!'

'Nor do you, Piggy.'

'How have you been all these years?'

'Pretty well. The lining of my stomach isn't all it should be.'

'Good Gad! You don't say so? I have trouble with the lining of *my* stomach.'

'It's a sort of heavy feeling after meals.'

'*I* get a sort of heavy feeling after meals. What are you trying for it?'

'I've been taking Perkins' Digestine.'

'My dear girl, no use! No use at all. Tried it myself for years and got no relief. Now, if you really want something that is some good—'

I slid away. The last I saw of them, Uncle George was down beside her on the Chesterfield, buzzing hard.

'Jeeves,' I said, tottering into the pantry.

'Sir?'

'There will only be two for lunch. Count me out. If they notice I'm not there, tell them I was called away by an urgent 'phone message. The situation has got beyond Bertram, Jeeves. You will find me at the Drones.'

'Very good, sir.'

It was lateish in the evening when one of the waiters came to me as I played a distrait game of snooker pool and informed me that Aunt Agatha was on the 'phone.

'Bertie!'

'Hullo?'

I was amazed to note that her voice was that of an aunt who feels that things are breaking right. It had the birdlike trill.

'Bertie, have you that cheque I gave you?'

'Yes.'

'Then tear it up. It will not be needed.'

'Eh?'

'I say it will not be needed. Your uncle has been speaking to me on the telephone. He is not going to marry that girl.'

'Not?'

'No. Apparently he has been thinking it over and sees how unsuitable it would have been. But what is astonishing is that he *is* going to be married!'

'He is?'

'Yes, to an old friend of his, a Mrs Wilberforce. A woman of a sensible age, he gave me to understand. I wonder which Wilberforces that would be. There are two main branches of the family—the Essex Wilberforces and the Cumberland Wilberforces. I believe there is also a cadet branch somewhere in Shropshire.'

'And one in East Dulwich.'

'What did you say?'

'Nothing,' I said. 'Nothing.'

I hung up. Then back to the old flat, feeling a trifle sandbagged.

'Well, Jeeves,' I said, and there was censure in the eyes. 'So I gather everything is nicely settled?'

'Yes, sir. His lordship formally announced the engagement between the sweet and cheese courses, sir.'

'He did, did he?'

'Yes, sir.'

I eyed the man sternly.

'You do not appear to be aware of it, Jeeves,' I said, in a cold, level voice, 'but this binge has depreciated your stock very considerably. I have always been accustomed to look upon you as a counsellor without equal. I have, so to speak, hung upon your lips. And now see what you have done. All this is the direct consequence of your scheme, based on the psychology of the individual. I should have thought, Jeeves, that, knowing the woman—meeting her socially, as you might say, over the afternoon cup of tea—you might have ascertained that she was Uncle George's barmaid.'

'I did, sir.'

'What!'

'I was aware of the fact, sir.'

'Then you must have known what would happen if she came to lunch and met him.'

'Yes, sir.'

'Well, I'm dashed!'

'If I might explain, sir. The young man Smethurst, who is greatly attached to the young person, is an intimate friend of mine. He applied to me some little while back in the hope that I might be able to do something to ensure that the young person followed the dictates of her heart and refrained from permitting herself to be lured by gold and the glamour of his lordship's position. There will now be no obstacle to their union.'

'I see. "Little acts of unremembered kindness", what?'

'Precisely, sir.'

'And how about Uncle George? You've landed him pretty nicely in the cart.'

'No, sir, if I may take the liberty of opposing your view. I fancy that Mrs Wilberforce should make an ideal mate for his lordship. If there was a defect in his lordship's mode of life, it was that he was a little unduly attached to the pleasures of the table—'

'Ate like a pig, you mean?'

'I would not have ventured to put it in quite that way, sir, but the expression does meet the facts of the case. He was also inclined to drink rather more than his medical adviser would have approved of. Elderly bachelors who are wealthy and without occupation tend somewhat frequently to fall into this error, sir. The future Lady Yaxley will check this. Indeed, I overheard her ladyship saying as much as I brought in the fish. She was commenting on a certain puffiness of the face which had been absent in his lordship's appearance in the earlier days of their acquaintanceship, and she observed that his lordship needed looking after. I fancy, sir, that you will find the union will turn out an extremely satisfactory one.'

It was—what's the word I want?—it was plausible, of course, but still I shook the onion.

'But, Jeeves!'

'Sir?'

'She *is*, as you remarked not long ago, definitely of the people."

He looked at me in a reproachful sort of way.

'Sturdy lower middle class stock, sir.'

'H'm!'

'Sir?'

'I said "H'm!", Jeeves.'

'Besides, sir, remember what the poet Tennyson said: "Kind hearts are more than coronets".'

'And which of us is going to tell Aunt Agatha that?'

'If I might make the suggestion, sir, I would advise that we omitted to communicate with Mrs Spenser Gregson in any way. I have your suitcase practically packed. It would be a matter of but a few minutes to bring the car round from the garage—'

'And off over the horizon to where men are men?'

'Precisely, sir.'

'Jeeves,' I said, 'I'm not sure that even now I can altogether see eye to eye with you regarding your recent activities. You think you have scattered light and sweetness on every side. I am not so sure. However, with this latest suggestion you have rung the bell. I examine it narrowly and I find no flaw in it. It is the goods. I'll get the car at once.'

'Very good, sir.'

'Remember what the poet Shakespeare said, Jeeves.'

'What was that, sir?'

'"Exit hurriedly, pursued by a bear". You'll find it in one of his plays. I remember drawing a picture of it on the side of the page, when I was at school.'

11

THE ORDEAL OF YOUNG TUPPY

'What-ho, Jeeves!' I said, entering the room where he waded knee-deep in suitcases and shirts and winter suitings, like a sea-beast among rocks. 'Packing?'

'Yes, sir,' replied the honest fellow, for there are no secrets between us.

'Pack on!' I said approvingly. 'Pack, Jeeves, pack with care. Pack in the presence of the passenjare.' And I rather fancy I added the words 'Tra-la!' for I was in merry mood.

Every year, starting about the middle of November, there is a good deal of anxiety and apprehension among owners of the better class of country-house throughout England as to who will get Bertram Wooster's patronage for the Christmas holidays. It may be one or it may be another. As my Aunt Dahlia says, you never know where the blow will fall.

This year, however, I had decided early. It couldn't have been later than Nov. 10 when a sigh of relief went up from a dozen stately homes as it became known that the short straw had been drawn by Sir Reginald Witherspoon, Bart, of Bleaching Court, Upper Bleaching, Hants.

In coming to the decision to give this Witherspoon my custom, I had been actuated by several reasons, not counting the fact that, having married Aunt Dahlia's husband's younger sister Katherine, he is by way of being a sort of uncle of mine. In the first place, the Bart does one extraordinarily well, both browsing and sluicing being above criticism. Then, again, his stables always contain something worth riding, which is a consideration. And, thirdly, there is no danger of getting lugged into a party of amateur Waits and having to tramp the countryside in the rain, singing, 'When Shepherds Watched Their Flocks by Night'. Or for the matter of that, 'Noel! Noel!'

All these things counted with me, but what really drew me to Bleaching Court like a magnet was the knowledge that young Tuppy Glossop would be among those present.

I feel sure I have told you before about this black-hearted bird, but I will give you the strength of it once again, just to keep the records straight. He was the fellow, if you remember, who, ignoring a lifelong friendship in the course of which he had frequently eaten my bread and salt, betted me one night at the Drones that I wouldn't swing myself across the swimming-bath by the ropes and rings and then, with almost inconceivable treachery, went and looped back the last ring, causing me to drop into the fluid and ruin one of the nattiest suits of dress-clothes in London.

To execute a fitting vengeance on this bloke had been the ruling passion of my life ever since.

'You are bearing in mind, Jeeves,' I said, 'the fact that Mr Glossop will be at Bleaching?'

'Yes, sir.'

'And, consequently, are not forgetting to put in the Giant Squirt?'

'No, sir.'

'Nor the Luminous Rabbit?'

'No, sir.'

'Good! I am rather pinning my faith on the Luminous Rabbit, Jeeves. I hear excellent reports of it on all sides. You wind it up and put it in somebody's room in the night watches, and it shines in the dark and jumps about, making odd, squeaking noises the while. The whole performance being, I should imagine, well calculated to scare young Tuppy into a decline.'

'Very possibly, sir.'

'Should that fail, there is always the Giant Squirt. We must leave no stone unturned to put it across the man somehow,' I said. 'The Wooster honour is at stake.'

I would have spoken further on this subject, but just then the front-door bell buzzed.

'I'll answer it,' I said. 'I expect it's Aunt Dahlia. She 'phoned that she would be calling this morning.'

It was not Aunt Dahlia. It was a telegraph-boy with telegram. I opened it, read it, and carried it back to the bedroom, the brow a bit knitted.

'Jeeves,' I said. 'A rummy communication has arrived. From Mr Glossop.'

'Indeed, sir?'

'I will read it to you. Handed in at Upper Bleaching. Message runs as follows:

'*"When you come to-morrow, bring my football boots. Also, if humanly possible, Irish water-spaniel. Urgent. Regards. Tuppy."*

'What do you make of that, Jeeves?'

'As I interpret the document, sir, Mr Glossop wishes you, when you come to-morrow, to bring his football boots. Also, if humanly possible, an Irish water-spaniel. He hints that the matter is urgent, and sends his regards.'

'Yes, that's how I read it, too. But why football boots?'

'Perhaps Mr Glossop wishes to play football, sir.'

I considered this.

'Yes,' I said. 'That may be the solution. But why would a man, staying peacefully at a country-house, suddenly develop a craving to play football?'

'I could not say, sir.'

'And why an Irish water-spaniel?'

'There again I fear I can hazard no conjecture, sir.'

'What *is* an Irish water-spaniel?'

'A water-spaniel of a variety bred in Ireland, sir.'

'You think so?'

'Yes, sir.'

'Well, perhaps you're right. But why should I sweat about the place collecting dogs—of whatever nationality—for young Tuppy? Does he think I'm Santa Claus? Is he under the impression that my feelings towards him, after that Drones Club incident, are those of kindly benevolence? Irish water-spaniels, indeed! Tchah!'

'Sir?'

'Tchah, Jeeves.'

'Very good, sir.'

The front-door bell buzzed again.

'Our busy morning, Jeeves.'

'Yes, sir.'

'All right. I'll go.'

This time it was Aunt Dahlia. She charged in with the air of a woman with something on her mind—giving tongue, in fact, while actually on the very doormat.

'Bertie,' she boomed, in that ringing voice of hers which cracks window-panes and upsets vases, 'I've come about that young hound, Glossop.'

'It's quite all right, Aunt Dahlia,' I replied soothingly. 'I have the situation well in hand. The Giant Squirt and the Luminous Rabbit are even now being packed.'

'I don't know what you're talking about, and I don't for a moment suppose you do, either,' said the relative somewhat brusquely, 'but, if you'll kindly stop gibbering, I'll tell you what I mean. I have had a most disturbing letter from Katherine. About this reptile. Of course, I haven't breathed a word to Angela. She'd hit the ceiling.'

This Angela is Aunt Dahlia's daughter. She and young Tuppy are generally supposed to be more or less engaged, though nothing definitely 'Morning Posted' yet.

'Why?' I said.

'Why what?'

'Why would Angela hit the ceiling?'

'Well, wouldn't you, if you were practically engaged to a fiend in human shape and somebody told you he had gone off to the country and was flirting with a dog-girl?'

'With a what was that, once again?'

'A dog-girl. One of these dashed open-air flappers in thick boots and tailor-made tweeds who infest the rural districts and go about the place followed by packs of assorted dogs. I used to be one of them myself in my younger days, so I know how dangerous they are. Her name is Dalgleish. Old Colonel Dalgleish's daughter. They live near Bleaching.'

I saw a gleam of daylight.

'Then that must be what his telegram was about. He's just wired, asking me to bring down an Irish water-spaniel. A Christmas present for this girl, no doubt.'

'Probably. Katherine tells me he seems to be infatuated with her. She says he follows her about like one of her dogs, looking like a tame cat and bleating like a sheep.'

'Quite the private Zoo, what?'

'Bertie,' said Aunt Dahlia—and I could see her generous nature was stirred to its depths—'one more crack like that out of you, and I shall forget that I am an aunt and hand you one.'

I became soothing. I gave her the old oil.

'I shouldn't worry,' I said. 'There's probably nothing in it. Whole thing no doubt much exaggerated.'

'You think so, eh? Well, you know what he's like. You remember the trouble we had when he ran after that singing-woman.'

I recollected the case. You will find it elsewhere in the archives. Cora Bellinger was the female's name. She was studying for Opera, and young Tuppy thought highly of her. Fortunately, however, she punched him in the eye during Beefy Bingham's clean, bright entertainment in Bermondsey East, and love died.

'Besides,' said Aunt Dahlia, 'There's something I haven't told you. Just before he went to Bleaching, he and Angela quarrelled.'

'They did?'

'Yes. I got it out of Angela this morning. She was crying her eyes out, poor angel. It was something about her last hat. As far as I could gather, he told her it made her look like a Pekingese, and she told him she never wanted to see him again in this world or the next. And he said "Right-ho!" and breezed off. I can see what has happened. This dog-girl has caught him on the rebound, and, unless something is done quick, anything may happen. So place the facts before Jeeves, and tell him to take action the moment you get down there.'

I am always a little piqued, if you know what I mean, at this assumption on the relative's part that Jeeves is so dashed essential on these occasions. My manner, therefore, as I replied, was a bit on the crisp side.

'Jeeves's services will not be required,' I said. 'I can handle this business. The programme which I have laid out will be quite sufficient to take young Tuppy's mind off love-making. It is my intention to insert the Luminous Rabbit in his room at the first opportunity that presents itself. The Luminous Rabbit shines in the dark and jumps about, making odd, squeaking noises. It will sound to young Tuppy like the Voice of Conscience, and I anticipate that a single treatment will make him retire into a nursing-home for a couple of weeks or so. At the end of which period he will have forgotten all about the bally girl.'

'Bertie,' said Aunt Dahlia, with a sort of frozen calm, 'you are the Abysmal Chump. Listen to me. It's simply because I am fond of you and have influence with the Lunacy Commissioners that you weren't put in a padded cell years ago. Bungle this business, and I withdraw my protection. Can't you understand that this thing is far too serious for any fooling about? Angela's whole happiness is at stake. Do as I tell you, and put it up to Jeeves.'

'Just as you say, Aunt Dahlia,' I said stiffly.

'All right, then. Do it now.'

I went back to the bedroom.

'Jeeves,' I said, and I did not trouble to conceal my chagrin, 'you need not pack the Luminous Rabbit.'

'Very good, sir.'

'Nor the Giant Squirt.'

'Very good, sir.'

'They have been subjected to destructive criticism, and the zest has gone. Oh, and, Jeeves.'

'Sir?'

'Mrs Travers wishes you, on arriving at Bleaching Court, to disentangle Mr Glossop from a dog-girl.'

'Very good, sir. I will attend to the matter and will do my best to give satisfaction.'

… … …

That Aunt Dahlia had not exaggerated the perilous nature of the situation was made clear to me on the following afternoon. Jeeves and I drove down to Bleaching in the two-seater, and we were tooling along about half-way between the village and the Court when suddenly there appeared ahead of us a sea of dogs and in the middle of it young Tuppy frisking round one of those largish, corn-fed girls. He was bending towards her in a devout sort of way, and even at a considerable distance I could see that his ears were pink. His attitude, in short, was unmistakably that of a man endeavouring to push a good thing along; and when I came closer and noted that the girl wore tailor-made tweeds and thick boots, I had no further doubts.

'You observe, Jeeves?' I said in a low, significant voice.

'Yes, sir.'

'The girl, what?'

'Yes, sir.'

I tootled amiably on the horn and yodelled a bit. They turned—Tuppy, I fancied, not any too pleased.

'Oh, hullo, Bertie,' he said.

'Hullo,' I said.

'My friend, Bertie Wooster,' said Tuppy to the girl, in what seemed to me rather an apologetic manner. You know—as if he would have preferred to hush me up.

'Hullo,' said the girl.

'Hullo,' I said.

'Hullo, Jeeves,' said Tuppy.

'Good afternoon, sir,' said Jeeves.

There was a somewhat constrained silence.

'Well, good-bye, Bertie,' said young Tuppy. 'You'll be wanting to push along, I expect.'

We Woosters can take a hint as well as the next man.

'See you later,' I said.

'Oh, rather,' said Tuppy.

I set the machinery in motion again, and we rolled off.

'Sinister, Jeeves,' I said. 'You noticed that the subject was looking like a stuffed frog?'

'Yes, sir.'

'And gave no indication of wanting us to stop and join the party?'

'No, sir.'

'I think Aunt Dahlia's fears are justified. The thing seems serious.'

'Yes, sir.'

'Well, strain the brain, Jeeves.'

'Very good, sir.'

It wasn't till I was dressing for dinner that night that I saw young Tuppy again. He trickled in just as I was arranging the tie.

'Hullo!' I said.

'Hullo!' said Tuppy.

'Who was the girl?' I asked, in that casual, snaky way of mine—off-hand, I mean.

'A Miss Dalgleish,' said Tuppy, and I noticed that he blushed a spot.

'Staying here?'

'No. She lives in that house just before you come to the gates of this place. Did you bring my football boots?'

'Yes. Jeeves has got them somewhere.'

'And the water-spaniel?'

'Sorry. No water-spaniel.'

'Dashed nuisance. She's set her heart on an Irish water-spaniel.'

'Well, what do you care?'

'I wanted to give her one.'

'Why?'

Tuppy became a trifle haughty. Frigid. The rebuking eye.

'Colonel and Mrs Dalgleish,' he said, 'have been extremely kind to me since I got here. They have entertained me. I naturally wish to make some return for their hospitality. I don't want them to look upon me as one of those ill-mannered modern young men you read about in the papers who grab everything they can lay their hooks on and never buy back. If people ask you to lunch and tea and what not, they appreciate it if you make them some little present in return.'

'Well, give them your football boots. In passing, why did you want the bally things?'

'I'm playing in a match next Thursday.'

'Down here?'

'Yes. Upper Bleaching versus Hockley-cum-Meston. Apparently it's the big game of the year.'

'How did you get roped in?'

'I happened to mention in the course of conversation the other day that, when in London, I generally turn out on Saturdays for the Old Austinians, and Miss Dalgleish seemed rather keen that I should help the village.'

'Which village?'

'Upper Bleaching, of course.'

'Ah, then you're going to play for Hockley?'

'You needn't be funny, Bertie. You may not know it, but I'm pretty hot stuff on the football field. Oh, Jeeves.'

'Sir?' said Jeeves, entering right centre.

'Mr Wooster tells me you have my football boots.'

'Yes, sir. I have placed them in your room.'

'Thanks. Jeeves, do you want to make a bit of money?'

'Yes, sir.'

'Then put a trifle on Upper Bleaching for the annual encounter with Hockley-cum-Meston next Thursday,' said Tuppy, exiting with swelling bosom.

'Mr Glossop is going to play on Thursday,' I explained as the door closed.

'So I was informed in the Servants' Hall, sir.'

'Oh? And what's the general feeling there about it?'

'The impression I gathered, sir, was that the Servants' Hall considers Mr Glossop ill-advised.'

'Why's that?'

'I am informed by Mr Mulready, Sir Reginald's butler, sir, that this contest differs in some respects from the ordinary football game. Owing to the fact that there has existed for many years considerable animus between the two villages, the struggle is conducted, it appears, on somewhat looser and more primitive lines than is usually the case when two teams meet in friendly rivalry. The primary object of the players, I am given to understand, is not so much to score points as to inflict violence.'

'Good Lord, Jeeves!'

'Such appears to be the case, sir. The game is one that would have a great interest for the antiquarian. It was played first in the reign of King Henry the Eighth, when it lasted from noon till sun-down over an area covering several square miles. Seven deaths resulted on that occasion.'

'Seven!'

'Not inclusive of two of the spectators, sir. In recent years, however, the casualties appear to have been confined to broken limbs and other minor injuries. The opinion of the Servants' Hall is that it would be more judicious on Mr Glossop's part, where he to refrain from mixing himself up in the affair.'

I was more or less aghast. I mean to say, while I had made it my mission in life to get back at young Tuppy for that business at the Drones, there still remained certain faint vestiges, if vestiges is the word I want, of the old friendship and esteem. Besides, there are limits to one's thirst for vengeance. Deep as my resentment was for the ghastly outrage he had perpetrated on me, I had no wish to see him toddle unsuspiciously into the arena and get all chewed up by wild villagers. A Tuppy scared stiff by a Luminous Rabbit—yes. Excellent business. The happy ending, in fact. But a Tuppy carried off on a stretcher in half a dozen pieces—no. Quite a different matter. All wrong. Not to be considered for a moment.

Obviously, then, a kindly word of warning, while there was yet time, was indicated. I buzzed off to his room forthwith, and found him toying dreamily with the football boots.

I put him in possession of the facts.

'What you had better do—and the Servants' Hall thinks the same,' I said, 'is fake a sprained ankle on the eve of the match.'

He looked at me in an odd sort of way.

'You suggest that, when Miss Dalgleish is trusting me, relying on me, looking forward with eager, girlish enthusiasm to seeing me help her village on to victory, I should let her down with a thud?'

I was pleased with his ready intelligence.

'That's the idea,' I said.

'Faugh!' said Tuppy—the only time I've ever heard the word.

'How do you mean, "Faugh!"?' I asked.

'Bertie,' said Tuppy, 'what you tell me merely makes me all the keener for the fray. A warm game is what I want. I welcome this sporting spirit on the part of the opposition. I shall enjoy a spot of roughness. It will enable me to go all out and give of my best. Do you realize,' said young Tuppy, vermilion to the gills, 'that She will be looking on? And do you know how that will make me feel? It will make me feel like some knight of old jousting under the eyes of his lady. Do you suppose that Sir Lancelot or Sir Galahad, when there was a tourney scheduled for the following Thursday, went and pretended they had sprained their ankles just because the thing was likely to be a bit rough?'

'Don't forget that in the reign of King Henry the Eighth—'

'Never mind about the reign of King Henry the Eighth. All I care about is that it's Upper Bleaching's turn this year to play in colours, so I shall be able to wear my Old Austinian shirt. Light blue, Bertie, with broad orange stripes. I shall look like something, I tell you.'

'But what?'

'Bertie,' said Tuppy, now becoming purely ga-ga, 'I may as well tell you that I'm in love at last. This is the real thing. I have found my mate. All my life I have dreamed of meeting some sweet, open-air girl with all the glory of the English countryside in her eyes, and I have found her. How different she is, Bertie, from these hot-house, artificial London girls! Would they stand in the mud on a winter afternoon, watching a football match? Would they know what to give an Alsatian for fits? Would they tramp ten miles a day across the fields and come back as fresh as paint? No!'

'Well, why should they?'

'Bertie, I'm staking everything on this game on Thursday. At the moment, I have an idea that she looks on me as something of a weakling, simply because I got a blister on my foot the other afternoon and had to take the bus back from Hockley. But when she sees me going through the rustic opposition like a devouring flame, will that make her think a bit? Will that make her open her eyes? What?'

'What?'

'I said "What?"'

'So did I.'

'I meant, "Won't it?"'

'Oh, rather.'

Here the dinner-gong sounded, not before I was ready for it.

… … …

Judicious inquiries during the next couple of days convinced me that the Servants' Hall at Bleaching Court, in advancing the suggestion that young Tuppy, born and bred in the gentler atmosphere of the metropolis, would do well to keep out of local disputes and avoid the football-field on which these were to be settled, had not spoken idly. It had weighed its words and said the sensible thing. Feeling between the two villages undoubtedly ran high, as they say.

You know how it is in these remote rural districts. Life tends at times to get a bit slow. There's nothing much to do in the long winter evenings but listen to the radio and brood on what a tick your neighbour is. You find yourself remembering how Farmer Giles did you down over the sale of your pig, and Farmer Giles finds himself remembering that it was your son, Ernest, who bunged the half-brick at his horse on the second Sunday before Septuagesima. And so on and so forth. How this particular feud had started, I don't know, but the season of peace and good will found it in full blast. The only topic of conversation in Upper Bleaching was Thursday's game, and the citizenry seemed to be looking forward to it in a spirit that can only be described as ghoulish. And it was the same in Hockley-cum-Meston.

I paid a visit to Hockley-cum-Meston on the Wednesday, being rather anxious to take a look at the inhabitants and see how formidable they were. I was shocked to observe that practically every second male might have been the Village Blacksmith's big brother. The muscles of their brawny arms were obviously strong as iron bands, and the way the company at the Green Pig, where I looked in incognito for a spot of beer, talked about the forthcoming sporting contest was enough to chill the blood of anyone who had a pal who proposed to fling himself into the fray. It sounded rather like Attila and a few of his Huns sketching out their next campaign.

I went back to Jeeves with my mind made up.

'Jeeves,' I said, 'you, who had the job of drying and pressing those dress-clothes of mine, are aware that I have suffered much at young Tuppy Glossop's hands. By rights, I suppose, I ought to be welcoming the fact that the Wrath of Heaven is now hovering over him in this fearful manner. But the view I take of it is that Heaven looks like overdoing it. Heaven's idea of a fitting retribution is not mine. In my most unrestrained moments I never wanted the poor blighter assassinated. And the idea in Hockley-cum-Meston seems to be that a good opportunity has arisen of making it a bumper Christmas for the local undertaker. There was a fellow with red hair at the Green Pig this afternoon who might have been the undertaker's partner, the way he talked. We must act, and speedily, Jeeves. We must put a bit of a jerk in it and save young Tuppy in spite of himself.'

'What course would you advocate, sir?'

'I'll tell you. He refuses to do the sensible thing and slide out, because the girl will be watching the game and he imagines, poor lizard, that he is going to shine and impress her. So we must employ guile. You must go up to London to-day, Jeeves, and to-morrow morning you will send a telegram, signed "Angela", which will run as follows. Jot it down. Ready?'

'Yes, sir.'

'"So sorry—" . . .' I pondered. 'What would a girl say, Jeeves, who, having had a row with the bird she was practically engaged to because he told her she looked like a Pekingese in her new hat, wanted to extend the olive-branch?'

'"So sorry I was cross", sir, would, I fancy, be the expression.'

'Strong enough, do you think?'

'Possibly the addition of the word "darling" would give the necessary verisimilitude, sir.'

'Right. Resume the jotting. "So sorry I was cross, darling . . ." 'No, wait, Jeeves. Scratch that out. I see where we have gone off the rails. I see where we are missing a chance to make this the real tabasco. Sign the telegram not "Angela" but "Travers".'

'Very good, sir.'

'Or, rather, "Dahlia Travers". And this is the body of the communication. "Please return at once."'

'"Immediately" would be more economical, sir. Only one word. And it has a stronger ring.'

'True. Jot on, then. "Please return immediately. Angela in a hell of a state."'

'I would suggest "seriously ill", sir.'

'All right. "Seriously ill". "Angela seriously ill. Keeps calling for you and says you were quite right about hat."'

'If I might suggest, sir—?'

'Well, go ahead.'

'I fancy the following would meet the case. "Please return immediately. Angela seriously ill. High fever and delirium. Keeps calling your name piteously and saying something about a hat and that you were quite right. Please catch earliest possible train. Dahlia Travers."'

'That sounds all right.'

'Yes, sir.'

'You like that "piteously"? You don't think "incessantly"?'

'No, sir. "Piteously" is the *mot juste*.'

'All right. You know. Well, send it off in time to get here at two-thirty.'

'Yes, sir.'

'Two-thirty, Jeeves. You see the devilish cunning?'

'No, sir.'

'I will tell you. If the telegram arrived earlier, he would get it before the game. By two-thirty, however, he will have started for the ground. I shall hand it to him the moment there is a lull in the battle. By that time he will have begun to get some idea of what a football match between Upper Bleaching and Hockley-cum-Meston is like, and the thing ought to work like magic. I can't imagine anyone who has been sporting awhile with those thugs I saw yesterday not welcoming any excuse to call it a day. You follow me?'

'Yes, sir.'

'Very good, Jeeves.'

'Very good, sir.'

You can always rely on Jeeves. Two-thirty I had said, and two-thirty it was. The telegram arrived almost on the minute. I was going to my room to change into something warmer at the moment, and I took it up with me. Then into the heavy tweeds and off in the car to the field of play. I got there just as the two teams were lining up, and half a minute later the whistle blew and the war was on.

What with one thing and another—having been at a school where they didn't play it and so forth—Rugby football is a game I can't claim absolutely to understand in all its niceties, if you know what I mean. I can follow the broad, general principles, of course. I mean to say, I know that the main scheme is to work the ball down the field somehow and deposit it over the line at the other end, and that, in order to squelch this programme, each side is allowed to put in a certain amount of assault and battery and do things to its fellow-man which, if done elsewhere, would result in fourteen days without the option, coupled with some strong remarks from the Bench. But there I stop. What you might call the science of the thing is to Bertram Wooster a sealed book. However, I am informed by experts that on this occasion there was not enough science for anyone to notice.

There had been a great deal of rain in the last few days, and the going appeared to be a bit sticky. In fact, I have seen swamps that were drier than this particular bit of ground. The red-haired bloke whom I had encountered in the pub paddled up and kicked off amidst cheers from the populace, and the ball went straight to where Tuppy was standing, a pretty colour-scheme in light blue and orange. Tuppy caught it neatly, and hoofed it back, and it was at this point that I understood that an Upper Bleaching versus Hockley-cum-Meston game had certain features not usually seen on the football-field.

For Tuppy, having done his bit, was just standing there, looking modest, when there was a thunder of large feet and the red-haired bird, galloping up, seized him by the neck, hurled him to earth, and fell on him. I had a glimpse of Tuppy's face, as it registered horror, dismay, and a general suggestion of stunned dissatisfaction with the scheme of things, and then he disappeared. By the time he had come to the surface, a sort of mob-warfare was going on at the other side of the field. Two assortments of sons of the soil had got their heads down and were shoving earnestly against each other, with the ball somewhere in the middle.

Tuppy wiped a fair portion of Hampshire out of his eye, peered round him in a dazed kind of way, saw the mass-meeting and ran towards it, arriving just in time for a couple of heavyweights to gather him in and give him the mud-treatment again. This placed him in an admirable position for a third heavyweight to kick him in the ribs with a boot like a violin-case. The red-haired man then fell on him. It was all good, brisk play, and looked fine from my side of the ropes.

I saw now where Tuppy had made his mistake. He was too dressy. On occasions such as this it is safest not to be conspicuous, and that blue and orange shirt rather caught the eye. A sober beige, blending with the colour of the ground, was what his best friends would have recommended. And, in addition to the fact that his costume attracted attention, I rather think that the men of Hockley-cum-Meston resented his being on the field at all. They felt that, as a non-local, he had butted in on a private fight and had no business there.

At any rate, it certainly appeared to me that they were giving him preferential treatment. After each of those shoving-bees to which I have alluded, when the edifice caved in and tons of humanity wallowed in a tangled mass in the juice, the last soul to be excavated always seemed to be Tuppy. And on the rare occasions when he actually managed to stand upright for a moment, somebody—generally the red-haired man—invariably sprang to the congenial task of spilling him again.

In fact, it was beginning to look as though that telegram would come too late to save a human life, when an interruption occurred. Play had worked round close to where I was standing, and there had been the customary collapse of all concerned, with Tuppy at the bottom of the basket, as usual; but this time, when they got up and started to count the survivors, a sizeable cove in what had once been a white shirt remained on the ground. And a hearty cheer went up from a hundred patriotic throats as the news spread that Upper Bleaching had drawn first blood.

The victim was carried off by a couple of his old chums, and the rest of the players sat down and pulled their stockings up and thought of life for a bit. The moment had come, it seemed to me, to remove Tuppy from the *abattoir*, and I hopped over the ropes and toddled to where he sat scraping mud from his wishbone. His air was that of a man who has been passed through a wringer, and his eyes, what you could see of them, had a strange, smouldering gleam. He was so crusted with alluvial deposits that one realized how little a mere bath would ever be able to effect. To fit him to take his place once more in polite society, he would certainly have to be sent to the cleaner's. Indeed, it was a moot point whether it wouldn't be simpler just to throw him away.

'Tuppy, old man,' I said.

'Eh?' said Tuppy.

'A telegram for you.'

'Eh?'

'I've got a wire here that came after you left the house.'

'Eh?' said Tuppy.

I stirred him up a trifle with the ferule of my stick, and he seemed to come to life.

'Be careful what you're doing, you silly ass,' he said, in part. 'I'm one solid bruise. What are you gibbering about?'

'A telegram has come for you. I think it may be important.'

He snorted in a bitter sort of way.

'Do you suppose I've time to read telegrams now?'

'But this one may be frightfully urgent,' I said. 'Here it is.'

But, if you understand me, it wasn't. How I had happened to do it, I don't know, but apparently, in changing the upholstery, I had left it in my other coat.

'Oh, my gosh,' I said, 'I've left it behind.'

'It doesn't matter.'

'But it does. It's probably something you ought to read at once. Immediately, if you know what I mean. If I were you, I'd just say a few words of farewell to the murder-squad and come back to the house right away.'

He raised his eyebrows. At least, I think he must have done, because the mud on his forehead stirred a little, as if something was going on underneath it.

'Do you imagine,' he said, 'that I would slink away under her very eyes? Good God! Besides,' he went on, in a quiet, meditative voice, 'there is no power on earth that could get me off this field until I've thoroughly disembowelled that red-haired bounder. Have you noticed how he keeps tackling me when I haven't got the ball?'

'Isn't that right?'

'Of course it's not right. Never mind! A bitter retribution awaits that bird. I've had enough of it. From now on I assert my personality.'

'I'm a bit foggy as to the rules of this pastime,' I said. 'Are you allowed to bite him?'

'I'll try, and see what happens,' said Tuppy, struck with the idea and brightening a little.

At this point, the pall-bearers returned, and fighting became general again all along the Front.

... ...

There's nothing like a bit of rest and what you might call folding of the hands for freshening up the shop-soiled athlete. The dirty work, resumed after this brief breather, started off with an added vim which it did one good to see. And the life and soul of the party was young Tuppy.

You know, only meeting a fellow at lunch or at the races or loafing round country-houses and so forth, you don't get on to his hidden depths, if you know what I mean. Until this moment, if asked, I would have said that Tuppy Glossop was, on the whole, essentially a pacific sort of bloke, with little or nothing of the tiger of the jungle in him. Yet here he was, running to and fro with fire streaming from his nostrils, a positive danger to traffic.

Yes, absolutely. Encouraged by the fact that the referee was either filled with the spirit of Live and Let Live or else had got his whistle choked up with mud, the result being that he appeared to regard the game with a sort of calm detachment, Tuppy was putting in some very impressive work. Even to me, knowing nothing of the finesse of the thing, it was plain that if Hockley-cum-Meston wanted the happy ending they must eliminate young Tuppy at the earliest possible moment. And I will say for them that they did their best, the red-haired man being particularly assiduous. But Tuppy was made of durable material. Every time the opposition talent ground him into the mire and sat on his head, he rose on stepping-stones of his dead self, if you follow me, to higher things. And in the end it was the red-haired bloke who did the dust-biting.

I couldn't tell you exactly how it happened, for by this time the shades of night were drawing in a bit and there was a dollop of mist rising, but one moment the fellow was hareing along, apparently without a care in the world, and then suddenly Tuppy had appeared from nowhere and was sailing through the air at his neck. They connected with a crash and a slither, and a little later the red-haired bird was hopping off, supported by a brace of friends, something having gone wrong with his left ankle.

After that, there was nothing to it. Upper Bleaching, thoroughly bucked, became busier than ever. There was a lot of earnest work in a sort of inland sea down at the Hockley end of the field, and then a kind of tidal wave poured over the line, and when the bodies had been removed and the tumult and the shouting had died, there was young Tuppy lying on the ball. And that, with the exception of a few spots of mayhem in the last five minutes, concluded the proceedings.

... ...

I drove back to the Court in rather what you might term a pensive frame of mind. Things having happened as they had happened, there seemed to me a goodish bit of hard thinking to be done. There was a servitor of sorts in the hall, when I arrived, and I asked him to send up a whisky-and-soda, strongish, to my room. The old brain, I felt, needed stimulating. And about ten minutes later there was a knock at the door, and in came Jeeves, bearing tray and materials.

'Hullo, Jeeves,' I said, surprised. 'Are you back?'

'Yes, sir.'

'When did you get here?'

'Some little while ago, sir. Was it an enjoyable game, sir?'

'In a sense, Jeeves,' I said, 'yes. Replete with human interest and all that, if you know what I mean. But I fear that, owing to a touch of carelessness on my part, the worst has happened. I left the telegram in my other coat, so young Tuppy remained in action throughout.'

'Was he injured, sir?'

'Worse than that, Jeeves. He was the star of the game. Toasts, I should imagine, are now being drunk to him at every pub in the village. So spectacularly did he play—in fact, so heartily did he joust—that I can't see the girl not being all over him. Unless I am greatly mistaken, the moment they meet, she will exclaim "My hero!" and fall into his bally arms.'

'Indeed, sir?'

I didn't like the man's manner. Too calm. Unimpressed. A little leaping about with fallen jaw was what I had expected my words to produce, and I was on the point of saying as much when the door opened again and Tuppy limped in.

He was wearing an ulster over his football things, and I wondered why he had come to pay a social call on me instead of proceeding straight to the bathroom. He eyed my glass in a wolfish sort of way.

'Whisky?' he said, in a hushed voice.

'And soda.'

'Bring me one, Jeeves,' said young Tuppy. 'A large one.'

'Very good, sir.'

Tuppy wandered to the window and looked out into the gathering darkness, and for the first time I perceived that he had got a grouch of some description. You can generally tell by a fellow's back. Humped. Bent. Bowed down with weight of woe, if you follow me.

'What's the matter?' I asked.

Tuppy emitted a mirthless.

'Oh, nothing much,' he said. 'My faith in woman is dead, that's all.'

'It is?'

'You jolly well bet it is. Women are a wash-out. I see no future for the sex, Bertie. Blisters, all of them.'

'Er—even the Dogsbody girl?'

'Her name,' said Tuppy, a little stiffly, 'is Dalgleish, if it happens to interest you. And, if you want to know something else, she's the worst of the lot.'

'My dear chap!'

Tuppy turned. Beneath the mud, I could see that his face was drawn and, to put it in a nutshell, wan.

'Do you know what happened, Bertie?'

'What?'

'She wasn't there.'

'Where?'

'At the match, you silly ass.'

'Not at the match?'

'No.'

'You mean, not among the throng of eager spectators?'

'Of course I mean not among the spectators. Did you think I expected her to be playing?'

'But I thought the whole scheme of the thing—'

'So did I. My gosh!' said Tuppy, laughing another of those hollow ones. 'I sweat myself to the bone for her sake. I allow a mob of homicidal maniacs to kick me in the ribs and stroll about on my face. And then, when I have braved a fate worse than death, so to speak, all to please her, I find that she didn't bother to come and watch the game. She got a 'phone-call from London from somebody who said he had located an Irish water-spaniel, and up she popped in her car, leaving me flat. I met her just now outside her house, and she told me. And all she could think of was that she was as sore as a sun-burnt neck because she had had her trip for nothing. Apparently it wasn't an Irish water-spaniel at all. Just an ordinary English water-spaniel. And to think I fancied I loved a girl like that. A nice life-partner she would make! "When pain and anguish wring the brow, a ministering angel thou"—I don't think! Why, if a man married a girl like that and happened to get stricken by some dangerous illness, would she smooth his pillow and press cooling drinks on him? Not a chance! She'd be off somewhere trying to buy Siberian eel-hounds. I'm through with women.'

I saw that the moment had come to put in a word for the old firm.

'My cousin Angela's not a bad sort, Tuppy,' I said, in a grave elder-brotherly kind of way. 'Not altogether a bad egg, Angela, if you look at her squarely. I had always been hoping that she and you . . . and I know my Aunt Dahlia felt the same.'

Tuppy's bitter sneer cracked the top-soil.

'Angela!' he woofed. 'Don't talk to me about Angela. Angela's a rag and a bone and a hank of hair and an A1 scourge, if you want to know. She gave me the push. Yes, she did. Simply because I had the manly courage to speak out candidly on the subject of that ghastly lid she was chump enough to buy. It made her look like a Peke, and I told her it made her look like a Peke. And instead of admiring me for my fearless honesty she bunged me out on my ear. Faugh!'

'She did?' I said.

'She jolly well did,' said young Tuppy. 'At four-sixteen p.m. on Tuesday the seventeenth.'

'By the way, old man,' I said, 'I've found that telegram.'

'What telegram?'

'The one I told you about.'

'Oh, that one?'

'Yes, that's the one.'

'Well, let's have a look at the beastly thing.'

I handed it over, watching him narrowly. And suddenly, as he read, I saw him wobble. Stirred to the core. Obviously.

'Anything important?' I said.

'Bertie,' said young Tuppy, in a voice that quivered with strong emotion, 'my recent remarks *re* your cousin Angela. Wash them out. Cancel them.

Look on them as not spoken. I tell you, Bertie, Angela's all right. An angel in human shape, and that's official. Bertie, I've got to get up to London. She's ill.'

'Ill?'

'High fever and delirium. This wire's from your aunt. She wants me to come up to London at once. Can I borrow your car?'

'Of course.'

'Thanks,' said Tuppy, and dashed out.

He had only been gone about a second when Jeeves came in with the restorative.

'Mr Glossop's gone, Jeeves.'

'Indeed, sir?'

'To London.'

'Yes, sir?'

'In my car. To see my cousin Angela. The sun is once more shining, Jeeves.'

'Extremely gratifying, sir.'

I gave him the eye.

'Was it you, Jeeves, who 'phoned to Miss What's-her-bally-name about the alleged water-spaniel?'

'Yes, sir.'

'I thought as much.'

'Yes, sir?'

'Yes, Jeeves, the moment Mr Glossop told me that a Mysterious Voice had 'phoned on the subject of Irish water-spaniels, I thought as much. I recognized your touch. I read your motives like an open book. You knew she would come buzzing up.'

'Yes, sir.'

'And you knew how Tuppy would react. If there's one thing that gives a jousting knight the pip, it is to have his audience walk out on him.'

'Yes, sir.'

'But, Jeeves.'

'Sir?'

'There's just one point. What will Mr Glossop say when he finds my cousin Angela full of beans and not delirious?'

'The point had not escaped me, sir. I took the liberty of ringing Mrs Travers up on the telephone and explaining the circumstances. All will be in readiness for Mr Glossop's arrival.'

'Jeeves,' I said, 'you think of everything.'

'Thank you, sir. In Mr Glossop's absence, would you care to drink this whisky-and-soda?'

I shook the head.

'No, Jeeves, there is only one man who must do that. It is you. If ever anyone earned a refreshing snort, you are he. Pour it out, Jeeves, and shove it down.'

'Thank you very much, sir.'

'Cheerio, Jeeves!'

'Cheerio, sir, if I may use the expression.'

RIGHT HO, JEEVES

TO RAYMOND NEEDHAM, K.C.

WITH AFFECTION AND ADMIRATION

1

'Jeeves,' I said, 'may I speak frankly?'

'Certainly, sir.'

'What I have to say may wound you.'

'Not at all, sir.'

'Well, then—'

No—wait. Hold the line a minute. I've gone off the rails.

I don't know if you have had the same experience, but the snag I always come up against when I'm telling a story is this dashed difficult problem of where to begin it. It's a thing you don't want to go wrong over, because one false step and you're sunk. I mean, if you fool about too long at the start, trying to establish atmosphere, as they call it, and all that sort of rot, you fail to grip and the customers walk out on you.

Get off the mark, on the other hand, like a scalded cat, and your public is at a loss. It simply raises its eyebrows, and can't make out what you're talking about.

And in opening my report of the complex case of Gussie Fink-Nottle, Madeline Bassett, my Cousin Angela, my Aunt Dahlia, my Uncle Thomas, young Tuppy Glossop, and the cook, Anatole, with the above spot of dialogue, I see that I have made the second of these two floaters.

I shall have to hark back a bit. And taking it for all in all, and weighing this against that, I suppose the affair may be said to have had its inception, if inception is the word I want, with that visit of mine to Cannes. If

I hadn't gone to Cannes, I shouldn't have met the Bassett or bought that white mess jacket, and Angela wouldn't have met her shark, and Aunt Dahlia wouldn't have played baccarat.

Yes, most decidedly, Cannes was the *point d'appui*.

Right ho, then. Let me marshal my facts.

I went to Cannes—leaving Jeeves behind, he having intimated that he did not wish to miss Ascot—round about the beginning of June. With me traveled my Aunt Dahlia and her daughter Angela. Tuppy Glossop, Angela's betrothed, was to have been of the party, but at the last moment couldn't get away. Uncle Tom, Aunt Dahlia's husband, remained at home, because he can't stick the South of France at any price.

So there you have the layout—Aunt Dahlia, Cousin Angela, and self off to Cannes round about the beginning of June.

All pretty clear so far, what?

We stayed at Cannes about two months, and except for the fact that Aunt Dahlia lost her shirt at baccarat and Angela nearly got inhaled by a shark while aquaplaning, a pleasant time was had by all.

On July the twenty-fifth, looking bronzed and fit, I accompanied aunt and child back to London. At seven p.m. on July the twenty-sixth we alighted at Victoria. And at seven-twenty or thereabouts we parted with mutual expressions of esteem—they to shove off in Aunt Dahlia's car to Brinkley Court, her place in Worcestershire, where they were expecting to entertain Tuppy in a day or two; I to go to the flat, drop my luggage, clean up a bit, and put on the soup and fish preparatory to pushing round to the Drones for a bite of dinner.

And it was while I was at the flat, toweling the torso after a much-needed rinse, that Jeeves, as we chatted of this and that—picking up the threads, as it were—suddenly brought the name of Gussie Fink-Nottle into the conversation.

As I recall it, the dialogue ran something as follows:

SELF: Well, Jeeves, here we are, what?

JEEVES: Yes, sir.

SELF: I mean to say, home again.

JEEVES: Precisely, sir.

SELF: Seems ages since I went away.

JEEVES: Yes, sir.

SELF: Have a good time at Ascot?

JEEVES: Most agreeable, sir.

SELF: Win anything?

JEEVES: Quite a satisfactory sum, thank you, sir.

SELF: Good. Well, Jeeves, what news on the Rialto? Anybody been phoning or calling or anything during my abs?

JEEVES: Mr Fink-Nottle, sir, has been a frequent caller.

I stared. Indeed, it would not be too much to say that I gaped.

'Mr Fink-Nottle?'

'Yes, sir.'

'You don't mean Mr Fink-Nottle?'

'Yes, sir.'

'But Mr Fink-Nottle's not in London?'

'Yes, sir.'

'Well, I'm blowed.'

And I'll tell you why I was blowed. I found it scarcely possible to give credence to his statement. This Fink-Nottle, you see, was one of those freaks you come across from time to time during life's journey who can't stand London. He lived year in and year out, covered with moss, in a remote village down in Lincolnshire, never coming up even for the Eton and Harrow match. And when I asked him once if he didn't find the time hang a bit heavy on his hands, he said, no, because he had a pond in his garden and studied the habits of newts.

I couldn't imagine what could have brought the chap up to the great city. I would have been prepared to bet that as long as the supply of newts didn't give out, nothing could have shifted him from that village of his.

'Are you sure?'

'Yes, sir.'

'You got the name correctly? Fink-Nottle?'

'Yes, sir.'

'Well, it's the most extraordinary thing. It must be five years since he was in London. He makes no secret of the fact that the place gives him the pip. Until now, he has always stayed glued to the country, completely surrounded by newts.'

'Sir?'

'Newts, Jeeves. Mr Fink-Nottle has a strong newt complex. You must have heard of newts. Those little sort of lizard things that charge about in ponds.'

'Oh, yes, sir. The aquatic members of the family Salamandridae which constitute the genus Molge.'

'That's right. Well, Gussie has always been a slave to them. He used to keep them at school.'

'I believe young gentlemen frequently do, sir.'

'He kept them in his study in a kind of glass-tank arrangement, and pretty niffy the whole thing was, I recall. I suppose one ought to have been able to see what the end would be even then, but you know what boys are. Careless, heedless, busy about our own affairs, we scarcely gave this kink in Gussie's character a thought. We may have exchanged an occasional remark about it taking all sorts to make a world, but nothing more. You can guess the sequel. The trouble spread.'

'Indeed, sir?'

'Absolutely, Jeeves. The craving grew upon him. The newts got him. Arrived at man's estate, he retired to the depths of the country and gave his life up to these dumb chums. I suppose he used to tell himself that he could take them or leave them alone, and then found—too late—that he couldn't.'

'It is often the way, sir.'

'Too true, Jeeves. At any rate, for the last five years he has been living at this place of his down in Lincolnshire, as confirmed a species-shunning hermit as ever put fresh water in the tank every second day and refused to see a soul. That's why I was so amazed when you told me he had suddenly risen to the surface like this. I still can't believe it. I am inclined to think that there must be some mistake, and that this bird who has been calling here is some different variety of Fink-Nottle. The chap I know wears horn-rimmed spectacles and has a face like a fish. How does that check up with your data?'

'The gentleman who came to the flat wore horn-rimmed spectacles, sir.'

'And looked like something on a slab?'

'Possibly there was a certain suggestion of the piscine, sir.'

'Then it must be Gussie, I suppose. But what on earth can have brought him up to London?'

'I am in a position to explain that, sir. Mr Fink-Nottle confided to me his motive in visiting the metropolis. He came because the young lady is here.'

'Young lady?'

'Yes, sir.'

'You don't mean he's in love?'

'Yes, sir.'

'Well, I'm dashed. I'm really dashed. I positively am dashed, Jeeves.'

And I was too. I mean to say, a joke's a joke, but there are limits.

Then I found my mind turning to another aspect of this rummy affair. Conceding the fact that Gussie Fink-Nottle, against all the ruling of the form book, might have fallen in love, why should he have been haunting my flat like this? No doubt the occasion was one of those when a fellow needs a friend, but I couldn't see what had made him pick on me.

It wasn't as if he and I were in any way bosom. We had seen a lot of each other at one time, of course, but in the last two years I hadn't had so much as a post card from him.

I put all this to Jeeves:

'Odd, his coming to me. Still, if he did, he did. No argument about that. It must have been a nasty jar for the poor perisher when he found I wasn't here.'

'No, sir. Mr Fink-Nottle did not call to see you, sir.'

'Pull yourself together, Jeeves. You've just told me that this is what he has been doing, and assiduously, at that.'

'It was I with whom he was desirous of establishing communication, sir.'

'You? But I didn't know you had ever met him.'

'I had not had that pleasure until he called here, sir. But it appears that Mr Sipperley, a fellow student of whose Mr Fink-Nottle had been at the university, recommended him to place his affairs in my hands.'

The mystery had conked. I saw all. As I dare say you know, Jeeves's reputation as a counselor has long been established among the cognoscenti, and the first move of any of my little circle on discovering themselves in any form of soup is always to roll round and put the thing up to him. And when he's got A out of a bad spot, A puts B on to him. And then, when he has fixed up B, B sends C along. And so on, if you get my drift, and so forth.

That's how these big consulting practices like Jeeves's grow. Old Sippy, I knew, had been deeply impressed by the man's efforts on his behalf at the time when he was trying to get engaged to Elizabeth Moon, so it was not to be wondered at that he should have advised Gussie to apply. Pure routine, you might say.

'Oh, you're acting for him, are you?'

'Yes, sir.'

'Now I follow. Now I understand. And what is Gussie's trouble?'

'Oddly enough, sir, precisely the same as that of Mr Sipperley when I was enabled to be of assistance to him. No doubt you recall Mr Sipperley's predicament, sir. Deeply attached to Miss Moon, he suffered from a rooted diffidence which made it impossible for him to speak.'

I nodded.

'I remember. Yes, I recall the Sipperley case. He couldn't bring himself to the scratch. A marked coldness of the feet, was there not? I recollect you saying he was letting—what was it?—letting something do something. Cats entered into it, if I am not mistaken.'

'Letting "I dare not" wait upon "I would", sir.'

'That's right. But how about the cats?'

'Like the poor cat i' the adage, sir.'

'Exactly. It beats me how you think up these things. And Gussie, you say, is in the same posish?'

'Yes, sir. Each time he endeavours to formulate a proposal of marriage, his courage fails him.'

'And yet, if he wants this female to be his wife, he's got to say so, what? I mean, only civil to mention it.'

'Precisely, sir.'

I mused.

'Well, I suppose this was inevitable, Jeeves. I wouldn't have thought that this Fink-Nottle would ever have fallen a victim to the divine p, but, if he has, no wonder he finds the going sticky.'

'Yes, sir.'

'Look at the life he's led.'

'Yes, sir.'

'I don't suppose he has spoken to a girl for years. What a lesson this is to us, Jeeves, not to shut ourselves up in country houses and stare into glass tanks. You can't be the dominant male if you do that sort of thing. In this life, you can choose between two courses. You can either shut yourself up in a country house and stare into tanks, or you can be a dasher with the sex. You can't do both.'

'No, sir.'

I mused once more. Gussie and I, as I say, had rather lost touch, but all the same I was exercised about the poor fish, as I am about all my pals, close or distant, who find themselves treading upon Life's banana skins. It seemed to me that he was up against it.

I threw my mind back to the last time I had seen him. About two years ago, it had been. I had looked in at his place while on a motor trip, and he had put me right off my feed by bringing a couple of green things with legs to the luncheon table, crooning over them like a young mother and eventually losing one of them in the salad. That picture, rising before my eyes, didn't give me much confidence in the unfortunate goof's ability to woo and win, I must say. Especially if the girl he had earmarked was one of these tough modern thugs, all lipstick and cool, hard, sardonic eyes, as she probably was.

'Tell me, Jeeves,' I said, wishing to know the worst, 'what sort of a girl is this girl of Gussie's?'

'I have not met the young lady, sir. Mr Fink-Nottle speaks highly of her attractions.'

'Seemed to like her, did he?'

'Yes, sir.'

'Did he mention her name? Perhaps I know her.'

'She is a Miss Bassett, sir. Miss Madeline Bassett.'

'What?'

'Yes, sir.'

I was deeply intrigued.

'Egad, Jeeves! Fancy that. It's a small world, isn't it, what?'

'The young lady is an acquaintance of yours, sir?'

'I know her well. Your news has relieved my mind, Jeeves. It makes the whole thing begin to seem far more like a practical working proposition.'

'Indeed, sir?'

'Absolutely. I confess that until you supplied this information I was feeling profoundly dubious about poor old Gussie's chances of inducing any spinster of any parish to join him in the saunter down the aisle. You will agree with me that he is not everybody's money.'

'There may be something in what you say, sir.'

'Cleopatra wouldn't have liked him.'

'Possibly not, sir.'

'And I doubt if he would go any too well with Tallulah Bankhead.'

'No, sir.'

'But when you tell me that the object of his affections is Miss Bassett, why, then, Jeeves, hope begins to dawn a bit. He's just the sort of chap a girl like Madeline Bassett might scoop in with relish.'

This Bassett, I must explain, had been a fellow visitor of ours at Cannes; and as she and Angela had struck up one of those effervescent friendships which girls do strike up, I had seen quite a bit of her. Indeed, in my moodier moments it sometimes seemed to me that I could not move a step without stubbing my toe on the woman.

And what made it all so painful and distressing was that the more we met, the less did I seem able to find to say to her.

You know how it is with some girls. They seem to take the stuffing right out of you. I mean to say, there is something about their personality that paralyses the vocal cords and reduces the contents of the brain to cauliflower. It was like that with this Bassett and me; so much so that I have known occasions when for minutes at a stretch Bertram Wooster might have been observed fumbling with the tie, shuffling the feet, and behaving in all other respects in her presence like the complete dumb brick. When, therefore, she took her departure some two weeks before we did, you may readily imagine that, in Bertram's opinion, it was not a day too soon.

It was not her beauty, mark you, that thus numbed me. She was a pretty enough girl in a droopy, blonde, saucer-eyed way, but not the sort of breath-taker that takes the breath.

No, what caused this disintegration in a usually fairly fluent prattler with the sex was her whole mental attitude. I don't want to wrong anybody, so I won't go so far as to say that she actually wrote poetry, but her conversation, to my mind, was of a nature calculated to excite the liveliest suspicions. Well, I mean to say, when a girl suddenly asks you out of a blue sky if you don't sometimes feel that the stars are God's daisy-chain, you begin to think a bit.

As regards the fusing of her soul and mine, therefore, there was nothing doing. But with Gussie, the posish was entirely different. The thing that had stymied me—viz. that this girl was obviously all loaded down with ideals and sentiment and what not—was quite in order as far as he was concerned.

Gussie had always been one of those dreamy, soulful birds—you can't shut yourself up in the country and live only for newts, if you're not—and I could see no reason why, if he could somehow be induced to get the low, burning words off his chest, he and the Bassett shouldn't hit it off like ham and eggs.

'She's just the type for him,' I said.

'I am most gratified to hear it, sir.'

'And he's just the type for her. In fine, a good thing and one to be pushed along with the utmost energy. Strain every nerve, Jeeves.'

'Very good, sir,' replied the honest fellow. 'I will attend to the matter at once.'

Now up to this point, as you will doubtless agree, what you might call a perfect harmony had prevailed. Friendly gossip between employer and employed, and everything as sweet as a nut. But at this juncture, I regret to say, there was an unpleasant switch. The atmosphere suddenly changed, the storm clouds began to gather, and before we knew where we were, the jarring note had come bounding on the scene. I have known this to happen before in the Wooster home.

The first intimation I had that things were about to hot up was a pained and disapproving cough from the neighbourhood of the carpet. For, during the above exchanges, I should explain, while I, having dried the frame, had been dressing in a leisurely manner, donning here a sock, there a shoe, and gradually climbing into the vest, the shirt, the tie, and the knee-length, Jeeves had been down on the lower level, unpacking my effects.

He now rose, holding a white object. And at the sight of it, I realized that another of our domestic crises had arrived, another of those unfortunate clashes of will between two strong men, and that Bertram, unless he remembered his fighting ancestors and stood up for his rights, was about to be put upon.

I don't know if you were at Cannes this summer. If you were, you will recall that anybody with any pretensions to being the life and soul of the party was accustomed to attend binges at the Casino in the ordinary evening-wear trouserings topped to the north by a white mess jacket with brass buttons. And ever since I had stepped aboard the Blue Train at Cannes station, I had been wondering, on and off, how mine would go with Jeeves.

In the matter of evening costumes, you see, Jeeves is hidebound and reactionary. I had had trouble with him before about soft-bosomed shirts. And while these mess jackets had, as I say, been all the rage—*tout ce qu'il y a de chic*—on the Côte d'Azur, I had never concealed it from myself, even when treading the measure at the Palm Beach Casino in the one I had hastened to buy, that there might be something of an upheaval about it on my return.

I prepared to be firm.

'Yes, Jeeves?' I said. And though my voice was suave, a close observer in a position to watch my eyes would have noticed a steely glint. Nobody has a greater respect for Jeeve's intellect than I have, but this disposition of his to dictate to the hand that fed him had got, I felt, to be checked. This mess jacket was very near to my heart, and I jolly well intended to fight for it with all the vim of grand old Sieur de Wooster at the Battle of Agincourt.

'Yes, Jeeves?' I said. 'Something on your mind, Jeeves?'

'I fear that you inadvertently left Cannes in the possession of a coat belonging to some other gentleman, sir.'

I switched on the steely a bit more.

'No, Jeeves,' I said, in a level tone, 'the object under advisement is mine. I bought it out there.'

'You wore it, sir?'

'Every night.'

'But surely you are not proposing to wear it in England, sir?'

I saw that we had arrived at the nub.

'Yes, Jeeves.'

'But sir—'

'You were saying, Jeeves?'

'It is quite unsuitable, sir.'

'I do not agree with you, Jeeves. I anticipate a great popular success for this jacket. It is my intention to spring it on the public tomorrow at Pongo Twistleton's birthday party, where I confidently expect it to be one long scream from start to finish. No argument, Jeeves. No discussion. Whatever fantastic objection you may have taken to it, I wear this jacket.'

'Very good, sir.'

He went on with his unpacking. I said no more on the subject. I had won the victory, and we Woosters do not triumph over a beaten foe. Presently, having completed my toilet, I bade the man a cheery farewell and in generous mood suggested that, as I was dining out, why didn't he take the evening off and go to some improving picture or something. Sort of olive branch, if you see what I mean.

He didn't seem to think much of it.

'Thank you, sir, I will remain in.'

I surveyed him narrowly.

'Is this dudgeon, Jeeves?'

'No, sir, I am obliged to remain on the premises. Mr Fink-Nottle informed me that he would be calling to see me this evening.'

'Oh, Gussie's coming, is he? Well, give him my love.'

'Very good, sir.'

'And a whisky and soda, and so forth.'

'Very good, sir.'

'Right ho, Jeeves.'

I then set off for the Drones.

At the Drones I ran into Pongo Twistleton, and he talked so much about this forthcoming merry-making of his, of which good reports had already reached me through my correspondents, that it was nearing eleven when I got home again.

And scarcely had I opened the door when I heard voices in the sitting-room, and scarcely had I entered the sitting-room when I found that these proceeded from Jeeves and what appeared at first sight to be the Devil.

A closer scrutiny informed me that it was Gussie Fink-Nottle, dressed as Mephistopheles.

2

'What-ho Gussie,' I said.

You couldn't have told it from my manner, but I was feeling more than a bit nonplussed. The spectacle before me was enough to nonplus anyone. I mean to say, this Fink-Nottle, as I remembered him, was the sort of shy, shrinking goop who might have been expected to shake like an aspen if invited to so much as a social Saturday afternoon at the vicarage. And yet here he was, if one could credit one's senses, about to take part in a fancy-dress ball, a form of entertainment notoriously a testing experience for the toughest.

And he was attending that fancy-dress ball, mark you—not, like every other well-bred Englishman, as a Pierrot, but as Mephistopheles—this involving, as I need scarcely stress, not only scarlet tights but a pretty frightful false beard.

Rummy, you'll admit. However, one masks one's feelings. I betrayed no vulgar astonishment, but, as I say, what-hoed with civil nonchalance.

He grinned through the fungus—rather sheepishly, I thought.

'Oh, hullo, Bertie.'

'Long time since I saw you. Have a spot?'

'No, thanks. I must be off in a minute. I just came round to ask Jeeves how he thought I looked. How do you think I look, Bertie?'

Well, the answer to that, of course, was 'perfectly foul'. But we Woosters are men of tact and have a nice sense of the obligations of a host. We do not tell old friends beneath our roof-tree that they are an offence to the eyesight. I evaded the question.

'I hear you're in London,' I said carelessly.

'Oh, yes.'

'Must be years since you came up.'

'Oh, yes.'

'And now you're off for an evening's pleasure.'

He shuddered a bit. He had, I noticed, a hunted air.

'Pleasure!'

'Aren't you looking forward to this rout or revel?'

'Oh, I suppose it'll be all right,' he said, in a toneless voice. 'Anyway, I ought to be off, I suppose. The thing starts round about eleven. I told my cab to wait . . . Will you see if it's there, Jeeves.'

'Very good, sir.'

There was something of a pause after the door had closed. A certain constraint. I mixed myself a beaker, while Gussie, a glutton for punishment, stared at himself in the mirror. Finally I decided that it would be best to let him know that I was abreast of his affairs. It might be that it would ease his mind to confide in a sympathetic man of experience. I have generally found, with those under the influence, that what they want more than anything is the listening ear.

'Well, Gussie, old leper,' I said, 'I've been hearing all about you.'

'Eh?'

'This little trouble of yours. Jeeves has told me everything.'

He didn't seem any too braced. It's always difficult to be sure, of course, when a chap has dug himself in behind a Mephistopheles beard, but I fancy he blushed a trifle.

'I wish Jeeves wouldn't go gassing all over the place. It was supposed to be confidential.'

I could not permit this tone.

'Dishing up the dirt to the young master can scarcely be described as gassing all over the place,' I said, with a touch of rebuke. 'Anyway, there it is. I know all. And I should like to begin,' I said, sinking my personal opinion that the female in question was a sloppy pest in my desire to buck and encourage, 'by saying that Madeline Bassett is a charming girl. A winner, and just the sort for you.'

'You don't know her?'

'Certainly I know her. What beats me is how you ever got in touch. Where did you meet?'

'She was staying at a place near mine in Lincolnshire the week before last.'

'Yes, but even so. I didn't know you called on the neighbours.'

'I don't. I met her out for a walk with her dog. The dog had got a thorn in its foot, and when she tried to take it out, it snapped at her. So, of course, I had to rally round.'

'You extracted the thorn?'

'Yes.'

'And fell in love at first sight?'

'Yes.'

'Well, dash it, with a thing like that to give you a send-off, why didn't you cash in immediately?'

'I hadn't the nerve.'

'What happened?'

'We talked for a bit.'

'What about?'

'Oh, birds.'

'Birds? What birds?'

'The birds that happened to be hanging round. And the scenery, and all that sort of thing. And she said she was going to London, and asked me to look her up if I was ever there.'

'And after that you didn't so much as press her hand?'

'Of course not.'

Well, I mean, it looked as though there was no more to be said. If a chap is such a rabbit that he can't get action when he's handed the thing on a plate, his case would appear to be pretty hopeless. Nevertheless, I reminded myself that this non-starter and I had been at school together. One must make an effort for an old school friend.

'Ah, well,' I said, 'we must see what can be done. Things may brighten. At any rate, you will be glad to learn that I am behind you in this enterprise. You have Bertram Wooster in your corner, Gussie.'

'Thanks, old man. And Jeeves, of course, which is the thing that really matters.'

I don't mind admitting that I winced. He meant no harm, I suppose, but I'm bound to say that this tactless speech nettled me not a little. People are always nettling me like that. Giving me to understand, I mean to say, that in their opinion Bertram Wooster is a mere cipher and that the only member of the household with brains and resources is Jeeves.

It jars on me.

And tonight it jarred on me more than usual, because I was feeling pretty dashed fed-up with Jeeves. Over that matter of the mess jacket, I mean. True, I had forced him to climb down, quelling him, as described, with the quiet strength of my personality, but I was still a trifle shirty at his having brought the thing up at all. It seemed to me that what Jeeves wanted was the iron hand.

'And what is he doing about it?' I inquired stiffly.

'He's been giving the position of affairs a lot of thought.'

'He has, has he?'

'It's on his advice that I'm going to this dance.'

'Why?'

'She is going to be there. In fact, it was she who sent me the ticket of invitation. And Jeeves considered—'

'And why not as a Pierrot?' I said, taking up the point which had struck me before. 'Why this break with a grand old tradition?'

'He particularly wanted me to go as Mephistopheles.'

I started.

'He did, did he? He specifically recommended that definite costume?'

'Yes.'

'Ha!'

'Eh?'

'Nothing. Just "Ha!"'

And I'll tell you why I said 'Ha!' Here was Jeeves making heavy weather about me wearing a perfectly ordinary white mess jacket, a garment not only *tout ce qu'il y a de chic*, but absolutely *de rigueur*, and in the same breath, as you might say, inciting Gussie Fink-Nottle to be a blot on the London scene in scarlet tights. Ironical, what? One looks askance at this sort of in-and-out running.

'What has he got against Pierrots?'

'I don't think he objects to Pierrots as Pierrots. But in my case he thought a Pierrot wouldn't be adequate.'

'I don't follow that.'

'He said that the costume of Pierrot, while pleasing to the eye, lacked the authority of the Mephistopheles costume.'

'I still don't get it.'

'Well, it's a matter of psychology, he said.'

There was a time when a remark like that would have had me snookered. But long association with Jeeves had developed the Wooster vocabulary considerably. Jeeves has always been a whale for the psychology of the individual, and I now follow him like a bloodhound when he snaps it out of the bag.

'Oh, psychology?'

'Yes. Jeeves is a great believer in the moral effect of clothes. He thinks I might be emboldened in a striking costume like this. He said a Pirate Chief would be just as good. In fact, a Pirate Chief was his first suggestion, but I objected to the boots.'

I saw his point. There is enough sadness in life without having fellows like Gussie Fink-Nottle going about in sea boots.

'Are you emboldened?'

'Well, to be absolutely accurate, Bertie, old man, no.'

A gust of compassion shook me. After all, though we had lost touch a bit of recent years, this man and I had once thrown inked darts at each other.

'Gussie,' I said, 'take an old friend's advice, and don't go within a mile of this binge.'

'But it's my last chance of seeing her. She's off tomorrow to stay with some people in the country. Besides, you don't know.'

'Don't know what?'

'That this idea of Jeeves's won't work. I feel a most frightful chump now, yes, but who can say whether that will not pass off when I get into a mob of other people in fancy dress. I had the same experience as a child, one year during the Christmas festivities. They dressed me up as a rabbit, and the shame was indescribable. Yet when I got to the party and found myself surrounded by scores of other children, many in costumes even ghastlier than my own, I perked up amazingly, joined freely in the revels, and was able to eat so hearty a supper that I was sick twice in the cab coming home. What I mean is, you can't tell in cold blood.'

I weighed this. It was specious, of course.

'And you can't get away from it that, fundamentally, Jeeves's idea is sound. In a striking costume like Mephistopheles, I might quite easily pull off something pretty impressive. Colour does make a difference. Look at newts. During the courting season the male newt is brilliantly coloured. It helps him a lot.'

'But you aren't a male newt.'

'I wish I were. Do you know how a male newt proposes, Bertie? He just stands in front of the female newt vibrating his tail and bending his body in a semicircle. I could do that on my head. No, you wouldn't find me grousing if I were a male newt.'

'But if you were a male newt, Madeline Bassett wouldn't look at you. Not with the eye of love, I mean.'

'She would, if she were a female newt.'

'But she isn't a female newt.'

'No, but suppose she was.'

'Well, if she was, you wouldn't be in love with her.'

'Yes, I would, if I were a male newt.'

A slight throbbing about the temples told me that this discussion had reached saturation point.

'Well, anyway,' I said, 'coming down to hard facts and cutting out all this visionary stuff about vibrating tails and what-not, the salient point that emerges is that you are booked to appear at a fancy-dress ball. And I tell you out of my riper knowledge of fancy-dress balls, Gussie, that you won't enjoy yourself.'

'It isn't a question of enjoying yourself.'

'I wouldn't go.'

'I must go. I keep telling you she's off to the country tomorrow.'

I gave it up.

'So be it,' I said. 'Have it your own way . . . Yes, Jeeves?'

'Mr Fink-Nottle's cab, sir.'

'Ah? The cab, eh? . . . Your cab, Gussie.'

'Oh, the cab? Oh, right. Of course, yes, rather . . . Thanks, Jeeves . . . Well, so long, Bertie.'

And giving me the sort of weak smile Roman gladiators used to give the Emperor before entering the arena, Gussie trickled off. And I turned to

Jeeves. The moment had arrived for putting him in his place, and I was all for it.

It was a little difficult to know how to begin, of course. I mean to say, while firmly resolved to tick him off, I didn't want to gash his feelings too deeply. Even when displaying the iron hand, we Woosters like to keep the thing fairly matey.

However, on consideration, I saw that there was nothing to be gained by trying to lead up to it gently. It is never any use beating about the b.

'Jeeves,' I said, 'may I speak frankly?'

'Certainly, sir.'

'What I have to say may wound you.'

'Not at all, sir.'

'Well, then, I have been having a chat with Mr Fink-Nottle, and he has been telling me about this Mephistopheles scheme of yours.'

'Yes, sir?'

'Now let me get it straight. If I follow your reasoning correctly, you think that, stimulated by being upholstered throughout in scarlet tights, Mr Fink-Nottle, on encountering the adored object, will vibrate his tail and generally let himself go with a whoop.'

'I am of opinion that he will lose much of his normal diffidence, sir.'

'I don't agree with you, Jeeves.'

'No, sir?'

'No. In fact, not to put too fine a point upon it, I consider that of all the dashed silly, drivelling ideas I ever heard in my puff this is the most blithering and futile. It won't work. Not a chance. All you have done is to subject Mr Fink-Nottle to the nameless horrors of a fancy-dress ball for nothing. And this is not the first time this sort of thing has happened. To be quite candid, Jeeves, I have frequently noticed before now a tendency of disposition on your part to become—what's the word?'

'I could not say, sir.'

'Eloquent? No, it's not eloquent. Elusive? No, it's not elusive. It's on the tip of my tongue. Begins with an "e" and means being a jolly sight too clever.'

'Elaborate, sir?'

'That is the exact word I was after. Too elaborate, Jeeves—that is what you are frequently prone to become. Your methods are not simple, not straightforward. You cloud the issue with a lot of fancy stuff that is not of the essence. All that Gussie needs is the elder-brotherly advice of a seasoned man of the world. So what I suggest is that from now onwards you leave this case to me.'

'Very good, sir.'

'You lay off and devote yourself to your duties about the home.'

'Very good, sir.'

'I shall no doubt think of something quite simple and straightforward yet perfectly effective ere long. I will make a point of seeing Gussie tomorrow.'

'Very good, sir.'

'Right ho, Jeeves.'

But on the morrow all those telegrams started coming in, and I confess that for twenty-four hours I didn't give the poor chap a thought, having problems of my own to contend with.

3

The first of the telegrams arrived shortly after noon, and Jeeves brought it in with the before-luncheon snifter. It was from my Aunt Dahlia, operating from Market Snodsbury, a small town of sorts a mile or two along the main road as you leave her country seat.

It ran as follows:

Come at once. Travers.

And when I say it puzzled me like the dickens, I am understating it, if anything. As mysterious a communication, I considered, as was ever flashed over the wires. I studied it in a profound reverie for the best part of two dry Martinis and a dividend. I read it backwards. I read it forwards. As a matter of fact, I have a sort of recollection of even smelling it. But it still baffled me.

Consider the facts, I mean. It was only a few hours since this aunt and I had parted, after being in constant association for nearly two months. And yet here she was—with my farewell kiss still lingering on her cheek, so to speak—pleading for another reunion. Bertram Wooster is not accustomed to this gluttonous appetite for his society. Ask anyone who knows me, and they will tell you that after two months of my company, what the normal person feels is that that will about do for the present. Indeed, I have known people who couldn't stick it out for more than a few days.

Before sitting down to the well-cooked, therefore, I sent this reply:

Perplexed. Explain. Bertie.

To this I received an answer during the after-luncheon sleep:

What on earth is there to be perplexed about, ass? Come at once. Travers.

Three cigarettes and a couple of turns about the room, and I had my response ready:

How do you mean come at once? Regards. Bertie.

I append the comeback:

I mean come at once, you maddening half-wit. What did you think I meant? Come at once or expect an aunt's curse first post tomorrow. Love. Travers.

I then dispatched the following message, wishing to get everything quite clear:

When you say 'Come' do you mean 'Come to Brinkley Court'? And when you say 'At once' do you mean 'At once'? Fogged. At a loss. All the best. Bertie.

I sent this one off on my way to the Drones, where I spent a restful afternoon throwing cards into a top-hat with some of the better element. Returning in the evening hush, I found the answer waiting for me:

Yes, yes, yes, yes, yes, yes, yes. It doesn't matter whether you understand or not. You just come at once, as I tell you, and for heaven's sake stop this backchat. Do you think I am made of money that I can afford to send you telegrams every ten minutes. Stop being a fat-head and come immediately. Love. Travers.

It was at this point that I felt the need of getting a second opinion. I pressed the bell.

'Jeeves,' I said, 'a V-shaped rumminess has manifested itself from the direction of Worcestershire. Read these,' I said, handing him the papers in the case.

He scanned them.

'What do you make of it, Jeeves?'

'I think Mrs Travers wishes you to come at once, sir.'

'You gather that too, do you?'

'Yes, sir.'

'I put the same construction on the thing. But why, Jeeves? Dash it all, she's just had nearly two months of me.'

'Yes, sir.'

'And many people consider the medium dose for an adult two days.'

'Yes, sir. I appreciate the point you raise. Nevertheless, Mrs Travers appears very insistent. I think it would be well to acquiesce in her wishes.'

'Pop down, you mean?'

'Yes, sir.'

'Well, I certainly can't go at once. I've an important conference on at the Drones tonight. Pongo Twistleton's birthday party, you remember.'

'Yes, sir.'

There was a slight pause. We were both recalling the little unpleasantness that had arisen. I felt obliged to allude to it.

'You're all wrong about that mess jacket, Jeeves.'

'These things are a matter of opinion, sir.'

'When I wore it at the Casino in Cannes, beautiful women nudged one another and whispered: "Who is he?"'

'The code at Continental casinos is notoriously lax, sir.'

'And when I described it to Pongo last night, he was fascinated.'

'Indeed, sir?'

'So were all the rest of those present. One and all admitted that I had got hold of a good thing. Not a dissentient voice.'

'Indeed, sir?'

'I am convinced that you will eventually learn to love this mess jacket, Jeeves.'

'I fear not, sir.'

I gave it up. It is never any use trying to reason with Jeeves on these occasions. 'Pig-headed' is the word that springs to the lips. One sighs and passes on.

'Well, anyway, returning to the agenda, I can't go down to Brinkley Court or anywhere else yet awhile. That's final. I'll tell you what, Jeeves. Give me form and pencil, and I'll wire her that I'll be with her some time next week or the week after. Dash it all, she ought to be able to hold out without me for a few days. It only requires will power.'

'Yes, sir.'

'Right ho, then. I'll wire "Expect me tomorrow fortnight" or words to some such effect. That ought to meet the case. Then if you will toddle round the corner and send it off, that will be that.'

'Very good, sir.'

And so the long day wore on till it was time for me to dress for Pongo's party.

Pongo had assured me, while chatting of the affair on the previous night, that this birthday binge of his was to be on a scale calculated to stagger humanity, and I must say I have participated in less fruity functions. It was well after four when I got home, and by that time I was about ready to turn in. I can just remember groping for the bed and crawling into it, and it seemed to me that the lemon had scarcely touched the pillow before I was aroused by the sound of the door opening.

I was barely ticking over, but I contrived to raise an eyelid.

'Is that my tea, Jeeves?'

'No, sir. It is Mrs Travers.'

And a moment later there was a sound like a mighty rushing wind, and the relative had crossed the threshold at fifty m.p.h. under her own steam.

4

It has been well said of Bertram Wooster that, while no one views his flesh and blood with a keener and more remorselessly critical eye, he is nevertheless a man who delights in giving credit where credit is due. And if you have followed these memoirs of mine with the proper care, you will be aware that I have frequently had occasion to emphasize the fact that Aunt Dahlia is all right.

She is the one, if you remember, who married old Tom Travers *en secondes noces*, as I believe the expression is, the year Bluebottle won the Cambridgeshire, and once induced me to write an article on What The Well-Dressed Man Is Wearing for that paper she runs—*Milady's Boudoir*. She is a large, genial soul, with whom it is a pleasure to hob-nob. In her spiritual make-up there is none of that subtle gosh-awfulness which renders such an exhibit as, say, my Aunt Agatha the curse of the Home Counties and a menace to one and all. I have the highest esteem for Aunt Dahlia, and have never wavered in my cordial appreciation of her humanity, sporting qualities, and general good-eggishness.

This being so, you may conceive of my astonishment at finding her at my bedside at such an hour. I mean to say, I've stayed at her place many a time and oft, and she knows my habits. She is well aware that until I have had my cup of tea in the morning, I do not receive. This crashing in at a moment when she knew that solitude and repose were of the essence was scarcely, I could not but feel, the good old form.

Besides, what business had she being in London at all? That was what I asked myself. When a conscientious housewife has returned to her home after an absence of seven weeks, one does not expect her to start racing off again the day after her arrival. One feels that she ought to be sticking round, ministering to her husband, conferring with the cook, feeding the cat, combing and brushing the Pomeranian—in a word, staying put. I was more than a little bleary-eyed, but I endeavoured, as far as the fact that my eyelids were more or less glued together would permit, to give her an austere and censorious look.

She didn't seem to get it.

'Wake up, Bertie, you old ass!' she cried, in a voice that hit me between the eyebrows and went out at the back of my head.

If Aunt Dahlia has a fault, it is that she is apt to address a *vis-à-vis* as if he were somebody half a mile away whom she had observed riding over hounds. A throwback, no doubt, to the time when she counted the day lost that was not spent in chivvying some unfortunate fox over the countryside.

I gave her another of the austere and censorious, and this time it registered. All the effect it had, however, was to cause her to descend to personalities.

'Don't blink at me in that obscene way,' she said. 'I wonder, Bertie,' she proceeded, gazing at me as I should imagine Gussie would have gazed at some newt that was not up to sample, 'if you have the faintest conception how perfectly loathsome you look? A cross between an orgy scene in the movies and some low form of pond life. I suppose you were out on the tiles last night?'

'I attended a social function, yes,' I said coldly. 'Pongo Twistleton's birthday party. I couldn't let Pongo down. *Noblesse oblige*.'

'Well, get up and dress.'

I felt I could not have heard her aright.

'Get up and dress?'

'Yes.'

I turned on the pillow with a little moan, and at this juncture Jeeves entered with the vital oolong. I clutched at it like a drowning man at a straw hat. A deep sip or two, and I felt—I won't say restored, because a birthday party like Pongo Twistleton's isn't a thing you get restored after with a mere mouthful of tea, but sufficiently the old Bertram to be able to bend the mind on this awful thing which had come upon me.

And the more I bent same, the less could I grasp the trend of the scenario.

'What is this, Aunt Dahlia?' I inquired.

'It looks to me like tea,' was her response. 'But you know best. You're drinking it.'

If I hadn't been afraid of spilling the healing brew, I have little doubt that I should have given an impatient gesture. I know I felt like it.

'Not the contents of this cup. All this. Your barging in and telling me to get up and dress, and all that rot.'

'I've barged in, as you call it, because my telegrams seemed to produce no effect. And I told you to get up and dress because I want you to get up and dress. I've come to take you back with me. I like your crust, wiring that you would come next year or whenever it was. You're coming now. I've got a job for you.'

'But I don't want a job.'

'What you want, my lad, and what you're going to get are two very different things. There is man's work for you to do at Brinkley Court. Be ready to the last button in twenty minutes.'

'But I can't possibly be ready to any buttons in twenty minutes. I'm feeling awful.'

She seemed to consider.

'Yes,' she said, 'I suppose it's only humane to give you a day or two to recover. All right, then, I shall expect you on the thirtieth at the latest.'

'But, dash it, what is all this? How do you mean, a job? Why a job? What sort of job?'

'I'll tell you if you'll only stop talking for a minute. It's quite an easy, pleasant job. You will enjoy it. Have you ever heard of Market Snodsbury Grammar School?'

'Never.'

'It's a grammar school at Market Snodsbury.'

I told her a little frigidly that I had divined as much.

'Well, how was I to know that a man with a mind like yours would grasp it so quickly?' she protested. 'All right, then. Market Snodsbury Grammar School is, as you have guessed, the grammar school at Market Snodsbury. I'm one of the governors.'

'You mean one of the governesses.'

'I don't mean one of the governesses. Listen, ass. There was a board of governors at Eton, wasn't there? Very well. So there is at Market Snodsbury Grammar School, and I'm a member of it. And they left the arrangements for the summer prize-giving to me. This prize-giving takes place on the last—or thirty-first—day of this month. Have you got that clear?'

I took another oz. of the life-saving and inclined my head. Even after a Pongo Twistleton birthday party, I was capable of grasping simple facts like these.

'I follow you, yes. I see the point you are trying to make, certainly. Market . . . Snodsbury . . . Grammar School . . . Board of Governors . . . Prize-giving . . . Quite. But what's it got to do with me?'

'You're going to give away the prizes.'

I goggled. Her words did not appear to make sense. They seemed the mere aimless vapouring of an aunt who has been sitting out in the sun without a hat.

'Me?'

'You.'

I goggled again.

'You don't mean me?'

'I mean you in person.'

I goggled a third time.

'You're pulling my leg.'

'I am not pulling your leg. Nothing would induce me to touch your beastly leg. The vicar was to have officiated, but when I got home I found a letter from him saying that he had strained a fetlock and must scratch his nomination. You can imagine the state I was in. I telephoned all over the place. Nobody would take it on. And then suddenly I thought of you.'

I decided to check all this rot at the outset. Nobody is more eager to oblige deserving aunts than Bertram Wooster, but there are limits, and sharply defined limits, at that.

'So you think I'm going to strew prizes at this bally Dothe-boys Hall of yours?'

'I do.'

'And make a speech?'

'Exactly.'

I laughed derisively.

'For goodness' sake, don't start gargling now. This is serious.'

'I was laughing.'

'Oh, were you? Well, I'm glad to see you taking it in this merry spirit.'

'Derisively,' I explained. 'I won't do it. That's final. I simply will not do it.'

'You will do it, young Bertie, or never darken my doors again. And you know what that means. No more of Anatole's dinners for you.'

A strong shudder shook me. She was alluding to her *chef*, that superb artist. A monarch of his profession, unsurpassed—nay, unequalled—at dishing up the raw material so that it melted in the mouth of the ultimate consumer, Anatole had always been a magnet that drew me to Brinkley Court with my tongue hanging out. Many of my happiest moments had been those which I had spent champing this great man's roasts and ragouts, and the prospect of being barred from digging into them in the future was a numbing one.

'No, I say, dash it!'

'I thought that would rattle you. Greedy young pig.'

'Greedy young pigs have nothing to do with it,' I said with a touch of hauteur. 'One is not a greedy young pig because one appreciates the cooking of a genius.'

'Well, I will say I like it myself,' conceded the relative. 'But not another bite of it do you get, if you refuse to do this simple, easy, pleasant job. No, not so much as another sniff. So put that in your twelve-inch cigarette-holder and smoke it.'

I began to feel like some wild thing caught in a snare.

'But why do you want me? I mean, what am I? Ask yourself that.'

'I often have.'

'I mean to say, I'm not the type. You have to have some terrific nib to give away prizes. I seem to remember, when I was at school, it was generally a prime minister or somebody.'

'Ah, but that was at Eton. At Market Snodsbury we aren't nearly so choosy. Anybody in spats impresses us.'

'Why don't you get Uncle Tom?'

'Uncle Tom!'

'Well, why not? He's got spats.'

'Bertie,' she said, 'I will tell you why not Uncle Tom. You remember me losing all that money at baccarat at Cannes? Well, very shortly I shall have to sidle up to Tom and break the news to him. If, right after that, I ask him to put on lavender gloves and a topper and distribute the prizes at Market Snodsbury Grammar School, there will be a divorce in the family. He would pin a note to the pincushion and be off like a rabbit. No, my lad, you're for it, so you may as well make the best of it.'

'But, Aunt Dahlia, listen to reason. I assure you, you've got hold of the wrong man. I'm hopeless at a game like that. Ask Jeeves about that time I got lugged in to address a girls' school. I made the most colossal ass of myself.'

'And I confidently anticipate that you will make an equally colossal ass of yourself on the thirty-first of this month. That's why I want you. The way I look at it is that, as the thing is bound to be a frost, anyway, one may as well get a hearty laugh out of it. I shall enjoy seeing you distribute those prizes, Bertie. Well, I won't keep you, as, no doubt, you want to do your Swedish exercises. I shall expect you in a day or two.'

And with these heartless words she beetled off, leaving me a prey to the gloomiest emotions. What with the natural reaction after Pongo's party and this stunning blow, it is not too much to say that the soul was seared.

And I was still writhing in the depths, when the door opened and Jeeves appeared.

'Mr Fink-Nottle to see you, sir,' he announced.

5

I gave him one of my looks.

'Jeeves,' I said, 'I had scarcely expected this of you. You are aware that I was up to an advanced hour last night. You know that I have barely had my tea. You cannot be ignorant of the effect of that hearty voice of Aunt Dahlia's on a man with a headache. And yet you come bringing me Fink-Nottles. Is this a time for Fink or any other kind of Nottle?'

'But did you not give me to understand, sir, that you wished to see Mr Fink-Nottle to advise him on his affairs?'

This, I admit, opened up a new line of thought. In the stress of my emotions, I had clean forgotten about having taken Gussie's interests in hand. It altered things. One can't give the raspberry to a client. I mean, you didn't find Sherlock Holmes refusing to see clients just because he had been out late the night before at Doctor Watson's birthday party. I could have wished that the man had selected some more suitable hour for approaching me, but as he appeared to be a sort of human lark, leaving his watery nest at daybreak, I supposed I had better give him an audience.

'True,' I said. 'All right. Bung him in.'

'Very good, sir.'

'But before doing so, bring me one of those pick-me-ups of yours.'

'Very good, sir.'

And presently he returned with the vital essence.

I have had occasion, I fancy, to speak before now of these pick-me-ups of Jeeves's and their effect on a fellow who is hanging to life by a thread on the morning after. What they consist of, I couldn't tell you. He says some kind of sauce, the yolk of a raw egg and a dash of red pepper, but nothing will convince me that the thing doesn't go much deeper than that. Be that as it may, however, the results of swallowing one are amazing.

For perhaps the split part of a second nothing happens. It is as though all Nature waited breathless. Then, suddenly, it is as if the Last Trump had sounded and Judgement Day set in with unusual severity.

Bonfires burst out in all parts of the frame. The abdomen becomes heavily charged with molten lava. A great wind seems to blow through the world, and the subject is aware of something resembling a steam hammer striking the back of the head. During this phase, the ears ring loudly, the eyeballs rotate and there is a tingling about the brow.

And then, just as you are feeling that you ought to ring up your lawyer and see that your affairs are in order before it is too late, the whole situation seems to clarify. The wind drops. The ears cease to ring. Birds twitter. Brass bands start playing. The sun comes up over the horizon with a jerk.

And a moment later all you are conscious of is a great peace.

As I drained the glass now, new life seemed to burgeon within me. I remember Jeeves, who, however much he may go off the rails at times in the matter of dress clothes and in his advice to those in love, has always had a neat turn of phrase, once speaking of someone rising on stepping-stones of his dead self to higher things. It was that way with me now. I felt that the Bertram Wooster who lay propped up against the pillows had become a better, stronger, finer Bertram.

'Thank you, Jeeves,' I said.

'Not at all, sir.'

'That touched the exact spot. I am now able to cope with life's problems.'

'I am gratified to hear it, sir.'

'What madness not to have had one of those before tackling Aunt Dahlia. However, too late to worry about that now. Tell me of Gussie. How did he make out at the fancy-dress ball?'

'He did not arrive at the fancy-dress ball, sir.'

I looked at him a bit austerely.

'Jeeves,' I said, 'I admit that after that pick-me-up of yours I feel better, but don't try me too high. Don't stand by my sick bed talking absolute rot.

We shot Gussie into a cab and he started forth, headed for wherever this fancy-dress ball was. He must have arrived.'

'No, sir. As I gather from Mr Fink-Nottle, he entered the cab convinced in his mind that the entertainment to which he had been invited was to be held at No. 17 Suffolk Square, whereas the actual rendezvous was No. 71 Norfolk Terrace. These aberrations of memory are not uncommon with those who, like Mr Fink-Nottle, belong essentially to what one might call the dreamer type.'

'One might also call it the fat-headed type.'

'Yes, sir.'

'Well?'

'On reaching No. 17 Suffolk Square, Mr Fink-Nottle endeavoured to produce money to pay the fare.'

'What stopped him?'

'The fact that he had no money, sir. He discovered that he had left it, together with his ticket of invitation, on the mantelpiece of his bedchamber in the house of his uncle, where he was residing. Bidding the cabman to wait, accordingly, he rang the door-bell, and when the butler appeared, requested him to pay the cab, adding that it was all right, as he was one of the guests invited to the dance. The butler then disclaimed all knowledge of a dance on the premises.'

'And declined to unbelt?'

'Yes, sir.'

'Upon which—'

'Mr Fink-Nottle directed the cabman to drive him back to his uncle's residence.'

'Well, why wasn't that the happy ending? All he had to do was go in, collect cash and ticket, and there he would have been, on velvet.'

'I should have mentioned, sir, that Mr Fink-Nottle had also left his latchkey on the mantelpiece of his bedchamber.'

'He could have rung the bell.'

'He did ring the bell, sir, for some fifteen minutes. At the expiration of that period he recalled that he had given permission to the caretaker—the house was officially closed and all the staff on holiday—to visit his sailor son at Portsmouth.'

'Golly, Jeeves.'

'Yes, sir.'

'These dreamer-types do live, don't they.'

'Yes, sir.'

'What happened then?'

'Mr Fink-Nottle appears to have realized at this point that his position as regards the cabman had become equivocal. The figures on the clock had already reached a substantial sum, and he was not in a position to meet his obligations.'

'He could have explained.'

'You cannot explain to cabmen, sir. On endeavouring to do so, he found the fellow sceptical of his bona fides.'

'I should have legged it.'

'That is the policy which appears to have commended itself to Mr Fink-Nottle. He darted rapidly away, and the cabman, endeavouring to detain him, snatched at his overcoat. Mr Fink-Nottle contrived to extricate himself from the coat, and it would seem that his appearance in the masquerade costume beneath it came as something of a shock to the cabman. Mr Fink-Nottle informs me that he heard a species of whistling gasp, and, looking round, observed the man crouching against the railings with his hands over his face. Mr Fink-Nottle thinks he was praying. No doubt an uneducated, superstitious fellow, sir. Possibly a drinker.'

'Well, if he hadn't been one before, I'll bet he started being one shortly afterwards. I expect he could scarcely wait for the pubs to open.'

'Very possibly, in the circumstances he might have found a restorative agreeable, sir.'

'And so, in the circumstances, might Gussie too, I should think. What on earth did he do after that? London late at night—or even in the daytime, for that matter—is no place for a man in scarlet tights.'

'No, sir.'

'He invites comment.'

'Yes, sir.'

'I can see the poor old bird ducking down side-streets, skulking in alleyways, diving into dust-bins.'

'I gathered from Mr Fink-Nottle's remarks, sir, that something very much on those lines was what occurred. Eventually, after a trying night, he found his way to Mr Sipperley's residence, where he was able to secure lodging and a change of costume in the morning.'

I nestled against the pillows, the brow a bit drawn. It is all very well to try to do old school friends a spot of good, but I could not but feel that in espousing the cause of a lunkhead capable of mucking things up as Gussie had done, I had taken on a contract almost too big for human consumption. It seemed to me that what Gussie needed was not so much the advice of a seasoned man of the world as a padded cell in Colney Hatch and a couple of good keepers to see that he did not set the place on fire.

Indeed, for an instant I had half a mind to withdraw from the case and hand it back to Jeeves. But the pride of the Woosters restrained me. When we Woosters put our hands to the plough, we do not readily sheathe the sword. Besides, after that business of the mess jacket, anything resembling weakness would have been fatal.

'I suppose you realize, Jeeves,' I said, for though one dislikes to rub it in, these things have to be pointed out, 'that all this was your fault?'

'Sir?'

'It's no good saying "Sir?" You know it was. If you had not insisted on his going to that dance—a mad project, as I spotted from the first—this would not have happened.'

'Yes, sir, but I confess I did not anticipate—'

'Always anticipate everything, Jeeves,' I said, a little sternly. 'It is the only way. Even if you had allowed him to wear a Pierrot costume, things would not have panned out as they did. A Pierrot costume has pockets. However,' I went on more kindly, 'we need not go into that now. If all this has shown you what comes of going about the place in scarlet tights, that is something gained. Gussie waits without, you say?'

'Yes, sir.'

'Then shoot him in, and I will see what I can do for him.'

6

Gussie, on arrival, proved to be still showing traces of his grim experience. The face was pale, the eyes gooseberrylike, the ears drooping, and the whole aspect that of a man who has passed through the furnace and been caught in the machinery. I hitched myself up a bit higher on the pillows and gazed at him narrowly. It was a moment, I could see, when first aid was required, and I prepared to get down to cases.

'Well, Gussie.'

'Hullo, Bertie.'

'What ho.'

'What ho.'

These civilities concluded, I felt that the moment had come to touch delicately on the past.

'I hear you've been through it a bit.'

'Yes.'

'Thanks to Jeeves.'

'It wasn't Jeeves's fault.'

'Entirely Jeeves's fault.'

'I don't see that. I forgot my money and latchkey—'

'And now you'd better forget Jeeves. For you will be interested to hear, Gussie,' I said, deeming it best to put him in touch with the position of affairs right away, 'that he is no longer handling your little problem.'

This seemed to slip it across him properly. The jaw fell, the ears drooped more limply. He had been looking like a dead fish. He now looked like a deader fish, one of last year's, cast up on some lonely beach and left there at the mercy of the wind and tides.

'What!'

'Yes.'

'You don't mean that Jeeves isn't going to—'

'No.'

'But, dash it—'

I was kind, but firm.

'You will be much better off without him. Surely your terrible experiences of that awful night have told you that Jeeves needs a rest. The keenest of thinkers strikes a bad patch occasionally. That is what has happened to Jeeves. I have seen it coming on for some time. He has lost his form. He wants his plugs decarbonized. No doubt this is a shock to you. I suppose you came here this morning to seek his advice?'

'Of course I did.'

'On what point?'

'Madeline Bassett has gone to stay with these people in the country, and I want to know what he thinks I ought to do.'

'Well, as I say, Jeeves is off the case.'

'But, Bertie, dash it—'

'Jeeves,' I said with a certain asperity, 'is no longer on the case. I am now in sole charge.'

'But what on earth can you do?'

I curbed my resentment. We Woosters are fair-minded. We can make allowances for men who have been parading London all night in scarlet tights.

'That,' I said quietly, 'we shall see. Sit down and let us confer. I am bound to say the thing seems quite simple to me. You say this girl has gone to visit friends in the country. It would appear obvious that you must go there too, and flock round her like a poultice. Elementary.'

'But I can't plant myself on a lot of perfect strangers.'

'Don't you know these people?'

'Of course I don't. I don't know anybody.'

I pursed the lips. This did seem to complicate matters somewhat.

'All that I know is that their name is Travers, and it's a place called Brinkley Court down in Worcestershire.'

I unpursed the lips.

'Gussie,' I said, smiling paternally, 'it was a lucky day for you when Bertram Wooster interested himself in your affairs. As I foresaw from the start, I can fix everything. This afternoon you shall go to Brinkley Court, an honoured guest.'

He quivered like a *mousse*. I suppose it must always be rather a thrilling experience for the novice to watch me taking hold.

'But, Bertie, you don't mean you know these Traverses?'

'They are my Aunt Dahlia.'

'My gosh!'

'You see now,' I pointed out, 'how lucky you were to get me behind you. You go to Jeeves, and what does he do? He dresses you up in scarlet tights and one of the foulest false beards of my experience, and sends you off to fancy-dress balls. Result, agony of spirit and no progress. I then take over and put you on the right lines. Could Jeeves have got you into Brinkley Court? Not a chance. Aunt Dahlia isn't his aunt. I merely mention these things.'

'By Jove, Bertie, I don't know how to thank you.'

'My dear chap!'

'But, I say.'

'Now what?'

'What do I do when I get there?'

'If you knew Brinkley Court, you would not ask that question. In those romantic surroundings you can't miss. Great lovers through the ages have fixed up the preliminary formalities at Brinkley. The place is simply ill with atmosphere. You will stroll with the girl in the shady walks. You will sit with her on the shady lawns. You will row on the lake with her. And gradually you will find yourself working up to a point where—'

'By Jove, I believe you're right.'

'Of course, I'm right. I've got engaged three times at Brinkley. No business resulted, but the fact remains. And I went there without the foggiest idea of indulging in the tender pash. I hadn't the slightest intention of proposing to anybody. Yet no sooner had I entered those romantic grounds than I found myself reaching out for the nearest girl in sight and slapping my soul down in front of her. It's something in the air.'

'I see exactly what you mean. That's just what I want to be able to do—work up to it. And in London—curse the place—everything's in such a rush that you don't get a chance.'

'Quite. You see a girl alone for about five minutes a day, and if you want to ask her to be your wife, you've got to charge into it as if you were trying to grab the gold ring on a merry-go-round.'

'That's right. London rattles one. I shall be a different man altogether in the country. What a bit of luck this Travers woman turning out to be your aunt.'

'I don't know what you mean, turning out to be my aunt. She has been my aunt all along.'

'I mean, how extraordinary that it should be your aunt that Madeline's going to stay with.'

'Not at all. She and my Cousin Angela are close friends. At Cannes she was with us all the time.'

'Oh, you met Madeline at Cannes, did you? By Jove, Bertie,' said the poor lizard devoutly, 'I wish I could have seen her at Cannes. How wonderful she must have looked in beach pyjamas! Oh, Bertie—'

'Quite,' I said, a little distantly. Even when restored by one of Jeeves's depth bombs, one doesn't want this sort of thing after a hard night. I touched the bell and, when Jeeves appeared, requested him to bring me telegraph form and pencil. I then wrote a well-worded communication to Aunt Dahlia, informing her that I was sending my friend, Augustus Fink-Nottle, down to Brinkley today to enjoy her hospitality, and handed it to Gussie.

'Push that in at the first post office you pass,' I said. 'She will find it waiting for her on her return.'

Gussie popped along, flapping the telegram and looking like a close-up of Joan Crawford, and I turned to Jeeves and gave him a précis of my operations.

'Simple, you observe, Jeeves. Nothing elaborate.'

'No, sir.'

'Nothing far-fetched. Nothing strained or bizarre. Just Nature's remedy.'

'Yes, sir.'

'This is the attack as it should have been delivered. What do you call it when two people of opposite sexes are bunged together in close association in a secluded spot, meeting each other every day and seeing a lot of each other?'

'Is "propinquity" the word you wish, sir?'

'It is. I stake everything on propinquity, Jeeves. Propinquity, in my opinion, is what will do the trick. At the moment, as you are aware, Gussie is a mere jelly when in the presence. But ask yourself how he will feel in a week or so, after he and she have been helping themselves to sausages out of the same dish day after day at the breakfast sideboard. Cutting the same ham, ladling out communal kidneys and bacon—why—'

I broke off abruptly. I had one of my ideas.

'Golly, Jeeves!'

'Sir?'

'Here's an instance of how you have to think of everything. You heard me mention sausages, kidneys and bacon and ham.'

'Yes, sir.'

'Well, there must be nothing of that. Fatal. The wrong note entirely. Give me that telegraph form and pencil. I must warn Gussie without delay. What he's got to do is to create in this girl's mind the impression that he is pining away for love of her. This cannot be done by wolfing sausages.'

'No, sir.'

'Very well, then.'

And, taking form and p., I drafted the following:

Fink-Nottle
Brinkley Court
Market Snodsbury
Worcestershire
Lay off the sausages. Avoid the ham.
Bertie

'Send that off, Jeeves, instanter.'

'Very good, sir.'

I sank back on the pillows.

'Well, Jeeves,' I said, 'you see how I am taking hold. You notice the grip I am getting on this case. No doubt you realize now that it would pay you to study my methods.'

'No doubt, sir.'

'And even now you aren't on to the full depths of the extraordinary sagacity I've shown. Do you know what brought Aunt Dahlia up here this morning? She came to tell me I'd got to distribute the prizes at some beastly seminary she's a governor of down at Market Snodsbury.'

'Indeed, sir? I fear you will scarcely find that a congenial task.'

'Ah, but I'm not going to do it. I'm going to shove it off on to Gussie.'

'Sir?'

'I propose, Jeeves, to wire to Aunt Dahlia saying that I can't get down, and suggesting that she unleashes him on these young Borstal inmates of hers in my stead.'

'But if Mr Fink-Nottle should decline, sir?'

'Decline? Can you see him declining? Just conjure up the picture in your mind, Jeeves. Scene, the drawing-room at Brinkley; Gussie wedged into a corner, with Aunt Dahlia standing over him making hunting noises. I put it to you, Jeeves, can you see him declining?'

'Not readily, sir, I agree. Mrs Travers's is a forceful personality.'

'He won't have a hope of declining. His only way out would be to slide off. And he can't slide off, because he wants to be with Miss Bassett. No, Gussie will have to toe the line, and I shall be saved from a job at which I confess the soul shuddered. Getting up on a platform and delivering a short, manly speech to a lot of foul school-kids! Golly, Jeeves. I've been through that sort of thing once, what? You remember that time at the girls' school?'

'Very vividly, sir.'

'What an ass I made of myself!'

'Certainly I have seen you to better advantage, sir.'

'I think you might bring me just one more of those dynamite specials of yours, Jeeves. This narrow squeak has made me come over all faint.'

I suppose it must have taken Aunt Dahlia three hours or so to get back to Brinkley, because it wasn't till well after lunch that her telegram arrived. It read like a telegram that had been dispatched in a white-hot surge of emotion some two minutes after she had read mine.

As follows:

Am taking legal advice to ascertain whether strangling an idiot nephew counts as murder. If it doesn't look out for yourself. Consider your conduct frozen limit. What do you mean by planting your loathsome friends on me like this? Do you think Brinkley Court is a leper colony or what is it? Who is this Spink-Bottle? Love. Travers.

I had expected some such initial reaction. I replied in temperate vein:

Not Bottle. Nottle. Regards. Bertie.

Almost immediately after she had dispatched the above heart cry, Gussie must have arrived, for it wasn't twenty minutes later when I received the following:

Cipher telegram signed by you has reached me here. Runs 'Lay off the sausages. Avoid the ham'. Wire key immediately. Fink-Nottle.

I replied:

Also Kidneys. Cheerio. Bertie.

I had staked all on Gussie making a favourable impression on his hostess, basing my confidence on the fact that he was one of those timid, obsequious, teacup-passing, thin-bread-and-butter-offering, yes-men whom women of my Aunt Dahlia's type nearly always like at first sight. That I had not overrated my acumen was proved by her next in order, which, I was pleased to note, assayed a markedly larger percentage of the milk of human kindness.

As follows:

Well, this friend of yours has got here, and I must say that for a friend of yours he seems less sub-human than I had expected. A bit of a pop-eyed bleater, but on the whole clean and civil, and certainly most informa-

tive about newts. Am considering arranging series of lectures for him in neighbourhood. All the same I like your nerve using my house as a summer-hotel resort and shall have much to say to you on subject when you come down. Expect you thirtieth. Bring spats. Love. Travers.

To this I riposted:

On consulting engagement book find it impossible come Brinkley Court. Deeply regret. Toodle-oo. Bertie.

Hers in reply struck a sinister note:

Oh, so it's like that, is it? You and your engagement book, indeed. Deeply regret my foot. Let me tell you, my lad, that you will regret it a jolly sight more deeply if you don't come down. If you imagine for one moment that you are going to get out of distributing those prizes you are very much mistaken. Deeply regret Brinkley Court hundred miles from London as unable hit you with a brick. Love. Travers.

I then put my fortune to the test, to win or lose it all. It was not a moment for petty economies. I let myself go regardless of expense:

No, but dash it, listen. Honestly, you don't want me. Get Fink-Nottle distribute prizes. A born distributor, who will do you credit. Confidently anticipate Augustus Fink-Nottle as Master of Revels on thirty-first inst. Would make genuine sensation. Do not miss this great chance, which may never occur again. Tinkerty-tonk. Bertie.

There was an hour of breathless suspense, and then the joyful tidings arrived:

Well, all right. Something in what you say, I suppose. Consider you treacherous worm and contemptible, spineless cowardy custard, but have booked Spink-Bottle. Stay where you are, then, and I hope you get run over by an omnibus. Love. Travers.

The relief, as you may well imagine, was stupendous. A great weight seemed to have rolled off my mind. It was as if somebody had been pouring Jeeves's pick-me-ups into me through a funnel. I sang as I dressed for dinner that night. At the Drones I was so gay and cheery that there were several complaints. And when I got home and turned into the old bed, I fell asleep like a little child within five minutes of inserting the person between the sheets. It seemed to me that the whole distressing affair might now be considered definitely closed.

Conceive my astonishment, therefore, when waking on the morrow and sitting up to dig into the morning tea-cup, I beheld on the tray another telegram.

My heart sank. Could Aunt Dahlia have slept on it and changed her mind? Could Gussie, unable to face the ordeal confronting him, have legged it during the night down a water-pipe? With these speculations racing through the bean, I tore open the envelope. And as I noted contents I uttered a startled yip.

'Sir?' said Jeeves, pausing at the door.

I read the thing again. Yes, I had got the gist all right. No, I had not been deceived in the substance.

'Jeeves,' I said, 'do you know what?'

'No, sir.'

'You know my Cousin Angela?'

'Yes, sir.'

'You know young Tuppy Glossop?'

'Yes, sir.'

'They've broken off their engagement.'

'I am sorry to hear that, sir.'

'I have here a communication from Aunt Dahlia, specifically stating this. I wonder what the row was about.'

'I could not say, sir.'

'Of course you couldn't. Don't be an ass, Jeeves.'

'No, sir.'

I brooded. I was deeply moved.

'Well, this means that we shall have to go down to Brinkley today. Aunt Dahlia is obviously all of a twitter, and my place is by her side. You had better pack this morning, and catch that 12.45 train with the luggage. I have a lunch engagement, so will follow in the car.'

'Very good, sir.'

I brooded some more.

'I must say this has come as a great shock to me, Jeeves.'

'No doubt, sir.'

'A very great shock. Angela and Tuppy . . . Tut, tut! Why, they seemed like the paper on the wall. Life is full of sadness, Jeeves.'

'Yes, sir.'

'Still, there it is.'

'Undoubtedly, sir.'

'Right ho, then. Switch on the bath.'

'Very good, sir.'

7

I meditated pretty freely as I drove down to Brinkley in the old two-seater that afternoon. The news of this rift or rupture of Angela's and Tuppy's had disturbed me greatly.

The projected match, you see, was one on which I had always looked with kindly approval. Too often, when a chap of your acquaintance is planning to marry a girl you know, you find yourself knitting the brow a bit and chewing the lower lip dubiously, feeling that he or she, or both, should be warned while there is yet time.

But I have never felt anything of this nature about Tuppy and Angela. Tuppy, when not making an ass of himself, is a soundish sort of egg. So is Angela a soundish sort of egg. And, as far as being in love was concerned, it had always seemed to me that you wouldn't have been far out in describing them as two hearts that beat as one.

True, they had had their little tiffs, notably on the occasion when Tuppy—with what he said was fearless honesty and I considered thorough goofiness—had told Angela that her new hat made her look like a Pekingese. But in every romance you have to budget for the occasional dust-up, and after that incident I had supposed that he had learned his lesson and that from then on life would be one grand, sweet song.

And now this wholly unforeseen severing of diplomatic relations had popped up through a trap.

I gave the thing the cream of the Wooster brain all the way down, but it continued to beat me what could have caused the outbreak of hostilities, and I bunged my foot sedulously on the accelerator in order to get to Aunt Dahlia with the greatest possible speed and learn the inside history straight from the horse's mouth. And what with all six cylinders hitting nicely, I made good time and found myself closeted with the relative shortly before the hour of the evening cocktail.

She seemed glad to see me. In fact, she actually said she was glad to see me—a statement no other aunt on the list would have committed herself to, the customary reaction of these near and dear ones to the spectacle of Bertram arriving for a visit being a sort of sick horror.

'Decent of you to rally round, Bertie,' she said.

'My place was by your side, Aunt Dahlia,' I responded.

I could see at a g. that the unfortunate affair had got in amongst her in no uncertain manner. Her usually cheerful map was clouded, and the genial smile conspic. by its a. I pressed her hand sympathetically, to indicate that my heart bled for her.

'Bad show this, my dear old flesh and blood,' I said. 'I'm afraid you've been having a sticky time. You must be worried.'

She snorted emotionally. She looked like an aunt who has just bitten into a bad oyster.

'Worried is right. I haven't had a peaceful moment since I got back from Cannes. Ever since I put my foot across this blasted threshold,' said Aunt Dahlia, returning for the nonce to the hearty *argot* of the hunting field, 'everything's been at sixes and sevens. First there was that mix-up about the prize-giving.'

She paused at this point and gave me a look. 'I had been meaning to speak freely to you about your behaviour in that matter, Bertie,' she said. 'I had some good things all stored up. But, as you've rallied round like this, I suppose I shall have to let you off. And, anyway, it is probably all for the best that you evaded your obligations in that sickeningly craven way. I have an idea that this Spink-Bottle of yours is going to be good. If only he can keep off newts.'

'Has he been talking about newts?'

'He has. Fixing me with a glittering eye, like the Ancient Mariner. But if that was the worst I had to bear, I wouldn't mind. What I'm worrying about is what Tom is going to say when he starts talking.'

'Uncle Tom?'

'I wish there was something else you could call him except "Uncle

Tom",' said Aunt Dahlia a little testily. 'Every time you do it, I expect to see him turn black and start playing the banjo. Yes, Uncle Tom, if you must have it. I shall have to tell him soon about losing all that money at baccarat, and, when I do, he will go up like a rocket.'

'Still, no doubt Time, the great healer—'

'Time, the great healer, be blowed. I've got to get a cheque for five hundred pounds out of him for *Milady's Boudoir* by August the third at the latest.'

I was concerned. Apart from a nephew's natural interest in an aunt's refined weekly paper, I had always had a soft spot in my heart for *Milady's Boudoir* ever since I contributed that article to it on What The Well-Dressed Man Is Wearing. Sentimental, possibly, but we old journalists do have these feelings.

'Is the *Boudoir* on the rocks?'

'It will be if Tom doesn't cough up. It needs help till it has turned the corner.'

'But wasn't it turning the corner two years ago?'

'It was. And it's still at it. Till you've run a weekly paper for women, you don't know what corners are.'

'And you think the chances of getting into Uncle—into my uncle by marriage's ribs are slight?'

'I'll tell you, Bertie. Up till now, when these subsidies were required, I have always been able to come to Tom in the gay, confident spirit of an only child touching an indulgent father for chocolate cream. But he's just had a demand from the income-tax people for an additional fifty-eight pounds, one and threepence, and all he's been talking about since I got back has been ruin and the sinister trend of socialistic legislation and what will become of us all.'

I could readily believe it. This Tom has a peculiarity I've noticed in other very oofy men. Nick him for the paltriest sum, and he lets out a squawk you can hear at Land's End. He has the stuff in gobs, but he hates giving it up.

'If it wasn't for Anatole's cooking, I doubt if he would bother to carry on. Thank God for Anatole, I say.'

I bowed my head reverently.

'Good old Anatole,' I said.

'Amen,' said Aunt Dahlia.

Then the look of holy ecstasy, which is always the result of letting the mind dwell, however briefly, on Anatole's cooking, died out of her face.

'But don't let me wander from the subject,' she resumed. 'I was telling you of the way hell's foundations have been quivering since I got home. First the prize-giving, then Tom, and now, on top of everything else, this infernal quarrel between Angela and young Glossop.'

I nodded gravely.

'I was frightfully sorry to hear of that. Terrible shock. What was the row about?'

'Sharks.'

'Eh?'

'Sharks. Or, rather, one individual shark. The brute that went for the poor child when she was aquaplaning at Cannes. You remember Angela's shark?'

Certainly I remembered Angela's shark. A man of sensibility does not forget about a cousin nearly being chewed by monsters of the deep. The episode was still green in my memory.

In a nutshell, what had occurred was this: You know how you aquaplane. A motor-boat nips on ahead, trailing a rope. You stand on a board, holding the rope, and the boat tows you along. And every now and then you lose your grip on the rope and plunge into the sea and have to swim to your board again.

A silly process it has always seemed to me, though many find it diverting.

Well, on the occasion referred to, Angela had just regained her board after taking a toss, when a great beastly shark came along and cannoned into it, flinging her into the salty once more. It took her quite a bit of time to get on again and make the motor-boat chap realize what was up and haul her to safety, and during that interval you can readily picture her embarrassment.

According to Angela, the finny denizen kept snapping at her ankles virtually without cessation, so that by the time help arrived, she was feeling more like a salted almond at a public dinner than anything human. Very shaken the poor child had been, I recall, and had talked of nothing else for weeks.

'I remember the whole incident vividly,' I said. 'But how did that start the trouble?'

'She was telling him the story last night.'

'Well?'

'Her eyes shining and her little hands clasped in girlish excitement.'

'No doubt.'

'And instead of giving her the understanding and sympathy to which she was entitled, what do you think this blasted Glossop did? He sat listening like a lump of dough, as if she had been talking about the weather, and when she had finished, he took his cigarette-holder out of his mouth and said, "I expect it was only a floating log!"'

'He didn't!'

'He did. And when Angela described how the thing had jumped and snapped at her, he took his cigarette-holder out of his mouth again, and said, "Ah! Probably a flatfish. Quite harmless. No doubt it was just trying to play." Well, I mean! What would you have done if you had been Angela? She has pride, sensibility, all the natural feelings of a good woman. She told him he was an ass and a fool and an idiot, and didn't know what he was talking about.'

I must say I saw the girl's viewpoint. It's only about once in a lifetime that anything sensational ever happens to one, and when it does, you don't want people taking all the colour out of it. I remember at school having to read that stuff where that chap, Othello, tells the girl what a hell of a time he'd been having among the cannibals and what not. Well, imagine his feelings if, after he had described some particularly sticky passage with a cannibal chief and was waiting for the awe-struck 'Oh-h! Not really?' she had said that the whole thing had no doubt been greatly exaggerated and that the man had probably really been a prominent local vegetarian.

Yes, I saw Angela's point of view.

'But don't tell me that when he saw how shirty she was about it, the chump didn't back down?'

'He didn't. He argued. And one thing led to another until, by easy stages, they had arrived at the point where she was saying that she didn't know if he was aware of it, but if he didn't knock off starchy foods and do exercises every morning, he would be getting as fat as a pig, and he was talking about this modern habit of girls putting make-up on their faces, of which he had always disapproved. This continued for a while, and then there was a loud pop and the air was full of mangled fragments of their engagement. I'm distracted about it. Thank goodness you've come, Bertie.'

'Nothing could have kept me away,' I replied, touched. 'I felt you needed me.'

'Yes.'

'Quite.'

'Or, rather,' she said, 'not you, of course, but Jeeves. The minute all this happened, I thought of him. The situation obviously cries out for Jeeves. If ever in the whole history of human affairs there was a moment when that lofty brain was required about the home, this is it.'

I think, if I had been standing up, I would have staggered. In fact, I'm pretty sure I would. But it isn't so dashed easy to stagger when you're sitting in an arm-chair. Only my face, therefore, showed how deeply I had been stung by these words.

Until she spoke them, I had been all sweetness and light—the sympathetic nephew prepared to strain every nerve to do his bit. I now froze, and the face became hard and set.

'Jeeves!' I said, between clenched teeth.

'Oom beroofen,' said Aunt Dahlia.

I saw that she had got the wrong angle.

'I was not sneezing. I was saying "Jeeves!"'

'And well you may. What a man! I'm going to put the whole thing up to him. There's nobody like Jeeves.'

My frigidity became more marked.

'I venture to take issue with you, Aunt Dahlia.'

'You take what?'

'Issue.'

'You do, do you?'

'I emphatically do. Jeeves is hopeless.'

'What?'

'Quite hopeless. He has lost his grip completely. Only a couple of days ago I was compelled to take him off a case because his handling of it was so footling. And, anyway, I resent this assumption, if assumption is the word I want, that Jeeves is the only fellow with brain. I object to the way everybody puts things up to him without consulting me and letting me have a stab at them first.'

She seemed about to speak, but I checked her with a gesture.

'It is true that in the past I have sometimes seen fit to seek Jeeves's advice. It is possible that in the future I may seek it again. But I claim the right to have a pop at these problems, as they arise, in person, without having everybody behave as if Jeeves was the only onion in the hash. I sometimes feel that Jeeves, though admittedly not unsuccessful in the past, has been lucky rather than gifted.'

'Have you and Jeeves had a row?'

'Nothing of the kind.'

'You seem to have it in for him.'

'Not at all.'

And yet I must admit that there was a modicum of truth in what she said. I had been feeling pretty austere about the man all day, and I'll tell you why.

You remember that he caught that 12.45 train with the luggage, while I remained on in order to keep a luncheon engagement. Well, just before I started out to the tryst, I was pottering about the flat, and suddenly—I don't know what put the suspicion into my head, possibly the fellow's manner had been furtive—something seemed to whisper to me to go and have a look in the wardrobe.

And it was as I had suspected. There was the mess jacket still on its hanger. The hound hadn't packed it.

Well, as anybody at the Drones will tell you, Bertram Wooster is a pretty hard chap to outgeneral. I shoved the thing in a brown-paper parcel and put it in the back of the car, and it was on a chair in the hall now. But that didn't alter the fact that Jeeves had attempted to do the dirty on me, and I suppose a certain what-d'you-call-it had crept into my manner during the above remarks.

'There has been no breach,' I said. 'You might describe it as a passing coolness, but no more. We did not happen to see eye to eye with regard to my white mess jacket with the brass buttons and I was compelled to assert my personality. But—'

'Well, it doesn't matter, anyway. The thing that matters is that you are talking piffle, you poor fish. Jeeves lost his grip? Absurd. Why, I saw him for a moment when he arrived, and his eyes were absolutely glittering with intelligence. I said to myself "Trust Jeeves", and I intend to.'

'You would be far better advised to let me see what I can accomplish, Aunt Dahlia.'

'For heaven's sake, don't you start butting in. You'll only make matters worse.'

'On the contrary, it may interest you to know that while driving here I concentrated deeply on this trouble of Angela's and was successful in formulating a plan, based on the psychology of the individual, which I am proposing to put into effect at an early moment.'

'Oh, my God!'

'My knowledge of human nature tells me it will work.'

'Bertie,' said Aunt Dahlia, and her manner struck me as febrile, 'lay off, lay off! For pity's sake, lay off. I know these plans of yours. I suppose you want to shove Angela into the lake and push young Glossop in after her to save her life, or something like that.'

'Nothing of the kind.'

'It's the sort of thing you would do.'

'My scheme is far more subtle. Let me outline it for you.'

'No, thanks.'

'I say to myself—'

'But not to me.'

'Do listen for a second.'

'I won't.'

'Right ho, then. I am dumb.'

'And have been from a child.'

I perceived that little good could result from continuing the discussion. I waved a hand and shrugged a shoulder.

'Very well, Aunt Dahlia,' I said, with dignity, 'if you don't want to be in on the ground floor, that is your affair. But you are missing an intellectual treat. And, anyway, no matter how much you may behave like the deaf adder of Scripture which, as you are doubtless aware, the more one piped, the less it danced, or words to that effect, I shall carry on as planned. I am extremely fond of Angela, and I shall spare no effort to bring the sunshine back into her heart.'

'Bertie, you abysmal chump, I appeal to you once more. Will you please lay off? You'll only make things ten times as bad as they are already.'

I remember reading in one of those historical novels once about a chap—a buck he would have been, no doubt, or a macaroni or some such bird as that—who, when people said the wrong thing, merely laughed down from lazy eyelids and flicked a speck of dust from the irreproachable Mechlin lace at his wrists. This was practically what I did now. At least, I straightened my tie and smiled one of those inscrutable smiles of mine. I then withdrew and went out for a saunter in the garden.

And the first chap I ran into was young Tuppy. His brow was furrowed, and he was moodily bunging stones at a flowerpot.

8

I think I have told you before about young Tuppy Glossop. He was the fellow, if you remember, who, callously ignoring the fact that we had been friends since boyhood, betted me one night at the Drones that I couldn't swing myself across the swimming bath by the rings—a childish feat for one of my lissomness—and then, having seen me well on the way, looped back the last ring, thus rendering it necessary for me to drop into the deep end in formal evening costume.

To say that I had not resented this foul deed, which seemed to me deserving of the title of the crime of the century, would be paltering with the truth. I had resented it profoundly, chafing not a little at the time and continuing to chafe for some weeks.

But you know how it is with these things. The wound heals. The agony abates.

I am not saying, mind you, that had the opportunity presented itself of dropping a wet sponge on Tuppy from some high spot or of putting an eel in his bed or finding some other form of self-expression of a like nature, I would not have embraced it eagerly; but that let me out. I mean to say, grievously injured though I had been, it gave me no pleasure to feel that the fellow's bally life was being ruined by the loss of a girl whom, despite all that had passed, I was convinced he still loved like the dickens.

On the contrary, I was heart and soul in favour of healing the breach and rendering everything hotsy-totsy once more between these two young sundered blighters. You will have gleaned that from my remarks to Aunt

Dahlia, and if you had been present at this moment and had seen the kindly commiserating look I gave Tuppy, you would have gleaned it still more.

It was one of those searching, melting looks, and was accompanied by the hearty clasp of the right hand and the gentle laying of the left on the collar-bone.

'Well, Tuppy, old chap,' I said. 'How are you, old man?'

My commiseration deepened as I spoke the words, for there had been no lighting up of the eye, no answering pressure of the palm, no sign whatever, in short, of any disposition on his part to do spring dances at the sight of an old friend. The man seemed sand-bagged.

Melancholy, as I remember Jeeves saying once about Pongo Twistleton when he was trying to knock off smoking, had marked him for her own. Not that I was surprised, of course. In the circs, no doubt, a certain moodiness was only natural.

I released the hand, ceased to knead the shoulder, and, producing the old case, offered him a cigarette.

He took it dully.

'Are you here, Bertie?' he asked.

'Yes, I'm here.'

'Just passing through, or come to stay?'

I thought for a moment. I might have told him that I had arrived at Brinkley Court with the express intention of bringing Angela and himself together once more, of knitting up the severed threads, and so on and so forth; and for perhaps half the time required for the lighting of a gasper I had almost decided to do so. Then, I reflected, better, on the whole, perhaps not. To broadcast the fact that I proposed to take him and Angela and play on them as on a couple of stringed instruments might have been injudicious. Chaps don't always like being played on as on a stringed instrument.

'It all depends,' I said. 'I may remain. I may push on. My plans are uncertain.'

He nodded listlessly, rather in the manner of a man who did not give a damn what I did, and stood gazing out over the sunlit garden. In build and appearance, Tuppy somewhat resembles a bulldog, and his aspect now was that of one of these fine animals who has just been refused a slice of cake.

It was not difficult for a man of my discernment to read what was in his mind, and it occasioned me no surprise, therefore, when his next words had to do with the subject marked with a cross on the agenda paper.

'You've heard of this business of mine, I suppose? Me and Angela?'

'I have, indeed, Tuppy, old man.'

'We've bust up.'

'I know. Some little friction, I gather, *in re* Angela's shark.'

'Yes. I said it must have been a flatfish.'

'So my informant told me.'

'Who did you hear it from?'

'Aunt Dahlia.'

'I suppose she cursed me properly?'

'Oh, no. Beyond referring to you in one passage as "this blasted Glossop", she was, I thought, singularly temperate in her language for a woman who at one time hunted regularly with the Quorn. All the same, I could see, if you don't mind me saying so, old man, that she felt you might have behaved with a little more tact.'

'Tact!'

'And I must admit I rather agreed with her. Was it nice, Tuppy, was it quite kind to take the bloom off Angela's shark like that? You must remember that Angela's shark is very dear to her. Could you not see what a sock on the jaw it would be for the poor child to hear it described by the man to whom she had given her heart as a flatfish?'

I saw that he was struggling with some powerful emotion.

'And what about my side of the thing?' he demanded, in a voice choked with feeling.

'Your side?'

'You don't suppose,' said Tuppy, with rising vehemence, 'that I would have exposed this dashed synthetic shark for the flatfish it undoubtedly was if there had not been causes that led up to it? What induced me to speak as I did was the fact that Angela, the little squirt, had just been most offensive, and I seized the opportunity to get a bit of my own back.'

'Offensive?'

'Exceedingly offensive. Purely on the strength of my having let fall some casual remark—simply by way of saying something and keeping the conversation going—to the effect that I wondered what Anatole was going to give us for dinner, she said that I was too material and ought not always to be thinking of food. Material, my elbow! As a matter of fact, I'm particularly spiritual.'

'Quite.'

'I don't see any harm in wondering what Anatole was going to give us for dinner. Do you?'

'Of course not. A mere ordinary tribute of respect to a great artist.'

'Exactly.'

'All the same—'

'Well?'

'I was only going to say that it seems a pity that the frail craft of love should come a stinker like this when a few manly words of contrition—'

He stared at me.

'You aren't suggesting that I should climb down?'

'It would be the fine, big thing, old egg.'

'I wouldn't dream of climbing down.'

'But, Tuppy—'

'No. I wouldn't do it.'

'But you love her, don't you?'

This touched the spot. He quivered noticeably, and his mouth twisted. Quite the tortured soul.

'I'm not saying I don't love the little blighter,' he said, obviously moved. 'I love her passionately. But that doesn't alter the fact that I consider that what she needs most in this world is a swift kick in the pants.'

A Wooster could scarcely pass this.

'Tuppy, old man!'

'It's no good saying "Tuppy, old man".'

'Well, I do say "Tuppy, old man". Your tone shocks me. One raises the eyebrows. Where is the fine, old, chivalrous spirit of the Glossops?'

'That's all right about the fine, old, chivalrous spirit of the Glossops. Where is the sweet, gentle, womanly spirit of the Angelas? Telling a fellow he was getting a double chin!'

'Did she do that?'

'She did.'

'Oh, well, girls will be girls. Forget it, Tuppy. Go to her and make it up.'

He shook his head.

'No. It is too late. Remarks have been passed about my tummy which it is impossible to overlook.'

'But, Tummy—Tuppy, I mean—be fair. You once told her her new hat made her look like a Pekingese.'

'It did make her look like a Pekingese. That was not vulgar abuse. It was sound, constructive criticism, with no motive behind it but the kindly desire to keep her from making an exhibition of herself in public. Wantonly to accuse a man of puffing when he goes up a flight of stairs is something very different.'

I began to see that the situation would require all my address and ingenuity. If the wedding bells were ever to ring out in the little church of Market Snodsbury, Bertram had plainly got to put in some shrewdish work. I had gathered, during my conversation with Aunt Dahlia, that there had been a certain amount of frank speech between the two contracting parties, but I had not realized till now that matters had gone so far.

The pathos of the thing gave me the pip. Tuppy had admitted in so many words that love still animated the Glossop bosom, and I was convinced that, even after all that occurred, Angela had not ceased to love him. At the moment, no doubt, she might be wishing that she could hit him with a bottle, but deep down in her I was prepared to bet that there still lingered all the old affection and tenderness. Only injured pride was keeping these two apart, and I felt that if Tuppy would make the first move, all would be well.

I had another whack at it.

'She's broken-hearted about this rift, Tuppy.'

'How do you know? Have you seen her?'

'No, but I'll bet she is.'

'She doesn't look it.'

'Wearing the mask, no doubt. Jeeves does that when I assert my authority.'

'She wrinkles her nose at me as if I were a drain that had got out of order.'

'Merely the mask. I feel convinced she loves you still, and that a kindly word from you is all that is required.'

I could see that this had moved him. He plainly wavered. He did a sort of twiddly on the turf with his foot. And, when he spoke, one spotted the tremolo in the voice:

'You really think that?'

'Absolutely.'

'H'm.'

'If you were to go to her—'

He shook his head.

'I can't do that. It would be fatal. Bing, instantly, would go my prestige. I know girls. Grovel, and the best of them get uppish.' He mused. 'The only way to work the thing would be by tipping her off in some indirect way that I am prepared to open negotiations. Should I sigh a bit when we meet, do you think?'

'She would think you were puffing.'

'That's true.'

I lit another cigarette and gave my mind to the matter. And first crack out of the box, as is so often the way with the Woosters, I got an idea. I remembered the counsel I had given Gussie in the matter of the sausages and ham.

'I've got it, Tuppy. There is one infallible method of indicating to a girl that you love her, and it works just as well when you've had a row and want to make it up. Don't eat any dinner tonight. You can see how impressive that would be. She knows how devoted you are to food.'

He started violently.

'I am not devoted to food!'

'No, no.'

'I am not devoted to food at all.'

'Quite. All I meant—'

'This rot about me being devoted to food,' said Tuppy warmly, 'has got to stop. I am young and healthy and have a good appetite, but that's not the same as being devoted to food. I admire Anatole as a master of his craft, and am always willing to consider anything he may put before me, but when you say I am devoted to food—'

'Quite, quite. All I meant was that if she sees you push away your dinner untasted, she will realize that your heart is aching, and will probably be the first to suggest blowing the all clear.'

Tuppy was frowning thoughtfully.

'Push my dinner away, eh?'

'Yes.'

'Push away a dinner cooked by Anatole?'

'Yes.'

'Push it away untasted?'

'Yes.'

'Let us get this straight. Tonight, at dinner, when the butler offers me a *ris de veau à la financière* or whatever it may be, hot from Anatole's hands, you wish me to push it away untasted?'

'Yes.'

He chewed his lip. One could sense the struggle going on within. And then suddenly a sort of glow came into his face. The old martyrs probably used to look like that.

'All right.'

'You'll do it?'

'I will.'

'Fine.'

'Of course, it will be agony.'

I pointed out the silver lining.

'Only for the moment. You could slip down tonight, after everyone is in bed, and raid the larder.'

He brightened.

'That's right. I could, couldn't I?'

'I expect there would be something cold there.'

'There is something cold there,' said Tuppy, with growing cheerfulness. 'A steak-and-kidney pie. We had it for lunch today. One of Anatole's ripest. The thing I admire about that man,' said Tuppy reverently, 'the thing I admire so enormously about Anatole is that, though a Frenchman, he does not, like so many of these *chefs*, confine himself exclusively to French dishes, but is always willing and ready to weigh in with some good old simple English fare such as this steak-and-kidney pie to which I have alluded. A masterly pie, Bertie, and it wasn't more than half finished. It will do me nicely.'

'And at dinner you will push, as arranged?'

'Absolutely as arranged.'

'Fine.'

'It's an excellent idea. One of Jeeves's best. You can tell him from me, when you see him, that I'm much obliged.'

The cigarette fell from my fingers. It was as though somebody had slapped Bertram Wooster across the face with a wet dish-rag.

'You aren't suggesting that you think this scheme I have been sketching out is Jeeves's?'

'Of course it is. It's no good trying to kid me, Bertie. You wouldn't have thought of a wheeze like that in a million years.'

There was a pause. I drew myself up to my full height; then, seeing that he wasn't looking at me, lowered myself again.

'Come, Glossop,' I said coldly, 'we had better be going. It is time we were dressing for dinner.'

9

Tuppy's fat-headed words were still rankling in my bosom as I went up to my room. They continued rankling as I shed the form-fitting, and had not ceased to rankle when, clad in the old dressing-gown, I made my way along the corridor to the *salle de bain*.

It is not too much to say that I was piqued to the tonsils.

I mean to say, one does not court praise. The adulation of the multitude means very little to one. But, all the same, when one has taken the trouble to whack out a highly juicy scheme to benefit an in-the-soup friend in his hour of travail, it's pretty foul to find him giving the credit to one's personal attendant, particularly if that personal attendant is a man who goes about the place not packing mess jackets.

But after I had been splashing about in the porcelain for a bit, composure began to return. I have always found that in moments of heart-bowed-downness there is nothing that calms the bruised spirit like a good go at the soap and water. I don't say I actually sang in the tub, but there were times when it was a mere spin of the coin whether I would do so or not.

The spiritual anguish induced by that tactless speech had become noticeably lessened.

The discovery of a toy duck in the soap dish, presumably the property of some former juvenile visitor, contributed not a little to this new and happier frame of mind. What with one thing and another, I hadn't played with toy ducks in my bath for years, and I found the novel experience most invigorating. For the benefit of those interested, I may mention that if you shove the thing under the surface with the sponge and then let go, it shoots out of the water in a manner calculated to divert the most careworn. Ten minutes of this and I was enabled to return to the bedchamber much more the old merry Bertram.

Jeeves was there, laying out the dinner disguise. He greeted the young master with his customary suavity.

'Good evening, sir.'

I responded in the same affable key.

'Good evening, Jeeves.'

'I trust you had a pleasant drive, sir.'

'Very pleasant, thank you, Jeeves. Hand me a sock or two, will you?'

He did so, and I commenced to don.

'Well, Jeeves,' I said, reaching for the under-linen, 'here we are again at Brinkley Court in the country of Worcestershire.'

'Yes, sir.'

'A nice mess things seem to have gone and got themselves into in this rustic joint.'

'Yes, sir.'

'The rift between Tuppy Glossop and my cousin Angela would appear to be serious.'

'Yes, sir. Opinion in the servants' hall is inclined to take a grave view of the situation.'

'And the thought that springs to your mind, no doubt, is that I shall have my work cut out to fix things up?'

'Yes, sir.'

'You are wrong, Jeeves. I have the thing well in hand.'

'You surprise me, sir.'

'I thought I should. Yes, Jeeves, I pondered on the matter most of the way down here, and with the happiest results. I have just been in conference with Mr Glossop, and everything is taped out.'

'Indeed, sir? Might I inquire—'

'You know my methods, Jeeves. Apply them. Have you,' I asked, slipping into the shirt and starting to adjust the cravat, 'been gnawing on the thing at all?'

'Oh, yes, sir. I have always been much attached to Miss Angela, and I felt that it would afford me great pleasure were I to be able to be of service to her.'

'A laudable sentiment. But I suppose you drew blank?'

'No, sir. I was rewarded with an idea.'

'What was it?'

'It occurred to me that a reconciliation might be effected between Mr Glossop and Miss Angela by appealing to that instinct which prompts gentlemen in time of peril to hasten to the rescue of—'

I had to let go of the cravat in order to raise a hand. I was shocked.

'Don't tell me you were contemplating descending to that old he-saved-her-from-drowning gag? I am surprised, Jeeves. Surprised and pained. When I was discussing the matter with Aunt Dahlia on my arrival, she said in a sniffy sort of way that she supposed I was going to shove my Cousin Angela into the lake and push Tuppy in to haul her out, and I let her see pretty clearly that I considered the suggestion an insult to my intelligence. And now, if your words have the meaning I read into them, you are mooting precisely the same drivelling scheme. Really, Jeeves!'

'No, sir. Not that. But the thought did cross my mind, as I walked in the grounds and passed the building where the fire-bell hangs, that a sudden alarm of fire in the night might result in Mr Glossop endeavouring to assist Miss Angela to safety.'

I shivered.

'Rotten, Jeeves.'

'Well, sir—'

'No good. Not a bit like it.'

'I fancy, sir—'

'No, Jeeves. No more. Enough has been said. Let us drop the subj.'

I finished tying the tie in silence. My emotions were too deep for speech. I knew, of course, that this man had for the time being lost his grip, but I had never suspected that he had gone absolutely to pieces like this. Remembering some of the swift ones he had pulled in the past, I shrank with horror from the spectacle of his present ineptitude. Or is it ineptness? I mean this frightful disposition of his to stick straws in his hair and talk like a perfect ass. It was the old, old story, I supposed. A man's brain whizzes along for years exceeding the speed limit, and then something suddenly goes wrong with the steering-gear and it skids and comes a smeller in the ditch.

'A bit elaborate,' I said, trying to put the thing in as kindly a light as possible. 'Your old failing. You can see that it's a bit elaborate?'

'Possibly the plan I suggested might be considered open to that criticism, sir, but *faute de mieux*—'

'I don't get you, Jeeves.'

'A French expression, sir, signifying "for want of anything better".'

A moment before, I had been feeling for this wreck of a once fine thinker nothing but a gentle pity. These words jarred the Wooster pride, inducing asperity.

'I understand perfectly well what *faute de mieux* means, Jeeves. I did not recently spend two months among our Gallic neighbours for nothing. Besides, I remember that one from school. What caused my bewilderment was that you should be employing the expression, well knowing that there is no bally *faute de mieux* about it at all. Where do you get that *faute-de-mieux* stuff? Didn't I tell you I had everything taped out?'

'Yes, sir, but—'

'What do you mean—but?'

'Well, sir—'

'Push on, Jeeves. I am ready, even anxious, to hear your views.'

'Well, sir, if I may take the liberty of reminding you of it, your plans in the past have not always been uniformly successful.'

There was a silence—rather a throbbing one—during which I put on my waistcoat in a marked manner. Not till I had got the buckle at the back satisfactorily adjusted did I speak.

'It is true, Jeeves,' I said formally, 'that once or twice in the past I may have missed the bus. This, however, I attribute purely to bad luck.'

'Indeed, sir?'

'On the present occasion I shall not fail, and I'll tell you why I shall not fail. Because my scheme is rooted in human nature.'

'Indeed, sir?'

'It is simple. Not elaborate. And, furthermore, based on the psychology of the individual.'

'Indeed, sir?'

'Jeeves,' I said, 'don't keep saying "Indeed, sir?" No doubt nothing is further from your mind than to convey such a suggestion, but you have a way of stressing the "in" and then coming down with a thud on the "deed" which makes it virtually tantamount to "Oh, yeah?" Correct this, Jeeves.'

'Very good, sir.'

'I tell you I have everything nicely lined up. Would you care to hear what steps I have taken?'

'Very much, sir.'

'Then listen. Tonight at dinner I have recommended Tuppy to lay off the food.'

'Sir?'

'Tut, Jeeves, surely you can follow the idea, even though it is one that would never have occurred to yourself. Have you forgotten that telegram I sent to Gussie Fink-Nottle, steering him away from the sausages and ham? This is the same thing. Pushing the food away untasted is a universally recognized sign of love. It cannot fail to bring home the gravy. You must see that?'

'Well, sir—'

I frowned.

'I don't want to seem always to be criticizing your methods of voice production, Jeeves,' I said, 'but I must inform you that that "Well, sir" of yours is in many respects fully as unpleasant as your "Indeed, sir?" Like the latter, it seems to be tinged with a definite scepticism. It suggests a lack of faith in my vision. The impression I retain after hearing you shoot it at me a couple of times is that you consider me to be talking through the back of my neck, and that only a feudal sense of what is fitting restrains you from substituting for it the words "Says you!"'

'Oh, no, sir.'

'Well, that's what it sounds like. Why don't you think this scheme will work?'

'I fear Miss Angela will merely attribute Mr Glossop's abstinence to indigestion, sir.'

I hadn't thought of that, and I must confess it shook me for a moment. Then I recovered myself. I saw what was at the bottom of all this. Mortified by the consciousness of his own ineptness—or ineptitude—the fellow was simply trying to hamper and obstruct. I decided to knock the stuffing out of him without further preamble.

'Oh?' I said. 'You do, do you? Well, be that as it may, it doesn't alter the fact that you've put out the wrong coat. Be so good, Jeeves,' I said, indicating with a gesture the gent's ordinary dinner jacket, or *smoking*, as we call it on the Côte d'Azur, which was suspended from the hanger on the knob of the wardrobe, 'as to shove that bally black thing in the cupboard and bring out my white mess jacket with the brass buttons.'

He looked at me in a meaning manner. And when I say a meaning manner, I mean there was a respectful but at the same time uppish glint in his eye and a sort of muscular spasm flickered across his face which wasn't quite a quiet smile and yet wasn't quite not a quiet smile. Also the soft cough.

'I regret to say, sir, that I inadvertently omitted to pack the garment to which you refer.'

The vision of that parcel in the hall seemed to rise before my eyes, and I exchanged a merry wink with it. I may even have hummed a bar or two. I'm not quite sure.

'I know you did, Jeeves,' I said, laughing down from lazy eyelids and flicking a speck of dust from the irreproachable Mechlin lace at my wrists. 'But I didn't. You will find it on a chair in the hall in a brown-paper parcel.'

The information that his low manoeuvres had been rendered null and void and that the thing was on the strength after all, must have been the nastiest of jars, but there was no play of expression on his finely chiselled to indicate it. There very seldom is on Jeeves's f-c. In moments of discomfort, as I had told Tuppy, he wears a mask, preserving throughout the quiet stolidity of a stuffed moose.

'You might just slide down and fetch it, will you?'

'Very good, sir.'

'Right ho, Jeeves.'

And presently I was sauntering towards the drawing-room with the good old j. nestling snugly abaft the shoulder blades.

Aunt Dahlia was in the drawing-room. She glanced up at my entrance.

'Hullo, eyesore,' she said. 'What do you think you're made up as?'

I did not get the purport.

'The jacket, you mean?' I queried, groping.

'I do. You look like one of the chorus of male guests at Abernethy Towers in Act 2 of a touring musical comedy.'

'You do not admire this jacket?'

'I do not.'

'You did at Cannes.'

'Well, this isn't Cannes.'

'But, dash it—'

'Oh, never mind. Let it go. If you want to give my butler a laugh, what does it matter? What does anything matter now?'

There was a death-where-is-thy-sting-fulness about her manner which I found distasteful. It isn't often that I score off Jeeves in the devastating fashion just described, and when I do I like to see happy, smiling faces about me.

'Tails up, Aunt Dahlia,' I urged buoyantly.

'Tails up be dashed,' was her sombre response. 'I've just been talking to Tom.'

'Telling him?'

'No, listening to him. I haven't had the nerve to tell him yet.'

'Is he still upset about that income-tax money?'

'Upset is right. He says that Civilization is in the melting-pot and that all thinking men can read the writing on the wall.'

'What wall?'

'Old Testament, ass. Belshazzar's feast.'

'Oh, that, yes. I've often wondered how that gag was worked. With mirrors, I expect.'

'I wish I could use mirrors to break it to Tom about this baccarat business.'

I had a word of comfort to offer here. I had been turning the thing over in my mind since our last meeting, and I thought I saw where she had got twisted. Where she made her error, it seemed to me, was in feeling she had got to tell Uncle Tom. To my way of thinking, the matter was one on which it would be better to continue to exercise a quiet reserve.

'I don't see why you need mention that you lost that money at baccarat.'

'What do you suggest, then? Letting *Milady's Boudoir* join Civilization in the melting-pot. Because that is what it will infallibly do unless I get a cheque by next week. The printers have been showing a nasty spirit for months.'

'You don't follow. Listen. It's an understood thing, I take it, that Uncle Tom foots the *Boudoir* bills. If the bally sheet has been turning the corner for two years, he must have got used to forking out by this time. Well, simply ask him for the money to pay the printers.'

'I did. Just before I went to Cannes.'

'Wouldn't he give it to you?'

'Certainly he gave it to me. He brassed up like an officer and a gentleman. That was the money I lost at baccarat.'

'Oh? I didn't know that.'

'There isn't much you do know.'

A nephew's love made me overlook the slur.

'Tut!' I said.

'What did you say?'

'I said "Tut!"'

'Say it once again, and I'll biff you where you stand. I've enough to endure without being tutted at.'

'Quite.'

'Any tutting that's required, I'll attend to myself. And the same applies to clicking the tongue, if you were thinking of doing that.'

'Far from it.'

'Good.'

I stood awhile in thought. I was concerned to the core. My heart, if you remember, had already bled once for Aunt Dahlia this evening. It now bled again. I knew how deeply attached she was to this paper of hers. Seeing it go down the drain would be for her like watching a loved child sink for the third time in some pond or mere.

And there was no question that, unless carefully prepared for the touch, Uncle Tom would see a hundred *Milady's Boudoirs* go phut rather than take the rap.

Then I saw how the thing could be handled. This aunt, I perceived, must fall into line with my other clients. Tuppy Glossop was knocking off dinner to melt Angela. Gussie Fink-Nottle was knocking off dinner to impress the Bassett. Aunt Dahlia must knock off dinner to soften Uncle Tom. For the beauty of this scheme of mine was that there was no limit to the number of entrants. Come one, come all, the more the merrier, and satisfaction guaranteed in every case.

'I've got it,' I said. 'There is only one course to pursue. Eat less meat.'

She looked at me in a pleading sort of way. I wouldn't swear that her eyes were wet with unshed tears, but I rather think they were. Certainly she clasped her hands in piteous appeal.

'Must you drivel, Bertie? Won't you stop it just this once? Just for tonight, to please Aunt Dahlia.'

'I'm not drivelling.'

'I dare say that to a man of your high standards it doesn't come under the head of drivel, but—'

I saw what had happened. I hadn't made myself quite clear.

'It's all right,' I said. 'Have no misgivings. This is the real Tabasco. When I said "Eat less meat", what I meant was that you must refuse your oats at dinner tonight. Just sit there, looking blistered, and wave away each course as it comes with a weary gesture of resignation. You see what will happen. Uncle Tom will notice your loss of appetite, and I am prepared to bet that at the conclusion of the meal he will come to you and say "Dahlia, darling"—I take it he calls you "Dahlia"—"Dahlia, darling," he will say, "I noticed at dinner tonight that you were a bit off your feed. Is anything the matter, Dahlia, darling?" "Why, yes, Tom, darling," you will reply. "It is kind of you to ask, darling. The fact is, darling, I am terribly worried." "My darling," he will say—'

Aunt Dahlia interrupted at this point to observe that these Traverses seemed to be a pretty soppy couple of blighters, to judge by their dialogue. She also wished to know when I was going to get to the point.

I gave her a look.

'"My darling," he will say tenderly, "is there anything I can do?" To which your reply will be that there jolly well is—viz. reach for his cheque-book and start writing.'

I was watching her closely as I spoke, and was pleased to note respect suddenly dawn in her eyes.

'But, Bertie, this is positively bright.'

'I told you Jeeves wasn't the only fellow with brain.'

'I believe it would work.'

'It's bound to work. I've recommended it to Tuppy.'

'Young Glossop?'

'In order to soften Angela.'

'Splendid!'

'And to Gussie Fink-Nottle, who wants to make a hit with the Bassett.'

'Well, well, well! What a busy little brain it is.'

'Always working, Aunt Dahlia, always working.'

'You're not the chump I took you for, Bertie.'

'When did you ever take me for a chump?'

'Oh, some time last summer. I forget what gave me the idea. Yes, Bertie, this scheme is bright. I suppose, as a matter of fact, Jeeves suggested it?'

'Jeeves did not suggest it. I resent these implications. Jeeves had nothing to do with it whatsoever.'

'Well, all right, no need to get excited about it. Yes, I think it will work. Tom's devoted to me.'

'Who wouldn't be?'

'I'll do it.'

And then the rest of the party trickled in, and we toddled down to dinner.

Conditions being as they were at Brinkley Court—I mean to say, the place being loaded down above the Plimsoll mark with aching hearts and standing room only as regarded tortured souls—I hadn't expected the evening meal to be particularly effervescent. Nor was it. Silent. Sombre. The whole thing more than a bit like Christmas dinner on Devil's Island.

I was glad when it was over.

What with having, on top of her other troubles, to rein herself back from the trough, Aunt Dahlia was a total loss as far as anything in the shape of brilliant badinage was concerned. The fact that he was fifty quid in the red and expecting Civilization to take a toss at any moment had caused Uncle Tom, who always looked a bit like a pterodactyl with a secret sorrow, to take on a deeper melancholy. The Bassett was a silent bread crumbler. Angela might have been hewn from the living rock. Tuppy had the air of a condemned murderer refusing to make the usual hearty breakfast before tooling off to the execution shed.

And as for Gussie Fink-Nottle, many an experienced undertaker would have been deceived by his appearance and started embalming him on sight.

This was the first glimpse I had had of Gussie since we parted at my flat, and I must say his demeanour disappointed me. I had been expecting something a great deal more sparkling.

At my flat, on the occasion alluded to, he had, if you recall, practically given me a signed guarantee that all he needed to touch him off was a rural setting. Yet in his aspect now I could detect no indication whatsoever that he was about to round into mid-season form. He still looked like a cat in an adage, and it did not take me long to realize that my very first act on escaping from this morgue must be to draw him aside and give him a pep talk.

If ever a chap wanted the clarion note, it looked as if it was this Fink-Nottle.

In the general exodus of mourners, however, I lost sight of him, and, owing to the fact that Aunt Dahlia roped me in for a game of backgammon, it was not immediately that I was able to institute a search. But after we had been playing for a while, the butler came in and asked her if she would speak to Anatole, so I managed to get away. And some ten minutes later, having failed to find scent in the house I started to throw out the drag-net through the grounds, and flushed him in the rose garden.

He was smelling a rose at the moment in a limp sort of way, but removed the beak as I approached.

'Well, Gussie,' I said.

I had beamed genially upon him as I spoke, such being my customary policy on meeting an old pal; but instead of beaming back genially, he gave me a most unpleasant look. His attitude perplexed me. It was as if he were not glad to see Bertram. For a moment he stood letting this unpleasant look play upon me, as it were, and then he spoke.

'You and your "Well, Gussie"!'

He said this between clenched teeth, always an unmatey thing to do, and I found myself more fogged than ever.

'How do you mean—me and my "Well, Gussie"?'

'I like your nerve, coming bounding about the place, saying "Well, Gussie". That's about all the "Well, Gussie" I shall require from you, Wooster. And it's no good looking like that. You know what I mean. That damned prize-giving! It was a dastardly act to crawl out as you did and shove it off on to me. I will not mince my words. It was the act of a hound and a stinker.'

Now, though, as I have shown, I had devoted most of the time on the journey down to meditating upon the case of Angela and Tuppy, I had not neglected to give a thought or two to what I was going to say when I encountered Gussie. I had foreseen that there might be some little temporary unpleasantness when we met, and when a difficult interview is in the offing Bertram Wooster likes to have his story ready.

So now I was able to reply with a manly, disarming frankness. The sudden introduction of the topic had given me a bit of a jolt, it is true, for in the stress of recent happenings I had rather let that prize-giving business slide to the back of my mind; but I had speedily recovered and, as I say, was able to reply with a manly d.f.

'But, my dear chap,' I said, 'I took it for granted that you would understand that that was all part of my schemes.'

He said something about my schemes which I did not catch.

'Absolutely. "Crawling out" is entirely the wrong way to put it. You don't suppose I didn't want to distribute those prizes, do you? Left to myself, there is nothing I would find a greater treat. But I saw that the square, generous thing to do was to step aside and let you take it on, so I did so. I felt that your need was greater than mine. You don't mean to say you aren't looking forward to it?'

He uttered a coarse expression which I wouldn't have thought he would have known. It just shows that you can bury yourself in the country and still somehow acquire a vocabulary. No doubt one picks up things from the neighbours—the vicar, the local doctor, the man who brings the milk, and so on.

'But, dash it,' I said, 'can't you see what this is going to do for you? It will send your stock up with a jump. There you will be, up on that platform, a romantic, impressive figure, the star of the whole proceedings, the what-d'you-call-it of all eyes. Madeline Bassett will be all over you. She will see you in a totally new light.'

'She will, will she?'

'Certainly she will. Augustus Fink-Nottle, the newts' friend, she knows. She is acquainted with Augustus Fink-Nottle, the dogs' chiropodist. But

Augustus Fink-Nottle, the orator—that'll knock her sideways, or I know nothing of the female heart. Girls go potty over a public man. If ever anyone did anyone else a kindness, it was I when I gave this extraordinarily attractive assignment to you.'

He seemed impressed by my eloquence. Couldn't have helped himself, of course. The fire faded from behind his horn-rimmed spectacles, and in its place appeared the old fish-like goggle.

''Myes,' he said meditatively. 'Have you ever made a speech, Bertie?'

'Dozens of times. It's pie. Nothing to it. Why, I once addressed a girls' school.'

'You weren't nervous?'

'Not a bit.'

'How did you go?'

'They hung on my lips. I held them in the hollow of my hand.'

'They didn't throw eggs, or anything?'

'Not a thing.'

He expelled a deep breath, and for a space stood staring in silence at a passing slug.

'Well,' he said, at length, 'it may be all right. Possibly I am letting the thing prey on my mind too much. I may be wrong in supposing it the fate that is worse than death. But I'll tell you this much: the prospect of that prize-giving on the thirty-first of this month has been turning my existence into a nightmare. I haven't been able to sleep or think or eat . . . By the way, that reminds me. You never explained that cipher telegram of yours about the sausages and ham.'

'It wasn't a cipher telegram. I wanted you to go light on the food, so that she would realize you were in love.'

He laughed hollowly.

'I see. Well, I've been doing that, all right.'

'Yes, I was noticing at dinner. Splendid.'

'I don't see what's splendid about it. It's not going to get me anywhere. I shall never be able to ask her to marry me. I couldn't find the nerve to do that if I lived on wafer biscuits for the rest of my life.'

'But, dash it, Gussie. In these romantic surroundings. I should have thought the whispering trees alone—'

'I don't care what you would have thought. I can't do it.'

'Oh, come!'

'I can't. She seems so aloof, so remote.'

'She doesn't.'

'Yes, she does. Especially when you see her sideways. Have you seen her sideways, Bertie? That cold, pure profile. It just takes all the heart out of one.'

'It doesn't.'

'I tell you it does. I catch sight of it, and the words freeze on my lips.'

He spoke with a sort of dull despair, and so manifest was his lack of ginger and the spirit that wins to success that for an instant, I confess, I felt a bit stymied. It seemed hopeless to go on trying to steam up such a human jellyfish. Then I saw the way. With that extraordinary quickness of mine, I realized exactly what must be done if this Fink-Nottle was to be enabled to push his nose past the judges' box.

'She must be softened up,' I said.

'Be what?'

'Softened up. Sweetened. Worked on. Preliminary spadework must be put in. Here, Gussie, is the procedure I propose to adopt: I shall now return to the house and lug this Bassett out for a stroll. I shall talk to her of hearts that yearn, intimating that there is one actually on the premises. I shall pitch in strong, sparing no effort. You, meanwhile, will lurk on the outskirts, and in about a quarter of an hour you will come along and carry on from there. By that time, her emotions having been stirred, you ought to be able to do the rest on your head. It will be like leaping on to a moving bus.'

I remember when I was a kid at school having to learn a poem of sorts about a fellow named Pig-something—a sculptor he would have been, no doubt—who made a statue of a girl, and what should happen one morning but that the bally thing suddenly came to life. A pretty nasty shock for the chap, of course, but the point I'm working round to is that there were a couple of lines that went, if I remember correctly:

She starts. She moves. She seems to feel
The stir of life along her keel.

And what I'm driving at is that you couldn't get a better description of what happened to Gussie as I spoke these heartening words. His brow cleared, his eyes brightened, he lost that fishy look, and he gazed at the slug, which was still on the long, long trail, with something approaching bonhomie. A marked improvement.

'I see what you mean. You will sort of pave the way, as it were.'

'That's right. Spadework.'

'It's a terrific idea, Bertie. It will make all the difference.'

'Quite. But don't forget that after that it will be up to you. You will have to haul up your slacks and give her the old oil, or my efforts will have been in vain.'

Something of his former Gawd-help-us-ness seemed to return to him. He gasped a bit.

'That's true. What the dickens shall I say?'

I restrained my impatience with an effort. The man had been at school with me.

'Dash it, there are hundreds of things you can say. Talk about the sunset.'

'The sunset?'

'Certainly. Half the married men you meet began by talking about the sunset.'

'But what can I say about the sunset?'

'Well, Jeeves got off a good one the other day. I met him airing the dog in the park one evening, and he said, "Now fades the glimmering landscape on the sight, sir, and all the air a solemn stillness holds." You might use that.'

'What sort of landscape?'

'Glimmering. *G* for "gastritis", *l* for "lizard"—'

'Oh, glimmering? Yes, that's not bad. Glimmering landscape . . . solemn stillness . . . Yes, I call that pretty good.'

'You could then say that you have often thought that the stars are God's daisy-chain.'

'But I haven't.'

'I dare say not. But she has. Hand her that one, and I don't see how she can help feeling that you're a twin soul.'

'God's daisy-chain?'

'God's daisy-chain. And then you go on about how twilight always makes you sad. I know you're going to say it doesn't, but on this occasion it has jolly well got to.'

'Why?'

'That's just what she will ask, and you will then have got her going. Because you will reply that it is because yours is such a lonely life. It wouldn't be a bad idea to give her a brief description of a typical home evening at your Lincolnshire residence, showing how you pace the meadows with a heavy tread.'

'I generally sit indoors and listen to the wireless.'

'No, you don't. You pace the meadows with a heavy tread, wishing that you had someone to love you. And then you speak of the day when she came into your life.'

'Like a fairy princess.'

'Absolutely,' I said with approval. I hadn't expected such a hot one from such a quarter. 'Like a fairy princess. Nice work, Gussie.'

'And then?'

'Well, after that it's easy. You say you have something you want to say to her, and then you snap into it. I don't see how it can fail. If I were you, I should do it in this rose garden. It is well established that there is no sounder move than to steer the adored object into rose gardens in the gloaming. And you had better have a couple of quick ones first.'

'Quick ones?'

'Snifters.'

'Drinks, do you mean? But I don't drink.'

'What?'

'I've never touched a drop in my life.'

This made me a bit dubious, I must confess. On these occasions it is pretty generally conceded that a moderate skinful is of the essence.

However, if the facts were as he had stated, I supposed there was nothing to be done about it.

'Well, you'll have to make out as best you can on ginger pop.'

'I always drink orange juice.'

'Orange juice, then. Tell me, Gussie, to settle a bet, do you really like that muck?'

'Very much.'

'Then there is no more to be said. Now, let's just have a run through, to see that you've got the lay-out straight. Start off with the glimmering landscape.'

'Stars God's daisy-chain.'

'Twilight makes you feel sad.'

'Because mine lonely life.'

'Describe life.'

'Talk about the day I met her.'

'Add fairy-princess gag. Say there's something you want to say to her. Heave a couple of sighs. Grab her hand. And give her the works. Right.'

And confident that he had grasped the scenario and that everything might now be expected to proceed through the proper channels, I picked up the feet and hastened back to the house.

It was not until I had reached the drawing-room and was enabled to take a square look at the Bassett that I found the debonair gaiety with which I had embarked on this affair beginning to wane a trifle. Beholding her at close range like this, I suddenly became cognizant of what I was in for. The thought of strolling with this rummy specimen undeniably gave me a most unpleasant sinking feeling. I could not but remember how often, when in her company at Cannes, I had gazed dumbly at her, wishing that some kindly motorist in a racing car would ease the situation by coming along and ramming her amidships. As I have already made abundantly clear, this girl was not one of my most congenial buddies.

However, a Wooster's word is his bond. Woosters may quail, but they do not edge out. Only the keenest ear could have detected the tremor in the voice as I asked her if she would care to come out for half an hour.

'Lovely evening,' I said.

'Yes, lovely, isn't it?'

'Lovely. Reminds me of Cannes.'

'How lovely the evenings were there.'

'Lovely,' I said.

'Lovely,' said the Bassett.

'Lovely,' I agreed.

That completed the weather and news bulletin for the French Riviera. Another minute, and we were out in the great open spaces, she cooing a bit about the scenery, and self replying, 'Oh, rather, quite,' and wondering how best to approach the matter in hand.

10

How different it all would have been, I could not but reflect, if this girl had been the sort of girl one chirrups cheerily to over the telephone and takes for spins in the old two-seater. In that case, I would simply have said, 'Listen,' and she would have said, 'What?' and I would have said, 'You know Gussie Fink-Nottle,' and she would have said, 'Yes,' and I would have said, 'He loves you,' and she would have said either, 'What, that mutt? Well, thank heaven for one good laugh today!' or else, in more passionate vein, 'Hot dog! Tell me more.'

I mean to say, in either event the whole thing over and done with in under a minute.

But with the Bassett something less snappy and a good deal more glutinous was obviously indicated. What with all this daylight-saving stuff, we had hit the great open spaces at a moment when the twilight had not yet begun to cheese it in favour of the shades of night. There was a fag-end of sunset still functioning. Stars were beginning to peep out, bats were fooling round, the garden was full of the aroma of those niffy white flowers which only start to put in their heavy work at the end of the day—in short, the glimmering landscape was fading on the sight and all the air held a solemn stillness, and it was plain that this was having the worst effect on her. Her eyes were enlarged, and her whole map a good deal too suggestive of the soul's awakening for comfort.

Her aspect was that of a girl who was expecting something fairly fruity from Bertram.

In these circs, conversation inevitably flagged a bit. I am never at my best when the situation seems to call for a certain soupiness, and I've heard other members of the Drones say the same thing about themselves. I remember Pongo Twistleton telling me that he was out in a gondola with a girl by moonlight once, and the only time he spoke was to tell her that old story about the chap who was so good at swimming that they made him a traffic cop in Venice.

Fell rather flat, he assured me, and it wasn't much later when the girl said she thought it was getting a little chilly and how about pushing back to the hotel.

So now, as I say, the talk rather hung fire. It had been all very well for me to promise Gussie that I would cut loose to this girl about aching hearts, but you want a cue for that sort of thing. And when, toddling along, we reached the edge of the lake and she finally spoke, conceive my chagrin when I discovered that what she was talking about was stars.

Not a bit of good to me.

'Oh, look,' she said. She was a confirmed Oh-looker. I had noticed this at Cannes, where she had drawn my attention in this manner on various occasions to such diverse objects as a French actress, a Provençal filling station, the sunset over the Estorels, Michael Arlen, a man selling coloured spectacles, the deep velvet blue of the Mediterranean, and the late Mayor of New York in a striped one-piece bathing suit. 'Oh, look at that sweet little star up there all by itself.'

I saw the one she meant, a little chap operating in a detached sort of way above a spinney.

'Yes,' I said.

'I wonder if it feels lonely.'

'Oh, I shouldn't think so.'

'A fairy must have been crying.'

'Eh?'

'Don't you remember? "Every time a fairy sheds a tear, a wee bit star is born in the Milky Way." Have you ever thought that, Mr Wooster?'

I never had. Most improbable, I considered, and it didn't seem to me to check up with her statement that the stars were God's daisy-chain. I mean, you can't have it both ways.

However, I was in no mood to dissect and criticize. I saw that I had been wrong in supposing that the stars were not germane to the issue. Quite a decent cue they had provided, and I leaped on it promptly:

'Talking of shedding tears—'

But she was now on the subject of rabbits, several of which were messing about in the park to our right.

'Oh, look. The little bunnies!'

'Talking of shedding tears—'

'Don't you love this time of the evening, Mr Wooster, when the sun has gone to bed and all the bunnies come out to have their little suppers? When I was a child, I used to think that rabbits were gnomes, and that if I held my breath and stayed quite still, I should see the fairy queen.'

Indicating with a reserved gesture that this was just the sort of loony thing I should have expected her to think as a child, I returned to the point.

'Talking of shedding tears,' I said firmly, 'it may interest you to know that there is an aching heart in Brinkley Court.'

This held her. She cheesed the rabbit theme. Her face, which had been aglow with what I supposed was a pretty animation, clouded. She unshipped a sigh that sounded like the wind going out of a rubber duck.

'Ah, yes. Life is very sad, isn't it?'

'It is for some people. This aching heart, for instance.'

'Those wistful eyes of hers! Drenched irises. And they used to dance like elves of delight. And all through a foolish misunderstanding about a shark. What a tragedy misunderstandings are. That pretty romance broken and over just because Mr Glossop would insist that it was a flatfish.'

I saw that she had got the wires crossed.

'I'm not talking about Angela.'

'But her heart is aching.'

'I know it's aching. But so is somebody else's.'

She looked at me, perplexed.

'Somebody's else? Mr Glossop's, you mean?'

'No, I don't.'

'Mrs Travers's?'

The exquisite code of politeness of the Woosters prevented me clipping her one on the ear-hole, but I would have given a shilling to be able to do it. There seemed to me something deliberately fat-headed in the way she persisted in missing the gist.

'No, not Aunt Dahlia's, either.'

'I'm sure she is dreadfully upset.'

'Quite. But this heart I'm talking about isn't aching because of Tuppy's row with Angela. It's aching for a different reason altogether. I mean to say—dash it, you know why hearts ache!'

She seemed to shimmy a bit. Her voice, when she spoke, was whispery:

'You mean—for love?'

'Absolutely. Right on the bull's-eye. For love.'

'Oh, Mr Wooster!'

'I take it you believe in love at first sight?'

'I do, indeed.'

'Well, that's what happened to this aching heart. It fell in love at first sight, and ever since it's been eating itself out, as I believe the expression is.'

There was a silence. She had turned away and was watching a duck out on the lake. It was tucking into weeds, a thing I've never been able to understand anyone wanting to do. Though I suppose, if you face it squarely, they're no worse than spinach. She stood drinking it in for a bit, and then it suddenly stood on its head and disappeared, and this seemed to break the spell.

'Oh, Mr Wooster!' she said again, and from the tone of her voice, I could see that I had got her going.

'For you, I mean to say,' I proceeded, starting to put in the fancy touches. I dare say you have noticed on these occasions that the difficulty is to plant the main idea, to get the general outline of the thing well fixed. The rest is mere detail work. I don't say I became glib at this juncture, but I certainly became a dashed sight glibber than I had been.

'It's having the dickens of a time. Can't eat, can't sleep—all for love of you. And what makes it all so particularly rotten is that it—this aching heart—can't bring itself up to the scratch and tell you the position of affairs, because your profile has gone and given it cold feet. Just as it is about to speak, it catches sight of you sideways, and words fail it. Silly, of course, but there it is.'

I heard her give a gulp, and I saw that her eyes had become moistish. Drenched irises, if you care to put it that way.

'Lend you a handkerchief?'

'No, thank you. I'm quite all right.'

It was more than I could say for myself. My efforts had left me weak. I don't know if you suffer in the same way, but with me the act of talking anything in the nature of real mashed potatoes always induces a sort of prickly sensation and a hideous feeling of shame, together with a marked starting of the pores.

I remember at my Aunt Agatha's place in Hertfordshire once being put on the spot and forced to enact the role of King Edward III saying goodbye to that girl of his, Fair Rosamund, at some sort of pageant in aid of the Distressed Daughters of the Clergy. It involved some rather warmish medieval dialogue, I recall, racy of the days when they called a spade a spade, and by the time the whistle blew, I'll bet no Daughter of the Clergy was half as distressed as I was. Not a dry stitch.

My reaction now was very similar. It was a highly liquid Bertram who, hearing his *vis-à-vis* give a couple of hiccups and start to speak, bent an attentive ear.

'Please don't say any more, Mr Wooster.'

Well, I wasn't going to, of course.

'I understand.'

I was glad to hear this.

'Yes, I understand. I won't be so silly as to pretend not to know what you mean. I suspected this at Cannes, when you used to stand and stare at me without speaking a word, but with whole volumes in your eyes.'

If Angela's shark had bitten me in the leg, I couldn't have leaped more convulsively. So tensely had I been concentrating on Gussie's interests that it hadn't so much as crossed my mind that another and an unfortunate construction could be placed on those words of mine. The persp., already bedewing my brow, became a regular Niagara.

My whole fate hung upon a woman's word. I mean to say, I couldn't back out. If a girl thinks a man is proposing to her, and on that understanding books him up, he can't explain to her that she has got hold of entirely the wrong end of the stick and that he hadn't the smallest intention of suggesting anything of the kind. He must simply let it ride. And the thought of being engaged to a girl who talked openly about fairies being born because stars blew their noses, or whatever it was, frankly appalled me.

She was carrying on with her remarks, and as I listened I clenched my fists till I shouldn't wonder if the knuckles didn't stand out white under the strain. It seemed as if she would never get to the nub.

'Yes, all through those days at Cannes I could see what you were trying to say. A girl always knows. And then you followed me down here, and there was that same dumb, yearning look in your eyes when we met this evening. And then you were so insistent that I should come out and walk with you in the twilight. And now you stammer out those halting words. No, this does not come as a surprise. But I am sorry—'

The word was like one of Jeeves's pick-me-ups. Just as if a glassful of meat sauce, red pepper, and the yolk of an egg—though, as I say, I am convinced that these are not the sole ingredients—had been shot into me, I expanded like some lovely flower blossoming in the sunshine. It was all right, after all. My guardian angel had not been asleep at the switch.

'— but I am afraid it is impossible.'

She paused.

'Impossible,' she repeated.

I had been so busy feeling saved from the scaffold that I didn't get on to it for a moment that an early reply was desired.

'Oh, right ho,' I said hastily.

'I'm sorry.'

'Quite all right.'

'Sorrier than I can say.'

'Don't give it another thought.'

'We can still be friends.'

'Oh, rather.'

'Then shall we just say no more about it; keep what has happened as a tender little secret between ourselves?'

'Absolutely.'

'We will. Like something lovely and fragrant laid away in lavender.'

'In lavender—right.'

There was a longish pause. She was gazing at me in a divinely pitying sort of way, much as if I had been a snail she had happened accidentally to bring her short French vamp down on, and I longed to tell her that it was all right, and that Bertram, so far from being the victim of despair, had never felt fizzier in his life. But, of course, one can't do that sort of thing. I simply said nothing, and stood there looking brave.

'I wish I could,' she murmured.

'Could?' I said, for my attensh had been wandering.

'Feel towards you as you would like me to feel.'

'Oh, ah.'

'But I can't. I'm sorry.'

'Absolutely O.K. Faults on both sides, no doubt.'

'Because I am fond of you, Mr—no, I think I must call you Bertie. May I?'

'Oh, rather.'

'Because we are real friends.'

'Quite.'

'I do like you, Bertie. And if things were different—I wonder—'

'Eh?'

'After all, we are real friends . . . We have this common memory . . . You have a right to know . . . I don't want you to think—Life is such a muddle, isn't it?'

To many men, no doubt, these broken utterances would have appeared mere drooling and would have been dismissed as such. But the Woosters are quicker-witted than the ordinary and can read between the lines. I suddenly divined what it was that she was trying to get off the chest.

'You mean there's someone else?'

She nodded.

'You're in love with some other bloke?'

She nodded.

'Engaged, what?'

This time she shook the pumpkin.

'No, not engaged.'

Well, that was something, of course. Nevertheless, from the way she spoke, it certainly looked as if poor old Gussie might as well scratch his name off the entry list, and I didn't at all like the prospect of having to break the bad news to him. I had studied the man closely, and it was my conviction that this would about be his finish.

Gussie, you see, wasn't like some of my pals—the name of Bingo Little is one that springs to the lips—who, if turned down by a girl, would simply say, 'Well, bung-ho!' and toddle off quite happily to find another. He was so manifestly a bird who, having failed to score in the first chukker, would turn the thing up and spend the rest of his life brooding over his newts and growing long grey whiskers, like one of those chaps you read about in novels, who live in the great white house you can just see over there through the trees and shut themselves off from the world and have pained faces.

'I'm afraid he doesn't care for me in that way. At least, he has said nothing. You understand that I am only telling you this because—'

'Oh, rather.'

'It's odd that you should have asked me if I believed in love at first sight.' She half-closed her eyes. '"Who ever loved that loved not at first sight?"' she said in a rummy voice that brought back to me—I don't know why—the picture of my Aunt Agatha, as Boadicea, reciting at that pageant I was speaking of. 'It's a silly little story. I was staying with some friends in the country, and I had gone for a walk with my dog, and the poor wee mite got a nasty thorn in his little foot and I didn't know what to do. And then suddenly this man came along—'

Harking back once again to that pageant, in sketching out for you my emotions on that occasion, I showed you only the darker side of the picture. There was, I should now mention, a splendid aftermath when, having climbed out of my suit of chain mail and sneaked off to the local pub, I entered the saloon bar and requested mine host to start pouring. A moment later, a tankard of their special home-brewed was in my hand, and the ecstasy of that first gollup is still green in my memory. The recollection of the agony through which I had passed was just what was needed to make it perfect.

It was the same now. When I realized, listening to her words, that she must be referring to Gussie—I mean to say, there couldn't have been a whole platoon of men taking thorns out of her dog that day; the animal wasn't a pin-cushion—and became aware that Gussie, who an instant before had, to all appearances, gone so far back in the betting as not to be worth a quotation, was the big winner after all, a positive thrill permeated the frame and there escaped my lips a 'Wow!' so crisp and hearty that the Bassett leaped a liberal inch and a half from terra firma.

'I beg your pardon?' she said.

I waved a jaunty hand.

'Nothing,' I said. 'Nothing. Just remembered there's a letter I have to write tonight without fail. If you don't mind, I think I'll be going in. Here,' I said, 'comes Gussie Fink-Nottle. He will look after you.'

And, as I spoke, Gussie came sidling out from behind a tree.

I passed away and left them to it. As regards these two, everything was beyond a question absolutely in order. All Gussie had to do was keep his head down and not press. Already, I felt, as I legged it back to the house, the happy ending must have begun to function. I mean to say, when you leave a girl and a man, each of whom has admitted in set terms that she and he loves him and her, in close juxtaposition in the twilight, there doesn't seem much more to do but start pricing fish slices.

Something attempted, something done, seemed to me to have earned two-penn'orth of wassail in the smoking-room.

I proceeded thither.

11

The makings were neatly laid out on a side-table, and to pour into a glass an inch or so of the raw spirit and shoosh some soda-water on top of it was with me the work of a moment. This done, I retired to an arm-chair and put my feet up, sipping the mixture with carefree enjoyment, rather like Caesar having one in his tent the day he overcame the Nervii.

As I let the mind dwell on what must even now be taking place in that peaceful garden, I felt bucked and uplifted. Though never for an instant faltering in my opinion that Augustus Fink-Nottle was Nature's final word in cloth-headed guffins, I liked the man, wished him well, and could not have felt more deeply involved in the success of his wooing if I, and not he, had been the bloke under the ether.

The thought that by this time he might quite easily have completed the preliminary *pourparlers* and be deep in an informal discussion of honeymoon plans, was very pleasant to me.

Of course considering the sort of girl Madeline Bassett was—stars and rabbits and all that, I mean—you might say that a sober sadness would have been more fitting. But in these matters you have got to realize that tastes differ. The impulse of right-thinking men might be to run a mile when they saw the Bassett, but for some reason she appealed to the deeps in Gussie, so that was that.

I had reached this point in my meditations, when I was aroused by the sound of the door opening. Somebody came in and started moving like a leopard towards the side-table and, lowering the feet, I perceived that it was Tuppy Glossop.

The sight of him gave me a momentary twinge of remorse, reminding me, as it did, that in the excitement of getting Gussie fixed up I had rather forgotten about this other client. It is often that way when you're trying to run two cases at once.

However, Gussie now being off my mind, I was prepared to devote my whole attention to the Glossop problem.

I had been much pleased by the way he had carried out the task assigned him at the dinner-table. No easy one, I can assure you, for the browsing and sluicing had been of the highest quality, and there had been one dish in particular—I allude to the *nonnettes de poulet Agnès Sorel*—which might well have broken down the most iron resolution. But he had passed it up like a professional fasting man, and I was proud of him.

'Oh, hullo, Tuppy,' I said, 'I wanted to see you.'

He turned, snifter in hand, and it was easy to see that his privations had tried him sorely. He was looking like a wolf on the steppes of Russia which has seen its peasant shin up a high tree.

'Yes?' he said, rather unpleasantly. 'Well, here I am.'

'Well?'

'How do you mean—well?'

'Make your report.'

'What report?'

'Have you nothing to tell me about Angela?'

'Only that she's a blister.'

I was concerned.

'Hasn't she come clustering round you yet?'

'She has not.'

'Very odd.'

'Why odd?'

'She must have noted your lack of appetite.'

He barked raspingly, as if he were having trouble with the tonsils of the soul.

'Lack of appetite! I'm as hollow as the Grand Canyon.'

'Courage, Tuppy! Think of Gandhi.'

'What about Gandhi?'

'He hasn't had a square meal for years.'

'Nor have I. Or I could swear I hadn't. Gandhi, my left foot.'

I saw that it might be best to let the Gandhi *motif* slide. I went back to where we had started.

'She's probably looking for you now.'

'Who is? Angela?'

'Yes. She must have noticed your supreme sacrifice.'

'I don't suppose she noticed it at all, the little fat-head. I'll bet it didn't register in any way whatsoever.'

'Come, Tuppy,' I urged, 'this is morbid. Don't take this gloomy view. She must at least have spotted that you refused those *nonnettes de poulet Agnès Sorel*. It was a sensational renunciation and stuck out like a sore thumb. And the *cèpes à la Rossini*—'

A hoarse cry broke from his twisted lips:

'Will you stop it, Bertie! Do you think I am made of marble? Isn't it bad enough to have sat watching one of Anatole's supremest dinners flit by, course after course, without having you making a song about it? Don't remind me of those *nonnettes*. I can't stand it.'

I endeavoured to hearten and console.

'Be brave, Tuppy. Fix your thoughts on that cold steak-and-kidney pie in the larder. As the Good Book says, it cometh in the morning.'

'Yes, in the morning. And it's now about half past nine at night. You would bring that pie up, wouldn't you? Just when I was trying to keep my mind off it.'

I saw what he meant. Hours must pass before he could dig into that pie. I dropped the subject, and we sat for a pretty good time in silence. Then he rose and began to pace the room in an overwrought sort of way, like a zoo lion who has heard the dinner-gong go and is hoping the keeper won't forget him in the general distribution. I averted my gaze tactfully, but I could hear him kicking chairs and things. It was plain that the man's sould was in travail and his blood pressure high.

Presently he returned to his seat, and I saw that he was looking at me intently. There was that about his demeanour that led me to think that he had something to communicate.

Nor was I wrong. He tapped me significantly on the knee and spoke:

'Bertie.'

'Hullo?'

'Shall I tell you something?'

'Certainly, old bird,' I said cordially. 'I was just beginning to feel that the scene could do with a bit more dialogue.'

'This business of Angela and me.'

'Yes?'

'I've been putting in a lot of solid thinking about it.'

'Oh, yes?'

'I have analysed the situation pitilessly, and one thing stands out as clear as dammit. There has been dirty work afoot.'

'I don't get you.'

'All right. Let me review the facts. Up to the time she went to Cannes Angela loved me. She was all over me. I was the blue-eyed boy in every sense of the term. You'll admit that?'

'Indisputably.'

'And directly she came back we had this bust-up.'

'Quite.'

'About nothing.'

'Oh, dash it, old man, nothing? You were a bit tactless, what, about her shark.'

'I was frank and candid about her shark. And that's just my point. Do you seriously believe that a trifling disagreement about sharks would make a girl hand a man his hat, if her heart were really his?'

'Certainly.'

It beat me why he couldn't see it. But then poor old Tuppy has never been very hot on the finer shades. He's one of those large, tough, football-playing blokes who lack the more delicate sensibilities, as I've heard Jeeves call them. Excellent at blocking a punt or walking across an opponent's face in cleated boots, but not so good when it comes to understanding the highly-strung female temperament. It simply wouldn't occur to him that a girl might be prepared to give up her life's happiness rather than waive her shark.

'Rot! It was just a pretext.'

'What was?'

'This shark business. She wanted to get rid of me, and grabbed at the first excuse.'

'No, no.'

'I tell you she did.'

'But what on earth would she want to get rid of you for?'

'Exactly. That's the very question I asked myself. And here's the answer: because she has fallen in love with somebody else. It sticks out a mile. There's no other possible solution. She goes to Cannes all for me, she comes back all off me. Obviously, during those two months, she must have transferred her affections to some foul blister she met out there.'

'No, no.'

'Don't keep saying "No, no." She must have done. Well, I'll tell you one thing, and you can take this as official. If ever I find this slimy, slithery snake in the grass, he had better make all the necessary arrangements at his favourite nursing-home without delay, because I am going to be very rough with him. I propose, if and when found, to take him by his beastly neck, shake him till he froths, and pull him inside out and make him swallow himself.'

With which words he biffed off; and I, having given him a minute or two to get out of the way, rose and made for the drawing-room. The tendency of females to roost in drawing-rooms after dinner being well marked, I expected to find Angela there. It was my intention to have a word with Angela.

To Tuppy's theory that some insinuating bird had stolen the girl's heart from him at Cannes I had given, as I have indicated, little credence, considering it the mere unbalanced apple sauce of a bereaved man. It was, of course, the shark, and nothing but the shark, that had caused love's young dream to go temporarily off the boil, and I was convinced that a word or two with the cousin at this juncture would set everything right.

For, frankly, I thought it incredible that a girl of her natural sweetness and tender-heartedness should not have been moved to her foundations by what she had seen at dinner that night. Even Seppings, Aunt Dahlia's butler, a cold, unemotional man, had gasped and practically reeled when Tuppy waved aside those *nonnettes de poulet Agnès Sorel*, while the footman, standing by with the potatoes, had stared like one seeing a vision. I simply refused to consider the possibility of the significance of the thing having been lost on a nice girl like Angela. I fully expected to find her in the drawing-room with her heart bleeding freely, all ripe for an immediate reconciliation.

In the drawing-room, however, when I entered, only Aunt Dahlia met the eye. It seemed to me that she gave me rather a jaundiced look as I hove in sight, but this, having so recently beheld Tuppy in his agony, I attributed to the fact that she, like him, had been going light on the menu. You can't expect an empty aunt to beam like a full aunt.

'Oh, it's you, is it?' she said.

Well it was, of course.

'Where's Angela?' I asked.

'Gone to bed.'

'Already?'

'She said she had a headache.'

'H'm.'

I wasn't so sure that I liked the sound of that so much. A girl who has observed the sundered lover sensationally off his feed does not go to bed with headaches if love has been reborn in her heart. She sticks around and gives him the swift, remorseful glance from beneath the drooping eyelashes and generally endeavours to convey to him that, if he wants to get together across a round table and try to find a formula, she is all for it. Yes, I am bound to say I found that going-to-bed stuff a bit disquieting.

'Gone to bed, eh?' I murmured musingly.

'What did you want her for?'

'I thought she might like a stroll and a chat.'

'Are you going for a stroll?' said Aunt Dahlia, with a sudden show of interest. 'Where?'

'Oh, hither and thither.'

'Then I wonder if you would mind doing something for me.'

'Give it a name.'

'It won't take you long. You know that path that runs past the greenhouses into the kitchen garden. If you go along it you come to a pond.'

'That's right.'

'Well, will you get a good, stout piece of rope or cord and go down that path till you come to the pond—'

'To the pond. Right.'

'— and look about you till you find a nice, heavy stone. Or a fairly large brick would do.'

'I see,' I said, though I didn't, being still fogged. 'Stone or brick. Yes. And then?'

'Then,' said the relative, 'I want you, like a good boy, to fasten the rope to the brick and tie it round your damned neck and jump into the pond and drown yourself. In a few days I will send and have you fished up and buried because I shall need to dance on your grave.'

I was more fogged than ever. And not only fogged—wounded and resentful. I remember reading a book where a girl 'suddenly fled from the room, afraid to stay for fear dreadful things would come tumbling from her lips; determined that she would not remain another day in this house to be insulted and misunderstood'. I felt much about the same.

Then I reminded myself that one has got to make allowances for a woman with only about half a spoonful of soup inside her, and I checked the red-hot crack that rose to the lips.

'What,' I said gently, 'is this all about? You seem pipped with Bertram.'

'Pipped!'

'Noticeably pipped. Why this ill-concealed animus?'

A sudden flame shot from her eyes, singeing my hair.

'Who was the ass, who was the chump, who was the dithering idiot who talked me, against my better judgement, into going without my dinner? I might have guessed—'

I saw that I had divined correctly the basic cause of her strange mood.

'It's all right, Aunt Dahlia. I know just how you're feeling. A bit on the hollow side, what? But the agony will pass. If I were you, I'd sneak down and raid the larder, after the household have gone to bed. I am told there's a pretty good steak-and-kidney pie there which will repay inspection. Have faith, Aunt Dahlia,' I urged. 'Pretty soon Uncle Tom will be along, full of sympathy and anxious inquiries.'

'Will he? Do you know where he is now?'

'I haven't seen him.'

'He is in the study with his face buried in his hands, muttering about Civilization and melting-pots.'

'Eh? Why?'

'Because it has just been my painful duty to inform him that Anatole has given notice.'

I own that I reeled.

'What?'

'Given notice. As the result of that drivelling scheme of yours. What did you expect a sensitive, temperamental French cook to do, if you went about urging everybody to refuse all food? I hear that when the first two courses came back to the kitchen practically untouched, his feelings were so hurt that he cried like a child. And when the rest of the dinner followed, he came to the conclusion that the whole thing was a studied and calculated insult, and decided to hand in his portfolio.'

'Golly!'

'You may well say "Golly!" Anatole, God's gift to the gastric juices, gone like the dew off the petal of a rose, all through your idiocy. Perhaps you understand now why I want you to go and jump in that pond. I might have known that some hideous disaster would strike this house like a thunderbolt if once you wriggled your way into it and started trying to be clever.'

Harsh words, of course, as from aunt to nephew, but I bore her no resentment. No doubt, if you looked at it from a certain angle, Bertram might be considered to have made something of a floater.

'I am sorry.'

'What's the good of being sorry?'

'I acted for what I deemed the best.'

'Another time try acting for the worst. Then we may possibly escape with a mere flesh wound.'

'Uncle Tom's not feeling too bucked about it all, you say?'

'He's groaning like a lost soul. And any chance I ever had of getting that money out of him has gone.'

I stroked the chin thoughtfully. There was, I had to admit, reason in what she said. None knew better than I how terrible a blow the passing of Anatole would be to Uncle Tom.

I have stated earlier in this chronicle that this curious object of the seashore with whom Aunt Dahlia has linked her lot is a bloke who habitually looks like a pterodactyl that has suffered, and the reason he does so is that all those years he spent in making millions in the Far East put his digestion on the blink, and the only cook that has ever been discovered capable of pushing food into him without starting something like Old Home Week in Moscow under the third waistcoat button is this uniquely gifted Anatole. Deprived of Anatole's services, all he was likely to give the wife of his b. was a dirty look. Yes, unquestionably, things seemed to have struck a somewhat rocky patch, and I must admit that I found myself, at moment of going to press, a little destitute of constructive ideas.

Confident, however, that these would come ere long, I kept the stiff upper lip.

'Bad,' I conceded. 'Quite bad, beyond a doubt. Certainly a nasty jar for one and all. But have no fear, Aunt Dahlia, I will fix everything.'

I have alluded earlier to the difficulty of staggering when you're sitting down, showing that it is a feat of which I, personally, am not capable. Aunt Dahlia, to my amazement, now did it apparently without an effort. She was well wedged into a deep arm-chair, but, nevertheless, she staggered like billy-o. A sort of spasm of horror and apprehension contorted her face.

'If you dare to try any more of your lunatic schemes—'

I saw that it would be fruitless to try to reason with her. Quite plainly, she was not in the vein. Contenting myself, accordingly, with a gesture of loving sympathy, I left the room. Whether she did or did not throw a handsomely bound volume of the Works of Alfred, Lord Tennyson, at me, I am not in a position to say. I had seen it lying on the table beside her, and as I closed the door I remember receiving the impression that some blunt instrument had crashed against the woodwork, but I was feeling too preoccupied to note and observe.

I blamed myself for not having taken into consideration the possible effects of a sudden abstinence on the part of virtually the whole strength of the company on one of Anatole's impulsive Provençal temperament. These Gauls, I should have remembered, can't take it. Their tendency to fly off the handle at the slightest provocation is well known. No doubt the man had put his whole soul into those *nonnettes de poulet*, and to see them come homing back to him must have gashed him like a knife.

However, spilt milk blows nobody any good, and it is useless to dwell upon it. The task now confronting Bertram was to put matters right, and I was pacing the lawn, pondering to this end, when I suddenly heard a groan so lost-soulish that I thought it must have proceeded from Uncle Tom, escaped from captivity and come to groan in the garden.

Looking about me, however, I could discern no uncles. Puzzled, I was about to resume my meditations, when the sound came again. And peering into the shadows I observed a dim form seated on one of the rustic benches which so liberally dotted this pleasance and another dim form standing beside same. A second and more penetrating glance, and I had assembled the facts.

These dim forms were, in the order named, Gussie Fink-Nottle and Jeeves. And what Gussie was doing, groaning all over the place like this, was more than I could understand.

Because, I mean to say, there was no possibility of error. He wasn't singing. As I approached, he gave an encore, and it was beyond question a groan. Moreover, I could now see him clearly, and his whole aspect was definitely sand-bagged.

'Good evening, sir,' said Jeeves. 'Mr Fink-Nottle is not feeling well.'

Nor was I. Gussie had begun to make a low, bubbling noise, and I could no longer disguise it from myself that something must have gone seriously wrong with the works. I mean, I know marriage is a pretty solemn business and the realization that he is in for it frequently churns a chap up a bit, but I had never come across a case of a newly-engaged man taking it on the chin quite so completely as this.

Gussie looked up. His eye was dull. He clutched the thatch.

'Good-bye, Bertie,' he said, rising.

I seemed to spot an error.

'You mean "Hullo", don't you?'

'No, I don't. I mean good-bye. I'm off.'

'Off where?'

'To the kitchen garden. To drown myself.'

'Don't be an ass.'

'I'm not an ass . . . Am I an ass, Jeeves?'

'Possibly a little injudicious, sir.'

'Drowning myself, you mean?'

'Yes, sir.'

'You think, on the whole, not drown myself?'

'I should not advocate it, sir.'

'Very well, Jeeves. I accept your ruling. After all, it would be unpleasant for Mrs Travers to find a swollen body floating in her pond.'

'Yes, sir.'

'And she has been very kind to me.'

'Yes, sir.'

'And you have been very kind to me, Jeeves.'

'Thank you, sir.'

'So have you, Bertie. Very kind. Everybody has been very kind to me. Very, very kind. Very kind indeed. I have no complaints to make. All right, I'll go for a walk instead.'

I followed him with bulging eyes as he tottered off into the darkness.

'Jeeves,' I said, and I am free to admit that in my emotion I bleated like a lamb drawing itself to the attention of the parent sheep, 'what the dickens is all this?'

'Mr Fink-Nottle is not quite himself, sir. He has passed through a trying experience.'

I endeavoured to put together a brief synopsis of previous events.

'I left him out there with Miss Bassett.'

'Yes, sir.'

'I had softened her up.'

'Yes, sir.'

'He knew exactly what he had to do. I had coached him thoroughly in lines and business.'

'Yes, sir. So Mr Fink-Nottle informed me.'

'Well, then—'

'I regret to say, sir, that there was a slight hitch.'

'You mean, something went wrong?'

'Yes, sir.'

I could not fathom. The brain seemed to be tottering on its throne.

'But how could anything go wrong? She loves him, Jeeves.'

'Indeed, sir?'

'She definitely told me so. All he had to do was propose.'

'Yes, sir.'

'Well, didn't he?'

'No, sir.'

'Then what the dickens did he talk about?'

'Newts, sir.'

'Newts?'

'Yes, sir.'

'Newts?'

'Yes, sir.'

'But why did he want to talk about newts?'

'He did not want to talk about newts, sir. As I gather from Mr Fink-Nottle, nothing could have been more alien to his plans.'

I simply couldn't grasp the trend.

'But you can't force a man to talk about newts.'

'Mr Fink-Nottle was the victim of a sudden unfortunate spasm of nervousness, sir. Upon finding himself alone with the young lady, he admits to having lost his morale. In such circumstances, gentlemen frequently talk at random, saying the first thing that chances to enter their heads. This, in Mr Fink-Nottle's case, would seem to have been the newt, its treatment in sickness and in health.'

The scales fell from my eyes. I understood. I had had the same sort of thing happen to me in moments of crisis. I remember once detaining a dentist with the drill at one of my lower bicuspids and holding him up for nearly ten minutes with a story about a Scotchman, an Irishman, and a Jew. Purely automatic. The more he tried to jab, the more I said 'Hoots, mon', 'Begorrah', and 'Oy, oy'. When one loses one's nerve, one simply babbles.

I could put myself in Gussie's place. I could envisage the scene. There he and the Bassett were, alone together in the evening stillness. No doubt, as I had advised, he had shot the works about sunsets and fairy princesses, and so forth, and then had arrived at the point where he had to say that bit about having something to say to her. At this, I take it, she lowered her eyes and said, 'Oh, yes?'

He then, I should imagine, said it was something very important; to which her response would, one assumes, have been something on the lines of 'Really?' or 'Indeed?' or possibly just the sharp intake of the breath. And then their eyes met, just as mine met the dentist's, and something suddenly seemed to catch him in the pit of the stomach and everything went black and he heard his voice starting to drool about newts. Yes, I could follow the psychology.

Nevertheless, I found myself blaming Gussie. On discovering that he was stressing the newt note in this manner, he ought, of course, to have tuned out, even if it had meant sitting there saying nothing. No matter how much of a twitter he was in, he should have had sense enough to see that he was throwing a spanner into the works. No girl, when she has been led to expect that a man is about to pour forth his soul in a fervour of passion, likes to find him suddenly shelving the whole topic in favour of an address on aquatic Salamandridae.

'Bad, Jeeves.'

'Yes, sir.'

'And how long did this nuisance continue?'

'For some not inconsiderable time, I gather, sir. According to Mr Fink-Nottle, he supplied Miss Bassett with very full and complete information not only with respect to the common newt, but also the crested and palmated varieties. He described to her how newts, during the breeding season, live in the water, subsisting upon tadpoles, insect larvae, and crustaceans; how, later, they make their way to the land and eat slugs and worms; and how the newly born newt has three pairs of long, plumelike, external gills. And he was just observing that newts differ from salamanders in the shape of the tail, which is compressed, and that a marked sexual dimorphism prevails in most species, when the young lady rose and said that she thought she would go back to the house.'

'And then—'

'She went, sir.'

I stood musing. More and more, it was beginning to be borne in upon me what a particularly difficult chap Gussie was to help. He seemed to so marked an extent to lack snap and finish. With infinite toil, you manoeuvred him into a position where all he had to do was charge ahead, and he didn't charge ahead, but went off sideways, missing the objective completely.

'Difficult, Jeeves.'

'Yes, sir.'

In happier circs, of course, I would have canvassed his views on the matter. But after what had occurred in connexion with that mess jacket, my lips were sealed.

'Well, I must think it over.'

'Yes, sir.'

'Burnish the brain a bit and endeavour to find the way out.'

'Yes, sir.'

'Well, good night, Jeeves.'

'Good night, sir.'

He shimmered off, leaving a pensive Bertram Wooster standing motionless in the shadows. It seemed to me that it was hard to know what to do for the best.

12

I don't know if it has happened to you at all, but a thing I've noticed with myself is that, when I'm confronted by a problem which seems for the moment to stump and baffle, a good sleep will often bring the solution in the morning.

It was so on the present occasion.

The nibs who study these matters claim, I believe, that this has got something to do with the subconscious mind, and very possibly they may be right. I wouldn't have said off-hand that I had a subconscious mind, but I suppose I must without knowing it, and no doubt it was there, sweating away diligently at the old stand, all the while the corporeal Wooster was getting his eight hours.

For directly I opened my eyes on the morrow, I saw daylight. Well, I don't mean that exactly, because naturally I did. What I mean is that I found I had the thing all mapped out. The good old subconscious m. had delivered the goods, and I perceived exactly what steps must be taken in order to put Augustus Fink-Nottle among the practising Romeos.

I should like you, if you can spare me a moment of your valuable time, to throw your mind back to that conversation he and I had had in the garden on the previous evening. Not the glimmering landscape bit, I don't mean that, but the concluding passages of it. Having done so, you will recall that when he informed me that he never touched alcoholic liquor, I shook the head a bit, feeling that this must inevitably weaken him as a force where proposing to girls was concerned.

And events had shown that my fears were well founded.

Put to the test, with nothing but orange juice inside him, he had proved a complete bust. In a situation calling for words of molten passion of a nature calculated to go through Madeline Bassett like a red-hot gimlet through half a pound of butter, he had said not a syllable that could bring a blush to the cheek of modesty, merely delivering a well-phrased but, in the circumstances, quite misplaced lecture on newts.

A romantic girl is not to be won by such tactics. Obviously, before attempting to proceed further, Augustus Fink-Nottle must be induced to throw off the shackling inhibitions of the past and fuel up. It must be a primed, confident Fink-Nottle who squared up to the Bassett for Round No. 2.

Only so could the *Morning Post* make its ten bob, or whatever it is, for printing the announcement of the forthcoming nuptials.

Having arrived at this conclusion I found the rest easy, and by the time Jeeves brought me my tea I had evolved a plan complete in every detail. This I was about to place before him—indeed, I had got as far as the preliminary 'I say, Jeeves'—when we were interrupted by the arrival of Tuppy.

He came listlessly into the room, and I was pained to observe that a night's rest had effected no improvement in the unhappy wreck's appearance. Indeed, I should have said, if anything, that he was looking rather more moth-eaten than when I had seen him last. If you can visualize a bulldog which has just been kicked in the ribs and had its dinner sneaked by the cat, you will have Hildebrand Glossop as he now stood before me.

'Stap my vitals, Tuppy, old corpse,' I said, concerned, 'you're looking pretty blue round the rims.'

Jeeves slid from the presence in that tactful, eel-like way of his, and I motioned the remains to take a seat.

'What's the matter?' I said.

He came to anchor on the bed, and for a while sat picking at the coverlet in silence.

'I've been through hell, Bertie.'

'Through where?'

'Hell.'

'Oh, hell? And what took you there?'

Once more he became silent, staring before him with sombre eyes.

Following his gaze, I saw that he was looking at an enlarged photograph of my Uncle Tom in some sort of Masonic uniform which stood on the mantelpiece. I've tried to reason with Aunt Dahlia about this photograph for years, placing before her two alternative suggestions: (*a*) to burn the beastly thing; or (*b*) if she must preserve it, to shove me in another room when I come to stay. But she declines to accede. She says it's good for me. A useful discipline, she maintains, teaching me that there is a darker side to life and that we were not put into this world for pleasure only.

'Turn it to the wall, if it hurts you, Tuppy,' I said gently.

'Eh?'

'That photograph of Uncle Tom as the bandmaster.'

'I didn't come here to talk about photographs. I came for sympathy.'

'And you shall have it. What's the trouble? Worrying about Angela, I suppose? Well, have no fear. I have another well-laid plan for encompassing that young shrimp. I'll guarantee that she will be weeping on your neck before yonder sun has set.'

He barked sharply.

'A fat chance!'

'Tup, Tushy!'

'Eh?'

'I mean "Tush, Tuppy". I tell you I will do it. I was just going to describe this plan of mine to Jeeves when you came in. Care to hear it?'

'I don't want to hear any more of your beastly plans. Plans are no good. She's gone and fallen in love with this other bloke, and now hates my gizzard.'

'Rot.'

'It isn't rot.'

'I tell you, Tuppy, as one who can read the female heart, that this Angela loves you still.'

'Well, it didn't look much like it in the larder last night.'

'Oh, you went to the larder last night?'

'I did.'

'And Angela was there?'

'She was. And your aunt. Also your uncle.'

I saw that I should require foot-notes. All this was new stuff to me. I had stayed at Brinkley Court quite a lot in my time, but I had no idea the larder was such a social vortex. More like a snack bar on a race-course than anything else, it seemed to have become.

'Tell me the whole story in your own words,' I said, 'omitting no detail, however apparently slight, for one never knows how important the most trivial detail may be.'

He inspected the photograph for a moment with growing gloom.

'All right,' he said. 'This is what happened. You know my views about that steak-and-kidney pie.'

'Quite.'

'Well, round about one a.m. I thought the time was ripe. I stole from my room and went downstairs. The pie seemed to beckon to me.'

I nodded. I knew how pies do.

'I got to the larder. I fished it out. I set it on the table. I found knife and fork. I collected salt, mustard, and pepper. There were some cold potatoes. I added those. And I was about to pitch in when I heard a sound behind me, and there was your aunt at the door. In a blue-and-yellow dressing gown.'

'Embarrassing.'

'Most.'

'I suppose you didn't know where to look.'

'I looked at Angela.'

'She came in with my aunt?'

'No. With your uncle, a minute or two later. He was wearing mauve pyjamas and carried a pistol. Have you ever seen your uncle in pyjamas and a pistol?'

'Never.'

'You haven't missed much.'

'Tell me, Tuppy,' I asked, for I was anxious to ascertain this, 'about Angela. Was there any momentary softening in her gaze as she fixed it on you?'

'She didn't fix it on me. She fixed it on the pie.'

'Did she say anything?'

'Not right away. Your uncle was the first to speak. He said to your aunt, "God bless my soul, Dahlia, what are you doing here?" To which she replied, "Well, if it comes to that, my merry somnambulist, what are you?" Your uncle then said that he thought there must be burglars in the house, as he had heard noises.'

I nodded again. I could follow the trend. Ever since the scullery window was found open the year Shining Light was disqualified in the Cesarewitch for boring, Uncle Tom has had a marked complex about burglars. I can still recall my emotions when, paying my first visit after he had had bars put on all the windows and attempting to thrust the head out in order to get a sniff of country air, I nearly fractured my skull on a sort of iron grille, as worn by the tougher kinds of medieval prison.

'"What sort of noises?" said your aunt. "Funny noises," said your uncle. Whereupon Angela—with a nasty, steely tinkle in her voice, the little buzzard—observed, "I expect it was Mr Glossop eating." And then she did give me a look. It was the sort of wondering, revolted look a very spiritual woman would give a fat man gulping soup in a restaurant. The kind of look that makes a fellow feel he's forty-six round the waist and has great rolls of superfluous flesh pouring down over the back of his collar. And, still speaking in the same unpleasant tone, she added, "I ought to have told you, father, that Mr Glossop always likes to have a good meal three or four times during the night. It helps to keep him going till breakfast. He has the most amazing appetite. See, he has practically finished a large steak-and-kidney pie already."'

As he spoke these words, a feverish animation swept over Tuppy. His eyes glittered with a strange light, and he thumped the bed violently with his fist, nearly catching me a juicy one on the leg.

'That was what hurt, Bertie. That was what stung. I hadn't so much as started on that pie. But that's a woman all over.'

'The eternal feminine.'

'She continued her remarks. "You've no idea," she said, "how Mr Glossop loves food. He just lives for it. He always eats six or seven meals a day, and then starts in again after bedtime. I think it's rather wonderful." Your aunt seemed interested, and said it reminded her of a boa constrictor. Angela said, didn't she mean a python? And then they argued as to which of the two it was. Your uncle, meanwhile, poking about with that damned pistol of his till human life wasn't safe in the vicinity. And the pie lying there on the table, and me unable to touch it. You begin to understand why I said I had been through hell.'

'Quite. Can't have been at all pleasant.'

'Presently your aunt and Angela settled their discussion, deciding that Angela was right and that it was a python that I reminded them of. And shortly after that we all pushed back to bed, Angela warning me in a motherly voice not to take the stairs too quickly. After seven or eight solid meals, she said a man of my build ought to be very careful, because of the danger of apoplectic fits. She said it was the same with dogs. When they became very fat and overfed, you had to see that they didn't hurry upstairs, as it made them puff and pant, and that was bad for their hearts. She asked your aunt if she remembered the late spaniel, Ambrose; and your aunt said, "Poor old Ambrose, you couldn't keep him away from the garbage pail"; and Angela said, "Exactly, so do please be careful, Mr Glossop." And you tell me she loves me still!'

I did my best to encourage.

'Girlish banter, what?'

'Girlish banter be dashed. She's right off me. Once her ideal, I am now less than the dust beneath her chariot wheels. She became infatuated with this chap, whoever he was, at Cannes, and now she can't stand the sight of me.'

I raised the eyebrows.

'My dear Tuppy, you are not showing your usual good sense in this Angela-chap-at-Cannes matter. If you will forgive me saying so, you have got an *idée fixe*.'

'A what?'

'An *idée fixe*. You know. One of those things fellows get. Like Uncle Tom's delusion that everybody who is known even slightly to the police is lurking in the garden, waiting for a chance to break into the house. You keep talking about this chap at Cannes, and there never was a chap at Cannes, and I'll tell you why I'm so sure about this. During those two months on the Riviera, it so happens that Angela and I were practically inseparable. If there had been somebody nosing round her, I should have spotted it in a second.'

He started. I could see that this had impressed him.

'Oh, she was with you all the time at Cannes, was she?'

'I don't suppose she said two words to anybody else, except, of course, idle conv. at the crowded dinner-table or a chance remark in a throng at the Casino.'

'I see. You mean that anything in the shape of mixed bathing and moonlight strolls she conducted solely in your company?'

'That's right. It was quite a joke in the hotel.'

'You must have enjoyed that.'

'Oh, rather. I've always been devoted to Angela.'

'Oh, yes?'

'When we were kids, she used to call herself my little sweetheart.'

'She did?'

'Absolutely.'

'I see.'

He sat plunged in thought, while I, glad to have set his mind at rest, proceeded with my tea. And presently there came the banging of a gong from the hall below, and he started like a war horse at the sound of the bugle.

'Breakfast!' he said, and was off to a flying start, leaving me to brood and ponder. And the more I brooded and pondered, the more did it seem to me that everything now looked pretty smooth. Tuppy, I could see, despite that painful scene in the larder, still loved Angela with all the old fervour.

This meant that I could rely on that plan to which I had referred to bring home the bacon. And as I had found the way to straighten out the Gussie–Bassett difficulty, there seemed nothing more to worry about.

It was with an uplifted heart that I addressed Jeeves as he came in to remove the tea tray.

13

'Jeeves,' I said.

'Sir?'

'I've just been having a chat with young Tuppy, Jeeves. Did you happen to notice that he wasn't looking very roguish this morning?'

'Yes, sir. It seemed to me that Mr Glossop's face was sicklied o'er with the pale cast of thought.'

'Quite. He met my Cousin Angela in the larder last night, and a rather painful interview ensued.'

'I am sorry, sir.'

'Not half so sorry as he was. She found him closeted with a steak-and-kidney pie, and appears to have been a bit caustic about fat men who lived for food alone.'

'Most disturbing, sir.'

'Very. In fact, many people would say that things had gone so far between these two that nothing now could bridge the chasm. A girl who could make cracks about human pythons who ate nine or ten meals a day and ought to be careful not to hurry upstairs because of the danger of apoplectic fits is a girl, many people would say, in whose heart love is dead. Wouldn't many people say that, Jeeves?'

'Undeniably, sir.'

'They would be wrong.'

'You think so, sir?'

'I am convinced of it. I know these females. You can't go by what they say.'

'You feel that Miss Angela's strictures should not be taken too much *au pied de la lettre*, sir?'

'Eh?'

'In English, we should say "literally".'

'Literally. That's exactly what I mean. You know what girls are. A tiff occurs, and they shoot their heads off. But underneath it all the old love still remains. Am I correct?'

'Quite correct, sir. The poet Scott—'

'Right ho, Jeeves.'

'Very good, sir.'

'And in order to bring that old love whizzing to the surface once more, all that is required is the proper treatment.'

'By "proper treatment", sir, you mean—'

'Clever handling, Jeeves. A spot of the good old snaky work. I see what must be done to jerk my Cousin Angela back to normalcy. I'll tell you, shall I?'

'If you would be so kind, sir.'

I lit a cigarette, and eyed him keenly through the smoke. He waited respectfully for me to unleash the words of wisdom. I must say for Jeeves that—till, as he is so apt to do, he starts shoving his oar in and cavilling and obstructing—he makes a very good audience. I don't know if he is actually agog, but he looks agog, and that's the great thing.

'Suppose you were strolling through the illimitable jungle, Jeeves, and happened to meet a tiger cub.'

'The contingency is a remote one, sir.'

'Never mind. Let us suppose it.'

'Very good, sir.'

'Let us now suppose that you sloshed that tiger cub, and let us suppose further that word reached its mother that it was being put upon. What would you expect the attitude of that mother to be? In what frame of mind do you consider that that tigress would approach you?'

'I should anticipate a certain show of annoyance, sir.'

'And rightly. Due to what is known as the maternal instinct, what?'

'Yes, sir.'

'Very good, Jeeves. We will now suppose that there has recently been some little coolness between this tiger cub and this tigress. For some days, let us say, they have not been on speaking terms. Do you think that that would make any difference to the vim with which the latter would leap to the former's aid?'

'No, sir.'

'Exactly. Here, then, in brief, is my plan, Jeeves. I am going to draw my Cousin Angela aside to a secluded spot and roast Tuppy properly.'

'Roast, sir?'

'Knock. Slam. Tick off. Abuse. Denounce. I shall be very terse about Tuppy, giving it as my opinion that in all essentials he is more like a wart-hog than an ex-member of a fine old English public school. What will ensue? Hearing him attacked, my Cousin Angela's womanly heart will be as sick as mud. The maternal tigress in her will awake. No matter what differences they may have had, she will remember only that he is the man she loves, and will leap to his defence. And from that to falling into his arms and burying the dead past will be but a step. How do you react to that?'

'The idea is an ingenious one, sir.'

'We Woosters are ingenious, Jeeves, exceedingly ingenious.'

'Yes, sir.'

'As a matter of fact, I am not speaking without a knowledge of the form book. I have tested this theory.'

'Indeed, sir?'

'Yes, in person. And it works. I was standing on the Eden rock at Antibes last month, idly watching the bathers disport themselves in the water, and a girl I knew slightly pointed at a male diver and asked me if I didn't think his legs were about the silliest-looking pair of props ever issued to a human being. I replied that I did, indeed, and for the space of perhaps two minutes was extraordinarily witty and satirical about this bird's underpinning. At the end of that period, I suddenly felt as if I had been caught up in the tail of a cyclone.

'Beginning with a *critique* of my own limbs, which she said, justly enough, were nothing to write home about, this girl went on to dissect my manners, morals, intellect, general physique, and method of eating asparagus with such acerbity that by the time she had finished the best you could say of Bertram was that, so far as was known, he had never actually committed murder or set fire to an orphan asylum. Subsequent investigation proved that she was engaged to the fellow with the legs and had had a slight disagreement with him the evening before on the subject of whether she should or should not have made an original call of two spades, having seven, but without the ace. That night I saw them dining together with every indication of relish, their differences made up and the lovelight once more in their eyes. That shows you, Jeeves.'

'Yes, sir.'

'I expect precisely similar results from my Cousin Angela when I start roasting Tuppy. By lunchtime, I should imagine, the engagement will be on again and the diamond-and-platinum ring glittering as of yore on her third finger. Or is it the fourth?'

'Scarcely by luncheon time, sir. Miss Angela's maid informs me that Miss Angela drove off in her car early this morning with the intention of spending the day with friends in the vicinity.'

'Well, within half an hour of whatever time she comes back, then. These are mere straws, Jeeves. Do not let us chop them.'

'No, sir.'

'The point is that, as far as Tuppy and Angela are concerned, we may say with confidence that everything will shortly be hotsy-totsy once more. And what an agreeable thought that is, Jeeves.'

'Very true, sir.'

'If there is one thing that gives me the pip, it is two loving hearts being estranged.'

'I can readily appreciate the fact, sir.'

I placed the stub of my gasper in the ash tray and lit another, to indicate that that completed Chap. I.

'Right ho, then. So much for the western front. We now turn to the eastern.'

'Sir?'

'I speak in parables, Jeeves. What I mean is, we now approach the matter of Gussie and Miss Bassett.'

'Yes, sir.'

'Here, Jeeves, more direct methods are required. In handling the case of Augustus Fink-Nottle, we must keep always in mind the fact that we are dealing with a poop.'

'A sensitive plant would, perhaps, be a kinder expression, sir.'

'No, Jeeves, a poop. And with poops one has to employ the strong, forceful, straightforward policy. Psychology doesn't get you anywhere. You, if I may remind you without wounding your feelings, fell into the error of mucking about with psychology in connexion with this Fink-Nottle, and the result was a washout. You attempted to push him over the line by rigging him out in a Mephistopheles costume and sending him off to a fancy-dress ball, your view being that scarlet tights would embolden him. Futile.'

'The matter was never actually put to the test, sir.'

'No. Because he didn't get to the ball. And that strengthens my argument. A man who can set out in a cab for a fancy-dress ball and not get there is manifestly a poop of no common order. I don't think I have ever known anybody else who was such a dashed silly ass that he couldn't even get to a fancy-dress ball. Have you, Jeeves?'

'No, sir.'

'But don't forget this, because it is the point I wish, above all, to make: even if Gussie had got to that ball; even if those scarlet tights, taken in conjunction with his horn-rimmed spectacles, hadn't given the girl a fit of some kind; even if she had rallied from the shock and he had been able to dance and generally hobnob with her; even then your efforts would have been fruitless, because Mephistopheles costume or no Mephistopheles costume, Augustus Fink-Nottle would never have been able to summon up the courage to ask her to be his. All that would have resulted would have been that she would have got that lecture on newts a few days earlier. And why, Jeeves? Shall I tell you why?'

'Yes, sir.'

'Because he would have been attempting the hopeless task of trying to do the thing on orange juice.'

'Sir?'

'Gussie is an orange-juice addict. He drinks nothing else.'

'I was not aware of that, sir.'

'I have it from his own lips. Whether from some hereditary taint, or because he promised his mother he wouldn't, or simply because he doesn't like the taste of the stuff, Gussie Fink-Nottle has never in the whole course of his career pushed so much as the simplest gin and tonic over the larynx. And he expects—this poop expects, Jeeves—this wabbling, shrinking, diffident rabbit in human shape expects under these conditions to propose to the girl he loves. One hardly knows whether to smile or weep, what?'

'You consider total abstinence a handicap to a gentleman who wishes to make a proposal of marriage, sir?'

The question amazed me.

'Why, dash it,' I said, astounded, 'you must know it is. Use your intelligence, Jeeves. Reflect what proposing means. It means that a decent, self-respecting chap has got to listen to himself saying things which, if spoken on the silver screen, would cause him to dash to the box-office and demand his money back. Let him attempt to do it on orange juice, and what ensues? Shame seals his lips, or, if it doesn't do that, makes him lose his morale and start to babble. Gussie, for example, as we have seen, babbles of syncopated newts.'

'Palmated newts, sir.'

'Palmated or syncopated, it doesn't matter which. The point is that he babbles and is going to babble again, if he has another try at it. Unless—and this is where I want you to follow me very closely, Jeeves—unless steps are taken at once through the proper channels. Only active measures, promptly applied, can provide this poor, pusillanimous poop with the proper pep. And that is why, Jeeves, I intend tomorrow to secure a bottle of gin and lace his luncheon orange juice with it liberally.'

'Sir?'

I clicked the tongue.

'I have already had occasion, Jeeves,' I said rebukingly, 'to comment on the way you say "Well, sir" and "Indeed, sir?" I take this opportunity of informing you that I object equally strongly to your "Sir?" pure and simple. The word seems to suggest that in your opinion I have made a statement or mooted a scheme so bizarre that your brain reels at it. In the present instance, there is absolutely nothing to say "Sir?" about. The plan I have put forward is entirely reasonable and icily logical, and should excite no sirring whatsoever. Or don't you think so?'

'Well, sir—'

'Jeeves?'

'I beg your pardon, sir. The expression escaped me inadvertently. What

I intended to say, since you press me, was that the action which you propose does seem to me somewhat injudicious.'

'Injudicious? I don't follow you, Jeeves.'

'A certain amount of risk would enter into it, in my opinion, sir. It is not always a simple matter to gauge the effect of alcohol on a subject unaccustomed to such stimulant. I have known it to have distressing results in the case of parrots.'

'Parrots?'

'I was thinking of an incident of my earlier life, sir, before I entered your employment. I was in the service of the late Lord Brancaster at the time, a gentleman who owned a parrot to which he was greatly devoted, and one day the bird chanced to be lethargic, and his lordship, with the kindly intention of restoring it to its customary animation, offered it a portion of seed cake steeped in the '84 port. The bird accepted the morsel gratefully and consumed it with every indication of satisfaction. Almost immediately afterwards, however, its manner became markedly feverish. Having bitten his lordship in the thumb and sung part of a sea-chanty, it fell to the bottom of the cage and remained there for a considerable period of time with its legs in the air, unable to move. I merely mention this, sir, in order to—'

I put my finger on the flaw. I had spotted it all along.

'But Gussie isn't a parrot.'

'No, sir, but—'

'It is high time, in my opinion, that this question of what young Gussie really is was threshed out and cleared up. He seems to think he is a male newt, and you appear to suggest that he is a parrot. The truth of the matter being that he is just a plain, ordinary poop and needs a snootful as badly as ever man did. So no more discussion, Jeeves. My mind is made up. There is only one way of handling this difficult case, and that is the way I have outlined.'

'Very good, sir.'

'Right ho, Jeeves. So much for that, then. Now, here's something else: you noticed that I said I was going to put this project through tomorrow, and no doubt you wondered why I said tomorrow. Why did I, Jeeves?'

'Because you feel that if it were done when 'tis done, then 'twere well it were done quickly, sir?'

'Partly, Jeeves, but not altogether. My chief reason for fixing the date as specified is that tomorrow, though you have doubtless forgotten it, is the day of the distribution of prizes at Market Snodsbury Grammar School, at which, as you know, Gussie is to be the male star and master of the revels. So you see we shall, by lacing that juice, not only embolden him to propose to Miss Bassett, but also put him so into shape that he will hold that Market Snodsbury audience spellbound.'

'In fact, you will be killing two birds with one stone, sir.'

'Exactly. A very neat way of putting it. And now here is a minor point. On second thoughts, I think the best plan will be for you, not me, to lace the juice.'

'Sir?'

'Jeeves!'

'I beg your pardon, sir.'

'And I'll tell you why that will be the best plan. Because you are in a position to obtain ready access to the stuff. It is served to Gussie daily, I have noticed, in an individual jug. This jug will presumably be lying about the kitchen or somewhere before lunch tomorrow. It will be the simplest of tasks for you to slip a few fingers of gin in it.'

'No doubt, sir, but—'

'Don't say "but", Jeeves.'

'I fear, sir—'

'"I fear, sir" is just as bad.'

'What I am endeavouring to say, sir, is that I am sorry, but I am afraid I must enter an unequivocal *nolle prosequi*.'

'Do what?'

'The expression is a legal one, sir, signifying the resolve not to proceed with a matter. In other words, eager though I am to carry out your instructions, sir, as a general rule, on this occasion I must respectfully decline to cooperate.'

'You won't do it, you mean?'

'Precisely, sir.'

I was stunned. I began to understand how a general must feel when he has ordered a regiment to charge and has been told that it isn't in the mood.

'Jeeves,' I said, 'I had not expected this of you.'

'No, sir?'

'No, indeed. Naturally, I realize that lacing Gussie's orange juice is not one of those regular duties for which you receive the monthly stipend, and if you care to stand on the strict letter of the contract, I suppose there is nothing to be done about it. But you will permit me to observe that this is scarcely the feudal spirit.'

'I am sorry, sir.'

'It is quite all right, Jeeves, quite all right. I am not angry, only a little hurt.'

'Very good, sir.'

'Right ho, Jeeves.'

14

Investigation proved that the friends Angela had gone to spend the day with were some stately-home owners of the name of Stretchley-Budd, hanging out in a joint called Kingham Manor, about eight miles distant in the direction of Pershore. I didn't know these birds, but their fascination must have been considerable, for she tore herself away from them only just in time to get back and dress for dinner. It was, accordingly, not until coffee had been consumed that I was able to get matters moving. I found her in the drawing-room and at once proceeded to put things in train.

It was with very different feelings from those which had animated the bosom when approaching the Bassett twenty-four hours before in the same manner in this same drawing-room, that I headed for where she sat. As I had told Tuppy, I have always been devoted to Angela, and there is nothing I like better than a ramble in her company.

And I could see by the look of her now how sorely in need she was of my aid and comfort.

Frankly, I was shocked by the unfortunate young prune's appearance. At Cannes she had been a happy, smiling English girl of the best type, full of beans and buck. Her face now was pale and drawn, like that of a hockey centre-forward at a girls' school who, in addition to getting a fruity one on the shin, has just been penalized for 'sticks'. In any normal gathering, her demeanour would have excited instant remark, but the standard of gloom at Brinkley Court had become so high that it passed unnoticed. Indeed, I shouldn't wonder if Uncle Tom, crouched in his corner waiting for the end, didn't think she was looking indecently cheerful.

I got down to the agenda in my debonair way.

'What ho, Angela, old girl.'

'Hullo, Bertie, darling.'

'Glad you're back at last. I missed you.'

'Did you, darling?'

'I did, indeed. Care to come for a saunter?'

'I'd love it.'

'Fine. I have much to say to you that is not for the public ear.'

I think at this moment poor old Tuppy must have got a sudden touch of cramp. He had been sitting hard by, staring at the ceiling, and he now gave a sharp leap like a gaffed salmon and upset a small table containing a vase, a bowl of potpourri, two china dogs, and a copy of Omar Khayyàm bound in limp leather.

Aunt Dahlia uttered a startled hunting cry. Uncle Tom, who probably imagined from the noise that this was civilization crashing at last, helped things along by breaking a coffee-cup.

Tuppy said he was sorry. Aunt Dahlia, with a deathbed groan, said it didn't matter. And Angela, having stared haughtily for a moment like a princess of the old regime confronted by some notable example of gaucherie on the part of some particularly foul member of the underworld, accompanied me across the threshold. And presently I had deposited her and self on one of the rustic benches in the garden, and was ready to snap into the business of the evening.

I considered it best, however, before doing so, to ease things along with a little informal chitchat. You don't want to rush a delicate job like the one I had in hand. And so for a while we spoke of neutral topics. She said that what had kept her so long at the Stretchley-Budds was that Hilda Stretchley-Budd had made her stop on and help with the arrangements for their servants' ball tomorrow night, a task which she couldn't very well decline, as all the Brinkley Court domestic staff were to be present. I said that a jolly night's revelry might be just what was needed to cheer Anatole up and take his mind off things. To which she replied that Anatole wasn't going. On being urged to do so by Aunt Dahlia, she said, he had merely shaken his head sadly and gone on talking of returning to Provence, where he was appreciated.

It was after the sombre silence induced by this statement that Angela said the grass was wet and she thought she would go in.

This, of course, was entirely foreign to my policy.

'No, don't do that. I haven't had a chance to talk to you since you arrived.'

'I shall ruin my shoes.'

'Put your feet up on my lap.'

'All right. And you can tickle my ankles.'

'Quite.'

Matters were accordingly arranged on these lines, and for some minutes we continued chatting in desultory fashion. Then the conversation petered out. I made a few observations *in re* the scenic effects, featuring the twilight hush, the peeping stars, and the soft glimmer of the waters of the lake, and she said yes. Something rustled in the bushes in front of us, and I advanced the theory that it was possibly a weasel, and she said it might be. But it was plain that the girl was distrait, and I considered it best to waste no more time.

'Well, old thing,' I said, 'I've heard all about your little dust-up. So those wedding bells are not going to ring out, what?'

'No.'

'Definitely over, is it?'

'Yes.'

'Well, if you want my opinion, I think that's a bit of goose for you, Angela, old girl. I think you're extremely well out of it. It's a mystery to me how you stood this Glossop so long. Take him for all in all, he ranks very low down among the wines and spirits. A washout, I should describe him as. A frightful oik, and a mass of side to boot. I'd pity the girl who was linked for life to a bargee like Tuppy Glossop.'

And I emitted a hard laugh—one of the sneering kind.

'I always thought you were such friends,' said Angela.

I let go another hard one, with a bit more top spin on it than the first time:

'Friends. Absolutely not. One was civil, of course, when one met the fellow, but it would be absurd to say one was a friend of his. A club acquaintance, and a mere one at that. And then one was at school with the man.'

'At Eton?'

'Good heavens, no. We wouldn't have a fellow like that at Eton. At a kids' school before I went there. A grubby little brute he was, I recollect. Covered with ink and mire generally, and washing only on alternate Thursdays. In short, a notable outsider, shunned by all.'

I paused. I was more than a bit perturbed. Apart from the agony of having to talk in this fashion of one who, except when he was looping back rings and causing me to plunge into swimming baths in correct evening costume, had always been a very dear and esteemed crony, I didn't seem to be getting anywhere. Business was not resulting. Staring into the bushes without a yip, she appeared to be bearing these slurs and innuendoes of mine with an easy calm.

I had another pop at it:

'"Uncouth" about sums it up. I doubt if I've ever seen an uncouther kid than this Glossop. Ask anyone who knew him in those days to describe him in a word, and the word they will use is "uncouth". And he's just the same today. It's the old story. The boy is the father of the man.'

She appeared not to have heard.

'The boy,' I repeated, not wishing her to miss that one, 'is the father of the man.'

'What are you talking about?'

'I'm talking about this Glossop.'

'I thought you said something about somebody's father.'

'I said the boy was the father of the man.'

'What boy?'

'The boy Glossop.'

'He hasn't got a father.'

'I never said he had. I said he was the father of the boy—or, rather, of the man.'

'What man?'

I saw that the conversation had reached a point where, unless care was taken, we should be muddled.

'The point I am trying to make,' I said, 'is that the boy Glossop is the father of the man Glossop. In other words, each loathsome fault and blemish that led the boy Glossop to be frowned upon by his fellows is present in the man Glossop, and causes him—I am speaking now of the man

Glossop—to be a hissing and a byword at places like the Drones, where a certain standard of decency is demanded from the inmates. Ask anyone at the Drones, and they will tell you that it was a black day for the dear old club when this chap Glossop somehow wriggled into the list of members. Here you will find a man who dislikes his face; there one who could stand his face if it wasn't for his habits. But the universal consensus of opinion is that the fellow is a bounder and a tick, and that the moment he showed signs of wanting to get into the place he should have been met with a firm *nolle prosequi* and heartily blackballed.'

I had to pause again here, partly in order to take in a spot of breath, and partly to wrestle with the almost physical torture of saying these frightful things about poor old Tuppy.

'There are some chaps,' I resumed, forcing myself once more to the nauseous task, 'who, in spite of looking as if they had slept in their clothes, can get by quite nicely because they are amiable and suave. There are others who, for all that they excite adverse comment by being fat and uncouth, find themselves on the credit side of the ledger owing to their wit and sparkling humour. But this Glossop, I regret to say, falls into neither class. In addition to looking like one of those things that come out of hollow trees, he is universally admitted to be a dumb brick of the first water. No soul. No conversation. In short, any girl who, having been rash enough to get engaged to him, has managed at the eleventh hour to slide out is justly entitled to consider herself dashed lucky.'

I paused once more, and cocked an eye at Angela to see how the treatment was taking. All the while I had been speaking, she had sat gazing silently into the bushes, but it seemed to me incredible that she should not now turn on me like a tigress, according to specifications. It beat me why she hadn't done it already. It seemed to me that a mere tithe of what I had said, if said to a tigress about a tiger of which she was fond, would have made her—the tigress, I mean—hit the ceiling.

And the next moment you could have knocked me down with a toothpick.

'Yes,' she said, nodding thoughtfully, 'you're quite right.'

'Eh?'

'That's exactly what I've been thinking myself.'

'What!'

'"Dumb brick." It just describes him. One of the six silliest asses in England, I should think he must be.'

I did not speak. I was endeavouring to adjust the faculties, which were in urgent need of a bit of first-aid treatment.

I mean to say, all this had come as a complete surprise. In formulating the well-laid plan which I had just been putting into effect, the one contingency I had not budgeted for was that she might adhere to the sentiments which I expressed. I had braced myself for a gush of stormy emotion. I was expecting the tearful ticking off, the girlish recriminations and all the rest of the bag of tricks along those lines.

But this cordial agreement with my remarks I had not foreseen, and it gave me what you might call pause for thought.

She proceeded to develop her theme, speaking in ringing, enthusiastic tones, as if she loved the topic. Jeeves could tell you the word I want. I think it's 'ecstatic', unless that's that sort of rash you get on your face and have to use ointment for. But if that is the right word, then that's what her manner was as she ventilated the subject of poor old Tuppy. If you had been able to go simply by the sound of her voice, she might have been a court poet cutting loose about an Oriental monarch, or Gussie Fink-Nottle describing his last consignment of newts.

'It's so nice, Bertie, talking to somebody who really takes a sensible view about this man Glossop. Mother says he's a good chap, which is simply absurd. Anybody can see that he's absolutely impossible. He's conceited and opinionative and argues all the time, even when he knows perfectly well that he's talking through his hat, and he smokes too much and eats too much and drinks too much, and I don't like the colour of his hair. Not that he'll have any hair in a year or two, because he's pretty thin on the top already, and before he knows where he is he'll be as bald as an egg, and he's the last man who can afford to go bald. And I think it's simply disgusting, the way he gorges all the time. Do you know, I found him in the larder at one o'clock this morning, absolutely wallowing in a steak-and-kidney pie? There was hardly any of it left. And you remember what an enormous dinner he had. Quite disgusting, I call it. But I can't stop out here all night, talking about men who aren't worth wasting a word on and haven't even enough sense to tell sharks from flatfish. I'm going in.'

And gathering about her slim shoulders the shawl which she had put on as a protection against the evening dew, she buzzed off, leaving me alone in the silent night.

Well, as a matter of fact, not absolutely alone, because a few moments later there was a sort of upheaval in the bushes in front of me, and Tuppy emerged.

15

I gave him the eye. The evening had begun to draw in a bit by now and the visibility, in consequence, was not so hot, but there still remained ample light to enable me to see him clearly. And what I saw convinced me that I should be a lot easier in my mind with a stout rustic bench between us. I rose, accordingly, modelling my style on that of a rocketing pheasant, and proceeded to deposit myself on the other side of the object named.

My prompt agility was not without its effect. He seemed somewhat taken aback. He came to a halt, and, for about the space of time required to allow a bead of persp. to trickle from the top of the brow to the tip of the nose, stood gazing at me in silence.

'So!' he said, at length, and it came as a complete surprise to me that fellows ever really do say 'So!' I had always thought it was just a thing you read in books. Like 'Quotha!' I mean to say, or 'Odds bodikins!' or even 'Eh ba goom!'

Still, there it was. Quaint or not quaint, bizarre or not bizarre, he had said 'So!' and it was up to me to cope with the situation on those lines.

It would have been a duller man than Bertram Wooster who had failed to note that the dear old chap was a bit steamed up. Whether his eyes were actually shooting forth flame, I couldn't tell you, but there appeared to me to be a distinct incandescence. For the rest, his fists were clenched, his ears quivering, and the muscles of his jaw rotating rhythmically, as if he were making an early supper off something.

His hair was full of twigs, and there was a beetle hanging to the side of his head which would have interested Gussie Fink-Nottle. To this, however, I paid scant attention. There is a time for studying beetles and a time for not studying beetles.

'So!' he said again.

Now, those who know Bertram Wooster best will tell you that he is always at his shrewdest and most level-headed in moments of peril. Who was it who, when gripped by the arm of the law on boat-race night not so many years ago and hauled off to Vine Street police station, assumed in a flash the identity of Eustace H. Plimsoll, of The Laburnums, Alleyn Road, West Dulwich, thus saving the grand old name of Wooster from being dragged in the mire and avoiding wide publicity of the wrong sort? Who was it . . .

But I need not labour the point. My record speaks for itself. Three times pinched, but never once sentenced under the correct label. Ask anyone at the Drones about this.

So now, in a situation threatening to become every moment more scaly, I did not lose my head. I preserved the old sang-froid. Smiling a genial and affectionate smile, and hoping that it wasn't too dark for it to register, I spoke with a jolly cordiality:

'Why, hallo, Tuppy. You here?'

He said, yes, he was here.

'Been here long?'

'I have.'

'Fine. I wanted to see you.'

'Well, here I am. Come out from behind that bench.'

'No, thanks, old man. I like leaning on it. It seems to rest the spine.'

'In about two seconds,' said Tuppy, 'I'm going to kick your spine up through the top of your head.'

I raised the eyebrows. Not much good, of course, in that light, but it seemed to help the general composition.

'Is this Hildebrand Glossop speaking?' I said.

He replied that it was, adding that if I wanted to make sure I might move a few feet over in his direction. He also called me an opprobrious name.

I raised the eyebrows again.

'Come, come, Tuppy, don't let us let this little chat become acrid. Is "acrid" the word I want?'

'I couldn't say,' he replied, beginning to sidle round the bench.

I saw that anything I might wish to say must be said quickly. Already he had sidled some six feet. And though, by dint of sidling, too, I had managed to keep the bench between us, who could predict how long this happy state of affairs would last?

I came to the point, therefore.

'I think I know what's on your mind, Tuppy,' I said. 'If you were in those bushes during my conversation with the recent Angela, I dare say you heard what I was saying about you.'

'I did.'

'I see. Well, we won't go into the ethics of the thing. Eavesdropping, some people might call it, and I can imagine stern critics drawing in the breath to some extent. Considering it—I don't want to hurt your feelings, Tuppy—but considering it un-English. A bit un-English, Tuppy, old man, you must admit.'

'I'm Scotch.'

'Really?' I said. 'I never knew that before. Rummy how you don't suspect a man of being Scotch unless he's Mac-something and says "Och, aye" and things like that. I wonder,' I went on, feeling that an academic discussion on some neutral topic might ease the tension, 'if you can tell me something that has puzzled me a good deal. What exactly is it that they put into haggis? I've often wondered about that.'

From the fact that his only response to the question was to leap over the bench and make a grab at me, I gathered that his mind was not on haggis.

'However,' I said, leaping over the bench in my turn, 'that is a side issue. If, to come back to it, you were in those bushes and heard what I was saying about you—'

He began to move round the bench in a nor'-nor'-easterly direction. I followed his example, setting a course sou'-sou'-west.

'No doubt you were surprised at the way I was talking.'

'Not a bit.'

'What? Did nothing strike you as odd in the tone of my remarks?'

'It was just the sort of stuff I should have expected a treacherous, sneaking hound like you to say.'

'My dear chap,' I protested, 'this is not your usual form. A bit slow in the uptake, surely? I should have thought you would have spotted right away that it was all part of a well-laid plan.'

'I'll get you in a jiffy,' said Tuppy, recovering his balance after a swift clutch at my neck. And so probable did this seem that I delayed no longer, but hastened to place all the facts before him.

Speaking rapidly and keeping moving, I related my emotions on receipt of Aunt Dahlia's telegram, my instant rush to the scene of the disaster, my meditations in the car, and the eventual framing of this well-laid plan of mine. I spoke clearly and well, and it was with considerable concern, consequently, that I heard him observe—between clenched teeth, which made it worse—that he didn't believe a damned word of it.

'But, Tuppy,' I said, 'why not? To me the thing rings true to the last drop. What makes you sceptical? Confide in me, Tuppy.'

He halted and stood taking a breather. Tuppy, pungently though Angela might have argued to the contrary, isn't really fat. During the winter months you will find him constantly booting the football with merry shouts, and in the summer the tennis racket is seldom out of his hand.

But at the recently concluded evening meal, feeling, no doubt, that after that painful scene in the larder there was nothing to be gained by further abstinence, he had rather let himself go and, as it were, made up leeway; and after really immersing himself in one of Anatole's dinners, a man of his sturdy build tends to lose elasticity a bit. During the exposition of my plans for his happiness a certain animation had crept into this round-and-round-the-mulberry-bush jamboree of ours—so much so, indeed, that for the last few minutes we might have been a rather oversized greyhound and a somewhat slimmer electric hare doing their stuff on a circular track for the entertainment of the many-headed.

This, it appeared, had taken it out of him a bit, and I was not displeased. I was feeling the strain myself, and welcomed a lull.

'It absolutely beats me why you don't believe it,' I said. 'You know we've been pals for years. You must be aware that, except at the moment when you caused me to do a nose dive into the Drones' swimming bath, an incident which I long since decided to put out of my mind and let the dead past bury its dead about, if you follow what I mean—except on that one occasion, as I say, I have always regarded you with the utmost esteem.

Why, then, if not for the motives I have outlined, should I knock you to Angela? Answer me that. Be very careful.'

'What do you mean, be very careful?'

Well, as a matter of fact, I didn't quite know myself. It was what the magistrate had said to me on the occasion when I stood in the dock as Eustace Plimsoll, of The Laburnums: and as it had impressed me a good deal at the time, I just bunged it in now by way of giving the conversation a tone.

'All right. Never mind about being careful, then. Just answer me that question. Why, if I had not your interests sincerely at heart, should I have ticked you off, as stated?'

A sharp spasm shook him from base to apex. The beetle, which, during the recent exchanges, had been clinging to his head, hoping for the best, gave it up at this and resigned office. It shot off and was swallowed in the night.

'Ah!' I said. 'Your beetle,' I explained. 'No doubt you were unaware of it, but all this while there has been a beetle of sorts parked on the side of your head. You have now dislodged it.'

He snorted.

'Beetles!'

'Not beetles. One beetle only.'

'I like your crust!' cried Tuppy, vibrating like one of Gussie's newts during the courting season. 'Talking of beetles, when all the time you know you're a treacherous, sneaking hound.'

It was a debatable point, of course, why treacherous, sneaking hounds should be considered ineligible to talk about beetles, and I dare say a good cross-examining counsel would have made quite a lot of it.

But I let it go.

'That's the second time you've called me that. And,' I said firmly, 'I insist on an explanation. I have told you that I acted throughout from the best and kindliest motives in roasting you to Angela. It cut me to the quick to have to speak like that, and only the recollection of our lifelong friendship would have made me do it. And now you say you don't believe me and call me names for which I am not sure I couldn't have you up before a beak and jury and mulct you in very substantial damages. I should have to consult my solicitor, of course, but it would surprise me very much if an action did not lie. Be reasonable, Tuppy. Suggest another motive I could have had. Just one.'

'I will. Do you think I don't know? You're in love with Angela yourself.'

'What?'

'And you knocked me in order to poison her mind against me and finally remove me from your path.'

I had never heard anything so absolutely loopy in my life. Why, dash it, I've known Angela since she was so high. You don't fall in love with close relations you've known since they were so high. Besides, isn't there something in the book of rules about a man may not marry his cousin? Or am I thinking of grandmothers?

'Tuppy, my dear old ass,' I cried, 'this is pure banana oil! You've come unscrewed.'

'Oh, yes?'

'Me in love with Angela? Ha-ha!'

'You can't get out of it with any ha-ha's. She called you "darling".'

'I know. And I disapproved. This habit of the younger g. of scattering "darlings" about like birdseed is one that I deprecate. Lax is how I should describe it.'

'You tickled her ankles.'

'In a purely cousinly spirit. It didn't mean a thing. Why, dash it, you must know that in the deeper and truer sense I wouldn't touch Angela with a barge pole.'

'Oh? And why not? Not good enough for you?'

'You misunderstand me,' I hastened to reply. 'When I say I wouldn't touch Angela with a barge pole, I intend merely to convey that my feelings towards her are those of distant, though cordial, esteem. In other words, you may rest assured that between this young prune and myself there never has been and never could be any sentiment warmer and stronger than that of ordinary friendship.'

'I believe it was you who tipped her off that I was in the larder last night, so that she could find me there with that pie, thus damaging my prestige.'

'My dear Tuppy! A Wooster?' I was shocked. 'You think a Wooster would do that?'

He breathed heavily.

'Listen,' he said. 'It's no good your standing there arguing. You can't get away from the facts. Somebody stole her from me at Cannes. You told me yourself that she was with you all the time at Cannes and hardly saw anybody else. You gloated over the mixed bathing, and those moonlight walks you had together—'

'Not gloated. Just mentioned them.'

'So now you understand why, as soon as I can get you clear of this damned bench, I am going to tear you limb from limb. Why they have these bally benches in gardens,' said Tuppy discontentedly, 'is more than I can see. They only get in the way.'

He ceased, and, grabbing out, missed me by a hair's breadth.

It was a moment for swift thinking, and it is at such moments, as I have already indicated, that Bertram Wooster is at his best. I suddenly remembered the recent misunderstanding with the Bassett, and with a flash of clear vision saw that this was where it was going to come in handy.

'You've got it all wrong, Tuppy,' I said, moving to the left. 'True, I saw a lot of Angela, but my dealings with her were on a basis from start to finish of the purest and most wholesome camaraderie. I can prove it. During that sojourn in Cannes my affections were engaged elsewhere.'

'What?'

'Engaged elsewhere. My affections. During that sojourn.'

I had struck the right note. He stopped sidling. His clutching hand fell to his side.

'Is that true?'

'Quite official.'

'Who was she?'

'My dear Tuppy, does one bandy a woman's name?'

'One does if one doesn't want one's ruddy head pulled off.'

I saw that it was a special case.

'Madeline Bassett,' I said.

'Who?'

'Madeline Bassett.'

He seemed stunned.

'You stand there and tell me you were in love with that Bassett disaster?'

'I wouldn't call her "that Bassett disaster", Tuppy. Not respectful.'

'Dash being respectful. I want facts. You deliberately assert that you loved that weird Gawd-help-us?'

'I don't see why you should call her a weird Gawd-help-us, either. A very charming and beautiful girl. Odd in some of her views, perhaps—one does not quite see eye to eye with her in the matter of stars and rabbits—but not a weird Gawd-help-us.'

'Anyway, you stick to it that you were in love with her?'

'I do.'

'It sounds thin to me, Wooster, very thin.'

I saw that it would be necessary to apply the finishing touch.

'I must ask you to treat this as entirely confidential, Glossop, but I may as well inform you that it is not twenty-four hours since she turned me down.'

'Turned you down?'

'Like a bedspread. In this very garden.'

'Twenty-four hours?'

'Call it twenty-five. So you will readily see that I can't be the chap, if any, who stole Angela from you at Cannes.'

And I was on the brink of adding that I wouldn't touch Angela with a barge pole, when I remembered I had said it already and it hadn't gone frightfully well. I desisted, therefore.

My manly frankness seemed to be producing good results. The homicidal glare was dying out of Tuppy's eyes. He had the aspect of a hired assassin who had paused to think things over.

'I see.' he said, at length. 'All right, then. Sorry you were troubled.'

'Don't mention it, old man,' I responded courteously.

For the first time since the bushes had begun to pour forth Glossops, Bertram Wooster could be said to have breathed freely. I don't say I actually came out from behind the bench, but I did let go of it, and with something of the relief which those three chaps in the Old Testament must have experienced after sliding out of the burning fiery furnace, I even groped tentatively for my cigarette case.

The next moment a sudden snort made me take my fingers off it as if it had bitten me. I was distressed to note in the old friend a return of the recent frenzy.

'What the hell did you mean by telling her that I used to be covered with ink when I was a kid?'

'My dear Tuppy—'

'I was almost finickingly careful about my personal cleanliness as a boy. You could have eaten your dinner off me.'

'Quite. But—'

'And all that stuff about having no soul. I'm crawling with soul. And being looked on as an outsider at the Drones—'

'But, my dear old chap, I explained that. It was all part of my ruse or scheme.'

'It was, was it? Well, in future do me a favour and leave me out of your foul ruses.'

'Just as you say, old boy.'

'All right, then. That's understood.'

He relapsed into silence, standing with folded arms, staring before him rather like a strong, silent man in a novel when he's just been given the bird by the girl and is thinking of looking in at the Rocky Mountains and bumping off a few bears. His manifest pippedness excited my compash, and I ventured a kindly word.

'I don't suppose you know what *au pied de la lettre* means, Tuppy, but that's how I don't think you ought to take all that stuff Angela was saying just now too much.'

He seemed interested.

'What the devil,' he asked, 'are you talking about?'

I saw that I should have to make myself clearer.

'Don't take all that guff of hers too literally, old man. You know what girls are like.'

'I do,' he said, with another snort that came straight up from his insteps. 'And I wish I'd never met one.'

'I mean to say, it's obvious that she must have spotted you in those bushes and was simply talking to score off you. There you were, I mean, if you follow the psychology, and she saw you, and in that impulsive way girls have, she seized the opportunity of ribbing you a bit—just told you a few home truths, I mean to say.'

'Home truths?'

'That's right.'

He snorted once more, causing me to feel rather like royalty receiving a twenty-one-gun salute from the fleet. I can't remember ever having met a better right-and-left-hand snorter.

'What do you mean, "home truths"? I'm not fat.'

'No, no.'

'And what's wrong with the colour of my hair?'

'Quite in order, Tuppy, old man. The hair, I mean.'

'And I'm not a bit thin on the top . . . What the dickens are you grinning about?'

'Not grinning. Just smiling slightly. I was conjuring up a sort of vision, if you know what I mean, of you as seen through Angela's eyes. Fat in the middle and thin on the top. Rather funny.'

'You think it funny, do you?'

'Not a bit.'

'You'd better not.'

'Quite.'

It seemed to me that the conversation was becoming difficult again. I wished it could be terminated. And so it was. For at this moment something came shimmering through the laurels in the quiet evenfall, and I perceived that it was Angela.

She was looking sweet and saintlike, and she had a plate of sandwiches in her hand. Ham, I was to discover later.

'If you see Mr Glossop anywhere, Bertie,' she said, her eyes resting dreamily on Tuppy's façade, 'I wish you would give him these. I'm so afraid he may be hungry, poor fellow. It's nearly ten o'clock, and he hasn't eaten a morsel since dinner. I'll just leave them on this bench.'

She pushed off, and it seemed to me that I might as well go with her. Nothing to keep me there, I mean. We moved towards the house, and presently from behind us there sounded in the night the splintering crash of a well-kicked plate of ham sandwiches, accompanied by the muffled oaths of a strong man in his wrath.

'How still and peaceful everything is,' said Angela.

16

Sunshine was gilding the grounds of Brinkley Court and the ear detected a marked twittering of birds in the ivy outside the window when I woke next morning to a new day. But there was no corresponding sunshine in Bertram Wooster's soul and no answering twitter in his heart as he sat up in bed, sipping his cup of strengthening tea. It could not be denied that to Bertram, reviewing the happenings of the previous night, the Tuppy–Angela situation seemed more or less to have slipped a cog. With every desire to look for the silver lining, I could not but feel that the rift between these two haughty spirits had now reached such impressive proportions that the task of bridging same would be beyond even my powers.

I am a shrewd observer, and there had been something in Tuppy's manner as he booted that plate of ham sandwiches that seemed to tell me that he would not lightly forgive.

In these circs, I deemed it best to shelve their problem for the nonce and turn the mind to the matter of Gussie, which presented a brighter picture.

With regard to Gussie, everything was in train. Jeeves's morbid scruples about lacing the chap's orange juice had put me to a good deal of trouble, but I had surmounted every obstacle in the old Wooster way. I had secured an abundance of the necessary spirit, and it was now lying in its flask in the drawer of the dressing table. I had also ascertained that the jug, duly filled, would be standing on a shelf in the butler's pantry round about the hour of one. To remove it from that shelf, sneak it up to my room, and return it, laced, in good time for the midday meal would be a task calling, no doubt, for address, but in no sense an exacting one.

It was with something of the emotions of one preparing a treat for a deserving child that I finished my tea and rolled over for that extra spot of sleep which just makes all the difference when there is man's work to be done and the brain must be kept clear for it.

And when I came downstairs an hour or so later, I knew how right I had been to formulate this scheme for Gussie's bucking up. I ran into him on the lawn, and I could see at a glance that if ever there was a man who needed a snappy stimulant, it was he. All nature, as I have indicated, was smiling, but not Augustus Fink-Nottle. He was walking round in circles, muttering something about not proposing to detain us long, but on this auspicious occasion feeling compelled to say a few words.

'Ah, Gussie,' I said, arresting him as he was about to start another lap. 'A lovely morning, is it not?'

Even if I had not been aware of it already, I could have divined from the abruptness with which he damned the lovely morning that he was not in merry mood. I addressed myself to the task of bringing the roses back to his cheeks.

'I've got good news for you, Gussie.'

He looked at me with a sudden sharp interest.

'Has Market Snodsbury Grammar School burned down?'

'Not that I know of.'

'Have mumps broken out? Is the place closed on account of measles?'

'No, no.'

'Then what do you mean you've got good news?'

I endeavoured to soothe.

'You mustn't take it so hard, Gussie. Why worry about a laughably simple job like distributing prizes at a school?'

'Laughably simple, eh? Do you realize I've been sweating for days and haven't been able to think of a thing to say yet, except that I won't detain them long. You bet I won't detain them long. What the devil am I to say, Bertie? What do you say when you're distributing prizes?'

I considered. Once, at my private school, I had won a prize for Scripture knowledge, so I suppose I ought to have been full of inside stuff. But memory eluded me.

Then something emerged from the mists.

'You say the race is not always to the swift.'

'Why?'

'Well, it's a good gag. It generally gets a hand.'

'I mean, why isn't it? Why isn't the race to the swift?'

'Ah, there you have me. But the nibs say it isn't.'

'But what does it mean?'

'I take it it's supposed to console the chaps who haven't won prizes.'

'What's the good of that to me? I'm not worrying about them. It's the ones that have won prizes that I'm worrying about, the little blighters who will come up on the platform. Suppose they make faces at me.'

'They won't.'

'How do you know they won't? It's probably the first thing they'll think of. And even if they don't—Bertie, shall I tell you something?'

'What?'

'I've a good mind to take that tip of yours and have a drink.'

I smiled subtly. He little knew, about summed up what I was thinking.

'Oh, you'll be all right,' I said.

He became fevered again.

'How do you know I'll be all right? I'm sure to blow up in my lines.'

'Tush!'

'Or drop a prize.'

'Tut!'

'Or something. I can feel it in my bones. As sure as I'm standing here, something is going to happen this afternoon which will make everybody laugh themselves sick at me. I can hear them now. Like hyenas . . . Bertie!'

'Hullo?'

'Do you remember that kids' school we went to before Eton?'

'Quite. It was there I won my Scripture prize.'

'Never mind about your Scripture prize. I'm not talking about your Scripture prize. Do you recollect the Bosher incident?'

I did, indeed. It was one of the high spots of my youth.

'Major-General Sir Wilfred Bosher came to distribute the prizes at that school,' proceeded Gussie in a dull, toneless voice. 'He dropped a book. He stooped to pick it up. And, as he stooped, his trousers split up the back.'

'How we roared!'

Gussie's face twisted.

'We did, little swine that we were. Instead of remaining silent and exhibiting a decent sympathy for a gallant officer at a peculiarly embarrassing moment, we howled and yelled with mirth. I loudest of any. That is what will happen to me this afternoon, Bertie. It will be a judgement on me for laughing like that at Major-General Sir Wilfred Bosher.'

'No, no, Gussie, old man. Your trousers won't split.'

'How do you know they won't? Better men than I have split their trousers. General Bosher was a DSO, with a fine record of service on the north-western frontier of India, and his trousers split. I shall be a mockery and a scorn. I know it. And you, fully cognizant of what I am in for, come babbling about good news. What news could possibly be good to me at this moment except the information that bubonic plague had broken out among the scholars of Market Snodsbury Grammar School, and that they were all confined to their beds with spots?'

The moment had come for me to speak. I laid a hand gently on his shoulder. He brushed it off. I laid it on again. He brushed it off once more. I was endeavouring to lay it on for the third time, when he moved aside and desired, with a certain petulance, to be informed if I thought I was a ruddy osteopath.

I found his manner trying, but one has to make allowances. I was telling myself that I should be seeing a very different Gussie after lunch.

'When I said I had good news, old man, I meant about Madeline Bassett.'

The febrile gleam died out of his eyes, to be replaced by a look of infinite sadness.

'You can't have good news about her. I've dished myself there completely.'

'Not at all. I am convinced that if you take another whack at her, all will be well.'

And, keeping it snappy, I related what had passed between the Bassett and myself on the previous night.

'So all you have to do is play a return date, and you cannot fail to swing the voting. You are her dream man.'

He shook his head.

'No.'

'What?'

'No use.'

'What do you mean?'

'Not a bit of good trying.'

'But I tell you she said in so many words—'

'It doesn't make any difference. She may have loved me once. Last night will have killed all that.'

'Of course it won't.'

'It will. She despises me now.'

'Not a bit of it. She knows you simply got cold feet.'

'And I should get cold feet if I tried again. It's no good, Bertie. I'm hopeless, and there's an end of it. Fate made me the sort of chap who can't say "bo" to a goose.'

'It isn't a question of saying "bo" to a goose. The point doesn't arise at all. It is simply a matter of—'

'I know, I know. But it's no good. I can't do it. The whole thing is off. I am not going to risk a repetition of last night's fiasco. You talk in a light way of taking another whack at her, but you don't know what it means. You have not been through the experience of starting to ask the girl you love to marry you and then suddenly finding yourself talking about the plumelike external gills of the newly-born newt. It's not a thing you can do twice. No, I accept my destiny. It's all over. And now, Bertie, like a good chap, shove off. I want to compose my speech. I can't compose my speech with you mucking around. If you are going to continue to muck around, at least give me a couple of stories. The little hell hounds are sure to expect a story or two.'

'Do you know the one about—'

'No good. I don't want any of your off-colour stuff from the Drones' smoking-room. I need something clean. Something that will be a help to them in their after lives. Not that I care a damn about their after lives, except that I hope they'll all choke.'

'I heard a story the other day. I can't quite remember it, but it was about a chap who snored and disturbed the neighbours, and it ended, "It was his adenoids that adenoid them."'

He made a weary gesture.

'You expect me to work that in, do you, into a speech to be delivered to an audience of boys, every one of whom is probably riddled with adenoids? Damn it, they'd rush the platform. Leave me, Bertie. Push off. That's all I ask you to do. Push off . . . Ladies and gentlemen,' said Gussie, in a low, soliloquizing sort of way, 'I do not propose to detain this auspicious occasion long—'

It was a thoughtful Wooster who walked away and left him at it. More than ever I was congratulating myself on having had the sterling good sense to make all my arrangements so that I could press a button and set things moving at an instant's notice.

Until now, you see, I had rather entertained a sort of hope that when I had revealed to him the Bassett's mental attitude, Nature would have done the rest, bracing him up to such an extent that artificial stimulants would not be required. Because, naturally, a chap doesn't want to have to sprint about country houses lugging jugs of orange juice, unless it is absolutely essential.

But now I saw that I must carry on as planned. The total absence of pep, ginger, and the right spirit which the man had displayed during these conversational exchanges convinced me that the strongest measures would be necessary. Immediately upon leaving him, therefore, I proceeded to the pantry, waited till the butler had removed himself elsewhere, and nipped in and secured the vital jug. A few moments later, after a wary passage of the stairs, I was in my room. And the first thing I saw there was Jeeves, fooling about with trousers.

He gave the jug a look which—wrongly, as it was to turn out—I diagnosed as censorious. I drew myself up a bit. I intended to have no rot from the fellow.

'Yes, Jeeves?'

'Sir?'

'You have the air of one about to make a remark, Jeeves.'

'Oh, no, sir. I note that you are in possession of Mr Fink-Nottle's orange juice. I was merely about to observe that in my opinion it would be injudicious to add spirit to it.'

'That is a remark, Jeeves, and it is precisely—'

'Because I have already attended to the matter, sir.'

'What?'

'Yes, sir. I decided, after all, to acquiesce in your wishes.'

I stared at the man, astounded. I was deeply moved. Well, I mean, wouldn't any chap who had been going about thinking that the old feudal spirit was dead, and then suddenly found it wasn't, have been deeply moved?

'Jeeves,' I said, 'I am touched.'

'Thank you, sir.'

'Touched and gratified.'

'Thank you very much, sir.'

'But what caused this change of heart?'

'I chanced to encounter Mr Fink-Nottle in the garden, sir, while you were still in bed, and we had a brief conversation.'

'And you came away feeling that he needed a bracer?'

'Very much so, sir. His attitude struck me as defeatist.'

I nodded.

'I felt the same. "Defeatist" sums it up to a nicety. Did you tell him his attitude struck you as defeatist?'

'Yes, sir.'

'But it didn't do any good?'

'No, sir.'

'Very well, then, Jeeves. We must act. How much gin did you put in the jug?'

'A liberal tumblerful, sir.'

'Would that be a normal dose for an adult defeatist, do you think?'

'I fancy it should prove adequate, sir.'

'I wonder. We must not spoil the ship for a ha'porth of tar. I think I'll add just another fluid ounce or so.'

'I would not advocate it, sir. In the case of Lord Brancaster's parrot—'

'You are falling into your old error, Jeeves, of thinking that Gussie is a parrot. Fight against this. I shall add the oz.'

'Very good, sir.'

'And, by the way, Jeeves, Mr Fink-Nottle is in the market for bright, clean stories to use in his speech. Do you know any?'

'I know a story about two Irishmen, sir.'

'Pat and Mike?'

'Yes, sir.'

'Who were walking along Broadway?'

'Yes, sir.'

'Just what he wants. Any more?'

'No, sir.'

'Well, every little helps. You had better go and tell it to him.'

'Very good, sir.'

He passed from the room, and I unscrewed the flask and tilted into the jug a generous modicum of its contents. And scarcely had I done so, when there came to my ears the sound of footsteps without. I had only just time to shove the jug behind the photograph of Uncle Tom on the mantelpiece before the door opened and in came Gussie, curveting like a circus horse.

'What-ho, Bertie,' he said. 'What-ho, what-ho, what-ho, and again what-ho. What a beautiful world this is, Bertie. One of the nicest I ever met.'

I stared at him, speechless. We Woosters are as quick as lightning, and I saw at once that something had happened.

I mean to say, I told you about him walking round in circles. I recorded what passed between us on the lawn. And if I portrayed the scene with anything like adequate skill, the picture you will have retained of this Fink-Nottle will have been that of a nervous wreck, sagging at the knees, green about the gills, and picking feverishly at the lapels of his coat in an ecstasy of craven fear. In a word, defeatist. Gussie, during that interview, had, in fine, exhibited all the earmarks of one licked to a custard.

Vastly different was the Gussie who stood before me now. Self-confidence seemed to ooze from the fellow's every pore. His face was flushed, there was a jovial light in his eyes, the lips were parted in a swashbuckling smile. And when with a genial hand he sloshed me on the back before I could sidestep, it was as if I had been kicked by a mule.

'Well, Bertie,' he proceeded, as blithely as a linnet without a thing on his mind, 'you will be glad to hear that you were right. Your theory has been tested and proved correct. I feel like a fighting cock.'

My brain ceased to reel. I saw all.

'Have you been having a drink?'

'I have. As you advised. Unpleasant stuff. Like medicine. Burns your throat, too, and makes one as thirsty as the dickens. How anyone can mop it up, as you do, for pleasure beats me. Still, I would be the last to deny that it tunes up the system. I could bite a tiger.'

'What did you have?'

'Whisky. At least, that was the label on the decanter, and I have no reason to suppose that a woman like your aunt—staunch, true-blue, British—would deliberately deceive the public. If she labels her decanters Whisky, then I consider that we know where we are.'

'A whisky and soda, eh? You couldn't have done better.'

'Soda?' said Gussie thoughtfully. 'I knew there was something I had forgotten.'

'Didn't you put any soda in it?'

'It never occurred to me. I just nipped into the dining-room and drank out of the decanter.'

'How much?'

'Oh, about ten swallows. Twelve, maybe. Or fourteen. Say sixteen medium-sized gulps. Gosh, I'm thirsty.'

He moved over to the wash-hand stand and drank deeply out of the water bottle. I cast a covert glance at Uncle Tom's photograph behind his back. For the first time since it had come into my life, I was glad that it was so large. It hid its secret well. If Gussie had caught sight of that jug of orange juice, he would unquestionably have been on to it like a knife.

'Well, I'm glad you're feeling braced,' I said.

He moved buoyantly from the wash-hand stand, and endeavoured to slosh me on the back again. Foiled by my nimble footwork, he staggered to the bed and sat down upon it.

'Braced? Did I say I could bite a tiger?'

'You did.'

'Make it two tigers. I could chew holes in a steel door. What an ass you must have thought me out there in the garden. I see now you were laughing in your sleeve.'

'No, no.'

'Yes,' insisted Gussie. 'That very sleeve,' he said, pointing. 'And I don't blame you. I can't imagine why I made all that fuss about a potty job like distributing prizes at a rotten little country grammar school. Can you imagine, Bertie?'

'No.'

'Exactly. Nor can I imagine. There's simply nothing to it. I just shin up on the platform, drop a few gracious words, hand the little blighters their prizes, and hop down again, admired by all. Not a suggestion of split trousers from start to finish. I mean, why should anybody split his trousers? I can't imagine. Can you imagine?'

'No.'

'Nor can I imagine. I shall be a riot. I know just the sort of stuff that's needed—simple, manly, optimistic stuff straight from the shoulder. This shoulder,' said Gussie, tapping. 'Why I was so nervous this morning I can't imagine. For anything simpler than distributing a few footling books to a bunch of grimy-faced kids I can't imagine. Still, for some reason I can't imagine, I was feeling a little nervous, but now I feel fine, Bertie—fine, fine, fine—and I say this to you as an old friend. Because that's what you are, old man, when all the smoke has cleared away—an old friend. I don't think I've ever met an older friend. How long have you been an old friend of mine, Bertie?'

'Oh, years and years.'

'Imagine? Though, of course, there must have been a time when you were a new friend . . . Hullo, the luncheon gong. Come on, old friend.'

And, rising from the bed like a performing flea, he made for the door.

I followed rather pensively. What had occurred was, of course, so much velvet, as you might say. I mean, I had wanted a braced Fink-Nottle—indeed, all my plans had had a braced Fink-Nottle as their end and aim—but I found myself wondering a little whether the Fink-Nottle now sliding down the banister wasn't, perhaps, a shade too braced. His demeanour seemed to me that of a man who might quite easily throw bread about at lunch.

Fortunately, however, the settled gloom of those round him exercised a restraining effect upon him at the table. It would have needed a far more plastered man to have been rollicking at such a gathering. I had told the Bassett that there were aching hearts in Brinkley Court, and it now looked probable that there would shortly be aching tummies. Anatole, I learned, had retired to his bed with a fit of the vapours, and the meal now before us had been cooked by the kitchen maid—as C3 a performer as ever wielded a skillet.

This, coming on top of their other troubles, induced in the company a pretty unanimous silence—a solemn stillness, as you might say—which even Gussie did not seem prepared to break. Except, therefore, for one short snatch of song on his part, nothing untoward marked the occasion, and presently we rose, with instructions from Aunt Dahlia to put on festal raiment and be at Market Snodsbury not later than 3.30. This leaving me ample time to smoke a gasper or two in a shady bower beside the lake, I did so, repairing to my room round about the hour of three.

Jeeves was on the job, adding the final polish to the old topper, and I was about to apprise him of the latest developments in the matter of Gussie, when he forestalled me by observing that the latter had only just concluded an agreeable visit to the Wooster bedchamber.

'I found Mr Fink-Nottle seated here when I arrived to lay out your clothes, sir.'

'Indeed, Jeeves? Gussie was in here, was he?'

'Yes, sir. He left only a few moments ago. He is driving to the school with Mr and Mrs Travers in the large car.'

'Did you give him your story of the two Irishmen?'

'Yes, sir. He laughed heartily.'

'Good. Had you any other contributions for him?'

'I ventured to suggest that he might mention to the young gentlemen that education is a drawing out, not a putting in. The late Lord Brancaster was much addicted to presenting prizes at schools, and he invariably employed this dictum.'

'And how did he react to that?'

'He laughed heartily, sir.'

'This surprised you, no doubt? This practically incessant merriment, I mean.'

'Yes, sir.'

'You thought it odd in one who, when you last saw him, was well up in Group A of the defeatists.'

'Yes, sir.'

'There is a ready explanation, Jeeves. Since you last saw him, Gussie has been on a bender. He's as tight as an owl.'

'Indeed, sir?'

'Absolutely. His nerve cracked under the strain, and he sneaked into the dining-room and started mopping the stuff up like a vacuum cleaner. Whisky would seem to be what he filled the radiator with. I gather that he used up most of the decanter. Golly, Jeeves, it's lucky he didn't get at that laced orange juice on top of that, what?'

'Extremely, sir.'

I eyed the jug. Uncle Tom's photograph had fallen into the fender, and it was standing there right out in the open, where Gussie couldn't have helped seeing it. Mercifully, it was empty now.

'It was a most prudent act on your part, if I may say so, sir, to dispose of the orange juice.'

I stared at the man.

'What? Didn't you?'

'No, sir.'

'Jeeves, let us get this clear. Was it not you who threw away that o.j.?'

'No, sir. I assumed, when I entered the room and found the pitcher empty, that you had done so.'

We looked at each other, awed. Two minds with but a single thought.

'I very much fear, sir—'

'So do I, Jeeves.'

'It would seem almost certain—'

'Quite certain. Weigh the facts. Sift the evidence. The jug was standing on the mantelpiece, for all eyes to behold. Gussie had been complaining of thirst. You found him in here, laughing heartily. I think that there can be little doubt, Jeeves, that the entire contents of that jug are at this moment reposing on top of the existing cargo in that already brilliantly lit man's interior. Disturbing, Jeeves.'

'Most disturbing, sir.'

'Let us face the position, forcing ourselves to be calm. You inserted in that jug—shall we say a tumblerful of the right stuff?'

'Fully a tumblerful, sir.'

'And I added of my plenty about the same amount.'

'Yes, sir.'

'And in two shakes of a duck's tail Gussie, with all that lapping about inside him, will be distributing the prizes at Market Snodsbury Grammar School before an audience of all that is fairest and most refined in the county.'

'Yes, sir.'

'It seems to me, Jeeves, that the ceremony may be one fraught with considerable interest.'

'Yes, sir.'

'What, in your opinion, will the harvest be?'

'One finds it difficult to hazard a conjecture, sir.'

'You mean imagination boggles?'

'Yes, sir.'

I inspected my imagination. He was right. It boggled.

17

'And yet, Jeeves,' I said, twiddling a thoughtful steering wheel, 'there is always the bright side.'

Some twenty minutes had elapsed, and having picked the honest fellow up outside the front door, I was driving in the two-seater to the picturesque town of Market Snodsbury. Since we had parted—he to go to his lair and fetch his hat, I to remain in my room and complete the formal costume—I had been doing some close thinking.

The results of this I now proceeded to hand on to him.

'However dark the prospect may be, Jeeves, however murkily the storm clouds may seem to gather, a keen eye can usually discern the blue bird. It is bad, no doubt, that Gussie should be going, some ten minutes from now, to distribute prizes in a state of advanced intoxication, but we must never forget that these things cut both ways.'

'You imply, sir—'

'Precisely. I am thinking of him in his capacity of wooer. All this ought to have put him in rare shape for offering his hand in marriage. I shall be vastly surprised if it won't turn him into a sort of caveman. Have you ever seen James Cagney in the movies?'

'Yes, sir.'

'Something on those lines.'

I heard him cough, and sniped him with a sideways glance. He was wearing that informative look of his.

'Then you have not heard, sir?'

'Eh?'

'You are not aware that a marriage has been arranged and will shortly take place between Mr Fink-Nottle and Miss Bassett?'

'What?'

'Yes, sir.'

'When did this happen?'

'Shortly after Mr Fink-Nottle had left your room, sir.'

'Ah! In the post-orange-juice era?'

'Yes, sir.'

'But are you sure of your facts? How do you know?'

'My informant was Mr Fink-Nottle himself, sir. He appeared anxious to confide in me. His story was somewhat incoherent, but I had no difficulty in apprehending its substance. Prefacing his remarks with the statement that this was a beautiful world, he laughed heartily and said that he had become formally engaged.'

'No details?'

'No, sir.'

'But one can picture the scene.'

'Yes, sir.'

'I mean, imagination doesn't boggle.'

'No, sir.'

And it didn't. I could see exactly what must have happened. Insert a liberal dose of mixed spirits in a normally abstemious man, and he becomes a force. He does not stand round, twiddling his fingers and stammering. He acts. I had no doubt that Gussie must have reached for the Bassett and clasped her to him like a stevedore handling a sack of coals. And one could readily envisage the effect of that sort of thing on a girl of romantic mind.

'Well, well, well, Jeeves.'

'Yes, sir.'

'This is splendid news.'

'Yes, sir.'

'You see now how right I was.'

'Yes, sir.'

'It must have been rather an eye-opener for you, watching me handle this case.'

'Yes, sir.'

'The simple, direct method never fails.'

'No, sir.'

'Whereas the elaborate does.'

'Yes, sir.'

'Right ho, Jeeves.'

We had arrived at the main entrance of Market Snodsbury Grammar School. I parked the car, and went in, well content. True, the Tuppy–Angela problem still remained unsolved and Aunt Dahlia's five hundred quid seemed as far off as ever, but it was gratifying to feel that good old Gussie's troubles were over, at any rate.

The Grammar School at Market Snodsbury had, I understood, been built somewhere in the year 1416, and, as with so many of these ancient foundations, there still seemed to brood over its Great Hall, where the afternoon's festivities were to take place, not a little of the fug of the centuries. It was the hottest day of the summer, and though somebody had opened a tentative window or two, the atmosphere remained distinctive and individual.

In this hall the youth of Market Snodsbury had been eating its daily lunch for a matter of five hundred years, and the flavour lingered. The air was sort of heavy and languorous, if you know what I mean, with the scent of Young England and boiled beef and carrots.

Aunt Dahlia, who was sitting with a bevy of the local nibs in the second row, sighted me as I entered and waved to me to join her, but I was too smart for that. I wedged myself in among the standees at the back, leaning up against a chap who, from the aroma, might have been a corn chandler or something of that order. The essence of strategy on these occasions is to be as near the door as possible.

The hall was gaily decorated with flags and coloured paper, and the eye was further refreshed by the spectacle of a mixed drove of boys, parents, and what not, the former running a good deal to shiny faces and Eton collars, the latter stressing the black-satin note rather when female, and looking as if their coats were too tight, if male. And presently there was some applause—sporadic, Jeeves has since told me it was—and I saw Gussie being steered by a bearded bloke in a gown to a seat in the middle of the platform.

And I confess that as I beheld him and felt that there but for the grace of God went Bertram Wooster, a shudder ran through the frame. It all reminded me so vividly of the time I had addressed that girls' school.

Of course, looking at it dispassionately, you may say that for horror and peril there is no comparison between an almost human audience like the one before me and a mob of small girls with pigtails down their backs, and this, I concede, is true. Nevertheless, the spectacle was enough to make me feel like a fellow watching a pal going over Niagara Falls in a barrel, and the thought of what I had escaped caused everything for a moment to go black and swim before my eyes.

When I was able to see clearly once more, I perceived that Gussie was now seated. He had his hands on his knees, with his elbows out at right angles, like a nigger minstrel of the old school about to ask Mr Bones why a chicken crosses the road, and he was staring before him with a smile so fixed and pebble-beached that I should have thought that anybody could have guessed that there sat one in whom the old familiar juice was splashing up against the back of the front teeth.

In fact, I saw Aunt Dahlia, who, having assisted at so many hunting dinners in her time, is second to none as a judge of the symptoms, give a start and gaze long and earnestly. And she was just saying something to Uncle Tom on her left when the bearded bloke stepped to the footlights and started making a speech. From the fact that he spoke as if he had a hot potato in his mouth without getting the raspberry from the lads in the ringside seats, I deduced that he must be the headmaster.

With his arrival in the spotlight, a sort of perspiring resignation seemed to settle on the audience. Personally, I snuggled up against the chandler and let my attention wander. The speech was on the subject of the doings of the school during the past term, and this part of a prize-giving is always apt rather to fail to grip the visiting stranger. I mean, you know how it is. You're told that J. B. Brewster has won an Exhibition for Classics at Cat's, Cambridge, and you feel that it's one of those stories where you can't see how funny it is unless you really know the fellow. And the same applies to G. Bullett being awarded the Lady Jane Wix Scholarship at the Birmingham College of Veterinary Science.

In fact, I and the corn chandler, who was looking a bit fagged, I thought, as if he had had a hard morning chandling the corn, were beginning to doze lightly when things suddenly brisked up, bringing Gussie into the picture for the first time.

'Today,' said the bearded bloke, 'we are all happy to welcome as the guest of the afternoon Mr Fitz-Wattle—'

At the beginning of the address, Gussie had subsided into a sort of daydream, with his mouth hanging open. About halfway through, faint signs of life had begun to show. And for the last few minutes he had been trying to cross one leg over the other and failing and having another shot and failing again. But only now did he exhibit any real animation. He sat up with a jerk.

'Fink-Nottle,' he said, opening his eyes.

'Fitz-Nottle.'

'Fink-Nottle.'

'I should say Fink-Nottle.'

'Of course you should, you silly ass,' said Gussie genially. 'All right, get on with it.'

And closing his eyes, he began trying to cross his legs again.

I could see that this little spot of friction had rattled the bearded bloke a bit. He stood for a moment fumbling at the fungus with a hesitating hand. But they make these headmasters of tough stuff. The weakness passed. He came back nicely and carried on.

'We are all happy, I say, to welcome as the guest of the afternoon Mr Fink-Nottle, who has kindly consented to award the prizes. This task, as you know, is one that should have devolved upon that well-beloved and vigorous member of our board of governors, the Rev. William Plomer, and we are all, I am sure, very sorry that illness at the last moment should have prevented him from being here today. But, if I may borrow a familiar metaphor from the—if I may employ a homely metaphor familiar to you all—what we lose on the swings we gain on the roundabouts.'

He paused, and beamed rather freely, to show that this was comedy. I could have told the man it was no use. Not a ripple. The corn chandler leaned against me and muttered 'Whoddidesay?' but that was all.

It's always a nasty jar to wait for the laugh and find that the gag hasn't got across. The bearded bloke was visibly discomposed. At that, however,

I think he would have got by, had he not, at this juncture, unfortunately stirred Gussie up again.

'In other words, though deprived of Mr Plomer, we have with us this afternoon Mr Fink-Nottle. I am sure that Mr Fink-Nottle's name is one that needs no introduction to you. It is, I venture to assert, a name that is familiar to us all.'

'Not to you,' said Gussie.

And the next moment I saw what Jeeves had meant when he had described him as laughing heartily. 'Heartily' was absolutely the *mot juste*. It sounded like a gas explosion.

'You didn't seem to know it so dashed well, what, what?' said Gussie. And, reminded apparently by the word 'what' of the word 'Wattle', he repeated the latter some sixteen times with a rising inflexion.

'Wattle, Wattle, Wattle,' he concluded. 'Right-ho. Push on.'

But the bearded bloke had shot his bolt. He stood there, licked at last; and, watching him closely, I could see that he was now at the crossroads. I could spot what he was thinking as clearly as if he had confided it to my personal ear. He wanted to sit down and call it a day, I mean, but the thought that gave him pause was that, if he did, he must then either uncork Gussie or take the Fink-Nottle speech as read and get straight on to the actual prize-giving.

It was a dashed tricky thing, of course, to have to decide on the spur of the moment. I was reading in the paper the other day about those birds who are trying to split the atom, the nub being that they haven't the foggiest as to what will happen if they do. It may be all right. On the other hand, it may not be all right. And pretty silly a chap would feel, no doubt, if, having split the atom, he suddenly found the house going up in smoke and himself torn limb from limb.

So with the bearded bloke. Whether he was abreast of the inside facts in Gussie's case, I don't know, but it was obvious to him by this time that he had run into something pretty hot. Trial gallops had shown that Gussie had his own way of doing things. Those interruptions had been enough to prove to the perspicacious that here, seated on the platform at the big binge of the season, was one who, if pushed forward to make a speech, might let himself go in a rather epoch-making manner.

On the other hand, chain him up and put a green-baize cloth over him, and where were you? The proceeding would be over about half an hour too soon.

It was, as I say, a difficult problem to have to solve, and, left to himself, I don't know what conclusion he would have come to. Personally, I think he would have played it safe. As it happened, however, the thing was taken out of his hands, for at this moment, Gussie, having stretched his arms and yawned a bit, switched on that pebble-beached smile again and tacked down to the edge of the platform.

'Speech,' he said affably.

He then stood with his thumbs in the armholes of his waistcoat, waiting for the applause to die down.

It was some time before this happened, for he had got a very fine hand indeed. I suppose it wasn't often that the boys of Market Snodsbury Grammar School came across a man public-spirited enough to call their headmaster a silly ass, and they showed their appreciation in no uncertain manner. Gussie may have been one over the eight, but as far as the majority of those present were concerned he was sitting on top of the world.

'Boys,' said Gussie, 'I mean ladies and gentlemen and boys, I will not detain you long, but I propose on this occasion to feel compelled to say a few auspicious words. Ladies—boys and ladies and gentlemen—we have all listened with interest to the remarks of our friend here who forgot to shave this morning—I don't know his name, but then he didn't know mine—Fitz-Wattle, I mean, absolutely absurd—which squares things up a bit—and we are all sorry that the Reverend What-ever-he-was-called should be dying of adenoids, but after all, here today, gone tomorrow, and all flesh is as grass, and what not, but that wasn't what I wanted to say. What I wanted to say was this—and I say it confidently—without fear of contradiction—I say, in short, I am happy to be here on this auspicious occasion and I take much pleasure in kindly awarding the prizes, consisting of the handsome books you see laid out on that table. As Shakespeare says, there are sermons in books, stones in the running brooks, or, rather, the other way about, and there you have it in a nutshell.'

It went well, and I wasn't surprised. I couldn't quite follow some of it, but anybody could see that it was real ripe stuff, and I was amazed that even the course of treatment he had been taking could have rendered so normally tongue-tied a dumb brick as Gussie capable of it.

It just shows, what any member of Parliament will tell you, that if you want real oratory, the preliminary noggin is essential. Unless pie-eyed, you cannot hope to grip.

'Gentlemen,' said Gussie, 'I mean ladies and gentlemen and, of course, boys, what a beautiful world this is. A beautiful world, full of happiness on every side. Let me tell you a little story. Two Irishmen, Pat and Mike, were walking along Broadway, and one said to the other, "Begorrah, the race is not always to the swift," and the other replied, "Faith and begob, education is a drawing out, not a putting in."'

I must say it seemed to me the rottenest story I had ever heard, and I was surprised that Jeeves should have considered it worth shoving into a speech. However, when I taxed him with this later, he said that Gussie had altered the plot a good deal, and I dare say that accounts for it.

At any rate, that was the *conte* as Gussie told it, and when I say that it got a very fair laugh, you will understand what a popular favourite he had become with the multitude. There might be a bearded bloke or so on the platform and a small section in the second row who were wishing the speaker would conclude his remarks and resume his seat, but the audience as a whole was for him solidly.

There was applause, and a voice cried: 'Hear, hear!'

'Yes,' said Gussie, 'it is a beautiful world. The sky is blue, the birds are singing, there is optimism everywhere. And why not, boys and ladies and gentlemen? I'm happy, you're happy, we're all happy, even the meanest Irishman that walks along Broadway. Though as I say, there were two of them—Pat and Mike, one drawing out, the other putting in. I should like you boys, taking the time from me, to give three cheers for this beautiful world. All together now.'

Presently the dust settled down and the plaster stopped falling from the ceiling, and he went on.

'People who say it isn't a beautiful world don't know what they are talking about. Driving here in the car today to award the kind prizes, I was reluctantly compelled to tick off my host on this very point. Old Tom Travers. You will see him sitting there in the second row next to the large lady in beige.'

He pointed helpfully, and the hundred or so Market Snodsburyians who craned their necks in the direction indicated were able to observe Uncle Tom blushing prettily.

'I ticked him off properly, the poor fish. He expressed the opinion that the world was in a deplorable state. I said, "Don't talk rot, old Tom Travers." "I am not accustomed to talk rot," he said. "Then, for a beginner," I said, "you do it dashed well." And I think you will admit, boys and ladies and gentlemen, that that was telling him.'

The audience seemed to agree with him. The point went big. The voice that had said 'Hear, hear' said 'Hear, hear' again, and my corn chandler hammered the floor vigorously with a large-size walking stick.

'Well, boys,' resumed Gussie, having shot his cuffs and smirked horribly, 'this is the end of the summer term, and many of you, no doubt, are leaving the school. And I don't blame you, because there's a froust in here you could cut with a knife. You are going out into the great world. Soon many of you will be walking along Broadway. And what I want to impress upon you is that, however much you may suffer from adenoids, you must all use every effort to prevent yourselves becoming pessimists and talking rot like old Tom Travers. There in the second row. The fellow with a face rather like a walnut.'

He paused to allow those wishing to do so to refresh themselves with another look at Uncle Tom, and I found myself musing in some little perplexity. Long association with the members of the Drones has put me pretty well in touch with the various ways in which an overdose of the blushful Hippocrene can take the individual, but I had never seen anyone react quite as Gussie was doing.

There was a sort of snap about his work which I had never witnessed before, even in Barmy Fotheringay-Phipps on New Year's Eve.

Jeeves, when I discussed the matter with him later, said it was something to do with inhibitions, if I caught the word correctly, and the suppression of, I think he said, the ego. What he meant, I gathered, was that, owing to the fact that Gussie had just completed a five years' stretch of blameless seclusion among the newts, all the goofiness which ought to have been spread out thin over those five years and had been bottled up during that period came to the surface on this occasion in a lump—or, if you prefer to put it that way, like a tidal wave.

There may be something in this. Jeeves generally knows.

Anyway, be that as it may, I was dashed glad I had had the shrewdness to keep out of that second row. It might be unworthy of the prestige of a Wooster to squash in among the proletariat in the standing-room-only section, but at least, I felt, I was out of the danger zone. So thoroughly had Gussie got it up his nose by now that it seemed to me that had he sighted me he might have become personal about even an old school friend.

'If there's one thing in the world I can't stand,' proceeded Gussie, 'it's a pessimist. Be optimists, boys. You all know the difference between an optimist and a pessimist. An optimist is a man who—well, take the case of two Irishmen walking along Broadway. One is an optimist and one is a pessimist, just as one's name is Pat and the other's Mike . . . Why, hullo, Bertie; I didn't know you were here.'

Too late, I endeavoured to go to earth behind the chandler, only to discover that there was no chandler there. Some appointment, suddenly remembered—possibly a promise to his wife that he would be home to tea—had caused him to ooze away while my attention was elsewhere, leaving me right out in the open.

Between me and Gussie, who was now pointing in an offensive manner, there was nothing but a sea of interested faces looking up at me.

'Now, there,' boomed Gussie, continuing to point, 'is an instance of what I mean. Boys and ladies and gentlemen, take a good look at that object standing up there at the back—morning coat, trousers as worn, quiet grey tie, and carnation in buttonhole—you can't miss him. Bertie Wooster, that is, and as foul a pessimist as ever bit a tiger. I tell you I despise that man. And why do I despise him? Because, boys and ladies and gentlemen, he is a pessimist. His attitude is defeatist. When I told him I was going to address you this afternoon, he tried to dissuade me. And do you know why he tried to dissuade me? Because he said my trousers would split up the back.'

The cheers that greeted this were the loudest yet. Anything about splitting trousers went straight to the simple hearts of the young scholars of Market Snodsbury Grammar School. Two in the row in front of me turned purple, and a small lad with freckles seated beside them asked me for my autograph.

'Let me tell you a story about Bertie Wooster.'

A Wooster can stand a good deal, but he cannot stand having his name bandied in a public place. Picking my feet up softly, I was in the very process of executing a quiet sneak for the door, when I perceived that the bearded bloke had at last decided to apply the closure.

Why he hadn't done so before is beyond me. Spellbound, I take it. And, of course, when a chap is going like a breeze with the public, as Gussie had been, it's not so dashed easy to chip in. However, the prospect of hearing another of Gussie's anecdotes seemed to have done the trick. Rising rather as I had risen from my bench at the beginning of that painful scene with Tuppy in the twilight, he made a leap for the table, snatched up a book and came bearing down on the speaker.

He touched Gussie on the arm, and Gussie, turning sharply and seeing a large bloke with a beard apparently about to bean him with a book, sprang back in an attitude of self-defence.

'Perhaps, as time is getting on, Mr Fink-Nottle, we had better—'

'Oh, ah,' said Gussie, getting the trend. He relaxed. 'The prizes, eh? Of course, yes. Rightho. Yes, might as well be shoving along with it. What's this one?'

'Spelling and dictation—P. K. Purvis,' announced the bearded bloke.

'Spelling and dictation—P. K. Purvis,' echoed Gussie, as if he were calling coals. 'Forward, P. K. Purvis.'

Now that the whistle had been blown on his speech, it seemed to me that there was no longer any need for the strategic retreat which I had been planning. I had no wish to tear myself away unless I had to. I mean, I had told Jeeves that this binge would be fraught with interest, and it was fraught with interest. There was a fascination about Gussie's methods which gripped and made one reluctant to pass the thing up provided personal innuendoes were steered clear of. I decided, accordingly, to remain, and presently there was a musical squeaking and P. K. Purvis climbed the platform.

The spelling-and-dictation champ was about three foot six in his squeaking shoes, with a pink face and sandy hair.

Gussie patted this hair. He seemed to have taken an immediate fancy to the lad.

'You P. K. Purvis?'

'Sir, yes, sir.'

'It's a beautiful world, P. K. Purvis.'

'Sir, yes, sir.'

'Ah, you've noticed it, have you? Good. You married, by any chance?'

'Sir, no, sir.'

'Get married, P. K. Purvis,' said Gussie earnestly. 'It's the only life . . . Well, here's your book. Looks rather bilge to me from a glance at the title page, but, such as it is, here you are.'

P. K. Purvis squeaked off amidst sporadic applause, but one could not fail to note that the sporadic was followed by a rather strained silence. It was evident that Gussie was striking something of a new note in Market Snodsbury scholastic circles. Looks were exchanged between parent and parent. The bearded bloke had the air of one who had drained the bitter cup. As for Aunt Dahlia, her demeanour now told only too clearly that her last doubts had been resolved and her verdict was in. I saw her whisper to the Bassett, who sat on her right, and the Bassett nodded sadly and looked like a fairy about to shed a tear and add another star to the Milky Way.

Gussie, after the departure of P. K. Purvis, had fallen into a sort of daydream and was standing with his mouth open and his hands in his pockets·. Becoming abruptly aware that a fat kid in knickerbockers was at his elbow, he started violently.

'Hullo!' he said, visibly shaken. 'Who are you?'

'This,' said the bearded bloke, 'is R. V. Smethurst.'

'What's he doing here?' asked Gussie suspiciously.

'You are presenting him with the drawing prize, Mr Fink-Nottle.'

This apparently struck Gussie as a reasonable explanation. His face cleared.

'That's right too,' he said . . . 'Well, here it is, cocky. You off?' he said, as the kid prepared to withdraw.

'Sir, yes, sir.'

'Wait, R. V. Smethurst. Not so fast. Before you go, there is a question I wish to ask you.'

But the bearded bloke's aim now seemed to be to rush the ceremonies a bit. He hustled R. V. Smethurst off stage rather like a chucker-out in a pub regretfully ejecting an old and respected customer, and starting paging G. G. Simmons. A moment later the latter was up and coming, and conceive my emotion when it was announced that the subject on which he had clicked was Scripture knowledge. One of us, I mean to say.

G. G. Simmons was an unpleasant, perky-looking stripling, mostly front teeth and spectacles, but I gave him a big hand. We Scripture-knowledge sharks stick together.

Gussie, I was sorry to see, didn't like him. There was in his manner, as he regarded G. G. Simmons, none of the chumminess which had marked it during his interview with P. K. Purvis or, in a somewhat lesser degree, with R. V. Smethurst. He was cold and distant.

'Well, G. G. Simmons.'

'Sir, yes, sir.'

'What do you mean—sir, yes, sir? Dashed silly thing to say. So you've won the Scripture-knowledge prize, have you?'

'Sir, yes, sir.'

'Yes,' said Gussie, 'you look just the sort of little tick who would. And yet,' he said, pausing and eyeing the child keenly, 'how are we to know that this has all been open and above board? Let me test you, G. G. Simmons. Who was What's-His-Name—the chap who begat Thingummy? Can you answer me that, Simmons?'

'Sir, no, sir.'

Gussie turned to the bearded bloke.

'Fishy,' he said. 'Very fishy. This boy appears to be totally lacking in Scripture knowledge.'

The bearded bloke passed a hand across his forehead.

'I can assure you, Mr Finkle-Nottle, that every care was taken to ensure a correct marking and that Simmons outdistanced his competitors by a wide margin.'

'Well, if you say so,' said Gussie doubtfully. 'All right, G. G. Simmons, take your prize.'

'Sir, thank you, sir.'

'But let me tell you that there's nothing to stick on side about in winning a prize for Scripture knowledge. Bertie Wooster—'

I don't know when I've had a nastier shock. I had been going on the assumption that, now that they had stopped him making his speech, Gussie's fangs had been drawn, as you might say. To duck my head down and resume my edging towards the door was with me the work of a moment.

'Bertie Wooster won the Scripture-knowledge prize at a kids' school we were at together, and you know what he's like. But, of course, Bertie frankly cheated. He succeeded in scrounging that Scripture-knowledge trophy over the heads of better men by means of some of the rawest and most brazen swindling methods ever witnessed even at a school where such things were common. If that man's pockets, as he entered the examination-room, were not stuffed to bursting point with lists of the kings of Judah—'

I heard no more. A moment later I was out in God's air, fumbling with a fevered foot at the self-starter of the old car.

The engine raced. The clutch slid into position. I tooted and drove off.

My ganglions were still vibrating as I ran the car into the stables of Brinkley Court, and it was a much shaken Bertram who tottered up to his room to change into something loose. Having donned flannels, I lay down on the bed for a bit, and I suppose I must have dozed off, for the next thing I remember is finding Jeeves at my side.

I sat up.

'My tea, Jeeves?'

'No, sir. It is nearly dinner-time.'

The mists cleared away.

'I must have been asleep.'

'Yes, sir.'

'Nature taking its toll of the exhausted frame.'

'Yes, sir.'

'And enough to make it.'

'Yes, sir.'

'And now it's nearly dinner-time, you say? All right. I am in no mood for dinner, but I suppose you had better lay out the clothes.'

'It will not be necessary, sir. The company will not be dressing tonight. A cold collation has been set out in the dining-room.'

'Why's that?'

'It was Mrs Travers's wish that this should be done in order to minimize the work for the staff, who are attending a dance at Sir Percival Stretchley-Budd's residence tonight.'

'Of course, yes. I remember. My Cousin Angela told me. Tonight's the night, what? You going, Jeeves?'

'No, sir. I am not very fond of this form of entertainment in the rural districts, sir.'

'I know what you mean. These country binges are all the same. A piano, one fiddle, and a floor like sandpaper. Is Anatole going? Angela hinted not.'

'Miss Angela was correct, sir. Monsieur Anatole is in bed.'

'Temperamental blighters, these Frenchmen.'

'Yes, sir.'

There was a pause.

'Well, Jeeves,' I said, 'it was certainly one of those afternoons, what?'

'Yes, sir.'

'I cannot recall one more packed with incident. And I left before the finish.'

'Yes, sir. I observed your departure.'

'You couldn't blame me for withdrawing.'

'No, sir. Mr Fink-Nottle had undoubtedly become embarrassingly personal.'

'Was there much more of it after I went?'

'No, sir. The proceedings terminated very shortly. Mr Fink-Nottle's remarks with reference to Master G. G. Simmons brought about an early closure.'

'But he had finished his remarks about G. G. Simmons.'

'Only temporarily, sir. He resumed them immediately after your departure. If you recollect, sir, he had already proclaimed himself suspicious of Master Simmons's bona fides, and he now proceeded to deliver a violent verbal attack upon the young gentleman, asserting that it was impossible for him to have won the Scripture-knowledge prize without systematic cheating on an impressive scale. He went so far as to suggest that Master Simmons was well known to the police.'

'Golly, Jeeves!'

'Yes, sir. The words did create a considerable sensation. The reaction of those present to this accusation I should describe as mixed. The young students appeared pleased and applauded vigorously, but Master Simmons's mother rose from her seat and addressed Mr Fink-Nottle in terms of strong protest.'

'Did Gussie seem taken aback? Did he recede from his position?'

'No, sir. He said that he could see it all now, and hinted at a guilty liaison between Master Simmons's mother and the headmaster, accusing the latter of having cooked the marks, as his expression was, in order to gain favour with the former.'

'You don't mean that?'

'Yes, sir.'

'Egad, Jeeves! And then—'

'They sang the national anthem, sir.'

'Surely not?'

'Yes, sir.'

'At a moment like that?'

'Yes, sir.'

'Well, you were there and you know, of course, but I should have thought the last thing Gussie and this woman would have done in the circs would have been to start singing duets.'

'You misunderstand me, sir. It was the entire company who sang. The headmaster turned to the organist and said something to him in a low tone. Upon which the latter began to play the national anthem, and the proceedings terminated.'

'I see. About time, too.'

'Yes, sir. Mrs Simmons's attitude had become unquestionably menacing.'

I pondered. What I had heard was, of course, of a nature to excite pity and terror, not to mention alarm and despondency, and it would be paltering with the truth to say that I was pleased about it. On the other hand, it was all over now, and it seemed to me that the thing to do was not to mourn over the past but to fix the mind on the bright future. I mean to say, Gussie might have lowered the existing Worcestershire record for goofiness and definitely forfeited all chance of becoming Market Snodsbury's favourite son, but you couldn't get away from the fact that he had proposed to Madeline Bassett, and you had to admit that she had accepted him.

I put this to Jeeves.

'A frightful exhibition,' I said, 'and one which will very possibly ring down history's pages. But we must not forget, Jeeves, that Gussie, though now doubtless looked upon in the neighbourhood as the world's worst freak, is all right otherwise.'

'No, sir.'

I did not quite get this.

'When you say "No, sir", do you mean "Yes, sir"?'

'No, sir. I mean "No, sir".'

'He is not all right otherwise?'

'No, sir.'

'But he's betrothed.'

'No longer, sir. Miss Bassett has severed the engagement.'

'You don't mean that?'

'Yes, sir.'

I wonder if you have noticed a rather peculiar thing about this chronicle. I allude to the fact that at one time or another practically everybody playing a part in it has had occasion to bury his or her face in his or her hands. I have participated in some pretty glutinous affairs in my time, but I think that never before or since have I been mixed up with such a solid body of brow clutchers.

Uncle Tom did it, if you remember. So did Gussie. So did Tuppy. So, probably, though I have no data, did Anatole, and I wouldn't put it past the Bassett. And Aunt Dahlia, I have no doubt, would have done it, too, but for the risk of disarranging the carefully fixed coiffure.

Well, what I am trying to say is that at this juncture I did it myself. Up went the hands and down went the head, and in another jiffy I was clutching as energetically as the best of them.

And it was while I was still massaging the coconut and wondering what the next move was that something barged up against the door like the delivery of a ton of coals.

'I think this may very possibly be Mr Fink-Nottle himself, sir,' said Jeeves.

His intuition, however, had led him astray. It was not Gussie but Tuppy. He came in and stood breathing asthmatically. It was plain that he was deeply stirred.

18

I eyed him narrowly. I didn't like his looks. Mark you, I don't say I ever had, much, because Nature, when planning this sterling fellow, shoved in a lot more lower jaw than was absolutely necessary and made the eyes a bit too keen and piercing for one who was neither an Empire builder nor a traffic policeman. But on the present occasion, in addition to offending the aesthetic sense, this Glossop seemed to me to be wearing a distinct air of menace, and I found myself wishing that Jeeves wasn't always so dashed tactful.

I mean, it's all very well to remove yourself like an eel sliding into mud when the employer has a visitor, but there are moments—and it looked to me as if this was going to be one of them—when the truer tact is to stick round and stand ready to lend a hand in the free-for-all.

For Jeeves was no longer with us. I hadn't seen him go, and I hadn't heard him go, but he had gone. As far as the eye could reach, one noted nobody but Tuppy. And in Tuppy's demeanour, as I say, there was a certain something that tended to disquiet. He looked to me very much like a man who had come to reopen that matter of my tickling Angela's ankles.

However, his opening remark told me that I had been alarming myself unduly. It was of a pacific nature, and came as a great relief.

'Bertie,' he said, 'I owe you an apology. I have come to make it.'

My relief on hearing these words, containing as they did no reference of any sort to tickled ankles, was, as I say, great. But I don't think it was any greater than my surprise. Months had passed since that painful episode at the Drones, and until now he hadn't given a sign of remorse and contrition. Indeed, word had reached me through private sources that he frequently told the story at dinners and other gatherings and, when doing so, laughed his silly head off.

I found it hard to understand, accordingly, what could have caused him to abase himself at this later date. Presumably he had been given the elbow by his better self, but why?

Still, there it was.

'My dear chap,' I said, gentlemanly to the gills, 'don't mention it.'

'What's the sense of saying, "Don't mention it"? I have mentioned it.'

'I mean, don't mention it any more. Don't give the matter another thought. We all of us forget ourselves sometimes and do things which, in our calmer moments, we regret. No doubt you were a bit tight at the time.'

'What the devil do you think you're talking about?'

I didn't like his tone. Brusque.

'Correct me if I am wrong,' I said, with a certain stiffness, 'but I assumed that you were apologizing for your foul conduct in looping back the last ring that night in the Drones, causing me to plunge into the swimming b. in the full soup and fish.'

'Ass! Not that, at all.'

'Then what?'

'This Bassett business.'

'What Bassett business?'

'Bertie,' said Tuppy, 'when you told me last night that you were in love with Madeline Bassett, I gave you the impression that I believed you, but I didn't. The thing seemed too incredible. However, since then I have made inquiries and the facts appear to square with your statement. I have now come to apologize for doubting you.'

'Made inquiries?'

'I asked her if you had proposed to her, and she said, yes, you had.'

'Tuppy! You didn't?'

'I did.'

'Have you no delicacy, no proper feeling?'

'No.'

'Oh? Well, right-ho, of course, but I think you ought to have.'

'Delicacy be dashed. I wanted to be certain that it was not you who stole Angela from me. I now know it wasn't.'

So long as he knew that, I didn't so much mind him having no delicacy.

'Ah,' I said. 'Well, that's fine. Hold that thought.'

'I have found out who it was.'

'What?'

He stood brooding for a moment. His eyes were smouldering with a dull fire. His jaw stuck out like the back of Jeeves's head.

'Bertie,' he said, 'do you remember what I swore I would do to the chap who stole Angela from me?'

'As nearly as I recall, you planned to pull him inside out—'

'— and make him swallow himself. Correct. The programme still holds good.'

'But, Tuppy, I keep assuring you, as a competent eyewitness, that nobody snitched Angela from you during that Cannes trip.'

'No. But they did after she got back.'

'What?'

'Don't keep saying, "What?" You heard.'

'But she hasn't seen anybody since she got back.'

'Oh, no? How about that newt bloke?'

'Gussie?'

'Precisely. The serpent Fink-Nottle.'

This seemed to me absolute gibbering.

'But Gussie loves the Bassett.'

'You can't all love this blighted Bassett. What astonishes me is that anyone can do it. He loves Angela, I tell you. And she loves him.'

'But Angela handed you your hat before Gussie ever got here.'

'No, she didn't. Couple of hours after.'

'He couldn't have fallen in love with her in a couple of hours.'

'Why not? I fell in love with her in a couple of minutes. I worshipped her immediately we met, the pop-eyed little excrescence.'

'But, dash it—'

'Don't argue, Bertie. The facts are all docketed. She loves this newt-nuzzling blister.'

'Quite absurd, laddie—quite absurd.'

'Oh?' He ground a heel into the carpet—a thing I've often read about, but had never seen done before.

'Then perhaps you will explain how it is that she happens to come to be engaged to him?'

You could have knocked me down with a f.

'Engaged to him?'

'She told me herself.'

'She was kidding you.'

'She was not kidding me. Shortly after the conclusion of this afternoon's binge at Market Snodsbury Grammar School he asked her to marry him, and she appears to have right-hoed without a murmur.'

'There must be some mistake.'

'There was. The snake Fink-Nottle made it, and by now I bet he realizes it. I've been chasing him since 5.30.'

'Chasing him?'

'All over the place. I want to pull his head off.'

'I see. Quite.'

'You haven't seen him, by any chance?'

'No.'

'Well, if you do, say good-bye to him quickly and put in your order for lilies . . . Oh, Jeeves.'

'Sir?'

I hadn't heard the door open, but the man was on the spot once more. My private belief, as I think I have mentioned before, is that Jeeves doesn't have to open doors. He's like one of those birds in India who bung their astral bodies about—the chaps, I mean, who having gone into thin air in Bombay, reassemble the parts and appear two minutes later in Calcutta. Only some such theory will account for the fact that he's not there one moment and is there the next. He just seems to float from Spot A to Spot B like some form of gas.

'Have you seen Mr Fink-Nottle, Jeeves?'

'No, sir.'

'I'm going to murder him.'

'Very good, sir.'

Tuppy withdrew, banging the door behind him, and I put Jeeves abreast.

'Jeeves,' I said, 'do you know what? Mr Fink-Nottle is engaged to my Cousin Angela.'

'Indeed, sir?'

'Well, how about it? Do you grasp the psychology? Does it make sense? Only a few hours ago he was engaged to Miss Bassett.'

'Gentlemen who have been discarded by one young lady are often apt to attach themselves without delay to another, sir. It is what is known as a gesture.'

I began to grasp.

'I see what you mean. Defiant stuff.'

'Yes, sir.'

'A sort of "Oh, right-ho, please yourself, but if you don't want me, there are plenty who do."'

'Precisely, sir. My cousin George—'

'Never mind about your Cousin George, Jeeves.'

'Very good, sir.'

'Keep him for the long winter evenings, what?'

'Just as you wish, sir.'

'And, anyway, I bet your Cousin George wasn't a shrinking, non-goose-bo-ing jellyfish like Gussie. That is what astounds me, Jeeves—that it should be Gussie who has been putting in all this heavy gesture-making stuff.'

'You must remember, sir, that Mr Fink-Nottle is in a somewhat inflamed cerebral condition.'

'That's true. A bit above par at the moment, as it were?'

'Exactly, sir.'

'Well, I'll tell you one thing—he'll be in a jolly sight more inflamed cerebral condition if Tuppy gets hold of him . . . What's the time?'

'Just on eight o'clock, sir.'

'Then Tuppy has been chasing him for two hours and a half. We must save the unfortunate blighter, Jeeves.'

'Yes, sir.'

'A human life is a human life, what?'

'Exceedingly true, sir.'

'The first thing, then, is to find him. After that we can discuss plans and schemes. Go forth, Jeeves, and scour the neighbourhood.'

'It will not be necessary, sir. If you will glance behind you, you will see Mr Fink-Nottle coming out from beneath your bed.'

And, by Jove, he was absolutely right.

There was Gussie, emerging as stated. He was covered with fluff and looked like a tortoise popping forth for a bit of a breather.

'Gussie!' I said.

'Jeeves,' said Gussie.

'Sir?' said Jeeves.

'Is that door locked, Jeeves?'

'No, sir, but I will attend to the matter immediately.'

Gussie sat down on the bed, and I thought for a moment that he was going to be in the mode by burying his face in his hands. However, he merely brushed a dead spider from his brow.

'Have you locked the door, Jeeves?'

'Yes, sir.'

'Because you can never tell that that ghastly Glossop may not take it into his head to come—'

The word 'back' froze on his lips. He hadn't got any further than a *b*-ish sound, when the handle of the door began to twist and rattle. He sprang from the bed, and for an instant stood looking exactly like a picture my Aunt Agatha has in her dining-room—The Stag at Bay—Landseer. Then he made a dive for the cupboard and was inside it before one really got on to it that he had started leaping. I have seen fellows late for the 9.15 move less nippily.

I shot a glance at Jeeves. He allowed his right eyebrow to flicker slightly, which is as near as he ever gets to a display of the emotions.

'Hullo?' I yipped.

'Let me in, blast you!' responded Tuppy's voice from without. 'Who locked this door?'

I consulted Jeeves once more in the language of the eyebrow. He raised one of his. I raised one of mine. He raised his other. I raised my other. Then we both raised both. Finally, there seeming no other policy to pursue, I flung wide the gates and Tuppy came shooting in.

'Now what?' I said, as nonchalantly as I could manage.

'Why was the door locked?' demanded Tuppy.

I was in pretty good eyebrow-raising form by now, so I gave him a touch of it.

'Is one to have no privacy, Glossop?' I said coldly. 'I instructed Jeeves to lock the door because I was about to disrobe.'

'A likely story!' said Tuppy, and I'm not sure he didn't add 'Forsooth!' 'You needn't try to make me believe that you're afraid people are going to run excursion trains to see you in your underwear. You locked that door because you've got the snake Fink-Nottle in here. I suspected it the moment I'd left, and I decided to come back and investigate. I'm going to search this room from end to end. I believe he's in that cupboard . . . What's in this cupboard?'

'Just clothes,' I said, having another stab at the nonchalant, though extremely dubious as to whether it would come off. 'The usual wardrobe of the English gentleman paying a country-house visit.'

'You're lying!'

Well, I wouldn't have been if he had only waited a minute before speaking, because the words were hardly out of his mouth before Gussie was out of the cupboard. I have commented on the speed with which he had gone in. It was as nothing to the speed with which he emerged. There was a sort of whir and blur, and he was no longer with us.

I think Tuppy was surprised. In fact, I'm sure he was. Despite the confidence with which he had stated his view that the cupboard contained Fink-Nottle, it plainly disconcerted him to have the chap fizzing out at him like this. He gargled sharply, and jumped back about five feet. The next moment, however, he had recovered his poise and was galloping down the corridor in pursuit. It only needed Aunt Dahlia after them, shouting 'Yoicks!' or whatever is customary on these occasions, to complete the resemblance to a brisk run with the Quorn.

I sank into a handy chair. I am not a man whom it is easy to discourage, but it seemed to me that things had at last begun to get too complex for Bertram.

'Jeeves,' I said, 'all this is a bit thick.'

'Yes, sir.'

'The head rather swims.'

'Yes, sir.'

'I think you had better leave me, Jeeves. I shall need to devote the very closest thought to the situation which has arisen.'

'Very good, sir.'

The door closed. I lit a cigarette and began to ponder.

19

Most chaps in my position, I imagine, would have pondered all the rest of the evening without getting a bite, but we Woosters have an uncanny knack of going straight to the heart of things, and I don't suppose it was much more than ten minutes after I had started pondering before I saw what had to be done.

What was needed to straighten matters out, I perceived, was a heart-to-heart talk with Angela. She had caused all the trouble by her mutton-headed behaviour in saying 'Yes' instead of 'No' when Gussie, in the grip of mixed drinks and cerebral excitement, had suggested teaming up. She must obviously be properly ticked off and made to return him to store. A quarter of an hour later, I had tracked her down to the summer-house in which she was taking a cooler, and was seating myself by her side.

'Angela,' I said, and if my voice was stern, well, whose wouldn't have been, 'this is all perfect drivel.'

She seemed to come out of a reverie. She looked at me inquiringly.

'I'm sorry, Bertie, I didn't hear. What were you talking drivel about?'

'I was not talking drivel.'

'Oh, sorry, I thought you said you were.'

'Is it likely that I would come out here in order to talk drivel?'

'Very likely.'

I thought it best to haul off and approach the matter from another angle.

'I've just been seeing Tuppy.'

'Oh?'

'And Gussie Fink-Nottle.'

'Oh, yes?'

'It appears that you have gone and got engaged to the latter.'

'Quite right.'

'Well, that's what I meant when I said it was all perfect drivel. You can't possibly love a chap like Gussie.'

'Why not?'

'You simply can't.'

Well, I mean to say, of course she couldn't. Nobody could love a freak like Gussie except a similar freak like the Bassett. The shot wasn't on the board. A splendid chap, of course, in many ways—courteous, amiable, and just the fellow to tell you what to do till the doctor came, if you had a sick newt on your hands—but quite obviously not of Mendelssohn's March timber. I have no doubt that you could have flung bricks by the hour in England's most densely-populated districts without endangering the safety of a single girl capable of becoming Mrs Augustus Fink-Nottle without an anaesthetic.

I put this to her, and she was forced to admit the justice of it.

'All right, then. Perhaps I don't.'

'Then what,' I said keenly, 'did you want to go and get engaged to him for, you unreasonable young fat-head?'

'I thought it would be fun.'

'Fun!'

'And so it has been. I've had a lot of fun out of it. You should have seen Tuppy's face when I told him.'

A sudden bright light shone upon me.

'Ha! A gesture!'

'What?'

'You got engaged to Gussie just to score off Tuppy?'

'I did.'

'Well, then, that was what I was saying. It was a gesture.'

'Yes, I suppose you could call it that.'

'And I'll tell you something else I'll call it—viz. a dashed low trick. I'm surprised at you, young Angela.'

'I don't see why.'

I curled the lip about half an inch. 'Being a female, you wouldn't. You gentler sexers are like that. You pull off the rawest stuff without a pang. You pride yourselves on it. Look at Jael, the wife of Heber.'

'Where did you ever hear of Jael, the wife of Heber?'

'Possibly you are not aware that I once won a Scripture-knowledge prize at school?'

'Oh, yes. I remember Augustus mentioning it in his speech.'

'Quite,' I said, a little hurriedly. I had no wish to be reminded of Augustus's speech. 'Well, as I say, look at Jael, the wife of Heber. Dug spikes into the guest's coconut while he was asleep, and then went swanking about the place like a Girl Guide. No wonder they say "Oh, woman, woman!"'

'Who?'

'The chaps who do. Coo, what a sex! But you aren't proposing to keep this up, of course?'

'Keep what up?'

'This rot of being engaged to Gussie.'

'I certainly am.'

'Just to make Tuppy look silly.'

'Do you think he looks silly?'

'I do.'

'So he ought to.'

I began to get the idea that I wasn't making real headway. I remember when I won that Scripture-knowledge prize, having to go into the facts about Balaam's ass. I can't quite recall what they were, but I still retain a sort of general impression of something digging its feet in and putting its ears back and refusing to co-operate; and it seemed to me that this was what Angela was doing now. She and Balaam's ass were, so to speak, sisters under the skin. There's a word beginning with *r*—'re' something—'recal' something—No, it's gone. But what I am driving at is that is what this Angela was showing herself.

'Silly young geezer,' I said.

She pinkened.

'I'm not a silly young geezer.'

'You are a silly young geezer. And, what's more, you know it.'

'I don't know anything of the kind.'

'Here you are, wrecking Tuppy's life, wrecking Gussie's life, all for the sake of a cheap score.'

'Well, it's no business of yours.'

I sat on this promptly:

'No business of mine when I see two lives I used to go to school with wrecked? Ha! Besides, you know you're potty about Tuppy.'

'I'm not!'

'Is that so? If I had a quid for every time I've seen you gaze at him with the lovelight in your eyes—'

She gazed at me, but without the lovelight.

'Oh, for goodness' sake, go away and boil your head, Bertie!'

I drew myself up.

'That,' I replied, with dignity, 'is just what I am going to go away and boil. At least, I mean, I shall now leave you. I have said my say.'

'Good.'

'But permit me to add—'

'I won't.'

'Very good,' I said coldly. 'In that case, tinkerty tonk.'

And I meant it to sting.

'Moody' and 'discouraged' were about the two adjectives you would have selected to describe me as I left the summer-house. It would be idle to deny that I had expected better results from this little chat.

I was surprised at Angela. Odd how you never realize that every girl is at heart a vicious specimen until something goes wrong with her love affair. This cousin and I had been meeting freely since the days when I wore sailor suits and she hadn't any front teeth, yet only now was I beginning to get on to her hidden depths. A simple, jolly, kindly young pimple she had always struck me as—the sort you could more or less rely on not to hurt a fly. But here she was now laughing heartlessly—at least, I seemed to remember hearing her laugh heartlessly—like something cold and callous out of a sophisticated talkie, and fairly spitting on her hands in her determination to bring Tuppy's grey hairs in sorrow to the grave.

I've said it before, and I'll say it again—girls are rummy. Old Pop Kipling never said a truer word than when he made that crack about the f. of the s. being more d. than the m.

It seemed to me in the circs that there was but one thing to do—that is head for the dining-room and take a slash at that cold collation of which Jeeves had spoken. I felt in urgent need of sustenance, for the recent interview had pulled me down a bit. There is no gainsaying the fact that all this naked-emotion stuff reduces a chap's vitality and puts him in the vein for a good whack at the beef and ham.

To the dining-room, accordingly, I repaired, and had barely crossed the threshold when I perceived Aunt Dahlia at the sideboard, tucking into salmon mayonnaise.

The spectacle drew from me a quick 'Oh, ah,' for I was somewhat embarrassed. The last time this relative and I had enjoyed a *tête-à-tête*, it will be remembered, she had sketched out plans for drowning me in the kitchen-garden pond, and I was not quite sure what my present standing with her was.

I was relieved to find her in genial mood. Nothing could have exceeded the cordiality with which she waved her fork.

'Hallo, Bertie, you old ass,' was her very matey greeting. 'I thought I shouldn't find you far away from the food. Try some of this salmon. Excellent.'

'Anatole's?' I queried.

'No. He's still in bed. But the kitchen maid has struck an inspired streak. It suddenly seems to have come home to her that she isn't catering for a covey of buzzards in the Sahara Desert, and she has put out something quite fit for human consumption. There is good in the girl, after all, and I hope she enjoys herself at the dance.'

I ladled out a portion of salmon, and we fell into pleasant conversation, chatting of this servants' ball at the Stretchley-Budds and speculating idly, I recall, as to what Seppings, the butler, would look like, doing the rumba.

It was not till I had cleaned up the first platter and was embarking on a second that the subject of Gussie came up. Considering what had passed at Market Snodsbury that afternoon, it was one which I had been expecting her to touch on earlier. When she did touch on it, I could see that she had not yet been informed of Angela's engagement.

'I say, Bertie,' she said, meditatively chewing fruit salad. 'This Spink-Bottle.'

'Nottle.'

'Bottle,' insisted the aunt firmly. 'After that exhibition of his this afternoon, Bottle, and nothing but Bottle, is how I shall always think of him.

However, what I was going to say was that, if you see him, I wish you would tell him that he has made an old woman very, very happy. Except for the time when the curate tripped over a loose shoelace and fell down the pulpit steps, I don't think I have ever had a more wonderful moment than when good old Bottle suddenly started ticking Tom off from the platform. In fact, I thought his whole performance in the most perfect taste.'

I could not but demur.

'Those references to myself—'

'Those were what I liked next best. I thought they were fine. Is it true that you cheated when you won that Scripture-knowledge prize?'

'Certainly not. My victory was the outcome of the most strenuous and unremitting efforts.'

'And how about this pessimism we hear of? Are you a pessimist, Bertie?'

I could have told her that what was occurring in this house was rapidly making me one, but I said no, I wasn't.

'That's right. Never be a pessimist. Everything is for the best in this best of all possible worlds. It's a long lane that has no turning. It's always darkest before the dawn. Have patience and all will come right. The sun will shine, although the day's a grey one . . . Try some of this salad.'

I followed her advice, but even as I plied the spoon my thoughts were elsewhere. I was perplexed. It may have been the fact that I had recently been hobnobbing with so many bowed-down hearts that made this cheeriness of hers seem so bizarre, but bizarre was certainly what I found it.

'I thought you might have been a trifle peeved,' I said.

'Peeved?'

'By Gussie's manoeuvres on the platform this afternoon. I confess that I had rather expected the tapping foot and the drawn brow.'

'Nonsense. What was there to be peeved about? I took the whole thing as a great compliment, proud to feel that any drink from my cellars could have produced such a majestic jag. It restores one's faith in post-war whisky. Besides, I couldn't be peeved at anything tonight. I am like a little child clapping its hands and dancing in the sunshine. For though it has been some time getting a move on, Bertie, the sun has at last broken through the clouds. Ring out those joy bells. Anatole has withdrawn his notice.'

'What? Oh, very hearty congratulations.'

'Thanks. Yes. I worked on him like a beaver after I got back this afternoon, and finally, vowing he would ne'er consent, he consented. He stays on, praises be, and the way I look at it now is that God's in His heaven and all's right with—'

She broke off. The door had opened, and we were plus a butler.

'Hullo, Seppings,' said Aunt Dahlia. 'I thought you had gone.'

'Not yet, madam.'

'Well, I hope you will all have a good time.'

'Thank you, madam.'

'Was there something you wanted to see me about?'

'Yes, madam. It is with reference to Monsieur Anatole. Is it by your wish, madam, that Mr Fink-Nottle is making faces at Monsieur Anatole through the skylight of his bedroom?'

20

There was one of those long silences. Pregnant, I believe, is what they're generally called. Aunt looked at butler. Butler looked at aunt. I looked at both of them. An eerie stillness seemed to envelop the room like a linseed poultice. I happened to be biting on a slice of apple in my fruit salad at the moment, and it sounded as if Carnera had jumped off the top of the Eiffel Tower on to a cucumber frame.

Aunt Dahlia steadied herself against the sideboard, and spoke in a low, husky voice:

'Faces?'

'Yes, madam.'

'Through the skylight?'

'Yes, madam.'

'You mean he's sitting on the roof?'

'Yes, madam. It has upset Monsieur Anatole very much.' I suppose it was that word 'upset' that touched Aunt Dahlia off. Experience had taught her what happened when Anatole got upset. I had always known her as a woman who was quite active on her pins, but I had never suspected her of being capable of the magnificent burst of speed which she now showed. Pausing merely to get a rich hunting-field expletive off her chest, she was out of the room and making for the stairs before I could swallow a sliver of—I think—banana. And feeling, as I had felt when I got that telegram of hers about Angela and Tuppy, that my place was by her side, I put down my plate and hastened after her. Seppings following at a loping gallop.

I say that my place was by her side, but it was not so dashed easy to get there, for she was setting a cracking pace. At the top of the first flight she must have led by a matter of half a dozen lengths, and was still shaking off my challenge when she rounded into the second. At the next landing, however, the gruelling going appeared to tell on her, for she slackened off a trifle and showed symptoms of roaring, and by the time we were in the straight we were running practically neck and neck. Our entry into Anatole's room was as close a finish as you could have wished to see.

Result:

1. Aunt Dahlia.
2. Bertram.
3. Seppings.
Won by a short head. Half a staircase separated second and third.

The first thing that met the eye on entering was Anatole. This wizard of the cooking-stove is a tubby little man with a moustache of the outsize or soup-strainer type, and you can generally take a line through it as to the state of his emotions. When all is well, it turns up at the ends like a sergeant-major's. When the soul is bruised, it droops.

It was drooping now, striking a sinister note. And if any shadow of doubt had remained as to how he was feeling, the way he was carrying on would have dispelled it. He was standing by the bed in pink pyjamas, waving his fists at the skylight. Through the glass, Gussie was staring down. His eyes were bulging and his mouth was open, giving him so striking a resemblance to some rare fish in an aquarium that one's primary impulse was to offer him an ant's egg.

Watching this fist-waving cook and this goggling guest, I must say that my sympathies were completely with the former. I considered him thoroughly justified in waving all the fists he wanted to.

Review the facts, I mean to say. There he had been, lying in bed, thinking idly of whatever French cooks do think about when in bed, and he had suddenly become aware of that frightful face at the window. A thing to jar the most phlegmatic. I know I should hate to be lying in bed and have Gussie popping up like that. A chap's bedroom—you can't get away from it—is his castle, and he has every right to look askance if gargoyles come glaring in at him.

While I stood musing thus, Aunt Dahlia, in her practical way, was coming straight to the point:

'What's all this?'

Anatole did a sort of Swedish exercise, starting at the base of the spine, carrying on through the shoulder-blades and finishing up among the back hair.

Then he told her.

In the chats I have had with this wonder man, I have always found his English fluent, but a bit on the mixed side. If you remember, he was with Mrs Bingo Little for a time before coming to Brinkley, and no doubt he picked up a good deal from Bingo. Before that, he had been a couple of years with an American family at Nice and had studied under their chauffeur, one of the Maloneys of Brooklyn. So, what with Bingo and what with Maloney, he is, as I say, fluent but a bit mixed.

He spoke, in part, as follows:

'Hot dog! You ask me what is it? Listen. Make some attention a little. Me, I have hit the hay, but I do not sleep so good, and presently I wake and up I look, and there is one who make faces against me through the dashed window. Is that a pretty affair? Is that convenient? If you think I like it, you jolly well mistake yourself. I am so mad as a wet hen. And why not? I am somebody, isn't it? This is a bedroom, what-what, not a house for some apes? Then for what do blighters sit on my window so cool as a few cucumbers, making some faces?'

'Quite,' I said. Dashed reasonable, was my verdict.

He threw another look up at Gussie, and did Exercise 2—the one where you clutch the moustache, give it a tug and then start catching flies.

'Wait yet a little. I am not finish. I say I see this type on my window, making a few faces. But what then? Does he buzz off when I shout a cry, and leave me peaceable? Not on your life. He remain planted there, not giving any damns, and sit regarding me like a cat watching a duck. He make faces against me and again he make faces against me, and the more I command that he should get to hell out of here, the more he do not get to hell out of here. He cry something towards me, and I demand what is his desire, but he do not explain. Oh, no, that arrives never. He does but shrug his head. What damn silliness! Is this amusing for me? You think I like it? I am not content with such folly. I think the poor mutt's loony. *Je me fiche de ce type infect. C'est idiot de faire comme ça l'oiseau . . . Allez-vous-en, louffier . . .* Tell the boob to go away. He is mad as some March hatters.'

I must say I thought he was making out a jolly good case, and evidently Aunt Dahlia felt the same. She laid a quivering hand on his shoulder.

'I will, Monsieur Anatole, I will,' she said, and I couldn't have believed that robust voice capable of sinking to such an absolute coo. More like a turtle dove calling to its mate than anything else. 'It's quite all right.'

She had said the wrong thing. He did Exercise 3.

'All right? *Nom d'un nom d'un nom!* The hell you say it's all right? Of what use to pull stuff like that? Wait one half-moment. Not yet quite so quick, my old sport. It is by no means all right. See yet again a little. It is some very different dishes of fish. I can take a few smooths with a rough, it is true, but I do not find it agreeable when one play larks against me on my windows. That cannot do. A nice thing, no. I am a serious man. I do not wish a few larks on my windows. I enjoy larks on my windows worse as any. It is very little all right. If such rannygazoo is to arrive, I do not remain any longer in this house no more. I buzz off and do not stay planted.'

Sinister words, I had to admit, and I was not surprised that Aunt Dahlia, hearing them, should have uttered a cry like the wail of a master of hounds seeing a fox shot. Anatole had begun to wave his fists again at Gussie, and she now joined him. Seppings, who was puffing respectfully in the background, didn't actually wave his fists, but he gave Gussie a pretty austere look. It was plain to the thoughtful observer that this Fink-Nottle, in getting on to that skylight, had done a mistaken thing. He couldn't have been more unpopular in the home of G. G. Simmons.

'Go away, you crazy loon!' cried Aunt Dahlia, in that ringing voice of hers which had once caused nervous members of the Quorn to lose stirrups and take tosses from the saddle.

Gussie's reply was to waggle his eyebrows. I could read the message he was trying to convey.

'I think he means,' I said—reasonable old Bertram, always trying to throw oil on the troubled w's—'that if he does he will fall down the side of the house and break his neck.'

'Well, why not?' said Aunt Dahlia.

I could see her point, of course, but it seemed to me that there might be a neater solution. This skylight happened to be the only window in the house which Uncle Tom had not festooned with his bally bars. I suppose he felt that if a burglar had the nerve to climb up as far as this, he deserved what was coming to him.

'If you opened the skylight, he could jump in.'

The idea got across.

'Seppings, how does this skylight open?'

'With a pole, madam.'

'Then get a pole. Get two poles. Ten.'

And presently Gussie was mixing with the company. Like one of those chaps you read about in the papers, the wretched man seemed deeply conscious of his position.

I must say Aunt Dahlia's bearing and demeanour did nothing to assist towards a restored composure. Of the amiability which she had exhibited when discussing this unhappy chump's activities with me over the fruit salad, no trace remained, and I was not surprised that speech more or less froze on the Fink-Nottle lips. It isn't often that Aunt Dahlia, normally as genial a bird as ever encouraged a gaggle of hounds to get their noses down to it, lets her angry passions rise, but when she does, strong men climb trees and pull them up after them.

'Well?' she said.

In answer to this, all that Gussie could produce was a sort of strangled hiccough.

'Well?'

Aunt Dahlia's face grew darker. Hunting, if indulged in regularly over a period of years, is a pastime that seldom fails to lend a fairly deepish tinge to the patient's complexion, and her best friends could not have denied that even at normal times the relative's map tended a little towards the crushed strawberry. But never had I seen it take on so pronounced a richness as now. She looked like a tomato struggling for self-expression.

'Well?'

Gussie tried hard. And for a moment it seemed as if something was going to come through. But in the end it turned out nothing more than a sort of death-rattle.

'Oh, take him away, Bertie, and put ice on his head,' said Aunt Dahlia, giving the thing up. And she turned to tackle what looked like the rather man's size job of soothing Anatole, who was now carrying on a muttered conversation with himself in a rapid sort of way.

Seeming to feel that the situation was one to which he could not do justice in Bingo-cum-Maloney Anglo-American, he had fallen back on his native tongue. Words like '*marmiton de Domange*', '*pignouf*', '*burluberlu*', and '*roustisseur*' were fluttering from him like bats out of a barn. Lost on me, of course, because, though I sweated a bit at the Gallic language during that Cannes visit, I'm still more or less in the Esker-vous-avez stage. I regretted this, for they sounded good.

I assisted Gussie down the stairs. A cooler thinker than Aunt Dahlia, I had already guessed the hidden springs and motives which had led him to the roof. Where she had seen only a cockeyed reveller indulging himself in a drunken prank or whimsy, I had spotted the hunted fawn.

'Was Tuppy after you?' I asked sympathetically.

What I believe is called a *frisson* shook him.

'He nearly got me on the top landing. I shinned out through a passage window and scrambled along a sort of ledge.'

'That baffled him, what?'

'Yes. But then I found I had stuck. The roof sloped down in all directions. I couldn't go back. I had to go on, crawling along this ledge. And then I found myself looking down the skylight. Who was that chap?'

'That was Anatole, Aunt Dahlia's chef.'

'French?'

'To the core.'

'That explains why I couldn't make him understand. What asses these Frenchmen are. They don't seem able to grasp the simplest thing. You'd have thought if a chap saw a chap on a skylight, the chap would realize the chap wanted to be let in. But no, he just stood there.'

'Waving a few fists.'

'Yes. Silly idiot. Still, here I am.'

'Here you are, yes—for the moment.'

'Eh?'

'I was thinking that Tuppy is probably lurking somewhere.'

He leaped like a lamb in springtime.

'What shall I do?'

I considered this.

'Sneak back to your room and barricade the door. That is the manly policy.'

'Suppose that's where he's lurking?'

'In that case, move elsewhere.'

But on arrival at the room, it transpired that Tuppy, if anywhere, was infesting some other portion of the house. Gussie shot in, and I heard the key turn. And feeling that there was no more that I could do in that quarter, I returned to the dining-room for further fruit salad and a quiet think. And I had barely filled my plate when the door opened and Aunt Dahlia came in. She sank into a chair, looking a bit shopworn.

'Give me a drink, Bertie.'

'What sort?'

'Any sort, so long as it's strong.'

Approach Bertram Wooster along these lines, and you catch him at his best. St Bernard dogs doing the square thing by Alpine travellers could not have bustled about more assiduously. I filled the order, and for some moments nothing was to be heard but the sloshing sound of an aunt restoring her tissues.

'Shove it down, Aunt Dahlia,' I said sympathetically. 'These things take it out of one, don't they? You've had a toughish time, no doubt, soothing Anatole,' I proceeded, helping myself to anchovy paste on toast. 'Everything pretty smooth now, I trust?'

She gazed at me in a long, lingering sort of way, her brow wrinkled as if in thought.

'Attila,' she said at length. 'That's the name. Attila the Hun.'

'Eh?'

'I was trying to think who you reminded me of. Somebody who went about strewing ruin and desolation and breaking up homes which, until he came along, had been happy and peaceful. Attila is the man. It's amazing,' she said, drinking me in once more. 'To look at you, one would think you were just an ordinary sort of amiable idiot—certifiable, perhaps, but quite harmless. Yet, in reality, you are a worse scourge than the Black Death. I tell you, Bertie, when I contemplate you I seem to come up against all the underlying sorrow and horror of life with such a thud that I feel as if I had walked into a lamp post.'

Pained and surprised, I would have spoken, but the stuff I had thought was anchovy paste had turned out to be something far more gooey and adhesive. It seemed to wrap itself round the tongue and impede utterance like a gag. And while I was still endeavouring to clear the vocal cords for action, she went on:

'Do you realize what you started when you sent that Spink-Bottle man down here? As regards his getting blotto and turning the prize-giving ceremonies at Market Snodsbury Grammar School into a sort of two-reel comic film, I will say nothing, for frankly I enjoyed it. But when he comes leering at Anatole through skylights, just after I had with infinite pains and tact induced him to withdraw his notice, and makes him so temperamental that he won't hear of staying on after tomorrow—'

The paste stuff gave way. I was able to speak.

'What?'

'Yes, Anatole goes tomorrow, and I suppose poor old Tom will have indigestion for the rest of his life. And that is not all. I have just seen Angela, and she tells me she is engaged to this Bottle.'

'Temporarily, yes,' I had to admit.

'Temporarily be blowed. She's definitely engaged to him and talks with a sort of hideous coolness of getting married in October. So there it is. If the prophet Job were to walk into the room at this moment, I could sit swapping hard-luck stories with him till bedtime. Not that Job was in my class.'

'He had boils.'

'Well, what are boils?'

'Dashed painful, I understand.'

'Nonsense. I'd take all the boils on the market in exchange for my troubles. Can't you realize the position? I've lost the best cook in England. My husband, poor soul, will probably die of dyspepsia. And my only daughter, for whom I had dreamed such a wonderful future, is engaged to be married to an inebriated newt fancier. And you talk about boils!'

I corrected her on a small point:

'I don't absolutely talk about boils. I merely mentioned that Job had them. Yes, I agree with you, Aunt Dahlia, that things are not looking too oojah-cum-spiff at the moment, but be of good cheer. A Wooster is seldom baffled for more than the nonce.'

'You rather expect to be coming along shortly with another of your schemes?'

'At any minute.'

She sighed resignedly.

'I thought as much. Well, it needed but this. I don't see how things could possibly be worse than they are, but no doubt you will succeed in making them so. Your genius and insight will find the way. Carry on, Bertie. Yes, carry on. I am past caring now. I shall even find a faint interest in seeing into what darker and profounder abysses of hell you can plunge this home. Go to it, lad . . . What's that stuff you're eating?'

'I find it a little difficult to classify. Some sort of paste on toast. Rather like glue flavoured with beef extract.'

'Gimme,' said Aunt Dahlia listlessly.

'Be careful how you chew,' I advised. 'It sticketh closer than a brother . . . Yes, Jeeves?'

The man had materialized on the carpet. Absolutely noiseless, as usual.

'A note for you, sir.'

'A note for me, Jeeves?'

'A note for you, sir.'

'From whom, Jeeves?'

'From Miss Bassett, sir.'

'From whom, Jeeves?'

'From Miss Bassett, sir.'

'From Miss Bassett, Jeeves?'

'From Miss Bassett, sir.'

At this point, Aunt Dahlia, who had taken one nibble at her whatever-it-was-on-toast and laid it down, begged us—a little fretfully, I thought—for heaven's sake to cut out the cross-talk vaudeville stuff, as she had enough to bear already without having to listen to us doing our imitation of the Two Macs. Always willing to oblige, I dismissed Jeeves with a nod, and he flickered for a moment and was gone. Many a spectre would have been less slippy.

'But what,' I mused, toying with the envelope, 'can this female be writing to me about?'

'Why not open the damn thing and see?'

'A very excellent idea,' I said, and did so.

'And if you are interested in my movements,' proceeded Aunt Dahlia, heading for the door, 'I propose to go to my room, do some Yogi deep breathing, and try to forget.'

'Quite,' I said absently, skimming p.1. And then, as I turned over, a sharp howl broke from my lips, causing Aunt Dahlia to shy like a startled mustang.

'Don't do it!' she exclaimed, quivering in every limb.

'Yes, but dash it—'

'What a pest you are, you miserable object,' she sighed. 'I remember years ago, when you were in your cradle, being left alone with you one day and you nearly swallowed your rubber comforter and started turning purple. And I, ass that I was, took it out and saved your life. Let me tell you, young Bertie, it will go very hard with you if you ever swallow a rubber comforter again when only I am by to aid.'

'But, dash it!' I cried. 'Do you know what's happened? Madeline Bassett says she's going to marry me!'

'I hope it keeps fine for you,' said the relative, and passed from the room looking like something out of an Edgar Allan Poe story.

21

I don't suppose I was looking so dashed unlike something out of an Edgar Allan Poe story myself, for, as you can readily imagine, the news item which I have just recorded had got in amongst me properly. If the Bassett, in the belief that the Wooster heart had long been hers and was waiting ready to be scooped in on demand, had decided to take up her option, I should, as a man of honour and sensibility, have no choice but to come across and kick in. The matter was obviously not one that could be straightened out with a curt *nolle prosequi*. All the evidence, therefore, seemed to point to the fact that the doom had come upon me and, what was more, had come to stay.

And yet, though it would be idle to pretend that my grip on the situation was quite the grip I would have liked it to be, I did not despair of arriving at a solution. A lesser man, caught in this awful snare, would no doubt have thrown in the towel at once and ceased to struggle; but the whole point about the Woosters is that they are not lesser men.

By way of a start, I read the note again. Not that I had any hope that a second perusal would enable me to place a different construction on its contents, but it helped to fill in while the brain was limbering up. I then, to assist thought, had another go at the fruit salad, and in addition ate a slice of sponge cake. And it was as I passed on to the cheese that the machinery started working. I saw what had to be done.

To the question which had been exercising the mind—viz., can Bertram cope?—I was now able to reply with a confident 'Absolutely'.

The great wheeze on these occasions of dirty work at the crossroads is not to lose your head but to keep cool and try to find the ringleaders. Once find the ringleaders, and you know where you are.

The ringleader here was plainly the Bassett. It was she who started the whole imbroglio by chucking Gussie, and it was clear that before anything could be done to solve and clarify, she must be induced to revise her views and take him on again. This would put Angela back into circulation, and that would cause Tuppy to simmer down a bit, and then we could begin to get somewhere.

I decided that as soon as I had had another morsel of cheese I would seek this Bassett out and be pretty eloquent.

And at this moment in she came. I might have foreseen that she would be turning up shortly. I mean to say, hearts may ache, but if they know that there is a cold collation set out in the dining-room, they are pretty sure to come popping in sooner or later.

Her eyes, as she entered the room, were fixed on the salmon mayonnaise, and she would no doubt have made a bee-line for it and started getting hers, had I not, in the emotion of seeing her, dropped a glass of the best with which I was endeavouring to bring about a calmer frame of mind. The noise caused her to turn, and for an instant embarrassment supervened. A slight flush mantled the cheek, and the eyes popped a bit.

'Oh!' she said.

I have always found that there is nothing that helps to ease you over one of these awkward moments like a spot of stage business. Find something to do with your hands, and it's half the battle. I grabbed a plate and hastened forward.

'A touch of salmon?'

'Thank you.'

'With a suspicion of salad?'

'If you please.'

'And to drink? Name the poison.'

'I think I would like a little orange juice.'

She gave a gulp. Not at the orange juice, I don't mean, because she hadn't got it yet, but at all the tender associations those two words provoked. It was as if someone had mentioned spaghetti to the relict of an Italian organ-grinder. Her face flushed a deeper shade, she registered anguish, and I saw that it was no longer within the sphere of practical politics to try to confine the conversation to neutral topics like cold boiled salmon.

So did she, I imagine, for when I, as a preliminary to getting down to brass tacks, said 'Er', she said 'Er', too, simultaneously, the brace of 'Ers' clashing in mid-air.

'I'm sorry.'

'I beg your pardon.'

'You were saying—'

'You were saying—'

'No, please go on.'

'Oh, right-ho.'

I straightened the tie, my habit when in this girl's society, and had at it:

'With reference to yours of even date—'

She flushed again, and took a rather strained forkful of salmon.

'You got my note?'

'Yes, I got your note.'

'I gave it to Jeeves to give it to you.'

'Yes, he gave it to me. That's how I got it.'

There was another silence. And as she was plainly shrinking from talking turkey, I was reluctantly compelled to do so. I mean, somebody had got to. Too dashed silly, a male and female in our position simply standing eating salmon and cheese at one another without a word.

'Yes, I got it all right.'

'I see. You got it.'

'Yes, I got it. I've just been reading it. And what I was rather wanting to ask you, if we happened to run into each other, was—well, what about it?'

'What about it?'

'That's what I say: What about it?'

'But it was quite clear.'

'Oh, quite. Perfectly clear. Very well expressed and all that. But—I mean—Well, I mean, deeply sensible of the honour, and so forth—but—Well, dash it!'

She had polished off her salmon, and now put the plate down.

'Fruit salad?'

'No, thank you.'

'Spot of pie?'

'No, thanks.'

'One of those glue things on toast?'

'No, thank you.'

She took a cheese straw. I found a cold egg which I had overlooked. Then I said 'I mean to say' just as she said 'I think I know', and there was another collision.

'I beg your pardon.'

'I'm sorry.'

'Do go on.'

'No, you go on.'

I waved my cold egg courteously, to indicate that she had the floor, and she started again:

'I think I know what you are trying to say. You are surprised.'

'Yes.'

'You are thinking of—'

'Exactly.'

'— Mr Fink-Nottle.'

'The very man.'

'You find what I have done hard to understand.'

'Absolutely.'

'I don't wonder.'

'I do.'

'And yet it is quite simple.'

She took another cheese straw. She seemed to like cheese straws.

'Quite simple, really. I want to make you happy.'

'Dashed decent of you.'

'I am going to devote the rest of my life to making you happy.'

'A very matey scheme.'

'I can at least do that. But—may I be quite frank with you, Bertie?'

'Oh, rather.'

'Then I must tell you this. I am fond of you. I will marry you. I will do my best to make you a good wife. But my affection for you can never be the flame-like passion I felt for Augustus.'

'Just the very point I was working round to. There, as you say, is the snag. Why not chuck the whole idea of hitching up with me? Wash it out altogether. I mean, if you love old Gussie—'

'No longer.'

'Oh, come.'

'No. What happened this afternoon has killed my love. A smear of ugliness has been drawn across a thing of beauty, and I can never feel towards him as I did.'

I saw what she meant, of course. Gussie had bunged his heart at her feet; she had picked it up, and, almost immediately after doing so, had discovered that he had been stewed to the eyebrows all the time. The shock must have been severe. No girl likes to feel that a chap has got to be thoroughly plastered before he can ask her to marry him. It wounds the pride.

Nevertheless, I persevered.

'But have you considered,' I said, 'that you may have got a wrong line on Gussie's performance this afternoon? Admitted that all the evidence points to a more sinister theory, what price him simply having got a touch of the sun? Chaps do get touches of the sun, you know, especially when the weather's hot.'

She looked at me, and I saw that she was putting in a bit of the old drenched-irises stuff.

'It was like you to say that, Bertie. I respect you for it.'

'Oh, no.'

'Yes. You have a splendid, chivalrous soul.'

'Not a bit.'

'Yes, you have. You remind me of Cyrano.'

'Who?'

'Cyrano de Bergerac.'

'The chap with the nose?'

'Yes.'

I can't say I was any too pleased. I felt the old beak furtively. It was a bit on the prominent side, perhaps, but, dash it, not in the Cyrano class. It began to look as if the next thing this girl would do would be to compare me to Schnozzle Durante.

'He loved, but pleaded another's cause.'

'Oh, I see what you mean now.'

'I like you for that, Bertie. It was fine of you—fine and big. But it is no use. There are things which kill love. I can never forget Augustus, but my love for him is dead. I will be your wife.'

Well, one has to be civil.

'Right ho,' I said. 'Thanks awfully.'

Then the dialogue sort of poofed out once more, and we stood eating cheese straws and cold eggs respectively in silence. There seemed to exist some little uncertainty as to what the next move was.

Fortunately, before embarrassment could do much more supervening, Angela came in, and this broke up the meeting. The Bassett announced our engagement, and Angela kissed her and said she hoped she would be very, very happy, and the Bassett kissed her and said she hoped she would be very, very happy with Gussie, and Angela said she was sure she would, because Augustus was such a dear, and the Bassett kissed her again, and Angela kissed her again, and, in a word, the whole thing got so bally feminine that I was glad to edge away.

I would have been glad to do so, of course, in any case, for if ever there was a moment when it was up to Bertram to think, and think hard, this moment was that moment.

It was, it seemed to me, the end. Not even on the occasion, some years earlier, when I had inadvertently become betrothed to Tuppy's frightful Cousin Honoria, had I experienced a deeper sense of being waist high in the gumbo and about to sink without trace. I wandered out into the garden, smoking a tortured gasper, with the iron well embedded in the soul. And I had fallen into a sort of trance, trying to picture what it would be like having the Bassett on the premises for the rest of my life and at the same time, if you follow me, trying not to picture what it would be like, when I charged into something which might have been a tree, but was not—being, in point of fact, Jeeves.

'I beg your pardon, sir,' he said. 'I should have moved to one side.'

I did not reply. I stood looking at him in silence. For the sight of him had opened up a new line of thought.

This Jeeves, now, I reflected. I had formed the opinion that he had lost his grip and was no longer the force he had been, but was it not possible, I asked myself, that I might be mistaken? Start him off exploring avenues and might he not discover one through which I would be enabled to sneak off to safety, leaving no hard feelings behind? I found myself answering that it was quite on the cards that he might.

After all, his head still bulged out at the back as of old. One noted in the eyes the same intelligent glitter.

Mind you, after what had passed between us in the matter of that white mess jacket with the brass buttons, I was not prepared absolutely to hand over to the man. I would, of course, merely take him into consultation. But, recalling some of his earlier triumphs—the Sipperley Case, the Episode of My Aunt Agatha and the Dog McIntosh, and the smoothly handled Affair of Uncle George and The Barmaid's Niece were a few that sprang to my mind—I felt justified at least in offering him the opportunity of coming to the aid of the young master in his hour of peril.

But before proceeding further, there was one thing that had got to be understood between us, and understood clearly.

'Jeeves,' I said, 'a word with you.'

'Sir?'

'I am up against it a bit, Jeeves.'

'I am sorry to hear that, sir. Can I be of any assistance?'

'Quite possibly you can, if you have not lost your grip. Tell me frankly, Jeeves, are you in pretty good shape mentally?'

'Yes, sir.'

'Still eating plenty of fish?'

'Yes, sir.'

'Then it may be all right. But there is just one point before I begin. In the past, when you have contrived to extricate self or some pal from some little difficulty, you have frequently shown a disposition to take advantage of my gratitude to gain some private end. Those purple socks, for instance. Also the plus fours and the Old Etonian spats. Choosing your moment with subtle cunning, you came to me when I was weakened by relief and got me to get rid of them. And what I am saying now is that if you are successful on the present occasion there must be no rot of that description about that mess jacket of mine.'

'Very good, sir.'

'You will not come to me when all is over and ask me to jettison the jacket?'

'Certainly not, sir.'

'On that understanding then, I will carry on. Jeeves, I'm engaged.'

'I hope you will be very happy, sir.'

'Don't be an ass. I'm engaged to Miss Bassett.'

'Indeed, sir? I was not aware—'

'Nor was I. It came as a complete surprise. However, there it is. The official intimation was in that note you brought me.'

'Odd, sir.'

'What is?'

'Odd, sir, that the contents of that note should have been as you describe. It seemed to me that Miss Bassett, when she handed me the communication, was far from being in a happy frame of mind.'

'She is far from being in a happy frame of mind. You don't suppose she really wants to marry me, do you? Pshaw, Jeeves! Can't you see that this is simply another of those bally gestures which are rapidly rendering Brinkley Court a hell for man and beast? Dash all gestures, is my view.'

'Yes, sir.'

'Well, what's to be done?'

'You feel that Miss Bassett, despite what has occurred, still retains a fondness for Mr Fink-Nottle, sir?'

'She's pining for him.'

'In that case, sir, surely the best plan would be to bring about a reconciliation between them.'

'How? You see. You stand silent and twiddle the fingers. You are stumped.'

'No, sir. If I twiddled my fingers, it was merely to assist thought.'

'Then continue twiddling.'

'It will not be necessary, sir.'

'You don't mean you've got a bite already?'

'Yes, sir.'

'You astound me, Jeeves. Let's have it.'

'The device which I have in mind is one that I have already mentioned to you, sir.'

'When did you ever mention any device to me?'

'If you will throw your mind back to the evening of our arrival, sir. You were good enough to inquire of me if I had any plan to put forward with a view to bringing Miss Angela and Mr Glossop together, and I ventured to suggest—'

'Good Lord! Not the old fire-alarm thing?'

'Precisely, sir.'

'You're still sticking to that?'

'Yes, sir.'

It shows how much the ghastly blow I had received had shaken me when I say that, instead of dismissing the proposal with a curt 'Tchah!' or anything like that, I found myself speculating as to whether there might not be something in it, after all.

When he had first mooted this fire-alarm scheme of his, I had sat upon it, if you remember, with the maximum of promptitude and vigour. 'Rotten' was the adjective I had employed to describe it, and you may recall that I mused a bit sadly, considering the idea conclusive proof of the general breakdown of a once fine mind. But now it somehow began to look as if it might have possibilities. The fact of the matter was that I had about reached the stage where I was prepared to try anything once, however goofy.

'Just run through that wheeze again, Jeeves,' I said thoughtfully. 'I remember thinking it cuckoo, but it may be that I missed some of the finer shades.'

'Your criticism of it at the time, sir, was that it was too elaborate, but I do not think it is so in reality. As I see it, sir, the occupants of the house, hearing the fire bell ring, will suppose that a conflagration has broken out.'

I nodded. One could follow the train of thought.

'Yes, that seems reasonable.'

'Whereupon, Mr Glossop will hasten to save Miss Angela, while Mr Fink-Nottle performs the same office for Miss Bassett.'

'Is that based on psychology?'

'Yes, sir. Possibly you may recollect that it was an axiom of the late Sir Arthur Conan Doyle's fictional detective, Sherlock Holmes, that the instinct of everyone, upon an alarm of fire, is to save the object dearest to them.'

'It seems to me that there is a grave danger of seeing Tuppy come out carrying a steak-and-kidney pie, but resume, Jeeves, resume. You think that this would clean everything up?'

'The relations of the two young couples could scarcely continue distant after such an occurrence, sir.'

'Perhaps you're right. But, dash it, if we go ringing fire bells in the night watches, shan't we scare half the domestic staff into fits? There is one of the housemaids—Jane, I believe—who already skips like the high hills if I so much as come on her unexpectedly round a corner.'

'A neurotic girl, sir, I agree. I have noticed her. But by acting promptly we should avoid such a contingency. The entire staff, with the exception of Monsieur Anatole, will be at the ball at Kingham Manor tonight.'

'Of course. That just shows the condition this thing has reduced me to. Forget my own name next. Well, then, let's just try to envisage. Bong goes the bell. Gussie rushes and grabs the Bassett . . . Wait. Why shouldn't she simply walk downstairs?'

'You are overlooking the effect of sudden alarm on the feminine temperament, sir.'

'That's true.'

'Miss Bassett's impulse, I would imagine, sir, would be to leap from her window.'

'Well, that's worse. We don't want her spread out in a sort of *purée* on the lawn. It seems to me that the flaw in this scheme of yours, Jeeves, is that it's going to litter the garden with mangled corpses.'

'No, sir. You will recall that Mr Travers's fear of burglars has caused him to have stout bars fixed to all the windows.'

'Of course, yes. Well, it sounds all right,' I said, though still a bit doubtfully. 'Quite possibly it may come off. But I have a feeling that it will slip up somewhere. However, I am in no position to cavil at even a 100 to 1 shot. I will adopt this policy of yours, Jeeves, though, as I say, with misgivings. At what hour would you suggest bonging the bell?'

'Not before midnight, sir.'

'That is to say, some time after midnight.'

'Yes, sir.'

'Right-ho, then. At 12.30 on the dot, I will bong.'

'Very good, sir.'

22

I don't know why it is, but there's something about the rural districts after dark that always has a rummy effect on me. In London I can stay out till all hours and come home with the milk without a tremor, but put me in the garden of a country house after the strength of the company has gone to roost and the place is shut up, and a sort of goose-fleshy feeling steals over me. The night wind stirs the treetops, twigs crack, bushes rustle, and before I know where I am, the morale has gone phut and I'm expecting the family ghost to come sneaking up behind me, making groaning noises.

Dashed unpleasant, the whole thing, and if you think it improves matters to know that you are shortly about to ring the loudest fire bell in England and start an all-hands-to-the-pumps panic in that quiet, darkened house, you err.

I knew all about the Brinkley Court fire bell. The dickens of a row it makes. Uncle Tom, in addition to not liking burglars, is a bloke who has always objected to the idea of being cooked in his sleep, so when he bought the place he saw to it that the fire bell should be something that might give you heart failure, but which you couldn't possibly mistake for the drowsy chirping of a sparrow in the ivy.

When I was a kid and spent my holidays at Brinkley, we used to have fire drills after closing time, and many is the night I've had it jerk me out of the dreamless like the Last Trump.

I confess that the recollection of what this bell could do when it buckled down to it gave me pause as I stood that night at 12.30 a.m. prompt beside the outhouse where it was located. The sight of the rope against the whitewashed wall and the thought of the bloodsome uproar which was about to smash the peace of the night into hash served to deepen that rummy feeling to which I have alluded.

Moreover, now that I had had time to meditate upon it, I was more than ever defeatist about this scheme of Jeeves's.

Jeeves seemed to take it for granted that Gussie and Tuppy, faced with a hideous fate, would have no thought beyond saving the Bassett and Angela.

I could not bring myself to share his sunny confidence.

I mean to say, I know how moments when they're faced with a hideous fate affect chaps. I remember Freddie Widgeon, one of the most chivalrous birds in the Drones, telling me how there was an alarm of fire once at a seaside hotel where he was staying and, so far from rushing about saving women, he was down the escape within ten seconds of the kick-off, his mind concerned with but one thing—viz., the personal well-being of F. Widgeon.

As far as any idea of doing the delicately nurtured a bit of good went, he tells me, he was prepared to stand underneath and catch them in blankets, but no more.

Why, then, should this not be so with Augustus Fink-Nottle and Hildebrand Glossop?

Such were my thoughts as I stood toying with the rope, and I believe I should have turned the whole thing up, had it not been that at this juncture there floated into my mind a picture of the Bassett hearing that bell for the first time. Coming as a wholly new experience, it would probably startle her into a decline.

And so agreeable was this reflection that I waited no longer, but seized the rope, braced the feet, and snapped into it.

Well, as I say, I hadn't been expecting that bell to hush things up to any great extent. Nor did it. The last time I had heard it, I had been in my room on the other side of the house, and even so it had hoiked me out of bed as if something had exploded under me. Standing close to it like this, I got the full force and meaning of the thing, and I've never heard anything like it in my puff.

I rather enjoy a bit of noise, as a general rule. I remember Catsmeat

Potter-Pirbright bringing a police rattle into the Drones one night and loosing it off behind my chair, and I just lay back and closed my eyes with a pleasant smile, like someone in a box at the opera. And the same applies to the time when my Aunt Agatha's son, young Thos, put a match to the parcel of Guy Fawkes Day fireworks to see what would happen.

But the Brinkley Court fire bell was too much for me. I gave about half a dozen tugs, and then, feeling that enough was enough, sauntered round to the front lawn to ascertain what solid results had been achieved.

Brinkley Court had given of its best. A glance told me that we were playing to capacity. The eye, roving to and fro, noted here Uncle Tom in a purple dressing gown, there Aunt Dahlia in the old blue and yellow. It also fell upon Anatole, Tuppy, Gussie, Angela, the Bassett, and Jeeves, in the order named. There they all were, present and correct.

But—and this was what caused me immediate concern—I could detect no sign whatever that there had been any rescue work going on.

What I had been hoping, of course, was to see Tuppy bending solicitously over Angela in one corner, while Gussie fanned the Bassett with a towel in the other. Instead of which, the Bassett was one of the group which included Aunt Dahlia and Uncle Tom and seemed to be busy trying to make Anatole see the bright side, while Angela and Gussie were, respectively, leaning against the sundial with a peeved look and sitting on the grass rubbing a barked shin. Tuppy was walking up and down the path, all by himself.

A disturbing picture, you will admit. It was with a rather imperious gesture that I summoned Jeeves to my side.

'Well, Jeeves?'

'Sir?'

I eyed him sternly. 'Sir?' forsooth!

'It's no good saying "Sir?", Jeeves. Look round you. See for yourself. Your scheme has proved a bust.'

'Certainly it would appear that matters have not arranged themselves quite as we anticipated, sir.'

'We?'

'As I had anticipated, sir.'

'That's more like it. Didn't I tell you it would be a flop?'

'I remember that you did seem dubious, sir.'

'Dubious is no word for it, Jeeves. I hadn't a scrap of faith in the idea from the start. When you first mooted it, I said it was rotten, and I was right. I'm not blaming you, Jeeves. It is not your fault that you have sprained your brain. But after this—forgive me if I hurt your feelings, Jeeves—I shall know better than to allow you to handle any but the simplest and most elementary problems. It is best to be candid about this, don't you think? Kindest to be frank and straightforward?'

'Certainly, sir.'

'I mean, the surgeon's knife, what?'

'Precisely, sir.'

'I consider—'

'If you will pardon me for interrupting you, sir, I fancy Mrs Travers is endeavouring to attract your attention.'

And at this moment a ringing 'Hoy!' which could have proceeded only from the relative in question, assured me that his view was correct.

'Just step this way a moment, Attila, if you don't mind,' boomed that well-known—and under certain conditions, well-loved—voice, and I moved over.

I was not feeling unmixedly at my ease. For the first time it was beginning to steal upon me that I had not prepared a really good story in support of my questionable behaviour in ringing fire bells at such an hour, and I have known Aunt Dahlia to express herself with a hearty freedom upon far smaller provocation.

She exhibited, however, no signs of violence. More a sort of frozen calm, if you know what I mean. You could see that she was a woman who had suffered. 'Well, Bertie, dear,' she said, 'here we all are.'

'Quite,' I replied guardedly.

'Nobody missing, is there?'

'I don't think so.'

'Splendid. So much healthier for us out in the open like this than frowsting in bed. I had just dropped off when you did your bell-ringing act. For it was you, my sweet child, who rang that bell, was it not?'

'I did ring the bell, yes.'

'Any particular reason, or just a whim?'

'I thought there was a fire.'

'What gave you that impression, dear?'

'I thought I saw flames.'

'Where, darling? Tell Aunt Dahlia.'

'In one of the windows.'

'I see. So we have all been dragged out of bed and scared rigid because you have been seeing things.'

Here Uncle Tom made a noise like a cork coming out of a bottle, and Anatole, whose moustache had hit a new low, said something about 'some apes', and, if I am not mistaken, a '*rogommier*'—whatever that is.

'I admit I was mistaken. I am sorry.'

'Don't apologize, ducky. Can't you see how pleased we all are. What were you doing out here, anyway?'

'Just taking a stroll.'

'I see. And are you proposing to continue your stroll?'

'No, I think I'll go in now.'

'That's fine. Because I was thinking of going in, too, and I don't believe I could sleep knowing you were out here giving rein to that powerful imagination of yours. The next thing that would happen would be that you would think you saw a pink elephant sitting on the drawing-room window-sill and start throwing bricks at it . . . Well, come on, Tom, the entertainment seems to be over . . . Yes, Mr Fink-Nottle?'

Gussie, as he joined our little group, seemed upset about something.

'I say!'

'Say on, Augustus.'

'I say, what are we going to do?'

'Speaking for myself, I intend to return to bed.'

'But the door's shut.'

'What door?'

'The front door. Somebody must have shut it.'

'Then I shall open it.'

'But it won't open.'

'Then I shall try another door.'

'But all the other doors are shut.'

'What? Who shut them?'

'I don't know.'

I advanced a theory:

'The wind?'

Aunt Dahlia's eye met mine.

'Don't try me too high,' she begged. 'Not now, precious.' And, indeed, even as I spoke, it did strike me that the night was pretty still.

Uncle Tom said we must get in through a window. Aunt Dahlia sighed a bit.

'How? Could Lloyd George do it, could Winston do it, could Baldwin do it? No. Not since you had those bars of yours put on.'

'Well, well, well. God bless my soul, ring the bell, then.'

'The fire bell?'

'The door bell.'

'To what end, Thomas? There's nobody in the house. The servants are all at Kingham.'

'But, confound it all, we can't stop out here all night.'

'Can't we? You just watch us. There is nothing—literally nothing—which a country house party can't do with Attila here operating on the premises. Seppings presumably took the back-door key with him. We must just amuse ourselves till he comes back.'

Tuppy made a suggestion:

'Why not take out one of the cars and drive over to Kingham and get the key from Seppings?'

It went well. No question about that. For the first time, a smile lit up Aunt Dahlia's drawn face. Uncle Tom grunted approvingly. Anatole said something in Provençal that sounded complimentary. And I thought I detected even on Angela's map a slight softening.

'A very excellent idea,' said Aunt Dahlia. 'One of the best. Nip round to the garage at once.'

After Tuppy had gone, some extremely flattering things were said about his intelligence and resource, and there was a disposition to draw rather invidious comparisons between him and Bertram. Painful for me, of course, but the ordeal didn't last long, for it couldn't have been more than five minutes before he was with us again.

Tuppy seemed perturbed.

'I say, it's all off.'

'Why?'

'The garage is locked.'

'Unlock it.'

'I haven't the key.'

'Shout, then, and wake Waterbury.'

'Who's Waterbury?'

'The chauffeur, ass. He sleeps over the garage.'

'But he's gone to the dance at Kingham.'

It was the final wallop. Until this moment, Aunt Dahlia had been able to preserve her frozen calm. The dam now burst. The years rolled away from her, and she was once more the Dahlia Wooster of the old yoicks-and-tantivy days—the emotional, free-speaking girl who had so often risen in her stirrups to yell derogatory personalities at people who were heading hounds.

'Curse all dancing chauffeurs! What on earth does a chauffeur want to dance for? I mistrusted that man from the start. Something told me he was a dancer. Well, this finishes it. We're out here till breakfast-time. If those blasted servants come back before eight o'clock, I shall be vastly surprised. You won't get Seppings away from a dance till you throw him out. I know him. The jazz'll go to his head, and he'll stand clapping and demanding encores till his hands blister. Damn all dancing butlers! What is Brinkley Court? A respectable English country house or a crimson dancing school? One might as well be living in the middle of the Russian Ballet. Well, all right. If we must stay out here, we must. We shall all be frozen stiff, except'—here she directed at me not one of her friendliest glances—'except dear old Attila, who is, I observe, well and warmly clad. We will resign ourselves to the prospect of freezing to death like the Babes in the Wood, merely expressing a dying wish that our old pal Attila will see that we are covered with leaves. No doubt he will also toll that fire bell of his as a mark of respect—And what might you want, my good man?'

She broke off, and stood glaring at Jeeves. During the latter portion of her address, he had been standing by in a respectful manner, endeavouring to catch the speaker's eye.

'If I might make a suggestion, madam.'

I am not saying that in the course of our long association I have always found myself able to view Jeeves with approval. There are aspects of his character which have frequently caused coldnesses to arise between us. He is one of those fellows who, if you give them a thingummy, take a what-d' you-call-it. His work is often raw, and he has been known to allude to me as 'mentally negligible'. More than once, as I have shown, it has been my painful task to squelch in him a tendency to get uppish and treat the young master as a serf or peon.

These are grave defects.

But one thing I have never failed to hand the man. He is magnetic. There is about him something that seems to soothe and hypnotize. To the best of my knowledge, he has never encountered a charging rhinoceros, but should this contingency occur, I have no doubt that the animal, meeting his eye, would check itself in mid-stride, roll over and lie purring with its legs in the air.

At any rate he calmed down Aunt Dahlia, the nearest thing to a charging rhinoceros, in under five seconds. He just stood there looking respectful, and though I didn't time the thing—not having a stop-watch on me—I should say it wasn't more than three seconds and a quarter before her whole manner underwent an astounding change for the better. She melted before one's eyes.

'Jeeves! You haven't got an idea?'

'Yes, madam.'

'That great brain of yours has really clicked as ever in the hour of need?'

'Yes, madam.'

'Jeeves,' said Aunt Dahlia in a shaking voice, 'I am sorry I spoke so abruptly. I was not myself. I might have known that you would not come simply trying to make conversation. Tell us this idea of yours, Jeeves. Join our little group of thinkers and let us hear what you have to say. Make yourself at home, Jeeves, and give us the good word. Can you really get us out of this mess?'

'Yes, madam, if one of the gentlemen would be willing to ride a bicycle.'

'A bicycle?'

'There is a bicycle in the gardener's shed in the kitchen garden, madam. Possibly one of the gentlemen might feel disposed to ride over to Kingham Manor and procure the backdoor key from Mr Seppings.'

'Splendid, Jeeves!'

'Thank you, madam.'

'Wonderful!'

'Thank you, madam.'

'Attila!' said Aunt Dahlia, turning and speaking in a quiet, authoritative manner.

I had been expecting it. From the very moment those ill-judged words had passed the fellow's lips, I had had a presentiment that a determined effort would be made to elect me as the goat, and I braced myself to resist and obstruct.

And as I was about to do so, while I was in the very act of summoning up all my eloquence to protest that I didn't know how to ride a bike and couldn't possibly learn in the brief time at my disposal, I'm dashed if the man didn't go and nip me in the bud.

'Yes, madam, Mr Wooster would perform the task admirably. He is an expert cyclist. He has often boasted to me of his triumphs on the wheel.'

I hadn't. I hadn't done anything of the sort. It's simply monstrous how one's words get twisted. All I had ever done was to mention to him—casually, just as an interesting item of information, one day in New York when we were watching the six-day bicycle race—that at the age of fourteen, while spending my holidays with a vicar of sorts who had been told off to teach me Latin, I had won the Choir Boys' Handicap at the local school treat.

A very different thing from boasting of one's triumphs on the wheel.

I mean, he was a man of the world and must have known that the form at school treats is never of the hottest. And, if I'm not mistaken, I had specifically told him that on the occasion referred to I had received half a lap start and that Willie Punting, the odds-on favourite to whom the race was expected to be a gift, had been forced to retire, owing to having pinched his elder brother's machine without asking the elder brother, and the elder brother coming along just as the pistol went and giving him one on the side of the head and taking it away from him, thus rendering him a scratched-at-the-post non-starter. Yet, from the way he talked, you would have thought I was one of those chaps in sweaters with medals all over them, whose photographs bob up from time to time in the illustrated press on the occasion of their having ridden from Hyde Park Corner to Glasgow in three seconds under the hour, or whatever it is.

And as if this were not bad enough, Tuppy had to shove his oar in.

'That's right,' said Tuppy. 'Bertie has always been a great cyclist. I remember at Oxford he used to take all his clothes off on bump-supper nights and ride around the quad, singing comic songs. Jolly fast he used to go too.'

'Then he can go jolly fast now,' said Aunt Dahlia with animation. 'He can't go too fast for me. He may also sing comic songs, if he likes . . . And if you wish to take your clothes off, Bertie, my lamb, by all means do so. But whether clothed or in the nude, whether singing comic songs or not singing comic songs, get a move on.'

I found speech:

'But I haven't ridden for years.'

'Then it's high time you began again.'

'I've probably forgotten how to ride.'

'You'll soon get the knack after you've taken a toss or two. Trial and error. The only way.'

'But it's miles to Kingham.'

'So the sooner you're off, the better.'

'But—'

'Bertie, dear.'

'But, dash it—'

'Bertie, darling.'

'Yes, but dash it—'

'Bertie, my sweet.'

And so it was arranged. Presently I was moving sombrely off through the darkness, Jeeves at my side, Aunt Dahlia calling after me something about trying to imagine myself the man who brought the good news from Aix to Ghent. The first I had heard of the chap.

'So, Jeeves,' I said, as we reached the shed, and my voice was cold and bitter, 'this is what your great scheme has accomplished! Tuppy, Angela, Gussie and the Bassett not on speaking terms, and self faced with an eight-mile ride—'

'Nine, I believe, sir.'

'— a nine-mile ride, and another nine-mile ride back.'

'I am sorry, sir.'

'No good being sorry now. Where is this foul bone-shaker?'

'I will bring it out, sir.'

He did so. I eyed it sourly.

'Where's the lamp?'

'I fear there is no lamp, sir.'

'No lamp?'

'No, sir.'

'But I may come a fearful stinker without a lamp. Suppose I barge into something.'

I broke off and eyed him frigidly.

'You smile, Jeeves. The thought amuses you?'

'I beg your pardon, sir. I was thinking of a tale my Uncle Cyril used to tell me as a child. An absurd little story, sir, though I confess that I have always found it droll. According to my Uncle Cyril, two men named Nicholls and Jackson set out to ride to Brighton on a tandem bicycle, and were so unfortunate as to come into collision with a brewer's van. And when the rescue party arrived on the scene of the accident, it was discovered that they had been hurled together with such force that it was impossible to sort them out at all adequately. The keenest eye could not discern which portion of the fragments was Nicholls and which Jackson. So they collected as much as they could, and called it Nixon. I remember laughing very much at that story when I was a child, sir.'

I had to pause a moment to master my feelings.

'You did, eh?'

'Yes, sir.'

'You thought it funny?'

'Yes, sir.'

'And your Uncle Cyril thought it funny?'

'Yes, sir.'

'Golly, what a family! Next time you meet your Uncle Cyril, Jeeves, you can tell him from me that his sense of humour is morbid and unpleasant.'

'He is dead, sir.'

'Thank heaven for that . . . Well, give me the blasted machine.'

'Very good, sir.'

'Are the tyres inflated?'

'Yes, sir.'

'The nuts firm, the brakes in order, the sprockets running true with the differential gear?'

'Yes, sir.'

'Right ho, Jeeves.'

In Tuppy's statement that, when at the University of Oxford, I had been known to ride a bicycle in the nude about the quadrangle of our mutual college, there had been, I cannot deny, a certain amount of substance. Correct, however, though his facts were, so far as they went, he had not told all. What he had omitted to mention was that I had invariably been well oiled at the time, and when in that condition a chap is capable of feats at which in cooler moments his reason would rebel.

Stimulated by the juice, I believe, men have even been known to ride alligators.

As I started now to pedal out into the great world, I was icily sober, and the old skill, in consequence, had deserted me entirely. I found myself wobbling badly, and all the stories I had ever heard of nasty bicycle accidents came back to me with a rush, headed by Jeeves's Uncle Cyril's cheery little anecdote about Nicholls and Jackson.

Pounding wearily through the darkness, I found myself at a loss to fathom the mentality of men like Jeeves's Uncle Cyril. What on earth he could see funny in a disaster which had apparently involved the complete extinction of a human creature—or, at any rate, of half a human creature and half another human creature—was more than I could understand. To me, the thing was one of the most poignant tragedies that had ever been brought to my attention, and I have no doubt that I should have continued to brood over it for quite a time, had my thoughts not been diverted by the sudden necessity of zigzagging sharply in order to avoid a pig in the fairway.

For a moment it looked like being real Nicholls-and-Jackson stuff, but, fortunately, a quick zig on my part, coinciding with an adroit zag on the part of the pig, enabled me to win through, and I continued my ride safe, but with the heart fluttering like a captive bird.

The effect of this narrow squeak upon me was to shake the nerve to the utmost. The fact that pigs were abroad in the night seemed to bring home to me the perilous nature of my enterprise. It set me thinking of all the other things that could happen to a man out and about on a velocipede without a lamp after lighting-up time. In particular, I recalled the statement of a pal of mine that in certain sections of the rural districts goats were accustomed to stray across the road to the extent of their chains, thereby forming about as sound a booby trap as one could well wish.

He mentioned, I remember, the case of a friend of his whose machine got entangled with a goat chain and who was dragged seven miles—like skijoring in Switzerland—so that he was never the same man again. And there was one chap who ran into an elephant, left over from a travelling circus.

Indeed, taking it for all in all, it seemed to me that, with the possible exception of being bitten by sharks, there was virtually no front-page disaster that could not happen to a fellow, once he had allowed his dear ones to override his better judgement and shove him out into the great unknown on a push-bike, and I am not ashamed to confess that, taking it by and large, the amount of quailing I did from this point on was pretty considerable.

However, in respect to goats and elephants, I must say things panned out unexpectedly well.

Oddly enough, I encountered neither. But when you have said that you have said everything, for in every other way the conditions could scarcely have been fouler.

Apart from the ceaseless anxiety of having to keep an eye skinned for elephants, I found myself much depressed by barking dogs, and once I received a most unpleasant shock when, alighting to consult a signpost, I saw sitting on top of it an owl that looked exactly like my Aunt Agatha. So agitated, indeed, had my frame of mind become by this time that I thought at first it was Aunt Agatha, and only when reason and reflection told me how alien to her habits it would be to climb signposts and sit on them, could I pull myself together and overcome the weakness.

In short, what with all this mental disturbance added to the more purely physical anguish in the billowy portions and the calves and ankles, the Bertram Wooster who eventually toppled off at the door of Kingham Manor was a very different Bertram from the gay and insouciant *boulevardier* of Bond Street and Piccadilly.

Even to one unaware of the inside facts, it would have been evident that Kingham Manor was throwing its weight about a bit tonight. Lights shone in the windows, music was in the air, and as I drew nearer my ear detected the sibilant shuffling of the feet of butlers, footmen, chauffeurs, parlourmaids, housemaids, tweenies, and, I have no doubt, cooks, who were busily treading the measure. I suppose you couldn't sum it up much better than by saying that there was a sound of revelry by night.

The orgy was taking place in one of the ground-floor rooms which had French windows opening on to the drive, and it was to these French windows that I now made my way. An orchestra was playing something with a good deal of zip to it, and under happier conditions I dare say my feet would have started twitching in time to the melody. But I had sterner work before me than to stand hoofing it by myself on gravel drives.

I wanted that back-door key, and I wanted it instanter.

Scanning the throng within, I found it difficult for a while to spot Seppings. Presently, however, he hove in view, doing fearfully lissom things in mid-floor. I 'Hi-Seppings!'-ed a couple of times, but his mind was too much on his job to be diverted, and it was only when the swirl of the dance had brought him within prodding distance of my forefinger that a quick one to the lower ribs enabled me to claim his attention.

The unexpected buffet caused him to trip over his partner's feet, and it was with marked austerity that he turned. As he recognized Bertram, however, coldness melted, to be replaced by astonishment.

'Mr Wooster!'

I was in no mood for bandying words.

'Less of the "Mr Wooster" and more back-door keys,' I said curtly. 'Give me the key of the back door, Seppings.'

He did not seem to grasp the gist.

'The key of the back door, sir?'

'Precisely. The Brinkley Court back-door key.'

'But it is at the Court, sir.'

I clicked the tongue, annoyed.

'Don't be frivolous, my dear old butler,' I said. 'I haven't ridden nine miles on a push-bike to listen to you trying to be funny. You've got it in your trousers pocket.'

'No, sir. I left it with Mr Jeeves.'

'You did—what?'

'Yes, sir. Before I came away. Mr Jeeves said that he wished to walk in the garden before retiring for the night. He was to place the key on the kitchen window-sill.'

I stared at the man dumbly. His eye was clear, his hand steady. He had none of the appearance of a butler who has had a couple.

'You mean that all this while the key has been in Jeeves's possession?'

'Yes, sir.'

I could speak no more. Emotion had overmasted my voice. I was at a loss and not abreast; but of one thing, it seemed to me, there could be no doubt. For some reason, not to be fathomed now, but most certainly to be gone well into as soon as I had pushed this infernal sewing-machine of mine over those nine miles of lonely country road and got within striking distance of him, Jeeves had been doing the dirty. Knowing that at any given moment he could have solved the whole situation, he had kept Aunt Dahlia and others roosting out on the front lawn *en déshabille* and, worse still, had stood calmly by and watched his young employer set out on a wholly unnecessary eighteen-mile bicycle ride.

I could scarcely believe such a thing of him. Of his Uncle Cyril, yes. With that distorted sense of humour of his, Uncle Cyril might quite conceivably have been capable of such conduct. But that it should be Jeeves—

I leaped into the saddle and, stifling the cry of agony which rose to the lips as the bruised person touched the hard leather, set out on the homeward journey.

23

I remember Jeeves saying on one occasion—I forget how the subject had arisen—he may simply have thrown the observation out, as he does sometimes, for me to take or leave—that hell hath no fury like a woman scorned. And until tonight I had always felt that there was a lot in it. I had never scorned a woman myself, but Pongo Twistleton once scorned an aunt of his, flatly refusing to meet her son Gerald at Paddington and give him lunch and see him off to school at Waterloo, and he never heard the end of it. Letters were written, he tells me, which had to be seen to be believed. Also two very strong telegrams and a bitter picture post card with a view of the Little Chilbury War Memorial on it.

Until tonight, therefore, as I say, I had never questioned the accuracy of the statement. Scorned women first and the rest nowhere, was how it had always seemed to me.

But tonight I revised my views. If you want to know what hell can really do in the way of furies, look for the chap who has been hornswoggled into taking a long and unnecessary bicycle ride in the dark without a lamp.

Mark that word 'unnecessary'. That was the part of it that really jabbed the iron into the soul. I mean, if it was a case of riding to the doctor's to save the child with croup, or going off to the local pub to fetch supplies in the event of the cellar having run dry, no one would leap to the handlebars more readily than I. Young Lochinvar, absolutely. But this business of being put through it merely to gratify one's personal attendant's diseased sense of the amusing was a bit too thick, and I chafed from start to finish.

So, what I mean to say, although the providence which watches over good men saw to it that I was enabled to complete the homeward journey unscathed except in the billowy portions, removing from my path all goats, elephants and even owls that looked like my Aunt Agatha, it was a frowning and jaundiced Bertram who finally came to anchor at the Brinkley Court front door. And when I saw a dark figure emerging from the porch to meet me, I prepared to let myself go and uncork all that was fizzing in the mind.

'Jeeves!' I said.

'It is I, Bertie.'

The voice which spoke sounded like warm treacle, and even if I had not recognized it immediately as that of the Bassett, I should have known that it did not proceed from the man I was yearning to confront. For this figure before me was wearing a simple tweed dress and had employed my first name in its remarks. And Jeeves, whatever his moral defects, would never go about in skirts calling me Bertie.

The last person, of course, whom I would have wished to meet after a long evening in the saddle, but I vouchsafed a courteous 'What ho!'

There was a pause, during which I massaged the calves. Mine, of course, I mean.

'You got in, then?' I said, in allusion to the change of costume.

'Oh, yes. About a quarter of an hour after you left Jeeves went searching about and found the back-door key on the kitchen window-sill.'

'Ha!'

'What?'

'Nothing.'

'I thought you said something.'

'No, nothing.'

And I continued to do so. For at this juncture, as had so often happened when this girl and I were closeted, the conversation once more went blue on us. The night breeze whispered, but not the Bassett. A bird twittered, but not so much as a chirp escaped Bertram. It was perfectly amazing, the way her mere presence seemed to wipe speech from my lips—and mine, for that matter, from hers. It began to look as if our married life together would be rather like twenty years among the Trappist monks.

'Seen Jeeves anywhere?' I asked, eventually coming through.

'Yes, he is in the dining-room.'

'The dining-room?'

'Waiting on everybody. They are having eggs and bacon and champagne . . . What did you say?'

I had said nothing—merely snorted. There was something about the thought of these people carelessly revelling at a time when, for all they knew, I was probably being dragged about the countryside by goats or chewed by elephants, that struck home at me like a poisoned dart. It was the sort of thing you read about as having happened just before the French Revolution—the haughty nobles in their castles callously digging in and quaffing while the unfortunate blighters outside were suffering frightful privations.

The voice of the Bassett cut in on these mordant reflections:

'Bertie.'

'Hullo!'

Silence.

'Hullo!' I said again.

No response. Whole thing rather like one of those telephone conversations where you sit at your end of the wire saying: 'Hullo! Hullo!' unaware that the party of the second part has gone off to tea.

Eventually, however, she came to the surface again:

'Bertie, I have something to say to you.'

'What?'

'I have something to say to you.'

'I know. I said "What?"'

'Oh, I thought you didn't hear what I said.'

'Yes, I heard what you said, all right, but not what you were going to say.'

'Oh, I see.'

'Right-ho.'

So that was straightened out. Nevertheless, instead of proceeding, she took time off once more. She stood twisting the fingers and scratching the gravel with her foot. When finally she spoke, it was to deliver an impressive boost:

'Bertie, do you read Tennyson?'

'Not if I can help it.'

'You remind me so much of those Knights of the Round Table in the *Idylls of the King*.'

Of course I had heard of them—Lancelot, Galahad, and all that lot, but I didn't see where the resemblance came in. It seemed to me that she must be thinking of a couple of other fellows.

'How do you mean?'

'You have such a great heart, such a fine soul. You are so generous, so unselfish, so chivalrous. I have always felt that about you—that you are one of the few really chivalrous men I have ever met.'

Well, dashed difficult, of course, to know what to say when someone is giving you the old oil on a scale like that. I muttered an 'Oh, yes?' or something on those lines, and rubbed the billowy portions in some embarrassment. And there was another silence, broken only by a sharp howl as I rubbed a bit too hard.

'Bertie.'

'Hullo?'

I heard her give a sort of gulp.

'Bertie, will you be chivalrous now?'

'Rather. Only too pleased. How do you mean?'

'I am going to try you to the utmost. I am going to test you as few men have ever been tested. I am going—'

I didn't like the sound of this.

'Well,' I said doubtfully, 'always glad to oblige, you know, but I've just had the dickens of a bicycle ride, and I'm a bit stiff and sore, especially in the—as I say, a bit stiff and sore. If it's anything to be fetched from upstairs—'

'No, no, you don't understand.'

'I don't, quite, no.'

'Oh, it's so difficult . . . How can I say it? . . . Can't you guess?'

'No, I'm dashed if I can.'

'Bertie—let me go!'

'But I haven't got hold of you.'

'Release me!'

'Re—'

And then I suddenly got it. I suppose it was fatigue that had made me so slow to apprehend the nub.

'What?'

I staggered, and the left pedal came up and caught me on the shin. But such was the ecstasy in the soul that I didn't utter a cry.

'Release you?'

'Yes.'

I didn't want any confusion on the point.

'You mean you want to call it all off? You're going to hitch up with Gussie, after all?'

'Only if you are fine and big enough to consent.'

'Oh, I am.'

'I gave you my promise.'

'Dash promises.'

'Then you really—'

'Absolutely.'

'Oh, Bertie!'

She seemed to sway like a sapling. It is saplings that sway, I believe.

'A very parfait knight!' I heard her murmur, and there not being much to say after that, I excused myself on the ground that I had got about two pecks of dust down my back and would like to go and get my maid to put me into something loose.

'You go back to Gussie,' I said, 'and tell him that all is well.'

She gave a sort of hiccup and, darting forward, kissed me on the forehead. Unpleasant, of course, but, as Anatole would say, I can take a few smooths with a rough. The next moment she was legging it for the dining-room, while I, having bunged the bicycle into a bush, made for the stairs.

I need not dwell upon my buckedness. It can be readily imagined. Talk about chaps with the noose round their necks and the hangman about to let her go and somebody galloping up on a foaming horse, waving the reprieve—not in it. Absolutely not in it at all. I don't know that I can give you a better idea of the state of my feelings than by saying that as I started to cross the hall I was conscious of so profound a benevolence towards all created things that I found myself thinking kindly thoughts even of Jeeves.

I was about to mount the stairs when a sudden 'What ho!' from my rear caused me to turn. Tuppy was standing in the hall. He had apparently been down to the cellar for reinforcements, for there were a couple of bottles under his arm.

'Hullo, Bertie,' he said. 'You back?' He laughed amusedly. 'You look like the Wreck of the Hesperus. Get run over by a steam-roller or something?'

At any other time I might have found his coarse badinage hard to bear. But such was my uplifted mood that I waved it aside and slipped him the good news.

'Tuppy, old man, the Bassett's going to marry Gussie Fink-Nottle.'

'Tough luck on both of them, what?'

'But don't you understand? Don't you see what this means? It means that Angela is once more out of pawn, and you have only to play your cards properly—'

He bellowed rollickingly. I saw now that he was in the pink. As a matter of fact, I had noticed something of the sort directly I met him, but had attributed it to alcoholic stimulant.

'Good Lord! You're right behind the times, Bertie. Only to be expected, of course, if you will go riding bicycles half the night. Angela and I made it up hours ago.'

'What?'

'Certainly. Nothing but a passing tiff. All you need in these matters is a little give and take, a bit of reasonableness on both sides. We got together and talked things over. She withdrew my double chin. I conceded her shark. Perfectly simple. All done in a couple of minutes.'

'But—'

'Sorry, Bertie. Can't stop chatting with you all night. There is a rather impressive beano in progress in the dining-room, and they are waiting for supplies.'

Endorsement was given to this statement by a sudden shout from the apartment named. I recognized—as who would not—Aunt Dahlia's voice:

'Glossop!'

'Hullo?'

'Hurry up with that stuff.'

'Coming, coming.'

'Well, come on, then, Yoicks! Hark for-rard!'

'Tallyho, not to mention tantivy. Your aunt,' said Tuppy, 'is a bit above herself. I don't know all the facts of the case, but it appears that Anatole gave notice and has now consented to stay on, and also your uncle has given her a cheque for that paper of hers. I didn't get the details, but she is much braced. See you later. I must rush.'

To say that Bertram was now definitely nonplussed would be but to state the simple truth. I could make nothing of this. I had left Brinkley Court a stricken home, with hearts bleeding wherever you looked, and I had returned to find it a sort of earthly paradise. It baffled me.

I bathed bewilderedly. The toy duck was still in the soap-dish, but I was too preoccupied to give it a thought. Still at a loss, I returned to my room, and there was Jeeves. And it is proof of my fogged condish that my first words to him were words not of reproach and stern recrimination but of inquiry:

'I say, Jeeves!'

'Good evening, sir. I was informed that you had returned. I trust you had an enjoyable ride.'

At any other moment, a crack like that would have woken the fiend in Bertram Wooster. I barely noticed it. I was intent on getting to the bottom of this mystery.

'But I say, Jeeves, what?'

'Sir?'

'What does all this mean?'

'You refer, sir—'

'Of course I refer. You know what I'm talking about. What has been happening here since I left? The place is positively stiff with happy endings.'

'Yes, sir. I am glad to say that my efforts have been rewarded.'

'What do you mean, your efforts? You aren't going to try to make out that that rotten fire bell scheme of yours had anything to do with it?'

'Yes, sir.'

'Don't be an ass, Jeeves. It flopped.'

'Not altogether, sir. I fear, sir, that I was not entirely frank with regard to my suggestion of ringing the fire bell. I had not really anticipated that it would in itself produce the desired results. I had intended it merely as a preliminary to what I might describe as the real business of the evening.'

'You gibber, Jeeves.'

'No, sir. It was essential that the ladies and gentlemen should be brought from the house, in order that, once out of doors, I could ensure that they remained there for the necessary period of time.'

'How do you mean?'

'My plan was based on psychology, sir.'

'How?'

'It is a recognized fact, sir, that there is nothing that so satisfactorily unites individuals who have been so unfortunate as to quarrel amongst themselves as a strong mutual dislike for some definite person. In my own family, if I may give a homely illustration, it was a generally accepted axiom that in times of domestic disagreement it was necessary only to invite my Aunt Annie for a visit to heal all breaches between the other members of the household. In the mutual animosity excited by Aunt Annie, those who had become estranged were reconciled almost immediately. Remembering this, it occurred to me that were you, sir, to be established as the person responsible for the ladies and gentlemen being forced to spend the night in the garden, everybody would take so strong a dislike to you that in this common sympathy they would sooner or later come together.'

I would have spoken, but he continued.

'And such proved to be the case. All, as you see, sir, is now well. After your departure on the bicycle, the various estranged parties agreed so heartily in their abuse of you that the ice, if I may use the expression, was broken, and it was not long before Mr Glossop was walking beneath the trees with Miss Angela, telling her anecdotes of your career at the university in exchange for hers regarding your childhood; while Mr Fink-Nottle, leaning against the sundial, held Miss Bassett enthralled with stories of your school-days. Mrs Travers, meanwhile, was telling Monsieur Anatole—'

I found speech.

'Oh?' I said. 'I see. And now, I suppose, as the result of this dashed psychology of yours, Aunt Dahlia is so sore with me that it will be years before I can dare to show my face here again—years, Jeeves, during which, night after night, Anatole will be cooking those dinners of his—'

'No, sir. It was to prevent any such contingency that I suggested that you should bicycle to Kingham Manor. When I informed the ladies and gentlemen that I had found the key, and it was borne in upon them that you were having that long ride for nothing, their animosity vanished immediately, to be replaced by cordial amusement. There was much laughter.'

'There was, eh?'

'Yes, sir. I fear you may possibly have to submit to a certain amount of good-natured chaff, but nothing more. All, if I may say so, is forgiven, sir.'

'Oh?'

'Yes, sir.'

I mused awhile.

'You certainly seem to have fixed things.'

'Yes, sir.'

'Tuppy and Angela are once more betrothed. Also Gussie and the Bassett. Uncle Tom appears to have coughed up that money for *Milady's Boudoir*. And Anatole is staying on.'

'Yes, sir.'

'I suppose you might say that all's well that ends well.'

'Very apt, sir.'

I mused again.

'All the same, your methods are a bit rough, Jeeves.'

'One cannot make an omelette without breaking eggs, sir.'

I started.

'Omelette! Do you think you could get me one?'

'Certainly, sir.'

'Together with half a bot. of something?'

'Undoubtedly, sir.'

'Do so, Jeeves, and with all speed.'

I climbed into bed and sank back against the pillows. I must say that my generous wrath had ebbed a bit. I was aching the whole length of my body, particularly towards the middle, but against this you had to set the fact that I was no longer engaged to Madeline Bassett. In a good cause one is prepared to suffer. Yes, looking at the thing from every angle, I saw that

Jeeves had done well, and it was with an approving beam that I welcomed him as he returned with the needful.

He did not check up with this beam. A bit grave, he seemed to me to be looking, and I probed the matter with a kindly query:

'Something on your mind, Jeeves?'

'Yes, sir. I should have mentioned it earlier, but in the evening's disturbance it escaped my memory. I fear I have been remiss, sir.'

'Yes, Jeeves?' I said, champing contentedly.

'In the matter of your mess jacket, sir.'

A nameless fear shot through me, causing me to swallow a mouthful of omelette the wrong way.

'I am sorry to say, sir, that while I was ironing it this afternoon I was careless enough to leave the hot instrument upon it. I very much fear that it will be impossible for you to wear it again, sir.'

One of those old pregnant silences filled the room.

'I am extremely sorry, sir.'

For a moment, I confess, that generous wrath of mine came bounding back, hitching up its muscles and snorting a bit through the nose, but, as we say on the Riviera, *à quoi sert-il*? There was nothing to be gained by g. w. now.

We Woosters can bite the bullet. I nodded moodily and speared another slab of omelette.

'Right ho, Jeeves.'

'Very good, sir.'